The forests awaken . . .

They could hear a rustling and soughing like a storm through pine-branches, then they saw a great army of faeries marching toward them. Through the forest of tree-changers prowled slinky shadow-hounds and sharp-horned satyricorns, while a screech of gravenings circled overhead, their harsh shrieks echoing. Leathery-skinned corrigans grasped clubs of stone, hobgoblins scampering behind, while the horse-eel pranced at their head, swollen to his largest size. It was an army the like of which had never been seen before in Eileanan. . . .

Praise for *The Pool of Two Moons*

"Good fun, with a surprisingly strong conclusion . . . lots of hairbreadth escapes . . . intriguing." —*Locus*

Praise for *The Witches of Eileanan*

"With lost twins, underground rebellions, enchanted princes, and witches with cheeky familiars, this first novel is firmly based in genre fantasy and fairy tale, yet surprisingly original, well-developed, and a lot of fun." —*Locus*

"Kate Forsyth spices up a suitably complex power struggle with vividly depicted imagery and a worthy heroine in the beginning volume of what promises to be a most interesting fantasy series."

—*Romantic Times*

The Cursed Towers

Book Three of *The Witches of Eileanan*

KATE FORSYTH

A ROC BOOK

ROC
Published by New American Library, a division of
Penguin Putnam Inc., 375 Hudson Street,
New York, New York 10014, U.S.A.
Penguin Books Ltd, 27 Wrights Lane,
London W8 5TZ, England
Penguin Books Australia Ltd, Ringwood,
Victoria, Australia
Penguin Books Canada Ltd, 10 Alcorn Avenue,
Toronto, Ontario, Canada M4V 3B2
Penguin Books (N.Z.) Ltd, 182–190 Wairau Road,
Auckland 10, New Zealand

Penguin Books Ltd, Registered Offices:
Harmondsworth, Middlesex, England

Published in the United States by Roc, an imprint of New American Library,
a division of Penguin Putnam Inc. Previously published in an Arrow Book edition
by Random House Australia Pty Ltd.

First Roc Printing, May 2000
10 9 8 7 6 5 4 3 2

for my Nonnie,
Joy Mackenzie-Wood

"Thou shall not suffer a sorceress to live."
EXODUS 22:18

"If any person or persons shall . . . consult, covenant with, entertain, employ, feed or reward any evil or wicked spirit for any intent or purpose, or take up any dead man, woman or child out of their grave or any other place where the dead body resteth, to be employed or used in any manner of witchcraft, sorcery, charm or enchantment whereby any person shall be killed, destroyed, wasted, consumed, pined or lamed in his or her body, every such offender . . . shall suffer death."

"An Act Against Conjuration, Witchcraft, and Dealing with Evil and Wicked Spirits"
—A Statute Made in the First Year of the Reign of King James the First (1603)

The
Cursed Towers

THE SHINING CITY

Snow drifted down from the darkening sky, mantling the horses' manes. Lilanthe huddled into the rough blanket. She hated winter. Ordinarily she would have found a sheltered valley some weeks ago, with rich, dark soil in which to dig her roots. There she would have dreamed the winter away, her sap quiescent, the winter storms shaking her boughs but barely penetrating her slumbering senses. Only when the snow had melted and her sap quickened, new buds swelling along her twigs, would she have stirred and stretched and opened her long eyes, smelling the sharp spring wind. Only then would she have shaken the earth from her roots and taken her first trembling steps after the long winter rest.

Instead the tree-shifter was perched on the hard wooden bench of Gwilym the Ugly's caravan, trying to keep her balance as the cart lurched over the ruts of the dirt road. Her twiggy hair was hidden beneath a plaid, and her broad, gnarled feet were wrapped in sheepskins. Lilanthe was taking no risks despite the success of the Samhain rebellion which had restored the Coven of Witches. Already they had encountered trouble along the road, her uncanny green eyes arousing suspicion among crofters whose hatred of faeries had been encouraged for sixteen long years.

Enit Silverthroat's brightly painted caravan swayed ahead of them, while behind rattled her son Morrell the Fire-Eater's caravan and an old canvas-covered wagon driven by a slim young man with a crimson velvet cap and very bright, black eyes. Lilanthe turned to gaze back at him, clenching her jaw a little when she saw the pretty blonde girl who sat beside him, laughing at one of his jokes. Lilanthe would much rather have been sitting beside Dide the Juggler, singing and laughing, than beside the taciturn Gwilym. Somehow Gilliane NicAislin always managed to get there first, however, and Lilanthe was too shy to insist on having her turn.

Huddled under the meager shelter of the canvas were a cluster of children, the youngest only nine, and a young, fair-haired woman in the final months of pregnancy. She was whey-faced and her eyes were closed, her hand gripping the side of the wagon as she tried to brace herself against its lurch and sway. One of the young men walking beside the wagon turned often to glance up at her, his face creased with anxiety, and once he reached up to touch her in reassurance. Iain MacFóghnan and Elfrida NicHilde had not been married very long and, although theirs had been a marriage of convenience, it had soon blossomed into love.

Lilanthe clung to the side board as the mare's hooves slipped on a patch of ice, causing the caravan to slide sideways. Gwilym the Ugly gripped the reins tighter, urging the mare on. Ahead, Enit's caravan was almost invisible in the snowy dusk, and Gwilym said anxiously, "We had best find somewhere to camp soon, for it'll be another bitter night by the looks o' it."

The old jongleur did not pull her caravan over, however, not even when they passed a field with running water and a tall stand of trees where they might have sheltered. They began to see the occasional cottage, orange warmth glinting through the shutters, then lights pricked the gloom ahead. Gently Gwilym shook Lilanthe, who had dozed off to sleep. She woke with a start, straightening hurriedly and rubbing her eyes with one hand.

"There's a town ahead, thank Eà!" Gwilym said. "Hot stew and soft beds for us tonight! Keep your plaid over your head, there's a good lass. We dinna want to be chased out o' town again, that be for sure!"

Lilanthe gave a shudder and rubbed the bruise on her cheekbone where she had been a hit by a stone at a

village a few days earlier. She pulled the plaid close
about her face as they drove over the bridge and into
the town square, the wheels of the caravans rattling
loudly against the cobblestones. Dide handed the reins
of the great carthorse to Iain and leapt down from the
wagon, his guitar in his hand. He began to strum it melo-
diously, while his father shouted:

"Come watch the jongleurs sing for ye and play;
Let us chase the winter miseries away.
We'll sing for ye tunes both wistful and gay,
Amuse ye, enthrall ye and lead ye astray!"

The doors of the Glenmorven Inn swung open, and curious faces peered out. Children tumbled out of the cottages, followed by their bright-eyed mothers, while the
few merchants still packing up their stalls glanced up in
interest. The innkeeper beckoned the jongleurs in with
a broad grin splitting his bearded face. His tavern would
be packed to the rafters tonight with such a large troupe!

Iain helped Elfrida down from the wagon and supported her as she took faltering steps into the inn. Neither was used to the rough life of the jongleurs, and so
both were glad that custom dictated the inn offer free
food and lodgings for the itinerant performers. With only
four months until her babe was due, Elfrida was particularly grateful for the chance to spend a night indoors.
Morrell lifted Enit down from her driving seat and carried her into the inn's common room, Dide playing a
well-known folk song as he sauntered behind.

Gwilym the Ugly, unable to perform because of his
wooden leg and harsh voice, busied himself stabling the
horses, leaving the wagon and caravans drawn up in the
courtyard outside the inn's barn. Lilanthe helped him,
unwilling to leave the sheltering darkness. The cluricaun
Brun stayed within the safety of Enit's caravan, unwilling
even to poke his furry face out the door in case he should
be seen. Both faeries were very nervous of being discovered, even though the first action of the new rìgh had
been to overturn his brother's decrees against witchcraft

and the faeries. Lilanthe and Brun had suffered too much
in the past to trust easily to the good nature of the countryfolk, despite the strict new laws that forbade any violence to those of faery blood.

The traveling troupe had first heard of the rebels' victory as they traveled out of Aslinn and into the wide
valleys of upper Blèssem. A peddler had been holding
court among a rapt crowd, his cart piled high with pots
and saucepans, rolls of bright material, rakes, spades and
wooden sabots. Voice shrill with excitement, arms gestic-
ulating wildly, he had described how the rebels had
stormed Lucescere Palace after the death of the former
rìgh, Jaspar MacCuinn. The rebel army had been led by
a winged warrior who—the peddler had paused theatri-
cally—was none other than Lachlan Owein MacCuinn,
the youngest son of Parteta the Brave and Jaspar's long-
lost brother.

Ripples of excitement, bewilderment and dismay had
run over the crowd. Rumors of the winged prionnsa had
been burning like wildfire all over the country for almost
a year, but the countryfolk had always been loyal to the
Crown and many had loved the former Banrìgh and could
not believe the tales now told of her. Maya the Blessed,
born of the dreaded Fairgean, the fierce sea-dwelling faeries who had terrorized the coastline for centuries? Maya
the Blessed an evil sorceress who had transformed the
lost prionnsachan into blackbirds and then cruelly hunted
them down? It was too strange and horrible for the people to believe, and there was much muttering among
the throng.

The jongleurs and their companions had been thrilled
at the news. Since rescuing Gilliane and the other children kidnapped by Margrit of Arran, the jongleurs had
been hurrying to join Lachlan and give him their support.
Until they had purchased the wagon, the children had
had to walk and so their progress had been painfully
slow. The delay had frustrated them all, but particularly
Dide, who longed to be with Lachlan in the center of
the action.

Dide and his grandmother Enit had worked closely

with the young prionnsa, coordinating the rebellion and undermining the Banrìgh's powers. They had given him shelter for five long years as he struggled to adapt to life as a man again after so many years trapped in the body of a blackbird. Now Dide was impatient to reach Lucescere and greet his friend, the new Rìgh of all Eileanan. The young jongleur had urged the convoy on at a dangerous pace, pushing on well into the snowy nights and waking them before the dawn to hitch up the horses again.

On their journey to Rionnagan, the jongleurs had heard many different rumors. There was talk of the Fairgean rising, invasions of Bright Soldiers from beyond the Great Divide, regicide and civil war. Some of the villages had been attacked by bands of soldiers, some from Tìrsoilleir and some the former Banrìgh's own guards fleeing the new order. Sometimes on the horizon they saw pillars of smoke rising as another town fell to the invaders. It had been a time of great anxiety for the jongleurs, and Enit had dared not use her witch skills to seek news of their friends with the countryside in such turmoil. Although every town had pinned to the door of its meeting hall a copy of the Rìgh's new decrees announcing the restoration of the Coven of Witches, it would take some time before those with faery blood felt safe to openly walk the streets or enter a village tavern.

It was cold out in the courtyard tonight, however, and from the inn came the sound of music and laughter. Lilanthe stared longingly at the brightly lit windows and wondered how long it would be before one of the children remembered she and Gwilym were out here and brought them some food. Despite the shelter it gave her, she hated being left out in the darkness while the others were free to relax and enjoy themselves inside by the fire. She wondered whether Dide had even noticed her absence.

Gwilym was busy cleaning the horses' tack and checking their hooves for stones, balancing himself with a club under one arm to compensate for his wooden leg. After a while the tree-shifter looked at him rather shyly and said, "Happen they may want me to perform tonight?"

"Ye'd be better staying out here," Gwilym said tersely. "The jongleurs dinna need ye. They have plenty o' support from the bairns, and besides, ye ken it be dangerous."

Lilanthe said nothing for a while, then replied rather sulkily, "The last village we were at liked my mimicry."

"And the village before that chased us out o' town with stones and rotten fruit," Gwilym said, scowling at her. He was a thickset man with pockmarked skin, a hooked nose and a sardonic mouth, and Lilanthe was secretly rather afraid of him.

"Ye could cast a spell o' glamourie over me," she suggested after a moment. "It'll be dim in there, and it is no' likely that there'll be anyone with enough Talent to see through the illusion."

Gwilym refused gruffly, but she looked at him so pleadingly he eventually relented with a shrug and a mutter. Glancing around the courtyard to make sure they were unobserved, he pointed two fingers at her and intoned the spell, smoothing and flattening Lilanthe's features so she looked much like any other country lass. Her twiggy hair, bare now of any leaves and flowers, he transformed into flowing brown locks that Lilanthe wished fervently were really hers.

"Ye had better hope there's none around who can sense the working o' witchcraft," the sorcerer said gruffly. "It's a cruel night to be chased out o' town."

She thanked him fervently and left him alone in the snowy night. Inside the inn the townsfolk were listening with rapture to Dide as he sang.

> "Och if my love was a bonny red rose,
> Growing upon some barren wall,
> And I myself a drop o' dew,
> Down into that red rose I would fall."

Then Enit and Nina joined in to sing the refrain, their voices so sweet that Lilanthe felt tears prickle her eyes.

"Och my love's bonny, bonny, bonny, my love's bonny
and fair to see."

> "Och if my love was a coffer o' gold
> And I the keeper o' the kcy,
> Then I would open it when I lost
> And into that coffer I would be."

Those of the children who could not sing so sweetly were
accompanying the jongleurs on hand-made drums and
tambourines tied up with brightly colored ribbons. Morrell was playing the fiddle, and Gilliane was accompanying him on a wooden flute the cluricaun had made for
her. As the jongleurs sang the chorus, many among the
audience joined in enthusiastically, so the words rang:
"Och my love's bonny, bonny, bonny, my love's bonny
and fair to see."

When the song ended, Morrell began to display his
tricks with fire as Dide circulated through the crowd with
his feathered cap, listening carefully to the talk of the
townsfolk and giving them what news he had of the
court. Lilanthe made her way to his side, her pacc has-
tening when she saw his expression darken.

"They say the new Rìgh has already set his seed in
her belly, which at least shows he is more o' a man than
his brother. Sixteen years it took Jaspar the Ensorcelled
to get his wife wi' babe, and they say now it were naught
but a spell that did it at all."

"But this is news indeed!" Dide cried, catching the
coins being flung in his cap. "Ye say the new Banrìgh is
a warrior maid wi' hair as red as fire? Who is she? Wha'
is her name?"

A surly-faced crofter with huge, hard hands and lank,
greasy hair gave a contemptuous shrug. "I heard she be
born o' Faodhagan the Red's line, though indeed we had
all thought that clan had long ago died out. Then someone said the foul, flying sorceress Ishbel the Winged was
her mother, and one o' the horned snow-faeries her father, but surely that canna be true, the Rìgh would no'

be marrying a blaygird halfbreed, witch-lover though he may be."

"I heard she was brought up as a foundling babe by the horned snow-faeries, no' that she was one o' them," another crofter said.

"Nay, she was Meghan o' the Beasts' foster child, do ye no' remember? That was wha' the peddler said," a young man in a shabby kilt cut in.

"Either way, she be a witch-lover and faery-friend," an old man with cropped gray hair said with disapproval cold in his voice.

Dide gave a light laugh that sounded artificial to Lianthe's ears. "Och, they say the Rìgh is returning us to the auld days," he said. "They say anyone who raises a hand against the faeries shall be punished severely."

"Well, it's been a long time syne we've seen any o' those demon spawn in Glenmorven," the innkeeper said fervently, "and let's hope it's a long time until we do."

Lilanthe felt the blood rise to her face. Dide noticed her behind him and flashed her a warning glance. He could see through Gwilym's glamourie, having the gift of clear-seeing which could penetrate a spell of illusion, unless it was very cunningly cast.

"If the Grand-Seeker has his way, we shall no' have to endure the rule o' the witch-lovers for long," the surly-faced crofter said with a sidelong look at the jongleur. "They say he is gathering together a force to put Jaspar's wee daughter back on the throne and restore the Awl."

"The Grand-Seeker?" Dide said casually, trying not to show that mention of the Anti-Witchcraft League had caught his interest. "I thought he had perished in the taking o' Lucescere Palace or had been taken captive wi' the others."

"Och, Grand-Seeker Renshaw be as wily as a fox," the man said, raking Lilanthe over with a glance that made her fidget. "No way he was going to be caught by a handful o' rebellious ruffians."

"Do no' let anyone hear ye speak o' the new rìgh in such terms," Dide said in a lowered voice, covering his anger with a friendly face. "He be a MacCuinn, ye ken, and one with witch powers too. It's a new order now, and my granddam always said a new broom sweeps clean."

"Aye, Jock, ye should keep a still tongue in your head," the old man said with a wary glance around.

The man spat loudly. "To think we need suffer a witch-lover on the throne again! It's enough to make a Truth-fearing man's bluid boil!"

"Careful, my man," the other said in an undertone, so Dide had to strain his ears to catch the words. "Ye ken all loyal men were told to keep mumchance till we heard the word."

"Och, no need to fraitch, I'll keep my tongue between my teeth, dinna ye fear," Jock replied, swallowing his ale and pulling his tam-o'-shanter back on over his greasy hair. As he turned to go, he tripped over one of Lilanthe's spreading feet. He glanced down in surprise but saw nothing that could have caused him to stumble, since the tree-shifter's feet, so like gnarled tree roots, were hidden by the illusion of wooden sabots. Jock scowled in puzzlement and muttered something under his breath.

Lilanthe moved away, her feet crossing over each other involuntarily, color rising in her cheeks. She tried to maintain an expression of unconcern but could not help her breath coming unevenly as the crofter's glance deepened to uneasy suspicion. He looked her over with a bleary gaze, shrugged and went out into the snowy night. Lilanthe breathed more easily, and followed Dide as he tossed off a light-hearted jest, juggled the copper coins till they disappeared one by one, then made his way through the crowd again. His face was somber and rather pale, and his knuckles white as he gripped the edge of his crimson cap.

"Things will never change, will they?" Lilanthe whispered to him. "They still hate the faeries and think them *uile-bheistean*."

"It takes time to change, ye canna expect them to throw off sixteen years o' hatred overnight," Dide answered bleakly. "In the meantime, ye mun be more careful, Lilanthe!"

"Do ye think it was Isabeau they were speaking o'?"

the tree-shifter asked, excitement warming her voice. "They say hair as red as flame, and Meghan's apprentice. Surely it mun be Isabeau? Would that no' be wonderful, Isabeau the new Banrìgh?"

"Wonderful," Dide responded blankly.

She cast him a doubtful glance but before she could say anything she was called upon to perform. Taking a deep breath, she began to mimic the sounds of the forest birds, warbling as sweetly as any woodlark. For some reason her mimicry was always immensely popular, though often she was asked to imitate the sound of a rooster or duck, something she always found hard to understand. These crofters could listen to their farmyard fowls any time they wished; why they found it so amusing to hear a young woman make the same sounds was beyond her.

Suddenly her voice faltered as terror seized her throat muscles. Standing in the doorway was a very tall, very thin man dressed in a long robe of rich crimson. His face was gaunt and extremely pale, as if he was ill, and he was staring straight at her with the intense hatred of a fanatic. Behind him was the crofter Jock, a gloating expression on his face. The shoulders and heads of both men were covered in snow, and a bitter wind was swirling through the open door into the smoke-filled room. Already people were turning to look in irritation, though their expressions turned quickly to fearful respect when they caught sight of the seeker. Many moved out of his way as he stepped forward and pointed his thin fingers at Lilanthe, intoning, "Your foul arts canna deceive me, *uile-bheist*! I see ye for what ye are—monster and demon-spawn!"

Lilanthe gave a strangled moan, and stepped back, looking for a way out. Her knees felt weak, her heart was pounding so loudly she thought it must boom like a drum. The seeker turned to the crowd, and cried, "Ye shall no' suffer an *uile-bheist* to live! She is no lassie but a blaygird tree-faery. Seize her!"

The crowd glanced from the seeker to Lilanthe, some in disbelief, others in horror and fear. Then the group

of crofters that had talked of the Grand-Seeker sprang
into action, charging the open area where the jongleurs
had been performing. Immediately Morrell swallowed his
burning brand and spat out a long plume of fire that
had them scrambling backward to avoid being scorched.
Before the crowd had time to react, Dide's long daggers
were out of his belt and flashing dangerously through the
air. Those nearest to the young jongleur ducked back
with cries of alarm. Dide grasped Lilanthe's hand and
dragged her back toward the inn's kitchens, calling to his
sister, "Get the others, Nina, we mun get out o' here
fast!"

Quick as a squirrel, the little girl somersaulted over
the table and darted up the stairs, while Morrell again
spat out fire that sent the crofters diving for cover. Enit
hit out with her walking sticks, breaking one over the
back of an attacker. Douglas MacSeinn, the eldest of the
children rescued from the Tower of Mists, threw a chair
that knocked over another two men advancing from the
side. Confusion reigned on all sides as belligerent farmers
and townsfolk tried to seize the jongleurs but were forced
back by Morrell's blasts of fire or Dide's wicked knives.
Then someone threw a chair which hit the fire-eater in
the back. He staggered and fell. Someone leapt onto his
back and pinned him to the ground, but the jongleur
threw him off and leapt to his feet. With a sweep of his
palm he conjured a handful of fire, and threw it at the
attacking crowd.

Fire blossomed in the curtains, and the screams intensified as people began to struggle toward the door. The
push of those trying to escape slowed down the advance
of the seeker's followers long enough for the youngest
of the children to escape to the kitchen. Morrell caught
up his mother and carried her out of the common room
at a run, Enit still brandishing her walking stick. Dide
and Lilanthe were close behind, the tree-shifter weeping
with shock and fear.

Out in the courtyard Gwilym and two of the older
children were frantically harnessing the horses to the caravans. Iain had seized a pitchfork and was keeping off

two burly crofters while his wife tried to heave her bulk
into the wagon. She was dressed only in her shift, with
a plaid thrown over her shoulders, and she shivered violently in the freezing air. Gilliane was sobbing with fear
as she tried to help her, while the other children were
throwing buckets and pots at the advancing mob. Nina
was kicking and screaming in the brutal grasp of one
man, while Douglas was only just managing to fend off
two burly men wielding clubs. A lurid red light from the
burning inn hung over the scene, giving the faces of the
shouting men a demonic look.

Dide dropped Lilanthe's wrist and threw one of his
daggers straight through the breast of the man holding
his sister. The attacker dropped like a stone, and Nina
scrambled onto the step of the caravan as Morrell threw
his mother up into the driving seat. Enit seized the reins,
and her brown mare, rearing in terror at the smell of
smoke, plunged forward, knocking several crofters to the
ground. One man reached up and grasped the little girl,
trying to drag her back, but the caravan door flew open
and a small, furry arm wielding a frying pan flashed out
and smashed him over the head. He stumbled back with
a groan, and the cluricaun pulled Nina into the safety of
the caravan's interior.

As Enit's caravan raced out of the courtyard, Morrell
came to Douglas's rescue, knocking one of his attackers
to the ground with a well-aimed punch and kicking the
other in the groin. The boy was able to scramble into
the driver's seat of the wagon just as Gilliane whipped
the old carthorse forward. With the other children battering
at the many hands gripping the side of the wagon, the
carthorse broke into a ponderous gallop. There were
screams of anguish as men fell beneath his great hooves.

Behind them the Grand-Seeker was standing stiff and
tall, his red robes vivid in the blazing firelight, his face
distorted as he screamed to his followers to stop them.
Gwilym turned and pointed two fingers directly at him,
and the Grand-Seeker stumbled back, shouting in alarm
as snakes hissed and writhed up his arms. The next instant the illusion was gone, but the distraction had been

enough to allow Morrell's and Gwilym's caravans to escape the courtyard as well. The crowd surged along behind them, throwing stones and shouting invective, but they were unable to keep up with the galloping mares and soon the town of Glenmorven was left far behind in the snowy darkness.

During the night the jongleurs, anxious to avoid any further pursuit, left the highway and turned into the maze of back lanes that wound through the countryside. For the next few weeks they rarely stopped to rest, walking when they could to lighten the horses' load and steering clear of the villages. Dide was somber and quiet, barely speaking to Lilanthe at all. The tree-shifter tried to show she was sorry for talking Gwilym into casting the spell of illusion, but the young jongleur only nodded and said tersely, "Och, well, it canna be helped. Least said, soonest mended."

It was another month before the cavalcade at last saw the domes and spires of Lucescere rising out of the bleak hills. A lone ray of sunlight broke through the heavy clouds and fell upon the minarets so they gleamed bronze-gold. Lilanthe gazed in amazement—she had never seen such a great city, piled high upon an island between two rivers which together poured over the edge of a cliff. A cloud of spray hung about the curve of the waterfall so it looked as though the glowing city floated on mist, while behind the city brooded snow-draped mountains.

"Look, the Shining City," Dide cried, walking alongside the caravan. "Even in the midst o' the winter gloom, it shines like a star."

The road was crowded with travelers; caravans jostled on all sides. Lilanthe pulled her plaid closer about her head, for many carried vicious-looking pitchforks or scythes, as well as expressions of fierce determination.

"Lachlan the Winged is gathering himself an army." A twisted smile lifted Gwilym's lean, pock-marked cheek. "I wonder how he plans to feed and house them all."

By the time the cavalcade reached the end of the long

bridge that arched over the river, it was well past sunset. The stream of refugees stretched for miles behind them, and harassed-looking guards directed groups of people in one direction or another. Enit leant down from her driving-bench and spoke to the sentinel before the city portal. He directed the jongleurs straight up the wide road that led toward the palace, but it was so crowded it was another few hours before they at last came out into the great square before the palace gates.

The gates stood wide open, a steady flow of people hurrying in and out, their credentials checked by rows of hard-faced soldiers wrapped in thick, blue cloaks. There were gaudily dressed lairds with swords at their hips, artisans carrying the tools of their trades, a boy with a herd of lean pigs, women carrying massive loops of wool, wagons piled high with sacks of meal and cages of anxiously squawking chickens. With a sigh and a grimace, Enit urged her mare to the end of the line, the other caravans falling into place behind her.

When at last the jongleurs' cavalcade reached the line of guards, there was a joyous reunion. Dide clapped the captain on the back, and Gwilym reached down and gripped hands with those of the soldiers he knew. Jokes and anecdotes of the Samhain uprising flew back and forth, as did grim news of the state of affairs in Eileanan.

"Meghan has been most anxious about ye," the huge, ham-fisted captain said. "She's been ailing wi' the cold and the effects o' her wound and worried indeed that ye may have had trouble in the countryside."

"Aye, it's been a slow journey," Enit replied, her voice sweet and melodious as ever. "I thought we would have been here long ago, but as ye can see, we have unexpected company." With a sweep of her hand she indicated the children hanging wide-eyed over the side of the wagon.

It was close on midnight before they were finally trundling up the long drive to the palace, their way lit with flaming torches. Beneath the bare branches of the trees on either side were hundreds of tents and makeshift shelters, campfires twinkling before them. Light flurries of snow were falling, and Lilanthe shivered, huddling deeper into her plaid.

Despite the late hour, the palace was a hive of activity. Lights flared from every window, and hammering and shouting could be heard beyond the courtyard wall. Grooms rushed out from the stables to help the jongleurs unharness their horses and unpack their belongings. There was no room in the stables for their horses or carts, but the exhausted mares were rapidly rubbed down, covered in horse blankets and led into a yard where hay was scattered on the snow for them.

An eager-faced lad was sent to show the party the way, and he marched before them, casting curious glances at them from under his sandy thatch of hair. Morrell swung the crippled Enit into his strong arms and carried her easily, a mere bundle of shawls, amber jewelry and dark, liquid eyes.

The palace corridors were as crowded as the streets and square had been. Everyone hurried about his or her business with purposeful faces. Dide's face lit up as he gazed about him. One long hall had been converted into a military training ground, and young men and women sparred together with wooden swords, a blue-kilted soldier shouting orders from what had once been a musicians' platform.

Through another set of doors sleeping forms huddled in blankets covered the floor. One man leant on his elbow to cough harshly, and a girl knelt by his side and gave him something to drink from a beaker. Another hall had been turned into an indoor garden, seedlings growing in pots covered by sheets of glass. Growing from dark, rich soil were the feathery tops of carrots, the writhing vines of pumpkins, the spindly stems of oats and barley, all flourishing despite the snow whirling against the steamed-up windows. Another young woman was spraying the plants with water, her face flushed, her sleeves rolled up past her elbow.

The boy led the jongleurs through into the main wing of the palace where another blue-clad soldier relieved him of his task. Servants hurried past, arms full of scrolls, while men in furred cloaks and velvet doublets conferred in low voices at the foot of the wide, marble stairs. They were taken up to the top floor, Morrell panting as he carried his mother's frail form up the many flights of steps.

Dide was tense now, his fingers clenching the strap of his guitar. Overwhelmed by the grandeur of the palace and the crowds of richly dressed people, Lilanthe hung close to the young jonglcur's shoulder, Gwilym stumping behind, while the children chattered in nervous excitement. Only Iain, Douglas and the NicAislin sisters seemed at ease—they had grown up in castles as grand as this and were used to the magnificence of the furnishings.

The party was shown into a long hall hung with blue and silver brocade, the ceiling lavishly painted with clouds, rainbows and the lissom shapes of dancing nisses. Pacing the floor at one end was a tall, powerfully built man with black curly hair and an aquiline nose. He was scowling ferociously, one hand clenched around a scepter in which a large round orb of glowing white was set in claws of silver. He was dressed in a dark green kilt and plaid and fidgeting bchind him were a pair of long, glossy black wings.

"Even if we get the recruits trained by the spring thaw, we still have no' got enough weapons or horses to arm even a third o' them!" he exclaimed.

"Lachlan, ye ken we have every forge in Rionnagan fired up night and day! I shall no' let ye start melting down plough-shares and shovels to make swords—come the spring, we shall need to be planting the crops and preparing for the harvest. Too many people are starving already." The speaker was a small, thin woman, her gray hair streaked with white, her face heavily lined. She was sitting bolt upright on a cushioned chair, a donbeag curled on her lap.

The room was lined with an odd selection of people. There were courtiers in velvet doublets, soldiers in the blue kilts and mail-shirts of the Rìgh's own bodyguard, a bow-legged old man in the leather gaiters of a groom. A frail old man in a blue robe sat near the throne, a raven on his shoulder. His eyes were milky white, his snowy beard reaching to his knees. On the other side of the throne sat a shaggy wolf leaning against the knee of a tall man in a black kilt. By the fireplace a woman with cropped red-gold curls was sitting, cushions at her back, the folds of her white tunic failing to conceal the great mound of her abdomen. She looked to be only a few days away from giving birth.

"Isabeau," Lilanthe whispered in delight and nudged Dide, standing stiff-backed before her. He nodded once, brusquely.

"Lachlan, is there no' some other way to get the metal ye need?" the red-haired woman asked wearily, and both Lilanthe and Dide started at the sound of her voice. It had an odd, stilted intonation, quite unlike the eager tones of the Isabeau they both knew. Lilanthe leant forward, staring at her intently, then, at Dide's raised eyebrow, shrugged.

Dide and Lilanthe had first been drawn together by their friendship with the red-haired Isabeau. It was only because of Isabeau's capture by the Anti-Witchcraft League that Lilanthe had left the safety of the sheltering forests and joined the rebel movement. It was partly the hope of seeing Isabeau that had persuaded Lilanthe to accompany the jongleurs to Lucescere rather than staying in Aslinn with the other tree-shifter, Corissa. It had cost her dearly to leave Corissa for, until she had helped rescue her in Arran, Lilanthe had thought she was the only one of her kind—half human, half tree-changer, and welcomed by neither. She would happily have stayed in Aslinn, sleeping away the winter in the shape of a tree, had she not hoped to see Isabeau again, and had her secret feelings for Dide the Juggler not meant she wished to stay by his side.

"We shall just have to try and find the men to work the iron mines," the old woman said, stroking the don beag's brown fur. "Though it be cruel work in this bitter weather, with the rations so short."

"Make all those that refused to submit to us work the mines," the redhead said. "All those prisoners o' war

that Tòmas insisted on healing should be put to good
use. We have little enough food for our supporters without feeding and housing all those still championing Maya
the Ensorcellor. Perhaps a few months digging in the
darkness will make them regret their defiance!''

The ruthless note in her voice made Lilanthe frown in
puzzlement, for it was so unlike the tender-hearted Isabeau she knew. Tentatively she probed the mind of the
white-robed girl. Immediately the bright blue eyes turned
her way, meeting Lilanthe's perplexed gaze with no hint
of recognition. "But we have guests!'' the woman said,
rising awkwardly, one hand bracing her back, the other
trying in vain to support the weight of her enormously
swollen stomach.

Lachlan swung round and his scowl disappeared at the
sight of the jongleurs. "Enit! Dide!'' he cried and strode
forward, the kilt swinging. "Glad indeed I am to see ye!
What in Eà's name has kept ye?''

He seized Dide's hands and embraced him, then took
Enit's clawlike hand, kissing her withered cheek. From
the group of courtiers by the fire came an inarticulate
cry, and a tall man with a haggard face came stumbling
forward. "Douglas, is it ye?'' he cried.

"Dai-dein!'' Douglas rushed forward and was pulled
into a fierce embrace.

His father, Linley MacSeinn, said brokenly, "I thought
I had lost ye as well! Douglas, where have ye been?
What happened to ye?''

Ghislaine and Gilliane NicAislin were being as eagerly
greeted, for their parents had also been among those to
flee the siege of Rhyssmadill. The other children shifted
unhappily and wished they too were being reunited with
their families. They had all been kidnapped by Margrit
of Arran for her Theurgia, and many were a long way
from home.

"What a crowd! Where's my wee Nina? Heavens, how
ye've shot up, lassie!'' Dide's younger sister Nina laughed
and dimpled, her black eyes dancing at the Rìgh's words.
She made a pert response, and Lachlan picked her up in
his powerful arms and spun her around.

"But, Lachlan my lad, wha' is this?" Enit asked in a trembling voice. "Your claws, they are gone! Ye move as gracefully as any young man should. Wha' happened? How did ye break the enchantment?"

"A long story and one I hope ye will write a ballad about to woo the people to my side!" He laughed. "Come, Morrell, set your mother down, ye must be dying for a dram on this wicked cold night."

"That I am!" the fire-eater said. "But wha' do ye do holding war councils at midnight? Surely all good people should be abed at this hour?"

"Sleep is the one thing we have little time for," Lachlan responded, the laughter dying from his face, leaving it haggard with tiredness. "I am glad indeed ye have come, for we need all the help we can get."

In the whirl of explanations and introductions which followed, Lilanthe stood to one side, tired and bewildered. She did not understand how the redhead could look so much like Isabeau but be so unlike her in voice and temperament. She wondered if such a profound change could be the result of the torture Isabeau had suffered at the hands of the Awl during her imprisonment. Then Lachlan introduced the woman as his wife, Iseult NicFaghan, and Meghan said, "She's Isabeau's twin sister, Enit. Ye must remember Isabeau from that time in the woods, when we labored so hard together to release Lachlan from his enchantment? She was only a bairn then, and Dide a mere lad."

"O' course I remember her," Enit exclaimed. "So this is her twin? I remember ye hinting at such, last time we were able to speak."

The two old women gossiped on, but Lilanthe did not listen. She was gripping her hands together in sudden dread. She had seen the relief and gladness that had transformed Dide's face at Meghan's words. With a sharp pang she wondered whether his quietness this past month had been because he was afraid his one-time playmate was married and with child rather than because he was concerned about the ill will in the countryside. When a door at the end of the hall opened quietly and Isabeau

slipped inside, Lilanthe saw the nervous anticipation that
flashed over the jongleur's expressive face and knew her
suspicions to be true.

Then she heard her name called in joy, and Isabeau
had seized her hands and embraced her. "Thank Eà!"
Isabeau cried. "I have so wondered about ye these
months. What are ye doing here, Lilanthe?"

All Lilanthe's anxiety and loneliness melted away, and
she hugged her friend tightly. "I'm here to join the rebels," she answered gruffly and heard Isabeau's familiar
laugh peal out.

"We're no' rebels anymore," Isabeau said. "We won
the Lodestar at Samhain and now we rule the land, as
the auld proverb says—"

"Those parts o' the land no' overrun by the Bright
Soldiers or held by supporters o' the Awl," Meghan said
dryly and held out her hand to the tree-shifter. "Welcome to Lucescere, Lilanthe. I have heard much about
ye. Glad we are indeed to have ye with us."

Outside, the howling wind threw handfuls of snow
against the palace windows, but inside Isabeau's chamber
everything was warm and quiet. The young witch had
ordered a tub of earth from the conservatory for Lilanthe
to sink her roots in, and the tree-shifter's feet were
thankfully buried. Her slender torso looked more like a
tree trunk than a human form, her arms stretched into
lissom branches that dangled toward the ground. Only
her face still retained its humanlike characteristics,
though occasionally a shiver ran over her like a susurration of wind, and then it seemed as if Isabeau was con-
fiding in a weeping greenberry tree instead of her best
friend.

It was very late and the palace had at last quietened.
Lilanthe resisted the temptation to shift entirely into her
tree shape and listened intently as Isabeau finished the
tale of her adventures. The red-haired witch kept her
hands tucked close under the silken bedclothes, not ges-
ticulating as she once would have done. Lilanthe knew
she hid her maimed hand and wondered how else her

torture and imprisonment had changed the carefree girl she had known.

In a cradle by the bed, a baby whimpered in her sleep and immediately Isabeau turned to look within the canopy and murmur soothingly.

"So that is the Ensorcellor's babe?" Lilanthe whispered, and Isabeau flashed her a quick glance.

"Aye," she answered, a defensive note in her voice.

"In the villages, there is much talk o' raising an army to restore her to the throne. They say she was named heir and Lachlan the Winged had no right to seize the Crown."

"That is bad news indeed," Isabeau whispered back. "Lachlan already looks on the babe with distrust. If he sees her as a threat to the throne, who kens what he will do."

"Who has the right o' it?" Lilanthe asked, her voice almost inaudible as she stifled a timber-cracking yawn.

Isabeau shrugged and slid down the bed, her face troubled. "Who is to say? The Lodestar went to Lachlan's hand, no' the babe's, and by Aedan Whitelock's law it is he who wields the Lodestar who rules the land. Yet Jaspar named his daughter heir, and there are many who do no' wish the days o' the Coven to return and will seek to undermine Lachlan's charter. We had hoped the saving o' the Lodestar would prevent civil war, yet it seems we canna escape it."

Isabeau glanced at the tree-shifter and saw she had closed her long eyes so they looked like mere knots in the smooth bark of her trunk. "Go to sleep, Lilanthe," she said affectionately. "I canna sit here talking to a tree, for Eà's sake. And ye'll need your rest—none o' us are getting much sleep these days."

The only answer was a slight shiver of Lilanthe's bare twigs, and with a small hand gesture Isabeau snuffed the candles on the mantelpiece and caused the fire to sink down to embers. She did not close her eyes, however, but stared into the darkness with a grimly set mouth. She was so tired her bones ached, but she was too troubled to sleep easily.

It was the fourth week of winter, almost a month since the success of the Samhain rebellion and the winning of the Lodestar. That month had been crammed with activity. On the winter solstice, Lachlan had been crowned Rìgh of Eileanan in a grand ceremony, with Iseult causing an absolute sensation by turning the white velvet Toireasa the Seamstress had brought her into a trouser suit instead of the trailing, clinging gown the seamstress had imagined.

The new Coven had been reinstalled at the ruined Tower of Two Moons, Meghan of the Beasts leading the solemn procession with the sacred Key hanging at her breast. It had been a bittersweet day for Meghan, for she had been unable to muster the thirteen sorcerers and sorceresses required for the full council of the Coven. After sixteen years of persecution, any witch who had not died in the Awl's fires was still in hiding, and there had not been time for more than a few to make their way to the Shining City.

Jorge the Seer had been chosen as the Keybearer's second, pacing close behind Meghan in the procession, his ancient face wet with tears. Behind him walked Feld of the Dragons, who had flown down from the mountains for the ceremony, though Ishbel the Winged had not woken, despite all his entreaties, instead remaining deep in her grief-troubled sleep. Arkening the Dreamwalker had arrived in the train of the rebels, having been rescued from the fire in Siantan, and a sorcerer named Daillas the Lame limped along behind her. He had been cruelly tortured by the Awl and was yet another frail figure in the pitiful parade of elderly, blind and crippled sorcerers.

Behind the five members of the council had walked those few fully trained witches who did not have either the power or the training to have won their sorcerer's ring. Toireasa the Seamstress and Riordan Bowlegs were accompanied by a wizened old woman called Wise Tully who had trained at the Tower of Ravens many years earlier, and a gloomy-visaged man called Matthew the Lean who had escaped the burning of the Tower of

Blessed Fields. With them, her face lowered in shame, walked Latifa the Cook, who had been pardoned for her betrayal during the Samhain rebellion after much pleading by Meghan. As the Keybearer said, there were very few witches of any ability left at all, and they were in much need of Latifa's culinary magic with so many hungry mouths to feed.

Altogether they only made ten, and Meghan was bitterly conscious of the gaps in their ranks. The former Keybearer Tabithas was still trapped in the shape of a wolf, while hundreds of her former friends and colleagues had been burnt to death.

Still, all journeys began with the first step. Meghan hoped that more witches would emerge from hiding and return to the Tower of Two Moons as word of the successful rebellion spread.

Meanwhile behind the witches walked a small flock of apprentices, Isabeau among them. Close behind were the Theurgia, those children aged between eight and sixteen who had joined the witches' school. Many of the city's young had joined, while the school's numbers had been further swelled by the children of refugees only too glad to know their offspring would be housed and fed. At their head marched the League of the Healing Hand under a fluttering banner of blue and gold carried by Tòmas the Healer.

The procession had been a brave sight, and it brought a lump to the throats of many of the elderly among the crowd, who well remembered the great days of the Coven. Isabeau had been deeply affected too, for she had been raised by Meghan of the Beasts and had dreamt of the return of the Coven all her life. As she lay awake, mulling over all Lilanthe had told her, Isabeau dreaded the difficult days that lay ahead of them. The only one of their enemies who had been satisfactorily dealt with was Sani the Seer, Maya's servant and the High-Priestess of Jor, whose crumpled body had been found in the garden of the Pool of Two Moons, a white-fletched arrow through her heart. Maya had not been found anywhere, and they feared she had returned to her Fairgean father with many secrets about Eileanan's defenses and strengths. Many people were suspicious of the news of Maya's evil deeds, thinking them mere propaganda spread by the new Rìgh to absolve him of any wrongdoing. And now there was all this talk of restoring Maya's daughter, Bronwen, to the throne, the baby who had been Banrìgh for a few short hours before being dispossessed by Lachlan. Loving the baby as she did, and fearing for her future, Isabeau did not sleep at all that night.

Isabeau woke Lilanthe at dawn and they did not return to their sleeping spots until the wee small hours of the next day, a pattern that was to become their routine over the coming weeks. The red-haired apprentice witch was teaching a large troupe of trainee healers everything she knew about herb lore, and much of the morning was spent foraging in the snowy forest for anything that had curative or nutritional value. Nuts were shaken out of trees, roots of all kinds were dug up, and bark was carefully stripped from the winter-bare trees. Isabeau even begged the donbeags and squirrels to part with some of their precious winter hoards to help feed the thousands of refugees who crowded the streets of Lucescere.

What was not made into soups and coarse bread and ladled out twice a day to the crowds at the gate was distilled into healing potions to help cure the many illnesses that plagued the city. With the help of the League of the Healing Hand, Isabeau cared for the sick and injured, offering comfort and restorative medicines and trying to prevent Tòmas the Healer from exhausting himself too much. The young boy spent all day in the hospital, but they had limited him to healing only those who would have otherwise died. Nonetheless, he was as delicate as a bellfruit seed, with dark shadows under his sky-blue eyes.

Isabeau also assisted Matthew the Lean in the conservatory, where young plants in all stages of growth were carefully nurtured, their development coaxed along with magic so that the scanty food supplies would soon be supplemented. Anyone who showed any ability with plants was being trained to feed the seedlings with their own powers, and Lilanthe found she was soon spending many hours in the conservatory's warm, steamy interior, crooning the plants to spurts of unnatural growth.

The two friends spent their afternoons in study at the Tower of Two Moons, under the tutelage of whatever witch could be spared to take the class. Shivering with cold and exhaustion, they struggled to understand and use the One Power, the energy force that existed in all living things and which the witches drew upon to work their magic. Lilanthe also found herself lecturing about the ways of the forest faeries, for although she considered herself appallingly ignorant about her mother's people, she still knew more than anyone else in Lucescere. Along with the cluricaun Brun, she did what she could to change the attitude of the common people to the faery folk.

There were no idle hands in the city that winter. Every beggar, thief and refugee was put to work. Many an abandoned warehouse in the city was turned into a weaving factory where women toiled to produce cloaks and kilts for the growing army, blankets for the shivering homeless and oiled tents to shelter them in. Blacksmiths labored at the forges, shaping swords, daggers, pikes, and arrowheads from every spare scrap of metal that could be found. Stonemasons sweated through the wintry days, repairing the city walls and rebuilding the burnt-out shell of the Tower of Two Moons, which had been destroyed by Maya's soldiers so many years before. Even the jongleurs were only able to catch a rare hour of sleep, singing themselves hoarse in every inn and tavern in the city. Ballads were composed honoring Lachlan the Winged and describing the beauty of the faeries and the valor of the witches. Old songs about Aedan Whitelock and old tales about the great days of the Coven were dug out, and new ones composed.

Even the prionnsachan and great lairds spent the days hunting stag and wild boar to feed the people, and the evenings teaching the finer points of the craft of war. Everyone between the ages of sixteen and forty was being taught to fight, for Lucescere was a city under siege. Although no army had yet attempted to broach its walls, the entire countryside beyond the Rhyllster was occupied by the Bright Soldiers of Tìrsoilleir, with legions camped outside every walled town and castle.

"The only consolation," Lachlan said moodily one night, "is that the blaygird Fairgean seem to have disappeared. I canna understand why. All o' Clachan and lower Rionnagan lay open before them, yet they swam out to open seas again and we have no' seen them since."

"They went north again," Isabeau said, rocking Bronwen against her shoulder. "They spend the winter in the polar seas."

"But why? It is all icebergs up there at this time o' year. Why do they no' stay down here in the south where at least the seas do no' freeze over?"

"They follow the blue whale," Isabeau said. "The tiny creatures the whales eat live only in the icy seas, and the Fairgean hunt the whales for their meat and bone. In the spring the whales swim south so they can breed in the warmer waters, and so the Fairgean follow in their trail. When the tides turn in the autumn, the whales head north again, and so do the Fairgean. They do no' feel the cold as we do."

Lachlan shuddered and cast her a look of suspicious dislike. "How do ye ken so much about the blaygird cold-blooded fish-people then, Isabeau?"

Isabeau was not foolish enough to tell him that Maya the Ensorcellor had told her much about the Fairgean when they had first met on the shores of Clachan. Instead she said blandly, "I have been reading all the scrolls and books I can find on them, for Iseult says one must ken one's enemy to defeat them."

"Very true," Isabeau's twin said and cast her husband a quelling look. "So when can we expect the Fairgean again, Isabeau?"

"They'll come again in the spring," she answered. "The tides run highest at the spring equinox and that is when we'll have the most to fear. But as long as we keep away from the rivers and lochan they canna do too much damage. Most can only keep their land shape a few hours, I have read—"

"What about the Ensorcellor?" Lachlan sneered. "Six-

teen years she lived amongst us and none but I knew
she was a Fairge!"

"Did she no' tell ye she was born o' a human mother?"
Meghan said. "Happen being half human made it easier
for her."

"What about her blaygird servant?" Lachlan pointed
out. "She was a true Fairge and yet she also lived among
us for sixteen years. Even with the seawater pool in
Maya's quarters, she must have been able to retain her
landshape for many hours."

"That's true," Isabeau conceded anxiously. "Perhaps
the books are wrong . . ."

"Or perhaps Sani the Sinister was unusual among her
kind," Meghan said. "I have heard the Priestesses o' Jor
have a cruel apprenticeship, and are taught to suffer all
manner o' pain and deprivation. And we ken this plan
o' theirs was years in the making, so happen she had a
long time to learn to survive above water."

"I wish I knew where the Ensorcellor has fled," Lachlan mused, pacing the floor in his usual restless way. "It
troubles me that she is lurking somewhere out there,
plotting against us and spinning her foul enchantments."

"Do no' fear," Meghan said wearily. "She would have
returned to her own kind; besides, did Isabeau no' say
we have a few months before we need to worry about
them? Let us plan how best to oust the Bright Soldiers,
for it is they who concern us more nearly."

"And this time let us lance the boil altogether," Lachlan said grimly. "Too long Tirsoilleir has been a shadow
on our borders, with their bizarre rites and cruel prac-
tices. Why Aedan Whitelock ever allowed them to stay
independent is beyond me. They should have signed the
Pact o' Peace and joined with the rest o' Eileanan. Arran
should have too!"

Iain bowed a trifle stiffly. He was the son of Margrit
NicFóghnan, the Banprionnsa of Arran, whose clan had
always been the traditional enemy of the MacCuinns.
Having no great love for his cold and disdainful mother,
Iain had fled Arran with the pupils of his mother's

Theurgia to warn the Rìgh of the Bright Soldiers' planned invasion.

"The Thistle has always s-s-stood alone," he responded. "But perhaps the t-t-time has come when the M-M-MacFóghnan and MacCuinn clans c-c-can be friends and allies instead o' enemies." There was a gentle reproof in his voice, and Lachlan flushed a little and fidgeted his wings.

"Indeed, Iain, and I'm sorry if I sounded surly. I am glad indeed to have ye and your wife here, and I see clearly what aid ye can give us in bringing peace to Eileanan. At least we know now how the Bright Soldiers are flooding into the land, and your knowledge o' the fenlands will help us indeed in driving them back, no' to mention your witch skills. I did no' mean to sound as if I did no' appreciate your offers o' help and support, nor as if I did no' understand how difficult it must be to stand against your own mother."

Both Isabeau and Iseult glanced at the Rìgh in surprise, for it was unusual for him to be so conciliatory. He was looking at Iain with genuine sympathy and friendliness, however, and the prionnsa flushed and took the hand Lachlan held out to him, gripping it fervently and muttering something in response.

Iain's wife, Elfrida, leant forward. "Am I to understand by your words, Your Highness, that ye intend to invade Tìrsoilleir and overthrow the Fealde?"

Lachlan looked at her warily. "I suppose I do, my lady." He knew, of course, that Elfrida was the last of the MacHilde clan, one-time rulers of Tìrsoilleir, who had long ago been ousted by the militant religious leaders of that country.

Although it would have been easy to assume Elfrida was a bitter opponent of the Fealde, Lachlan also knew she had for eighteen years been indoctrinated with the philosophy of the Kirk. The army camped throughout southern Eileanan was made up of her countryfolk, and it was entirely possible she felt some qualms at the talk of war against them. Most tellingly, she had several times exclaimed in bemusement and even horror at some tenet of the Coven's beliefs. Like the others, she had spent many hours of the past few weeks at the Tower of Two Moons, being taught about the history of the land and the philosophy of the witches. There was no doubt it was far different to what she had been taught. The Tìrsoilleirean believed in one god and one god only. They believed all who chose to worship a different deity or in a different way were condemned to eternal agony in a fiery realm. Their god was a cruel and jealous god who rode the sky in a flaming chariot, sweeping the land with fierce eyes in search of sinners and heretics.

The Coven of Witches, however, believed only in the natural forces of the world. Everyone was free to seek their own path to wisdom and to worship in whatever way they pleased. If they prayed, it was to Eà, who encompassed both light and darkness, life and death, the creative and the destructive. Eà was neither good nor evil, male or female. Eà was both and neither.

The tensions between Arran and the rest of Eileanan had always been both personal and political, but the differences with Tìrsoilleir were religious, and therefore far more dangerous. It was no wonder Lachlan looked at Elfrida warily as he spoke of invading her homeland and overthrowing the ruling council.

"And what do ye plan to do with my country once ye have conquered it?"

Lachlan flushed and gripped his scepter tightly, the Lodestar mounted at its crest glowing brighter in response. "I will demolish its evil temples and free the people from the tyranny o' the Fealde," he retorted hotly. "Everyone should have the right to believe as they please, and no' be forced to sacrifice their children and mutilate their bodies at the direction o' a passel o' filthy, pain-loving priests!"

"It is only the berhtildes who must mutilate themselves and that is the command o' the Fealde and no' the General Assembly," Elfrida replied hotly, before blushing in confusion and stammering, "I beg your pardon, Your Highness, but indeed it is no' true what ye say. The pastors do no' sacrifice children, though it is true many mortify their flesh in repentance for their sins."

"But are there no' cruel punishments for those who do no' agree with your priests' teaching?" Meghan asked in interest.

Elfrida nodded. "Aye, indeed, many are maimed in reprisal for confessions o' heresy, or burnt alive, or drawn and quartered. But ye should no' call them priests, my lady, that is an heretical term. There are the pastors and the elders and the berhtildes who together make up the General Assembly who rule the land."

"I can see it is a blessing the Spinners have brought our threads to cross," Meghan said. "Indeed, it has been so many years since we've heard from beyond the Great Divide that we really know very little about your countryfolk. If it is true that ye must ken your enemies to defeat them, as Iseult says, then whatever you can teach us shall be a boon indeed."

"And what shall ye do with my people once ye have conquered them?" Elfrida asked, color rising again in her pale cheeks.

"We shall rebuild the witches' tower in Bride and bring Tìrsoilleir back into the fold o' the Coven," Meghan said calmly, stroking the soft brown fur of her donbeag. "If Eà permits that we prevail."

"And who shall rule?" Elfrida asked, back straight as a ramrod, hands folded over the swell of the child she carried within.

"Ye shall," Meghan responded, her voice drowning Lachlan's. "Ye are the last o' your line, the direct descendant o' Berhtilde herself. We shall restore the monarchy in Tìrsoilleir and ye shall swear fealty to Lachlan MacCuinn in return for our support and sign the Pact o' Peace on behalf o' your people."

Lachlan relaxed and nodded his head as Elfrida inclined hers. "Then I shall do what I can to help ye. Ye know nothing about the Bright Soldiers or why they follow the berhtildes. I shall tell ye what ye need to know, if ye swear to restore my throne to me."

"I shall do my best," Lachlan promised with a relieved

smile. "But first we must drive them from my land and the lands o' my people, and that shall no' be easy to do. They occupy most o' Blèssem and Clachan and have access to all their storehouses o' grain and meat while we live off nuts and porridge. They bombard the walls o' our cities with their foul-smelling balls o' iron and fire, while we are lucky to have a sword in the hand o' half our soldiers. Worst o' all, the only trained soldiers were all in the pay o' the Ensorcellor and many remain faithful to her, while the Bright Soldiers are taught the craft o' war with their mother's milk. How are we to stand against them?"

"I ken ye only have a small troop, and that badly equipped and poorly trained," Elfrida said slowly, "but canna ye trick them into thinking ye have greater forces at your command? And they are afraid o' the powers o' witchcraft, thinking them the works o' the Archfiend. If ye use magic against them, it will throw them into superstitious terror."

"Both Iain and Gwilym have the power o' illusion," Dide cried eagerly. "With a little trickery, we could conjure an army from thin air!"

"And surely we could turn this foul weather to our advantage?" Iseult suggested.

Excited murmurs ran around the room, with suggestions thrown from every corner. Lachlan's yellow eyes blazed with excitement. "They need no' know we have only a handful o' fully trained witches," he cried. "If we can just relieve Rhyssmadill, then we shall have the royal treasury back in our hands and all its food and weapon stores. Our contacts in the blue city say the palace has no' yet fallen, though fighting has been fierce on all sides. Once we have Rhyssmadill back in our hands, then we can march on the rest o' Blèssem and free Dùn Eidean and the other towns."

The Prionnsa of Blèssem, Alasdair MacThanach, cheered. He and his family had been caught at Rhyssmadill when the Bright Soldiers had attacked and had fled to Lucescere with Jaspar. A practical man, he had quickly thrown his lot in with Lachlan and the rebels after Jaspar's death, despite his long-held views against witchcraft. Better a strong Rìgh with a few witch tricks up his sleeve than a bawling babe, he had decided.

"If we are to have the Bright Soldiers in flight before the Fairgean return with the spring tides, we are going to have to move fast," Iseult said, frowning.

"Let us start planning a strike against them now, then." Lachlan stretched out his wings, flexing them so the candles danced in the breeze he created. "They shall no' expect us to strike through the snow storms, and if we are canny, we may be able to steal some o' their supply wagons and have ourselves a real feast for the New Year!"

THE THREADS DIVIDE

HOGMANAY

Iseult stood before the tall mirror, frowning ferociously at her reflection. The light of many candles bathed her naked body in a warm, golden glow. Her skin was white as snow, the damp curls on her head and at the junction of her thighs red-bright as the flames on the hearth. Over her swollen breasts and the great mound of her stomach, veins ran blue as spring water.

"I canna bear this anymore, Isabeau!" she cried. "When will these babes be born? I should be with Lachlan, no' lying about, huge and ponderous as a woolly bear."

"They'll come soon enough, fear no'," her twin replied. She lay Bronwen back in her cradle and wrapped Iseult in her furred robe. "It's too cold to be standing about like this, even with the fire built so high. Do no' fret, Lachlan will return soon. He promised he'd be back as quickly as he could. He wants to be here for the birth, ye ken that, and he kens it is time. Besides, there are all the New Year festivities tonight and he kens how important they are to keep up the spirits o' the people."

"I should be there, helping him. I canna believe he rode out without me!" Iseult walked restlessly to the window, pulling aside the brocade curtains so she could stare out at the grim afternoon, the sky so heavy with snow clouds it was as dark as evening. "Ye ken he kens little about war, and the Yeomen o' the Guard are so happy to be back in the Rìgh's service, they would do anything he said, never mind how foolish."

"Come, ye canna say that is true o' Duncan Ironfist, and he's there at Lachlan's side. Sit down, Iseult, all this

fretting is no' doing ye or the babes any good. Ye couldna
have ridden into battle only a few days before the babes
were due!"

"Ye dinna understand—I promised Lachlan I would
always be with him."

"I am sure he did no' mean on the battlefield . . ."

"Where better to protect him!" Iseult cried, pacing
back and forth. "I should be there with him, why did he
ride out without me?"

"Come, Iseult, ye ken he thinks only o' ye and the
babes. That is why he rode out while ye were sleeping,
no' because he does no' wish ye with him."

Iseult sighed and allowed Isabeau to lead her back to
the armchair before the fire. Isabeau passed her some
warm slippers, and rang the bell for the maids to come
and take away the hipbath.

Lying in her cradle, Bronwen kicked her feet and
wailed thinly. She shook little crumpled fists in the air
and screwed up her silvery-blue eyes, tears leaking from
the corners. A white tuft stuck up out of her dark thatch
of hair, the result of her bonding with the Lodestar on
the night of the dead.

"Hush, my wee one," Isabeau said. "Ye can have your
bath later."

"Let her use the bath if she wishes," Iseult said. "We
can ask the maids to bring fresh water."

Isabeau shook her head. "Nay, she can bathe later. I
have no desire to get wet from head to foot just yet."
She kept her eyes lowered. Although Iseult regarded the
baby with casual indifference, Isabeau had no wish to
remind her of Bronwen's Fairge ancestry. As soon as the
child was submerged in water, she transformed into her
quicksilver seashape, glimmering with scales and fins, the
gills in her neck fluttering. Bronwen's wish to swim beat
at Isabeau's consciousness, but she kept her attention
turned firmly away.

Although only three months old, the baby banprionnsa
had an imperious will which saw those about her dance
to a soundless tune. Isabeau's maid Sukey would feel a
shiver of cold and build up the fire, not noticing that the

baby's silken coverlet had fallen to the floor. Courtiers in velvet doublets would bend and retrieve her jeweled rattle, though had they dropped their own handkerchief they would have waited for their manservant to pick it up for them. The wet nurse, a large placid woman named Ketti, came hurrying from the kitchen as soon as the baby woke, even though Bronwen had had no time to utter more than a few wailing cries. "I thought the wee one would be waking by now," she would say, not thinking it odd that she should have been happily drinking ale by the fire until the very moment the child woke.

Only Isabeau and Meghan knew Bronwen was already showing powers far beyond her age. Sometimes, when they were alone in the nursery, Isabeau resisted the urge to do things for the baby so she could watch the child and ascertain the limits of her abilities. She had seen toys float from the shelves to the cradle, and the baby's brightly painted mobile often spun in a nonexistent wind. Once she sat silently in the shadows as Ketti came in with two pitchers of water which she poured into the baby's porcelain bath, her face empty of all thought. No-one but Isabeau was allowed to bathe the baby, and the wet nurse flushed in chagrin when Isabeau made her presence known. "I be sorry, my lady, I canna think what I was doing," she had stammered. "I was taking the water to the Prionnsa o' Rurach, I do no' see how I came to bring it here. I mun have been woolgathering, my lady."

Isabeau knew Bronwen was happiest when submerged in salted water, but she only let her bathe once a day and then only in seclusion. Lachlan barely tolerated his niece at all; Bronwen was a constant reminder to him of her enchantress mother, who had transformed him into a blackbird when he was only a young boy. His sable wings were all that were left of the enchantment, but he blamed Maya for the death of his three brothers and for the current unrest tearing Eileanan apart.

When the chambermaids came to take away the hip-bath, Isabeau called for her maid Sukey. The young girl had been a scullery maid with Isabeau back in Rhyssmadill and had recently become Isabeau's personal maid, a massive promotion for a country lass who would normally have spent many years scrubbing iron pots and turning the spits. Like most of the palace servants, she had been astounded to discover Isabeau's true identity and was now rather in awe of the young apprentice witch.

"Would ye please send a messenger down to the barracks to see if there has been any word o' His Highness, Sukey," said Isabeau. The Rìgh and three hundred of his men had ridden off to Dunwallen several weeks previously to strike a blow against the Bright Soldiers and had been expected back the previous afternoon to prepare for the New Year festivities.

Sukey's round, pink cheeks flushed even brighter at Isabeau's words, and she bobbed her head shyly, murmuring, "Yes, my lady, at once, my lady."

Isabeau sighed as Sukey scurried away. She wished they had been able to remain friends, but the apple-cheeked maid was all too well aware of Isabeau's newly discovered noble ancestry and treated her with nervous deference.

She returned some time later, her blue eyes bright with excitement. "His Highness has just ridden into the city, my lady! They say the skirmish went off just as planned, and they have wagons full o' oats and barley, and flocks o' goats and barrels o' ale and everything, my lady! Everyone is dancing and laughing, and they say it is a good omen indeed to win such a blow on Near Year's Eve!"

Iseult sighed with relief. "Thank the gods! Was His Highness well, Sukey? No sign o' any wounds?"

"I did no' see him, Your Highness, but they say our casualties were light indeed, and the Bright Soldiers in retreat from Dunwallen in much confusion, and the town ours again!"

Isabeau laughed in relief and pleasure. Dunwallen was a small town on the far side of the Rhyllster, which had been overrun by the Tìrsoilleirean soldiers only a few weeks previously. Built close on the banks of the river, it was in a strategic position, controlling both the river

and the main road from Blèssem, and therefore much of
the highlands' supply routes. For the Rìgh's first blow
against the enemy to have met with such success would
greatly hearten the whole countryside and was bound to
swing popular opinion toward Lachlan. Best of all, it
would do much to relieve the food shortage in the city,
for Dunwallen's storehouses had been well stocked with
the produce of the autumn harvest.

Together Iseult and Isabeau went down from the royal
quarters to greet Lachlan, leaving the baby banprionnsa
in Sukey's care. The grand hall was filled with the tired
and dirty lairds who had ridden out with the Rìgh, all
toasting Lachlan with whiskey and talking over the battle. The winged Rìgh was lounging in his carved chair,
his shirt stiff with blood and grime, his mail-shirt much
battered and stained. He was alight with the thrill of the
battle, his topaz-yellow eyes blazing in his swarthy face.
At the sight of the twins he leapt to his feet and rushed
excitedly into an account of the skirmish, the blows he
had struck, the tactics they had employed.

". . . Iain called up a mist so they could no' even see
their own hand in front o' their face, and we crept right
up to the walls under its cover. They hardly knew what
hit them, *leannan* . . ."

"Gwilym and Dide sent fireballs w-w-whizzing about
so the Bright Soldiers were th-th-thrown into c-c-confu-
sion," Iain stammered, his Adam's apple bobbing madly.

"Your husband fought like a pride o' elven cats," Anghus MacRuraich called. Duncan Ironfist, the captain of
the Yeomen and seanalair of Lachlan's army, came to
make his bow to Iseult and assure her he had watched
over the Rìgh well. "Though I was hard put to keep up
with him," the huge soldier said. "Especially when he
flew to the top o' the barbican. I thought my heart would
fail in my chest, but he had the guard disarmed and the
portcullis raised in moments!"

As Iseult fired questions at Duncan and Lachlan, Isabeau ordered some food for the lairds and prionnsachan
and sent a page to find Meghan, who would be busy
preparing for the Hogmanay festivities. The old sorceress

was determined that all the key dates in the witches' calendar would once again be properly celebrated. Traditionally the last day of the year was a time of feasting and first-footing, a difficult event to arrange with their food stocks so low.

The victorious soldiers spent most of the evening drinking and carousing, while out in the city long tables were set out in the squares with breads and stews, barrels of well-watered ale on either side. The palace was ablaze with lights, the trees in the gardens strung with lanterns. Overhead the stars were diamond hard, diamond bright in a clear, frosty sky, while the snow underfoot was crisp and white. The children of the Theurgia ran whooping through the palace grounds, beating each other's bare arms and legs with holly till the blood sprang up, for all knew that every drop of blood meant another clear year of life assured.

By midnight the streets were virtually empty and everyone had gone home. Much misfortune in the coming year could be caused by the wrong person being the first to cross a house's threshold. That privilege was reserved for the First Foot, usually a young man chosen for his strength and health and comeliness, who went from house to house in his street, laying evergreen branches upon the mantelpiece and a fresh piece of peat upon the fire. Only then would he break the silence, gravely greeting the household and handing over his gifts of bread, salt and whiskey. Once the ritual had been observed, jests and laughter would again break out, and the First Foot would be toasted with a heady mixture of hot spiced ale, whiskey, eggs and honey known as the Het Pint.

Up at the palace the First Foot had been chosen with great care, for everyone wanted to make sure all omens for the coming year were as auspicious as possible. Cathmor the Nimble won the privilege for, apart from his tall, well-muscled stature and dark, handsome looks, he had again and again proven himself a loyal supporter of the new rìgh. Stiff-backed and crimson-cheeked, he solemnly crossed the threshold on the last stroke of midnight, laid his evergreen wreath on the mantel and his handful of coal upon the flames, then presented his gifts to Lachlan. Apart from the usual, he carried combs of honey to ensure a year full of sweetness and peace, flower-scented candles to fill it with light, and a pouch of gold to bring prosperity.

Cheers and laughter rang out as the big wooden bowl of Het Pint was passed from mouth to mouth. Then the musicians started to play again, the hall began to fill with dancers, and the servants refilled empty goblets with wine or ale or passed around trays of sweetmeats. New Year gifts which had been carefully chosen for their luck-bringing qualities were exchanged. Meghan gave Isabeau and Iseult snowy white plaids she had woven with her own hands from the soft fur of the *geal'teas*. The fine material had pale bands of red and blue running through it, and the old sorceress said with great solemnity, "It is the MacFaghan tartan, my dears. Ye are the first to wear it in a thousand years, so wear it with pride."

Lachlan must have known what she was planning for he gave them both a gold brooch to pin it with—a circle made from the writhing form of a winged dragon rising from two single-petaled roses. The dragons' eyes were made from tiny, perfect dragoneye jewels which matched the rose-carved rings the twins wore on their left hands.

Isabeau pinned the plaid about her shoulders with a constriction in her throat and a burning in her eyes. She had only just discovered the secret of her parentage after sixteen years of wondering, for Meghan had found her as a baby, abandoned in the forest. Isabeau now knew she and Iseult were the daughters of Ishbel the Winged, the flying sorceress of legend, and her faery lover Khan'gharad the Dragon-Laird. The lovers had been cruelly separated on the Day of Betrayal, Khan'gharad falling into a pit that Meghan had opened below his feet. Her intention had been to kill Maya, but somehow the Ensorcellor had escaped and the sacrifice of Khan'gharad's life had been in vain.

Although the queen-dragon had told Meghan Khan'gharad still lived, Ishbel had refused to believe her, fall-

ing back into her enchanted sleep that had lasted for
sixteen years.

Although her father was lost and her mother was sunk
in grief-stricken sleep, it meant a great deal to Isabeau
to know she was no longer a foundling child without a
name or ancestry, but a banprionnsa, the descendant of
Faodhagan the Red, one of the First Coven of Witches.
This meant she was of the very finest blood, as nobly
born as Lachlan himself.

Isabeau was still examining her plaid with pride and
satisfaction when Dide found her. She looked up at him
and said huskily, "It is odd what a difference it makes,
knowing my real name and who my parents are."

He gave her a shadowed smile and bowed deeply to
her. "May I have this dance, Isabeau NicFaghan o'
Tìrlethan? If ye are no' too proud to dance with a mere
jongleur now that ye ken ye are a banprionnsa."

"Thank ye indeed, Dide the Juggler, I would love it,
as long as ye do no' mind me stomping on your toes,"
she replied wryly. "I never had much chance to learn to
dance in the depths o' the Sithiche Mountains!"

"I shall be glad to teach ye," he cried and swept her
away into a vigorous reel. Panting and laughing, Isabeau
skipped down the room, Dide's arm about her waist. She
waved to Lilanthe who was watching enviously from one
corner. Although tree-changers loved to dance, theirs
was a far statelier promenade, and Lilanthe was too self-
conscious about her broad, gnarled feet to ever display
them so freely.

As the fiddles and flutes began another tune, Cathmor
the Nimble leapt up onto the musicians' platform. "Come
join the wassail," he cried, lifting the over-brimming bowl
of Het Pint. "Wassail, wassail, all over the town!"

With cries of delight, many of the younger people left
the floor, streaming out behind Cathmor as he danced
out of the hall and through the great front doors. Dide
caught Isabeau's hand and dragged her after, lifting up
his voice and singing.

> "Here we come a-wassailing
> among the leaves so green

> Here we come a-wandering
> so bonny to be seen.
> Here we come a-wassailing
> wi' our bowl o' ashen tree
> Here we come a-wandering
> love and peace to all o' ye.
> For it's your wassail and it's our wassail,
> wassail, wassail, all over the town,
> wi' the wassailing bowl we'll drink to thee!
> Love and peace to all o' ye!"

Through the snowy streets of the city they ran, trailing
colored ribbons. Everyone whose paths they crossed was
invited to drink from the great bowl of hot spiced ale,
which was replenished frequently from the bubbling cauldrons set up in every square. They met other wassailing
parties, not so grandly dressed but with as much good
cheer and enthusiasm as the young lairds and ladies from
the palace. The lantern-hung streets of the city resounded with song, as voices both rough and refined car-
oled the refrain.

> "For it's your wassail and it's our wassail,
> wassail, wassail, all over the town,
> wi' the wassailing bowl we'll drink to thee!
> Love and peace to all o' ye!"

Isabeau danced and laughed with genuine pleasure, her
doubts and anxieties melting away in the atmosphere of
joy and expectancy that had transfigured the war-stricken
city. She thought how wise it was of Meghan to plan this
night of celebration which had fallen out of favor under
Maya's rule. Everywhere she heard people toasting the
new Rìgh and Banrìgh, the return of the Coven, the birth
of a new year and a new era.

The heady warmth of the spiced ale pervaded Isabeau's body, making her head spin and her throat bubble
with laughter. Dide's arm was warm and strong around
her back, his black eyes, bright as polished jet, smiling
into hers. As he spun her into another strathspey she felt

how lithe and slim his body was against hers, how fluidly they moved together.

Through the icy darkness of the palace gardens the dancing promenade wound, then back into the hot, crowded hall. The flaming torches and laughing faces spun in a whirl as Dide swept Isabeau around. She was helplessly dizzy, having to clutch at his arms to keep her feet. He laughed and kissed her. Somehow they danced out of the ballroom and into the shadowed halls behind. His mouth on her throat was hot as a brand. He spoke broken words of love she hardly heard, so feverish was her response.

They were lying entwined together on her bed when Lilanthe opened the door. Unable to find her friends and shy of so many strangers, the tree-shifter had thought to seek her tub of earth and go to sleep. The light from the open door streamed across the bedchamber, and Lilanthe was unable to stifle an exclamation as she saw Dide and Isabeau tangled together in a welter of unfastened clothing. The jongleur lifted his mouth from Isabeau's breast while she stared dazedly at Lilanthe across his bare back. The tree-shifter stood frozen for a moment, color flaming into her face, then she turned and ran.

With a cry Isabeau clutched her clothes to her and scrambled after, calling "Lilanthe!" Dide cursed, and struggled to pull on his shirt.

The tree-shifter ran down the corridor and plunged down the stairs, only just managing to avoid colliding with the numerous couples who stood chatting on the landings or kissing in the corners. Trying desperately to do up her bodice, Isabeau hurried after, still calling her friend's name.

Dide caught her at the top of the stairs. "Come back to bed, *leannan*," he murmured, sliding his arm about her waist. "There is nothing we can do now . . ."

"But did ye no' see her face? She looked absolutely stricken."

"It was just the shock. She was no' expecting to find us so. Let it be, *leannan*. She'll be a wee embarrassed, but she'll get over it. Come back." He pulled her toward the bedroom, his other hand sliding up her back to cup the nape of her neck. Isabeau hesitated, staring down the stairs. The candles were all guttering in their sconces, but enough light remained to show there was no sign of Lilanthe. With a sigh she let Dide lead her back toward her bedchamber.

Suddenly a ripple of pain ran over Isabeau and she cried out, clutching her abdomen.

"Wha' is it, wha' be wrong?" Dide cried, and had to support her as she swayed, her face bleached of color.

She bent over, arms crossed over her stomach. "It's Iseult," she moaned. "The babes must be on their way."

A door at the other end of the corridor swung open, and Lachlan burst out, clutching a sheet to him, his black hair wildly tousled. His eyes were bloodshot and he smelt of stale alcohol. "Isabeau!" he cried. "Quickly! It's Iseult! I think her time has come."

Another undulation of pain washed through her, and she groaned. "Call . . . Meghan," she said through stiff lips. "Quickly!"

Reluctantly Dide let her go and hurried to call the guards. The pain passed, and Isabeau followed her distraught brother-in-law into the royal bedchamber. Iseult was sitting up in the great bed, her face white, her blue eyes dilated. She cried out in relief at the sight of her sister and held out her hand. Isabeau ran to her side, gripping her fingers tightly.

"Did ye feel it?" Iseult whispered, and Isabeau nodded.

"The babes are getting ready to be born," she said. "I've sent for Meghan, she'll be here soon. If I am to feel all ye do, I do no' think I'll be much help to ye."

"It'll be enough to have ye here," Iseult answered.

Isabeau nodded and kissed her sister's tense fingers. She knew how much the admission must have cost her proud twin. "I know, dearling," she whispered back. "But everything will be fine and soon ye shall have two bonny babies to show for your effort." She busied herself stoking up the fire and rang the bell for her sister's maid.

Another sharp ripple of pain swept through her and she groaned, clutching her stomach. Glancing up, she saw

Iseult bowed over, her hands mirroring Isabeau's. "They come quickly," she managed to say. "Fear no', Iseult, it shall be a swift birthing."

Iseult's maid hurried in, rubbing her eyes and exclaiming, her face anxious under the frilled cap she had pulled on askew in her hurry. Isabeau told her to call Sukey and ask her to bring her mistress's herb bag as quickly as she could. "We shall need clean linen and a kettle to boil water, and see if ye can find any raspberry leaf tea in the cellar, it is helpful indeed with the contractions. Oh, and send someone to wake Johanna—if she truly wishes to be a healer, she may as well witness her first birthing!"

Another contraction saw Iseult clutch at Lachlan's hand. Isabeau had to hold the mantelpiece to keep on her feet, biting her lip hard. Then Meghan was there, her gray-white hair streaming about her shoulders, her plaid clutched around her nightgown. She ordered Lachlan away from the bed, telling him sharply to get out of her way. "Wash yourself and dress, for Eà's sake!" she snapped. "Ye stink o' the brewery."

Scowling, Lachlan went through to his dressing-room, catching up his kilt and shirt from where they lay on the floor. Meghan picked up the scepter from where it had rolled against the wall and put it on the chair, muttering under her breath. Then she bent over Iseult, feeling her grossly distended stomach with delicate fingers, murmuring reassurance.

The maids arrived laden down with water jugs, baskets of herbs and tinctures, and piles of clean linen. Sukey carried a wailing Bronwen in one arm and Isabeau's herb bag in the other, her face flushed with anxiety. "I be sorry indeed, my lady, but I couldna wake Ketti from her sleep, and the babe is that upset, I dared no' leave her . . ."

"Has Ketti had too much o' the Het Pint that ye canna be waking her?" Meghan asked sharply.

Sukey blushed even pinker and bit her lip, nodding and shrugging at once. "Indeed, she snores and snores, and there is an empty mug fallen from her hand . . ."

"We shall have to find ourselves another wet nurse," the old sorceress snapped. "Never mind, Sukey, ye have done well. Ask Latifa to make a weak gruel to feed the wee one with, then give her some poppy syrup to soothe her and bring her cradle in here. Be quick, though, I can feel these babes are ready to be born!"

Indeed, by the time Sukey had returned and put a sleepy Bronwen to bed in her silk-hung cradle, Iseult was in the last stages of her contractions, her red curls wet with perspiration. She was pacing the room, magnificent in her swollen nakedness, her jaw set with determination. It was just on dawn; through the half-drawn curtains the flowers of frost on the windowpane were stained rose. Isabeau, limp from sharing her twin's pain, paced with her, arm about her back, as Meghan explained to Johanna, the eldest of the League of the Healing Hand, exactly what she was doing.

Iseult smothered a groan and clung to the mantelpiece. Isabeau supported her weight as her twin bore down with all her strength.

"I can see its head!" Johanna cried. "Look!" Iseult bit her lip and pushed again, and Johanna knelt behind her. Her plain face transfigured with amazement, she cradled the baby's head between her work-worn hands and, under Meghan's watchful eye, guided the baby out. "It's a boy!"

They heard the cock crow the coming of the dawn, and light illuminated the window as the sun rose. The baby gulped for breath and uttered a thin, wailing cry.

"Ye have a bonny son," Meghan said gently, "and how this can be, I do no' know, but he has wings, Iseult, just like his father."

Tears leaking from the corners of her eyes, Iseult strained to see. Meghan held up the naked child to show her the tiny, wet wings glued to his back. They were the same burnished gold as the downy hair on his head.

"Winged," she sighed in wonderment, then another convulsion of pain wracked her and she gripped Isabeau's hand tightly, biting her lip so she would not cry out. Scarred Warriors did not scream in pain, not even in childbirth.

"The second one should come quickly," Meghan said, giving the baby boy to Sukey to wash and swaddle. "It'll soon be over, my dear. Johanna, give Iseult some more o' that feverfew syrup."

Despite the old sorceress's words, the birth of the second babe was a long, slow, painful process, and Meghan's face was creased with concern. Iseult was white as the icicles framing the window, and blood from her bitten lip ran down her chin. At last the second child was born, but her umbilical cord was wrapped tight around her throat and she was blue as ice shadows. Meghan bent and put her mouth to the baby's, breathing her own breath into the tiny lungs, gently pumping her chest to try and make her heart start beating, but it was no use. "I'm sorry, my dear," the sorceress said, tears standing in her eyes. "I'm so sorry. It's too late. She does no' live."

Rocking her baby boy against her breast, Iseult gave a strange, wailing cry. "Curse ye, Gods o' White, for taking my daughter!" she cried. She shook her fist at the window, where the first rays of sun were melting the frost so the snow-humped branches outside could be seen.

Tears wet on her own cheeks, Isabeau tried to soothe her while Johanna somberly wrapped the dead baby in linen. "Let me hold her," Iseult said quietly, resting her cheek on the soft head of her son. "Let me hold her afore ye take her away."

With the little boy cradled in one arm and his dead sister in the other, she crooned over their heads, speaking to them in the strange, guttural language of the Khan'-cohbans. Where the boy's head was only faintly touched with fire, the little girl's hair was as bronze-red as newly minted pennies.

The sorceress opened the door and let a haggard, white-faced Lachlan in. He had been able to hear Iseult's cry from the corridor, and he was sick with anxiety and fear. Jorge the Seer was there as well, his lined face wet with tears, a serious-faced Tòmas huddled by his side.

Both knew there was nothing that could be done for the dead baby.

"Do no' grieve so bitterly, *leannan*," Lachlan murmured, holding Iseult in his arms and rocking back and forth. "We have a fine, strong son, bonny as the day is new. We've been blessed indeed. Look at our wee bonny boy."

At last Meghan took the little girl away, leaving Iseult to nurse her son. Exhausted with emotion, Isabeau moved about the room, tidying away the blood-stained linen and packing up her herbal potions. Wondering that Bronwen should have remained so quiet during the uproar, she bent over the cradle and what she saw made her suck her breath in sharply. Bronwen was awake, her silvery-blue eyes wide open, babbling happily to herself. In her tiny hands she held the Lodestar, shining white.

Panic rushed through Isabeau's veins. She glanced up and saw Lachlan's scepter still lying on the chair where Meghan had left it, though now the silver claws were empty. Somehow Bronwen had called the Lodestar to her while everyone else was distracted with the birthing. Her pulses pounding, Isabeau wondered what to do. Lachlan rarely let the scepter out of his hand, and he would be greatly enraged if he realized what Bronwen had done. Isabeau could not take the Lodestar from the baby, though, for it was death to anyone but a MacCuinn to touch it. If Meghan had still been in the room, she could perhaps have taken the Lodestar without Lachlan noticing it had gone missing, but the sorceress had taken the dead baby away to prepare for burial.

Just then the Rìgh glanced up and saw her hovering in indecision over the cradle. Even as he frowned in interrogation, his eyes followed hers to the scepter and he saw at once that the Lodestar was gone. Color rose in his swarthy cheeks and just as quickly drained away, leaving him a sickly yellow. With a falcon's shriek he leapt to his feet, his wings extending, and was across the room. Isabeau shrank back. He seized the glowing orb and wrested it from the baby, who at once began to wail. To Lachlan's horror, the Lodestar slipped from his fingers and flew back to the baby's outstretched hands. He grasped it again, while Bronwen bellowed with disappointment, her face turning scarlet.

Isabeau darted forward and snatched Bronwen from the cradle. Lachlan's face was set in a mask of fury, his eyes glaring. "Do no' dare touch her!" Isabeau cried, cuddling the little girl to her chest. She saw his hands clench into fists, every tendon in his body taut with anger. With a cry, Isabeau turned and fled the room, Bronwen sobbing disconsolately. Outside all the bells in the city began to ring in triumph at the birth of the new heir to the throne, but to Isabeau they seemed to toll a warning.

The House of Wanton Delights was the most exclusive brothel in all of Lucescere. Within its crimson-hung walls the most beautiful and exotic of whores were available to anyone who could afford the exorbitant prices charged by Black Donagh, the proprietor. An immensely fat man, he lounged at his ease on a couch among gold-tasseled cushions, fondling a slender young boy with one ringladen, pudgy hand, the other toying with the embroidered hose of a tall hookah. An exquisitely dressed young laird lounged opposite, swirling whiskey in a glass of cut crystal. Diamonds glittered at his shoulder and in one ear. Candlelight flickered over the ornate fabrics of the curtains, pillows and silk-hung walls, deepening the shadowed cleavages of scantily dressed girls and the rouge-enhanced muscles of slim boys. From the smoky corners of embrasures came low laughs and murmurs, and in the center of the room danced an exceedingly well-fleshed woman, dressed only in jewels and gold chains.

Under a velvet embossed canopy a woman sat strumming the gilded strings of a clàrsach. Although her dress was buttoned high around her throat and wrists, it was cut away from collarbone to navel, revealing a shapely expanse of very pale skin. Her silky black hair curved onto her cheekbones, shadowing her features, though occasionally her eyes glinted blue in the candlelight. She sang of love in a husky voice as rose-clad servitors poured wine into the goblets of the customers and brought trays of sweetmeats and comfits to lay upon the delicate little tables.

"She is new since I was last here," the young laird said languidly, reaching out one white hand to select a little spiced cake from the tray. "Where did ye find her, Donagh my dear?"

"Is she no' delectable?" the fat man responded. "As pale as the blue moon, as ethereal as sea mists . . ."

"And no doubt as expensive as moonbane," the young laird responded dryly.

Black Donagh blew out a long plume of smoke, smiling enigmatically. "But o' course, my sweet. She is choosy indeed about whom she bestows her favors upon, and if she likes no' the cut o' your doublet or the smell o' your armpits, she'll give ye naught but her very smooth, very cold shoulder. She is the most exclusive o' all our courtesans."

The laird raised a perfectly shaped eyebrow. "Indeed? She is bonny, it is true, but even the dim lighting ye have in here shows me she is past the first flush o' her youth."

"Ah, yes, but she has talents, my sweet. I can promise ye will no' be disappointed should ye choose to . . . ah, sample her wares."

The young laird lay back on his cushion and observed the clàrsach-player through heavy-lidded eyes. His long, white fingers played with the circle of diamonds securing his plaid so they flashed with brilliant light. Gently, sensuously, the musician swept her fingers over the strings and began another song, one of hoarse longing and husky promise. He moistened his lip, then smiled. "Very well, Donagh my dear," he said. "Just how much do ye wish for your mysterious siren?"

He was the son of one of the richest of the Rìonnagan lairds and used to paying highly for his pleasures. Nonetheless, the amount named was enough for him to lift his eyebrow. "Ye had best hope she does no' disappoint me, my sweet," he said softly.

Black Donagh waved the spiced cake in his hand with an expression of bliss on his face. "Disappoint?" he purred. "I think no', my laird."

When dawn finally fingered its way through the heavy velvet curtains of the upstairs boudoir, the young laird lay sweat-dampened and satiated in the tangled sheets, his eyes hungry on the pale shape of the woman dressing before him. "Will ye no' stay with me?" he said throatily. "I will set ye up in your own house, ye can have a houseful o' servants to attend ye and none but me to satisfy."

"But do ye no' live in the highlands, my laird?" she answered in her deep, husky voice. "It would no' amuse me to live so far away from the city."

"Ye can have anything ye want, anything," he answered.

She tossed the heavy bag of coins he had flung at her to make her stay with him till dawn. "This is what I want," she answered, "and I have taken all that ye have."

"I can get more," the laird said eagerly. "I just need to speak with my father . . ."

"Then come back when ye have more," she answered indifferently.

He lunged across the bed and caught her arm, dragging her back onto the bed and ripping open her bodice so he could kiss her breasts. Suddenly he stilled, looking at her with dread. In the dim light filtering through the curtains, he could see three thin, translucent slits on the side of her throat, which fluttered gently as she breathed. She did not attempt to resist as he tore the dress from her shoulders, revealing the wide, serrated fin that curved out of her spine, the frills of fin that ran from elbow to wrist. He understood now why she had insisted on snuffing all the candles before disrobing, despite his pleas for light, and why she had not allowed him free play with her body, teasing him unbearably by withdrawing each time he tried to caress her. He had thought it a game and it had excited him immensely. Now he knew there was a deeper reason for her teasing and tantalizing, but his lust for her was only heightened. He pressed his hot, urgent mouth to her flesh, and she lay still, watching him with mocking coolness.

"Ye are an *uile-bheist*!" he cried. "They will stone ye

to death if they should find out. If ye will no' come with me, I shall tell Donagh, I shall betray your secret!"

She smiled and ran her webbed fingers through his sweat-damped hair. "Ye think Black Donagh does no' ken? Why do ye think I am so expensive? It is no' every day that ye can spill your seed into one o' the sea folk, ye ken. Do no' be a fool. This new rìgh o' yours has outlawed the stoning o' faeries, ye ken that. Besides, who shall suffer the most once it is kent ye have lain with one o' the Fairgean? I shall just slip once more into the back ways o' the city and find myself a new protector. Ye shall be branded forever."

He lay still, dry sobs shaking his ribcage. She slid out from under him and rebuttoned her dress, hiding the heavy coin-pouch in her clothing. Then she picked up her clàrsach from where it had fallen to the floor, and began to strum a lullaby. "Sleep, my honeyed sweet, sleep," she sang, tender emotion thrilling through every note.

> "Rocked in the cradle o' my arms
> forget all your fears and qualms,
> dream only o' precious love,
> rocked in my wings like a dove,
> forget, my honeyed sweet, forget,
> sleep, my honeyed sweet, sleep."

His head cradled on his arms, a tear slipping from the corner of his eye, the young laird slipped into sleep. When he woke at the clamor of bells, he remembered nothing but the sweetness of her voice, the thrill of her embrace, and his own helpless longing.

The baby girl was named Lavinya, after Lachlan's mother, and buried in the MacCuinn graveyard at one end of the palace garden. White as the snow, Iseult held her little boy closely, the two of them well wrapped against the bitter cold. He had been named Donncan Feargus, after Lachlan's two brothers who had been transformed into blackbirds and hunted down by Maya's hawk.

The Banrìgh did not weep as her baby daughter was buried in the iron-hard earth; her face was set as cold as if it were carved from marble. Isabeau wept for her, bitter tears that scalded the skin of her face.

"It is the price the Gods o' White have demanded for my betrayal," Iseult said as they walked back toward the palace. "I should have known they would no' let me go so easily."

Dide the Juggler had been among the mourners gathered at the burial ground, and he came up and took Isabeau's elbow as she walked by her sister's side. "I'm terribly sorry about the wee lassie," he said awkwardly.

"Aye, is it no' sad?" Isabeau replied, tears springing again. "Still, they have a bonny wee boy, and he seems strong and healthy."

Dide pulled her away from the procession of mourners and kissed her in the shadow of a snow-laden yew tree. She stood quiescent in his arms for a moment, then pulled back. "Dide, what news had ye o' Bronwen in the countryside? What is the mood toward her?"

He was startled. "Ye mean the Ensorcellor's babe? There were some who supported her, o' course. We heard talk o' a move to put her on the throne, but that be only talk . . ."

"Did ye tell Lachlan?"

"O' course I told him," Dide replied irritably. "Is he no' my master? What is all this talk o' the Ensorcellor's babe?" He tried to kiss her again, his mouth rigid with desire, but she moved her face away so he could only reach her cheek.

"What are his feelings toward her?" she asked.

"What does it matter?" he answered.

She pulled out of his arms so she could look up into his face. "It matters because I fear he means harm to the babe!" she replied hotly.

"Well, she shall always be a threat while she lives, I suppose," he answered, sliding one arm about her waist. "Come, Isabeau, will ye no' kiss me?"

She submitted to his embrace again, but he could only rouse a half-hearted response from her. "Did ye find Lilanthe?" she asked, and he gave a sigh of frustration. "Nay, I did no' really look for her," he answered. "Did ye want me to?"

"I just be worried about her," Isabeau responded, and the color ran hot into her cheeks. "I mean, after she found us like that."

"Her timing was no' the best," he agreed with a chuckle. She could not look at him, and began to mumble something, but he stopped her mouth with his hand. "Do no' be saying it, Isabeau," he said roughly. "'I am no' sorry at all, except that I wish she had stayed away longer. Do no' be saying ye wish it had no' happened, or that ye should no' have done it. I've wanted nothing else since I saw ye again in Caeryla . . ."

"So what *was* ye in the square?"

"Aye, and sorry I am indeed that I could no' be rescuing ye!" he cried. "I've been thinking o' nothing else since I heard it was ye. I wish I had known ye had been captured! I saw only the glimpse o' ye and could no' get any closer, what wi' the crowds—"

Her downturned face was bitter. "Aye, throwing their rotten vegetables and stones," she said, and unconsciously she cradled her maimed hand in her other.

Dide grasped it, peeling back her glove so he could kiss the pitted scars, but she snatched her hand away and would not let him see. He tried to draw her back into his arms, but she resisted, saying, "I had best be getting back, Iseult will be wanting me. Will ye see if ye can find Lilanthe, it's worried indeed I am about her."

Dide watched her go, a troubled expression on his face, then kicked the tree with his shabby boot so snow fell in a shower onto his head and shoulders. With a curse he shook it from his crimson cap and followed after.

It was several days before Isabeau at last found a weeping greenberry tree huddled in the shelter of a wall in the garden. She leant her hand against the smooth bark and called Lilanthe's name, but there was no quiver of the bare branches in answer, no indication that the tree was anything but a tree. Softly Isabeau pleaded with the greenberry tree, stumbling to explain and reassure, but there was no response and at last she left the tree-shifter to rest dormant in peace.

THE RED STALLION

I sabeau was in the classroom at the Tower of Two Moons, her head bent over a scorched textbook, when she heard a timid knock at the door. All the pupils looked up as their teacher Daillas the Lame gave an impatient grunt and called, "Come in!"

The freckled face of one of the stablehands peered rather nervously round the heavy door. "Be Isabeau the Red here?" the boy asked. "She's wanted at the palace."

Isabeau got to her feet with a resigned shrug, the other apprentice witches looking at her enviously. They would have welcomed any interruption to their struggles with the alchemical tables, but few ever had the chance to escape their classes. Isabeau was often called away, however, to solve a problem in the infirmary or to assist the Keybearer Meghan.

Isabeau cast a longing glance at the book and Daillas said gruffly, "Take it with ye, lassie. Ye may get a chance to study it, and it be a shame indeed to interrupt your lesson when ye were so close to solving the problem."

She gave him a quick smile of thanks and tucked it under her arm as she followed the boy back through the snowy boulevard. Isabeau loved her lessons at the tower and wished she could devote more time to her studies, but it seemed someone always needed her elsewhere. Unlike the other apprentice witches her age, Isabeau found the hours at the Tower of Two Moons were never long enough. She had already progressed far beyond her classmates, thanks to her thorough grounding by Meghan of the Beasts, who had raised her. Although Meghan had rarely given her any lessons in witchcraft and witchcunning, Isabeau had been taught much about the theory and philosophy of the One Power, which her fellow apprentices were now struggling to understand. Most importantly, she had been raised to think of magic as natural and intrinsic, while the others all had to overcome a lifetime of indoctrination against the use of sorcery.

To her surprise, Isabeau was led to the stables. Although she loved horses, she had had little time to visit the mews since her arrival at Lucescere Palace. Gladly she breathed in the rich odor of horse, hay and manure, lifting her skirts clear of the straw-strewn cobblestones. In the central courtyard ostlers were rubbing down steaming horses, carrying buckets of water and vigorously cleaning tack, while a group of excited grooms surrounded a bent, bow-legged old man sitting on a barrel. At the sight of Isabeau they fell back in confusion. Once they would have shouted ribald greetings, but now that they knew Isabeau was the Banrìgh's sister, they bowed and touched their tam-o'-shanters and murmured shy courtesies.

"Riordan!" she cried. "It's grand to see ye!"

The old groom gave her a gap-toothed grin and waved away the others with a testy comment. Once the stablehands had gone back to their work, he struggled to his feet, leaning heavily on his gnarled staff. "Grand to see ye too, my lassie. Sorry indeed I am to be calling ye away from your book learning, but I thought ye might like to ken the lairds are taking out a hunting party to ride down a herd o' horses that's been running wild through yon Ban-Bharrach hills. They say a red stallion is leading the herd . . ."

Isabeau, following the old man into his quarters beside the carriage house, stopped with an exclamation.

Riordan Bowlegs looked back at her with a knowing grin on his wrinkled face. "Aye, if I remember rightly, ye often came back to Rhyssmadill wi' red hairs on your skirt after one o' your trips into the forest, no' to mention a strong smell o' horse."

The apprentice witch sat down by Riordan's fire with

a troubled expression on her face. "I wonder if it is La-sair," she murmured.

"Is that your horse?" he asked. "The one ye used to ride?"

"Aye," she answered, "though he is no' *mine*. He is a free horse."

He nodded wisely. "Ye sound like a thigearn when ye say that. They too think o' horses as friends and col-leagues, no' slaves to their will. The Rìgh's cavalry mas-ter does no' think so, though, and ye ken the Rìgh, Eà bless his heart, needs horses for his army. They ride out tomorrow at dawn wi' whips and ropes to capture them and mean to break them this week."

"I canna let them do that," Isabeau said, distressed.

"I canna see how ye can stop them," Riordan replied. "They need the horses, and the red stallion has been stealing mares from the farms for his herd and breaking into barns in search o' oats and corn. They say he is a rogue indeed."

"I must warn him," Isabeau said, getting to her feet.

He glanced at her quickly. "Obh obh! It's talking to the horses, are we?"

She nodded. "Lasair is my friend. I promised him he'd never again be subject to whip or spur."

"But that is the way o' the world, lassie," Riordan said, troubled. "The cavalry master will be angry indeed if ye stand in his way—it's a fine herd o' mares the stal-lion has gathered together and we need them for the war. I have a better thought. If ye and the stallion have a connection, why do ye no' ride out wi' us in the morn and speak to him? It's hard pickings in the mountains this winter and here we have hay and corn. Happen he'll be happy to bring the mares in and that'd save us all a might o' trouble."

Isabeau hesitated. Already an early dusk was dropping, bringing with it a flurry of sleet. She had been up since before dawn and she had no wish to ride out into the chill darkness in search of the stallion, even if she could persuade the head groom to lend her a pony. Under her arm was the book Daillas had lent her, and her inclination was to curl up with it by her fire. So she nodded and agreed, hoping Lasair would not find her arrival with a mob of men a betrayal.

Isabeau and the stallion had been friends and comrades from the time she had first seen him in the Sithiche Mountains, soon after she had set out alone from the secret valley where she had grown up. The chestnut stallion had helped her rescue Lachlan the Winged from the Awl and had carried her willingly in her desperate flight to Rhyssmadill with one third of the Key that Meghan now wore at her breast. They had always understood each other easily, and had achieved that deeper level of communication normally reserved for witches and their familiars. There was some strange link between them that kept the stallion near her, despite his hatred of men and his determination to run free.

Early the next morning, Isabeau dressed in a pair of sturdy breeches, pulled on a woolly tam-o'-shanter, and wrapped herself up in her plaid before venturing out into the freezing darkness. In the stable yard horses were neighing and prancing as the men mounted up, well pleased to be riding out of the city in search of some sport. Since the hunting of wild boar and deer had become a task of necessity rather than pleasure, many of the lairds had lost their taste for it and were looking forward to a different quarry.

Isabeau caused some comment by refusing to ride with bridle and saddle, particularly since Riordan Bowlegs had led out a feisty, high-spirited mare for her. She controlled the horse easily, however, whickering in her ear before vaulting smoothly on her back. Some of the lairds whistled in appreciation, and Isabeau smiled and pulled off her tam-o'-shanter to bow in acknowledgment, the mare rearing in a graceful levade. They rode out of the courtyard with a clatter of hooves and trotted through the quiet city toward the Bridge of Sorrows which crossed the Ban-Bharrach River to the south. By the time they had ridden into the forest on the other side of the river, the sun was rising over the snowy hills.

Isabeau nudged her sorrel mare up beside the black

stallion of Anghus MacRuraich, the Prionnsa of Rurach, and one of Lachlan's most trusted advisers. The MacRuraich had been instrumental in the success of the Samhain rebellion and was spending the winter at Lucescere with his daughter, Fionnghal. Like many in the MacRuraich clan, Anghus had a Talent for searching, and it was his responsibility to lead the hunting party to the wild horses. Isabeau wanted to make sure she was among the first to find the herd and had already used her authority as the Banrìgh's sister to make the cavalry master promise he would not try to lasso the stallion until she had first tried to use her influence upon him.

It was long past noon when the MacRuraich at last reined his stallion to a halt. "The herd is just beyond that rise," he said softly.

The cavalry master tested the wind, then nodded. "We're downwind still, which is a bonus," he said. "Come, let us ride to the top o' the rise and see what we find there."

He nodded rather brusquely at Isabeau. "Ye may try and approach the stallion then, but I warn ye, if the herd runs, we'll be quick in pursuit, no matter your objections," he said shortly. "The Rìgh needs those horses!"

She nodded and whickered to the mare who broke into a light trot which took them rapidly to the copse of trees on the hill. From their shelter she looked down into a wide, open valley where a large herd of horses grazed. Many were the rough-coated, nimble-footed horses that had roamed these hills for many years, but here and there among them she saw the glossy hides of domesticated mares, some still with halters trailing a broken rope. A tall chestnut stallion was scraping away the snow with his forefoot to reach the thin grass below, and Isabeau's face brightened at the sight of him. She dismounted and warned the mare to keep quiet with a pat of her hand. Then she slowly began the descent into the valley, carrying with her a small sack of oats.

Lasair's head immediately lifted, and he sniffed the air with flared nostrils. Isabeau gave a welcoming whinny, and the stallion tossed his bright mane and broke into a

canter which took him round the herd of mares, urging
them closer together. She whinnied again, and he danced
a little and whinnied in response. From the copse of trees
on the slope another whinny came, and Isabeau cursed
under her breath, for she had hoped to keep her companions hidden for the time being. Lasair's head swung in
that direction, and he gave a cry of challenge, rearing
back on his hind hooves. Isabeau whickered placatingly,
moving slowly and steadily across the valley floor toward
him. He cantered back and forth, and she spoke with
him softly and confidently, slowly undoing the neck of
the sack so he could smell the oats. He came to her
willingly, pushing his nose against her breast before burying it in the sack. She made no attempt to hold him or
mount him, just told him with her voice and her mind
what she wanted him to do. He was quick to understand
there were men nearby, and his eyes rolled back and he
danced away skittishly.

Isabeau spoke on, her voice as soothing as she knew
how, her body movements slow and assured. In her
mind's eye she pictured the cozy stables, the mangers
filled with oats, the loose straw in which to roll. A few of
the mares clustered close, whickering, their ears pricked
forward. Lasair was undecided, and Isabeau had to make
many reassurances and promises before he at last lowered his head and allowed her to mount. With the herd
of mares streaming behind, they cantered across the valley to where the cavalry master and his men waited.

Many of the lairds were rather disgruntled that the
expected chase and tussle had not been necessary, but
the cavalry master was pleased, and his tone was far
more respectful on the long ride back to the city. He
had no wish to risk his horses in a gallop across rough
terrain, or any desire to spend a night out in the forests, which were still infested with bandits. Most
importantly, he reserved his respect for those who could
manage a horse, and Isabeau had more than proven herself in his eyes.

It was dark by the time they came back across the
Bridge of Sorrows, and they had to hammer on the gates

to be allowed back into the city. Lasair tossed his head nervously, and many of the mares grew skittish as the reek of the city met their nostrils. The tall, narrow houses loomed over them, almost meeting overhead in some places, and Isabeau had to exert all her will to keep the herd of wild horses from breaking and running. At last they reached the open space of the palace grounds, and the horses were herded into a large meadow where hay and fresh oats were scattered for them. The stallion's eyes rolled white as the bars of the gate slid into place, but Isabeau stayed with him, rubbing him down with a twist of hay and soothing him with her voice. At last the horses were settled for the night and, stiff, sore and tired, Isabeau was able to make her way back to the palace.

The next morning Isabeau was down at the meadow before dawn. Lasair was waiting for her by the gate, his mane and tail bright in the light of the rising sun. She rode him through the quiet garden, cantering along the boulevard. He had been pleased to see her, but as they went further away from the home meadow, he grew tense and nervy, shying at the rattle of bare twigs in the wind. She held him steady with her knees, but as the ruins of the Tower of Two Moons loomed up through the trees, he bucked and reared, tossing back his head. Isabeau was almost thrown and had to cling to the stallion's mane with both hands. He gave a terrified whinny, rearing again. She soothed him with her hand and voice, but he bolted, hooves ringing sharply on the pavement. For a while she could only cling to his back as he galloped wildly away from the ruins, while in her mind's eye she saw visions of fire and death, and felt the stallion's uncontrollable dread. *Danger!* Lasair shrieked. *Betrayal!*

At last she was able to slow his headlong gallop and direct him back toward the stable. He was trembling, his flanks flecked with foam. Isabeau made him warm mash and rubbed him down well, leaving him at last in the warmth of the stall, his head hanging down in exhaustion. Usually she looked in on the infirmary first thing every morning, but today she made her way back to the Tower instead.

"I canna understand it," she said to Meghan, sharing her morning porridge. "He had such a strong reaction to being close to the Tower. I ken horses are meant to have a strong extrasensory perception, but sixteen years have passed since the tragedy there, would he have been able to sense the fear and horror so clearly after all that time?"

"I do no' ken," Meghan answered, holding up a nut for Gitâ the donbeag to nibble. "The woodland creatures have always been my specialty, no' horses. I would ask Riordan, he spent some years in Tìreich, ye ken, and has a true Talent with horses."

"I saw it all so clearly," Isabeau mused. "There were soldiers hacking down witches, others carrying burning torches. People were running and screaming, and smoke was billowing everywhere. It was horrible! It was almost as if I was there."

"Happen horses are like people, and some have a greater sixth sense than others," Meghan suggested. "Still, it would be a rare Talent in a human to see so clearly. This be an uncommon horse indeed. I have always wanted to ken how it is he came to find ye in Aslinn when ye were sick indeed with the fever. Cloudshadow was convinced he traveled the Auld Ways, and indeed he had sense enough to take ye to the Tower o' Dreams where Cloudshadow and Brun could tend ye. I will come down today to speak with him and see if I can read his mind. Has Riordan looked in on him?"

"I do no' think so," Isabeau responded, "but I can ask him to." She finished the last of her porridge and reluctantly stood up to go. She loved Meghan's rooms in the Tower of Two Moons. The spinning wheel in the corner, the piles of books and scrolls, the crystal ball on its clawed feet, and the faded globe of the world on its wooden stand, all reminded her of the treehouse where she had grown up. Isabeau missed the serene beauty of the secret valley, where all the animals were her friends and every track and cave familiar to her. She would have liked to stay with the Keybearer, listening to her tales of the heroic past and playing with the little donbeag, but

Isabeau's day stretched before her, crammed with duties and responsibilities.

"Bide a wee, Beau," Meghan said suddenly. "I wish to talk with ye a moment." Isabeau gladly sat down again, though the old sorceress's face was creased with concern. "I am troubled in my heart about the Ensorcellor's babe," she said. Immediately Isabeau stiffened. "Ye did no' come to the meeting last night and so ye missed the latest news from the countryside. It was no' good. Ye remember Renshaw the Ruthless, the last Grand-Seeker? Well, news came in last night from Blèssem. Apparently he's gathered together an army and raised Blairgowrie against us. They have proclaimed Bronwen the true Banrìgh, and call Lachlan the Pretender. The Rìgh was in such a rage last night, I have never seen him so black and bitter."

Isabeau clenched her fingers together, fear coiled cold as an adder in her stomach. Gitâ crawled from Meghan's lap to hers, patting her wrist with his black-tipped paw and nestling his silky head into her palm. She ignored him. "Do ye think he means to harm Bronwen?" she asked harshly.

Meghan hesitated. "I do no' ken. My heart rebels at the thought that he might harm her, his own niece, but he has always hated the very thought o' her and indeed he casts dark looks at her, especially since wee Donncan was born. He thinks o' her as Maya's spawn, no' Jaspar's, and indeed she will always be a threat to him while she lives."

"But she is only a babe!"

"That does no' matter, Isabeau. Have ye forgotten all I have taught ye o' history and politics? Do no' forget Jaspar named her heir and she was proclaimed Banrìgh at his death. Banrìgh for only a few hours, it is true, but Banrìgh nonetheless. Lachlan's hold on the throne is slender indeed with the countryside torn by war and famine and the threat o' the Fairgean closer than ever. He canna afford rivals to the Crown."

"So ye think he is right to fear and hate her!" Isabeau cried.

"O' course he is right to fear her, he is Rìgh, Isabeau, and must always be thinking o' the future. Eileanan needs a strong Rìgh, and one with a secure claim to the throne. We canna afford to be fighting our own people as well as threats from without! If he canna settle such counterclaims and rebellions, Eileanan will be at war for many a long year. Nay, Isabeau, he is right to be angry."

"What will he do?" she whispered.

"First he must put down the uprising and wipe out Renshaw once and for all. The Grand-Seeker is a dangerous man indeed, and we canna afford to allow sympathy for the seekers to run unchecked. Lachlan will have to ride into Blèssem and take back Blairgowrie, a distraction we could do without at this time, for Blairgowrie lies right on the edge o' the land held by the Bright Soldiers, and we have no' the strength to be taking Blèssem back piece by piece just yet."

"I mean about the babe."

Meghan sighed. "What the young fool should do is keep Bronwen by his knee and treat her kindly, raise her to love him so that she would never want to stand against him. She and Donncan would grow up together, and happen they would grow into love and be married, then any dispute over the throne be laid to rest, for they would rule together. But I fear Lachlan is no' a man to see so clearly. He has always had a bitter, impatient temper and his hatred o' Maya is so deep, so profound, I canna see him laying aside his prejudices so easily."

"What am I to do?" Isabeau whispered.

Meghan reached out her thin, gnarled hand and patted Isabeau's knee. "Watch her well and keep her safe, my dear, it is all ye can do. I will speak to Lachlan and remind him that any misfortune to befall the babe would always be suspect and would turn many against him who would otherwise support his rule. He is no' entirely a fool and has much to occupy him these next few years. Once the country lies easy under his hand, he will no' fear her so much."

Isabeau nodded and gave the velvety fur of the donbeag a final stroke before passing him back to Meghan.

"I must go," she said. "My students in herb lore will be waiting and I have no' yet looked in on the infirmary. What time shall I meet ye at the stables?"

"I have much to do today," the Keybearer replied. "Make it just before sunset, for I have to be at the palace soon after anyway." Isabeau nodded and hurried away, much troubled in her heart.

She made her way back to her rooms to gather up her herb bag, hurrying through the palace halls which were as always thronged with people. Her gait hastened as she reached the upper corridor, for she could hear Bronwen wailing in distress. She swung open the door and halted in shock on the threshold. The Rìgh stood inside, scowling angrily, holding the baby awkwardly above a deep bowl of water, one hand gripping her neck so tightly the flesh bulged between his fingers. Water dripped from her naked limbs all over the floor. The golden red light of the leaping flames played over her scaled body making her gleam opal and mother-of-pearl and sharply defining her delicate, flowing fins. Bronwen twisted her head toward the door, recognizing Isabeau's step, and the young witch could clearly see the gills fluttering just below her ear. Her mouth was wide open and roaring, her whole face wrinkled in distress, her eyes squeezed shut.

"What are ye doing?" Isabeau cried.

"Seeing if my memory served me well," Lachlan snarled. "I thought I had no' been mistaken at Samhain! See, she is clearly a Fairge, this niece o' mine. This is the babe they wish to place on the throne, this black-blooded *uile-bheist*!" His fingers tightened and Bronwen screamed louder, her scrunched-up face red as beet.

Isabeau flew across the room and tried to seize the baby, but Lachlan would not release her.

"This is the babe they wish to rule the land!" he cried, shaking her. "For this, they would disinherit me and my laddic?"

Isabeau managed to wrest the screaming child from him, clutching her to her breast. Lachlan picked up the scepter from the table, the Lodestar blazing white, and held it before him like a sword. "Keep her away from me," he said through clenched teeth. "By the Centaur's Beard, keep that *uile-bheist* away from me and my son!"

Once he was gone, Isabeau sank down into her chair, wrapping the wailing child in a warm shawl and soothing her with rhythmic pats. Fear held her throat closed so she could hardly breathe. The soft sound of the door opening made her jerk her head up in fear. It was only Sukey, though, hurrying back inside with her arms full of linen, her pretty, apple-cheeked face pink and rather anxious.

"Where have ye been?" Isabeau asked harshly. "What made ye leave the babe all alone?"

"It was the Rìgh, my lady. He sent me off to run an errand for him and said he'd mind the babe while I was gone. I did no' want to leave her, men never knowing wha' to do wi' a babe, but he insisted." She hesitated, then said stumblingly, "I be sorry, my lady, if I did wrong, but he was so insistent, and he was in such a temper I dared no' argue but just tried to be quick as I could."

"His Highness was in a temper?" Isabeau asked carefully.

"Black as thunder, he were, my lady," Sukey answered earnestly. "Prowling about as he does and clutching the scepter so tightly I feared the hilt would break. And the babe were bawling her wee heart out, bless her soul."

Bronwen stirred, rubbing her closed eyes with tiny fists and making a whimper of protest. Isabeau stroked the baby's damp, soft hair and tried to keep her voice level as she thanked the maid and dismissed her. Despite the warmth of the fire, she was cold and huddled her shoulders into her plaid. She would never leave Bronwen again, she vowed, rocking her. From now on, the baby banprionnsa would go everywhere she did.

Isabeau made her way to the mews just as the sun was settling down behind the tall rampart; the baby was on her back, wrapped in a shawl Isabeau had tied over her shoulder. She could hear Lasair's shrill whinnies and the stamp of his hooves on the cobblestones as she entered the dim stables.

Riordan Bowlegs was leaning over the side of the stallion's stall, smoking a long pipe. He looked up as she came in and gave her a gap-toothed smile. "How are ye yourself, Red?" he asked. "Looking a wee pale. Did ye no' sleep well last night?"

"I be well, Riordan, and ye?" Isabeau answered, mustering a smile.

"Och, I be right dandy," he replied. "Fine horse ye have here, though nervy and bad-tempered. He will no' let anyone near him, no' even myself, and ye ken I learnt the horse-whispering from a thigearn himself."

Isabeau nodded absent-mindedly, and the old groom went on, "He almost killed one o' the lads today when he tried to slip a halter on him. We wanted to check his hooves, but there was no getting near him. He just about kicked the back wall, and puir Owen got a right nasty blow to the stomach."

"Is he all right?" Isbeau asked, whickering to the red stallion to quieten him as he reared and tested his weight against the wooden wall.

"Aye, he'll be just grand. Lucky he's a nimble lad and got out o' the way fast enough. The head groom is no' happy, though, he says all the neighing and rearing is disturbing the other horses and he fears for his men."

Isabeau laid the baby down in a nest of hay and slipped into the stall, whickering reassuringly. Lasair danced nervously, backing away from her. "He does no' like being confined to the stall," she answered. "And he has no desire to be harnessed by a strange man."

"Ye had best keep him calm," Riordan said, "for the stable master will no' allow him to distress the other horses."

Isabeau nodded and ran her hands over the nervous stallion, soothing him and telling him all was well. He leant against her, shoving his head urgently against her breast. The sound of a halting step on the cobblestones made him start and back away nervously, and Isabeau stroked his nose gently with her hand.

"So this is the one?" Meghan said, coming to stand next to Riordan.

Immediately Lasair reared, eyes rolling white, hooves threshing the air. Isabeau staggered back and fell as the stallion bucked wildly, smashing his hooves into the wooden wall behind him. Again and again he plunged, and deep in Isabeau's mind, she heard him scream: *It is ye! False, treacherous witch! Breaker o' faith!*

He threw his weight against the wall, then spun and kicked the door. The wood splintered and broke. Again and again he kicked out with his powerful hindquarters, until the door was smashed into fragments. Then, with a wild toss of his mane, he leapt over Isabeau and out of the stall. He reared over Meghan, hooves flailing the air as she scrambled back in shock and fear, Gitâ shrieking from her shoulder. Foam flew from his bared teeth, and he neighed in resounding challenge, sending the other horses whinnying and plunging. Isabeau scrambled to her feet and ran to catch his head, but he was bucking and rearing so wildly she could not get near him. He kicked out viciously; but with a cry, the old sorceress had fallen. He pawed the air over her prostrate body and would have brought his heavy hooves pounding down upon her if Riordan had not seized a long pitchfork and menaced him with it. In utter shock and dismay, Isabeau called his name and tried to get near him to calm him, but the stallion leapt away from the sharp tines of the pitchfork, eyes staring white, and galloped down the stable. One of the grooms tried to stand in his way but the stallion knocked him over and fled out into the courtyard. Isabeau could hear screams and frantic neighs as he churned through the yard.

"Lasair!" she cried despairingly. "Whatever can be wrong?"

Far across the mountains, curled in a nest of her own hair, Ishbel the Winged stirred in her sleep. "Khan'gharad?" she murmured. Slowly her eyes opened and she looked blankly about the tower room. Gray stone curved about her, sculpted round the tall windows with the delicate shape of single-petalled roses. Impossibly long strands of silver hair floated about her. "Khan'gharad?" she said more firmly.

Deep in her mind she heard a stifled cry of hatred and fear. *False, treacherous witch! Breaker o' faith!*

Ishbel sat bolt upright. "Khan'gharad!" she called. "Where are ye, my love?"

She caught only a fading echo of that frantic voice, but her blue eyes lit with ardor. "Wait, Khan'gharad!" she cried. "I'm coming!"

"Meghan!" Isabeau cried and knelt by the crumpled body of the sorceress. Meghan sighed faintly, and one hand groped for her heart, then she slid into unconsciousness again. White as whey, Isabeau called desperately for help and the grooms came running. A wet cloth failed to revive the old witch, and Isabeau was distraught to see a red patch growing on the shoulder of her dress. Meghan had been stabbed in the heart by Maya the Ensorcellor during the Samhain rebellion and had only been saved from death by Tòmas's powers. The jolt of her fall must have pulled apart the lips of the slowly healing wound.

The anxious donbeag crooned over Meghan as she was carried to the Tower on a stretcher made from an old door. Isabeau was hanging over her in distress, the baby clutched tightly in her arms.

Tòmas came and laid his hands upon the old sorceress, and the bleeding stopped, the lips of the wound slowly sealing over again. He shook his head, though, and said in his solemn way, "She is auld and has no' much strength. I do no' know how many more times I can heal her. She should lie quietly and rest and try to restore her strength."

Isabeau wept silently, for she knew Meghan would never submit to lying quietly in her bed. Lachlan and Iseult had hurried to the witch's side as soon as they had heard she had fallen, and the Rìgh turned on Isabeau as soon as the young Tòmas had left the room. "Ye cause nothing but trouble and strife!" he cried. "Ye should

never have let Meghan near such a savage creature as
that horse o' yours! Ye think o' nothing but yourself."

Isabeau was too distressed to defend herself, but Iseult
uttered a quiet reproof. Lachlan would not listen. The
shock of Meghan's last encounter with Gearradh, the
goddess of death, was too fresh in his mind and he was
tired and bitterly disappointed with the latest news from
the countryside. Isabeau's protection of the little banprionnsa was an unacknowledged goad to his anger, and he
lashed out at her in sullen frustration.

"The horse shall be shot!" he cried, slamming one fist
into his hand. "He is a danger to us all! Meghan could
have been killed, and six grooms were injured in his subduing! I canna allow him to rampage through the stables
any longer. I'll have him put to death in the morning!"
He turned and left the room, slamming the door behind him.

Meghan turned her head, muttering in her sleep, and
Iseult rose to follow her husband. "I'm sorry, Isabeau,
but indeed it would be for the best," she said. "Truly he
is a savage and unpredictable horse."

"I do no' understand it," Isabeau cried, but her twin's
mind was already turning back to her sleeping son, and
she smiled a little wearily and left the room.

Isabeau dropped her head into her arms and wept, so
tired and upset she could not think straight. A soft touch
on her arm made her jump, and she raised her head to
see Meghan staring at her with dazed black eyes. "A
most strange and unaccountable horse," the sorceress
whispered. "Almost I remember . . . he seems . . ."

"Hush, Meghan," Isabeau whispered, scrubbing her
hot eyes. "Ye must rest."

"I seem to remember . . . but surely he canna be . . ."

Isabeau lifted her guardian's head and gave her some
soothing poppy syrup to sip. "Sleep, Meghan," she said
in a choked voice. "Ye must rest and get well. We need
ye."

The sorceress looked as if she was going to say more,
but then her wrinkled eyelids slowly closed and she
sighed, slipping again into sleep.

*   *   *

The whore slipped out the back door of the brothel, a shawl wrapped close about her head, and struggled down the back alley, her boots sinking deep into the mire. Despite all her efforts, she could not keep her skirts from dragging in the thick mud. Flaring her nostrils in distaste, she toiled on, stepping when she could on the broken crates and sacks that littered the ground. Deeper into the maze of stinking alleys she went, down into the slums that clustered like a suppurating sore on the lip of the cliff. The stench of refuse, urine and excrement almost made her gag, but she pushed on grimly, holding the shawl close about her face.

At last she came to a warehouse, built so close under the surge of the waterfall that the spray dampened her face. Casting a quick glance about her, she pushed open the door and slipped inside. Within was a long room, piled high with trash and treasure from the back streets and sewers. There was a strange smell, like long-dead mice, mingled with a sharper scent, like pungent bay leaves. From the shadows an old man came shuffling, his hands clasped high before him, his bleary eyes peering to make out her face hidden behind the fold of her shawl.

"And wha' can I be finding for ye, missus? A bolt o' cloth, hardly mildewed at all, or a pot for the porridge? A stool for your weary bones, or a spindle for the spinning?"

"Ye know what it is I want, auld man," the whore said, and at the husky tones of her voice, he cringed back.

"Aye, aye, I ken, I ken wha' it is ye want. Cantrips and curses, spells and soothsaying, that be all they want, the fine ladies. Philtres and potions, glamouries and ghost-raising, that be all they want, the fine ladies."

She followed his bent muttering form through a dusty, cobwebbed shop, piled high with broken furniture and damaged goods, to a cupboard pushed in one back corner. Casting a furtive glance about him, the old man opened the wardrobe door and ushered the whore inside, closing the door behind her.

She felt forward with her hand, found the secret catch

and lifted it, her heart beating rapidly. The back of the
wardrobe slid noiselessly aside and she stumbled forward
in the darkness, climbing a narrow flight of stairs, steep
as a ladder. The secret door closed instantly behind her.

Above was a long, overheated room hung with rich
silks and furnished as richly as any merchant's house.
A gilded candelabra hung from the ceiling, while bright
tapestries covered every wall. The woman made her way
forward, lifting her mud-stained skirts clear of the intricately woven carpet.

"Look at ye, tracking mud and filth into my fine
house," a high, petulant voice said. "Obh, obh! Could
ye no' have left your boots at the door?"

From a low chaise-longue pushed against the wall, a
gaudily dressed dwarf hopped to his feet and came fuss-
ing around the whore, insisting she remove her caked
boots and brush the mud from her skirts down the stairwell. He came no higher than her waist and wore a crimson doublet slashed with purple and green. His head was
far too large for his body, the effect exaggerated by a
huge round cap of purple velvet embellished with bha-
nais feathers. With the matt white skin of his face dusted
with no more than a few fine, fair hairs, he looked like
an absurd child.

He reclined back on the chaise-longue, his short legs
taking up barely half of its velvet-upholstered length, and
looked her over with a lewd glance. "So it be Majasma
the Mysterious come to visit her auld friend, the Wizard
Wilmot, master o' the magical mysteries. Wha' is it this
time, my bonny?"

The whore sat on the chair opposite, letting the shawl
drop from her head. The light fell full on her face, revealing its alien cast—the flat nose with its flaring nostrils,
the thin, almost lipless mouth. Her pale skin was moist
and had a iridescent shimmer like mother-of-pearl. One
cheek was marred with a fine spider's web of scars. She
cast the dwarf a scornful glance from her pale eyes and
lifted one webbed hand to her cheek.

"Another spell o' glamourie to wrap your fair features
in youthful charm, my bonny? To hide the cruel scars

that mar your perfection?" He gave a high-pitched chuckle. "Do your lovers cringe at the sight o' ye, my bonny?"

"No' as much as all who see ye, my wee manikin," she replied harshly. "Ye ken why I am here, let us cease these pleasantries and get down to business."

"Aye," he answered with another shrill giggle. "Show me your gold and we will begin to spin ye the spell."

"What do ye need gold for, Willie the Wee?" She waved one hand at the richness that surrounded them. "Ye have a house stuffed with every imaginable luxury, ye wear the finest silks and the rarest perfumes and drink only the best whiskey. What more could ye possibly want?"

A look of petulant anger screwed up his hairless face and he cried shrilly, "Ye want my wizardry, ye must pay the price!"

The whore pulled a small, jingling bag from her basket and tossed it to him with a scornful gesture. He caught it nimbly, and at once began to count it into his tiny hand. Twice he counted it, and then he snapped his fingers and the coins disappeared.

"It is no' enough, my bonny," he said with a lewd sneer. "I find the price o' my expertise has risen. Times are hard in Lucescere, and the winter has been long."

"We agreed on the price!" she cried, and he answered with another chuckle, "That was then, this is now, my bonny. Pay the price or find yourself another spell-mongerer."

Reluctantly she fished another small bag out of the basket, and he counted the coins with glee, tossing them between his pudgy little fingers and letting them disappear one by one. Only then did he swing his legs round and begin to rummage in a chest by his side. She leant forward and watched what he did intently, and he turned his gaudy body so she could not see.

With another snap of his fingers he extinguished the candles so only the four-branched candelabra on the table between them was still alight. The light of the black and white candles danced over the paraphernalia arranged on the table's gilded surface. There was a three-dimensional circle and pentagram, a brazier of odd-smelling incense, bowls of water and sea salt, an urn of ashes, piles of crystals and colored stones, and bottles of dried dragon's blood, powdered herbs and desiccated insects.

When he turned to face the whore, the dwarf held in his arms a fat book bound with leather so old it was cracking and discolored. He propped it on a stand held ready for it, his eyes gleaming with excitement, and held out his childlike hand for the whore to reluctantly pass him one of her silky black hairs. Just as reluctantly she unbuttoned her dress and drew it down over her arms until she was naked to the waist. He glanced at her, giggled obscenely, and licked his lips. Swaying back and forth, muttering strings of rhymes, he threw pinches from many different bottles and jars into the brass bowl, then waved his hands over it. Foul-smelling smoke billowed up, and he threw the disgusting mixture over the whore's face and body.

Although she had braced herself for it, she still gagged and choked, wiping her face and torso clean with a look of distaste. The wizard chortled, rocking back and forth still, the feathers on his absurd hat nodding. At last her skin was clean and she held out one imperious hand for the mirror.

The gills at her neck and the little frills of fin that ran from her elbow to wrist were both gone, and her face was free of scarring. Subtly her features and figure had altered so she looked both younger and more human. She nodded her head abruptly and pulled her clothes about her, buttoning her dress again with rapid fingers. The dwarf stared at her with undisguised lust, muttering to himself once again.

Although she was clearly anxious to be gone from this hot, crimson room, she hesitated before she rose, fingering the handle of her basket. "I have heard tell, Wilmot the Wizard, that ye can cast curses as well as spells," she said, her voice more conciliatory than it had been since her arrival.

He laughed and twisted the many rings on his fingers.

"Ye ken curses are like chickens, my bonny, they come home to roost. If Wilmot the Wizard is to take such a risk, it's a high price he wants, a high price indeed."

"Name it," she said harshly.

He giggled. "It be ye yourself," he answered, raking her with such a lascivious glance there was no mistaking his meaning.

She drew back, making no attempt to hide her distaste. "Ye canna be serious," she replied, lip curling.

The dwarf scowled like a sulky child, and said, "Ye think I jest, my bonny? I jest no'. If ye wish me to cast curses for ye, it is more than gold I want. As ye say, what need have I o' gold? I be one o' the richest men in Lucescere, with so many whores to buy my spells o' glamouries and so many fine ladies anxious to ken their futures. It is no' more gold I want from ye, Maya the Ensorcellor, but your own white body. Ye see, I ken who ye are, my bonny. Ye think me a mere bairn and a bagatelle, but I am the Wizard Wilmot and I see what other blind fools canna see. It will please me mightily to cast my seed into the MacCuinn's furrow."

Maya gave an involuntary jerk, unable to prevent the blanching of her lips and cheeks.

The wizard chortled with amusement, sliding off the chaise-longue to come and press his squat body against her legs. "Aye, indeed. Ye canna tell me the new Rìgh will no' pay highly to ken where his brother's wife is hiding—more gold than ye can earn even with your fair face and your songs o' love. Ye see, I ken more about ye than ye kent, my proud lady o' the sea. So if ye wish me to keep my knowledge to myself, ye will open your legs to me as ye open them to any young laird with a pouch o' gold. Aye, and ye will moan and sob for me too and tell me I be the finest lover ye ever had." As he spoke, he scrabbled under her skirt, stroking her legs with his hot little hands.

Maya was rigid, her face as white as chalk, her eyes downcast. "And if I lie with ye, will ye cast this curse for me? A curse that shall no' fail?"

"Aye, I'll cast the curse," he sniggered. "I will need a

lock o' hair or a scale o' their skin or a paring o' fingernail, do ye understand? It needs to be part o' their living
flesh for the curse to work."

She shook her head involuntarily. "I canna get anything like that," she replied. "Do ye no' understand, this
is my bitterest enemy I wish to curse. I canna come that
close to him!"

"Ye shall have to if ye wish me to cast a curse o' any
power," he said. "If ye canna manage a tuft o' hair or a
turd from his chamberpot, some clothing still warm from
his flesh, or dust from his footprints, or even the shape o'
his sleeping form in his bedclothes, is better than naught,
though I canna ensure the curse will stick that way. The
more ye bring me, the better the curse, understand?"
She nodded, straining away from him.

He squeezed her inner thigh, saying sharply, "Ye will
moan for me, do ye understand? Ye will be hot and wet
and willing, and ye will cry my name."

"Cast me a curse o' power that will shrivel their house
forever and I'll do whatever ye wish," she replied coldly.
"Though if I am to pay such a high price, there is one
more thing I want."

His rosebud mouth pouted and he stepped back.
"What is it?" he asked sulkily.

"I wish ye to teach me how ye cast such spells and
glamouries," Maya said cajolingly, casting a longing look
at his fat book of spells.

He laughed mockingly. "So ye can cast the spell o'
illusion yourself, ye mean? No' likely, my fair lady! I
would soon be out o' business if I revealed my secrets
to my clients. Besides, ye need to have the talent to cast
such things. The craft is o' no use if ye do no' have
the cunning."

She frowned. "I do no' understand."

"The spells and incantations are just noise and babble
if ye do no' have the power," he said dismissively. "They
focus the will and name the desire precisely, which is
what ye need if such things are to work. Yet without the
Talent, they are just words. The Talent must be born
in ye."

He did not notice the sudden gleam in Maya's ice-blue eyes as he wrapped the great book up and slid it back into the chest. "I see," she said and gathered her mud-stained skirts up in her hand.

He looked up at her, his ungainly head held to one side. "Till we meet again, my lady," he said. "I look forward to it very much."

"Till we meet again," Maya replied meekly.

It was the darkest hour of the night, several hours before dawn, when Isabeau slipped out of one of the back doors and made her way through the kitchen gardens. She carried the baby banprionnsa on her back and two bulging satchels in her arms. She was dressed for traveling in breeches and boots, with her tam o'shanter crammed over her curls.

Two little dogs, flop-eared and skewbald, came running to her heels, yelping in excitement.

"Sssh, Spot, sssh, Blackie," she whispered. "Ye canna come with me. Stay here with Latifa." They whined and sank down, wriggling after her on their bellies.

Isabeau said sternly, "No. Stay." They obeyed, the stumps of their tails sinking. She patted their heads as best she could with her laden arms, then left them, a little ache in her breast.

She hid the satchels behind the snow-domed beehives, then made her way through the dark park. The light of the two moons shone brightly on the white lawn, the shadows of the yew trees black and impenetrable. She made her way to the small garden where the bare branches of the weeping greenberry tree dangled above the frozen surface of a small pool.

"Lilanthe," she whispered. "Can ye hear me?"

There was no response. She knelt before the tree. "I'm so sorry, Lilanthe, I never meant to hurt ye," she said, as she had said every time she had come. "He means naught to me—it was the spiced ale, and being so lonely, and jealous of Iseult, who has everything now. Please forgive me. If I had kent . . ." Her voice trailed off, then she groped within the pouch at her waist and pulled out a long snake of plaited hair which glinted red even in the colorless light of the moons.

"I have to leave, Lilanthe. I wish ye could come with me but I canna wait for ye to wake in the spring. It's too dangerous . . ." Carefully she hid the long braid within the tree-shifter's branches. "So ye can find me," she whispered and gave the smooth bark a soft caress. Then she rose, dusted her knees free of snow, and made her silent way back through the silver and black parkland.

The mews were dark, and the stable-lad on guard in the main stables slept in the straw. Seeing as easily in the darkness as any elven cat, Isabeau made her way to the stall where Lasair was confined. He was hobbled and harnessed so tightly he could barely move, his head hanging listlessly. She gave a low whicker as she approached and his ears pricked forward. She put down the satchels and laid her hand over the velvety bridge of his nose to warn him to keep quiet. He nudged her urgently, almost unbalancing her.

Within moments she had unbuckled his halter and hobbles. He gave a restless shudder, but followed her quietly out of the stall. One of the other horses gave a questioning hurrumph, but Isabeau quietened it with a soft reassurance, waiting until the stable lad had sighed and turned in his sleep before going on. She had to heave open the stable door to allow Lasair's great bulk through, and the sound of the wood grating on the stone woke the boy. She heard him make an exclamation, and she urged Lasair outside, crashing the door closed behind him. Rapidly she slid a rake through the handles, locking the stable-lad in, before leading Lasair away as quickly as she could.

Within moments the stable hand was banging on the door and calling the alarm. Isabeau muttered a curse and clambered on to Lasair's back, using a garden seat as a mounting block. The satchels flopped against the stallion's withers as she urged him into a trot, and she had to hold them with one hand to keep them from sliding off.

It had been in Isabeau's mind to slip out through the

secret gateway in the back wall of the palace grounds and disappear into the mountains behind, so she urged Lasair deeper into the garden. She had hoped to get away without raising an alarm, however, and so was dismayed when she heard the clamor of bells behind her. It was unlikely the stable-hands had any idea who had slipped into the stalls and stolen a horse, or that the thief carried with her the Banprionnsa Bronwen NicCuinn, but they seemed determined to catch her nonetheless. And since it was a crisp, cold night, and Lasair's hoofprints were clear behind them, black against the moonlit snow, Isabeau soon had the palace guard close on her trail.

Lasair broke into a smooth gallop that took him rapidly through the park. Isabeau tried to urge him up the side promenade toward the secret gateway, but he veered deeper into the garden. When she saw soldiers running down the walkways, carrying flaring torches, she thought he was wise and gave him his head. He twisted through a copse of winter-bare trees, leapt over a hedge and cantered through a small parterre garden where his hooves would leave no trail. She saw they were coming near the Tower of Two Moons and clung tighter with her knees, afraid he would have another attack of the jitters at the proximity of the ghost-haunted ruins. He turned, though, and sped along the tall, thorny hedge that marked the boundary of the maze at the heart of the garden. There was a shout, and Isabeau saw horsemen were racing close behind. Some carried bright torches, while others had crossbows already armed and lifted. Fear flashed through her, and she urged Lasair on desperately. He leapt another hedge, spun on his haunches and bounded through the archway that led into the enchanted maze. Isabeau could only cling on desperately.

The maze of hedges had been planted many years before to conceal and protect the sacred tarn at its center, the Pool of Two Moons. Isabeau, Iseult and Lachlan had penetrated its labyrinthine heart on Samhain Day to rescue the Lodestar and restore its waning powers in the pool. Isabeau had only been able to crack the secrets of the maze with the help of *The Book of Shadows,* an

ancient and magical book that contained within it all the
lore of the witches. Although she had memorized the
intricate twists and turns of the hedge-lined paths that
day, she doubted she would be able to remember them
in the panic of flight and with every landmark masked
by the darkness.

The stallion seemed to know exactly where to go, however. Without slacking his pace, he wove his way between
the tall hedges, while their pursuers fell back in baf-
flement. Occasionally they heard shouting or saw the
light of flaming torches through the yew branches, but
as they worked their way deeper and deeper into the
heart of the maze, the pursuit grew further and further
behind.

At last they trotted out of the tall corridors of yew
and into the garden that surrounded the Pool of Two
Moons. At one end was the dark, round bulk of the
observatory, its dome black against the paling sky.

"The maze will no' protect us," Isabeau whispered,
leaning down to stroke the stallion's damp flank. "It has
only thrown the soldiers off, but others ken its secrets.
They will come in search o' us."

Lasair whickered softly in reply, then deep in her mind
Isabeau heard him say, *Trust me.* He moved forward,
hooves crunching the snow, then climbed the broad steps,
halting just beyond the arched colonnade that circled the
pool. He followed the circle round until he came to the
north-facing arch, and there he waited, muzzle raised to
sniff the wind. Isabeau sat wearily, the weight of the child
heavy on her back, her heart still troubled with misgivings. The sky along the horizon was brushed with the
first unfurling of color, while the shapes of trees and
hedges were lifting from the amorphous darkness. The
stallion waited until the very moment the sun lifted over
the horizon, then bent his head and nudged his nose
against the ancient, pockmarked stone. Only then did he
step through.

To her amazement Isabeau saw the long neck and
proudly raised head of the stallion disappear into a silvery haze that materialized between the pillars. Before

she could do more than gasp, the glinting, hazy curtain had passed over her with a tingling chill that sent electric shocks down every nerve fiber. Shot through with fiery green, the silvery haze was all about her. Isabeau could only cling to his back as the stallion cantered into a tunnel of gauzy fire. Although she could see the dim shapes of trees through the glimmer, they seemed to blur with every step the stallion took. She heard a rushing in her ears and her whole body stung and twitched. Only the warmth of the stallion beneath her and the sweet weight on her back stopped her senses from reeling.

Behind her she heard a strange shrieking and looked over her shoulder to see the shredded shapes of ghosts racing after them. She screamed, and the baby gave a long, wailing cry. The stallion stretched his neck and galloped faster, and the ghosts fell back, faces contorted in utter grief and horror, their plaintive cries lingering in Isabeau's brain. Dark, hunched shadows fell over their path, but the stallion leapt over them. Something clutched at Isabeau's ankle with bitter-cold claws, but she kicked it away frantically and heard a harsh cry as the shadowy figure tumbled down. Terror pounded through her blood, but she could do nothing but crouch low against the stallion's neck as he raced along. Below them, the silvery-green path heaved and palpitated, while the shimmering walls and ceiling shook and rustled as if disturbed by a constant, restless wind. Dimly she saw hills blur into forest, and trees blur into craggy mountains. There was a circle of blazing pillars ahead. She saw a tall, pale figure with a long mane of white hair raise a three-eyed face towards them. Lasair did not slow, however; he galloped through with a ringing neigh, though Isabeau turned and stared back with a name unuttered on her lips.

The path grew darker, and the hunched, shadowy shapes lurched towards them more often. Only Lasair's fleetness and nimbleness kept them from being dragged down. Beyond the glimmering curtain of silver fire, Isabeau could see the sharp points of mountains rearing all about them. The pain in her joints and nerve endings grew fiercer; she could barely keep her fingers clenched in the stallion's mane or her legs gripping his heaving sides.

There was a sudden, unexpected whoosh of sound, and absolute terror flooded through her, weakening her bowels and sending every muscle into spasm. Overhead a great, golden-scaled creature flew on widespread wings as thin and translucent as stretched silk. Isabeau screamed, and the creature swept down so that the wind of its passing blasted her face. The angular head turned and a golden eye—larger than the stallion itself—stared at them, its pupil like a pit of blackness. Isabeau screamed and kept on screaming. With a lissom twist, the dragon spread its wings and soared back into the sky. Isabeau's whole body slackened and she would have fallen from the stallion's back if he had not swerved to follow the arc of her body. Somehow she managed to cling on, then the path was tumbling down and they went with it, green sparks hissing from the stallion's hooves.

TO BE A RÌGH AT WAR

It wanted only a few hours to midnight and only a few days to the end of winter. Out in the palace gardens the many campfires had winked out as the Rìgh's army settled down for their night's rest. Most of the palace was sleeping but lights still blazed from the windows of the top floor. The long conference room was crowded with the Rìgh's councillors, the blue-kilted general staff of the Yeomen of the Guards, and all the prionnsachan and lairds gathered in Lucescere.

Anghus MacRuraich was seated close to the Rìgh's chair, the black wolf that had once been his sister Tabithas lying at his feet, his young daughter leaning against her shaggy side. Next to him sat Linley MacSeinn, the Prionnsa of Carraig, with his son Douglas on a stool at his feet. Iain and Elfrida sat together on a small couch on the other side, while Dughall MacBrann reclined in a satin-upholstered chair on the Rìgh's right hand, playing with his silver-embossed wand.

The thickset figure of Alasdair MacThanach, Prionnsa of Blèssem and Aslinn, stood before the fire, feet planted firmly, square hands thrust through his belt. As usual, his loud voice dominated the room, easily drowning out the speech of the others. "When are we going to drive those blaygird Bright Soldiers out o' the countryside for good?" he boomed. "Every strike we've made against them has been successful, but I canna help noticing it is only lower Rionnagan that we have freed so far. What about Blèssem? I've been away from my land for nigh on six months now!"

"What about Carraig?" the MacSeinn cried. "Six years

I've been in exile, MacThanach, and no' a move have we made to regain my lands!"

"Peace, my lairds!" Lachlan leant forward, hands outspread. "Ye ken we can only fight one battle at a time. We may have driven the Bright Soldiers out o' Rionnagan but they occupy all o' Aslinn, Blèssem and Clachan, and control the river and every major road. We are all here tonight to plan the summer campaign, but we canna fight the Tìrsoilleirean if we fight among ourselves."

When the prionnsachan had quieted down, maps were flung out across the table, the Rìgh using his scepter to weigh down one end, the MacThanach moving his great tankard of ale to weigh down the other. "As ye can see, we are beset on all sides," Lachlan said. "Bright Soldiers are still pouring in through Arran and Aslinn, and I have heard another fleet o' galleons has sailed into the Berhtfane, with near six hundred men on board. We have had no news from Ravenshaw or Tìreich, so do no' ken whether they have also been attacked from the coast. If they have no', we may be able to raise support for our armies there, but if they too are under duress, there will be little they can do to help us."

"We have another problem," the quartermaster said. "The forests are still infested with bandits, who attack our supply wagons as well as those o' the enemy. We canna be planning a strong push into Blèssem and Clachan if we canna secure our supply routes. Ye ken the NicHilde has told us the Bright Soldiers burn the fields and barns in their wake."

A pained expression crossed the MacThanach's face, and he cast an imploring glance at Elfrida who nodded gravely, and said, "Aye, what they canna use or carry, they'll burn. The only way to prevent it is to drive them so quickly they have no' got time to burn too thoroughly."

Iseult nodded gravely. "To triumph in war, starve your enemy," she said.

"All very good advice," the MacThanach said, annoyed, "but it seems it is us who are starving, Your Highness. Tell me how we can cause the blaygird Bright Soldiers to go hungry and I'll thank ye for the advice."

"We have no' got the men to be subduing the outlaws," Lachlan said, troubled. "They have run wild in the forests for years now and ken them far better than we do."

"Can we no' offer the outlaws amnesty?" the MacRuraich said. "Were no' many o' them turned out o' their crofts by the Red Guards or charged with plotting against the Ensorcellor's rule?"

"Some, it is true, but most are thieves and murderers, and rightly accused," the MacThanach protested.

"It would be one way o' swelling the ranks o' our armies," the MacRuraich argued. "True, they're rough and undisciplined, but I am sure many o' them would rather be pardoned for the past and given a chance to start afresh than be hanged as outlaws."

"No' a bad idea," Lachlan said. "If they steal or murder while under our command, we can punish them then. Cameron, make a note! We shall send out messengers to every village and town offering to pardon outlaws and bandits as long as they present themselves to our army for active service."

The chancellor nodded, scribbling industriously. Lachlan paced the floor thoughtfully, then said, "Make it clear the amnesty is also extended to all former Red Guards, Cameron. Any we can swing to our cause will make our job o' subduing the countryside that much easier, and we could do with their military experience."

Daillas the Lame said, "Is that wise, Your Highness? The Red Guards have spent the last sixteen years burning witches and fairies. Surely we canna be pardoning their wicked crimes so easily?"

There was a mutter of agreement from the other witches, and Gwilym the Ugly cried, "They never showed any mercy to the witches, why should we offer it to them?"

Both Daillas and Gwilym had suffered cruel torture at the hands of the Awl and were crippled as a result, so a murmur of sympathy arose at their words. Iseult leant forward and said, "Why blame the common soldier for the misdeeds o' their leaders? Many were just following orders, and indeed that is a trait ye should encourage in your troopers. If we offer them pardon, they may tip the balance toward victory; otherwise they are just more power to our enemies."

They argued the point for some time, Gwilym pointing out that the Red Guards had been indoctrinated with the philosophy of the Awl for sixteen years and were unlikely to serve under a rìgh who had reinstated the Coven of Witches.

Iseult shrugged rather wearily and replied, "In that case, they are likely to join Renshaw the Ruthless at Blairgowrie anyway. Surely we should offer them an alternative? Too many have gone to swell his ranks as it is."

There was a subdued murmur, for all had heard the reports of the army the former Grand-Seeker was gathering together at Blairgowrie. The subject made the lairds uneasy, for the disappearance of Maya's child from the court had given rise to many rumors. Lachlan MacCuinn may have said the Banrìgh's sister, Isabeau the Red, had taken her to a place of safety, but many suspected a darker reason for her absence.

Lachlan flushed at the mutters but held a tight rein on his temper, saying merely, "That is one nest o' gravenings that must be cleaned out, and soon!"

"Aye," Iseult agreed. "I think it should be our first target. If we strike them hard and fast, we can prevent them from gathering too great a force."

The MacThanach frowned. He strongly disapproved of his new Banrìgh, who did not speak or act in a way he thought appropriate for a young lass. After all, she was not yet seventeen, the same age as his fourth daughter, who would never dare put forth her opinions with such boldness. "Surely we should secure the harbor and river first, Your Highness," he said gruffly. "As it stands, the Bright Soldiers can simply sail into the Berhtfane any time they wish, bringing in reinforcements and controlling the supply routes up the river."

Iseult began to say something, but he cut across her, an indulgent tone in his voice. "No' that it is no' a good idea to nip the Renshaw rebellion in the bud, Your Highness, but happen we'd best relieve the siege at Rhyssmadill first, aye?"

Most of the other lairds nodded their heads in agreement, but Iseult said clearly, "Nay, my laird. Indeed, such action would be foolish at this point."

The MacThanach stiffened, his beard bristling. "Happen ye'd best look to your babe and your spinning and leave the scheming o' war to the men," he said brusquely. "I think I know better than a mere lassie like yourself."

"How could ye?" Iseult replied. "Blèssem has been fat and peaceful for decades, and your only training the tilting at stuffed dummies with a wooden lance. I am a Scarred Warrior and have fought many a battle and won them all. The fact that ye advise us to concentrate on relieving the siege at Rhyssmadill only proves to me ye have no' thought the matter through. We should no' send more men there but tell our forces in the city to retreat."

"Retreat?" A startled cry rose up, and the MacThanach drew himself up to his full height, clearly offended.

Before he could retort, Duncan Ironfist asked curiously, "Why do ye say so, Your Highness? I too would have thought the relieving o' Rhyssmadill one o' our first priorities."

"Have ye forgotten the Fairgean?" Iseult said impatiently. "We all ken they come with the rising o' the spring tides. We should arrive on the shores o' the Berhtfane in time to fight both the Bright Soldiers and the sea-fairies. Why do we no' just let the Fairgean do our work for us?"

"What do ye mean?" someone cried, and Iseult stifled a sigh.

"The Fairgean will sweep into the firth and river as soon as they have arrived on our shores," she said. "Since the Bright Soldiers destroyed the river gates, there is nothing to keep them out. They will swarm into the city and into the surrounding countryside, killing whatever they can. Surely ye can see it would be foolish to have any o' our forces there at that time? If we retreat, the Bright Soldiers will seize the chance to consolidate their position in the city and reinforce the assault on the palace. They will then take the brunt o' the Fairgean's attack, and we can move all our forces east instead, moving to attack Blairgowrie and to relieve the siege at Dùn Eidean . . ."

The MacThanach had opened his mouth to protest, but at Iseult's final words he closed it, fingering his beard thoughtfully. Some of the plum-red color in his cheeks died away, and he said rather reluctantly, "Well, there be some sense in that."

Lachlan could not help giving a chuckle, for he knew that MacThanach was most anxious that his home city be relieved and the Bright Soldiers driven out of Blèssem. He said quickly, to hide his amusement, "And even better, we show the people that no defiance will be tolerated! For us to bring peace to the land, we must have the unconditional support o' the countryside; while we allow seekers to roam the land, spreading vile rumors and causing disquiet, we shall never have peace."

So it was decided. The Rìgh's army would move east, striking deep into the heart of Blèssem, while Lachlan's supporters would be ordered to withdraw from the river and coast. After long discussion, Dide the Juggler and Cathmor the Nimble were given the dangerous job of riding for Dùn Gorm to spread the news. Dide had been close-lipped and gloomy since Hogmanay, and he seized upon the chance of action with disturbing alacrity.

Lachlan looked at him in some perturbation, saying, "But Dide, would ye no' rather ride with me for Blairgowrie?"

"Ye ken I be friends wi' all the lads in Dùn Gorm," Dide replied. "Many times we've worked together to rescue a witch or thwart some plan o' the Ensorcellor's. They ken me and trust me."

"True enough," Lachlan replied. "Still, I would like to have ye with me."

"I will come and join ye when I can, master," Dide

replied, with a lightening of his dour expression. "It has been some time since wc fought together. I shall take the news to the blue city first, though—they must be in hard straits there."

"I shall ride to Dùn Gorm with ye," Dughall Mac-Brann said, lifting his slumberous black eyes from the contemplation of his rings.

Dide and Cathmor looked at each other dubiously. Dughall was a slim, languid man, dressed always in black silks and velvets, with jewels on each finger and hanging from his ear lobe. "It will be dangerous, my laird," Cathmor said. "Dùn Gorm is occupied by the Bright Soldiers, and our men attack from the shadows when they can. We shall have to make our way through occupied land and sneak through their lines. If we are caught, all is lost."

Dughall yawned behind one delicate, white hand. "Indeed, I understand that," he answered in a fatigued voice. "Ye may remember I was at Rhyssmadill when the Bright Soldiers attacked, and I saw the city had been overrun. Besides, we have talked about little else for weeks. Strangely enough, I have managed to keep my attention on the war conference much o' the time."

"We shall have to travel rough, my laird," Dide said tentatively, trying to convey his concerns to the prionnsa without offending him. "Most probably we shall have to disguise ourselves as crofters, or even as beggars . . ."

Dughall raised one eyebrow. "You surprise me, lad. Did ye expect me to ride to war in my best silk? It might get damaged. Nay, rest assured, my lad, I'll change before we ride out."

Lachlan glanced at his cousin quizzically. "Why do ye wish to ride to Dùn Gorm, Dughall? Would ye no' rather ride east with me?"

Dughall spread his fingers so he could admire the flash of his rings. "As ye mentioned before, Your Highness, we have had no word from Ravenshaw. The last missive from my beloved father was six months ago, and it said only that the Bright Soldiers had approached him wanting to use Ravenshaw's harbors and bays. Naturally enough I feel some filial concern. It occurred to me that it might be time for a visit to the ancestral acres."

"Indeed, I would like to ken whether the Tìrsoilleirean have invaded Ravenshaw as well," Lachlan said.

Dughall shrugged. "I too feel some small interest in the matter, Your Highness."

"And ye will be able to scry to us with news," the Rìgh mused, remembering belatedly that the rings weighing down his cousin's hands were not just for decoration. Dughall MacBrann was a fully trained sorcerer, one of the few left in the land. He was as qualified to join the council of sorcerers as Daillas the Lame, but as heir to the throne of Ravenshaw he could not, for the council was designed to be independent of the prionnsachan.

Lachlan's cousin smiled. "Indeed I can, my dear. It also occurs to me that we should be sending messengers to Tìreich to see how they fare there and whether they can offer us support. The horsemen o' the plains would be most useful just now."

"Indeed they would," Lachlan agreed fervently. One of his most pressing problems was the lack of cavalry, for only the Red Guards had been trained to fight on horseback and most of them had fled the new regime.

"By all accounts, Kenneth McAhern is a proud man and protective o' his dignities. I met him when he came to Rhyssmadill for the Lammas Congress, and a haughty, stiff-backed prionnsa he was indeed. I think he would be more willing to help us if the Rìgh sent his own cousin to negotiate rather than a lowly messenger."

"True again," Lachlan said, eyeing his cousin with some scepticism. "Though surprised I am indeed to have ye offering for the role o' lowly messenger yourself, Dughall. Ye are sure ye would no' rather come and win glory on the battlefield at Blairgowrie?"

"I aim only to serve my Rìgh," he answered with a languid bow. "Though I must admit I hope to return with the forces o' both Ravenshaw and Tìreich at my back and win acclaim and your approval that way."

"Well, if ye can manage such a feat I shall be most

grateful," Lachlan replied. "Though I shall miss ye at my shoulder when we challenge Renshaw the Ruthless. By all accounts, we shall need every soldier and every sorcerer we can get!"

Anghus MacRuraich stirred uneasily and the wolf sat upright, dislodging the sleepy little girl who leant against her. The thud as she slid to the floor caught Lachlan's attention and he turned to glance in their direction. "My pardon, Your Highness," Anghus said, "but fear I may have to beg your forbearance as well. Now that the winter snows are melting, I am eager indeed to return to my own lands. Ye ken it is close on a year since I left Rurach, and I have no' seen my wife or my men in all that time."

"But I need ye with me when we lay siege to Blairgowrie," Lachlan cried in some dismay, having found the advice and support of the MacRuraich invaluable in the past.

Anghus returned his glance steadily. "I thank Your Highness for his regard and shall ride at his side if he so commands it. However, as ye ken, I have only a handful o' men with me. If I return to Rurach, I shall be able to secure peace in my lands, enforce the repealing o' the decrees against witchcraft and the faeries, and raise an army to bring to your assistance. Most importantly, I shall be able to return Fionnghal to the arms o' her mother. It is close on six years since she was stolen from us, my laird, and Gwyneth suffered her loss cruelly."

Lachlan glanced at Iseult, whose face had softened at the MacRuraich's words. A new mother herself, she could imagine how much Gwyneth NicSian had grieved when her young daughter had been stolen from her and held at ransom by the Anti-Witchcraft League. She gave a slight nod, and Lachlan reluctantly gave Anghus permission to return to Rurach.

"I shall need ye, though, Anghus, so be sure to put your affairs in order and return to me," he said. "Blairgowrie is only the first o' our objectives. It shall be a long and bloody war, never forget that, and I need all the prionnsachan behind me."

"I shall return as soon as I am able," Anghus replied. "And I shall bring an army with me, Your Highness, that I promise."

Lachlan nodded in thanks, though his face was drawn with worry. He had never had to plan a war before, for the years of rebellion had mostly been spent in small engagements and minor conflicts. For all their shrewdness, Meghan and Enit did not have the tactical or logistical knowledge to help him, and most of his brother's military advisers had fled to join Renshaw's forces. Iseult was well trained in the art of the Scarred Warrior, but her experience involved close hand-to-hand fighting and not the arming and deploying of almost six thousand soldiers.

With his small staff of officers, Lachlan not only had to command the army troops but also to organize efficient service corps, with farriers to tend the horses, carpenters to build siege machines, and engineers to plan and build fortifications. He also had to try and set up secure lines of communications between the various battalions, as well as organize supply trains with herds of sheep and goats to feed them all. Worst of all, he had to try and raise the funds to pay for it all. Most of the royal treasury had been left behind in the hurried escape from Rhyssmadill, and with the palace still under siege from the Tìrsoilleirean army, Lachlan had to find alternative sources of money.

Luckily Lucescere was a rich city, with over fifty different guilds ranging from silk weavers to clock-makers to potters. In return for promises of significant grants in the future, the young rìgh had managed to secure sufficient funds for the immediate future, but he knew all too well how much the merchants' support depended on quick success in the countryside.

His major problem remained the feeding of the soldiers, for he was determined not to simply take what he needed from the farmers and crofters, as the Red Guards had done. Rionnagan, Clachan and Blèssem were rich in grain and fruit and meat, but the Bright Soldiers had descended on the countryside like locusts, stripping what they needed and destroying the rest. Those parts of southern Eileanan that had not fallen to the invaders had already been plundered to feed the thousands of refugees who had fled to Lucescere and upper Rionnagan. Lachlan knew it was imperative that the spring planting went ahead if they were to have food for the winter, and so he had to deploy some of his troops to help the farmers and protect the crops.

With a frown etched deep into his brow, Lachlan wondered whether he would have gone ahead with the rebellion had he known exactly how much responsibility being the rìgh entailed. It was too late to balk now, though; he was the MacCuinn, Rìgh of all Eileanan and the Far Islands, bearer of the Lodestar, and the future of the land weighed on his shoulders. He sighed and turned back to the maps.

"It be a cold, raw morn," the weaver woman said with a shiver, holding the shawl close about her head with a bluish hand. Her feet on the icy cobblestones were bare, and she shifted from foot to foot in a vain attempt to keep warm. In her arms she carried long bolts of rough-woven gray cloth.

"Aye, that it is," the guard at the palace gate replied with a grin, "but I'd be happy to warm it for ye."

"Och, ye're a cheeky lad," she said. "Wha' would my man be saying if he heard ye?"

"He'd give him a mouthful o' knuckles, if I know Jimmy Cobbler," the other guard said, blowing on his hands. He glanced up at the sky, a dull gray behind the rooftops of the city. "Looks like we'll have a touch o' rain before too long."

"Looks like more than a touch, if those clouds close in," one of the other weaver women said, coughing hoarsely. "Och, it's been a hard winter this year!"

"Happen the spring'll bring better weather and better news," another said. "They say the highland lairds have pledged the Rìgh their support, which should bring the army another thousand men at least."

"Aye, but they say the blaygird Bright Soldiers have

twelve thousand camped through Blèssem, and still more marching through the fenlands. 'Tis twice as many as the Rìgh's been able to muster, by all accounts," her friend said with a sigh.

"Obh obh, woman!" the driver of the wagon behind said impatiently. "Do we have to wait all morn while ye wag your tongue about wha' ye ken naught!"

The weaver woman cast him a disdainful glance but moved on through the palace gates, her companions following close behind, their arms filled with bolts of gray cloth, their plaids over their heads against the chilly breeze. They walked with confidence down the long, tree-lined avenue, calling out greetings to the squads of soldiers practicing their maneuvers alongside. The weaver women were regular visitors to the palace, undertaking much labor on behalf of Toireasa Seamstress. The gray cloth they carried had been spun and woven in the weavers' hall in Lucescere and was to be made into kilts and cloaks for the soldiers. Joking and laughing, they bypassed the great entrance hall of the palace, heading instead across the quadrangle to the east wing, which had been converted into the army's headquarters.

None noticed as one fell back, her plaid clutched close about her face. The bolts of cloth she carried were held high so all that could be seen of her were two silvery-blue eyes. As the weaver women disappeared through the door into the crowded hall beyond, the lone figure darted across the yard and in through a side door.

Maya's heart was beating so fast she thought it would leap from her breast, but she kept her face low and the bolts of cloth high. If anyone challenged her, she would simply pretend to be lost and let them redirect her to the eastern wing. She was ready to croon the challenger to forgetfulness if they recognized her for she had not lost her ability to charm and compel with the breaking of the Mirror of Lela. Those of strong will or clear-hearing could withstand her charm, however, and so she carried a slim dagger in her sleeve on the off-chance her magic would not work, though she hoped rather desperately she would not have to use it. Maya had never murdered anyone with her own two hands, though she had ordered the deaths of many. She had an uneasy feeling that her mask of cold indifference would not be so easy to sustain if she had to strike the blow herself.

Maya made her way through the busy corridors of the palace without incident, though several times she recognized some of her former servants and counsellors and had to lift the bolts of cloth to cover her face. She wished she knew the spell of glamourie so that she could have disguised herself. She had not dared visit the dwarf again, for she was all too aware of his malicious nature and love of power. He could well decide to betray her in a moment of pique, and Maya did not want to give him any opportunity until after the curse against the MacCuinn had been cast.

The sight of Duncan Ironfist coming down the stairs threw her into a panic, and she ducked into an antechamber until she was sure he had passed. It took some time before her racing pulse slowed, for she had no doubt a trial and public humiliation would be hers if she was caught, followed inevitably by death. If she were lucky, it would be the quick death of beheading; if not, death by fire, as she had inflicted upon so many thousands of witches.

Her skin grew cold and clammy at the thought, and she had to steady herself with one hand on a table. She did not hesitate, though, checking the corridor beyond was clear and then hurrying on her way. A powerful impulse had driven her this far and she refused to allow fear to weaken her will.

Maya had escaped the Samhain assault with nothing but the clothes she had been standing in. By some ghastly misfortune she had even been forced to leave her daughter in the hands of her enemy. Diving into the heart of the Pool of Two Moons, she had expected the little girl to swim after her, as all Fairge babies did by instinct. Yet Isabeau the Red had seized Bronwen, and so Maya had lost her daughter and with her any chance of regaining power. Without Bronwen, Maya was merely the

Dowager Banrìgh, hated by her brother-in-law and an outlaw in the land that had once loved and feted her.

She had been sucked through the underground channels by the force of the retreating water, then spat out, bruised, cold and barely conscious, at the mouth of one of the great sewers. An old streetwalker, whose lost youth and beauty meant she was unable to find protection in any of the many brothels of Lucescere, had found her there. Molly Pockface had once been a highly paid whore, but age and syphilis had taken their toll, and she was severely wasted, with many sores and lesions disfiguring her face, lips and hands. Years of living on the streets, exchanging sexual favors for a crust of bread or copper coin, had not brutalized her kind heart, however, and Maya had found it easy to charm her. Overcome with pity, Molly Pockface had dragged Maya to her huddle of filthy blankets and cared for her until some sense and strength returned to her. Molly never thought to question her overwhelming desire to help and protect the Fairge, even though she came close to starvation as a result.

Maya's face had been badly gashed by the shattering of the enchanted mirror, but to her surprise she found the spider web of cuts on her face had miraculously healed, leaving only a faint tangle of scars. The illusion of human beauty she had created with the mirror was still gone, though, and the face that looked back at her from the whore's fragment of looking glass was clearly the face of a Fairge. Maya had been very afraid, for she knew a high price would be placed on her head and there were many in Lucescere only too glad to win the reward. She had no clothes, no money and no friends, and it was a bitter winter. The former banrìgh had had little choice but to take Molly Pockface's advice and seek shelter in a brothel. It was Molly who had taken her to the dwarf and paid for the first glamourie he cast with her own hard won pennies, and Molly who had introduced her to Black Donagh.

All winter Maya had swallowed her pride and her revulsion, and sold her body for gold. After all, she had told herself bitterly, what else had she been doing for the last sixteen years? She had seduced Jaspar MacCuinn when he was little more than a boy and had kept him tied to her all those years with the beauty of her body and skill of her lovemaking. Not for gold, of course, though the MacCuinns were wealthy and she had wanted for nothing as his wife. For power and for her father's revenge, she had seduced and married him, ensorcelled him and drained his life force. For power and the greatness of the Fairgean.

Yet those sixteen years of plotting and seducing were all for nothing. Jaspar was dead, as planned, but she did not rule in his place, and the hated Coven of Witches was somehow reunited and reinstalled as the power in the land. Maya had failed, and because of that she dared not return to her own people. The King of the Fairgean never forgave failure. The best she could hope for was again to be a pawn in her father's power games, a sexual plaything for whatever male was then in the king's favor. At worst, he would feed her to his sea serpent, taking his time over the task. Maya had ground her teeth at the thought of such a bleak future and hoarded her gold pieces, waiting for an opportunity to win back her daughter, and with her a chance at regaining power.

Although the palace corridors were crowded that icy morning, Maya was lucky enough to find her way to the laundries without incident. She filched a clean apron and cap from the neat piles on the shelves, leaving the bolts of cloth shoved behind a basket of dirty linen. Her pulse quickened as she made her way back into the main part of the palace, for she felt exposed indeed now she could no longer hide behind the reams of cloth. She knew that the nobility rarely spared a glance for the servants, however, and was confident she could easily penetrate the upper floors without being challenged. The only danger was that one of the stewards would see her and realize she was not one of the usual chambermaids. Seeing a bucket of soapy water and a mop left in one corner, she grabbed them, carrying the mop so its shaggy head concealed her face.

Maya had just taken a shirt from the wardrobe when she heard the door behind her open. She dropped to her knees and pretended to be polishing the floor as quick, light footsteps crossed the room behind her.

"Wha' are ye doing, cleaning the Rìgh's rooms now?" a young woman's voice scolded. "Do ye no' ken he'll be returning from the parade ground any minute now? This should have been done hours ago!"

Maya mumbled something in return, keeping her face down. It was all too clear to her that the rooms had already been cleaned thoroughly, for there was not a speck of dust under the bed, let alone a tuft of hair or a discarded crescent of fingernail. She had hoped to find the Rìgh's bed still unmade, or dirty clothes on the floor, but there was nothing. However, she was desperate to find something she could take to Wee Willie, so even though the shirts in the wardrobe were clean, she could tell from the long slits in the back that they belonged to Lachlan and had purloined one in the hope it would still retain something of his living essence.

The footsteps came up behind her, and a small, rough hand descended on her shoulder. "Get ye gone, lassie! The Rìgh'll be angry indeed to find ye here, ye ken he's in no gentle mood these days!"

Maya nodded and said, "Och, aye, I'll just finish this then."

She was hauled to her feet by a surprisingly strong grip. "Did I no' say ye had to be gone from here!" the voice cried. Then suddenly the hand dropped and there was a gasp of surprise. To Maya's amazement and delight, the chambermaid cried, "Your Highness! Wha' do ye do here! Do ye no' ken they will kill ye if ye are discovered?"

Maya looked down into a pair of worshipful blue eyes and felt pleasure and satisfaction well through her. It seemed not all of Lachlan the Winged's servants welcomed his rule. She had spent much of the sixteen years of her rule charming all those who came in contact with her, subtly casting spells of compulsion upon them so that they did as she willed without question. The Priestesses of Jor called such mindpower *leda,* and Maya had found it very useful in the past, most recently in the overwhelming of Latifa the Cook, who had showed her the way through the maze to the Pool of Two Moons.

"So ye ken who I am?" she said softly. "Ye ken who I am and shall no' betray me? Ye ken who I am yet will no' call the guards?"

"I ken who ye are," the chambermaid repeated obediently, "but shall no' betray ye."

"Will ye help me and serve me?" Maya asked, letting the power throb in her husky voice. "Will ye be loyal to me and help me?"

"I shall help ye and serve ye," she replied.

"And tell none that ye have seen me."

"And tell none that I have seen ye."

"And will ye come to me and tell me o' news?"

Again the chambermaid repeated what she had been told, and Maya felt herself relax. She need exert only a little power over this girl, for her will and desire were already aligned to Maya's. She must have been one of the many servants at Rhyssmadill who had been devoted to their Banrìgh, saving scraps of soap from her bath and squabbling over who would gain the honor of cleaning her boots. And if there was one among the Rìgh's servants and followers who loved her still, there would be more. Undermining the young *uile-bheist's* power was going to be much easier than she had expected.

Lilanthe opened her eyes and looked about her. Sunlight fell dappled upon her boughs and she felt the first burgeoning of buds beneath the smooth skin of her bark. A bird was singing lustily above her, but the tree-shifter felt only the weight of misery. It took her a long while to remember why, for the heaviness of winter was still upon her. Then she remembered and shut her eyes again, seeking to sink herself again in dormancy. The sun was warm, however, and the earth beneath her stirring with life. Lilanthe could sleep no longer.

Tentatively she stretched, then stirred her roots so the soil fell away, lifting her twigs to the warm wind. She became conscious of the green smell of spring and, despite herself, her sap quickened. She shook her long twiggy mane and took a deep breath, then eased her roots out of the soil. Despite her unhappiness, Lilanthe was very hungry.

As she took her first stiff steps, she felt something slither out of her branches and fall to the ground. Startled, she stepped back and saw a long snake of ruddy hair lying upon the ground. Tentatively she bent and picked it up, realizing at once that it was Isabeau's. In her mind's eye she saw moonlight-silvered snow and heard the whispered apology of the young apprentice witch as she hid the plait in Lilanthe's branches. Tears welled up in her slanted, green eyes. Such a bitter anger was in her that she almost threw the plait away. Lilanthe had loved Isabeau like a sister. Isabeau's warm and generous affection had filled a cold, aching hole in Lilanthe's spirit.

Yet ever since Lilanthe had met Dide the previous spring, the tree-shifter had focused all her longing for romance and passion and tenderness upon the merry-hearted, bright-eyed jongleur.

The secrecy and suppression of her feelings only intensified her ardor. Finding Isabeau and Dide in such a close and passionate entanglement had been a double betrayal, in no way alleviated by the fact neither had known of her feelings. Perversely, she blamed Isabeau the most. Isabeau had always had such a ready sympathy and understanding of the tree-shifter's feelings; she should have known, Lilanthe thought rebelliously. She should have guessed.

Her fingers clenched on the plait of ruddy hair and Lilanthe heard again Isabeau's remorseful whisper. Only then did she realize Isabeau had been bidding her farewell. Immediately her misery was submerged beneath a sharper, more immediate anxiety.

"Oh, Isabeau," she whispered. "Where have ye gone? Why?"

She paused, at a loss, wondering what to do. Her human stomach made a deep, rumbling noise, and she bent and picked up the green velvet gown she had worn on the night of the Hogmanay celebrations. It was crumpled and badly stained from lying in the gardens for so long, but it was all she had to wear. She pulled it on over her head and tucked the plait out of sight in one of the long, flowing sleeves.

The snow had almost melted and overhead the sky was a clear, pale blue. She made her way hesitantly to the kitchens, looking for a face she recognized among the crowds of people striding purposefully about. Although she had often been in the palace kitchens before, it had always been with Isabeau and she felt nervous asking for food from Latifa the Cook without Isabeau by her side. She stood awkwardly by the great doors, frightened by the bustle and noise of the many servants within.

"Lilanthe?" a voice asked tentatively. She looked up shyly and saw Isabeau's pretty maid coming toward her, a friendly smile on her face. She smiled back in relief, having met Sukey several times in the weeks before she had fled into the gardens.

"Ye've come back!" Sukey cried. "Indeed, they've been that worried about ye. Dide the Juggler's been searching for ye everywhere and the Keybearer Meghan was most concerned. Where have ye been?"

"Sleeping," Lilanthe answered and huddled her twig-thin arms about her, for it was cold in the shadow of the great building.

Sukey took off her goat-hair shawl and threw it around the tree-shifter's shoulders. "Come, let me get ye something to eat," she said. "It's been more than a month since ye disappeared, and indeed we were wondering if ye could have gone with Red, it seemed so odd ye should both disappear around the same time. But Red had said ye were in the garden . . . Ye ken that she has gone?"

Lilanthe nodded and showed Sukey the ruddy braid she carried. "She left me her plait, so I could find her if I needed."

"No one here is best pleased wi' Red at the moment," Sukey whispered, "for she took the baby Bronwen wi' her, and many among the lairds fear it's a plot by the Rìgh to get the banprionnsa out o' the way. 'Tis well known His Highness did no' . . . feel warmly toward the wee lassie, given the circumstances." Her voice hesitated only a moment, then she plunged on. "I ken it be no' true, though, for Red loved the wee banprionnsa and would never let harm come to her, that I be sure o'."

Lilanthe followed the apple-cheeked maid meekly as she led her to a seat at the long table. Tucking her gnarled feet under the hem of her dress, Lilanthe devoured the vegetable stew Sukey served her, listening intently as the little maid brought her up to date with the happenings at the palace.

"Now that Candlemas be past and the Banrìgh's birthday celebrations over, we all be busy getting ready for the army to ride out," she said. "I am to go wi' them, ye ken, for they have made me nursemaid to the wee prionnsa."

Lilanthe exclaimed at this, for she had not known of Donncan's birth or the death of his twin sister. Sukey sighed and shook her head over the sadness of the little stillborn girl, but rejoiced in the strength and beauty of the little boy. "He has wings, ye ken; is it no' marvelous strange? And his eyes are no' blue like a wee babe's should be, but yellow like a bird's."

"Like his father's,' Lilanthe said.

"Aye," Sukey said, a little hesitantly, before plunging on. "They are taking the babe wi' them, is that no' strange, taking a wee laddie to war? That is why I am going too, to mind the babe and wait on Her Highness." She giggled. "The MacThanach was livid when Her Highness said she was going; he said, 'What kind o' war campaign is this when we load ourselves down with women and babes?' She just looked him in the eye, and said, 'A triumphant one, since I will be there to ensure it is so.' She's an odd one, the new Banrìgh, is she no'?"

Lilanthe said, "I do no' really ken, I've only met her a few times."

Sukey blushed and twisted her apron in her fingers. "Och, I only mean she's no' like most fine ladies, who sit and gossip and ply their needle all day and never do much worth noting, while Her Highness oversees the training o' the longbowmen, and speaks in the war councils, and orders the Yeomen. It is only the funny way she says things, and her being so serious all the time, that's all I meant."

Lilanthe scraped the bowl with her spoon as Sukey continued. "Like when His Highness tried to make her stay here in Lucescere wi' the laddiekin. She fixed him wi' that look o' hers and said, 'But Lachlan, ye ken I canna stay behind while ye ride to war. I be in *geas* to ye, do ye no' remember? I swore never to leave ye.' "

"Wha' does *geas* mean?" Lilanthe asked, and the pretty maid shrugged and giggled, saying, "I do no' ken but the Rìgh went red and said no more, so I figure it mun be some pact they made, never to part. Is it no' romantic?" And she giggled again.

"Look, lassies, see who's lowered herself to come and visit us mere scrubbers in the kitchen," a loud voice sneered. "If it is no' Sukey the royal nursemaid! I'd have thought she'd be too proud now she be so grand."

Lilanthe looked up, shrinking a little into her chair, for she knew well that tone of voice. Standing before them, her hands on her hips, was a broad-hipped girl with a soiled apron and very red, chapped hands. Clustered behind her were several grinning scullery maids.

Sukey flushed and got to her feet. " 'Tis no' my fault they asked me to tend the wee laddie," she said defensively. "No need for ye to get nasty wi' me, Doreen, for ye ken I never put myself forward or said I was aught but wha' I am."

"Och, nay," the big girl replied contemptuously, "ye wi' your smug, smarmy ways, cozening your way in wi' the new rìgh and forgetting your auld friends, ye think we dinna see through ye?"

"It only be because I helped Red wi' the wee banprionnsa and so they knew I had a way wi' babes . . ."

"Och, sure," Doreen said. "A wee, skinny nippet like ye? I bet ye'd never dandled a babe in your life before. Nay, ye were just having an eye to the main chance."

Sukey started to say something, but one of the other scullery maids said in a high, piping voice, "And surprised I am that ye'd be willing to mind a witch-wean, Sukey. Are ye no' scared?"

"He's only a wee laddie, Elsie, ye shouldna say such things," Sukey said in a weak voice as the other maids glanced around nervously and shushed the girl.

"Button your lip, my lass," Doreen said, "else ye'll have that auld haggis-bag Latifa down on us all."

Elsie tossed her white-capped head, blue eyes defiant. "Say what ye like, he be a witch-wean, and *uile-bheist* too, wi' those wings and eyes."

Lilanthe felt blood rise to her cheeks, her feet crossing involuntarily, and saw how the scullery maids looked at her sideways. In her mud-bedraggled gown, her long mane of twiggy hair sprouting with new leaves, she knew she looked an *uile-bheist* indeed. Once again she wished she was safe in the forests, away from those who sneered at and hated those not of human blood.

Sukey must have sensed how she felt, for she said spiritedly, "Ye ken ye should no' talk like that, Elsie; the Rìgh has passed a decree against it, and ye'd be in trouble indeed if ye were reported."

"Listen to her," Elsie said admiringly, "all for the new order now, baint she? She changes her tune soon enough."

Sukey's round cheeks were red, her eyes bright with tears. "A new broom sweeps clean, my granddam always said," she replied, chin in the air. "And ye lassies would be best to remember it." She gathered her skirts together, and said, "Come, Lilanthe, I ken the Keybearer is wanting to see ye, and I'm sure His Highness is too. Dinna ye mind these jealous, cackling hens, they be just mean-minded and mean-hearted too." She swept past the other girls, and Lilanthe followed quietly, not looking any of them in the eye.

"Obh obh, a little pot's soon hot," Doreen called after them mockingly, but Sukey ignored her, taking Lilanthe swiftly through the corridors of the kitchen wing.

They eventually found Iseult and Lachlan in Meghan's

apartments at the Tower of Two Moons. The old sorceress had refused to stay in bed, despite her weakness, insisting she had too much to do to be fussed over and mollycoddled. She was sitting in her high-backed chair, as upright as ever, her narrow black eyes snapping with impatience as she listened to Lachlan's litany of complaints. Iseult was sitting in the window seat, Donncan feeding at her breast, while the little cluricaun Brun sat cross-legged on the hearth, mending a shirt with tiny, competent stitches.

"Well, Lachlan, if wishes were pots and pans, there'd be no need for tinkers," Meghan was saying briskly. "We canna conjure swords or arrowheads from thin air; Eà knows, I wish we could! We shall have to make do with what we have. Ye ken we have manned the iron mines in the Sithiche Mountains with the prisoners o' war and soon shall have more metal for the forge. Until then, your soldiers must make do with what weapons they have."

"But how am I to fight a war with a handful o' untrained, inexperienced, undisciplined and unarmed bairns?" Lachlan cried in exasperation.

"Wisely and boldly," Meghan said sharply. "How else should a MacCuinn fight?"

She stilled his bitter response with one hand and smiled at Lilanthe. "So ye have returned to us, my dear. I hope ye are refreshed after your winter sleep."

Wondering if the Keybearer knew why she had fled into the garden so precipitately, Lilanthe nodded, smiling shyly in response. The donbeag curled in Meghan's lap gave a reassuring chirrup, and automatically she chittered back.

"We missed your talks on the forest faeries at the Tower, though it did spur me to set some o' our young apprentices to researching tree-changers, nisses and cluricauns in the few books we have remaining," Meghan said. "I have found out some interesting things I did no' ken before. Tell me, Lilanthe, do ye ken o' the Summer Tree?"

The donbeag chittered in excitement and bounded up

Meghan's long, silver-streaked plait to sit on her shoulder. Lilanthe shrugged. "Nay, my lady."

Meghan sighed. "That's a shame, I was hoping ye'd be able to add to what little I have discovered. Never mind."

The cluricaun laid down his needle, his furry ears pricking forward. Solemnly he chanted:

> "Ten thousand bonny bairns I bred
> Yet still I live while they are dead.
> Fair my daughters bloomed,
> Even then their beauty doomed,
> Put to death by those who love them best.
> Vigorous and strong grow my sons,
> Soon to wither till I have none,
> I canna tell ye where they rest.
> Yet I do not grieve for long
> Bear more children fair and strong
> When again I hear midsummer's song."

They all stared at him and he said, "The Summer Tree, the Singing Tree."

Meghan said slowly, "One o' the references I've been able to find describes 'a garden with a great tree covered in blooms, sweet-scented as roses, which stands singing in the wind.'"

"The Summer Tree, the Singing Tree," the cluricaun repeated.

Meghan fell into a reverie. They all waited in silence, though Lachlan fidgeted a little, and the baby at Iseult's breast murmured. When Meghan roused herself, she looking a little startled to find them still all there. "Ye ken Isabeau has left us," she said abruptly.

Lilanthe nodded, and Sukey said breathlessly, "Red left her a plait o' hair, is that no' peculiar? To find her again, she said."

Meghan's gaze sharpened, and Lachlan balled his hands into fists. "Is that so?" the old witch asked. Reluctantly Lilanthe nodded and brought out the coiled braid to show them. Meghan held out an imperative hand. Even more reluctantly the tree-shifter passed the plait over. Something in the room had changed, she could sense a sharpening in the silence which made her uneasy. Meghan ran her hand over the braid dreamily.

"Can ye tell where she has gone?" Lachlan asked. When Meghan did not reply, he turned his intense yellow gaze to Lilanthe's face and she said hesitantly, "She's far, far away. To the north."

"She's heading for the secret valley?" He flashed a look at Meghan. "Could she have traveled so far so fast? Why is it none o' my patrols have found any trace o' her? Even if she had taken the cloak o' invisibility, could it have hidden all trace o' her and that damned horse?"

"The cloak o' invisibility can be as large or as small as is needed," Meghan said, "but I swear she did no' have it. Ye ken we searched the maze thoroughly for it after Maya swam free and could no' find it. Besides, ye ken we all saw the stallion's hoofprints in the maze and they went one way only. Even Isabeau could no' manage to make a horse walk backwards in its prints all the way out o' the maze."

"So how did she disappear into thin air like that?" Lachlan said furiously. "She must have the cloak o' invisibility, there's no other explanation."

"She would have told us had she found it, she was with us when we searched," Meghan said angrily, then frowned. "Though that cloak has strange, dark powers that can twist the mind and the will," she said softly. She pondered for a moment, then said, "No, I think she must somehow have traveled the Auld Ways. I know that stallion has the ability, though how any horse could, I canna fathom. It is clear he is no ordinary horse, that stallion o' Isabeau's."

"No, he's a wild, savage beastie," Lachlan said angrily. "He should have been shot!"

"It is odd," Meghan murmured, "but for a moment, when I saw the horse, I thought . . . but no, such a thing would surely be impossible. It has been almost seventeen years." She glared up at Lachlan, who was chewing his thumbnail, a ferocious frown on his face. "Do no' even be thinking o' wasting men on pursuit o' Isabeau," she warned. "It be a long and difficult journey to the secret valley, and besides, ye ken none but Isabeau and I know the way in and out o' the caves. Ye were complaining bitterly enough o' how few men ye have, ye canna be wasting them on a wild-goose chase. Isabeau is pursuing her own destiny; when it is time, the Spinners shall bring our threads to cross again." As she spoke, the old sorceress rolled the plait and went to tuck it in her pocket.

Lilanthe made an involuntary movement of protest. There were undercurrents in the room that she did not understand and they made her uneasy. The tree-shifter shuffled her feet self-consciously, but she said, "Isabeau left me the plait, Keybearer. It is all I have left o' her. She wanted me to have it." She held out her hand, though her freckled face burnt with embarrassment.

Meghan's fingers closed hard on the plait and her black eyes regarded Lilanthe steadily. Lilanthe forced herself to meet her gaze and Meghan sighed and reluctantly passed the braided hair back to the tree-shifter.

She said sternly, "Keep her plait safe, my dear, for much harm can be done to her if it should fall into the wrong hands. Ye should always guard the discards o' your living body carefully, for ye can be tracked or spied upon, or even have a curse cast upon ye, through naught but a crescent o' nail or a stain o' sweat." She passed back the ruddy braid, and Lilanthe stowed it away in her sleeve again.

"We have a task for ye, if ye be willing," the witch said. "Ye do still wish to work with us, do ye no'?" Lilanthe gave a very small nod, feeling her toes curl. "I ken ye are unhappy here in the palace," Meghan said, smiling at her. "Ye are a creature o' the forest, and despite all our decrees and declarations, there are many here who still distrust the faeries and are unkind. It occurs to me that ye may wish to return to the forest and perhaps search for your own kind."

Lilanthe listened incredulously. It was indeed a long-held dream of hers, but how had the Keybearer known? "I have often looked," she said softly, "but tree-changers are elusive creatures and rarely come together; they are hard to find."

"Happen if ye knew where to look, ye would have more luck," Meghan said persuasively. "I told ye I had set some o' the apprentices to researching the habits o' tree-changers and others o' those who dwell in the forests. It seems tree-changers do come together at least once a year, at midsummer, for the flowering o' the Summer Tree. What little I can find out about it suggests this tree blossoms but once a year, and then only for one day and one night. Its flowers are powerful in some way, or sacred."

"Is the Summer Tree no' the emblem o' the MacAislin family?" Lilanthe said, suddenly remembering something Dide had once told her. "Gilliane wears a little shield wi' the device o' a flowering tree around her neck."

"Aye, that she does," Meghan replied, pleased. "She and her mother and sister are all that remain o' the MacAislin clan; they are heirs to Aslinn and the Tower o' Dreamers, though it has been some decades since a MacAislin ruled Aslinn, thanks to the ambition o' the MacThanachs." Again she fell into silence, and Iseult passed the baby to Sukey to swaddle and rock to sleep, coming to stand beside Lachlan, her hand slipping through his tense arm.

"So ye want me to go to Aslinn in search o' tree-changers. Why? What is it that ye want with them?"

"I wish ye to seek the support o' the forest faeries for me," the old witch said. "In the past, tree-changers have been powerful allies o' the MacAislin clan and fought on their behalf. When my father Aedan Whitelock sought to bring peace to Eileanan, the tree-changers were amongst those o' faery kind who swore to abide by the Pact o' Peace, and one o' their number made his mark upon the proclamation. We wish to renew the Pact o' Peace, but after sixteen years of persecution, many o' the faeries are wary o' humankind, and with strong reason. It is in my mind that they would trust ye, Lilanthe, and that ye would be able to persuade them to give us their support and help."

"They will no' listen to me. They despise me as much

as ye humans do." Tears welled up in her slanted green eyes.

"They will no' fear ye, though, Lilanthe, and happen ye can teach them to trust ye and accept ye. Do ye no' think it is worth a try? Will ye think on it, for indeed we need them to come to trust us if we are ever to have true peace in this land."

Lilanthe looked unconvinced, but she nodded and said, "I'll think about it," her hand unconsciously creeping within her sleeve to caress Isabeau's braid of hair.

"In the planning and care o' crops and vegetables, the soil is one o' the most important considerations," Matthew the Lean droned. "Soil acts as a reservoir o' nutrients and water and absorbs the waste substances plants accumulate in the root system."

Dillon sighed and stared out the window at the trees waving in the garden. He had no interest in soil, but Matthew the Lean, a very earnest and well-meaning witch, thought it a subject of absorbing interest and was doing his best to pass on his enthusiasm to his pupils. He was an earth witch who had been trained in his youth at the Tower of Blessed Fields. After winning his moonstone and jade rings, he had settled in a small village where he blessed the farmers' crops every year, and researched ways of improving their seed yields.

When the witch-hunts began, he fled his village, at last finding a new home far to the south where none knew he was a witch. He had spent the seventeen years since the Day of Betrayal cultivating his small plot of land and growing vegetables of such size and deliciousness that his neighbors had grown very suspicious of him indeed. He may well have been accused of witchcraft if his demeanor had not been of such sober respectability, and if he had not been willing to pass on his knowledge of composting, seed raising and irrigation to his fellow gardeners.

He would have been quite happy living out his life in that small village, but Matthew the Lean had a strong sense of duty and he knew the Coven of Witches was in need of him. So when news came of the Samhain victory,

he had packed up his meager belongings and returned
to the Tower of Two Moons to help the witches in their
struggle. In a few days the younger, stronger witches
would be riding out with the Rìgh's army and Matthew
the Lean was determined to impart what knowledge he
could to the young students in the short time left to him.

The long schoolroom was filled with nearly fifty children aged between ten and fifteen. Most had the same
bored expression as Dillon. Some were carving into the
wooden desktops with their knives; some were whispering in low tones or passing globules of sweet sap to suck;
others were plaiting the fringe of their shawls or scraping
the mud off their bare feet with their fingernails. Dillon
cursed under his breath and wondered when he would
be allowed to join the older boys in weapons' practice.
It was Dillon's dream to become one of the Yeomen of
the Guards, the Rìgh's own elite company which rode
behind him into battle and guarded him during peace-
time. Knowledge of soil composition was of no use at all
to a Blue Guard, as the Yeomen were commonly called.

The door opened and a tall man with curly chestnut
hair and a full, red beard came striding in. At his side
was a young girl dressed in fur-trimmed velvet of forest
green, with a finely woven black plaid that matched the
man's kilt and plaid. A tiny black cat with tufted ears
rode in the crook of her arm, and at their heels loped a
large, shaggy wolf.

At once Matthew jumped to his feet, bowing and stammering greetings.

The Prionnsa of Rurach and Siantan inclined his head,
saying, "Thank ye, my good man. I am sorry to disturb
your class but we ride for Rurach this afternoon and my
daughter wishes to bid her friends goodbye."

"O' course, o' course," the witch replied and made a
vague gesture toward the classroom of wide-eyed children.

Dillon rose to his feet with alacrity, motioning to the
other members of the League of the Healing Hands to
follow suit. Jay the Fiddler was the first to his feet, his
thin cheeks crimsoning, while Anntoin and Artair were
quick to follow. Johanna was the only one to have been

listening to the lecture with any interest, for she knew a
sound knowledge of plant lore was necessary if her
dream of becoming a healer was to come true. Nonetheless, she was eager to see Finn, for they had hardly seen
her since the night of the Samhain rebellion, when she
had discovered she was the lost daughter of the MacRuraich, stolen by the Awl when she was only six years old.
Apprenticed to a thief and bounty hunter, she had been
taught many skills her royal parents would rather she did
not have, until she had run away to join the others on
the streets. They had been the swiftest, trickiest band of
beggar-children in Lucescere until they had joined forces
with Jorge the Seer and his young apprentice, Tòmas,
and formed the League of the Healing Hand. The
League had been instrumental in the success of the Samhain rebellion and had found the ensuing months rather
flat after all the action and excitement of the previous
year.

They stood around rather awkwardly, not quite sure
what to say to this girl with her velvets and furs, so
different to the ragged street bairn they had known before. Finn looked uncomfortable too, and said with a toss
of her head, "Well, I suppose this is goodbye, at least
for a while."

"It could be for years," Johanna said mournfully.
"Ye're a banprionnsa now and will no' have time for the
likes o' us."

"Do no' be so silly," Finn answered awkwardly. "O'
course I will."

"But ye'll be in Rurach and we'll be here," Jay pointed
out, "so who kens when we'll ever see ye again."

"I'll make them bring me back," she said. "After all,
this is the only Theurgia in the land now, and I suppose
I'll have to be educated." She looked rather miserable
at this prospect, but her expression only darkened as
Dillon said briskly, "Do no' be a fool, Finn, banprionnsa-
chan do no' go to school, they have tutors and governesses and stuff."

"Well, I will no'!" she cried. "It be bad enough that

I'm to be dragged off to the depths o' Rurach, without having to put up with that kind o' thing."

"Do ye no' wish to go?" Johanna said curiously. "I would have thought ye'd love it, being a banprionnsa, getting to wear velvet and jewels and having a maid to brush your hair and a page to carry your hankie . . ."

"That's just the sort o' sappy thing ye would like!" Finn said rudely. "It'd bore me to tears! I'd much rather be learning how to cast spells and shoot a bow, like ye."

Dillon's freckled face grew even sulkier. "Except we do no' learn that sort o' stuff, they say we're too young. Ye do no' get to learn about magic until ye're sixteen and then only if ye pass some stupid test. We just get taught useless stuff about dirt."

"Dirt?" Finn said blankly.

"That's what this old bore keeps droning on about. Dirt. Would ye believe it?"

"Och, Dillon, it's no' just about dirt, it's all about how to make plants grow," Johanna cried. "We get taught other stuff too, like history and mathematics," she said to Finn. "I do no' like that so much. Ye're lucky, getting to go off to Rurach and live in a castle."

Finn sighed. "I'd rather be here where everything is happening."

"But do ye no' want to meet your mother and be a family again?" Johanna was amazed. She and her young brother Connor were orphans, and Johanna's favorite daydream was discovering there had been some ghastly mistake and her mother and father really were alive and they could all be together again. Since this was exactly what had happened to Finn, she was troubled by the other girl's attitude.

Finn colored slightly and hunched one thin shoulder. "O' course I do," she replied. "It's just Rurach is so far away. And I do no' remember anything."

"Well, at least ye'll be living in a castle wi' servants waiting on ye and as much roast venison as ye like, while we'll be stuck here, learning stupid stuff like how to make compost," Dillon said sullenly.

"Aye, I suppose that'll be fun," Finn said. "And my

dai-dein says he'll teach me to hunt, so at least I'll get to learn how to shoot a bow like Iseult."

"That's so unfair!" Dillon burst out. "Ye're just a stupid lassie, why should ye be taught when they will no' let me or Anntoin learn just because we're too young! What use is archery to ye when ye're just going to marry some fat prionnsa and have lots o' babes? I'm the one who wants to be a soldier, yet since they stuck us in this daft Theurgia, we havena been allowed anywhere near a bow. They will no' even let me practice with the sword Lachlan gave me for helping win the rebellion!"

Both Anntoin and Artair made noises of agreement, the elder saying, " 'Tis no' bluidy fair!"

"Flaming dragon balls!" Finn cried. "Why shouldna a lassie learn to shoot? Look at Iseult! She's a better fighter than any o' those great soldiers. I'm no' surprised they're keeping ye in the Theurgia, so foolish and upstart ye are!"

They glared at each other, the elven cat in Finn's arms arching its back and hissing. The MacRuraich came and dropped his hand on Finn's shoulder. "Well, Fionnghal, are ye ready to leave?"

"Indeed I am," she replied disdainfully.

Her father smiled kindly at the others, saying, "Well, I know Fionnghal is sorry to leave ye all, but ye know ye're always welcome at Castle Rurach. I hope one day ye will come and visit."

They shuffled their feet and muttered as Finn followed him outside. She did not spare a backward glance for them, her back stiff.

Jay hesitated, then called after her, "If I learn to read, would ye write to me, Finn?"

She glanced over her shoulder and for a moment her old grin flashed out. "If ye can!" Then she was gone.

Lachlan and Iseult were walking in the garden, going over their plans one more time, when the tree branches above them suddenly rustled and a small figure dropped down out of the foliage and landed on all fours before them. Iseult immediately crouched into a defensive stance, only to lower her hands as she recognized who it was.

"Dillon!" Lachlan cried. "What are ye doing?"

The boy scrambled to his feet, oblivious of earth-stained knees and hands, and said, "Och, Lachlan, I mean, Your Highness, sorry I am to be startling ye but they would no' let me see ye."

"Well, we've been rather occupied, strangely enough," Lachlan replied dryly. "What was so urgent that ye needed to be skulking in the bushes in order to waylay me?"

Dillon's freckled face colored a little, but he said doggedly, "Your Highness, will ye please take me wi' ye when ye ride out in the morn? I wish to serve ye."

Lachlan's face, which had been looking rather stern, relaxed into a smile, though Iseult's expression remained intent and serious. "Well, my lad, I see why they call ye the Bold. I'm sorry, Dillon, but we ride to war, no' to a tea party. Far better that ye stay here and address yourself to your learning. There'll be time enough for ye to see war when ye are grown."

"I be grown," the boy replied angrily. "Besides, Jorge tells me ye are taking Tòmas, and he be only a laddiekin."

"But ye know we shall be needing Tòmas," Lachlan said, annoyed. "We have few enough men to be losing them to injury and infection. Tòmas can heal them and make them strong again." He turned to go, saying over his shoulder, "Ye should be at your lessons, my lad, no' climbing trees in the royal garden. Get ye back to your books."

Dillon flushed even redder and said respectfully, "I be a great lad for my age, Your Highness, and I can be useful, ye ken I can. Why, did I no' help ye on Samhain Eve?"

"Indeed, ye did," Iseult replied, unusual warmth in her voice.

Dillon said eagerly, "Ye will need squires, Your Highness, to run messages for ye, and hold your horse, and clean your armor . . ." Ideas failed him for a moment, and then he went on eagerly, "And we can carry your

standard into battle." His eyes glowed and it was clear
he was seeing a bold, heroic image of himself striding
ahead of the Rìgh into combat, carrying the MacCuinn
stag.

Lachlan would have laughed and told him again to
mind his books, but Iseult put her hand on his arm, sympathy in her eyes. "It is true ye will need squires, Lachlan," she said.

The Rìgh cast her a look of incredulity, then shrugged.
"I notice ye say 'we,' Dillon. I imagine then ye mean all
o' ye lads o' the League?"

"Aye, Your Highness."

"Well, Meghan will no' be pleased, nor Enit neither.
They think that Jay o' yours has Talent," Lachlan said.

"Does that mean we can ride wi' ye?" Dillon cried.

"Since I can see it's the only way to stop ye pestering
me, aye," Lachlan replied, amusement lighting his face.

Dillon gave a whoop of excitement and turned a
clumsy cartwheel, falling on his back amongst the bulbs.
"Flaming dragon balls, wait until I tell the lads!" he
cried.

As Dillon ran down the corridor, Anntoin, Artair and
young Parlan close behind and his shaggy dog Jed almost
tripping him up, he could hear the haunting strains of
Jay's viola. Even Dillon, who knew little about music,
could hear how his friend's playing had improved in the
few months that he had had the old jongleur as his
teacher. Enit Silverthroat had been reluctant to stay
within the shelter of the witches' Tower until she had
heard Jay play; then she had smiled and shrugged, saying,
"Well, I shall stay until my feet grow itchy, and at my
age, who kens when that shall be?"

Since she had taken on Jay as her pupil, Dillon and
the other boys had seen him only during the daily lessons
all pupils at the Theurgia attended. Otherwise Jay spent
all his time in the old jongleur's rooms, listening to her
as she sang or bade her son Morrell play his fiddle. Jay
had even refused to join his friends in their evening
weapon practice in the Tower's quadrangle when they

would get out the swords made from old wood and bash away at each other, pretending to be Blue Guards. "Enit may feel the urge to go traveling again once the spring is here," Jay had said, "and then what shall I do? She is the only one who kens the songs o' enchantment."

As Dillon hammered on the door, he heard the strains of viola music break off, and then Enit's soft, melodious voice. Jay, his viola in one hand, opened the door, the bow tucked under his arm. He did not look pleased to have been interrupted.

Dillon launched excitedly into explanations. He did not notice the expression on Jay's face until he had run out of words; then he said indignantly, "What's the matter with ye, ye great gowk! Cat got your tongue? Do ye no' want to come to war wi' us?"

"It's no' that," Jay said awkwardly. "It's just that I will no' be able to learn from Enit if I go. She's only staying so I can learn from her—she says she canna stand living in a house, the walls close in on her. If I go off wi' ye and the lads, she'll get in her caravan and go traveling again."

Dillon was incredulous. "Ye mean ye'd rather stay here and learn the fiddle than be the Rìgh's squire and carry his standard into battle?"

"It's no' just learning to play the fiddle," Jay replied, color rising in his thin, brown cheeks. He cradled his viola closer. "Ye ken this *viola d'amore* is one o' the great relics o' the MacSeinn clan. They think it was made by Gwenevyre NicSeinn herself, and she was the one who remade Seinneadair's Harp. It's a privilege for me to even touch it, let alone play it."

Dillon glanced at the viola in Jay's arms. He had never noticed it before, but it was indeed a most unusual fiddle, having nine strings raised over an elaborately carved wooden bridge. Its long neck had been carved into the form and face of a beautiful woman with flowing hair, her eyes blindfolded.

He knew the Keybearer Meghan had been very angry that Lachlan had given the League of the Healing Hand their choice of heirlooms from the relic room as a reward for their help at Samhain. Dillon had chosen a beautifully crafted sword which apparently had some historical significance. Anntoin had also chosen a sword and Artair a jeweled dagger, Johanna a pretty bracelet, and her brother Connor a cunning music box. Parlan had chosen a silver goblet with a crystal set in its stem, while Finn had taken a hunting horn which had proved to be the MacRuraich war horn, a relic of her own family and one that summoned the ghosts of warriors past. Though they had not known it at the time, she had also taken a cloak of invisibility which had first concealed Lachlan as he confronted his dying brother, then hidden Maya the Ensorcellor as she sneaked through the maze to the Pool of Two Moons. The cloak had disappeared after that and, although Meghan had instigated a thorough search for it, the cloak had not been recovered.

Meghan had been most perturbed by its disappearance, and had castigated Lachlan severely. She had taken away the swords and dagger, saying sharply that they were far too dangerous for children. Now they were to be the Rìgh's squires, Dillon had hoped they would be allowed to carry their own weapons, but Meghan had curtly forbidden it, much to the boys' disgust. Lachlan had taken pity on them, though, and said his squires could have small swords better suited to their age and stature, as long as they submitted to being taught how to use them properly. Since this was exactly what Dillon had dreamt of, he could not understand why Jay would rather learn how to play a viola, no matter how old or how sacred.

He said in disgust, "Well, stay here then and learn how to play your stupid auld fiddle. Ye canna be my lieutenant anymore, though. I'll have to promote Anntoin instead."

Jay went scarlet and said in a stifled voice, "All right then, if that's wha' ye want to do, fine. Though it seems unfair to throw me out of the League just because I do no' want to be a squire. The Keybearer says I will do more to help the Coven if I learn what I can. She says there are few who have the Talent to learn the songs o' enchantment and that one day I could be a great sorcerer and enchant people wi' my music."

"As if ye could," Dillon jeered.

"Well, Meghan thinks I could and she's the Keybearer, and Enit thinks I could and she's—"

"Naught but an auld gypsy," Dillon retorted, furious to have his lieutenant contradicting him.

Jay gripped his bow tighter, his lips thinning. Enit called out to him, and he said gruffly, "I have to go. I be sorry I canna go wi' ye, but my place is here. Be careful wi' yourselves."

Rather sorry he had lost his temper, Dillon searched for something to say, but Jay had gone back inside the room and shut the door.

Lilanthe woke with an acute sense of danger. She stood still, her branches held stiffly, and cast out her senses. Someone was close. Very close. She felt their breath on her bark. Fingers grazed her trunk, groped among her branches. Slowly she let the blood warm in her veins so that she could open her eyes and see. Suddenly agonizing pain jolted through her. Lilanthe screamed soundlessly. Again and again the cold fire bit into her wood and she flung up all her branches, almost falling. She felt Isabeau's plait of hair fall from the bole deep within her weeping branches where she had hidden it. Her attacker dropped the axe and seized the plait, then she heard their running footsteps.

She managed to effect the last stage of her shifting in time to see a tall figure slipping away into the dimness of the garden. It was no one she recognized. She bent over, sap-blood pouring from deep cuts in her thigh. She was so dizzy with pain she could barely stand. Wildly she cast out her mind. *Brun,* she called. *Help me . . .*

Clinging to another tree for support, trying to staunch the sticky green flow, she had to choke back tears of horror and pain. Why had she been attacked so viciously? Who had wanted Isabeau's plait of hair so badly? Whoever it was had known Lilanthe was to leave the palace the very next day, riding out with a squad of the Rìgh's soldiers to Aslinn and, hopefully, the Summer Tree.

Lilanthe had spent the last few weeks arguing with herself. Even if she was able to find any tree-changers in Aslinn, they would probably reject her, hating her for a half-breed, she thought. Even if they accepted her, they would not listen to her. Why would the faeries of the forest trust a representative of the hated humans, who cut down the trees and ploughed the earth, and raped it of its metals and minerals?

Yet Lilanthe longed to meet those of her mother's kind and secretly hoped they would embrace her as her father's people had failed to do. So Lilanthe had come to root herself in the rich soil of the palace gardens one last time, knowing that she may have difficulty shifting into her tree shape while riding through the often hostile countryside. She had hidden the plait deep in her trailing branches, now thick with new leaves, knowing how important it was to keep it safe. Yet now the plait was gone, and Lilanthe was sorely wounded. She pressed her hands into the gash and felt anguish knot up her throat so she could hardly breathe. As the little cluricaun came running to her aid, she thought miserably that the sooner she quit human society, the better. Humans had never brought her anything but grief and pain.

THE WARP AND THE WEFT

THE BATTLE OF BLAIRGOWRIE

The Rìgh stood on a dais high above the crowd, his wings spread proudly. Iseult stood at his side, dressed in a simple white gown, her hair covered with a linen snood. On either side were the prionnsachan, all dressed in their family tartans, their plaids flung back to show cuirasses of toughened leather. On their backs they carried their great claymores, with daggers at their belts and thrust into their boots. The council of sorcerers was gathered to one side, the wrinkled faces of the witches set in grim lines. Dillon, Anntoin, Artair, and Parlan stood proudly on either side, holding up square pennants depicting the white stag of the MacCuinns leaping against a background of forest green, a golden crown in its antlers.

In the great forecourt were gathered eight thousand men and women drawn up in lines and squares. One thousand carried long halberds or pikes of ash, with barbed metal heads specifically designed for piercing the heavy armor of the Tìrsoilleirean men-at-arms. On either side were lines of archers, some carrying curved bows as tall as themselves, others leaning on crossbows. Toward the back were the swordsmen, each carrying a great claymore strapped to their backs, the double-handled hilts high above their heads. The cavalrymen stood beside their mounts, their wooden lances bristling like a young forest.

Although the sun overhead shone down from a clear sky, the battalions did not glitter as might have been expected. There was no plate armor or chain mail to gleam in the bright light; no polished helms or metal

lances, not even steel bits or buckles in the horses' sad-
dlery. The great mass of men and women standing to
attention before their Rìgh were dressed plainly in their
own rough clothes of undyed wool, covered with cloaks
the gray of rocks and wild grasses and graygorse, hard
to see and easy to hide. Toireasa the Seamstress and her
team of weavers had woven spells of concealment and
camouflage into every cloak so that, even in the bright
light of day, the troops seemed to blend into the gray of
the palace stone. It had been Iseult's idea. She had never
been able to understand why the Red Guards wore such
bright colors when it made them such easy targets. On
the Spine of the World the Scarred Warriors all wore
white, even though it meant many wounded were never
recovered, lost among the blinding whiteness of the
glacier.

"The Scarred Warrior moves as swiftly and silently as
the wind, is as unfathomable as clouds when hidden, and
strikes as suddenly and as fatally as lightning," she had
said. "One should no' dress like a fool to fight."

Most importantly, no metal had been wasted on deco-
rative features or heavy plate armor that would only slow
the soldiers down in a campaign where every advantage
of surprise and mobility would have to be taken. Instead
the troops wore armor of toughened leather, with leather
gaiters to the knee, and all of their weapons were light
and easy to wield. Although many thought Lachlan's
army drab and rather dreary, nicknaming them the
Graycloaks, the result was an army that could move both
quickly and silently.

With Owein's Bow in one hand, the Lodestar gleaming
in the other, and the MacCuinn badge pinning together
the green folds of his plaid, Lachlan looked every inch
a rìgh. He stood proudly on the dais, his wings spread,
and addressed his army in ringing tones. As he reached
the crescendo of his speech, he raised the Lodestar so it
shone bright as a star, all who watched dazzled with its
brilliance. He beckoned Iseult forward, and she turned
and took her son from Sukey's arms so she could raise
him high. A great roar went up from the troops, and

they beat their leather shields with their daggers till the forecourt rang. The little boy, startled by the sound, flung up his hands, his tiny golden wings flying open. Again the crowd roared, and Lachlan moved to embrace his wife and child. Iseult leant her face into his shoulder, only to feel him jerk back with a cry.

"What is it?" she asked. "What's wrong?"

"Naught but a sudden pang," Lachlan replied, with a puzzled frown, one hand moving to rub a spot on one wing, his feathers fidgeting uneasily. "Happen I was stung by a bee."

"That is no' a good omen," Meghan said, frowning. "Bees are wise creatures indeed, and loyal. They revere their own queen and would no' sting the rìgh o' the land lightly. I wonder what this means."

He shrugged, and said, "It means I was stung by a bee, Meghan. It happens every day; no need to read more into it than that."

"I hope you are right," she said as he moved forward to give the order for the troops to ride out.

Blairgowrie rose gray-walled from the rolling meadows, built on a steep hill so it commanded a view of the countryside for miles around. Crowded within the town's thick walls were many peaked roofs. On each corner was a lofty tower made with massive protruding feet to frustrate any attempts at undermining the wall's foundations. From the battlements hundreds of crimson flags and pennants fluttered, each carrying the design of a golden clàrsach. Lachlan ground his teeth in rage at the sight.

"They are no' shy in declaring their allegiance," Duncan Ironfist observed as they rode up the winding road toward the town. The thin sunshine of early spring illuminated the freshly tilled and planted fields on either side, though along the low hills to the south, heavy clouds lay. "I wonder where they found so many o' Maya the Ensorcellor's pennons? There must be three or four hundred o' the things up there."

"If the gossip be true, every former Red Guard in the country has flocked to Renshaw's side, damn them," said

Hamish the Hot, one of Lachlan's most able officers. He was named for his quick temper and readiness to quarrel, unlike Hamish the Cool who was renowned for the calmness of his demeanor. Both had fought with Lachlan for some years, though they had known him as Bacaiche the Hunchback until only a few months previously.

Lachlan and Duncan had together appointed a general staff of twelve officers to the Yeomen of the Guard, rewarding the most faithful and able of those men who had helped the Rìgh gain the throne. As well as the two Hamishes, there was Iain of Arran, Dide the Juggler, Murdoch of the Axe, Cathmor the Nimble, Byrne Braveheart, Shane Mòr, Bald Deaglan, Niall the Bear, Finlay Fear-Naught and Barnard the Eagle. All but Dide, Cathmor and Niall had accompanied Lachlan and his battalion as they had marched through northern Blèssem, the first two riding for Dùn Gorm, the latter accompanying Lilanthe of the Forest in her journey to Aslinn.

Lachlan and his troops had encountered only a few companies of Bright Soldiers on their way to Blairgowrie, surprising them with sudden attacks and retreats so that the Tìrsoilleirean had been unsure how many men were involved or from which direction they had struck.

Meanwhile, the MacThanach had marched directly south with four thousand men, following the course of the Rhyllster as if heading straight for Dùn Gorm and the palace. In their train had been several long wagons, pulled by teams of six carthorses and piled high with the frames for siege machines and towers, which had been built within the safety of Lucescere's walls. Already Lachlan's reconnaissance officers had reported the Bright Soldiers were retreating from the surrounding countryside, preparing to defend Dùn Gorm and the harbor, and to reinforce their troops at Rhyssmadill. The MacThanach would change direction at the last moment and head away from the sea and the river before the spring tides brought the Fairgean to invade the coast.

Lachlan reined in his black stallion and stared up at Blairgowrie's forbidding gray walls now looming above him. He could see a handful of figures hurrying up the steep hill and smiled grimly. Even if the sentry guards had not seen the long line of soldiers approaching, the local crofters were making sure the town had ample warning of the Graycloaks' advance.

There were only two gates into the town, each topped by a heavy barbican and protected by a long passage and portcullis. Even from this distance they could see the gates were heavily guarded, with all who tried to enter being challenged and thoroughly questioned before being allowed through. As the troops came to a straggling halt behind Lachlan, they saw the massive, ironbound doors slammed shut behind the last of the peasants. Blairgowrie knew they were there.

"Set up camp, men, and this time try no' to make such a blithering mess o' it!" Duncan shouted. "Make sure ye encircle the entire town—we want to leave no weak positions, do ye hear me?"

The soldiers broke ranks, some running to the supply wagons at the rear of the cavalcade to fetch the tents, others attempting to picket the horses, most milling around, unsure of what to do.

Lachlan dismounted and waited for someone to take his horse, but his squires were staring up at the thick walls silhouetted ominously against swirling clouds. He spoke sharply to Dillon, who grasped the stallion's bridle and led him away, still overawed by the town's strong fortifications. Lachlan looked around, but there was no tent set up for him, not even a chair for him to sit on. Acutely aware of the many eyes watching from the battlements above, he shouted angrily for someone to attend him. At last the young Rìgh was brought a log to sit on while his attendants struggled to set up the royal pavilion.

Near sunset the camp was still in a state of chaos, with only half the tents raised, and the officers striding about, shouting orders, red-faced with exasperation. Lachlan watched sternly from the entrance to his tent, then raised the farseeing glass he had brought from the observatory at the Pool of Two Moons. He could clearly see dark figures crowded on the town's battlements,

watching them. He tucked the glass under his arm and
strode forward so he could berate a harassed-looking
Duncan. They stood arguing for some time then Lachlan
flung himself into his tent, calling for Anntoin to bring
him some wine. By the time darkness fell, the town was
ringed with the winking eyes of many campfires, but the
men slept rolled only in their cloaks, the wagons still
unloaded.

A few days later, when their camp was at last set up
and fortified with hastily dug ditches, Lachlan and his
officers rode up the steep, winding road to the town's
gates. Dillon proudly carried the Rìgh's standard, his
shaggy dog loping at his pony's heels. Lachlan was
dressed in the MacCuinn tartan, with a green velvet
jacket and cap, and carried Owein's Bow, the quiver of
arrows hanging down between his wings. He sat straight-
backed on his black stallion as Hamish the Cool shouted
up to the battlements, the other officers clustering close
about him to protect him from any fire from above. Their
approach was greeted by hoots of derisive laughter. Un-
daunted, Hamish took out a long parchment from which
he proceeded to read at the top of his voice.

" 'Ye, the citizens of Blairgowrie, have defied the royal
order o' Lachlan Owein MacCuinn, Rìgh o' all Eileanan
and the Far Islands, and are thus declared rebels and
outlaws. We demand that ye surrender to His Royal
Highness immediately. If ye do so, no action shall be
taken against this town, as long as those traitors and
rebels harbored within are taken into custody and submit
to the Rìgh's lawful authority. Any who wish may take
service with the Rìgh to fight against the invaders from
Tìrsoilleir; those who do no' choose to serve their Rìgh
and their country may go free, unhindered, as long as
they do no' again take up arms against His Royal Highness. The leaders o' this ill-fated rebellion will be tried
and judged in a court o' law by His Royal Highness, the
highest arbiter o' all justice in the land, and subject to
such punishment as he sees fit.' "

While he spoke, soldiers hanging over the battlements
and peering through the narrow slits in the walls con-

stantly mocked him. He ignored them, continuing to read out Lachlan's terms and demands. He finished by saying, "Ye have until dawn tomorrow to submit, else we shall raze this town to the ground."

"Wi' what?" one defender shouted. "Your fingernails?"

"Ye mun be joking!" another cried loudly. "Have ye no eyes in your head? Ride home, ye fools! Ye'll no' take Blairgowrie!"

"Look at the bonny laddie wi' his bow and arrow! Ye thinks ye'll get far wi' those, my pretty? Ye'll need bigger weapons than those to scare us."

The commander of the garrison leant over the wall, jeering as loudly as his men. "If it is no' the Pretender himself! Ye may as well ride home now, my bantling, else we'll come out and give ye a whipping ye shall no' forget. His Eminence the Grand-Seeker o' the Awl has a mind to be merciful and gives ye till dawn tomorrow to pack up and get ye gone. Else he shall ride out on behalf o' the rightful Banrìgh, Bronwen MacCuinn, and when we have dragged ye in like the traitorous cur that ye are, we shall hang ye from the battlements."

"I am the rightful Rìgh!" Lachlan's voice quavered with anger, and the soldiers jeered, "The laddiekin is going to greet, the poor wee bairn."

Lachlan clenched his hands and cried loudly, "I hold the Lodestar, and by the ancient law, he who holds the Lodestar holds the land. I am the Rìgh!"

"But what if the Lodestar was stolen?" a silky smooth voice called from above. Lachlan peered up to see a tall figure standing on the lowest battlement, dressed in a long robe of crimson. "Bronwen MacCuinn was named heir by her father on his deathbed, and ye only won the Lodestar and the throne with evil magic and treachery. Jaspar the Noble denounced ye and called ye fiend and *uile-bheist* . . ."

"No, that is no' true!" Lachlan cried, his voice breaking. "I won the Lodestar fairly, I am the rightful rìgh, no' that Fairge baby! She is the *uile-bheist,* no' I!"

Renshaw lifted up his arms, and they could see he

carried a baby girl, about six months old, dressed grandly
in red velvet with gold embroidery. A white lock was like
a blaze through her dark curly hair. "I give ye Bronwen
NicCuinn, rightful Banrìgh o' all o' Eileanan and the Far
Islands!" he shouted, and from the walls of the town
came cheering and the clanging of daggers on shields.
"She is no *uile-bheist,* this bonny babe. Does she have
wings like some evil fiend from the auld tales? Do her
eyes gleam yellow like a carrion bird? Nay, her eyes are
blue like any babe's should be, and ye can see she has
the white lock that shows she has held the Lodestar, as
only a true MacCuinn can. Ye stole it from her, a defenseless babe, and tried to murder her—"

"That's a lie!" Lachlan would have spurred his horse
toward the gate in fury if Duncan Ironfist had not
reached out and caught his bridle. He lashed at Duncan's
hand with his reins but the burly soldier did not relent.

Renshaw laughed mockingly. "Ye have till tomorrow to
withdraw, my arrogant young fool, else we shall ride out
and prove the Banrìgh's right to rule on the battlefield. Ye
think ye can prevail against us with your haggerty-taggerty
army? Ye think I do no' know your soldiers are naught
but peasants wielding pitchforks and foolish lads seeking
glory? Look at your camp! Ye canna even set up a circle
o' tents in an orderly fashion. Why, your mother's milk
has scarcely dried on your lips, and ye think ye can challenge the might o' the Awl?"

"The Awl is finished!" Lachlan spat. "It's dead and
gone!"

Renshaw laughed again. It was a cold, mocking sound.
"I think ye will find the Awl is alive and well," he replied. "It is your pitiful attempt at seizing the throne that
is finished. We shall give ye no quarter, *uile-bheist.* Ye
shall die, and all who stand with ye shall die as well."
Renshaw raised high the baby again, shouting, "Long
live Bronwen NicCuinn, long live the Banrìgh!"

The Red Guards cheered and shouted the words,
banging their daggers against their shields again so the
air rang with the sound. Lachlan and his party rode back
down the hill with the derisive sound loud in their ears.

That night, the circle of winking campfires around the town was far thinner, with dark gaps in its fiery garland.

Staring down at the besiegers, the commander of the Blairgowrie garrison smiled, leaning his elbows on the parapet. He said contemptuously to his captain, "See, already the cowardly curs are deserting the young Pretender. His Eminence was right when he said his army would flee at the might o' the Truth. It shall be like whipping a child, to break that young fool's blockade."

His captain grinned and poured them another dram of whiskey. "Let's drink then, to the triumph o' the Awl! We shall crack that laddie like a cockroach beneath our heel."

"To the triumph o' the Awl!" the commander echoed, swallowing down his dram with a ferocious smile.

Maya was careful to keep her exultation from showing on her face. Her daughter and victory so close! She had heard the rumors that Renshaw and the Red Guards had the little banprionnsa but had hardly dared give the stories credence until now. It had seemed so unlikely that Isabeau the Red had taken Bronwen to Lachlan's enemies. It had seemed far more likely that Bronwen had been murdered at the young Rìgh's behest, and Maya had been riven with anxiety at the thought. With Bronwen dead, all her hopes of regaining power would be smashed, for she was not naïve enough to think Eileanan would give her the throne when she was merely the widow of the former Rìgh.

She hid her mouth with her mug of ale, keeping her eyes lowered, as the soldiers around her discussed the confrontation between Lachlan and Renshaw and the likelihood of victory on the morrow. The Graycloaks were edgily confident, reminding each other that the young Rìgh had a few witch tricks up his sleeve, though Maya could tell much of their confidence was mere bravado. She herself was feeling more assured of success than she had been since Jaspar had died. She had overseen many a confrontation in the past sixteen years and had been surprised and rather disgusted by the confusion of Lachlan's ragtag army. True, he was only young and untried, but many of his advisers had served under his father, Parteta the Brave, and should have known better.

Maya had left Lucescere on the heels of the army, as had many of her fellow whores. The Shining City was to be left with only a skeleton garrison, and there was good money to be made as a camp follower, though the work was dirty and undignified. She and the other whores had found lodgings in a small town some miles north of Blairgowrie and had hired a cart to take them out to the army encampment once darkness fell. They knew that many a young soldier would pay well for what could be their last embrace. Maya was not really interested in the money, though any coin she could add to her jealously guarded hoard was welcomed. It was news of her daughter she was seeking, and she knew she had to stay near Meghan and the young MacCuinn for that.

Maya had been horrified when the palace chambermaid had told her about Browen's disappearance. All that was left of the little banprionnsa were a few clothes and a jeweled rattle, which Maya had hidden under her skirt in the hope Wee Willie would be able to use it to find Bronwen. She had taken the rattle to the wizard a few weeks after the army had left Lucescere, when she thought she would likely be safe from betrayal. She had had to wait until the waning moons were both dark, the best time for working black magic such as the casting of a curse.

The streets of Lucescere had been deserted that night, the only light shed by the occasional lantern hanging on a street corner. Maya had huddled her shawl close about her face, for the nights were still cold even though spring was well advanced. The stars swarmed thickly in the narrow gaps between the roofs but she had no glance to spare for their beauty. Every nerve in her body was coiled tight, and she had to consciously unclench her fingers from the neck of the sack she carried close to her body. If the sack was stolen, she would lose her chance of revenge against the young MacCuinn. However, if she was searched by any of the city soldiers, she would be arrested and executed. Inside the sack was a scrap of MacCuinn tartan, a tuft of black and silver hair taken from the Rìgh's brush and, most importantly, a long glossy feather plucked from the Rìgh's wing. The young chambermaid had done well.

The warehouse was dark, the surrounding streets empty. Maya could hear nothing above the roar of the waterfall, but she listened for a long moment anyway, unable to shake a sense of unease. Determinedly she told herself the dwarf would not betray her. The lust in his eyes at their last encounter had been hot and unfeigned, and Maya was used to inspiring obsessive love. Surely he would rather keep their bargain and have his chance at her than break faith for gold he could not use? She reminded herself that the Rìgh and his Coven of Witches were far away, then crossed the road and knocked gently on the door of the warehouse.

The old man let her in, holding a shaded lantern so only a thin ray of light fell on the ground. Muttering to himself, he led her through the piles of junk and broken furniture toward the secret door. Everything was silent. Not even a mouse scuffling disturbed the heavy hush. Maya tried to calm her racing pulse, holding her head high and listening with every nerve strained. As she closed the wardrobe door behind her she thought she heard a faint sound, like a breath being released. Slowly she climbed the stairs and, as she stepped into the dwarf's overheated room, nonchalantly pulled back a chair so it stood near the door.

The dwarf rose to meet her, smiling and rubbing his hands together. He wore a long dressing-gown of opulent silk, hanging open to reveal a hairless, sunken chest, and purple slippers on his feet.

Maya averted her eyes. "Ye see I am here, as arranged. Are ye already to do as ye promised?"

He poured wine for her, saying affably, "No need to be so hasty, my lady. Let us drink together, relax a little."

Reluctantly she took the wine and sipped it. He pulled her down beside him on the chaise-longue. One hand caressed her breast eagerly, and she drew away from him. "Business first," she said, trying to hide her revulsion.

"Nay, payment first," he leered. "I am looking forward to it very much."

Maya shook her head. "No. No' until ye have done as ye promised."

He tried to persuade her, but she stood up, saying, "I have heard there are many cursehags selling their wares in Lucescere. I shall go to them with my business if ye will no' help me."

He pouted and shrugged. "Well, if ye wish a mere cursehag to do the job . . . but they will no' have the strength or the subtlety o' the Wizard Wilmot."

"But their price is far lower," she replied harshly and picked up her sack as if to go.

He seized her wrist. "Nay, be no' so hasty," he said. "Tell me what it is ye wish me to do."

She eyed him suspiciously, then slowly drew the jeweled rattle out of the sack. "Can ye tell where the child who held this is?"

The dwarf took it, closing his eyes for a moment, then shook his head. "I canna tell where the child may be," he said. "She is too far away, or there is a sea or mountains between us, or some form o' magical shield."

Maya thinned her mouth in frustration and fear. "Can ye tell if the child is alive still?"

He squeezed his pudgy fingers over the rattle, concentrating, then shrugged. "Nay, I canna tell. Happen the babe was too young to give much o' her personal energies to the toy."

Maya took the rattle back with a cold feeling around her heart. She then drew out a long snake of copper hair. The wizard stared at it in surprise, but took it as she directed, and concentrated hard. After a moment he shrugged and said, "Certainly a braid o' hair is easier than a mere rattle, but still it is hard to tell. I sense cold . . . and loneliness . . . but where I canna tell. I am no MacRuraich."

Maya slipped the red-gold hair back into the sack with an acute sense of disappointment, wishing she could command the MacRuraich as she had once done. He had betrayed her, though, along with the other prionnsachan. Now she had to rely on such unreliable tools as the dwarf.

Wee Willie smirked at her and tried to fondle her breast again, saying, "So are ye ready to seal our bargain, my lady? I presume ye have no' changed your mind?"

Maya stepped away from him, saying, "Ye must cast the curse first."

"Have ye a lock o' hair for me, or some fingernail parings?"

Slowly she reached into her sack and withdrew the glossy black feather. He recognized it instantly. "But that would be treason!"

"Whom did ye think I meant when I said I wanted ye to curse my bitterest enemy? O' course I meant the Winged Pretender," Maya said impatiently, wondering at the odd note in his voice.

"I thought it were some other whore, or perhaps the brothel owner," Wilmot replied shrilly. "Do ye no' ken how dangerous it would be to curse the MacCuinn? The most powerful sorcerers in the land surround him, and it is said he has some witch skill himself. He would be closely guarded against such bad-wishing, and the curse would simply recoil on me. I will no' do it."

"We made a pact, Wilmot," Maya said cajolingly, leaning forward slightly so the curve of her cleavage deepened. "Are ye no' as clever as any o' those Tower witches? Are ye no' as strong?"

"I be stronger!" the dwarf boasted, and she sunk gracefully onto the chaise-longue in a billow of skirts so she no longer towered over him. Lowering her eyes, she crooned, "Shall ye no' help me, Willie? Shall ye no' save me from these desperate straits? I ken ye can cast a curse o' great power. Will ye no' help me?"

Unable to take his eyes from the pale skin revealed by her low-cut gown, the dwarf hesitated. "All bad-wishing can be turned away by a strong mind and will, no matter how strong the wizard casting the curse," he said slowly. "It takes subtlety as well as strength."

"Are ye no' the great Wizard Wilmot?" she cried. "I know ye can do it."

He frowned like a sulky child, flattered against his will. Very softly, so he had to lean forward to hear her, she crooned, "I need ye, Willie, please, shall ye no' help me?"

For a moment she thought she had won him, for he swayed a little, his eyes glazing. Then he flickered a quick glance toward the door and said loudly, "Nay, I will no' do it. I am a loyal citizen and shall do no harm to the rightful rìgh. Ye ask me to commit treason!"

All Maya's suspicions suddenly flared into life again. Quick as a thought, she leapt to her feet and kicked the chair hard against the door. "Ye think to betray me?" she hissed.

He cringed back in fear and cried shrilly, "Quickly! She has guessed! Come to me!"

Maya heard loud, hurried steps on the stairs, then a shoulder was thrust against the door, jammed closed by the chair. So livid with anger she could barely see, she dragged her dagger from her sleeve and brought it flashing down. It slipped easily through the flesh of the wizard's breast, hit bone, grated and slid sideways, embedding itself to the hilt. Blood spurted, and the dwarf looked up at her with a surprised expression on his face. For a moment she had to look into his eyes, then they rolled up and he fell.

Her stomach rebelled, and she had to stand very still, breathing heavily through her nose, to avoid vomiting. Her hand was stained with blood, the hem of her gown too. Mechanically she wiped her fingers on her skirt, then stood and stared down at the dead man at her feet. Although her mind screamed at her to hurry, she could not force her limbs to move.

Then the door splintered. She caught up the wing feather and thrust it back in her sack. Looking around her wildly, she swept the wizard's paraphernalia off the little table into his chest and slammed it shut, fastening the clasp. Then she picked up the chest, and with all her strength, hurled it through the windows at the far end of the room. As soldiers swarmed into the room, she dived out of the smashed window, falling down into the great surge of the waterfall that plunged past and down the cliff.

The Shining Waters fell more than two hundred feet into the loch below, and Maya fell with it. Even though she transformed into her seashape as soon as the water swallowed her, she was so pounded and bruised by its monumental force that she almost lost consciousness. She hit the water below with tremendous force, but automatically straightened her body and arms so that she cut through it like an arrow.

Deep below the surface she plunged, her nostrils automatically closing to keep the water out, the gills on either side of her neck opening wide. The Fairgean could dive deeper than three hundred feet without harm, a natural reflex slowing the heart rate and reducing their consumption of oxygen. Although Maya was thrust deep into the loch, she was only dazed and she eventually was able to slow her descent, then twist and strike for the surface.

Beneath the falls the water boiled like a maelstrom, and she had to fight to keep from being sucked under again. Kicking out with all her strength, her fingers touched the bobbing wizard's chest and she clung to it, using its buoyancy to help her swim clear of the pounding waters.

At last she crawled out onto the shore of the loch, shivering with cold and exhaustion. The strength her anger had lent her had dissipated, and she retched weakly, trying to thrust away the memory of the way her knife had slid into the dwarf's flesh, how he had stared at her like an astonished child. At last she fell asleep where she had fallen, soaking wet still and aching in every limb.

In the cold dawn she had woken and began rummaging through the wizard's chest. To her satisfaction, she had found it stuffed with bags of coins and jewels, the magical paraphernalia including bottles of rare dragons' blood, mandrake roots and, best of all, his thick spell book. So well made was the chest that everything had still been dry, and Maya had been able to read the spidery writing in his book quite easily.

Just the thought of the dwarf had been enough to turn her sick and cold. She had had to force herself to turn the pages as she struggled to understand the spells and incantations within. Maya had always thought it was the magic of the Mirror of Lela that had enabled her to disguise her Fairge features and transform her enemies into birds, horses, wolves, rats or whatever creature had most amused her. Since the dwarf had told her such magic was innate, she had tried many times to cast the spell of glamourie herself but had failed each time. The casting of illusions was not a skill of the Fairgean and so she had never been taught how to do it.

She had stolen the wizard's chest because she knew that was where he kept his spell book. She had thought all she would need to do was find the right spell in the book, follow its instructions and she would once again be safe behind the mask of glamourie. It was not so easy though. It took almost a month of constant study and repeated attempts before Maya was able to conjure the illusion and hold it for more than a few seconds. During that time, she held a shawl close about her face as if she was as horribly disfigured as Molly Pockface, sheltering in barns and under hedges where she could to avoid detection.

One day she had mumbled the spell while gazing in frustration at herself in a pool of still water. To her amazement and triumph, her features changed, though only for an instant. That afternoon she bought a hand mirror at a village market. By the end of the week, she had conquered the spell of glamourie and was once again able to travel abroad without fear.

Immediately, she had searched out the Rìgh's army, desperate for news of her daughter and for a chance to strike at her enemies.

Now that she had the dwarf's treasure trove as well as her own hoard of gold coins, she no longer needed to sell her body for funds. However, a whore was the perfect disguise. Not one of the soldiers drinking around the

campfires would ever believe she had once been their
Banrìgh. Still, if she did not start plying her trade, they
might grow suspicious, so when a young, pimple-faced soldier clumsily approached her, she smiled, drank down the
last of her ale and allowed him to lead her to his bedroll.
Tomorrow he could be dead, and Maya's fortunes transformed. She did not begrudge him one last night of
pleasure.

Dide yawned and stretched, hearing tired bones crack.
At the sound of marching feet, he crouched back down
in the shadows.

"Well, it seems we have at last put down those bluidy
insubordinate bastards," a soldier said in the clipped ac-
cent of the Tìrsoilleirean. "We have no' seen hair nor
hide o' one in three nights, and the sergeant said they've
been seen running from the city like the mangy curs
they are."

"Ye've got to worry about what they're up to," his
comrade said, boot heels clicking on the cobblestones.
"It's been six months since we landed in Dùn Gorm, and
in all that time they've been fierce as gutter rats. It seems
odd to me that they've turned tail and run like that."

"Happen they've realized they canna hope to defeat
us. The sergeant says there's naught to stop us controlling the city now, and soon we should break the siege o'
the palace," the first soldier said as they turned the corner and passed out of sight.

Dide smiled rather grimly. The retreat of the one-time
rebels from Dùn Gorm had gone as smoothly as planned,
and now the city was as empty as an abandoned house.
Only those merchants who were trading with the Bright
Soldiers and refused to give up the chance of making a
profit were left, and Dide was happy to leave them to
their fate. He, Cathmor the Nimble and a handful of
their men were making one last sweep of the city's docks
and warehouses to warn anyone who might still be in
hiding before they too retreated back into the countryside. They would then lead their forces to meet Lachlan
and the MacThanach at Dùn Eidean, the besieged capital

city of Blèssem, hopefully taking the Tìrsoilleirean army
there by surprise.

The once grand city of Dùn Gorm was a ruin. Constant
bombarding by the Bright Soldiers' cannons had reduced
many of the buildings to rubble, while many others had
been put to the torch. Wrecked and burnt-out ships littered the harbor, and the gates, which had once protected the Berhtfane from the sea, gaped like broken
teeth. Starving dogs roamed the streets looking for food,
and great mounds of earth in vacant lots were a testa-
ment to the many who had died in the fight against the
Bright Soldiers.

Dide moved silently along the wall, keeping a sharp
lookout for any more soldiers as he made his way to the
far end of the docks. The water gleamed in the gray
dawn light, lapping against the smashed stones below him
as the tide came sweeping in from the sea. He glanced
out through the mouth of the river and suddenly froze
in horror.

A sea serpent was swimming up the firth, its long green
body undulating through the waves, its tiny head held
high. On its neck rode a scaled figure with tusks like a
sea stirk, a long trident in its webbed hand. Trailing behind the serpent was a throng of Fairgean warriors
mounted on great horse-eels, their black snouts rising up
through the foam and sinking below it again as they galloped into shore. More Fairgean were swimming through
the waves on either side, and Dide could hear a high-
pitched whistling as the figure on the sea serpent pointed
up the river with his sharp-pronged trident. Out to sea
were several more serpents, while a long tentacle broke
the smooth surface of the water some distance out as a
giant octopus followed close behind. The waves were
thick with the sleek, dark heads of the Fairgean as they
bodysurfed to shore, long spears or tridents held close
to their opalescent bodies.

For a moment Dide could not move, blood pounding
in his ears, then he was running down the docks as fast
as his legs could carry him, not caring if anyone saw or
heard him. When he reached the corner he paused only

long enough to put two fingers in his mouth and whistle piercingly. Then he was running again. Behind him he heard an ululating wail as the sea serpent swam into the harbor, then alarm bells began ringing. Dide whistled again and was relieved to hear his call returned. Then Cathmor the Nimble was swinging down out of a burnt-out warehouse, his lean cheeks drained of all color.

"We have to get out o' here fast," he cried. "Have ye seen what the tide brings in?"

Together they raced through the streets, their comrades close behind. They reached their hide-out and untied the horses, hastily tying their packs behind the saddles. Three of their men were missing, but they did not hesitate in mounting and riding out at a gallop. They had all heard the stories of how the Fairgean had swept up the river last autumn, killing all living creatures on its shores. Fairgean warriors could survive out of water for up to six hours and they used that time to penetrate as far into the countryside as possible. They were as deadly on the ground as they were in the water, and nearly as swift. Even worse, the Fairgean had been known to swim through underground water and sewerage systems, emerging in farmyard wells to kill any human or animal within their reach. Dide and his men had no intention of staying in Dùn Gorm a moment longer than necessary. They only hoped they had time to escape the city before the onslaught of sea warriors reached the shore. Behind them they heard the ululation of the sea serpent, and then the sound of shouting and the clash of weapons.

"Well, at least that'll keep the Bright Soldiers out o' our hair for a while," Dide shouted to Cathmor with a grin, spurring his horse on with a wild whoop.

"Aye, but for how long?" Cathmor shouted back, and bent lower over his horse's neck.

With much blowing of trumpets, the gates of Blairgowrie opened soon after dawn. A cavalcade of Red Guards rode out, followed by a long line of men-at-arms carrying heavy pikes. Even Duncan Ironfist looked grim at the sheer size of the company. With so many of Lachlan's army leaving under the cover of darkness, they had little more than two thousand men, and only eight hundred of those were mounted. Grand-Seeker Renshaw had the advantage of numbers and position, with the hill at his back and the town to retreat to if things went badly. Lachlan and his army had only hastily dug fortifications and a tangle of tents and picket lines. Canvas walls were not much protection against a pike or a sword.

All the long morning the fighting surged around the walled town, the ground being churned into bloodied mud and littered with the bodies of the dead and injured. A heavy mist obscured the battlefield, and so for some hours Lachlan's troops held their own, fighting with reckless courage and ardor, their gray cloaks melting into the fog. Soon after noon, however, the superior skills and experience of Renshaw's men slowly and inexorably forced the Rìgh's army backward. Rain began to fall, making the footing even more treacherous. More and more of Lachlan's men fell, unable to withstand the charge of the cavalry. First one, then a few, then many of the Graycloaks began to flee the carnage, scrambling back over the bodies of their comrades. Lachlan tried to stem the tide, but at last, with a despairing cry, he too spurred his horse away from the battlefield, Iain galloping close behind.

The commander of the Red Guards smiled and whipped his horse after them. "Pursue!" he cried. "Ye can kill the rabble, but make sure ye catch the *uile-bheist* alive!"

The cavalry thundered down the fields, chasing Lachlan and his men as they scrambled toward a narrow pass in the surrounding hills. As the commander entered the ravine, he saw Lachlan only a few hundred yards ahead, disappearing into the drifting mist. He lifted his sword, urging his destrier into a canter with a triumphant shout. His troops surged after him, straining to see through the thickening rain.

Suddenly the commander felt himself pitched forward as his horse plunged into a quagmire up to its withers.

He shouted in alarm as another horse crashed into his mount's rump, driving him deeper into the mire. All round him were shouts as the Red Guards struggled to climb out of the thick, sucking mud. Only then did the commander remember that the small stream which ran through the ravine meandered through marshy ground for some distance. The heavy rain had turned the marsh into a veritable bog. Twisting in his saddle, he saw many of his men-at-arms had fallen into the marsh and were slowly being sucked under by the weight of their armor, some trampled by the panicking horses. Suddenly the long, slanting lines of rain became arrows, fired from above. The cries of alarm became screams of pain. As those who had been at the rear tried desperately to drag their comrades free of the swamp, gray-clad soldiers swarmed from their concealment behind rocks and bushes and fell on them from behind. As a narrow-tipped arrow smashed through his armor and into his breast, the commander realized he had been lured into a trap.

Lachlan reined in his horse to an abrupt halt and flung himself from the saddle. "Has it worked?" he cried anxiously. "Did they follow us into the marsh?"

"Aye, it worked," Meghan replied, opening her eyes and breaking her concentration.

They looked out into the rain and mist, which she and the witches had summoned, and smiled rather grimly. It had been a terrible risk, this plan of Iseult's, but they had not had the time or the resources for a long siege, and so trickery had been their only hope. If Renshaw had not sent his men out to engage with the Graycloaks, Lachlan would have had little hope to breaking the impasse. They could have spent a year camped outside Blairgowrie's stout walls, as the Bright Soldiers had been camped outside Rhyssmadill and Dùn Eidean. Gradually disease, lack of foodstuffs and clean water, and the diminishing of hope would have wreaked as great a havoc among Lachlan's men as among the defendants of the town. Lachlan had needed a resounding victory, and he had needed it fast. So, although it had been hard for him, he had swallowed his pride and allowed himself to look like a young, vainglorious fool who had more courage than sense. It had been Iseult who had convinced him. She had raised her serious blue eyes and said to the war council, "To win, deceive."

"What do ye mean?" the MacThanach had asked, impressed against his will.

"To win, deceive," she repeated. "If ye can attack, feign unfitness. If ye are active, feign inaction. If ye are near, make it appear ye are far away. When far away, make it appear ye are near. Thus will ye triumph."

The whole council stared at her, feeling uneasy for such tactics did not fit their ideas of chivalry. Iseult read their thoughts and smiled disdainfully. "Do ye wish to win this war?"

They nodded, and she again quoted dreamily, "To win, deceive."

So the Graycloaks had acted out an elaborate masquerade, designed to impress their lack of experience upon Renshaw and his men and to tempt them into rash action. The plan had worked beyond all expectations.

"I could no' believe it when I heard the Grand-Seeker had given ye till dawn to retreat, else he was riding out to engage," Meghan said, her gray hair plastered to her head despite the plaid she had lifted to protect her against the rain. "I thought we would have to spend some weeks pretending to build siege machines and to mine out the foundations before he finally lost patience. He was even more arrogant than we had thought!"

"He has reason for his arrogance," Lachlan raged. "Isabeau has betrayed us. She has taken the Fairge babe to our enemy! Half the countryside will flock to Renshaw's side if they fall for his filthy lies!"

"I do no' believe it!" Meghan cried.

"Well, believe it! I saw the babe wi' my own eyes, and so did my entire camp. Renshaw was no' surprised when he saw the number o' my men falling—he expected half the troops to desert at the news he had the babe. I am only surprised more did no' actually run away, instead o' merely pretending to!"

"I saw the babe t-t-too," Iain said somberly. "She had the M-M-MacCuinn white lock, no d-d-doubt about it."

"It must be a trick," Meghan said. "Isabeau would never deliver Bronwen into the hands o' your enemies. She knows the implications as well as ye do yourself."

"She could have been captured," Gwilym said, his face set in stern lines. "I am sure she would no' give the babe into Renshaw's hands o' her own free will."

"What could have happened to her?" Meghan asked anxiously. "I had no premonition o' danger."

"We must make haste to Blairgowrie before news o' the trap reaches Renshaw," Lachlan said. "I must get the babe back in my hands."

They turned back to the battlefield and saw the Graycloaks had won a decisive victory. Those of the Red Guards who had not drowned in the marsh had been cut down by the archers hidden in the rocks above the ravine, or by the foot soldiers who had waited for the Red Guards to charge past them before attacking from the rear. Quickly the Graycloaks tore the red flags from the hands of the standard bearers and dressed themselves in the torn and bloodied uniforms of the dead Red Guards. It was not enough to lure the garrison away from the town; Lachlan had to win the town itself and exact punishment on those who had defied him if he was to win the respect and support of those who still wavered in their allegiance.

They rode back to Blairgowrie through the pelting rain, singing and banging their daggers against their shields like a victorious army returning home. The streets were lined with townsfolk, cheering and waving banners, and the soldiers raised their hands and accepted the tribute, their helmets still lowered over their faces. They were not challenged until Lachlan dismounted within the inner bailey of the keep and flung back the commander's great red cloak to reveal his sable wings. There was some fierce fighting then as the few soldiers left to guard the Grand-Seeker tried desperately to hold the Graycloaks off. It was futile, though, with more than four thousand enemy soldiers having penetrated the town's defenses. With Duncan Ironfist wielding his claymore like a madman on one side, and Murdoch striking out with his double-headed war axe on the other, Lachlan fought his way into the great keep itself.

When he flung open the door to the main hall, there were screams as the servants ran to hide, or seized what weapons they could to defend themselves, hopelessness in their eyes. Traditionally, any besieged town or castle that was taken by assault was ransacked ruthlessly, and all inhabitants slaughtered for their defiance. The servants of the Blairgowrie Keep had no doubt this winged prionnsa, with his blazing golden eyes and dark look of fury, would have no mercy.

Lachlan seized a terrified page by the scruff of his neck and shook him. "Where is the traitor Renshaw?" he cried.

The boy shut his mouth and refused to answer, and Finlay Fear-Naught drew his dagger with a curse.

Duncan shook his head and said softly, "Do no' die for that piece o' worthless scum, lad. This is the true rìgh. We shall no' harm ye if ye tell the truth."

The page swallowed his terror and pointed with a shaking hand up the stairs. "The Grand-Seeker's rooms be on the third floor, through the gilded doors," he managed to say.

"Do no' call him the Grand-Seeker!" Lachlan flashed. "The Awl is dead, my lad, and shall never raise its cruel head again in my land!" He broke into a run, then to the astonishment of the cowering servants, spread his wings and soared up to the gallery above. With a glance at each other and a shrug, Duncan, Iain and Finlay hastened up the stairs, Bald Deaglan bringing up the rear with a curse at his rìgh's impetuosity. They found Lachlan standing in the center of an empty suite of rooms, his claymore in his hand, frustration and rage in every line of his taut body and wings. "The serpent has slithered away yet again," he spat.

On the floor was a crumpled heap of crimson where the Grand-Seeker had flung his robe. A cradle near the window showed the indentation of a small body. Duncan

Ironfist crossed the floor and laid his hand on the sheets. They were still warm. "He canna have gone far," he said. "Finlay, Deaglan, close the keep. Search every closet and every room, and examine the face o' every man, woman and child in this Eà-forsaken keep. And do it fast!"

It was too late, though. Renshaw the Ruthless had fled, and with him went the babe with the white lock, the child he had named Banrìgh.

ROSES AND THORNS

The Graycloaks took possession of Blairgowrie with disciplined ease. Contrary to the townsfolk's expectations, there was no looting, no rape and no executions. The local merchants and farmers were encouraged to bring in their produce to sell and were given a fair price for it. The dead from both sides were buried with the appropriate rituals, much to the relief of the local populous. They had dreaded the vermin and disease that invariably came after a major battle, since the dead and wounded of the defeated army were usually left to rot where they had fallen, prey to scavengers of both the human and animal kind.

Even more surprising, the wounded Red Guards were taken into Blairgowrie and given the same care as the injured Graycloaks. Usually those who were badly injured would lie among the corpses until they too were dead, sometimes killed by the scavengers who came hunting for anything of value but more often just kicked aside so the scavengers could seize their dagger or tear off their boots. Their bodies would then be picked clean by carrion birds or animals, until nothing was left but a few scattered bones to be turned up by a farmer's plow in centuries to come.

Lachlan's mercy astounded those used to the casual cruelty of the Awl, and stories soon spread of the miraculous healing hands of a young boy who traveled in Lachlan the Winged's train. Within a few days the local peasants were bringing in their sick and maimed for Tòmas the Healer to touch, and many who had believed that all witches were inherently evil found their assurance shaken.

Those Red Guards who refused to take service under Lachlan's banner were marched back to Lucescere under heavy guard to work in the mines and labor in the rebuilding of the Tower of Two Moons. Many were happy to throw their lot in with the young rìgh, however, impressed by the ease of his victory at Blairgowrie and pleased at his ready payment of their soldiers' shilling. Renshaw the Ruthless had not paid them anything, promising them recompense once the Awl was again in power. They found they were watched closely and any breach of discipline harshly punished, but this only increased their newfound respect for the Rìgh and his staff of officers.

Many of the Red Guards' horses had been rescued from the marsh, and the weapons had all been stripped from the corpses before burial, so Lachlan's troops were better equipped than ever before. They did not rest long after the Battle of Blairgowrie, for much of the surrounding countryside was occupied by the Bright Soldiers and Lachlan was eager to begin his campaign against them.

Meghan and Iain kept storm clouds low and heavy, for the Tìrsoilleirean burnt crops and farms as they retreated, and the witches wished to save as much of the land from the torch as possible. As a result, many of the battles in the following weeks were fought in rain and fog, the Bright Soldiers in their heavy armor struggling to keep their footing in the muddy battlefields.

The Tìrsoilleirean began to dread the sight of an ominous sky, for the Graycloaks materialized out of mist, giving no warning of their attack and disappearing as mysteriously as they had arrived. Worst of all, the Bright Soldiers' gunpowder was kept permanently damp, disabling their cannons and harquebuses and depriving them of one of their greatest advantages. As spring turned into summer, the Bright Soldiers were driven back toward the coast, squeezed between the Graycloaks and the Fairgean as if between the pincers of a giant crab.

The sea-faeries had swarmed into Dùn Gorm, taking the Tìrsoilleirean soldiers by surprise. Before they had had time to retreat into the countryside, most of the soldiers stationed at the blue city had been impaled on a Fairge trident or dragged into the water by a giant tentacle and drowned. The ships moored in the harbor had all been sunk by the sea serpents, which coiled their long bodies around the bows and crushed them to splinters.

Meanwhile, the crofters of Clachan had retreated to the rocky crags that thrust out of the flat coastal plains like petrified fingers. On the summits of these tall crags were ancient walled towns, built long ago when the high tides of early spring had swept in from the sea every year, drowning the land and bringing the Fairgean hordes in pursuit of the blue whale. In the four hundred years since Aedan's Wall had been built to keep the tides back, the Clachans had spread out across the plains, building towns and villages where they pleased. Now they crowded into the old towns, leaving their fields and villages untended.

For the Fairgean had set their sea serpents and giant octopi to tearing down great sections of the bulwark, crumbling from years of neglect, and the tide again flowed as it pleased. The battalions of Bright Soldiers marching through Clachan had been caught by surprise. Some were drowned as the sea raced in across the flat land; others died in fierce fighting as the Fairgean transformed into their land shapes and attacked in a wild, triumphant charge. In great confusion, the shocked and exhausted Tìrsoilleirean had retreated into Blèssem, only to be greeted by Lachlan's orderly and well-rested troops.

When the high tide had rushed into the Berhtfane, it had washed away many of the wrecked ships that littered the harbor and had split into the streets of the ravaged city of Dùn Gorm. The Fairgean rode the tide up the winding course of the Rhyllster to Lucescere Loch, so that the soldiers left to guard the city looked down from the garrison walls to see the loch far below seething with scaled bodies, like the palace fishpond. Some of the Fairgean tried to leap the Shining Waters, but the waterfalls fell almost two hundred feet down a sheer cliff-face, and not even the strongest Fairge could leap that high. Others left the water, transforming their shapes to attack the city from the land, but Lucescere was impregnable on its island between two great rivers. After many Fairgean had died trying to swarm over the Bridge of Seven Arches, the sea-faeries retreated and concentrated on killing Bright Soldiers, who had no such impregnable defenses.

With the seas thick with murderous sea-dwellers, the fleets of Tìrsoilleirean ships no longer sailed down the coast and into Dùn Gorm harbor to discharge their cargo of fresh troops and weaponry. Sea serpents or giant octopi sank many ships before the Fealde learnt her lesson and stopped sending out her navy. Instead, she concentrated on sending fresh battalions of Bright Soldiers into southern Eileanan through the marshes of Arran. As a result, Lachlan's army found itself attacked from the rear and had to retreat back into Rionnagan to avoid being caught between the two forces of Tìrsoilleirean, one desperate and angry at the reversal of its fortunes, the other untried but anxious to prove itself.

Iain MacFòghnan gazed through the window of Blairgowrie Keep and shook his head wearily at the burning blue sky. Now that summer had arrived, bringing long days of sunshine, it was harder for Meghan and him to control the weather. The clouds they summoned melted away in the warmth of the summer sun, and the Graycloaks were no longer able to hide their forces in mist and rain. The Bright Soldiers' gunpowder dried out and they were again able to fire their cannons and harquebuses upon Lachlan's troops. The tide retreated, and with it went the Fairgean warriors, to hunt the blue whale in the summer seas. All along the soft sand of the Strand, female Fairgean gave birth to their young, protected by the younger Fairgean males. Without the threat of Fairgean attack, the Bright Soldiers were again able to mobilize their forces and Lachlan's army found

themselves hard pressed. The fighting surged back and
forth across the meadows and fields of Blèssem, villages
being burnt to the ground, crofters intimidated and murdered, and the spring crops trampled.

Iain, his bony fingers clenching the windowsill, remembered the most recent disastrous engagement with a
heavy heart. Many good men had died, men he had come
to think of as friends. He could not understand what
obsession drove his mother. Why she should allow the
soldiers of Tìrsoilleir to march through her land and into
southern Eileanan, unleashing such death and devastation, was beyond him.

Arran was a beautiful and mysterious country, with
fens that rustled with bulrushes and cattails, diverse wa-
terways, slow-moving rivers and shallow lochan. Snow
geese and crimson-winged swans flew the skies; the song
of the giant frogs reverberated through the rushes, and
shy bog-faeries peered through the grasses with huge,
lustrous eyes. It was not a rich country, however. Most
of it was covered with lakes and marshes, so it did not
have much arable land that could be plowed and planted,
unlike Blèssem with its fields of wheat and corn, its lush
grazing meadows, its laden orchards. It had no abundant
lodes of iron or gold or any thriving industries like
Rionnagan.

Although it was not as rich as Blèssem or Rionnagan,
Arran was not a poor country however. Its marshes were
thick with fish and fowl, and it had a monopoly on the
export of rys seeds, the aphrodisiac honey of the golden
goddess flower, and the mysterious fungi called murk-
woad which grew nowhere else and had such remarkable
healing properties. These three commodities had made
Iain's mother a wealthy and powerful woman. The Tower
of Mists was filled with every imaginable luxury, and
Margrit NicFóghnan had many servants to cater to her
every whim.

Moreover, Margrit was a potent sorceress, with the
power of illusion at her fingertips and the ability to command air and water. Only Meghan of the Beasts was
more powerful, and the Keybearer was four hundred and

twenty-eight years old and showing her frailty. If she had wished, Margrit could have supported the Coven in its fight against the Ensorcellor and helped bring the witches back into power. Instead she had given aid to Maya and persuaded the gray-winged Mesmerdean to lend their strange powers to the Red Guards.

Even more unfathomable to Iain was the treaty she had signed with the Fealde of Tìrsoilleir, allowing the Bright Soldiers to march through the marshes and into Blèssem. The Tìrsoilleirean hated and feared witchcraft, as had Maya and her Anti-Witchcraft League, and were sworn to stamping it out; yet Margrit of Arran had given her support to them, instead of to the Coven.

She was even using her powers to thwart the Coven, keeping the mist and rain within her own borders and preventing Iain and Meghan from calling it to cover the Graycloaks' movements. Iain's mother was mistress of the Tower of Mists and none had her ability to control the patterns of wind and rain. All of the great weather witches had died in the Burning, and although Meghan had some ability to control air pressure, she was unable to match Margrit's skill. The banprionnsa of Arran kept Blèssem and southern Rionnagan baking under a hot sun, the sky clear of all but a few small clouds, while the fenlands remained shrouded in mist.

Iain sighed and glanced back into his suite, where Elfrida sat nursing their newborn son, her face soft with tenderness. His own heart contracted with a fierce, possessive love. All Iain wanted was a life of peace and tranquility; to read and study and laugh with his friends; to make love to his wife, whose pale, delicate body inspired him with a passion that surprised and sometimes frightened him; and to watch his son grow to manhood in peace and merriment, and the confidence of knowing he was loved. All the things that Iain had been denied in his own childhood.

Iain's mother had humiliated him, oppressed him, nullified him, all his life. As his love for his own family deepened, so did his hatred for his mother. He had thought he would be free of her malignant influence once he had escaped Arran, but he knew now he would never be free of her while she still ruled in the Tower of Mists, spinning her webs of malice and intrigue like a swarthyweb spider.

He came away from the window and knelt by Elfrida's chair, holding her tightly and laying his cheek against the downy head of his child. She stroked back his soft brown hair, knowing his thoughts.

"Fear no', my love," she whispered. "She shall never be able to harm ye or Neil. We shall win the war and her power shall be broken. Then we may all be at peace."

He nodded, though his face was still somber.

Neil Lachlan Strathclyde MacFóghnan had been born at Blairgowrie three weeks after their victory there, on Fool's Day, a date his parents hoped was not going to be indicative of his nature or his intelligence. Named after Iain's father and the Rìgh, Neil was a small, frail child with a fuzz of fair hair.

Iseult had brought Donncan to Blairgowrie Keep as soon as Lachlan and Meghan deemed it was safe enough for her to travel. With only three months in age between the two little boys, both Iain and Lachlan hoped that the two boys would grow into friendship as they had.

The MacFóghnan and MacCuinn clans had been bitter enemies for centuries, and Iain could only presume his mother's actions were driven by a desire to hurt the Mac-Cuinns. He did not share her obsessive hatred, however; quite the reverse, in fact. After two months fighting by Lachlan's side, Iain had formed a close friendship with the winged rìgh. They were close in age, and each was newly married with a newborn son. Both had inherited magical powers as well as a noble name and heritage, and were acutely aware of the weight of responsibilities such an inheritance gave them. Perhaps most tellingly, both were acutely self-conscious, Lachlan because of his years as a cripple, Iain because of his stutter.

Iseult and Elfrida, on the other hand, had not grown into friendship, despite their closeness in age and circumstances. The Banrìgh was disdainful of Elfrida's meekness and docility and often had to grip her hands

together to prevent irritable words from spilling out. Elfrida had not had an easy birth and took some time to
recover her strength and vitality, while Iseult was restless,
chafing at the proprieties which kept her confined to
Blairgowrie while Lachlan rode to war. Although she felt
tenderness towards her little winged son, she saw no reason why having a young child should prevent her from
fighting at her husband's side. She knew her attitudes
shocked and alienated many of the lairds, so she tried to
contain her impatience, turning her energies instead to
planning the war campaign and coordinating the logistics
of feeding and arming such a large force.

Iseult had been troubled indeed by the news that Renshaw the Ruthless had Maya's daughter Bronwen. She
refused to believe that Isabeau had betrayed them, as
Lachlan persisted in saying.

Finlay Fear-Naught had been sent on Renshaw's trail
and it was hoped he would be able to discover the truth
of how the Grand-Seeker had come by the little banprionn-
onnsa. It was a dangerous task, for the former Grand-
Seeker had ridden southeast, straight toward the heart of
the territory held by the Bright Soldiers. In the meantime
Meghan fretted about Isabeau and Bronwen's safety,
often trying to locate the young apprentice witch through
her crystal ball. All she could see were swirling clouds,
however, and this alarmed her more than ever.

"I canna understand it," she said to Iseult one morning, pacing the floor of the royal suite in Blairgowrie
Keep. "The seal I placed over Isabeau's third eye was
knocked away last year. I should have no trouble reaching her. Unless she is impossibly far away, or hidden
from me by some magical means, that is." She wrung
her vein-knotted hands together, Gitâ cuddling close to
her neck in comfort.

Elfrida looked up at the old witch in sympathy. She
was sitting on the floor playing with her son while Sukey
tried to change Donncan, a difficult task since the little
boy was just learning how to use his wings.

Meghan sighed. "I wish she had no' run away like that.
She should have trusted me to care for the wee lassie.

Och, well, happen if we win through to Dùn Eidean, I shall be able to use the scrying pool at the Tower o' Blessed Fields to see where she is. I just hope she is safe."

"Happen Finlay will return soon with news o' Renshaw, and we will ken if your sister is indeed a prisoner or ally o' the Red Guards," Gwilym said.

"Lachlan is still convinced Isabeau fled to his enemies," Iseult said, looking up from her notes.

Latifa sat next to her, helping her calculate what fresh supplies they would need to purchase before the Graycloaks again marched into Blèssem. The old cook's face puckered in distress and she said, "I do no' believe it. Isabeau would no' betray the Coven!"

"No, she would no'," Meghan said emphatically. "Lachlan should ken better. He has never forgiven Isabeau for rescuing him from the Awl, the foolish lad, and so he is always prone to think the worse o' her. Impetuous she may be, but Isabeau is no traitor. Iseult, ye and your sister have always had a close link. Canna ye tell where she may be?"

Iseult's thin, red brows drew together. "She is no' in pain, that I can tell. I would know if she'd been hurt or was dead, I am sure o' it. But no, I canna tell where she is. All I have is a sense o' loneliness, o' desolation. Wherever she is, I do no' think she is happy."

Isabeau moved slowly through the tangle of briars, clipping clusters of crimson rosehips and tucking them into the pouch at her belt. Every few steps she cut away long shoots of green, clearing a path before her. Although the sun shone, it was cool and she wore an old plaid around her shoulders.

Her face was pale and somber, and there were dark shadows under her eyes. Occasionally she sighed, looking about her with weary indifference before forcing herself to go on with her work. Behind her was a broken arch of gray stone, thick with moss at its base, which framed a square of freshly dug and planted soil. Beyond was a towering wall, many of its stones broken or missing.

Writhing all about the arch and the wall were long, tangled briars, wicked with thorns. Here and there tight buds had opened into single-petaled roses, their white petals fringed in red as if they had been dipped in blood.

It was almost three months since Lasair had galloped along the Old Way, Isabeau and Bronwen clinging to his back. After the dragon had flown down to investigate their passage, the red stallion had put on an extra burst of speed and fled down the magical roadway to another circle of flaming pillars like the one surrounding the Pool of Two Moons. Isabeau, her wet cheek pressed into Lasair's shoulder, had barely been able to breathe, so great was the pressure on her lungs and heart. Curtains of fiery silver-green had shivered over them, and Isabeau had sobbed at the sharp sting and prickle of her skin. Then the stallion had broken out of the tunnel of fire, and they were within a circle of ancient stones. Unable to hold on any longer, Isabeau had slid from the horse's back and fallen to her knees in the snow, the baby's shrill screams echoing in her ears.

It had been a long while before she had been able to recover her composure and look around her. Untying the baby and cradling her to her shoulder, she had scanned the horizon in bewilderment. Snowy meadows and forests stretched in all directions, overshadowed by the jagged peaks of mountains. Two great, crooked peaks thrust into the sky like gnarled fingers. The air was bitterly cold and burnt her lungs. Heady as greengage wine, it made her senses swim and her pulse quicken. Although the sky to the east was only just lightening, they had somehow managed to travel high into the mountains, so high that the abrupt change in altitude was making Isabeau giddy. She sat back in the snow, letting the dizziness pass, then slowly got to her feet. The two peaks towered over her, so like the narrow pinnacle of Dragonclaw that Isabeau was conscious of a dislocation within her. It seemed impossible that they could have traveled so far so quickly, yet the shape of the two mountains was so disturbingly familiar that Isabeau could only stare at them and believe. They were in the Cursed Valley, on the far side of Dragonclaw from the secret valley where she had lived with Meghan. They were in Tìrlethan, Isabeau's own land.

The red stallion was standing still, his head hanging, his heaving sides steaming. Isabeau saw his slender legs were trembling and laid the baby down on her shawl so she could rub him down. She felt sick and dizzy, but fought off her nausea so she could tend him. Somehow Lasair had once again brought her to safety, and she knew how dangerous the bitter air was to him in his hot and exhausted state. She filled her pewter bowl with snow and, using her powers, melted it so he could drink, leaving her plaid draped across his shoulders. Then she picked up the fractious baby, feeling how wet her swaddling cloths were. Somehow she had to find shelter so she could change and feed the wailing child, then build a fire to warm them all.

She was gazing about her rather helplessly when she saw a slender white figure flying toward them through the brightening sky. Isabeau shielded her eyes with her hand and watched in bemusement and growing delight. It was a woman, her long, silver hair floating behind her like a banrìgh's wedding veil. She flew as quickly and effortlessly as a snow goose, her hands stretched out before her, her flimsy dress fluttering about her. As Isabeau's eyes widened in recognition, the woman dropped down to the snowy mound with easy grace.

"Ishbel!" Isabeau cried and held out her hands, tears stinging her eyes. She had met her mother only once and had not then known who she was. Happiness flooded her—at last they could meet as mother and daughter and make up for the sixteen years they had lost.

But Ishbel seemed hardly to notice her. She took a few, faltering steps forward, hands stretched out to the stallion, who lifted his head and gave a long, echoing whinny.

"Khan'gharad?" Ishbel whispered. "No, it canna be!"

The stallion danced over to her, shaking his red mane. Ishbel put out her hand imploringly, then, to Isabeau's utter consternation, swayed and fell to the ground.

The red stallion had stepped up to her, nudging her with his nose and gently lipping her cheek. Then he had turned and stared at Isabeau with great dark eyes, saying: *Help her! Please, daughter, help her.*

Isabeau sighed as she recalled that day, then snipped back the last few briars so that she could see the waters of the loch lapping at the ground beneath her feet. She bent and brought a handful of the water to her lips. It was sweet and very cold. She drank deeply and looked across the still waters that reflected in perfect mirror-image the two snow-tipped pinnacles of the Cursed Peaks towering over the valley on the other side of the loch. Walking together on the far shore were Ishbel and the red stallion, her hand entwined in his mane. Isabeau sighed again and sat on the ground with her bare feet in the water, watching them.

Those first moments after Ishbel's appearance and collapse had passed in a dizzying whirl. After the terror and exhaustion of the long night and the frantic escape down the Old Way, it had all been too much for Isabeau to deal with. She simply knelt by her mother's side, staring from her pale, unconscious face to the restless stallion. The wailing of the baby at last roused her to action. Glancing around rather wildly, she realized she must indeed be in the Cursed Valley. Iseult had described the place to her, with its twin peaks, its river and loch, and the twin Towers hidden in the depths of a thorny forest. Isabeau could see the black, frozen surface of the loch stretching away from the foot of the hill, its far shore thick with tangled briar. The parapets of two tall, round towers rose from the winter-bare forest and Isabeau knew she would find refuge there.

First, though, she had to rest and eat and tend to the baby banprionnsa, so she covered the sleeping sorceress with blankets, gathered firewood and cooked up a pot of porridge which she and the baby shared. By the time they had eaten, clouds were pouring over the mountain ridges and the wind was freshening. Anxiously Isabeau hurried to make a rough litter from dead tree branches, lashing them together with rope from her pack and cov-

ering them with blankets and her plaid. When she finished heaving her mother's unconscious form on to the
litter, which she had tied behind the stallion, she was
trembling with exhaustion.

Her arduous journey had only just begun, however. It
was well after sunset when the weary procession at last
struggled through the snow to the forest's edge, their
progress hampered by the storm which had swept over
them during the afternoon. Isabeau may well have lost
her way in the swirling snowflakes had it not been for a
light burning in the windows of one of the towers. Whenever her knees threatened to give way beneath her or
her spirit flagged, she had only to fix her eyes on that
beacon and fresh energy would spur her on. Isabeau
knew they would all die if she were to give in to her
overwhelming desire to sink beneath that soft counterpane of snow.

Still, they might never have been able to fight their
way through the thorny forest if Feld of the Dragons had
not been out anxiously searching the darkness for Ishbel.
It was he who had put the beacon in the tower window
to help the witch find her way home and, as the storm
thickened, had come out into the bitter night, calling her
name, a lantern in his hand.

Isabeau was in such a daze of tiredness she was barely
stumbling along, her hand clenched around the rope that
bound the litter to Lasair. The stallion's neigh of recognition roused her and she raised her cold-numbed face to
peer around. She saw the swinging light of the lantern
and managed to raise her voice in a hoarse shout.

The old sorcerer hurried toward them, the light from
his upraised lantern illuminating his lined face and straggly beard so he looked like some strange demon. "By
the Centaur's Beard!" he exclaimed. "Iseult, is that ye?
What are ye doing here?"

The lantern's light fell upon the litter, where Ishbel
and Bronwen huddled together under a thick mound of
snow. Feld exclaimed again but managed to compose
himself enough to lead the miserable party back to the
Towers of Roses and Thorns, where he fed and tended

them all as tenderly as a mother her newborn babe. He soon realized the bedraggled young woman was not Iseult, but he could make no sense of her confused explanations.

"Never ye mind about that now, lassie," he said to her kindly. "Let's get ye into a warm bed with some nice hot posset to warm your insides, and we'll hear all about it tomorrow. Never mind about the horse, I'll have a care for him, I promise, and as for the wee babe, ye just leave her to me."

The old sorcerer carried Ishbel back to her room in the Tower. Isabeau followed him, unable to take her eyes off her mother's pale, sleeping face. Once he reached Ishbel's room, empty of all furniture, Feld simply let her go, and she floated there in mid-air, the silver-fair strands of her hair twisting themselves into a nest about her fragile form. Impossibly long, they brushed Isabeau's face and neck, and she pushed them away with one hand so they drifted back to twine about the sleeping woman. Ishbel sighed and lifted her hands to her thin cheek. "Khan'gharad," she murmured, then turned and nestled down into the cocoon of hair.

For the first two weeks after their arrival, Isabeau visited her mother every day and simply sat staring at her. She settled easily into a routine at the Tower, searching for food in the valley, digging and planting a garden, caring for the baby and reading books she found in the great library where Feld spent most of his time. It was a life very similar to the one she had lived with Meghan in the secret valley, and it increased her sense of unreality, as if time and space had slipped and she was again a young girl, eager for romance and adventure.

She found it almost impossible to comprehend that she was here, at the Towers of Roses and Thorns, her long-lost and much-longed-for mother floating before her, bound again in the depths of her enchanted sleep. Even harder to believe was the fact that the chestnut stallion who had carried her so far and so strangely was indeed her father, trapped as surely in equine shape as Lachlan had been in the form of a blackbird.

Although this would explain many things about Lasair—their instant rapport and slowly deepening connection, his few frantic words in her mind, his ability to
travel the Old Ways—her mind simply refused to grasp
that he was really her father. Again and again she tried to
grapple with the concept, only to have her heart quicken
and her palms dampen. She had stared into the stallion's
dark, liquid eyes and begged him for confirmation, or reassurance, but he had merely shied away, shaking his mane.
She had tried to reach him with her mind-voice, and he
had butted her with his nose, whickering softly. She had
reminded herself that Lasair was descended from An-
gharar, one of the six stallions Cuinn Lionheart had
brought with him in the Great Crossing, only to remember that it was Maya who had said so and she could not
be trusted.

Candlemas came to break the routine, and with it Isabeau's seventeenth birthday. It was a cold, rainy day, the
loch hidden in thick mist. Staring out the leaded window,
her plaid wrapped close about her, Isabeau chanted:

> "If Candlemas be fair and bright,
> Winter will have another flight.
> If Candlemas be shower and rain,
> Winter is gone and shall no' come again."

She gave a wry smile, repeating softly, "Winter is gone
and shall no' come again." The words filled her with
melancholy, her eyes with tears. So much had happened
in the year since her last birthday. She had carried the
Key of the Coven through the land, lost the two fingers
of her left hand in the torture-chambers of the Awl, and
spied for the rebels in Maya the Ensorcellor's own palace. She had guided Iseult and Lachlan through the maze
to the Pool of Two Moons and seen the moons being
eaten. She had watched as the Lodestar was restored in
the pool's enchanted waters, and had swam in it herself
as she tried to save the baby banprionnsa from drowning.
She had discovered she was a banprionnsa herself, heir

to the Towers of Roses and Thorns, and she had found her lost mother and father.

Pain, thin and cold as a needle of ice, pierced her. Her mother had not even spared her a glance. Isabeau had longed to be reunited with her mother ever since she had found out she still lived, but Ishbel only had eyes for the red stallion. And what a Pyrrhic victory that was, finding her father. Finding him trapped in the shape of a horse was almost worse than not knowing whether he was alive or dead. He had been a stallion for so long, Isabeau was very afraid that there was not much left of the man at all. She knew Lachlan had had great difficulty in adjusting to life as a human again, and he had spent only four years in the shape of a blackbird. What must it be like for Khan'gharad, who had been a horse for seventeen years?

Isabeau tried to shake off her gloomy thoughts as she and Feld celebrated the Candlemas rites together. When they had finished, the old sorcerer patted her shoulder kindly, wished her a happy birthday and went back to his huge, dark library which was lined with books a thousand years old, somehow preserved in the cold, dry air of the mountains.

Isabeau spent the rest of the day alone, wandering from one dusty, cobwebbed room to another, the baby sleeping in her sling on Isabeau's back. Unlike the other Towers Isabeau had seen, it was not fire that had destroyed the ancient beauty of the buildings, but centuries of neglect. Many of the rooms were furnished still, the tapestries on the walls so rotten a touch would dissolve them, the wood eaten out by burrowing insects so it was brittle as eggshells. Rats and mice had made their home in the cushions, and white owl guano covered everything.

Often the silent swoop of wings overhead would startle Isabeau so much that she would have to stifle a shriek. There were many owls roosting in the Towers—the huge white blizzard owls, large enough to seize Bronwen and swallow her whole; snowy horned owls that kept the rats and mice under control, and tiny elf owls that fed on moths and spiders. Their strange, haunting cries filled the

Towers at night as they flew through the dark halls in search of prey. During the day most slept in the rafters, pale hunched shapes, heads tucked under their wings. Isabeau had to be careful not to step in the many owl pellets that littered the floor.

She wandered down the sweeping spiral staircase to the lowest floor and went into the great throne-room. Brambles grew so thickly over the windows that a greenish gloom hung over everything, making it almost as dark as if it were night. Only Isabeau's acute eyesight made it possible for her to see. Filthy loops of cobwebs hung down from the vaulted ceiling, and she had to brush them away with her arm, though they clung to her sleeve stickily. She stood below the two tall thrones, staring at the shield carved into the stone above, with its device of roses and thorns entwining beneath the stylized shape of a dragon, wings and claws raised. Below this device was a banner with the motto of the MacFaghan clan inscribed in Latin. Although Isabeau could not yet read the ancient language, she knew what it meant, for Feld had translated it for her.

" 'Those who would gather roses must brave the thorns,' " she quoted and looked about her somberly. For a moment it was as if she could see the hall as it once must have been—full of people talking, laughing and dancing. Minstrels played lively music; the tapestries were rich and bright, and a young man was juggling bell-fruit from a bowl on the sideboard. On the right-hand throne an old man sat, throwing back his shaggy red-gray head to laugh before reaching out to move a knight on the red and white chessboard. The faery he played against shook back her white mane and shrugged, admitting defeat, then he bent and kissed her long, multi-jointed fingers.

Then Isabeau heard screaming and saw people running. She saw an old woman with long, wild, red-gray hair come striding through the room with a dagger in her hand, saw the dagger rise and fall, rise and fall. Then blood slid down the carved wood of the throne, pooling in the carvings and spilling out over the stones.

The next instant the vision had gone. Isabeau blinked and looked about her, seeing only shadowy arches, tattered tapestries and the heavy, dirty loops of cobwebs. She shivered, huddling her arms about her, and turned to go. Something near the foot of the thrones caught her eye and she bent and picked it up, dusting it off on her skirt. It was a chess piece, a horse's head cunningly carved from carnelian, with rubies for eyes.

Scratching around in the filth, Isabeau found a marble queen and a carnelian castle, and then her foot nudged the chessboard, broken in two at the foot of the throne steps. She fitted the pieces together wonderingly and for an instant heard again the sound of screaming. With a superstitious shudder, she tucked the chess pieces into her pocket and hurried away from the ghost-ridden throne-room.

Yet it seemed every room in the old Towers had a story of sorrow and madness to tell, and as the long, dreary hours passed, Isabeau's depression deepened, until she found herself weeping. This was her royal heritage, this ruined, cobwebby castle abandoned hundreds of years ago. This was her proud ancestry.

She sat on a step, looking about her at the decayed grandeur, and wondered what had happened to the bright future she had imagined. She was crippled, alone, in self-imposed exile from her friends, with no future except that of a nursemaid and drudge for a child who was not even her own.

Bronwen began to cry thinly, and Isabeau rose to her feet, trying to shake off her black mood. Both of them were cold and hungry, and she thought rather drearily of their bare larder. No birthday feast for her this year. She imagined the celebrations that must be occurring for Iseult in Lucescere and felt a shock of jealousy. *Ye could have stayed and shared in the feast,* she told herself, and tried to stifle the thought that came hard on its heels: *Though it would have been for Iseult the Banrìgh, no' for me.*

Suddenly anger filled her. Isabeau thought of her mother, floating asleep in her nest of hair. Seventeen years ago Ishbel had given birth to her twin daughters, with only dragons to assist her through her agony and fear. It had been in the week after the Day of Betrayal, and Ishbel had fled the burning of the Tower of Two Moons, flying halfway across the country, to seek her lover's people. Wracked by labor pains while flying across the mountains, she could have fallen to her death if the dragons had not caught her and taken her to safety. Ishbel had fallen into her uncanny sleep after the birth of her twins, and had slept for seventeen long years.

Anger hot in her veins, Isabeau marched up the great spiral staircase and threw open the door of her mother's room. Ishbel floated before her, all white, even her lips without color. For a moment Isabeau's courage failed her, then she reached through the cocoon of pale hair and shook her mother vigorously. At last Ishbel's eyes slowly opened and she looked about her dazedly.

"It's time to wake!" Isabeau cried. "Ye have slept long enough."

Ishbel looked at her and yawned, her arms stretching above her head. Her eyes, as intensely blue as Isabeau's, began to close again. Isabeau shook her even harder. "Ye must wake up!"

Slowly a look of recognition dawned. "Iseult?"

Isabeau almost wept with frustration. "No, it is me, Isabeau! Can ye no' tell us apart, your own daughters? Meghan can, and she is no' even our mother. Ye should no' have slept so long."

"Isabeau," Ishbel said softly and yawned again. "What do ye do here?" She looked about her at the stone walls and her eyes filled with tears. "I dreamt I found your father, but he was horribly changed . . . horribly changed." Her soft mouth trembled, and she cried, "Khan'gharad, why do ye no' answer me?"

Isabeau opened her mouth to say dryly, "Because he's a horse," but shut it, unable to speak the words. She stared at the thin, white face and said gently, "Mam, it is time for ye to wake. It has been seventeen years. Ye must face the reality o' what has happened. We, your daughters, need ye. Please do no' sleep anymore."

Ishbel rubbed at her wet eyes with her fists, saying pitifully, "Ye do no' understand . . ."

"Yes, I do, really I do. I ken ye loved our father and grieve for him still. He is here but he is no' as ye kent him, and I do no' think he ever will be again. Maya ensorcelled him and he is still under her enchantment."

"So it was no' a dream," Ishbel replied, shuddering. "Nay, I canna bear it! He canna be a horse. It is too awful! No' my Khan'gharad!"

"I think Maya would have thought it funny," Isabeau said wryly.

Ishbel shuddered again and covered her eyes with her hands. "No, no," she murmured.

Isabeau seized her shoulders again and shook her. "Do no' dare fall asleep again!" she warned. "I shall never forgive ye if ye fall asleep for another seventeen years. Will ye no' wake and let me get ye something to eat? Ye are so thin and cold."

"I must see Khan'gharad, I must see if it is true," Ishbel murmured. "Where is he?"

So Ishbel had woken. Although every morning Isabeau feared to find her bound in her enchanted sleep again, every morning her mother woke, ate the food Isabeau prepared for her, then walked by the loch with the red stallion, trying to reach him. Often Isabeau found her mother leaning against his chestnut flank, weeping, or staring into his large, dark eye as if trying to communicate mind to mind. Sometimes Khan'gharad responded with a few mind-spoken words; more often he merely shook his mane and whickered. It seemed only impending danger could reach the man trapped within and rouse him.

As the weeks passed, Ishbel seemed to accept her husband's enchantment. Although she spent nearly all the daylight hours with the stallion, the evenings were spent with Feld and Isabeau and the young apprentice-witch was at last able to begin building a relationship with her mother.

So, as the days lengthened and summer approached Isabeau found some measure of peace. Her days were so busy foraging for food and caring for Bronwen that she almost forgot Eileanan was at war. Feld had a small herd of goats which were staked out in the overgrown garden, so they had plenty of milk and cheese, and every few weeks the Khan'cohbans left a pile of roots, grains and vegetables at the edge of the valley as a sort of tithe. Feld said they had done so since he had first come to the Towers of Roses and Thorns to care for Ishbel. He never remembered to eat much himself; he said Iseult had hunted for them and prepared their meals when she had been with them. Once or twice a day he had tried to make Ishbel eat the thin porridge he made from the wild grains that the Khan'cohbans left him but mostly she only swallowed a few mouthfuls before turning her sleeping face away.

Now Ishbel was awake, she was regaining her appetite, and Isabeau took pleasure in cooking for them all. Luckily it was spring and the valley was rich with all sorts of herbs, mushrooms, roots, early berries and leafage. The apprentice witch had found a beehive and she managed to coax the bees to swarm to a new hive she had made for them in the garden. Many of the herbs and vegetables she found she transplanted into that part of the garden she had reclaimed from the weeds and rose briars, and she stripped seeds from many of the valley plants to sow later, when the earth was well warmed by the sun.

Isabeau's major problem was finding salt to add to Bronwen's bath water. The Fairgean were sea-dwelling creatures and died if away from salt water for too long. At Lucescere there had been no shortage of salt. It was one of Clachan's principal exports, used to cure fish, pickle vegetables, preserve hides and make glass and enameled jewelery. It had even become fashionable for fine ladies to add sea salt to their baths in imitation of Maya, and so it had been sold at the markets in little canvas bags, with rose petals or sweet herbs mixed through. There were no saltpans in Tìrlethan, however, and the sea was hundreds of miles away. Isabeau had packed a sack of salt, but that was almost all gone, and she worried about what she would do once it was empty.

She had wondered whether the loch at the foot of the Towers was, like many in the mountain region, rich in salt and minerals, but she now knew it was as pure and sweet as the loch in the secret valley.

Isabeau frowned, paddling her feet in the loch and smashing the serene reflection of red and white roses. She lifted her eyes from Ishbel and Lasair, still wandering together on the far shore, and gazed at the twin peaks of Dragonclaw.

A dragon soared far above the sharp-pointed mountains, gleaming as brightly as newly polished bronze in the sunshine. Instinctively, Isabeau's stomach muscles clenched and her heartbeat quickened. She lifted her numb feet out of the icy water and dried them on the edge of her plaid.

As she walked back to the Towers, Isabeau pondered her problem. If she did not find a source of salt soon, Bronwen would sicken and die. The only solution Isabeau could think of was to take Bronwen back to the secret valley. Deep beneath the mountain was an underground loch. Stalagmites and stalactites grew there in writhing columns, and the water was bitter. Hopefully bathing in its mineral-rich waters would help Bronwen avoid dehydration and fever. If it did not, Isabeau would have no choice but to head back toward the coast as fast as she could; she had not rescued Bronwen from danger in Lucescere only to place her in a far more life-threatening situation.

Isabeau was not sure how she was going to make the long and difficult journey back to the secret valley. From what Meghan had told her, it seemed the only road was the Great Stairway which led directly through the dragons' valley. She still felt a shiver of fear at the memory of the dragon she had seen while galloping the Old Way. Isabeau had not realized how huge or how fearsome the great, fire-breathing creatures were. Even though she had lived most of her life beneath Dragonclaw, she had only seen dragons twice, and even then they had been mere shadows passing over the moons. She knew Meghan had climbed the Great Stairway to seek counsel from the queen-dragon, but she was quite sure she did not have the courage to climb the stairs herself.

Isabeau washed the rosehips and put them on to boil with honey, then strained the syrup and laid it aside to cool. She then made her way through the cold, dark corridors to the library on the sixth floor where she was certain to find the old sorcerer.

It was a huge room with a fireplace at each end and two cunning spiral staircases made of iron lace which led to the upper galleries. Three stories high, the walls were lined with shelves which ran from the floor up to the ornately painted ceiling and were crammed with books, scrolls, letters and ledgers. The windows and fireplaces were bordered with the design of single-petaled roses and thorns, while above the mantelpieces were the stylized shapes of dragons, wings raised and tails writhing. Feld sat at a huge desk at one end of the room, dying coals in the grate behind him, a candle casting uncertain light over the page of the book he was reading. He peered through a pair of glasses, took them off, rubbed his eyes and peered again.

Isabeau waved her hand so the candelabra on the mantelpiece and the coals on the hearth leapt into life. "I made you a fresh batch o' candles especially so ye would no' strain your eyes, yet ye never think to light them," she scolded. "I might as well no' have bothered."

"Sorry, my dear. I'm afraid I always forget they are there," Feld replied absently. He was wearing a long velvet bed-gown, moth-eaten around the sleeves and hem, over a woolen jacket and breeches, with his stringy gray beard tucked through the gown's sash to stop it from hanging over the page. A badly knitted scarf was wrapped around his neck and dangled down his back, and he wore a mitten on one hand. On his feet were shabby slippers with holes in the soles. Bronwen lay on the floor beside him, kicking her legs vigorously in the air, her hands waving aimlessly.

Isabeau put the cup of tea she had made him by his elbow and perched on the side of the table. "Feld, do ye know o' any salt lakes or pools nearby, or any deposit o' rock salt?"

"The hot springs in the dragons' valley are salty," the sorcerer replied, putting his finger in the book so he would not lose his place. "I have seen salt encrusted on the rocks nearby, and many times have gathered some for use in ritual or to add to my porridge. Porridge is so tasteless without salt, do ye no' agree?"

Isabeau agreed rather defensively, having not used any of her or Feld's salt to add flavor to food since leaving Lucescere. She had saved it all for Bronwen. "Is that the only place, at the dragons' valley?" she asked.

He shrugged. "One can sometimes find deposits o' sodium chloride in volcanic regions like this, but it is no' common. I am sure there must be some rock salt somewhere in the mountains, but I have never seen it. My needs are simple, I rarely have much call for salt."

Isabeau sighed. It seemed her only choice was to brave the dragons. She knew her sister had served the great magical beasts for eight years and had often flown on the back of the youngest of the dragons. Many years before, her father had saved the life of the baby dragon and had won the creature's friendship as a result. Just because her father and sister were accepted by the dragons did not mean she would be, though. The thought of facing them was enough to make Isabeau feel rather sick.

She glanced down at the baby girl, who stared up at her intently, her pale eyes shining oddly in the firelight. Bronwen's face lit up with a wide smile. A pang of tenderness shot through Isabeau, and she knew she must make the journey to the dragons' valley. She only hoped she would be welcome.

"Make way for the Rìgh's soldiers!" a stentorian voice shouted. "Make way!"

Lilanthe parted the curtains of the window and peered out. On either side of the carriage were twelve straight-backed riders clad all in gray, their claymores strapped to their backs. Niall the Bear rode ahead, carrying the Rìgh's standard, his blue plaid and jacket showing he was one of Lachlan the Winged's Yeomen of the Guard. His great war-charger pranced as if enjoying the unusual warmth of the evening, and wide-eyed children stood and stared, their fingers in their mouths.

Ahead the village of Gilliebride was nestled in the dip of the valley, a small, prosperous-looking town that lay close to the borders of Aslinn. The road wound down the center of the wide strath, with golden barley fields stretching out on either side. A windmill turned lazily near the river, and to the west Lilanthe could see the blue waters of Loch Gillieslain lying at the foot of Tumbledown Ben. Forest grew thickly all round the stony feet of the hills, which rose steeply to the north. Lilanthe stared at the green trees with mixed feelings. In one way she longed to be under the thick canopy of leaves again, sinking her roots in the soil in peace and searching for her own kind without fear. But in another way she felt regret and a sense of failure, for Lilanthe had desperately wanted to be accepted by human society. She had hoped the victory of the Coven of Witches would enable that to happen, but it seemed the people of Eileanan were not yet ready to embrace faery kind again.

The cluricaun pushed his furry face out of the other carriage window so he could enjoy the evening breeze. She pulled him back, saying, "Best lie low, Brun, we do no' want anyone to see us."

His ears swiveled anxiously, and he said, "Why do they hate us, Lilanthe? We do no' hate them."

"Sometimes I do," she replied.

The carriage rattled into Gilliebride's large main square. Keeping her hood close about her leafy hair, Lilanthe gazed out rather wistfully at the stalls, bright with vegetables and pots of jam and marmalade. Gilliebride was high enough in the hills to have escaped assault from the Bright Soldiers, and so the marketplace was a peaceful scene. Women in rough plaids and wooden sabots stood gossiping in the warm dusk, their bare-legged children squatting on the cobblestones, tossing sheeps' knuckles. A wagon loaded with barrels stood outside a white-painted inn, the driver leaning down to talk to the innkeeper, a pipe stuck in the corner of his mouth. Above the town, the bare crown of Tumbledown Ben was fuzzed with golden light.

The party came to a halt before the inn, which had barley sheaves painted on its sign. Ostlers ran out to unhitch the horses and offer the outriders a dram of whiskey, and they dismounted thankfully, stretching and laughing.

Niall the Bear rapped on the door. "We had best stop here, lass," he said in his gruff, kind voice. "It is growing close to sundown and we need to make the Rìgh's proclamations and see the town council. Besides, the Barley Inn is famous for its whiskey, and my men are thirsty indeed after the dust o' the road."

"Ye do no' think there are too many people about? Wha' if they decide to try and stone us, like they did in Glenmorven?"

"Och, ye are in the highlands now, and highlanders were ever more comfortable wi' the faery than those stodgy Blèssem folk," he replied comfortingly. "Besides, the people o' Gilliebride have always been faithful to the MacCuinns and will no' want to start a rebellion over a tree-shifter and a wee cluricaun. Why, last time I was here they had a cluricaun turning tricks in the inn for pennies and the occasional wee dram."

"How many years ago was that, though, Niall?" Lilanthe asked wearily. "I'll wager ye there is no cluricaun here now."

"Happen ye're right, but there's a new broom sweeping clean now, and these folks will ken it. So do no' trouble yourself, we'll keep ye safe, lassie." Niall smiled at her kindly, his teeth flashing white through his beard. He was a tall, strongly built man with a great mane of dark brown hair grizzled with gray, and broad shoulders that threatened to split the cloth of his blue jacket. Unlike most men of his stature, he walked very lightly, with the grace of a swordsman.

Lilanthe smiled and thanked him. Wrapping her new green cloak tight about her, she let him open the door of the carriage so she could step out. Brun hopped out after her, pulling his own hood up to cover his furry ears. The soldiers formed a tight barrier around them and marched them into the inn, the tree-shifter walking with a halting step.

The innkeeper came placidly to greet them, showing no curiosity at the shrouded figures standing within the circle of gray-clad soldiers. He greeted them warmly, then called to his daughter to take them up to their rooms and bring them warm water and towels. Lilanthe's room was small but very clean, with a view over the town square. She sat there and watched the dusk deepen as the rattle-watch made his rounds and lanterns were kindled outside the inn. She felt uneasy. Although the scene was the very essence of rustic serenity, she felt an undercurrent of terror and pain. The smiling women, the children screeching with excitement as they played together by the pond in the village green, all hid some intense emotion which the tree-shifter's acute perceptions could sense.

She leant forward, scanning the crowd with both her eyesight and her more subtle senses. Her whole body tensed as she saw a rabble of children poking sticks at a cage hung from a willow tree. The cage swung wildly, and inside a little nisse huddled miserably, trying to protect herself from the sharp ends of the children's sticks.

Lilanthe struggled to her feet and limped as fast as she could out through the door, in her anger forgetting to catch up her new cloak. Niall heard her limping step and looked out his door. When he saw her hurrying down the stairs, he called after her, but Lilanthe ignored him, leaning on the balustrade and descending as fast as her crippled leg would let her.

Niall called to his men and followed her hastily, catching up his huge, double-edged sword. The little cluricaun heard the commotion and ran after, his tail waving excitedly.

There were eleven children in the group, ranging in age from four to thirteen. Barefoot and sunburnt, they were large, healthy children, armed with sticks and switches. As Lilanthe limped across the crowded square, calling to them to stop, they turned and faced her, lifting their sticks. For once she did not falter, coming straight up to them.

"Wha' do ye think ye are doing?" she cried. "Why do ye torment the puir wee nisse so? She does ye no harm. Look at her! It is cruel to keep her locked up in a wee cage like that and poke her with sticks and call her names."

The cage was so small the little faery was pressed in by wicker on all sides, unable to move more than a few inches. No larger than Lilanthe's hand, the nisse's triangular face was scarred with cuts and bruises. Only one bright eye peered through the tangle of filthy hair, the other glued shut with her sticky, greenish blood. Her water-bright wings were bent back by the walls of the cage, the iridescent gauze of one torn and lacerated. As Lilanthe spoke, the nisse screeched and threw herself desperately against the open weave of the cage.

The eldest of the children, a stocky, freckle faced girl, jeered loudly. "Look, it be a tree faery! Look at its hair, all leafy like the willow tree. Where's my father's axe? There's enough firewood there to feed our fires all winter!"

It was a familiar jeer, but for once it failed to send terror beating through Lilanthe's sap. She drew herself up. "How can some one so young be so mean?" she said. "It is true I am a tree faery, but I am no less than ye for that. Beware what ye say, lassie, for one day ye shall be walking in the forests and ye shall find the trees whose shade ye seek are no friends o' yours. Ye shall see the trees walking, and ye shall hear their terrible song and wish that ye had had more respect for those no' o' your kind. For the creatures o' the forest were here long before ye humankind came to our shores wi' your axes and your evil fires, and we shall be here long after your bones are food for our roots."

Silence had fallen over the busy square, and all faces were turned Lilanthe's way. The children looked afraid, and one or two were snivelling, their sticks fallen forgotten from their hands.

The tree-shifter shook back her mane of leaves defiantly and made her way through the silent children to break open the wicker cage. The nisse darted into her hand and quivered there, its broken wing trailing. Lilanthe cradled the faery tenderly. "Look at this puir wee thing!" she cried. "Look wha' ye have done to her! She should be flying free through the forest wi' her kin, sipping nectar from the flowers and teasing the squirrels."

"She be naught but a wicked faery who steals grain from the sacks and snatches bread from our hands," one of the women cried.

"I ken the nisses are cheeky wee things," Lilanthe replied, "but is this kind, to stuff her in a cage and let the children beat her wi' their sticks? All this land was once forest, rich wi' nuts and seeds for her to eat. Now it is all fields and there is no forest left for those who lived here first. She would starve if she did no' eat your grain and bread! Is that the way to thank those who are your hosts, who let ye take their land and believed ye when ye offered the hand o' friendship? Do ye think any o' us faeries would have let ye live if we had known what ye would do to us and ours? Once we were many and ye were but a few, and hungry. We thought the fruits o' the forest were plentiful and made ye welcome to take what ye needed. Instead ye cut down our homes and raped the land wi' your plows and axes, and infected us wi' your wasting sicknesses, and brought those greedy rats that fight the creatures o' the forest for what is rightfully theirs! And even that was no' enough; ye had to make it a sport to hunt us down and ye watched us burn on your fires for amusement! Ye wonder why we hate ye!"

Lilanthe stopped, panting, her cheeks burning. Niall the Bear and his men stood behind her, hands on their swords, but no one in the town square looked belligerent. They stood silently, their eyes downcast in shame. A few were resentful, but all had heard the town crier read out the new rìgh's decrees and had heard the penalties for those who defied them. Lilanthe stared around her, the anger draining out of her and leaving her perilously close to tears. Seeing nothing but rejection on the faces of the crowd, she turned and hurried back to the inn, the little faery safely cupped in her hands. The nisse pushed her tiny head out through Lilanthe's fingers and jeered mockingly at the villagers in her high, shrill voice.

Lilanthe did not have Isabeau's healing skills, but she bound up the torn wing as best she could and gave the faery water to drink and bread to chew on. The tree-shifter's cheeks were wet with tears wept for the pain the little faery had suffered and for her own loneliness and sorrow. She knew the nisse could never fly again with the fragile fabric of her wing so damaged, and so she crooned to her gently, in pity.

The nisse was exultant, however, and chattered non-stop in her own shrill language. *Let us sting stab those warm-blooded giants, let us piss in their waters and hurl poison berries into their food, let us goad them weeping and wailing into the sea!*

"Nay," Lilanthe said wearily. "We canna do that. The humans are here to stay. They have been here a thousand years now and have sunk their roots as deep into this soil as your kin or mine. And no' all are evil or ignorant. I have friends who are human."

The nisse squealed in disapproval.

Lilanthe said, "Better that we teach them to love and respect us, than let them taint us with their evil ways. Tree-changers are peace-loving creatures. All we wish for is to roam the land as we please, tasting the soil and celebrating the passing o' the seasons."

The nisse grinned wickedly, showing needle-sharp fangs. Lilanthe smiled despite herself. "I hope ye can forgive those foolish bairns, for indeed they did no' understand what they did. Happen they will think a wee now, and no' be so cruel next time."

The nisse was crouched on the table, licking her delicate little hands with a long, forked tongue and wiping her face clean. She trilled in derision.

"That is my task," Lilanthe explained softly. "I travel on behalf o' the Coven o' Witches, to win the faeries and humans to peace and understanding. I go in search o' the Summer Tree, hoping I can win the forest faeries to our cause and convince them the Coven means them only good."

The nisse cocked her head and looked up at Lilanthe speculatively. Her eye was as bright as a green flame. Lilanthe broke off a few more crumbs for her, and she snatched one up, cramming it into her mouth. *I know where the Summer Tree blooms blossoms. The juice of its flower will heal my wing so I can fly fleet once more.*

"Will ye take me there?" Lilanthe cried, her freckled face lighting up in hope.

Broken-winged I cannot soar swoop so far. So I will take you, as you shall take me. We must fly fleet, though, for the Summer Tree flowers only once, when the Celestines sing hum the sun to life. Only once a year the Summer Tree blossoms and blooms, and then its flowers wither wane on the branch and I must wait weep another year.

Lilanthe nodded. "Very well, we shall ride out tomorrow. Fear no', we shall find the Summer Tree now that we have ye to show us the way. It may take us a while, but in the end we shall find it."

PALACE OF THE DRAGONS

"**S**ee how the eagle uses the movement o' the wind to fly? See, he barely moves his wings, yet he soars hundreds o' feet above the earth. He understands the forces o' air and uses them. That is what ye must do if ye are to fly," Ishbel said.

She and Isabeau were sitting on a rocky ledge, watching an eagle soar through the air. Far below them the green meadows of the Cursed Valley undulated, cut in two by the blue snake of the river that wound away from the loch. On all sides the sharp pointed peaks rose, stretching as far as the eye could see. The snowy glacier swept away to the north, so bright in the sunshine it hurt the eye to gaze at it. With envious eyes Isabeau watched the eagle hover, wondering what it felt like to drift so effortlessly above the world. Suddenly the bird folded his wings and plummeted to earth. Moments later he rose with great strokes of his wings, a coney in his claws.

"How am I to learn to understand the wind, though?" Isabeau asked, watching longingly as her mother floated a foot off the ground, her legs tucked beneath her. Isabeau held Bronwen in her lap, the child tugging at her bright red-gold hair which hung in a plait over one shoulder. In the meadow behind them, Lasair cropped at the lush grass, while Feld lay in the shelter of a tree, reading a book.

"I do no' ken," Ishbel replied. "It is partly instinct, I suppose, and partly experience. Ye must watch the wind, and listen to it, and feel it with your skin."

"How am I meant to watch the wind?" Isabeau asked in some exasperation. "Air is invisible. It is no' like the

earth, which ye can touch and smell and taste." She
crumbled a sod of soil between her fingers, lifting it to
her nose to inhale its rich, peaty odor. Bronwen reached
out her grubby little hand, grabbing a clump of dirt and
trying to eat it. Isabeau smiled and cuddled her closer.

"Ye can touch and smell and taste the wind too," Ishbel replied. "Can ye no' feel it against your skin?"

Isabeau sat still for a moment, trying to understand
what her mother meant. "I suppose so," she said slowly.
"Though it's so still today, I canna feel much."

"That is one thing," Ishbel replied. "It is still and
warm, yet still the eagle finds currents o' air to fly with.
Where is the wind coming from?"

Isabeau noticed how the stems of the dandelions bent
and swayed in the meadow below them, how the leaves
of the trees turned up their silver undersides. She felt a
faint movement in the hairs on her bare arm. "From the
south," she replied hesitantly. "Maybe the southeast."

"Good," Ishbel said. "Now look at the clouds. Look
at their shape, their dimensions, their height, color and
texture. Clouds are water carried by air. They will tell
ye how the wind blows too. See how small and low the
clouds are? It shall no' rain today. Now smell the wind.
What does it smell of?"

"Grass," Isabeau said after a moment. "Warm grass."
She remembered her lessons with Latifa the Cook, and
how she had made her identify foods from smell and
taste alone. She shut her eyes and concentrated. "Hemlock leaves, from the tree down there," she said after a
while. "Clover, and dandelions, and harebells too, I
think. Soil, rich soil, filled with rotting vegetation. Water.
Still water, though, no' rain."

"Very good," Ishbel said. "Breathe it deeply into your
lungs. Taste it. Get to know every variation o' taste and
texture. Ye will soon know if the wind blows steady and
strong, or if it is a capricious breeze, and hard to fly
with."

"This reminds me of what Seychella told me about
whistling the wind," Isabeau said. "She told me I needed

to understand how the wind blows to be able to work the weather."

"I remember Seychella Wind-Whistler," Ishbel said rather dreamily. "She was Tabithas's apprentice when I was Meghan's. They thought she could one day be a great weather witch, like in the auld days. Whatever happened to her?"

"She was killed by a Mesmerd," Isabeau said grimly. "Do ye no' remember? She was one o' the witches at my Testing. She was killed when the Red Guards attacked. Ye flew away. I thought ye must die, the way ye stepped off the cliff, but ye just floated away, as easy as the seeds o' those dandelions."

"I remember," Ishbel said softly. "I am sorry to hear she died, though."

"Can ye work weather?" Isabeau asked. "Many o' the things ye say mirror what she said, but she could no' fly. I asked her."

Ishbel shrugged. "I have never really tried to use the forces o' air in that way. Weather magic has as much to do with the element o' water or fire. Ye might have some skill with the weather but I do no' think your Talent is to fly. I am sorry I canna teach ye more."

"You were able to teach Iseult," Isabeau said, her voice tight.

"She had the Talent," Ishbel replied. "She was just too used to using her own strength and vigor, rather than the forces o' air. Ye have power, I can sense that, and I know Meghan always thought so too. It is different from mine, though. Ye seem strong in all the elements, while I could never manage to manipulate fire or earth."

Ishbel looked down at her hands. On the heart finger of her right hand she wore a blue topaz, showing air was the element she was strongest in, and the moonstone ring Lachlan had given her at his Testing was on her middle finger. On her left hand she wore a sapphire and an opal, indicating that she had passed the Sorceress Tests of Air and Spirit.

"Ye must have been very young to win your sorceress rings," Isabeau said.

"Aye, I was. I was no' yet twenty, and as ye know, ye usually must wait until ye are twenty-four before ye are allowed to sit any o' the Tests o' Elements. My Talent was so strange and so strong, however, that the Coven made an exception. Some o' the other witches were no' pleased, but Meghan insisted."

Isabeau sighed and stretched, admiring the flash of the rings on her own hands. She too wore a moonstone ring on the middle finger of her right hand—that was the first ring any witch won—while on her left hand she wore the dragoneye stone the dragons had given her when she was born. The sight of it reassured her, and she stood. "We had best keep on climbing if we are to reach the Great Stairway by dawn tomorrow," she said abruptly.

Feld, Ishbel and Isabeau had set out the previous day to climb the mountain, Bronwen in a sling on Isabeau's back as usual. Somehow the young apprentice witch did not feel comfortable riding on Lasair's back now she knew he was really her father. So she walked, her arms filled with a great branch of sweet-scented roses, their white petals frilled with red. This was the rose-tithe, the payment the MacFaghans had to make to the dragons in return for their friendship and forbearance. One of the decaying tapestries hanging in the great hall showed Faodhagan the Red giving the queen-dragon a rose he had carelessly plucked and tucked in his buttonhole. The gift had so amused and pleased the queen-dragon she had allowed the cheeky human to live, and so the friendship between the sorcerer and the dragons had begun.

For centuries the rose-tithe had not been paid, but Feld had only been allowed to stay in the valley if he revived the ancient custom. When Iseult lived at the Towers, it had been her duty to cut a bunch of roses and carry it to the dragons' palace every midsummer, and now it was Isabeau's task. She had picked the roses while they were still tightly furled, then sprayed them with icy water to try and prevent them from wilting during the long climb to the Cursed Peaks. Their sweet, faint scent wafted around her as she clambered up the rocky path, and she wondered if she could distill the perfume for her candles and bath oil.

The way grew steep, but the view was so spectacular that Isabeau was content to climb slowly, occasionally pausing to wait for Feld, who often stopped to examine a flower or stone, or to read a passage from his book, which he carried under one arm. Feld was wearing a long coat of velvet, which Isabeau had brushed and darned for him, and had replaced his worn slippers with a pair of equally shabby boots. His long, striped scarf was wound around his neck, the ragged ends dangling down his back, while his beard was looped through his belt. On his head he wore a moth-eaten cap pulled low over his ears, and his gray hair stuck out from underneath it like straw spilling from an overstuffed sack. Behind his spectacles, Feld's eyes were vague and kind and, like a child's, always on the lookout for something new and wondrous.

Ishbel did not walk with them, but flew about as aimlessly as a sparrow, sometimes alighting in a tree to wait for them, sometimes dropping down to walk with the stallion. Lasair picked his way ahead of them up the path, breaking into a gallop when the way led into a meadow, wheeling around to call to them from the top of a hill, his bright mane flying.

They camped that night in the overhang of the cliff, Isabeau lighting a fire with a snap of her fingers and cooking them a nourishing stew from the supplies in the pack the stallion carried for her. Lasair lay down in the grass beside them, and Isabeau leant against his comforting bulk gratefully. Just around the bluff was the massive stone archway that marked the beginning of the Great Stairway. The stone dragons that spread their sculpted wings on either side of the archway were chilling reminders of what Isabeau had still to face. She tried hard to think of the coming confrontation with excitement and confidence, reminding herself again and again that the MacFaghans had always been friends to the dragons. Deep inside her was a niggling fear the great creatures would find her unworthy of their regard, however, maimed as she was and a failure.

Dawn across the icy peaks was a breathtaking sight, and Isabeau stood and watched the delicate splendor of the mountains with a sense of awe and humility. She drank her tea and ate her unsalted porridge in silence, and then picked up her armful of roses and made her way to the Great Stairway.

Isabeau stood alone under the shadow of the archway, looking up at the glowing sky with mingled apprehension and anticipation. Although she scanned the horizon constantly, the whistling dive of a dragon from above her still took her by surprise and she stumbled back with an inarticulate cry. Wings folded along his lissom body, he plunged down as fast as a flaming arrow, then flung open his wings just above her head. Isabeau was nearly knocked over by the force of his passing. When she recovered her balance, she saw the dragon was resting on the curve of the archway above her, his long serpentine tail wrapped several times around the camber of stone, his chain laid on his daintily crossed claws.

Close-lidded eyes of bright topaz regarded her with interest. Apart from the gentle swaying of the tip of his tail and the faint pulsing in his creamy throat, the dragon was still.

Isabeau had to fight down the terror that weakened every muscle and organ in her body. She took a deep breath and sank into a curtsey, keeping her eyes lowered. *Greetings, Great One,* she said haltingly, in the oldest and most difficult of languages. *I have brought ye the tithe o' roses in the name o' the MacFaghans, as the dragons decreed long ago, and hope that the long friendship between my clan and yours may grow and flourish as the roses do.*

To her consternation, the dragon yawned, his long, supple tongue, the color of the summer sky, curling out from between rows of needle-sharp teeth. He laid his angular head back on his claws and closed his eyes. Every line of his body suggested boredom and scorn.

Isabeau laid the branch of rosebuds on the first step and stepped back, waiting, though her palms were clammy and her knees weak. After a long period of silence, the dragon yawned again, and examined his claws through slitted eyes. The tip of his long, serrated tail began to swing more quickly.

Isabeau calmed her breathing and tried to remember everything Feld had told her. He had studied the lore of dragons ever since he was a young apprentice witch and knew more about the great, magical creatures than any human alive.

I know that I am o' as little account to the dragons as a gnat or a flea, a mere irritant in their flesh to be idly crushed between their claws. I humbly beg their indulgence, in the name o' my ancestor Faodhagan the Red, and beg that I may be allowed to pay homage to the Circle o' Seven, and receive the privilege o' their wisdom. I have brought gifts, insignificant though they are.

Moving slowly, her head still bent in supplication, Isabeau brought out the handful of artifacts she had chosen from the Towers. There was an armband set with an uncut ruby the size of a pigeon's egg, a solid gold statuette of a dragon in flight, a long string of milky pearls, a chalice carved with magical runes, and a silver dagger, so stained and notched that the fine workmanship was barely recognizable.

There were many such things in the Towers of Roses and Thorns—some piled in chests and cupboards, others lying among the dust and cobwebs and owl guano as if they had simply fallen from someone's hand. Feld had helped Isabeau choose a selection to bring for the dragons, passing his hands over the pile, his shaggy eyebrows drawn together in a frown of concentration. Isabeau had copied him and had been amazed to feel responses within her—some gave her a shiver of delight or distaste, others brought an image or sensation, so brief and frail that the insight was gone as soon as it came.

Isabeau was shaken with excitement. It seemed the veils that had covered her third eye were truly dropping away, giving her the clear-sight she had always longed for. A witch without the witch sense was no witch at all, and Isabeau had found it hard to swallow her resentment at Meghan for sealing up her third eye without her consent or knowledge.

The ruby armband had given her an impression of a tall man with a shaggy mane and beard of red hair turning to gray, quick to laughter and anger, with hands that spoke of a craftsman, strong and long-fingered. With it had been a square-cut ruby ring, which Feld had fingered for a long time and at last put back in the chest with a sigh, saying, "Happen we shall have need o' this in time, lassie. Take the dragons the pearls instead—they are finely matched and worth a rìgh's ransom, and as creatures o' air and flame, the dragons are always fascinated by things o' the sea."

The dagger Isabeau had found while clearing out the garden at the foot of the northern tower. As soon as she laid her hand upon it she was overcome by a vortex of emotion so intense she had grown dizzy for a moment. Obsessive hatred and jealousy, grief, fury, a stifling misery—all of these and more had washed over Isabeau so that she flung the dagger from her in panicked reflex. Later, when her hammering heart had slowed and the tumult of emotions had subsided, she went hunting through the undergrowth in search of it again. She picked it up through a fold in her plaid and carried it at arm's length into the library, able to feel it and smell it even through the thick wool.

Feld clambered down from the ladder, a book under his arm, and took it from her with a vague query in his myopic eyes. Immediately his eyebrows shot up and he dropped the dagger as if it had burnt his hand. "Obh obh!" he cried. "Where did ye find this!"

Isabeau explained, and he pursed up his mouth and examined the blackened knife closely. "I wonder . . ." he said. "Ye say ye found it at the foot o' the northern tower?"

Isabeau nodded, and he said thoughtfully, "That was Sorcha's tower, ye ken. Happen this was her knife. It seems steeped in murder to me." He gave a little shudder and they stared at the dagger with fascinated eyes. It seemed to throb with a malignant power that set all the hairs on the backs of their necks quivering.

"What shall we do with it?" Isabeau had asked. "I do

no' think I could bear to have it near me. Should we bury it, or throw it on the fire?"

"Let us give it to the dragons," Feld had replied. "It is just the sort o' thing to give them pleasure."

So Isabeau had wrapped the dagger in oiled cloth, trying not to touch it with her fingers, and pushed it to the very bottom of the pack. She brought it out just as reluctantly, laying it with the other artifacts on the stone, stepping back as if the notched blade truly stank of death and blood.

The dragon unwound his body from the archway with quick and sinuous grace, and flew down to the ground with such swiftness that Isabeau again scrambled backward in instinctive fear. Coiling his tail around his hindquarters, he bent down his great, square head to smell the dagger, his red, cavernous nostrils flaring.

The dragon's breath hissed. From under her lashes Isabeau could see his slitted pupil widen. Then the dragon shot her a glance and Isabeau was transfixed in the dart of his golden gaze like a butterfly on a pin.

Isabeau knew one should never meet a dragon's gaze. She knew one lost all will and sense, as helpless as a coney hypnotized by the stare of a sabre leopard. She had carefully kept her eyes averted all through their conversation, despite her fascination with the great, gleaming, scaled creature and its sinuous, menacing grace. That one quick glance undid her. Isabeau was drowning in the rough gold of his huge, steadfast eye, rapt in its fiery beauty.

She saw a fountain of fire, the sky raining ashes, a river of stone. She saw stars blooming, comets of ice soaring, suns collapsing into whirlpools of darkness in which time itself was bent.

The fiery darkness wheeled around her, blanking her senses. Isabeau felt the ground beneath her feet reeling. For the first time she knew, terrifyingly, in every fiber of her being, that the planet spun through space like a conker swung by a child. It seemed the ground rushed up to slam into her. She lost consciousness for only a moment but still experienced such a sense of dizzying dislocation and confusion when she opened her eyes that it seemed she did not know who she was or where. Then she saw her hand lying on the mossy stone, the two fingers and thumb slack and slightly curled, the scars of her torture white and shiny. Reason rushed back upon her.

She was lying on cold stone. Sharp pain was piercing her arm. Isabeau shifted and saw her arm had fallen upon the branch of roses, its thorns piercing her flesh. She sat up slowly, her hand to her head. By her foot was a great claw, arching over her like the vault of an ivory pillar. Fear chilled her blood. She glanced up and saw the dragon towering over her, as tall as the tallest tree in the forest. His scales gleamed like polished bronze, paling to satiny cream on his breast and belly. He bent his huge, angular head and regarded her with those beguiling golden eyes, and she stared back at him, unable to resist the desire to drown in his gaze again.

It is a brave human who meets the dragon's stare, he said in a surprisingly gentle voice. *Thou hast brought us kingly gifts indeed, and ones that I understand are of significance to thy clan. The gifts that are a wrench to give are the gifts that please us most. Rise, Isabeau the Red. Know that thou hast permission to climb the Great Stairway and take audience with the Circle of Seven. Thy companions must wait for thy return.*

Isabeau opened her mouth in some distress, knowing how much both Feld and Ishbel longed to take audience with the dragons' council also, but the words dried on her lips at the nearness of all that shining, dangerous beauty, and she merely bowed her head in acquiescence.

The dragon bent and gathered his strength, wings stretching wide, then he launched into the air, the wind as he passed almost knocking Isabeau over. She staggered and grasped at the stone pillar to keep herself balanced, then watched the dragon soar out of sight, a tightness akin to tears in her throat.

She bent and picked up the artifacts, packing them back into her satchel, gathered up the roses again and went to tell Feld and Ishbel what the dragon had said.

Feld was disappointed that he was not to accompany

her, both for her sake and his own. He had spent all his life studying and observing the dragons and yet could never get his fill. Only occasionally did they allow him to make the journey to their palace or answer the many questions he asked, and he was sorry that Isabeau's coming to Tīrlethan had relieved him of the rose-tithe duty. More importantly, however, he worried that Isabeau might forget his lessons or advice and so inadvertently anger the dragons.

Ishbel was rather relieved that she had to stay behind, even though she desperately wanted to ask the dragons how Khan'gharad could be freed from his enchantment. She gripped Isabeau's hands painfully tight and said in a quavering voice, "Ye will ask them for me, will ye no'? If anyone can break this evil spell, it will be the dragons."

Isabeau nodded and said, "Have a care for Bronwen. She will miss me while I am gone and may fret a wee." She bent and picked up the little girl and hugged her tightly. Bronwen pressed her warm face into Isabeau's neck, babbling, "Bo-Bo-Bo," the closest she could come to Isabeau's name.

"We shall look after her, dinna ye worry," Feld answered. "Be careful and canny, Isabeau, won't ye?"

She smiled rather wanly, shouldered her satchel again and left them with a wave. Then she crossed under the shadow of the arch once more and began to climb.

The road was built of large paving stones fitted together so closely that few weeds were able to find room in which to flourish. On either side was a high wall carved with scenes of men and animals and faeries, separated and bordered by an intricate frieze featuring the familiar design of roses and thorns. As Isabeau climbed she became absorbed in the bas-relief sculpture which seemed to be depicting stories from history and myth. She recognized one sequence as being the tale of Faodhagan and the dragon, for there was the tall man down on one knee presenting a perfectly carved rose to the great winged creature coiled above him. Isabeau saw the kneeling man wore an armband like the one she carried in her pack, and her eyes widened in amazement. So the

ruby ring and armband had belonged to the Red Sorcerer—no wonder the dragon had been pleased with
her gifts.

Higher up the road was a sequence of panels showing
the building of a city, directed by a man with a tall bow
and a grave face, a falling star carved overhead. Another
series of panels showed tree-changers dancing, their leafy
hair spread out in the wind, while an antlered man stood
with his head bowed beneath a flowering tree. Higher
still the bas-relief sculpture depicted a sea serpent coiling
its long body around a ship with a broken mast, the
towering waves all around thick with the sleek bodies
and tusked faces of the Fairgean.

Once or twice each day Isabeau scaled the wall to peer
over the edge, but she only saw variations of the grand
vista of snowy mountains stretching as far as the eye
could see.

The road crossed the mountain in three long, steep
lines, marked at each turn by another wide platform with
a tall archway guarded by two stone dragons. Isabeau
found that if she pushed herself hard enough, she was
able to reach each platform by nightfall, giving her a
more comfortable place in which to set up camp. By the
end of the third day she had reached the mountaintop
height, the jagged peak looming above her.

She stepped under the curving archway and saw that
this platform was much longer and wider than the others,
bounded to the east, north and west by a low wall. Her
heart beginning to pound with excitement, Isabeau hurried across the dais so she could get her first glimpse of
the dragons' valley.

She leant her elbows on the wall and stared down. The
peak opposite was still bright with sunset light, but the
pinnacle behind her shadowed the crater below, so that
Isabeau could see nothing but craggy walls descending
into a misty darkness. Disappointed, she unrolled her
blanket and stuck her finger in the pot of vegetable soup
to heat it up. She had made the soup before setting out
on her journey, filling it with as many different varieties
of vegetables, roots and grains as she could find. Since

Isabeau ate the soup several times a day, she was already heartily sick of the taste, but there was no food to be gathered on this stony road and she had no desire to bear the weight of a wide selection of different foods. For the same reason she carried no firewood and so was unable to light a fire to cheer up the dark nights. Once the sun set there was little she could do but lie on the hard paving stones and watch the stars wheel overhead. Luckily it was midsummer and so the skies were clear and the night air only just touched with chill. Isabeau knew Meghan had climbed this mountain while snow still lay thick on the ground and she thought how cold and grievous the old witch's journey must have been. She wondered whether Meghan had been nervous of meeting the dragons, but she could not imagine her indomitable guardian ever feeling anything so feeble as fear.

Meghan woke with all her senses preternaturally alert. All was dark and still. She lay quietly, casting out her witch sense, wondering what scent dread creeping down her spine like a trickle of cold water. After a moment she threw off her blanket and got stiffly to her feet. Gitâ protested sleepily and buried himself deeper under her pillow as the sorceress lifted the flap of her tent and looked out.

Mist drifted through the army camp, wreathing the tents and blurring the glow of the banked fires. Meghan frowned. It was midsummer and the weather had been hot and clear for weeks, making it difficult for the witches to call up rain to dampen the Bright Soldiers' fuses or to cover the Graycloaks' movements. There had been hard fighting indeed, with the Graycloaks winning back towns and villages one week, only to lose them again the next. This night they were camped on the shore of the River Arden, having pushed the Bright Soldiers back into southern Blèssem.

Although Meghan should have been pleased to see the weather change, her forehead was furrowed deeply and her seamed mouth was grim. After a moment she bent and caught up her staff and plaid. Wrapping the thick wool shawl around her shoulders, she walked out into the mist.

So quiet was she that the sentries sitting outside the royal pavilion did not hear her coming nor see her small, dark form slipping through the shadows. The sorceress came up behind them and startled one by dropping her hand on his shoulder. "Shane, have ye seen or heard anything?" she asked softly.

The burly man stifled a gasp and shook his head. "Nay, Keybearer, all is quiet," he answered.

"The mist began to rise about five, ten minutes ago," said the other sentry, a dark-haired man named Byrne Braveheart. "But otherwise we have no' heard even the squeak o' a mouse."

The sorceress nodded. "Keep a close eye and ear out and sound the alarm at the slightest hint o' trouble," she said. "I have a bad feeling indeed."

They nodded, hefting their weapons and scanning the mist with increased vigilance. She hesitated, then slipped away to another tent nearby, lifting its flap and calling softly, "Gwilym . . ."

He answered her softly.

"I'm sorry to wake ye, but I think I may need ye," she whispered.

"I was awake," he answered rather thickly. "I do no' ken why, for I was exhausted after all that spell-casting we did yesterday. I feel uneasy though . . ."

"So do I," she whispered as he came to the flap of the tent, leaning on his club.

"Mist," he said gruffly and sniffed the air. "Smells like the marsh," he said, his voice rising in sudden consternation.

She said softly, "I thought so too. Mesmerdean?"

"Let us pray to Eà that it is no' so," he replied grimly, a shadow of fear in his voice.

Suddenly there was a hoarse cry of alarm. Meghan whipped round. "The royal pavilion!" she cried. Both limping as fast as they could, the old sorceress and the one-legged warlock hurried back through the camp to the tall, white tent where Iseult and Lachlan slept. They could see nothing in the all-enveloping mist, then a silvery light sprang up which illuminated the camp all around. They saw a tall, alien-looking shadow bending over the drooping form of a broad-shouldered man. Behind the bent figure fluttered the shadow of long, gauzy wings. Meghan gave an inarticulate cry, terror leaping through her veins. Then she muttered, "Nay, Lachlan must be safe, it is the Lodestar shedding all that light and none can raise it but he!"

They reached the pavilion and saw Shane Mòr lying in the entrance to the royal pavilion. He was on his back, a smile of bliss on his dead face. Meghan and Gwilym did not pause to examine him, lifting their plaids to cover their mouths and noses instead and stepping over his corpse to rush inside the tent.

Ten of the winged creatures were hovering inside the perimeter of the tent, their stiff, translucent wings whirring, their great clusters of myriad eyes glittering a metallic green in the brightness of the Lodestar which shone like a star in Lachlan's hand. He and Iseult were backed against the tent pole, both naked. Lachlan was holding the faeries off with the threat of the Lodestar, a little eating knife in his other hand. Iseult had caught up her eight-sided *reil* but it hung from her fingers as she stared with fascination at the hovering marsh-faeries. Byrne Braveheart lay a few steps into the tent, the same rapturous smile on his upturned face.

As the witches rushed in, the Mesmerdean turned their handsome inhuman faces their way. Immediately Lachlan darted forward and ran his dagger through the eye of the marsh-faery nearest to him. It exploded into powder and Lachlan danced back, his hand cupped over his mouth and nose.

It was clear he had already killed two Mesmerdean, for their bodies had dissolved into two little pyramids of gray dust which Meghan and Gwilym were careful to keep well clear of.

Meghan took one look at Iseult's dreamy, contented face and clicked her tongue in annoyance. The sorceress would have liked to have shaken the young Banrìgh out

of her enthralled state, but half the marsh-faeries had
darted toward her and she had to move quickly to fight
them off. One she knocked away with her staff, another
exploded in mid-air with a flash of blue fire, and yet
another was blown off course by a wind that came
from nowhere.

Gwilym had killed one of the ghostly creatures with a
skillful thrust of his staff but had overbalanced and
fallen, his wooden leg unable to find purchase on the
earthen floor. Lying on his side, he sent blue witch's fire
arcing through the air, sizzling one as it dropped toward
him. He rolled to one side, covering his face with his
plaid as it fell to earth in a shower of dust.

Meanwhile, Meghan had gathered together a writhing
blue sphere of energy and thrown it at another Mesmerd
who had flitted down to grasp the warlock with its claws.
As the Mesmerd disintegrated, Gwilym was blown over
and over, slamming into Iseult's bare legs and bringing
her down in a tangle.

Lachlan leapt forward and brought the Lodestar slicing
through the middle of a Mesmerd threatening him from
the side. As it collapsed in a billow of gray draperies,
he followed through with the swing and the white light
of the glowing orb demolished another as if it were a
sword. As Gwilym and Iseult scrambled to recover their
balance, Lachlan and Meghan between them attacked
the three remaining Mesmerdean. The winged creatures
were wary now, however, moving with such sudden swiftness that time after time they escaped the fate of their
kindred.

Iseult had been shaken out of her dreamy fascination
by the fall. Although she was still rather dazed, she bent
her wrist and threw the bright eight-sided *reil*. It spun
round, cutting through the claw and hard shell of one,
the iridescent wing of another and the edge of the third's
robe before spinning back to her hand. Lachlan was able
to kill one of the wounded with a dagger thrust to the
eye, while Gwilym beat the other down with his staff.
Iseult threw her *reil* again, but the remaining Mesmerd

deftly avoided it, darting fast as a hornet out of the tent flap to disappear into the mist.

Choking and gasping in the dust-filled air, they stumbled out after them, neither Iseult nor Lachlan noticing they were still both stark naked. Meghan bent over her staff, coughing, then threw her plaid to Iseult to cover herself as Duncan Ironfist and Cathmor the Nimble came running half naked out of the mists, claymores drawn.

The camp had erupted, the sounds of fighting and the bright light of the Lodestar having roused the sleeping men.

"Where is the danger?" Duncan cried. "Who has attacked ye, Your Highness? How did they get into your tent? I shall gut those useless sentries myself!"

Gwilym caught his breath, saying harshly, "It is no' the sentries' fault, Duncan. Marsh-faeries come and go as they please, without making a sound. It is no' for nothing that they are called the Gray Ghosts."

Iseult huddled Meghan's dark green plaid around her, trying to still the little shudders that ran over her. She was leaning heavily on Lachlan, her face very white. She had been the worst affected by the stench of the dying Mesmerdean. Worst of all, she was ashamed and mortified by her failure to react to their attack.

"I'm the Scarred Warrior," she muttered, "but I stood and stared with my mouth hanging open like a foolish bairn. I canna understand it!"

Meghan said gruffly, "I think it mun be because ye almost died in their embrace that time in the Veiled Forest. They seem able to hypnotize their prey, and since ye have fallen into their embrace before, happen ye were more susceptible this time. Do no' trouble yourself about it, Iseult, they are powerful, uncanny creatures indeed."

"But what if they come at us again?" Iseult said. "It seems they have no' let go o' their vendetta against us. How am I to guard Lachlan if I fall into a swoon at the very sight and smell o' them?" She gave a little shudder at the remembrance of their dank, swampy odor.

"I shall guard ye," Lachlan said rather smugly. "It was

rather a nice change to have my Scarred Warrior clinging
and helpless for a change."

Iseult gave a snort of disgust and said rather curtly to
Duncan, "Can ye have someone clean out our tent for
us? I've had enough o' standing around half naked and
having the entire camp gawking at me."

Indeed, the plaid barely managed to cover much of
her at all and many of the soldiers were transfixed by
the sight of her long, bare legs and messy red hair.

"O' course, Your Highness," Duncan replied urbanely.

"Make sure they are careful no' to breathe in any o'
the dust or let it drift onto their skins," Meghan warned.
As he nodded and issued swift orders, she clenched her
fingers around her flower-carved staff and gazed out into
the mist. "That is another eleven Mesmerdean to be
added to our account," she said grimly. "Indeed, I do
no' think they will give up on this vendetta o' theirs."

"Mesmerdean never forgive and never forget," Gwilym said harshly. "As I know to my cost. Indeed, they
are fitting associates o' Margrit o' Arran."

Isabeau woke with a jerk, her plaid rumpled over her
face and smothering her. She fought it off, at first not
knowing where she was. Then she lay staring up at the
night sky, feeling vague and unsettled, her consciousness
not yet fully returned. She was still snared in her dream,
a dream she had had before. A face bending down over
hers, a beautiful alien face with great glittering eyes. A
face that was both lover and destroyer, that fascinated
as it repelled. She gave a little shudder, trying to shake
off the effects of the nightmare. After a while, she gathered up her things and began to walk on, afraid to fall
asleep again in case the dream returned.

Later that day Isabeau at last approached the end of
the Great Stairway. Her steps quickened with anticipation and apprehension, adrenaline beginning to pump
through her veins. She could see the great curve of the
archway and the shapes of the stone dragons, wings
spread wide. Beyond there was only rock and twisting
tendrils of mist. Isabeau came down to the platform with

a rush and then stopped, staring out into the valley with wide eyes. It was shaped like a deep bowl, as if some giant had scooped out the top of the mountain with a spoon. A vivid green loch filled most of the valley, its surface wisped with steam. Isabeau had to cover her nose with her hand for the air stank of rotten eggs. The surface of the water stirred and rippled as if touched by wind, but the air in the crater was still and heavy and warm. Occasionally bubbles rose to the surface, so that Isabeau wondered uneasily if some loch monster dwelt in its depths.

On the northern wall of the crater were seven great arched doorways all bordered by intricate knots and tendrils of stone. Wide circular steps spread out before the seven doorways like ripples cast from a stone and led down to a broad, paved square before the loch. The warm, sulphurous mist hung everywhere, giving the loch and the yawning dark doorways an uncanny, mysterious atmosphere.

Isabeau tried to gather the courage to step down from the dais into the valley but found her legs were unaccountably watery. She gripped the bunch of roses tightly and tried to remember all that Feld and Meghan had told her of dragons. Should she wait here until they gave her permission to enter, or should she brave the dragons' wrath by entering their domain without ceremony?

Suddenly a deafening bugle resounded around the valley and Isabeau saw a dragon soar out of the central doorway, her hooked and clawed wings spread wide, her tail whipping behind. The dragon circled the valley three times and then landed lightly before her, her wings folding along her side. She was smaller than the dragon Isabeau had seen earlier, and her silk-smooth scales were burnished green in color. Her topaz-gold eyes were slitted and her crested tail swished around like a cat's.

Without warning Isabeau's legs gave way and she dropped to her hands and knees.

Thou art wise for a human child, to kneel thus before me, the dragon said, her nose in the air. *Wiser than most of thy kind who think they are the lords of the earth and*

*sky. I see thou hast brought my queen-mother roses, as
the Great Circle decreed almost a thousand years ago.*

Isabeau nodded, staring down at the rose branch she
had dropped on the ground. The flowers were fully open
now and quite a few petals had dropped, scattering
across the stone like blood-edged snowflakes.

*The queen-mother feels some curiosity about thee and
is willing to spare thee a moment to kneel before her and
offer her thy homage.*

I thank ye, Great One, Isabeau answered rather shakily, keeping her head down. The closeness of the dragon
brought involuntary terror beating through her body and
she was conscious of sweat breaking out on her palms
and brow.

Thou hast our permission to enter the dragon's domain,
the dragon said. *I shall lead thee into the dragon's palace.
I am Caillec Asrohc Airi Telloch Cas.*

The name sank deep into Isabeau's mind with a rever-
beration of power that sent little shudders down her
body. She knew she would never forget the strange,
heavy syllables, which seemed to have burnt their way
into her memory like a brand.

*Thou must understand I do not give thee my name
lightly, but thou art the daughter of the great-hearted
Khan'gharad who saved me from death when I was a
mere damp-nosed kitten. I feel some measure of warmth
toward thy clan, who have always been of service to the
dragons. Therefore I give thee my name and my forbearance and shall allow thee to cross thy leg over my back
and to call me when thou wishest to fly the skies.*

Exultation flooded Isabeau. She was to fly by drag-
onback, as Iseult had, and call the dragon-princess friend.
Just as she was whispering her fervent thanks, the young
dragon yawned widely and added: *If I am not sleeping
or bathing or playing with my brothers, I may come, for I
find those of humankind somewhat amusing. Your womb-
sister was often quite diverting. Since she left I have none
to talk to except my brothers and, indeed, even a human
is better company than they.*

Isabeau nodded rather bemusedly, unable to help think-

ing the young dragon thought of her as a new sort of
pet. The dragon gave a little scamper and turned to lead
the way to the cavern mouths.

Within was a broad hall that descended into the mountain in a sweeping spiral. It was just as Iseult had described—the shadowy ceiling shining with stars and
moons and comets, the curving walls painted with trees
and flowers and faeries and all the creatures of the forest.
Below was the great cavern with its thick pillars and
vaulted ceiling, all dark with flowing shadows.

Isabeau's breath caught in her throat as she saw seven
great, bronze-backed dragons standing guard along its
length. One was the dragon that had spoken to her at
the beginning of the Great Stairway. He inclined his
head, topaz-golden eyes glinting mockingly. The others
ignored her, though their long, crested tails swayed back
and forth and their eyes narrowed.

Torches flamed in brackets all along the hall's length,
glimmering off dragon hide and the mound of treasure
heaped on the dais at the far end. Asleep on the pile of
tarnished coins and necklaces and cups and jewels was a
huge old dragon. As large as a hill or a building, her
humped back was lost in shadows, her thick tail writhing
out through the treasure and down the hall. As her nostrils flared to exhale, a sulphurous wind rushed down
toward Isabeau, blowing her hair away from her face and
causing her shirt to flutter. Then when the massive old
dragon breathed in, Isabeau felt her body tugged forward, her hair whipping over her face, obscuring her
vision.

Step by slow step, Isabeau walked down the hall, her
heart hammering, her palms sticky, her hair flowing first
back, then forward, then back again. The closer she came
to the sleeping queen-dragon, the more reluctant her
steps grew. She could feel the brooding presence of the
male dragons at her back, and once saw the vast shadow
of a hooked and clawed wing sweep across the wall before her as one stretched out languorously. The shock of
the movement caused every nerve in her body to jolt
and tingle, and her legs almost gave way beneath her.

Only a stubborn pride kept her upright, though she had to press her hands to her chest to calm the painful banging of her heart.

At last she came to the foot of the steps and knelt down with her head bent. There was a long, weighty silence, the only sound the sonorous rushing of the queen-dragon's breath and the occasional rustle of the other dragons. The young princess Asrohc had curled up at the side of the hall and was cleaning her sharp teeth with her claws. Isabeau finally got up the courage to glance upwards.

The queen-dragon was a dark bronze-green in color, the texture of her scales much rougher than those of her sons and daughter. Her head was the size of a cottage, her powerful forearms as thick as ancient trees, her claws nearly as long as Isabeau herself.

As Isabeau gazed at her wonderingly, a thick, wrinkled lid rolled back and she looked directly into the dragon's eye.

Again she felt a whirling dislocation, a loss of self. It seemed as if the dragon's eye held all the secrets of the universe. She saw life begin in a seed of fire which grew and spun like a wheel of flame. She saw time and space woven together in a gauzy sphere that hurtled past in a blur of galaxies and clusters of stars, her own world a tiny mote of dust in the universe's great eye. Within this fiery darkness, this whirling immensity, she was nothing, tinier and more insignificant than the larvae of mosquitoes clustering in a rain puddle.

Isabeau tried to cling to her sense of self, her sense of importance, but deep inside her was a lingering feeling of doubt which flowered and grew in the face of the immensity of the universe. A rush of tears came and she sobbed and covered her face, only to be reminded forcibly by the feel of her maimed hand against her skin. She clenched her fingers together, three on one hand, five on the other, raking the skin of her face with her nails, shaking her head from side to side. *Why, why?* Isabeau cried. Through the imperfect shelter of her fin-

gers she again met the queen-dragon's gaze, her eyes
dragged up against her will.

Isabeau saw a naked baby lying in the cleft of tree
roots, half covered in dead leaves, her head covered with
a fiery fuzz. She saw a little girl in an inn, pointing her
finger so a pair of dice tumbled over one more time. She
saw a young woman clamber out of a tree in the dark
to unbind a black-winged man. She saw a red horse running along the crest of a green hill.

Isabeau's breath tore in her throat as she lived again
her capture and torture, and her crippled hand flexed
and clenched. She saw herself wandering through the forest, crazy with fever, saw the Celestine heal her under
the stars in a broken tower. Faster and faster the scenes
came, replaying her life before her eyes. For a few moments the visions came so fast Isabeau was dizzy and
could make little sense of what she saw. An owl flying
over a snowy landscape, a white lion racing below. Fire
and ice devouring each other. Meghan's wrinkled face
wet with tears. A red-tailed comet soaring far above the
sea, waves rising to drown a dark forest. Feathers and
fire, water and leaves and red-gold hair all swirled together, then suddenly Isabeau saw a woman with a grave
face bending her head over the Key of the Coven which
she wore at her breast. With a startled jolt, Isabeau recognized the maimed hand cradling the star within the
circle and the intense blue eyes so full of sorrow and
wisdom.

At the very moment of recognition the vision faded.
Isabeau came back into her body, finding it tense and
quivering, the stone beneath her knees hard and cold. It
was difficult to tell how much time had passed. The
smoky torches still flared, the male dragons still watched
with slitted eyes, and Asrohc still groomed herself, her
snaky blue tongue lovingly polishing the pale scales of
her inner wrist.

Shakily Isabeau thought, *Do ye mean I am to be
Keybearer one day?*

The queen-dragon shifted her weight on the mound of

treasure, so coins and jewels went skipping away over the floor.

Do ye mean . . . ? Did I lose my fingers for some purpose? Did all this happen for some reason?

The queen-dragon half-closed her eyes. *Reason?* she said, the words so deep and ancient they were like thunder in Isabeau's mind. *Why must thou search for reasons? Thou thinkest of fate as a game played by some faceless master, the whole universe subject to his will. Yet thou chosest thy path freely and traveled it with set will.*

So ye are saying it is my own fault I was tortured and maimed, Isabeau said with cold dismay spreading through her.

The queen-dragon sighed, the blast of her exhalation blowing Isabeau's curls away from her tearstained face. *Why must thou look for faults and reasons? Thou chosest thine own path but not thy destination. Fate is woven together of will and the force of circumstances. It is one thread spun of many strands.*

Isabeau nodded. She could see how that was so. Although she may have been impulsive in rescuing Lachlan from the Awl so many months ago, she had not closed the pilliwinkes upon her own hand. That had been Baron Yutta's choice and he had died as a consequence. She felt something relax within her, some tension she had grown so used to, she had no longer known it was there. She looked down at her scarred hand and said softly, *So I will never be healed, will I?*

Thy soul-fabric will slowly heal, the queen-dragon said. *It is not like flesh or cloth, once torn, always torn. It is the stuff of the universe, like water or fire, without matter or shape. Thou wilt heal.*

Isabeau bent her head, showing she understood. Her thoughts flew back to the vision of herself cupping the Key of the Coven.

Perhaps, the queen-dragon answered.

But the dragons see both ways along the thread o' time, Isabeau protested.

All the dragons shifted and murmured and Asrohc laughed, a terrifying sound. Involuntarily Isabeau remembered Jorge crouched beside a fire, the shadows dancing over his blind old face. She had just asked him if he could see the future, and he had answered in his gentle voice: "I can see future possibilities. The future is like a tangled skein o' wool waiting for the first strands to be drawn and spun into a thread."

So it is a future possibility that ye see, Isabeau said thoughtfully. *That one day I will be Keybearer.* Excitement thrilled through her, ambition suddenly kindling in her heart.

This time all the dragons laughed, and Isabeau crouched down against the flagstones, her pulses hammering.

Mockingly the queen-dragon sent a vision of Isabeau burning and blistering in a blast of dragon fire, then another of her shot through the heart with an arrow, falling from a castle battlement like a dying swan.

But . . .

The dragons see many things, the queen-dragon said. *Why dost thou ask me things thou already knows? I tire of thy impatient curiosity. My son tells me thou hast brought gifts. Show me!*

Isabeau looked down and saw with dismay that she had dropped the branch of roses she had carried up the mountain so carefully. It lay crushed and broken at her feet. Horror filled her. *I'm sorry . . . I didn't . . .*

The queen-dragon reared up on her claws and sent a gust of fire shooting down the steps. Isabeau screamed and scrambled backward.

When she at last raised her face from the shelter of her arms, it was to see the roses all charred into ashes. She stared at the queen-dragon.

The blooming and dying of a rose is a mere passing of a moment to the dragons, the queen said coldly. *Stars blooming and dying are of greater consequence to us.*

But . . . Isabeau said, again fearful, remembering that vision of herself burnt to cinders.

It was the bringing of the tithe that was of importance, the dragon said. *Dost thou think I care for roses, when I sleep on a bed of jewels?*

Isabeau was so confused and afraid she could only

stare at the great, dark hulk. After a moment, she scrabbled open her satchel and took out the artifacts with trembling fingers. One by one she lay them on the stone steps and heard the hissing breath of the dragons behind her. The queen-dragon rose and came ponderously down the steps, treasure tumbling in all directions, her tail sweeping aside gold chalices, jeweled brooches, tarnished crowns and scepters as if they were mere rubbish.

Delicately she nudged and smelt the gifts, pushing the armband onto the tip of one claw, winding the pearls around another. She tossed the chalice in the air several times, then threw it nonchalantly over her back into the piles of treasure behind her. Then she licked the blood-stained dagger with her long, supple, sky-blue tongue and smiled a dragonish smile.

Well-chosen gifts indeed, she purred. Carrying the dagger in her mouth, she climbed back up the steps and turned round and round on the mound before again settling down. She lay curled as comfortably as if her bed was of silk and velvets rather than hard and knobbly treasure, and licked the dagger again and again, her eyes slitted with pleasure.

Isabeau took a deep breath. *I come bearing these gifts in homage to the wisdom and clear-sight of the dragons,* she said, grateful Feld had made her repeat this speech so many times. She did not think she could have found words otherwise. *My clan has always revered the dragons, knowing they are the greatest of all creatures, the most dangerous, the most powerful. I would very much like to seek counsel with ye, Queen o' the Great Ones, and hope that the centuries of goodwill between our clans will persist for centuries more.*

The queen-dragon inclined her head, pausing in her slow savoring of the dagger for a moment.

They say I have Talent, Isabeau said in a rush, *yet no one seems to ken what it is. I seem to have many o' the minor Skills, like the ability o' summoning flame or moving things around, yet many a skeelie or cunning man can do that. I canna fly, like my mother or Iseult; I canna charm beasts or see the future, or whistle up the wind, or conjure illusions. I canna do anything o' significance!*

There was a long pause and disappointment filled her. Then the queen-dragon tossed the knife in the air and caught it again. *To understand any living thing one must creep within and feel the beating of its heart,* she said. *To understand the deeper secrets of the universe thou must feel its heart beat too.*

The dragon turned her huge head and regarded Isabeau steadily. Isabeau stared back. The queen's eye was a fiery sea, her slitted pupil the deepest, most unfathomable space. Isabeau heard the rush of blood through the chambers of her own heart, heard its steady rhythm like the pound of drums. She thought she discerned a deeper echo pounding in her breast, a long, slow beat that shook her with its unstoppable force.

Thou must know thyself before thou canst know the universe, the queen-dragon said. *Thou must always be searching and asking and answering; thou must listen to the heart of the world; thou must listen to thine own heart. Thou must search out thine ancestors and listen to what they may teach thee; thou must know thy history before thou canst know thy future.*

Isabeau nodded.

Thy womb-sister was raised by thy father's kin, thou wert raised by thy mother's. Now thy womb-sister sits at the feet of Meghan of the Beasts and listens to her wisdom. It is time that thou sat at the feet of the Firemaker of the Fire-Dragon Pride. Thy womb-sister spent the white months of the year, the active months, with the Fire-Dragon Pride and the green months of the year, the rest months, with Feld of the Dragons and thy mother, Ishbel the Winged. Thou must do the same.

Isabeau's eyes widened. Even though she knew her father's people inhabited the snowy heights beyond the Cursed Valley, it had never occurred to her to seek them out. Immediately her thoughts flew to Bronwen.

I canna—she will die, she said incoherently.

The queen-dragon yawned and rested her head back on her claws. There was a long pause.

Isabeau said timidly, *Ye ken I have the Ensorcellor's babe? I canna let her die. She needs salt water to swim in, for she is o' the sea people. I have brought her so far, I must have a care for her. Will ye no' help me?*

There was no response from the queen-dragon and behind Isabeau the queen's sons stirred and hissed.

Isabeau gritted her teeth and thought defiantly: *Did ye know my father had been transformed into a horse? Why did ye no' tell Meghan when she was here? Or Iseult?*

Without opening her eyes, the queen-dragon replied, *For what purpose should I have told?*

Isabeau said, more incoherently than ever, *But ye must have kent that we would have wanted to ken . . .* Realizing how jumbled her thoughts must sound, she said more carefully, *For seventeen years my father has been trapped in the shape o' a horse, unable to tell anyone, unable to escape. If we had kent . . .*

What wouldst thou have done? There was mild curiosity in the queen-dragon's voice.

We could have tried to break the enchantment, Isabeau cried.

The tip of the queen-dragon's tail swayed. *The enchantment can only be lifted by she who cast it. Moreover, knowledge of Khan'gharad's fate may well have changed all of thy fates. To know what may happen is often to assure it does happen. We prefer not to meddle in the fates of foolish, muddling humans.*

There was a note of dismissal in her voice, and the great, crested tail was now swaying quite markedly.

Isabeau bowed her head. *I thank ye for your words and for your mercy.* After a long, sticky, heart-hammering moment, she found the courage to say, *Tell me, do ye think I did wrong in taking Bronwen away?*

There was no answer.

Desperately Isabeau cried, *I beg ye, tell me where I can find salt so she does no' die.*

The queen-dragon stirred and sighed, knocking Isabeau over with the force of the escaping air. *Thou mayst scrape salt off the rocks in the valley above and take it with thee for the moment. Then if thou lookest at the northern end of the Valley of the Two Towers, thou wilt find salt in the rocks and in a chain of bubbling pools akin to our lake above. Thou mayst let the Fairge child swim in those pools and she shall live.*

Thank ye, thank ye, Isabeau babbled, but the queen-dragon had closed her eyes again, her chin resting on the notched and blackened dagger. As Isabeau rather shakily made her way back down the long, vaulted hall she heard the sonorous roar of the queen-dragon's snores begin once again.

THE SPINE OF THE WORLD

Isabeau toiled up the snowy slope, her mittened hands huddled beneath her plaid, her tam-o'-shanter pulled down low over her ears. Behind her the deep, wavering line of her footsteps was the only mark on a pristine landscape, the fresh fall of snow covering everything with a soft drapery.

The sky overhead was blue but the air was bitterly cold, and Isabeau's panting breath hung before her face in white puffs like clouds. As far as the eye could see the tall white points of the mountains stretched, while behind her were the forest-filled valleys.

A wild whooping startled her and she glanced up. Down the slope sped a number of tall, white figures, swooping over the snow as swiftly and gracefully as birds in flight. Isabeau stopped in her tracks, half in fear and half in delight. She watched as first one then another leapt off a mound of snow and somersaulted like an acrobat before swooping on again at the same breakneck speed.

As they came closer she saw they rode small wooden sleighs, not much longer than their boots. The bottoms of the sleighs were painted with ferocious red dragons breathing fire. As they soared and spun through the air, it was as if the painted dragons took flight, only to be buried again in snow as the riders skidded to the ground again.

With another loud yell, the leader of the riders came to an abrupt, curving halt before Isabeau, spraying her with snow. He was a tall, lean man with a grim, dark face, all angles and hard planes, heavily hooded eyes, and a long braid of white, coarse hair. On either side of his forehead were two massive, tightly curled horns.

He inclined his head and gave the ritualistic Khan'cohban greeting—a sweep of two fingers to the brow, then to the heart, then out to the view. Hesitantly Isabeau returned the greeting and he frowned.

She wondered rather anxiously whether she had done something wrong. Feld had tried to teach her as much as he could of the Khan'cohban language, but it was a strange form of communication, as much gesture and intonation as sound. Luckily Isabeau was used to speaking the languages of beasts and birds, which were also composed more of body language than a complex system of vocal noises. She had a flair for languages and had studied hard, so by the time she left the Towers of Roses and Thorns to travel to the Spine of the World, she knew as much as Feld could teach her. She was still nervous of the winter ahead, however, knowing how different the Khan'cohbans' life was and already missing Bronwen, whom she had left in Feld's care.

The Khan'cohban warrior spoke to her then, uttering a few abrupt syllables that sounded more like grunts than words. He said something about the Firemaker, making a broad, sweeping gesture back up the hill. Isabeau nodded and smiled to show she understood, but he only stared at her haughtily.

The other Khan'cohbans had also swung to a halt around her and she heard them grunt to each other briefly, their hands making odd, brief gestures. Then they set off again in wide, curving swoops over the snow, some yelling with excitement. Their leader did not leave. Instead, he bent down, undid the straps tying the skimmer to his feet and tied it to his back. Without a word he gestured up the hill again and then began to walk swiftly and easily up the slope. Isabeau labored along behind him, her breath coming in short little gasps, her boots sinking deep into the snow. He turned often and waited for her, and Isabeau tried hard not to resent his calm, stern politeness.

It was close on sunset when they finally reached the crest of the mountain, and Isabeau's legs were on fire, her whole body shaking with cold and exhaustion. They had climbed slope after icy slope, leaving the valley floor

far behind them. The Khan'cohban had not spoken once
and Isabeau was grateful for that, having no breath to
spare. Above them a great outcropping of round boulders reared against the glowing sky, the long slopes falling away like the sweep of a white velvet gown. He
waited for her just below the gray bulging stone, his dark
face impassive. At last she reached his side and stood
panting harshly, holding her side with one hand and wiping her streaming nose with the other. He gave her only
long enough to catch her breath, then led her round the
side of the rock.

Isabeau's breath caught in amazement. The path they
trod led through an archway of ice-hung stone and round
to the mouth of a gigantic cave, the craggy head of the
mountain rearing above. Below was a wide valley, surrounded on three sides by towering cliffs. A waterfall fell
to one side of the cave mouth, the loch at its base frozen
over except where the plunging water churned. There
the water was a pure blue-green, its edges frothing into
great blocks of broken ice. A small boy had led a herd
of large, goat-like creatures with flat hooves and spreading horns down to drink, and they clustered at the water's edge, their woolly coats nearly as white as the snow.

Suddenly a tall Khan'cohban stepped out from the wall
of the archway. Isabeau stepped back with an exclamation, for in his white furs he had been invisible against
the snow. Her guide uttered a single, harsh word and the
guard struck the palm of one hand with the edge of the
other. Isabeau's guide nodded, once, and led her past.

The cave mouth yawned far above her head, all fringed
with icicles. Huddling her plaid around her numb cheeks,
Isabeau followed him inside. The cave stretched far back
into the mountain, with many shallow alcoves and
smaller caves leading off from the main chamber. A
stream ran down one side, some of its shallower pools
iced over at the edges. Many small campfires glowed
along its earthen floor, each surrounded by a pile of furs
and bundles of cooking utensils, weapons and rough
wooden bowls. At the very back was a large bonfire, its
smoke streaming up toward an aperture far above their

heads. Flaming torches were stuck here and there in the rough walls, but their light did not pierce very far into the gloom.

With the smoke from the fires stinging her eyes, Isabeau had to peer to see. She saw a number of straight-backed men and women sitting cross-legged around the bonfire. They were all dressed in long, tight leggings of soft, white leather, with white knitted shirts and leather jerkins over the top. Most wore long cloaks of animal furs huddled round their shoulders—Isabeau recognized woolly bear, timber wolf, arctic fox and the thick white wool of the *geal'teas*. There was even the rich spotted fur of a saber leopard, the ferocious head with its curving fangs still attached, and the white pelt of a snow lion.

The old woman wearing the snow-lion cloak sat on a thick pile of furs, the black-tipped mane and snarling muzzle hanging down her back. Unlike the other women sitting around the fire, her face was clearly that of a human, though strongly boned with high cheekbones. Her eyes were as blue as Isabeau's own, and the long hair bound back from her brow was gray with red intermingled. She looked up as Isabeau drew near the bonfire, and looked her over with an autocratic gaze.

Isabeau had been looking forward immensely to meeting her great-grandmother and her impulse was to rush forward and greet her with a kiss and a hug. The cold, autocratic face daunted her however, and so she merely made the gesture of greeting. Once again she wondered whether she had somehow made a mistake, for the faces of the warriors were all stiff and the Firemaker frowned in response. Then she pointed at Isabeau and then at the ground near her feet. "Sit," she said, the word stilted.

Obediently Isabeau sat, wondering what was to come. She felt very self-conscious and ill at ease, though none of the many Khan'cohbans in the cavern seemed to have noticed her presence. They kept on with their tasks of spinning, knitting, carving or hammering with not a single glance in her direction. Even the Council of Scarred Warriors paid her no attention, even though she sat so close to them she could smell their sharp odor and see the strange, colorless glint of their eyes.

Still the Firemaker subjected her to intense scrutiny and Isabeau returned her gaze with equal curiosity. The old woman's thin mouth thinned even further and her hand suddenly lashed out, striking Isabeau across the face.

"Rude, stare," she said.

Isabeau put her hand to her cheek. "But you're staring at me!"

Again the old woman slapped her. "Rude, answer back!"

Tears stung Isabeau's eyes but she lowered them and kept them lowered. After a long moment she felt rather than saw the Firemaker make an emphatic gesture and call, "Khan'kahlil?"

A Khan'cohban woman rose from a nearby fire and came to kneel at the old woman's side, her head lowered and her hands folded before her. Isabeau recognized the few guttural syllables she uttered as meaning, "Yes, Firemaker?"

The Firemaker issued a few orders too swift for Isabeau to understand. Khan'kahlil said, "Yes, Firemaker," again, but this time with a slight difference in intonation. Isabeau listened intently, determined to learn as much of the language as she could. Otherwise her life here for the next few months would be very difficult and lonely.

A quick stinging blow to her ear caught her by surprise. The Firemaker pointed at the Khan'cohban woman and said, "Go. Khan'kahlil teach manners. Return when polite."

Isabeau fought down her protest and, in exactly the same pose and manner as the Khan'cohban woman had, said, "Yes, Firemaker."

The Firemaker nodded in abrupt dismissal but Isabeau sensed her approval and followed the tall, lithe figure of the snow-faery in silence. Although her great-grandmother's cold welcome had brought her perilously close to tears, Isabeau managed to choke back her hurt and disappointment, determined not to show any weakness before these stern, grim-faced strangers. Khan'kahlil gestured to a pile of furs and Isabeau sat obediently. Without a word, the

Khan'cohban woman passed her a stone bowl and pestle and Isabeau began to ground the wild grains within to powder.

Khan'kahlil was, like the other Khan'cohbans, tall and olive-skinned, with an abundant white mane and long fingers with four joints. Only the male Khan'cohbans had the thick, down-curling horns, but the strong, prominent bone structure of her face and the deep-set eyes marked her clearly as a different race from Isabeau.

She soon realized Khan'kahlil was very low in the hierarchy, little more than a servant to the warriors, storytellers, metalsmiths and firekeepers, who were the most respected people in the pride. Khan'kahlil had only one scar, a crude arrow on her left cheek, and her name meant "little coney," a term of affectionate condescension. The fact that the Firemaker had spoken her name in front of Isabeau was a sign of how little respect she received. Names were secret, only revealed to kith and kin. As a stranger, Isabeau had no right to know any one's name. She learnt to call others by their title and position in the hierarchy.

The Firemaker was the most feared and respected person in the pride. The choicest pieces of meat were brought for her; she had the most favorable sleeping position, and everyone—even the First of the Scarred Warriors—approached her with bent head. He was the warrior who wore the saber-leopard cloak, and each cheek was slashed with three thin scars, another cutting down his forehead and between his eyes. Isabeau soon learnt he was the second most powerful person in the pride and she was beaten severely for showing disrespect to him by meeting his gaze.

Isabeau had never been beaten before and she found the Khan'cohbans' harshness the most shocking thing about her new life. There was no pity, no kindness, no forgiveness, no mercy. Betrayers of the Khan'cohbans' code of honor were staked out on a high rock for the Gods of White, meaning they died of cold and exposure, or were mauled to death by wild animals, or pecked to death by birds of prey. Even minor breaches were punished with blows or beatings or deprivation of warmth and food.

Over the next few weeks, Isabeau accompanied Khan'-kahlil everywhere, quietly watching and listening, learning very early on to keep her eyes lowered and her hands still. Since every gesture had a meaning, it was easy to be misunderstood by casual gesticulations, and Isabeau made many a stupid mistake before she learnt to keep her hands clasped in her lap at all times.

Her task of acquiring manners was made particularly difficult by her inability to ask questions or watch too closely. Any sign of curiosity was considered exceptionally rude. After repeated blows, Isabeau learnt not to ask for explanation or reasons, look directly at anyone or ask their name, approach another's campfire without an invitation, touch another person's arm or hand, eat before her superiors had eaten, or speak unless spoken to first. With so many people living in such close quarters, these rules ensured no one's personal space was invaded but, being of an affectionate and curious nature, Isabeau found herself constantly giving offense.

She had not realized either how strict the pride's social hierarchy was. Since Isabeau had not undergone her ordeal and initiation, she was considered a child and as such had lower status than every other adult in the group, even those younger than her in age. It did not matter that she was the Firemaker's great-granddaughter, and child of the revered Khan'gharad, who had been First Warrior and had flown on the dragon's back. She was a stranger to them and therefore ostracized; and uninitiated and therefore without a name or a place in the pride.

Like all other children, she was called simply Khan. She had to sleep on the furthermost edge of the fire, and was only allowed to eat once the rest of the pride was finished. The communal pot and her own plate and spoon were then ritualistically purified to remove the contamination of her touch. The only people Isabeau was allowed to address voluntarily were the other children who had not yet made their journey to the Skull of the World.

Since most undertook their ordeal and initiation in their thirteenth long darkness, this meant she spent a great deal of her time with the younger children. Most of the adult Khan'cohbans ignored her except to snap out the occasional terse order, but a few of those newly initiated took it upon themselves to humiliate her at every opportunity.

Although Isabeau worked hard to learn the customs of the pride and was now able to understand most of what was said, she was still treated like an outcast. Most of the time she felt as if she was invisible, some kind of ghost hovering at the edges of the pride. Sometimes she wanted to scream and shout, jump up and down and wave her arms, crying, "Look at me! I'm here, I exist!" Instead she bit her tongue, kept her eyes lowered and grew used to being called child.

Isabeau was desperately lonely and unhappy, though; often choked with tears that she concealed as best she could. Despite her isolation, she still had to work hard, as did all the people of the pride. She had to assist them in their daily tasks, which included digging through the snow for roots, spinning with a crude distaff, tending the woolly-coated *ulez*, grinding grain and picking up after the adults.

One bitterly cold day Isabeau was huddling into her plaid. The wind was howling outside, throwing handfuls of snow in through the cave-mouth and sending icy draughts sweeping through every corner. Khan'kahlil's fire was closest to the cave's entrance, a sign of her lowly status. With the freezing wind blowing straight at her back, Isabeau tried to spin the white wool of the *ulez* with hands so stiff with cold they felt as they were carved from stone.

The fire was losing its battle with the wind and Khan'-kahlil was busy chasing her impish young son, who had stolen one of her knives to pretend he was a Scarred Warrior. Without thought, Isabeau fed the dying embers with her own power. The flames leapt up warm and golden, and thankfully she held her hands to the blaze.

The Haven was usually quiet for the Khan'cohbans

were a silent people, but Isabeau was immediately aware of a change in the quality of the silence. She looked up and consternation filled her as she saw the anger on the face of the Firekeeper and the fear and horror on Khan'-kahlil's. Even the Firemaker had risen from her furs, her blue eyes cold with condemnation. Every Khan'cohban in the cave was staring at Isabeau, their hands for once frozen into stillness.

Hurried words of explanations and excuses rose to Isabeau's lips but she bit them back and bent her head in supplication.

The Firekeeper was a tall woman who guarded the central bonfire and carried burning coals in a little bag at her waist whenever the pride left the Haven on their migratory journeys, so that wherever they made camp the pride could always be sure of a fire for warmth and safety. Her position was one of the few in the prides that was hereditary, passed from mother to daughter for centuries, like that of the Old Mother.

Leaping to her feet, the Firekeeper pointed her long, multijointed finger at Isabeau. Her voice shrill with outrage she cried, "Khan has made fire! What of the law of the Firekeeper? She has flouted my law and spat scorn into my face."

She then turned to Khan'kahlil and said contemptuously, "That stupid coney did not guard her fire and in shame prevailed upon the Firemaker's kin to rekindle her fire instead of approaching me as is the custom and the law. I demand punishment and restitution for I have been belittled and overlooked."

Khan'kahlil had fallen on her knees, her arms spread out, her face pressed into the floor. She made no attempt to defend herself. Her little son threw himself down by her side, the make-believe sword fallen from his hand. The Firemaker limped down from her platform and stood over them and hastily Isabeau assumed the same position.

The Firemaker issued a few short, sharp orders and Isabeau heard the whistle and crack of Khan'kahlil being beaten by one of the Scarred Warriors. The Khan'cohban made no whimper or protest, though Isabeau cringed into the floor with every thwack. Then footsteps approached her. The apprentice witch tensed but no blow fell on her shoulders. Instead a cauldron of snow and icy water was flung over her, shocking her into a scream. Another cauldron of water was dumped on Khan'kahlil's fire, extinguishing Isabeau's bright flames.

Isabeau lay still, shuddering with fear and cold. The Firekeeper came and nudged her with her foot. "Rude Khan, presumptuous and proud. For three days no fire for you and no fire for the little coney and her family. In three days, if you still live, come to me with gifts and sorrow and I shall give you a live coal to cherish and coax into flame."

After the Firekeeper had stalked away, Isabeau sat up, weeping, trying to rub warmth into her cold wet arms. Khan'kahlil crept to her side, her son huddling into her side, and they all stared at the black, wet embers disconsolately.

Three days without a fire was harsh punishment indeed, particularly since their sleeping spot was so close to the cave mouth and so unprotected from the elements. Without a fire, they could not keep themselves warm or heat their food or have any light to cheer the bitter nights. The Firekeeper had not been exaggerating when she said, "If you still live."

Shivering violently in her wet clothes, already stiffening with ice, Isabeau did her best to express her remorse. Khan'kahlil shook her head, saying abruptly, "My fire, my responsibility." She dug around in her crude wooden chest and held out some dry clothes for Isabeau.

For the first few weeks of her stay at the pride's Haven, Isabeau had suffered terribly from the cold for she refused to wear the heavy skins and fur the Khan'cohbans swathed themselves in. She had sat huddled in her plaid trying to stop her shivering, determined not to wear the skins of murdered animals. Khan'kahlil had accepted her decision with a shrug, though her children had mocked Isabeau and called her "*ulez*-brain." Now, however, the Khan'cohban women insisted, saying gruffly, "*Ulez* not killed, *ulez* die when it is time."

Isabeau nodded and took the bundle of skins and furs with a gesture of gratefulness. There was no doubt she would die if she stayed in her damp clothes. She knew what Khan'-kahlil said was true. The *ulez* had died of old age, not by the knife.

The *ulez* were never killed, for they were too useful alive, providing wool and milk and pulling along the sleighs that the pride traveled in when they left the haven. Only when the *ulez* died were their skins cured and rubbed with fat to make the moisture-resistant leggings, jerkins and cloaks everyone wore.

The next three days were hard, bitter days. Only by huddling together in their furs and sharing their body warmth were they able to save themselves from freezing. Isabeau made them a thin porridge of grains and herbs and whenever their shivering grew too intense she made Khan'kahlil and her family drink a mouthful of her *mithuan*, which she always carried in her pack. The fiery liquid warmed their bodies and made their slowing hearts pound quickly again, and so they were able to endure the long, dark days of their punishment.

On the evening of the third day Isabeau went to the Firekeeper and debased herself, begging forgiveness for her folly and ignorance and offering her gifts—Khan'kahlil's best knife with a real metal blade, a pot of herbal cream she had made that would relieve the rheumatism in the Firekeeper's joints, and a string of fish Khan'kahlil's children had caught.

The Firekeeper accepted the gifts and, without one word or glance of acknowledgment, gave Isabeau a burning ember from her fire. Carefully Isabeau carried the coal back to Khan'kahlil's sleeping spot and tenderly they fed it dry leaves and twigs until at last their fire again leapt into life.

"Well, if it is no' Finlay the Fear-Naught! How are ye yourself, my lad?" Niall cried, pausing in the doorway of the Strathrowan tavern to shake the snow off his cloak.

The young man blowing smoke rings to the ceiling glanced over and lifted one well-shaped eyebrow. "Methinks I hear the roar o' a bear," he mused. "Indeed we are lost in the wilds that bears wander through villages at will. I wonder if I should call for help? But nay, they say one should stay perfectly still if one should encounter a woolly bear, and that seems sound advice to me."

He blew another smoke ring and watched it drift up and dissolve against the low beams. Although he was wearing the same blue officer's jacket as Niall, his was without a single stain or wrinkle, and fitted him like a glove. His boots were made of the softest kid, and his plaid was pinned over his shoulder with a diamond brooch. His beard was carefully clipped into a point, and his hair hung in silky curls to his shoulder.

"Look at ye, as pretty as if we were still in Lucescere and no' out here at the edge o' the forest! Do no' tell me ye brought your valet wi' ye!" Niall said jovially.

"Indeed I did," Finlay replied languidly. "What would he do if I left him at the Shining City? Spend all his wages on whores and whiskey, I am sure! Nay, far better that he rides with me and earns his keep. Besides, my sweet, surely ye do no' expect me to polish my own boots or brush my own hair?"

Niall snorted loudly and came to sit beside Finlay, the chair creaking under his weight. Lilanthe stood watching from the doorway, her cloak and hood covered in snow. After a moment she limped in shyly, putting back the hood, the nisse swinging from the bare twigs of her hair. The young soldier looked her over with a lift of his eyebrow. When Brun came bounding in, his eyebrow lifted ever further. "What do we have here?" he said. "Ye fraternizing with the faeries now, Niall?"

Lilanthe stiffened and the nisse bared her fangs. Niall leant back, stuffing his pipe with tobacco. "Aye, His Highness has given me the honor o' escorting the Lady Lilanthe and the cluricaun Brun into Aslinn. They go in search o' friends and allies who may well be the weight that swings the war our way. My lady, this mannerless young man is Laird Finlay James MacFinlay, the Marquess of Tullitay and Kirkcudbright, Viscount of Balmorran and Strathraer, and the only son o' the Duke of Falkglen. We call him Fear-Naught since he has no more sense than a foolhardy lad and is always running his neck into a noose o' trouble."

The young marquess rose and gave Lilanthe a courtly bow, sweeping the ground with his fingers. Her freckled face flushed and she nodded gravely, sensing his subtle mockery. It seemed even the Rìgh's own bodyguard contained those who did not favor creatures of faery blood.

"Have we no' met before, my laird?" she said.

He smiled and said charmingly, "No' that I remember, my lady, and I'm sure I would remember if I had."

Her color deepened, unsure whether he was mocking her still. He pulled out a chair for her and she sat, regarding him with puzzled eyes. His thoughts were carefully guarded so she could not read them and that in itself was enough to make her uneasy. He was a soldier, though, and trained into impassivity, so she turned to warm her hands at the fire while Laird Finlay poured her and Niall some hot whiskey toddy.

They had spent the autumn riding slowly from village to town, Lilanthe taking the opportunity to talk to the country folk about the faeries of the forest. Although there were some in the crowd who jeered her, the squad of soldiers standing stern-faced and straight-backed beside her prevented any real belligerence. As autumn passed, she grew more confident, her passion lending her eloquence so that many in the crowds were moved to regret their antipathy toward the faeries. As for Lilanthe, she found that the release of her pent-up emotions brought her some measure of peace and even contentment.

As they had followed the highway out of the lowlands of Rionnagan and into Blèssem, the mood had changed, however. They reached the outskirts of Aslinn with the onset of winter, and took refuge from the early snowstorms in the village of Crossmaglenn at the edge of the forest. Some of Lilanthe's nervousness returned, for they were only a week's ride from Glenmorven, the town where she had encountered the Grand-Seeker. The local populace was surly, casting looks of hostility at the faeries and pulling their children out of Lilanthe's path. Niall the Bear had to assert his authority before the innkeeper would allow them to stay under his roof, and then it was a frigid welcome he gave them. If it had not been for the snowy darkness outside and her tiredness, Lilanthe would have insisted on traveling on, but instead she accepted the food slapped in front of her and went despondently to bed.

In the morning Niall the Bear had greeted her cheerfully and told her they had heard a battalion of the Rìgh's soldiers had taken over the small village of Strathrowan to the south to use as their winter quarters. The innkeeper had suggested, none too courteously, that they go and join their comrades there. Glad to leave his inhospitable house, they had packed up and ridden on, for once not calling the townsfolk together for Lilanthe to address. It had been a gray cold day, the horses' hooves crunching snow underfoot, and Lilanthe felt some of her old misery return.

Soon they had seen a camp of soldiers outside a village, the MacCuinn stag flying from the pole along with a standard Lilanthe had not recognized. Niall obviously had, though, for he exclaimed in surprise and urged his destrier into a trot. He had exchanged greetings with the lieutenant overseeing the soldiers' maneuvers and then ridden into town to see their captain, who was now reclining back in his chair, blowing smoke rings and regarding his polished fingernails.

"But what do ye do here, Finlay?" Niall said after taking a deep swallow of the whiskey toddy. "Last I saw ye, ye were riding off to Blairgowrie with His Highness."

"Aye, and a grand fight that was! We tricked the renegades truly, and rode into the heart o' Blairgowrie as blithely as ye please!" Finlay's eyes glowed with excitement. "His Highness was magnificent! I swear half the men there were truly afraid his act o' a sulky young greenhorn was no sham, but he fought like a demon once we had lured the blaygird Red Guards out from behind the walls."

"So the Awl rebellion is nipped in the bud?"

"Nay, unfortunately. Renshaw the Ruthless fled with the babe he named Banrìgh. We've had reports he and his supporters are regrouping somewhere near the Aslinn and Blèssem border. That is what I do here, actually. I was set to track the Grand-Seeker down, but he's as cunning as a fox. It's been eight months and no hair nor hide o' him have I seen."

Niall frowned. "That is no' good news at all. I had hoped he would be caught quickly and we could get on with the task o' driving out the Bright Soldiers. What luck have ye had so far in tracking his movements?"

"I followed him to about twenty miles west o' here but he's got some hide somewhere and I canna find where. I suspect he fled this way because he has strong support in this part o' the country. The Bright Soldiers have not penetrated this far north yet, concentrating as they are on the highway to Blèssem, so the locals do no' look to the Rìgh for succor. Few are willing to give us any information, Eà damn them. I've had my fill o' rustic stupidity, I can tell ye. All I get when I ask for news are blank stares and dribble. It seems no one kens a thing about Renshaw and his movements, yet I know he came this way!"

Lilanthe moved uneasily, her long hair rustling. "I passed through upper Blèssem when I came up from Aslinn with Dide the Juggler and Enit Silverthroat," she said shyly. "The Grand-Seeker was hiding out in a town called Glenmorven, only a few days' ride from the edge o' the forest. A lot o' the men there seemed to be involved in his resistance against the Rìgh. Happen he fled back there?"

Finlay sat up. "Glenmorven, ye say? Ye may have given me the clue I need, my lady o' the forest, and for that I thank ye."

Lilanthe did not smile back. She sensed some trouble beneath his air of gay insouciance and was sorry for it. He rose gracefully to his feet and gave Niall a mocking bow. "Well, we ride for Glenmorven on the morrow and hope we find the ruthless one there! Will ye join us, my auld woolly bear?"

"We have another task," Niall replied gravely, rising so he could grasp Finlay's hand. "Will ye have a care for yourself? The Awl still has much support in the countryside, and there are many Red Guards who have flocked to Renshaw's banner. If ye find a sizable force has gathered at his side, do no' challenge him yourself. Send messengers to His Highness and he will send ye support. Promise me this?"

Finlay laughed. "Och, ye are just the same, ye auld fusspot. O' course I shall no'! Run back to Blairgowrie all because o' a few Red Guards? No' I! My men and I are all itching for another chance to run our swords through their tough auld hides. Nay, we shall triumph over Renshaw the Ruthless and his false Banrìgh, and take them back to the MacCuinn in chains. Then I shall be His Highness's favorite, ye shall see."

"I hope I do, my lad," Niall replied affably. "Let us hope that it is no' your bloodied corpse I see instead."

The young laird said mockingly, "Shall we have a wager on it, my woolly one? Though I canna promise I'll have the gold for ye should ye win. My father swears he has disinherited me for spending all my money on whores and jewelry and may no' honor any note I give ye. We shall just have to hope that I triumph, and then I can rest easy on the gold ye give me. What odds do ye give me, my sweet?"

"Nay, I shall no' toss dice with ye," Niall replied equably. "Ye have the luck o' the young and the foolish, and I have plans for what little gold I have! Just remember Renshaw the Ruthless is a wily auld fox and have a care for yourself, that's all I ask."

Finlay only laughed, and blew another smoke ring.

Snow swirled against the mullioned windows of the Tower of Two Moons, and the wind howled like a banshee. Lachlan shivered and rubbed his hands over his arms. "Eà blast it, I swear the winters are getting worse each year!"

Meghan glanced up from her spinning wheel. "Well, ye canna play all year with the weather patterns and no' expect some consequence," she replied calmly. "The Thistle kept southern Eileanan dry and cloudless all summer and autumn, while Arran stayed hidden behind its veil o' mist. All that had to flow on somehow."

"I just wish this bloody storm would blow over!" Lachlan said. Iseult glanced at him with a troubled expression. He was finding the enforced inactivity difficult, and every day his restlessness increased until Iseult feared he would do something mad and impulsive just to release his tension.

The last few months had been spent in hard fighting and all were tired and a little discouraged. Despite their clever tactics and bold courage, the Rìgh's army was still vastly outnumbered and undertrained, and they had suffered as many defeats as victories. With winter drawing its cold, dark mantle over the country, Lachlan and his retinue had withdrawn to Lucescere to recoup, leaving most of their troops to hold the land they had won.

"It be a bad night to be trying to use the scrying pool," Jorge said.

Meghan glanced at him affectionately. "Aye, all this turbulence will make it hard to connect, that is for sure. Still, the scrying pools were created for just this purpose, and Dughall at least is a powerful sorcerer, he should be able to throw his thoughts this far. I am no' so sure about Anghus, though he promised to ride to the Tower o' Searchers and try. I am eager indeed to hear news o' them and know what support they can lend us."

"What is a scrying pool?" Iseult asked, trying to detach her bright curls from her son's hand. He squealed and tugged harder.

"Ye can come with us if ye like," the old woman said. "A scrying pool was built in every Tower—it was the quickest and easiest way for the witches o' the Coven to communicate with each other, particularly for those who did not know each other."

Meghan glanced up at the clock on the wall. "It is near midnight," she said. "We may as well brave the cold and go down." She struggled to her feet and stood leaning on her staff, the iron-gray plait that hung down to her knees streaked with white. She looked at Jorge again, saying, "Shall ye come with us, auld friend?"

He shook his head, his wrinkled face somber. "Nay, ye ken the veils between the worlds are thinnest at Samhain. I shall do a sighting."

"Have a care then," she warned. "Ye ken the tower is thick still with ghosts." He nodded. "Happen Iseult had best stay with ye and watch over ye," the old sorceress said. Iseult tried not to look disappointed, for she was curious to see the scrying pool.

Jorge of course could sense her emotions and he smiled kindly at her. "Go with Meghan, lassie," he said. "The League of the Healing Hand shall stay with me and watch over me. It is time those squires o' Lachlan's did something apart from eat Latifa's good cooking and get into mischief!"

"Very well, I shall call for Dillon then," Meghan said and made her slow way toward the door, Gitâ poking his black nose out of her pocket before burrowing down again.

Leaving Donncan with Sukey, Iseult and Lachlan followed the old witch down the draughty stairs and through the great hall. It was crowded with students huddling near the fire, warming their hands or playing chess or trictrac at little low tables set between shabby but comfortable couches. Some serving maids had just brought in trays of steaming cider made from apples, honey, whiskey and spices, and many were drinking with enjoyment or eating the little Samhain cakes Latifa had made by the hundreds.

Iseult could not help but be struck by the difference a year had made. Last Samhain they had huddled here in this long hall, cold and afraid, Lachlan half mad with grief at the news his brother was dying. They had conjured a storm with the help of *The Book Of Shadows* and had flown through its icy gusts to confront the Ensorcellor. Now the great hall was warm and cheery, noisy with jokes and laughter, the windows steamed over so the cold night outside was forgotten. She glanced at Lachlan and he met her gaze with a little smile of shared remembrance.

After Lachlan's squires had been sent rather reluctantly up to Meghan's room, the small party made its way into a wide inner courtyard, surrounded on four sides by a graceful colonnade. Although a crystal dome had just been erected over the quadrangle, it was still bitterly cold once they stepped out from the shelter of the corridor.

In the very center of the courtyard was a round pool, enclosed within stone walls fretted with entwining lines and knots. At the four points of the compass were low stone benches, their edges carved with moons and stars.

Iseult sank down on one of the benches and looked into the heart of the pool, which glimmered blackly. Meghan sat beside her, while Lachlan prowled restlessly around the perimeter of the pool.

"There is a scrying pool at each of the thirteen Towers. They act as a focus for the will and the mind, just as my crystal ball does, or a bowl o' water, only the pools are designed to magnify the mind-voice one hundred fold," the old sorceress said. "Now, I ken ye have no' been practicing your scrying skills as ye ought . . . Nay, Lachlan, no need to bristle up, I ken ye have been busy fighting a war! I was no' accusing ye."

Lachlan made a face and sat down on the bench opposite. "What do ye want us to do?"

"Try and remember all I taught ye last year about the skill o' scrying. Ye must relax, clear your mind, empty your thoughts. Try and relax every muscle in your body. Watch the pool, let your mind drift free, think about who ye wish to see. Think o' your cousin Dughall, conjure his face in your mind's eye and his voice in your mind's ear."

As the three concentrated, the dark water in the pool slowly stirred, and the indistinct reflections of snow and crystal blurred into the white face and black hair and beard of Dughall MacBrann. Behind him Iseult could just make out the shape of a broken arch and the white of driving snow.

"Greetings, Lachlan," Dughall said. "Delightful night to be alone in a ghost-haunted ruin. I hope ye are as cold and uncomfortable as I am."

Lachlan grinned. "What sort o' manner is that to address your laird and rìgh with?" he said sternly. "Are ye no' going to call me 'Your Highness' and inquire after my health?"

"I hope ye have a snively head-cold and rheumatism o' the joints," Dughall replied. "Which is what I am going to have by the time I get back to a warm fire and a dram o' whiskey! Let us forget the courtesies, I beg ye. It's cold as Gearradh's womb out here, and this bloody pile o' stones simply reeks o' blood and murder. I want to get back to that dram as fast as I can."

"Well, it's glad I am to see ye alive and your usual charming self," Lachlan laughed. "Tell me then, what news?"

Dughall brushed a few icicles from his beard and launched into a terse account of how he had spent the nine months since leaving Lucescere. He had taken Owen MacBrann, one of the boys rescued from the Tower of Mists, as his squire, having learnt they shared a great-grandmother. The two of them had ridden for Ravenshaw, having a tricky time avoiding being captured by the many battalions of Bright Soldiers occupying the forests.

To their dismay they discovered the great ships of the Tirsoilleirean navy moored in the Firth of Seaforth, which could only mean the Bright Soldiers had coerced or bribed some local fishermen to guide them, for the bay was notoriously dangerous. The Soldiers' white banners were flying from the walls of the port town of Tullimuir, and a camp had been set up on the banks of the river.

Dughall and Owen rode on quickly and stealthily through the forest to Ravenscraig, the little castle that had been home to the MacBranns since the castle at Rhyssmadill had been abandoned. Ravenscraig was blockaded, however, the meadow below the tall crag filled with the Bright Soldiers' white tents and imposing siege towers.

When Dughall finally managed to communicate with his father—the MacBrann was adept at scrying through water or crystal, but he was so absent-minded that it was often difficult to reach him—he discovered that most of the seaside towns had been lost but that the Bright Soldiers had not yet won through to the highlands. However, the Fairgean invaded the firth and river each spring and autumn, so the Bright Soldiers found it difficult to hold the land they had won. The MacBrann was happy to let the Tìrsoilleirean fight off the sea-faeries for him while he busied himself in his laboratory and played with his many dogs.

"Och, we can hold them off for a good while yet, son," the MacBrann said comfortably. "In fact, it's glad I am to have them here for I've invented a new sort o' catapult that can throw boulders a good four hundred yards! It's much more fun peppering the blaygird berhtildes than trying to hit a painted target."

So Dughall had left his father to his amusements and had ridden off to Tìreich. It took him a long time to track down the MacAhern, for the Tìreichans were nomads and traveled the wide plains at their whim. In their grass-colored caravans pulled by the huge native dogs called zimbaras, they were as hard to pin down as will-o'-the-wisps. Finally, though, Dughall and Owen had caught up with Kenneth MacAhern, the Prionnsa of Tìreich, and had persuaded him to ride to the aid of Lachlan the Winged.

"So the horsemen ride to our aid?" the Rìgh cried. "Och, well done, Dughall!

"It shall take some time for them to gather an army and provision it for the campaign, but the MacAhern promised he would be with ye some time next year," Dughall said, blowing into his gloved hands. "They'll help drive the blaygird Bright Soldiers out o' Ravenshaw on the way, so happen we'll capture them between us like a flea between our nails."

"And have the Tìreichans no' seen any o' the Tìrsoilleirean in their land?" Iseult asked.

"Only some along the coast, but the horsemen say they

were easily led in circles until they were exhausted and then they crushed them. There are few towns or villages in Tìreich to conquer and, although I am sure the Bright Soldiers would have liked to have seized the horses for their cavalry, the thigearns were more than capable o' keeping their herds safe."

They exchanged a few more details of plans and dates, then Dughall MacBrann broke off the connection with a sweep of his hand.

"Well, that is good news indeed," Meghan said. "Now let us see if Rurach and Siantan ride to our aid as well."

The sorceress bent forward and stared into the black pool, her forehead furrowed. Through the glimmer they saw a face emerge and sink away, blur then emerge again. It was the MacRuraich, anxious and careworn. He had been trying to reach them for some minutes but had never before tried to scry and so had been unsure whether he would be able to summon them, despite the powers of the Scrying Pool.

Anghus had no good news for them. The Fairgean had been raiding and murdering all down the coastline and the hinterland was crowded with refugees. All the major rivers were impassable from early spring to late autumn, making it difficult to get supplies from one part of the country to another. To make matters worse, Siantan had erupted into rebellion and the MacRuraich had spent all summer trying to gather support from his lairds and barons to put the rebellion down.

"It's sorry I am indeed, Your Highness, but I can barely gather enough men to knock the rebellion on the head, let alone ride to your aid. On top o' that, there's a conclave o' seekers here stirring up trouble and calling for support for Renshaw and the baby banprionnsa. Even those who support me are uneasy about the wee Nic-Cuinn and I am having to argue your cause quite strongly. I am afraid I shall need ye to send men to help *me*, rather than being able to ride to your side as I had hoped."

Lachlan scowled and clenched his fist around the

Lodestar's shaft. "Eà damn these cursed seekers, am I never to be free o' them?"

"Anghus, what is the root o' the rebellion in Siantan? Is it still anger over the forming o' the Double Throne?" Meghan asked.

Anghus nodded. "Aye, I am afraid so. My parents thought they were doing what was best for the good o' both countries when they combined the thrones, but there has been naught but trouble since."

"Why do ye no' dissolve the Double Throne?" Meghan urged. "Your wife is a NicSian, why do ye no' let her rule in truth? Or what about her niece, what was her name? Brangaine or Breegeen? She grew up in Siantan, did she no'?"

Anghus shrugged, his mouth stubborn.

"Ye ken I never approved o' the joining o' the thrones—Siantan needs its own ruler, someone who puts its people first and understands their needs. Ye ken ye have never spent much time there or got to know the people."

"True," Anghus admitted.

"Well then. Think on it. Remember your wife is still a NicSian and it was she who was disenfranchised by the forming o' the Double Throne. I can never understand why she has no' insisted on ye giving it back before now."

"But she is my wife and banprionnsa with it," Anghus protested, then threw up his hands. "Obh obh! No need to glare at me like that! I'll think on it then."

"No other news?" Meghan said with a smile hovering on her grim old mouth.

Anghus grinned. "Och, I canna hide much from your witch eyes, can I, Meghan? Aye, it's true. Gwyneth is with child again, after twelve, long, barren years!"

"Och, happy news!" Lachlan cried. "Congratulations, Anghus."

"Well, there ye are then," Meghan said. "Ye'll have an heir for Rurach and another for Siantan. Problem solved."

A shadow settled on Anghus's face again. "Except my daughter Fionnghal insists she has no' the nature nor the inclination to be a banprionnsa. She swears she shall run away to sea and join the pirates before she accepts the throne."

Lachlan laughed and even Iseult gave a fleeting smile.

"Well, happen ye'll just have to breed up another heir," Meghan said. "I have a feeling that lassie o' yours may choose to enter the Coven anyway. She has a bright Talent indeed."

Anghus scowled. "But she is my eldest born!" he protested. "She should inherit the throne as I did."

"Anyone would think ye were dragging your heels at the idea o' breeding up more heirs," Lachlan teased. "Is the task no' to your liking?"

Anghus grinned in response and shrugged. "I only wish I had the leisure, Your Highness," he replied. "Truth is, I spend so much time out in the field, I rarely get to see Gwyneth or Fionnghal. The unborn babe was conceived the week I returned to Castle Rurach and I have been home again only twice in all these months."

"Let us pray to Eà that peace returns to Eileanan soon," Meghan said seriously. "So we may all rest and play with our children and have leisure to be with our loved ones."

They all made the sign of Eà's blessing, forming a circle with the fingers of their left hand and crossing it with one finger of their right. Then, after a somber-faced Lachlan had promised to send a battalion of soldiers to Rurach, Anghus bid them farewell and good luck, and the connection was broken. They sat for a while staring into the dark waters of the scrying pool, melancholy on their faces, then Meghan stirred and looked up.

"I shall look for Isabeau while we are here. My heart is troubled indeed about her. Happen I shall reach her, given that it is Samhain and the tide o' powers is on the turn."

"Why do ye bother? We know she has gone over to the enemy," Lachlan said bitterly.

"We know nothing o' the sort, ye great fool," Iseult snapped, losing her temper. "Why is it ye persist in thinking the worst o' her?"

Lachlan had the grace to look ashamed. He muttered something under his breath.

"It's because ye feel guilty about her hand," Iseult accused. "Ye ken she was tortured because she rescued ye from the Awl. Ye should be gentle to her because o' it, though, no' always so short-tempered and suspicious."

Lachlan scowled and looked away, his clenched fingers white. "Why did she have to go gaily riding into Caeryla like that?" he burst out. "She was tricky as a donbeag in shaking off that damned hard-mouthed bitch Glynelda before that. Why was she so stupid?"

"That was my fault," Meghan said grimly. "She knew nothing about ye or the rebellion or the state o' affairs in Eileanan. She thought it was all a game. I should never have sent her off on her own when she was such an innocent."

She sighed and stared into the water. Iseult could feel her gathering in her will and did the same. Then they heard footsteps pounding along the stone corridor and a white-faced Anntoin burst into the quadrangle. "Key-bearer Meghan, it's Jorge . . ."

"What's the matter wi' him?" Meghan cried.

"He did the sighting as he always does, but this time he sort o' stiffened all over and cried out, then just fell over, and now he's lying there all still and cold, and his eyes are just staring and white and oh Eà! I think he might be dead or dying," the boy gabbled, his freckled face frightened.

With a cry Meghan hoisted herself to her feet and hobbled out of the courtyard, Lachlan striding impatiently ahead. Iseult remained seated on the stone bench. Although she knew Meghan and Lachlan loved the old blind seer, she still had trouble overcoming her revulsion to his affliction. The scene just described by Anntoin was enough to send a shiver of disgust down her spine, and she had no wish to distress Meghan with these feelings. She knew she would only be in the way, so she sat still and gazed into the pool, thinking of Isabeau.

Slowly an image formed deep within the water. It was hard to focus on, a puzzle of shapes and shadows that kept slipping away as if a hand were passing before it.

Iseult stared intently into the pool, her heart beginning

to pound faster. She saw Isabeau sitting cross-legged before a fire, shadows gathering close about her. Her hands
were upturned on her lap and her eyes were closed, but
tears slid down her pale cheeks. Fire-shadows flickered
over her face, distorting it. Iseult received such a strong
sense of loneliness and desolation that instinctively she
leaned forward and called her sister's name. Isabeau's
eyes snapped open. *Iseult?* For a moment their eyes
seemed to meet and Iseult felt a surge of longing and
bitter homesickness. Then the image was blotted out
again, and Iseult could not summon it back.

She sat for a long while, not noticing the cold, thinking
and wondering. Then she rose and left the dark pool
slowly, her hand twisting the dragoneye ring on her left
hand.

When Iseult returned to Meghan's suite of rooms, it
was to find Jorge white and haggard in the old sorceress's
canopied bed, the Keybearer holding his hand and telling
him sternly to drink her *mithuan* and be quiet. The
League of the Healing Hand was clustered around with
anxious faces, Tòmas sitting on the bed with his hands
clasped in his lap. His blue eyes were brimming over with
tears and his bottom lip trembled. Although he knew he
could not lay hands on the old seer in case he healed his
blindness, Tòmas could not bear to see his beloved master so frail and he longed to give him the magic of his
touch.

Iseult touched Meghan briefly on the elbow and the
Keybearer turned to her impatiently. "What is it?" she
snapped.

"I saw Isabeau." Iseult spoke quietly so none but the
old sorceress could hear. Immediately Meghan's attention sharpened and she grasped Iseult's shoulder.
"Where was she? Was she safe? Was the Ensorcellor's
daughter with her? What could ye see?"

"I could see nothing but Isabeau. It was somewhere
cold, freezing cold, and she was very unhappy. The babe
was no' with her that I could see."

"Where? Where was she?"

Iseult hesitated for a moment, then shook her head.

"I do no' know. In some sort of cave. There was a fire—
I could see the flames dancing on her face and snow on
the ground."

The deep lines of worry deepened on Meghan's face
but then Jorge moved his head uneasily, muttering, and
she turned back to his side.

"Flames," the old seer muttered. "Flames leaping,
snow falling."

"Hush, auld friend," Meghan said. "Time enough to
tell me your visions when ye've regained your strength."
She lifted his head so he could drink from a silver-
embossed flask. He drank, then choked as the stimulant
burnt his throat. Johanna passed Meghan a flask of water
and Jorge sipped it gratefully, then fell back on the pillows with a sigh.

"I saw terrible things," he said pitifully. "This war is
to drag on for years, Meghan, and many, many people
will die. I saw the scaly sea rise and flood the land, the
Red Wanderer like a bloody gash in the sky. That is
when they will come . . . With the rising o' the red comet
the Fairgean shall come . . ." His voice rose and Meghan
stroked back the hair from his forehead, murmuring,
"Hush now, Jorge. Sleep."

Obediently the old man closed his eyes, though his
shaggy white brows were bunched together and his spindly fingers plucked at the coverlet unhappily. "Flames
leaping . . ." he murmured with a shudder.

Exactly one month after her arrival Isabeau was finally
allowed to eat from the communal pot, and for the first
time her plate and spoon were washed with the others
without being scoured with ashes and snow first. Isabeau
knew this meant she was no longer taboo and her
heart lifted.

That evening she was once again permitted into the
Firemaker's presence. This time she made no mistakes,
sitting cross-legged, her white-capped head bowed, her
hands still.

Her great-grandmother sat very straight on her furs
and looked Isabeau over. Her gaze lingered particularly

on Isabeau's maimed hand which was kept firmly clasped within the palm of her other hand. With an imperative gesture the Firemaker demanded that Isabeau spread it out for her to see. Her color rising, Isabeau obeyed. She knew that the Khan'cohbans regarded any disability with repugnance. It was considered more merciful to kill a badly wounded warrior than to allow him to live crippled. Weak, ailing or deformed babies were left out for the White Gods, and people too old and frail to tend for themselves were given a death drink made from poisonous berries.

The Firemaker examined Isabeau's hand closely, turning it over in her own two, thin, vein-knotted hands. She then lifted Isabeau's face and traced the shape of the scar between her brows.

"I would ask of you a question, Khan. Will you answer in fullness and in truth?" she asked in the Khan'cohbans' ritual phrasing.

"Yes, I will, Firemaker," Isabeau replied in the same language, her heart lifting. A question asked meant a question owed, and Isabeau had many things she would like to ask.

"You are scarred in hand and brow. Will you tell me how you came to be so disfigured."

Isabeau turned her palms upward in her lap and took a few deep breaths, calming and composing herself, gathering her thoughts and her words. When she spoke, it was not in her natural tone, but in a rhythmic singsong. Stumbling occasionally as she sought the right word or gesture, she explained how she had been captured and tortured, then put on trial.

When she had finished, the Firemaker pondered for a long moment. "So you underwent an ordeal to receive your scars," she said finally, then pointed at the scar on Isabeau's forehead. "And it is the seventh scar that you received. In the law of the people of the White Gods, this means you are powerful and to be respected."

Isabeau's eyes widened a little in surprise, though she tried hard not to show any reaction. It had never occurred to her that the little white triangular scar between her brows could be seen as one of the ritual disfigurements of the Khan'cohbans. She knew the forehead mark was only earned by the very finest in their field, like the First of the Scarred Warriors.

"Yet you are a stranger among us, crippled and nameless. The Soul-Sage and the Council of Scarred Warriors have pondered the dilemma you pose ever since your coming. Since your mark is that of the Soul-Sage, she who skims among the stars has been particularly perturbed. She has cast the bones and they have told her that you must seek your name and your totem, for though a child among us, you are marked by the White Gods and thus no child in their eyes."

Isabeau sat still, thinking over the Firemaker's words and puzzling out their meaning. She had never heard the term "Soul-Sage" before and was not sure whether she had interpreted the words correctly, though she had seen a woman throwing a handful of old bones before—a woman with triangular scars on her cheeks and forehead. She too slept at the back of the cave and was served first, along with the warriors and the storytellers. The description of her skimming among the stars was especially strange, particularly since Isabeau had never seen her leave the cave.

The suggestion that she was to seek her name and her totem excited Isabeau. She knew her sister Iseult had undergone her ordeal and initiation, and knew now that the second part of her name, the "derin" of "Khanderin," meant "savage like the saber leopard." This was a strong name, a highly respected name, indicating that Iseult had courage, strength and boldness.

"If you are to make the journey to the Skull of the World and ask the White Gods for your name, you must be properly prepared. Some among the Council of Scarred Warriors believe that you must set out now, for already you are highly marked. The First, the Soul-Sage and I the Firemaker disagree. Already the long darkness descends and you are a stranger in this land and still a child in our eyes. We would not send a child out to face the Gods of White without the right knowledge or tools and so we shall not send you. The children of the Gods of White are trained from birth, however. You are among us only a short time, so you shall begin your learning. Move your bed-roll from the fire of the little coney to the fire of the Soul-Sage. She shall teach you her craft, and the one who guided you to the haven shall teach you the art of the Scarred Warrior, and I shall teach you the wisdom and lore of the Firemaker. When you are ready, you shall make the journey to the Skull of the World."

Isabeau made the gesture of affirmation and understanding. The Firemaker said: "I asked of you a question which you answered fully and with truth. Do you wish a story in return?"

After some thought, Isabeau said, "Tell me the story of the Soul-Sage, if you please."

The Firemaker frowned and said reluctantly, "It is the story of the Soul-Sage to tell."

"I am but a stranger here and a child in your eyes. If I am to sit at the feet of the Soul-Sage, should I not know her story if I am not to offend from ignorance?"

The Firemaker bowed her head, turned her palms upward in her lap and said: "The Soul-Sage is the skimmer among stars, the speaker across distance, the caster of bones, the foreteller and foreboder. The Soul-Sage can hear the hidden thought and see the secret heart. Alone among the People does she hear the soundless speech of the Gods of White. The mark upon her brow is the scratch of their claw.

"Before the first Firemaker was born, each pride was equal in strength and cunning. The old mother, the soul-sages, the scarred warriors and the storytellers would consult and counsel together, and so direct the prides. The firekeepers carried the coals, the metalsmiths forged the weapons, the weavers made the clothes, and the children herded the *ulez* and gathered roots and leaves. Everyone in the pride had their place.

"Then the first Firemaker was born, and all places were turned upside down. She could conjure fire so the firekeepers' sacred duty was no longer of such vital importance. She could speak across distances and see into the hearts of those around her, so that the soul-sages were jealous and suspicious. She could turn aside the thrust of a *reil* or a dagger, or sense where game was hiding, so that the scarred warriors were made to seem small and stupid. All were angry, and wondered why the Gods of White had brought the red one to live among them.

"The Soul-Sage of the Fire Dragon Pride cast the bones and listened to the words of the gods, who told her that the red one was a gift to the people of the Spine of the World, in reward for their long exile. She was given to bring warmth and light to the howling night, and to protect the people of the prides from their enemies. She was not their master but their servant. So the old mothers and scarred warriors, soul-sages and storytellers came together and set laws and limits for the Firemaker which she must swear to uphold. This is why each pride still has its firekeeper, who carries the coals and keeps them safe, and only if the firekeeper fails may the Firemaker conjure fire for that pride and they must pay the price."

Isabeau bowed her head at these words, for at last she understood the consternation at her conjuring of fire. The Firemaker nodded and made a sweeping gesture with her thin, gnarled hand.

"There were some among the Firemakers who could skim the stars or foresee the future, however, and most can speak across distances or command the birds and beasts. So the soul-sages, who were once the wisdom of the pride, brood still about their lost power and glance askance at those of the Firemaker's get. This is the story of the Soul-Sage."

The Firemaker's hands dropped back into her lap and she met Isabeau's gaze for a moment before making the gesture of dismissal. Isabeau bowed her head, thanked her, then rose to obey her orders.

She rolled her blankets under her arm and went and knelt near the Soul-Sage's fire, her eyes downcast. She knew better than to make any gesture or word of greeting. She knelt in this way for close on ten minutes before the Soul-Sage lifted her eyes and brought her hand to her brow, her heart and then out. Isabeau crossed her hands over her breast and bowed her head. The Soul-Sage then indicated that Isabeau may sit, and she unrolled her blankets and sat down cross-legged once more.

The Soul-Sage was a woman of middle years, dark of skin with a long, narrow face and even more prominent facial structure than usual among her race. Her eyes were so heavily hooded, nothing could be seen of them but the occasional cold gleam. She was painfully thin, her arms and legs as spindly as the limbs of a bird. Hanging around her neck on a cord was a bird's talon, and in a bag of skin tied to her waist she carried her bones, an odd collection of animal knuckles, broken skeletons, claws and fossilized stones.

The Soul-Sage was a woman of long silences, but there was power in her every movement. Like the storytellers, she had a fable or proverb for every occasion. Since she was Isabeau's teacher, Isabeau was permitted to ask questions and request stories whenever she pleased. This meant, however, that she had to answer any question the Soul-Sage asked and some of these were deeply personal.

Isabeau had already learnt she must not fidget or prevaricate, but many of the Soul-Sage's questions caused scorching color to sweep over her face as she did her best to answer wholly and truthfully.

Her first question was whether Isabeau had preserved her virginity. This was rather puzzling because the Khan'-cohbans had a very straightforward and candid attitude to their sexuality. Since all lived in the same small area, there was almost no privacy and Isabeau had been rather shocked to discover Khan'cohbans were rarely monogamous, often sharing a different bed every night, with the only taboo being between children and parents or between siblings. Isabeau knew that the witches of the Coven rarely married, but those who did enter into relationships usually did so on a long-term basis and promiscuity was unusual.

After answering as best she could, feeling rather glad

now that Lilanthe had interrupted her and Dide when she had, Isabeau asked the Soul-Sage why her virginity was of such importance.

"You are still a child in our eyes and nameless," the woman replied, "but more importantly, the profoundest secrets of the gods are not revealed to those who too early distract themselves with thoughts of the flesh. Later, such things can lead to deeper levels of understanding, but at this stage one must think only of what is beyond one's body, not within. For now, learn and keep silence."

Isabeau nodded in understanding. She remembered Meghan once saying something similar to her about Ishbel the Winged, before Isabeau had known the fabled flying sorceress was her own mother. Meghan had said how disappointed she had been that Ishbel had fallen in love so early, for she might have been a great sorceress had she waited for her powers to flower fully.

Many of the Soul-Sage's lessons were similar to Meghan's, particularly the meditation and scrying exercises. Isabeau had always found it hard to sit still for prolonged periods and even harder to empty her mind of thoughts. Even if she had been able to subdue her natural restless energy, her mind would race on, filled with ideas, daydreams, random thoughts, stray memories and trivial worries. Meghan had always insisted on a short period of meditation each dawn and Isabeau had sat the nightlong Ordeal many times; but since parting ways with her guardian, Isabeau had fallen out of the habit of regular meditation.

She found the Soul-Sage a much harder taskmaster than Meghan had ever been. The Khan'cohban woman could sit still for hours at a time without fidgeting, sighing or altering the slow steady rhythm of her breathing. Since all her food was gathered and prepared for her, all her clothes woven, and all her tools and eating implements made for her, she had the leisure to spend her days in silent meditation.

Isabeau, however, was used to an active, busy life and at first she found it very difficult. The Soul-Sage kept a thin switch in her hand, however, and after being slashed every time she shifted her weight, moaned or peeked out through her eyelashes, Isabeau soon was able to sustain at least the semblance of immobility while her thoughts leapt and played.

One day the Soul-Sage brought out a little drum decorated with feathers and smears of ash and ocher. "As I beat, breathe," she ordered.

Obediently Isabeau sat, back straight, hands upturned on her thighs. Eyes shut, she heard the Soul-Sage slowly and rhythmically pound the drum with one hand. At first Isabeau found it difficult to regulate her breathing to the drumbeat. It was too slow, so that she was gasping for air by the time the sound came again. After a long while she caught the rhythm, inhaling very slowly, holding her breath for several strained moments when it felt as if every vein and capillary was swollen with oxygen, then slowly, quivering, exhaling until she was slack as a deflated bagpipe. When at last the drumbeat stopped, it took Isabeau a while to notice, so absorbed had she become in her own breathing. Then she felt rather light-headed and the cave around her seemed bright and noisy, when always before its gloom and silence had oppressed her.

"A beginning," the Soul-Sage said and put the drum away.

It was now the dark, cold depths of winter and the sun shone for only a few hours each day. Those few hours of dismal light were spent with the Khan'cohban who had guided her to the Haven, learning the treacherous nature of snow. To Isabeau's amazement, the otherwise taciturn Khan'cohbans had more than thirty words for frozen water. Words like snowflake, snowdrift, snowstorm, snowball, icicle, frost, sleet, slush, hail, blizzard and avalanche came nowhere near expressing the many subtleties of snow.

The Khan'cohban warrior taught her to know when it was only a few inches thick or many feet deep, when rocks were hidden beneath a deceptively soft slope, or when a mere breath of wind would be enough to cause an avalanche. Isabeau learnt to recognize the tracks of deer, coneys, marmots, foxes, squirrels, hoarweasels, native lynx, snow lions, bears and wolves—all of which looked quite different in snow than upon the bare earth. She learnt when a snowstorm was brewing and how to stay alive if caught in one.

She bruised herself black and blue trying to learn to stand on a skimmer. The first time she whizzed effortlessly down a slope was the most exhilarating experience of her life. For the first time she thought she knew how it felt to fly. That day was the first time Isabeau saw the Scarred Warrior smile, and it greatly lightened the grim darkness of his face. He punched his right fist into his left, a sign of triumph, and then sternly criticized her on her lack of grace and style. Isabeau only grinned in response and from that moment on practiced her skimming skills at every opportunity, despite the bruises and aching muscles.

It gradually occurred to Isabeau that her teacher was the only Scarred Warrior never to leave the Haven. The others spent much of their time out hunting meat for the pride, returning triumphantly with slaughtered deer, coneys, birds and the wide-antlered *geal'teas*. On their return the fires were built high, there were dances of jubilation, and everyone but Isabeau feasted with great enjoyment.

One day, as she and her Scarred Warrior teacher walked through the snowy forest, Isabeau asked tentatively, "Teacher, I would ask of you a question."

For a moment she thought he would refuse, then he made a curt gesture of assent.

"Teacher, why is it that you stay here in Haven when all the other Scarred Warriors are away hunting most of the time?"

There was silence for a moment, then he indicated she sit, unstrapping his skimmer from his back and sitting on it, cross-legged.

"Although I long to be out in the snowy fields, skimming with my comrades and feeling the hot lust of hunting and killing, I am under a *geas* to your kin, the

Firemaker. This is how she has commanded me to fulfill my debt of honor. Long ago my daughter was lost in a white storm of lightning and ice. I was far away, fighting against the Pride of the Woolly Bear. The Firemaker stilled the storm and my daughter, who is dear to my heart, was found. The effort exhausted the Firemaker and for a long time we thought her spirit was lost. Only the Soul-Sage was able to find her and heal her and bring her spirit back to the pride. The Firemaker was willing to surrender her life for my daughter and so a *geas* was laid upon me. So though it irks me greatly to stay behind like a mere child and lose a winter of fighting and hunting and thus a chance to win another scar, I stay in the Haven and teach you and guide you as the Firemaker has commanded."

Silence fell. He brought his hands back to lie still on his thighs and said, "I have answered your question in fullness and truth, now shall you answer mine."

Isabeau made the gesture of affirmation, though with some trepidation. She had learnt the questions of Khan'-cohbans were usually disconcerting and often embarrassing.

"Why do you scorn the White Gods' gift of blood and flesh? I have seen you grow sick and pale as we feast, and press your hand against your mouth and turn away into the shadows. You eat only seeds and wild grains like a sword-billed flutterwing. To eat flesh is to grow strong and fierce and hot-blooded. To eat seeds is to be weak and thin and defenseless."

Isabeau smiled rather ruefully. Indeed she had trouble finding enough to eat here in these snowy heights. Most of the pride's gathering of grains, fruits and nuts was done in the summer and stored in huge, stone jars in the Haven. Isabeau could not ask that she be given more than her fair share of this jealously guarded hoard, particularly since she had not shared in its gathering. She was often hungry, therefore, and had grown adept at finding fallen nuts and edible barks beneath the snow to give her the protein she needed.

Rhythmically, choosing her words and hand gestures

carefully, she replied, "My first teacher, wise as the Soul-Sage, powerful as the Firemaker, taught me to revere all life as sacred. Each bird, each seed, each stone, is filled with life force, the soul, both unique and universal. To destroy that life-force is to diminish the universe itself."

"But by eating a plant, does that not destroy it?" The Scarred Warrior struggled to understand.

Isabeau shook her head. "We eat only of its fruit and leaves, allowing the plant itself to grown and flourish. We never strip the plant completely or uproot it, so it may spread its seeds and continue the life cycle uninterrupted. We do not kill an animal for its skins but gather its wool for spinning. We do not cut down a tree for firewood but gather its discarded branches. We drink the milk of our goats and sheep but do not drain them dry so their young must thirst. I wear these skins only because I know the animal they belong to no longer has use for them, having died in its natural time, and if I did not accept its gift, I myself should die. I give thanks to Eà, our mother and our father, that this is so."

The Khan'cohban shook his head in puzzlement. "It is very odd," he said. "You shall never win your scars as a hunter and warrior with such philosophies."

Isabeau smiled at him. "I know."

He stood up and stretched down his many-jointed fingers to help her up. "You already wear the seventh scar of the Soul-Sage at your brow and I have observed the Soul-Sage often willfully starves herself before casting the bones or skimming the stars. As a Soul-Sage you shall not need to hunt or kill, so perhaps the Gods of White do not take offense at your strange beliefs, knowing you do not scorn them or their gifts."

"Indeed I hope so," Isabeau replied with a little shiver. Already she knew how cruel these mountains could be.

"You shall still need to know the art of the Scarred Warrior if you are to survive your initiation journey," the Khan'cohban said, leading the way on through the deep snow. "Soon the long darkness shall be here. When the ice storm blows without pause and the Gods of White roam the world, then I shall begin to teach you."

It was not very many more days until the brief hours of sunlight were swallowed into an incessant storm of ice and darkness that heaped the snow so high that the mouth of the cave was almost closed. Icicles hung down like transparent fangs, and the fires were guarded jealously. Isabeau's days were divided between the still meditations of the Soul-Sage and the moving meditations of the Scarred Warrior. In both, she was taught to control her every breath, to narrow down her consciousness to a single point of flame.

Isabeau found to her amazement that the slow, flowing movements of the Scarred Warrior were called *ahdayeh*, just like the fighting exercises she had been taught as a young girl. Each of the thirty-three stances or movements had the same title, named for the mountains' creatures of prey, the snow lions, saber leopards, lynxes, bears, wolves, and dragons. She wondered how it was the witches of the Coven had learnt *ahdayeh*, when humans and Khan'cohbans had lived so far apart for so many years. Then she remembered her own father had traveled down out of the mountains to the Towers of Roses and Thorns, years before she was born, and wondered if he had taught this art to the Coven.

Contrary to Isabeau's expectations, the art of the Scarred Warrior was not about pitting one's strength against one's adversary and trying to overcome them. It was instead a matter of stepping aside or back, tempting one's opponent to overreach and lose their balance. It was about maintaining one's own balance and own inner harmony, and confronting the other with their own chaos.

"Be as snow," the Scarred Warrior told her. "Snow is gentle, snow is silent, snow is inexorable. Fight hard against snow and it shall always smother you with its softness and silence. Submit to snow and it shall melt away before you."

So as the long darkness passed, Isabeau was as snow: quiet, gentle, inexorable, and cold.

ANGEL OF DEATH

"Rise up, bonny lassies, in your gowns o' green,
For summer is a-coming in today,
Ye're as fair a lady as any I've seen,
In the merry morn o' May."

Through the dim streets of Blairgowrie danced a long procession of men and women carrying torches. On their heads were crowns made of leaves and spring flowers. Dide the Juggler danced at the head of the cavalcade, leafy twigs tied to every limb, a thick garland of leaves on his head. As he spun and leapt he sang in his clear, strong voice:

"Rise up, rowdy laddies, we wish ye well and fine,
For summer is a-coming in today,
Ye've a shilling in your pocket and I wish it were
in mine,
In the merry morn o' May."

Lachlan and Iseult watched the procession from the wall of the great keep, smiling and waving to the crowd below. The young prionnsa Donncan sat on the Banrìgh's hip, laughing in delight as the passing men and women bowed and curtseyed before dancing on. Meghan and Jorge sat close behind, smiling as they watched the May Day procession winding through the town. It had been a long time since the Beltane fires had been lit on every hill at the rising of the sun, creating a chain of fire as far as the eye could see. Although the hills of Blèssem and Clachan would remain dark this morn, every hill in

Rionnagan was to be lit, and that made the Keybearer of the Coven a very proud and happy old woman.

"Be brave, my laddies, be canny and bold,
For summer is a-coming in today,
Let us build a mighty ship and gild her all wi' gold,
In the merry morn o' May."

Iseult leant closer to her husband and whispered: "The problem is we have the Bright Soldiers coming in from the east through Arran, through the north from Aslinn, and sailing up the coast and into the Berhtfane. No matter what we do, our forces are being split. If we could only find a way to plug one o' those approaches!"

"Eà curse it, the forests o' Aslinn are so thick and there are so few roads, we could spend years crashing around in there and then pass within a mile o' one o' their encampments and never ken it," Lachlan replied, his smile growing strained. "The fenlands are even worse, even if we do have Iain and Gwilym to show us the paths. And I'm no' sure we are strong enough to face Margrit and her blaygird Gray Ghosts yet. As long as the Mesmerdean guard the marshes, the potential cost is too great to even attempt an attack."

"Aye, it's true the Mesmerdean are no friends o' ours," Iseult replied with a little shiver. Even though it was two years since the marsh faeries had first attacked them in the Veiled Forest, she knew they would not have forgotten or forgiven the death of so many of their kin. Their attack last summer was proof enough of that.

"Be gay, my lassies, for ye may soon be wed,
And summer is a-coming in today,
Let us make a garland o' the white rose and the red,
In the merry morn o' May."

"Well, at least the Fairgean are on the rise again and are keeping the sea free o' the Bright Soldiers' ships," Lachlan said, bowing and smiling as some girls in the crowd threw him a handful of roses. "Who would have guessed we'd have occasion to be grateful to those black-blooded sea demons?"

"Well, I think we should push on for Dùn Eidean," Iseult said. "Ye ken Meghan is keen to win back as much o' Blèssem as we can so she and Matthew the Lean can plant the fields. And the MacThanach is worried indeed about his mother, who's been holed up for all this time. They must be close to starving in there, but the auld dowager has sworn she will no' give in."

"A feisty auld biddy," Lachlan said appreciatively. "Who would have thought she could keep the Bright Soldiers from Dùn Eidean for so long?"

"We need to keep the MacThanach's support," Iseult said, shifting her son to the other hip to ease her arm. "If we lose him, we lose the Blèssem lairds and all o' their men. That's almost half our troops. Besides, I think it will take the Bright Soldiers by surprise. They ken as well as we do that our forces are being split. They'll expect us to concentrate on driving them back one way or another, no' drive right down the middle and split *their* forces."

"Och, as long as we do something soon!" Lachlan cried, shaking his wings. "It's been a year since we won Blairgowrie, and since then we've been scuttling back and forth across Blèssem like crabs! It seems we cut off the head o' the monster only for it to grow two more."

"War is like that," Iseult replied somberly as the laughing, singing procession below them passed out of the gates and down the hill.

Lachlan bent down and picked up a rose to give her. "Happen we'll win peace in the end, *leannan*, and then we can rest and raise our son and have nothing to worry about save how to spend our Lammas tithes."

Iseult smiled slightly and tucked the rose into her bodice. "The Khan'cohbans say, 'If ye want peace, prepare for war,'" she answered. "Come, let us see if we can find a way to free Dùn Eidean and we'll worry about peace when we have it."

*   *   *

Meghan sighed and sipped from her goblet of wine. "Come, my lairds, must we always be arguing? The Rìgh has made his decision, now it is your job to help ensure his commands are carried out. This war has dragged on a year and a half as it is, and it is time we struck another decisive blow. Has anyone any ideas how we can break the blockade at Dùn Eidean?"

A chorus of angry voices answered her and she sighed and threw up her hands. The war council had been sitting for several days now, and all that the lairds did was argue and prevaricate.

To everyone's surprise, Elfrida leant forward and said in her clear, childish voice, "Ye will never make the Tìrsoilleirean turn and run merely by showing strength o' arms, Your Highness. They are taught to think the only honorable death is dying with a sword in their hand."

"Then if we canna make them retreat, we'll just have to beat them back by force," the MacThanach boomed.

"But, my laird, ye ken we have less than half their number, even if we pull all the MacSeinn's men away from the east and bring them in to reinforce us," Iseult said with the most patience she could muster.

The arguments broke out again and Elfrida had to raise her voice to cut across them. "But what if ye *could* make them run away?"

Iseult turned to her wearily. "But I thought ye just said they would never retreat and never surrender. They are like the Scarred Warriors then; it is no use dreaming o' what might be."

"I said force o' arms would no' make them flee. I did no' said *nothing* would."

Iseult's gaze sharpened. "If no' force, then what?"

Elfrida shrugged, a little discomfited. "Well, ye ken I have been spending time talking with the Tìrsoilleirean prisoners o' war and persuading them to our cause."

Iseult and Lachlan nodded, while Meghan stroked Gitâ's soft brown fur, her face tired. "Well, it seems the Bright Soldiers think ye are some incarnation o' Auld Clootie," Elfrida continued, color rising in her face.

Meghan looked up, her interest caught, though Lachlan frowned and said, "Auld who?"

"Auld Clootie," Elfrida repeated. "Ye ken, the Archfiend, the Prince o' Darkness."

The Rìgh and Banrìgh looked at each other, puzzled.

"The Tìrsoilleirean believe in omnipotent forces o' absolute good and absolute evil," Meghan said, a slight trace of sarcasm in her voice. "They call their idea o' evil manifest the Archfiend, among many other names."

Lachlan's skin darkened. "Ye mean they think me some sort o' spirit o' evil?"

Elfrida nodded, blushing even more.

"What have I ever done that's so evil?" Lachlan cried. "I did no' invade their country and burn their houses! I do no' ask my women soldiers to cut off their breasts or give up their family life! I do no' sacrifice bairns to a bloodthirsty god!"

"Neither do we!" Elfrida cried. "I've never seen the elders kill a baby!"

The Rìgh rose to his feet, his face ugly. "I will give them evil!" he cried, slamming his fist into his hand. "I will give them more wickedness than they ever dreamed o'!"

"Hush, *leannan*," Iseult murmured, rising also and laying her hand on his tense upper arm. "Ye always kent this was a holy war. O' course the priests and the berhtildes have tried to make ye seem evil and depraved. This is no surprise, and the lady Elfrida would no' bring it up if she did no' see how we could turn it to our advantage."

Elfrida's color subsided and she nodded her head once, jerkily. "Indeed, Her Highness is right. I did no' mean to insult ye, Your Highness, truly I did no'."

Lachlan remained standing, his jaw still gritted tight with anger. "Well, then, what advantage is it to us to have the Bright Soldiers calling me this Prince o' Darkness?"

"It is hard to explain because ye ken so little about what we . . . I mean, the Tìrsoilleirean believe," she said slowly. "It is true we are taught there is an evil force that spends its entire existence trying to overthrow our God the Father. As there are many angels that support our Holy God, so are there many demons that support the Archfiend. It is said the Prince o' Darkness is the first angel that sinned. The elders say he deceived the whole world and was cast out into the earth, and all his angels cast with him. Ever since, in his sinful pride and ambition, he has sought to regain his place in heaven."

"I do no' see what all that has to do with me!"

"It is because o' your wings," Elfrida said. "And all ken ye once had claws like a bird. In some auld drawings the Archfiend has hooves like a goat, in others they are like talons. In Tìrsoilleir we are taught we must resist this fallen angel, who seeks to turn us from the path o' righteousness. As long as the Bright Soldiers believe ye are the Prince o' Darkness, they will fight to the last breath in their body to overthrow ye, else they face eternal damnation."

Lachlan sat down heavily, his glossy black wings still tense and erect. "So it is a fight to the death."

"No' necessarily," Elfrida replied, leaning forward. "It is true we could use this to our advantage. Auld Clootie is regarded with such dread that we could cause absolute terror in the ranks, and some at least would break and run. I have a better idea though." She took a moment to gather her thoughts then said softly, "Ye ken I was raised in prison and had never walked freely or seen the whole wide sky until I was sent to Arran to marry Iain."

The lairds all nodded, many with open sympathy on their faces.

"A few years before I was released, another prisoner was brought to the Black Tower where I was incarcerated. Only the most important prisoners were kept there, the ones who were meant never to see daylight again. I heard much about this man from my gaolers. He was a prophet called Killian the Listener, for it was said he heard the voices o' the angels. Killian the Listener said the General Assembly had grown arrogant and corrupt. He said the elders had grown away from the true meaning o' the Word and sought only their own power and material comfort. He grew famous in Bride for standing on the steps o' the cathedral and denouncing the Fealde as she came to hear the service.

"Killian the Listener warned the elders that God our Father would no' tolerate their pride and corruption. He said the dark-winged angel o' death would come wi' his flaming sword and topple them from their gilded altars, and then the people o' the Bright Land would be free o' their terrible tyranny. He lost his ears and his liberty for his audacity, the elders saying the divine voice he heard was that o' the Archfiend and not o' our Holy God."

"They chopped off his ears?" Lachlan was aghast.

"Aye, even though he told them it was no' with the ears o' the body that he heard, but with the ears o' the soul."

"But what has this earless prophet to do with rescuing the people o' Dùn Eidean?" the MacThanach boomed.

"She means to make the Bright Soldiers think Lachlan is this angel," Iseult said, her serious blue gaze intent on the other woman's face. Elfrida nodded, glad to be understood so quickly.

"But did ye no' call it an angel o' death?" Lachlan cried. "How is that any better than this other angel ye spoke o', the fallen one."

"The angel o' death is no force o' evil," Elfrida replied. "He stands on God's right hand and is called the Prince o' Light, as the Archfiend is called the Prince o' Darkness. He is the warrior angel, the angel o' vengeance who fights for the faithful. He is God's messenger on earth. If we can make the Tìrsoilleirean army believe ye are the angel o' death, they will fall down before ye and throw down their arms. O' course, the berhtildes shall say it is more trickery on the part o' Auld Clootie and punish cruelly those who believe, but the Tìrsoilleirean have always been willing to be martyrs. Once they are convinced the Holy God our Father is angry with the Fealde and the elders, they shall take up arms against them, I am sure o' it!"

"And how are we to convince them?" Lachlan said

skeptically. "They have traveled hundreds o' miles on this crusade o' theirs. Ye think they will go home because I tell them to?"

"They might," Elfrida replied seriously. "Particularly if the ground is prepared by another seer. Prophets are much feared and respected in the Bright Land. Ye have told me how Jorge traveled around telling how a winged warrior would come to save the land. Could he no' do so again? If I taught him the language o' fire and brimstone, he could surely win the Bright Soldiers to our side wi' the telling of his prophecies."

"Nay!" Meghan exclaimed. "It is much too dangerous! What would the berhtildes do to him if they caught him? There must be another way!"

Jorge turned his blind head toward her. "There is no better way," he said gently. "Do no' fret, auld friend. I have seen what I must do. It shall be as the NicHilde decrees."

Meghan protested again, her face creased with worry, but the blind seer was adamant. Since his fainting fit in the winter, he was frailer than ever, his opaque eyes sunken back into his skull, his limbs as thin as sticks. His kindly old face was often shadowed in melancholy and he had confessed to Meghan that he slept uneasily, all his dreams filled with visions of blood and fire. He would not return to the safety of Lucescere though, despite all Meghan's urging, for he knew his powers would surely be needed. When Meghan once more protested that he was too precious to be risked, he shook his head at her and smiled. "Ye canna say that, my dear, when ye risk yourself each day. What would I do in Lucescere when all whom I hold dear are here at the battlefront? Nay, let me alone, Meghan. What Eà wills will be."

The war council broke up again into talk and argument. For some minutes the controversy raged, then Iseult leant forward, her scarred face a little flushed as she strove to repress her exasperation. "To win, deceive," she said. "Elfrida, how else can we trick these Bright Soldiers o' yours into believing Lachlan is this angel o' light?"

Elfrida smiled. "I shall need to teach him some new songs," she replied. "And can anyone here play a trumpet?"

Jorge leant on his staff, his old hands trembling, as he listened to the clatter of horses' hooves approaching along the road. He waited until they had drawn abreast of him, then stepped out from behind the shelter of the trees. The two horses in the lead shied, neighing loudly. Their riders cursed and dragged their mounts' heads back. Jorge raised his blind face and pointed directly at the berhtilde.

"Night-winged and flame-eyed, the angel o' death shall strike ye, for ye have forgotten the Word o' God," he cried. "The teeth o' beasts shall gnash ye, the claws o' birds shall slash ye, the venom o' things crawling in the dust shall sicken your blood. For ye have been led astray by false words and false promises! Oh, ye who call evil good and good evil, who mistake darkness for light and light for darkness, who put bitter for sweet and sweet for bitter! The arrows o' God the Father have been loosed against ye."

The berhtilde shrank back in superstitious terror, but almost immediately regained control of herself. She drew her sword and spurred her horse forward, crying, "Die, false prophet, creature o' the Archfiend! Deus vult!"

A raven screeched, beating its midnight-black wings around the berhtilde's head. To her consternation, the horse reared, then bucked her off. She landed heavily on the stones of the road, directly at Jorge's feet. He pointed his frail hand at her and said, "The anger o' God the Father knows no bounds. The very mountains shall quake, the sea shall rise up and sweep across the land, the whirlwind shall reap its bitter harvest, his wrath shall have no bounds until your false-hearted leaders are all swept away and truth and mercy again prevail."

The berhtilde struggled to rise but invisible chains held her prisoner. She tried to speak but her tongue was a stone in her mouth. Jorge bent over and touched her between the eyes and she fell back in a faint. He straightened and swept the rest of the company with white, clouded eyes. "The angel o' retribution comes," he said gently, then turned and stepped away.

The soldiers glanced at each other in fear and consternation. Most knew of Killian the Listener and were dismayed to hear another prophet spouting his words. They remembered, too, reports of the birds of the air and the beasts of the fields fighting at the command of their enemy. They had been told of rats swarming out of sewers to attack those battalions besieging towns, of swarms of wasps descending upon Bright Soldiers as they marched through fields, of cavalry horses becoming unaccountably spooked and throwing their riders in the midst of battle. They had heard that dogs of all shapes and sizes fought at the side of the heathen warriors, and that wolves obeyed their commands. Some had themselves seen the black winged warrior with the golden eyes and could not help wondering if the words of the prophet were true and this was indeed the messenger of God.

By the time the soldiers had gathered their wits, the old, blind man had disappeared into the forest. The captain sent scouts crashing through the undergrowth in search of him, but they found no bent twig, no footprint, not even a bruised leaf to show he had even been there. There was only the raven hovering far above them, like a hole torn in the blue of the sky, to prove it had not all been a dream. *One for sorrow*, the captain thought and felt a shudder run down his spine.

It was a red dawn, the thin clouds stained with the light of the blurred, crimson sun that crept up from behind the low hills. The Bright Soldiers camped in orderly rows and circles around Dùn Eidean glanced at the sky with troubled expressions. They had come to view the changes in the weather as omens for the future. When the sky was clear and the sun shone, it augured well. When the horizon was heavy with rain clouds or when mist rose from the fields, it meant only trouble.

The outer walls of Dùn Eidean lay in rubble, squads of soldiers in silver mail and long white cloaks patrolling the narrow streets of the town. Many of the buildings in the town had been burnt or demolished, but those still standing served as shelter for the berhtildes and the officers. White pennants marked with a scarlet fitché cross fluttered from the rooftops, and from the tents and pavilions that encircled the hill town. Only one flag defied the dominance of the scarlet cross. Green and gold, carrying the design of the MacThanach scythe, it flew defiantly from the castle battlements, mocking the soldiers who marched below.

Standing on the battlements was an old woman, a green and yellow plaid wrapped close about her body against the wind. Her face was very thin and pale, the bony nose standing out from the sunken cheeks like the prow of a ship, but her hazel eyes were alive with determination. She shook her clenched hand at the besiegers as if it were a gauntleted fist instead of a knob of thin, twisted, vein-knotted fingers. Standing with her was a middle-aged woman who had once been plump but whose skin now hung in folds. She was gray with exhaustion, but her jaw was set firmly, deep lines running from the corner of her compressed lips to her drooping chins.

"Come in from the cold, my lady," she implored. "It does ye no guid to stand here in this wind. If the Mac-Cuinn is riding to our aid, we shall hear soon enough. Ye mun rest and save your strength. If ye should fail, ye ken the hearts in our bodies shall fail too, and then the castle shall surely fall."

The old woman turned on her fiercely. "Do no' be a fool, Muire," she snapped. "We have withstood those cruel-hearted bastards for nigh on twenty-two months. Do ye think I would let ye give in now, even if I should die in my sleep tonight? I'd reach out from the very grave and throttle ye if such a thought should even cross your foolish mind. The MacCuinn shall come, never ye doubt, and he shall send these piddling soldier-lads whimpering home with their tail between their legs. Has no' that auld gypsy friend o' yours promised it?"

Muire nodded, though the lines of anxiety between her brows deepened. It had been almost a month since she

had last spoken with Enit Silverthroat through her scrying bowl, and Muire could not help the growing trepidation which gnawed at her every moment of every day.
Dùn Eidean had not been provisioned for such a long
siege, having been at peace for hundreds of years and
the attack of the Bright Soldiers having come with little
warning. The castle was crowded with folk from the surrounding countryside and the town, most of them old
and feeble, or young and weak. The flower of Dùn Eidean's youth and strength lay wasted on the battlefield
outside the town. Only a handful of soldiers remained to
protect the castle walls, and for all the Dowager Banprionnsa's brave words, Muire knew they could not withstand the Bright Soldiers much longer. Hunger and
illness were taking their toll. Every day more corpses
were tossed over the battlements in the hope disease
would spread through the encampment below and do the
job of the arrows Dùn Eidean no longer had.

"Whatever the cost, we must carry the yoke," the old
woman said. "Never let it be said the clan o' the Mac-
Thanach faltered under the load. My son shall come, and
the MacCuinn with him, and we shall rebuild Dùn
Eidean, stronger than ever."

"Aye, my lady," Muire said. "But will ye no' come
in? It looks like rain and ye shall do none o' us any guid
if ye fall ill and give me the trouble o' nursing ye."

The old woman gave a little laugh and let her maid
draw her away from the edge.

Blood red, the sun heaved itself clear of the horizon,
a gray, mizzling rain drifting across the ruins of the town.
The harquebusiers sighed and huddled into their cloaks,
knowing there would be no attack today. The rain would
dampen their gunpowder and their fuse, rendering their
harquebuses useless once again. Under their breaths they
cursed the Fealde who had described the golden fields
of Blèssem lying open and vulnerable under a warm sun.
Never had they known such a miserable climate or such
stubborn defendants, and they fervently wished they
were home again in Tìrsoilleir.

At the very edge of the camp, a squad of Bright Soldiers were making their dawn patrol, as unhappy and uncomfortable as the harquebusiers. Before them the trampled fields stretched as far as the eye could see, bloodied and charred. No living thing stirred, no bird sang or insect chirruped. The small loch that lay in the dip of the valley was choked with refuse, its shores all churned into mud. Piles of ash showed where the funeral pyres were lit each day. Not only were the casualties of both sides incinerated there, but also those Tìrsoilleirean soldiers who had tried to desert or had disobeyed orders or were too badly wounded to fight on. Although none of the squad discussed it, they had all heard of the lad with the miraculous healing hands who cured the sick and wounded, regardless of race or religion. All secretly hoped that, should they be wounded, the enemy would find them. If their own side retrieved them, all they could hope for would be a quick dagger thrust and a fiery mass funeral.

The morale of the Bright Soldiers was very low. They had not eaten a decent meal in months; they were sick of the war and uneasy about the reports of a blind prophet roaming the countryside south of Dùn Eidean. The prophet's words were repeated in mutters around the fires at night, and the pastor of the camp had begun to preach impassioned sermons against him. The berhtildes were harsher than ever in their punishments, anyone caught trying to run away dying a slow and horrible death. The patrols around the perimeter of the camp were as much to keep people in as to guard against attack from without, a duty that made the soldiers of the dawn squad most uncomfortable.

Suddenly the dim, damp silence was torn apart by the flourish of trumpets. The soldiers were jerked out of their apathetic trudge, their swords ringing out, their cloaks swinging as they stared around. They heard a choir of heavenly voices, all singing, "O praise him, O praise him, hallelujah, hallelujah, hallelujah!"

The clouds parted and a broad ray of sunlight struck down, dazzling their eyes. They shaded their faces with their hands, hearts pounding. Their pupils dilated as they saw a figure soaring through the light. Dressed all in white, he held aloft a great claymore, shining as bright as a lantern. His long wings were black and his blazing eyes were golden. He hovered in the air before them, holding up the sword like a cross. The singing voices reached a glorious crescendo and then tremored into silence.

"Fall down before the angel o' the Laird, for ye have sinned," the angel cried in a voice that echoed like thunder. As one the soldiers fell to their knees, arms across their faces. "What war and wickedness is this, what pursuit o' hatreds, contentions, jealousies, and selfish ambitions? I tell ye now, as I have told ye before, that those who practice such things shall no' inherit the Kingdom o' God, for the fruit o' the spirit is love, joy and peace. If we live in the Spirit, let us also walk in the Spirit!"

Again the trumpets rang out and the angel fixed the cowering soldiers with a fierce gaze. "Ye have become as children, tossed to and fro and carried about with every wind o' doctrine, by the trickery o' men, in the cunning craftiness o' deceitful plotting, lies and lust for power. Ye have been alienated from the life o' God because o' the blindness and folly o' your hearts."

The soldiers were sobbing with fear, their faces pressed into the mud. Again the trumpets rang out, and the angel raised the sword high, golden light pouring all around him.

"O pour out thy wrath on the false leaders who deceive ye; pour out thy indignation upon them and cause thy fierce anger to overtake them. Pursue them in wrath and remove them from under the heavens o' the Laird. O generation of vipers, they shall flee before the wrath that is to come!

"Put on the whole armor o' God that ye may be able to stand against the wiles o' the Archfiend. For we do no' wrestle against flesh and blood but against the rulers o' the darkness o' this age. Therefore take up the whole armor o' God that ye may withstand the evil day; stand therefore, having girded yourselves with truth, having put on the breastplate o' righteousness, and having shod your

feet with the gospel o' peace. Raise high the shield o'
faith with which to quench the fiery darts o' the wicked
one, who speaks through the loose lips o' your leaders.
Take the helmet o' salvation and the sword o' the spirit,
which is the word o' God our Father, and throw down
these false preachers, these proud, vain, deceitful
leaders!"

The angel lowered his sword, and held out his hand,
black wings curving around his body. "Put on tender
mercies, kindness, humility, meekness, long-suffering.
Bear with each other and forgive one another, as He
forgave ye. For by Him all things were created that are
in heaven and earth, visible and invisible, human and
unworldly. All things were created through Him and for
Him, He is before all things and of Him all things
consist."

The air was filled with sweet voices rejoicing. The
angel bowed his head and sang with such unearthly
beauty that tears started to the eyes of the soldiers
who listened.

> "Thou rushing wind that art so strong,
> Ye clouds in heaven that sail along,
> O praise him, hallelujah!
> Thou rising morn, in praise rejoice,
> Ye lights of heaven, find a voice,
> O praise him, O praise him
> Hallelujah, hallelujah, hallelujah!"

As he sang he slowly rose into the shining air. The clouds
closed about his body and he disappeared from their
sight. For a moment the sound of his song lingered, and
then there was silence again.

The soldiers staggered to their feet and ran toward the
camp, their faces transfigured, their swords lying forgotten in the mud behind them.

Their blundering run brought them among the tents
and picket lines. They were greeted with cries of alarm
and astonishment as their comrades jumped up to question them. Many had heard the trumpets and the singing,

and had seen the golden light on the hill. Some had seen the black-winged angel flying into the clouds. Stammering, half crying, the dawn patrol described what they had seen. Exclamations and queries were shouted, and a crowd soon gathered, shifting and murmuring with excitement. For months they had been hearing rumors of miracles and marvels. Indeed, the forces of the enemy fought as if God's might was behind them, clothed in storm and flame, striking as swiftly and fatally as lightning. The beasts of the field and forest and the birds of the air fought with them, and in their wake fields flourished and orchards bloomed. The soldiers looked about them at the charred meadows and broken buildings, and many felt the weariness and sickness in their hearts spark into anger.

A berhtilde strode out of her tent and demanded to know the meaning of all the noise and confusion. She was a tall, hard-faced woman, her nose broken out of shape. She wore chain-mail leggings but had replaced her breastplate with a shirt of rough goat's hair, a common act of mortification among the berhtildes. Without her armor, the asymmetry of her breasts was sharply defined. The soldiers told her what they had seen, stammering in sudden fear.

"Blasphemy!" she cried. "Ye have had dealings with the Archfiend! These cursed witches have sent false messengers to bewilder your mind. How dare ye doubt the word o' the elders? Ye shall kneel before the holy cross and swear that what ye have seen is an evil lie, and then ye shall whip yourself till ye are bloody in penance for your weak folly."

For a moment it looked as if her authority would be maintained, then one of the soldiers leapt forward with a cry. "Nay! We have seen the angel o' the Laird and it is ye who does the Archfiend's work!"

His hand had fallen to his hilt but found it empty, so, with one quick motion, he seized a stone from the ground and flung it at her. It hit her on the cheekbone, drawing blood. She stared at him in stupefaction, her fingers rising to touch the wound. The soldier's act fired the crowd. They shouted in gleeful excitement. Some found the courage to throw clods of mud or stones. One young soldier, who had often suffered the harshness of the berhtilde's punishments, drew his dagger and stabbed her in the side. She staggered back, then drew her own dagger with an oath, killing the young soldier with a single stroke. Her resistance inflamed the crowd. Although she shouted for help, she fell quickly, her blood soaking into the churned-up soil.

The frenzy of the crowd spread out like ripples from a stone flung into water. Soon the fighting was surging through the entire camp. The pastor was dragged out of his tent, naked and pleading for mercy, one of the camp whores beside him, sobbing and clutching the bedclothes to her. Both were beaten near to death, and the officers who tried to defend them killed. Several berhtildes were battered to insensibility or death, and the camp commandant found himself and his officers barricaded inside one of the inns as the riot spread through the town.

In the castle above, the Dowager Banprionnsa leant over the battlements, watching the fighting with amazement. "Have they gone mad?" she cried.

"Who kens?' the commander of the garrison replied, his one undamaged eye glaring bright among the bandages that swathed his head. "Happen they have eaten o' tainted grain, or breathed air all sickened by the dead. Whatever drives this madness, let us thank the Truth that it is so!"

"Let us thank *Eà*," the Dowager said sternly, and he nodded, meeting her eyes gravely.

"Aye, let us thank Eà," he agreed.

"Look, my lady!" Muire cried. "There on the hill!"

The dowager screwed up her eyes. At first all she could see was a dazzle of light on the rim of the low hills to the north, then she saw an army marching down the slope, swords drawn so they glittered in the sunlight that poured down from a rift in the clouds. Before them a light shower was still twisting here and there across the muddy fields, but where the Rìgh's army marched, no rain fell.

The garrison commander cried aloud in joy, and his soldiers—bruised, bandaged and gray with exhaustion— hung over the battlements with cries of excitement. They banged their shields with their daggers and the clan piper began rather shakily to play a triumphant tune. On and on the army marched, and soon they could hear the sound of their drums and trumpets, and see the colors of the pennants that fluttered at their head.

"See, it is the MacCuinn stag!" Muire cried. "And the dear green and gold—your son is there, my lady! The MacThanach is home!"

Tears ran down the wrinkles of the old woman's face though she said nothing. All the watchers on the battlements took up the cry. "The MacThanach is home! The MacThanach is home!" Down in the great hall many who had thought they had felt Gearradh's breath on their cheeks raised themselves on their elbows and listened, at first in fear and dread at the commotion and then in growing hope and elation.

Out in the Bright Soldiers' camp the turmoil grew. Some threw down their weapons and fled. Some knelt or threw themselves on their faces in the blood and the filth. Others tried to rally their comrades to defend the camp, only to find themselves standing alone or even attacked by their own side.

Lachlan and Iseult rode right to the very gates of the town without striking a single blow. The Rìgh was clad all in white still, his claymore held upright, his black wings spread proudly. Many of the Bright Soldiers called to him in fear and awe, begging for mercy and forgiveness, and he inclined his head majestically. Those few Tìrsoilleirean who still resisted were unarmed quickly and efficiently by his men and taken prisoner. Then the Rìgh's healers moved through the camp, tending the many sick and wounded. Tòmas laid his hands on those closest to death, miraculously returning life and health to their disease- and pain-wracked bodies, while Johanna and her team of healers worked to help those whose injuries were not so serious.

The MacThanach, riding on Lachlan's right hand,

looked about him at the ruins of the town with dismay clear on his broad, red face. Barely a building was left standing, most reduced to mere rubble. From the narrow streets below the castle hill came a sickening smell, and he had to cover his mouth with his gauntlet. They could see corpses lying in the mud like discarded dolls, their limbs twisted at unnatural angles, their skulls cracked open by the force of their fall. The MacThanach had to fight back his nausea and grief, his mouth clenched tight behind the shelter of his glove. Iseult looked at him with interest and noticed, somewhat to her surprise, that many others among their retinue were also pale and sweating, even her husband.

"It was wise to throw them over," Duncan Ironfist said in an attempt to comfort the MacThanach. "They could not have buried them properly within the castle walls and they must already have been fighting off disease."

"By the Centaur," the MacThanach breathed, "what they must have suffered! More than six hundred days they've been trapped in there. Och, it's a bad laird I've been to them indeed, to have waited so long to relieve them."

"What else could we have done?" Lachlan said irritably. "It is no' as if we've been sitting on our hands admiring the view. It's been hard fighting indeed this last year and I've lost many fine men winning back your land for ye."

"And here we are riding up to the very gates without striking a single blow," the MacThanach said with the wondering air of a child. "Look at all their siege machines! It is a wonder my castle is no' a mere pile o' stones like the rest o' the town."

"Aye, your ancestors chose their spot well," Duncan said, dismounting as they reached the castle gate. "It would be hard to attack, built on this hill, with all the town getting in the way. Look, can ye see where they've been digging, to try and undermine the walls? And by the looks o' it, they tried to tunnel right under the very hill there."

He went to hammer on the gates with his massive fist,

but before he had a chance to do so, they were opened from within and an emaciated old man fell to his knees before them. "Thank Eà ye are here at last, my laird!" he cried. "Och, but it was grand to see ye riding over the hill, with all the flags flying and the trumpets blowing." Tears were streaming down his sunken cheeks and his fingers were shaking uncontrollably as he clutched at the MacThanach's kilt. The prionnsa raised him and embraced him, his own face wet.

The defenders of the castle were crowding out through the gates, all of them painfully thin, the strain of the last twenty months evident in their sunken and shadowed eyes. They fell down on their knees before Lachlan and Iseult, weeping with gratitude and relief. Lachlan dismounted swiftly, helping many to their feet with his own hands, calling for his soldiers to bring in the cartloads of supplies they had brought with them.

"My mother, where is my mother?" the MacThanach cried.

"Och, my laird, so strong and steadfast she has been for all these months, and keeping the hope alive in our hearts even when it seemed we could no' keep them off for another night. And yet the moment it was sure we were saved . . ." The middle-aged woman clutched at the MacThanach's arm, tears pouring down her cheeks.

"What, Muire, what?"

"She fell where she stood, my laird, and we canna rouse her, though she breathes still. I fear . . ." But Muire was unable to finish her words, for the MacThanach had torn himself free of her grip and broken into a ponderous run, his leather armor creaking.

Lachlan turned and called to his squires. "Dillon, Artair, get me Tòmas, quickly! Tell him we need his healing powers in the castle. And bring Johanna and the healers also. Our own people must come first! Anntoin, ride down and find Meghan for me, and that fat auld cook too! We have starving people here and it is about time she proved her worth."

"Aye, Your Highness," the boys saluted and wheeled their ponies round to gallop back down the hill.

Lachlan and Iseult paused only long enough to give quick directives to the Yeomen of the Guard, then they followed Muire into the inner bailey. She led them through the castle, talking all the way, her mouth working in distress.

"Indeed, Your Highness, many times we would have all given in, no matter the cost, such despair o' the spirit we felt, but never would she allow us to falter. It was my dear lady who oversaw the rationing o' what little food we had, and ordered the punishment o' those who broke the rule. It was she who thought o' pulling up the cobblestones in the courtyards to catapult over the battlements, and she who tore up her own petticoats and bound the men's wounds wi' her own hands . . ."

They climbed the narrow stairs to the tower height and came out onto the wind-blown battlements. Overhead the square green flag of the MacThanach clan snapped in the breeze. A crowd was gathered near the doorway of the guardroom, and Iseult could hear the MacThanach's voice raised in entreaty.

Within lay an old woman, so thin the bones of her face pressed sharply against her parchment-colored skin. Her lips were stiff and twisted, and one side of her face seemed frozen, but her eyes beneath the discolored, wrinkled lids were bright as jewels. "We carried the yoke for ye, my son," she whispered, clutching at the MacThanach's sleeve with one clawlike hand. "Though the load was heavy indeed, we did no' falter."

The MacThanach was weeping. He bent and gathered the frail form close to his breast and whispered words of reassurance. Her bright eyes turned to Lachlan and she mumbled something, then seemed to gather strength. "So this is the young MacCuinn," she said clearly. "Indeed, we are glad to see ye, Your Highness. Though ye took your time in coming."

Lachlan bent over her and said, "We came as quickly as we could, though I wish it had no' been so long."

She gave a twisted smile and said, "No matter. We carried the yoke."

He smiled and squeezed her hand. "Indeed ye did,"

he said, but she did not return the pressure, and her eyes beneath her drooping lids were glassy.

As a weeping Muire drew the Dowager Banprionnsa's plaid over her face, the MacThanach dropped his head into his hands and sobbed. "Curse ye, Bright Soldiers!" he cried. "Ye have destroyed my home and taken my mother's life! I shall no' rest until ye are all as stiff and lifeless as she!"

The Walking Forest

It was cool under the overarching trees, and Lilanthe
stretched thankfully, lifting her long white arms to the
sky. The nisse Elala clung to the flowery tresses of
her hair, while Brun trotted purposefully ahead, the odd
collection of shiny objects around his neck jangling nois-
ily. Niall the Bear followed close behind, although the
nisse turned often to make rude faces at him and call
out insults in her own language. Although the big man
could not understand a word she said, the faery's tone
and expression were unmistakable, and his face was red
with embarrassment.

They had waited out the winter storms at Strathrowan,
the village where they had met Finlay Fear-Naught and
his company of soldiers. Once the thaw set in, they had
set off again for the Tower of Dreamers in Aslinn, the
nisse growing shrill with excitement as the forests grew
nearer.

The witches' Tower was just as Lilanthe remembered.
Sitting in the old kitchen while Brun pattered around,
preparing them all a meal, she grew quite nostalgic and
wondered where Dide was and what he was doing. Last
time she had been here he had slept, curled under a rag
of a blanket, his olive cheek flushed and warm. A pang
of tenderness shot through her at the memory, sharper
than grief. She sighed and her broad, spreading toes
curled together. Brun came and rubbed his head against
her arm and gave her a speckled blue bird's egg he
had found.

At the Tower of Dreamers they left the horses with
the rest of the soldiers to guard them, for the nisse said

the soldiers would not be welcome in the garden of the
Celestines. The little faery would have liked Niall to stay
behind as well, but the big man insisted on accompanying
them. His Rìgh had entrusted Lilanthe and Brun to his
care, he said, and he would not risk harm coming to
them in the dangerous forests of Aslinn. Lilanthe was
secretly glad, for she liked the big, slow-spoken man and
thought she would like to have him by their side should
they be attacked by the vicious satyricorns.

They had seen no sign of the horned faeries, however.
Niall thought the many battalions of Bright Soldiers
marching through Aslinn must have frightened them
away. They had passed a few Tìrsoilleirean encampments, but had had no difficulty in avoiding them. Although Niall was large, his woodcraft was near as good
as Lilanthe's. He explained placidly that he had grown
up in the forest, as his father had been a woodcutter.
This admission earned him a hiss of disapproval from
Elala and a little shiver from Lilanthe, but he merely
smiled and said, "No need to fear, lassie, he never took
his axe to a tree-changer that I ken o'."

There were only a few days till the summer solstice
left, and Lilanthe was conscious of both anxiety and anticipation. By now they were deep into the forest, having
left all roads and paths far behind them. The tree-shifter
knew Niall at times suspected the nisse of having led
them astray out of mischief or malevolence, but she herself trusted the little faery, knowing how desperately
Elala wished to have her wing healed so she could fly
again.

Suddenly they heard high shrieks of glee as a flock of
nisses swooped out of the canopy. They darted through
the group of travelers, swift as hornets, fragile as glass,
rainbow-bright as sun-dazzled water. As they shot past,
the nisses pulled Niall's hair and beard, tweaked the cluricaun's ears and pinched Lilanthe's arm so she cried out
in pain. Elala screeched in excited greeting. Her unbro-
ken wing fluttered madly as if she too wished to take off
into the air. The nisses turned and swerved past again,
their wings flashing silver.

The Celestines' grove garden is close, Elala said.

Lilanthe felt her pulse quicken. She had often longed to find one of the fabled gardens of the Celestines, but despite all her years of wandering in the forests, she had never yet stumbled across one. They were said to be beautiful indeed, full of peace and wonder. Her tree-changer mother had told her tales of the Celestines, and she knew that there had once been many gardens scattered through the forests, though only a few still survived.

The flight of nisses soared before them, leading them down an avenue of moss-oaks. The earth between the thick, upthrusting roots was rich with lichens and mosses which muffled their footsteps. They picked their way carefully through the tangle of roots, some slender and sinuous as snakes, others curving higher than their heads in a silver-gray surge. Here and there were the frail skeletons of trees that had managed to catch what little sunlight filtered through the lacy weavings of moss. They were all choked and tangled with the stuff, and the ground about was smothered by it.

Silence fell over the party as they looked about with reverence. It was hard to tell the passage of time under the great trees, for the sunlight barely filtered through, and all was quiet. It must have been at least six hours of difficult walking before the dim, green light at last gave way to golden sunlight, the avenue of moss-hung trees leading out into an open meadow where flowers grew in drifts of color. The cluricaun bounded ahead, his ears pricked forward with anticipation, while the nisses swooped back like a flight of flaming arrows.

To one side a dappled brown brook meandered, all overhung with trailing greenberry trees and branches of flowering may. A massive mossy rock was gently carved into the graceful form of a woman, her lap offering a comfortable seat. At the far end of the meadow an arrangement of three tall stones led the eye to a break in the trees where blue vistas of distance could be seen. Lilanthe had never seen anywhere as beautiful, and she drank in the scents and colors eagerly. Elala shrieked in excitement, swinging on Lilanthe's hair as if it were a flower-entwined rope.

Under one of the trees a Celestine was sitting, dressed in a loose robe of pale shimmering silk. The thick mane of hair that flowed down her back was as white as moonlight, while the eyes that regarded them serenely were as translucent as water, without iris or pupil. Her forehead was whorled in the center, like a whirlpool of skin.

Lilanthe could sense such a deep and profound sorrow in the Celestine that tears started to her own eyes in sympathy. The forest faery smiled gently when she saw the party of weary travelers, however, and rose to greet them with a low, sonorous humming, her thin, multi-jointed fingers rising to touch the whorl of wrinkles between her brows. The nisses hovered about her head, a crown of bright-winged faeries.

Welcome to the garden of the Celestines, she said. *We have been expecting you. It is almost time for the sun to sink to sleep. You must be weary. If you will come with me, we have prepared a place for you to rest and refresh yourselves. In two days' time, the sun shall reach its closest point above our world, and we shall sing the sun to life so all may flourish. Then shall the Summer Tree bloom and all the peoples of the forest come together to celebrate the green and growing season. You are all welcome, even the one of human blood, for we sense you are in harmony with this earth and wish none of us any ill. Do not fear the anger and hatred of the other creatures of the forest, for in our garden all are at peace.*

Lilanthe saw there were tears in Niall the Bear's eyes. "Thank ye indeed, my lady," he said huskily. "I ken I am privileged among men to be so welcomed into your garden. All my life I have wished to see one o' the Celestines, and now at last I have. My heart trembles at the sight, for indeed ye are bonny, even more so than I had imagined."

The Celestine smiled at him and reached up to touch him between the eyes, the tight whorl of wrinkles between her brows opening to reveal a dark, bright eye. Niall started and fell back a pace, and she hummed in reassurance. He let her touch him, and the tears flowed down and disappeared into his bushy beard.

You may call me Cloudshadow, the Celestine said, *for I know you of human blood set much store in naming and classifying.*

Cloudshadow then led them all to a flowery bower near the water, where a feast of nuts, berries and fruits was laid out for them on broad, curving plates of leaves. They drank water sweetened with honey from green leaf-cups and ate hungrily as the golden light slowly faded into dusk. That night they slept heavily and dreamlessly, then woke in the morning to find the leaf-plates again loaded with the delicious fruits of the forest.

The next few days were spent wandering the sunlit lawns and avenues of the garden, talking with the Celestines tending the flowers and trees, and laughing at the antics of the cheeky little nisses who waltzed about their heads wherever they went. Brun was elated to find many other cluricauns living in the garden, and he joined in their games and riddling competitions with delight. The cluricauns were all lovers of music and played drums, flutes and little round stringed instruments they called *banu*. Many of the cluricauns were wild, having never left the depths of the forest, though a number had lived for many years among humankind. They ran and hid with cries of alarm when they saw Niall, Brun having to reassure them that the big, bearded man meant them no harm.

There were many other types of faeries in the garden, some very shy, others as bold as the tiny nisses. Lilanthe saw a family of hobgoblins carrying rocks to build a flowerbed for the Celestines, and one-eyed corrigans crouched like craggy boulders under the trees. Every dusk a screech of gravenings swooped overhead, flying to their roosts in the tall mountain ashes, while shadow-hounds slinked through the undergrowth at the garden's edge, their green eyes as bright as candles. A herd of horned women fought and wrestled in a meadow, the male satyricorns resting in the shade and watching. Lilanthe's heart hammered at the sight of them, but they ignored her, whooping loudly as one horned woman threw another over her head and sent her crashing into the ground.

Nixies played in the water, tinier even than the nisses and far more timid, while a horse-eel lived in the small, deep loch in the heart of the garden. The hairy shapes of araks swung through the branches, while the ugly little faeries called brownies peered out from the bushes, ducking down if their gaze was returned. Although many of the faeries were carnivores, there seemed to be a covenant of peace in the Celestines' garden and no animal or faery was ever killed or hurt within its boundaries.

On the day before the summer solstice, Lilanthe was wandering through the garden when she saw a slim girl with green, leafy hair like her own, and a craggy, one-eyed boy sitting together by the brook. She exclaimed in joy and amazement and went up to greet them. "Corissa! Carrick! Wha' do ye do here?" she cried. She had met the two half-faeries in Arran, for they had been among those rescued from the Tower of Mists. They had escaped Arran with the other students of Margrit NicFóghnan's Theurgia but had decided not to travel to Rionnagan with the others, being too afraid of returning to human society.

Both the tree-shifter and the corrigan boy said they had been found in the forests by Cloudshadow and told to come for the flowering of the Summer Tree.

"Faeries from all over Eileanan have been traveling the Auld Ways to get here," Corissa cried, her clear green eyes alight with excitement. She looked far more like a tree-faery than did Lilanthe, her angular features bearing only the faintest trace of her human ancestry. "The Celestines are guiding them through, for no' all ken the secret o' the Auld Ways."

"Cloudshadow says the Auld Ways are still dangerous, despite the strength o' the summerbourne the last two years," Carrick said. He was a short, squat boy, his face gray and leathery-skinned, his one eye set deeply into his head. "They say the rites o' the Summer Tree have been difficult indeed to perform the last few years, with so few

Celestines remaining and most too afraid to travel the Auld Ways here. Most o' them have been content to stay within their own gardens and sing their own songs, and leave the singing o' the Summer Tree to the Stargazer's family. It has taken a hard toll on them, though, I hear."

"Who is the Stargazer?" Lilanthe asked.

Corissa looked at her in surprise. "Cloudshadow is the Stargazer's granddaughter," she replied. "They are the family o' Celestines who live here in this garden. It is the Stargazers who have borne the brunt o' the Summer Tree's consecration these last sixteen years, and I have heard only a few of them survived the Ensorcellor's Burning anyway. They were always too quick to trust those blaygird humans."

Lilanthe flushed a little, and the tree-shifter threw her a mocking glance. "Did your mother teach ye nothing?" she said.

"I did no' see her very often," Lilanthe replied gravely. "She left me wi' my father and wandered away. When I did see her, she was often shy and suspicious o' me, and thought I was far too much like a human for her taste." She sighed and asked no more questions, seeking out Niall the Bear's company instead. Like her friend Isabeau, he did not seem to care that she was neither human nor faery, liking her for her own sake.

As the day passed, Lilanthe's mixed feelings grew more intense, so she did not know whether she longed for the meeting with her own kind or dreaded it. The garden grew more crowded as sunset approached, until every glade and grove was brimming over with the faeries of the forest, each bringing a handful of nuts or a bunch of ripe berries to add to the feast. The nisses wove garlands of flowers which were hung from branch to branch, and clusters of fireflies fluttered around, their lights winking.

As the sun sank down into a blue haze, tree-changers began to wander in from the woods. Lilanthe was too shy to do more than stare at them, her feet crossing self-consciously. Some were as tall and thick as an ancient hemlock, their heads crowned with prickly leaves and bright golden berries, their feet as broad and gnarled as the roots of an oak tree. Some had bark all scribbled over like the doodlings of a child, while others were slim and pale and smooth, with flowing hair all tangled with tiny green flowers, just like Lilanthe herself. They danced that night, weaving all through the trees, bowing and swaying like a forest in a storm, while the cluricauns played their drums and flutes and the nisses darted through the canopy, shrieking in excitement.

Lilanthe watched, entranced. When the tree-changers began to sing their strange, stormy song, she found herself swaying in slow and stately rhythm, her roots lifting and tapping. One caught her hand, then another, and she bowed with gladness in her heart, dancing along with them, her sap surging in her veins. She saw Niall was dancing too, flowers tucked into his wild hair and beard, a hobgoblin clinging to each rough hand. Brun sat on the bough of a tree, playing his wooden flute, then somersaulted down to jig alongside her.

All night the faeries danced to the wild, haunting music, the chain of dancers leading them deeper and deeper into the garden. Once or twice, as she twirled and swayed, Lilanthe saw that a tall man led the procession, crowned with antlers like a stag. Illuminated only by moonlight and the fitful light of the tiny fireflies, his face was carved with shadows. By his side danced the youngest of the Celestines, the one named Cloudshadow, and she wept from all three of her eyes.

All through the sweet-scented night they danced, winding their way to the secret heart of the garden. Lilanthe had not explored so far, the Celestines having always gently but insistently guarded the paths which led that way. She looked about her with fascination as they danced along an avenue of moss-oaks and into a wide clearing. Tall stones stood sentinel all around the grove, each topped with another stone to form crude arches. Within the stones a tree soared upward, its leaves black against the star-crowded sky, its roots writhing outward like the tentacles of a giant octopus.

All through the standing stones the chain of dancers wound, at last collapsing panting and laughing onto the warm grass. As dawn began to finger the sky with delicate color, the Celestines stepped forward, their pale robes shimmering so it appeared they were haloed with starlight. Silence fell over the gathered faeries as the Celestines held hands around the massive tree. There were nearly fifty of the tall, slender faeries, but even with their arms stretched wide, they were barely able to encircle the tree.

The antlered faery stood with them, Cloudshadow clinging still to his hand. As he turned and bent his head, Lilanthe saw the antlers were bound to a mask which hid his eyes. The thick, white mane of a Celestine flowed down from beneath it, and his mouth was sad and stern.

Into the hush rose a low, melodic humming which thrilled all through Lilanthe's veins. She leant forward, listening intently, and by her side Niall clasped his big hands on his knees, his head bent. The hymn to the sun reverberated through the clearing, and slowly the darkness dissolved till the leaves crowning the tree were all gilded with sunshine. Broad and glossy, the leaves were colored purple and green with a silvery underside so that when the wind blew, they flashed like the bright scales of fish crowded together at the shore. Clustered within the leaves were hundreds of creamy buds as large as Lilanthe's head. As the sun spilled down upon them, they burst open, showering the air with perfume. An excited murmur arose.

The Celestines dropped their hands and stood with their heads bowed before the tree. Lilanthe breathed in the rich, spicy incense, feeling her whole being respond. Although she should have been exhausted after the night of dancing, she felt more alive and vibrant than ever before. Thousands of bright-winged nisses flew up into the branches, gathering the flowers and throwing them down so they covered the ground like a counterpane of snow.

The antlered faery dropped to his knees before the tree, spreading his arms wide. Another slow humming

arose, though this time it had the melancholy tempo of
a funeral dirge. Cloudshadow stepped forward and thrust
her hand into the smooth trunk of the tree until it was
submerged to the wrist. When she withdrew her hand,
she held a long, wavy dagger made of wood, the hilt
carved and set with mother-of-pearl. Lilanthe tensed,
feeling such profound grief and remorse in the Celestine
that tears again started involuntarily to her eyes.

"No," she whispered. "I thought the Celestines were
a peaceful people."

"Wha' is wrong?" Niall whispered, but the tree-shifter
did not answer, staring at the scene below her with painful intensity.

Cloudshadow brought the dagger to her mouth and
kissed it, then she bent and seized the prostrate Celestine
by his antlers, pulling back his head so she could slice
his throat with the dagger. Blood poured from the gash
onto the creamy petals of the flowers scattered before
him, and there was a collective gasp from the crowd.
Lilanthe sobbed out loud.

The antlered faery fell forward, his body slack. The
blood from his terrible wound soaked into the earth and
the Celestines all wept, their soft crooning changing to a
discordant wail. Cloudshadow wept also, falling to her
knees by the dead faery's side and trying to lift his body
into her arms, her pale robe stained with blood.

An old Celestine, his face seamed with wrinkles, came
and tried to raise her. She resisted for a moment, then
allowed him to help her stand. The tears on her face
shone with a silvery trace. The other Celestines clustered
around her, embracing her and trying to console her. She
composed herself and stood upright, raising her reddened
hands to the dawn sky. They tore the bloodied robe from
her shoulders until she was naked. Lilanthe saw with a
little shock that the Celestine had three pairs of breasts.
They were all swollen with milk above her distended
stomach, and Lilanthe realized Cloudshadow was gravid
with child.

The other Celestines used her robe to wrap the dead
faery in, the oldest removing the mask with reverent fin-

gers and placing it over Cloudshadow's weeping eyes. The victim was revealed as a young Celestine, his face smooth except for the corrugations of skin around his third eye. They heaped his breast with the blood-wet flowers and, chanting and humming, carried him away. Cloudshadow followed, her horned head downcast.

Lilanthe roused herself from her trance. Elala was perched on her knee and Lilanthe asked, with her eyes still hot with tears, *Why did she kill him? I thought the Celestine abhorred all violence! Who was he?*

He was the Treeblood, Elala answered, her tattered wings drooping. *The Celestines must always slay slaughter a lover beloved for the blooming of the Summer Tree.*

But I thought they hated violence o' any kind, Lilanthe protested.

The nisse nodded, her triangular face sad. *Sorrow suffer for the slaying of the Treeblood, truly they sorrow suffer.*

Who was he? Why did she have to do it? Lilanthe gazed after the drooping figure of the young Celestine as she followed the funeral procession out of the circle of stones.

Her lover beloved, her life-mate.

Ye mean that was her husband? The father o' the baby?

Always the lover beloved must slay slaughter the Treeblood, the nisse said and hunched her tattered wings around her.

What about your wing? Lilanthe asked. *Do the flowers o' the Summer Tree no' heal? Why did ye no' gather some o' the flowers?*

The Stargazers shall repair restore my wing, Elala answered. *The flowers belong to them, for it is their lifeblood bloodlife that was spilled to bless the tree.*

As the sun reached its apex in the sky, the forest faeries again assembled at the circle of stones. Again the long procession of Celestines gathered at the foot of the massive old tree. This time Cloudshadow led the procession, robed again in white silk, a child in her arms. There was a look of exhausted peace on her face, and her hair was bound back with the fragrant, white flowers of the Summer Tree. To the accompaniment of low, sonorous humming, she held the child aloft. The baby's three eyes were wide open and wondering, and the crowd all round erupted into talk and laughter.

See my daughter, Cloudshadow said in Lilanthe's mind. *One day she too may have to murder her beloved so the Summer Tree shall continue to grow and blossom. Such is the heavy task laid upon us, and indeed my heart is burdened with sorrow.*

Lilanthe's heart swelled in sympathy, and she saw Niall the Bear was choking back tears. She took his hand and he gripped it tightly.

Come, bring me Elala, Cloudshadow said. *Now I have eaten of the Summer Tree's flowers, my powers are stronger than ever. This is the reward for the price I have paid.*

Lilanthe carried the quivering little nisse through the crowd and across the lawn to where the Celestines were grouped. She saw many other faeries were following her, all with wounds or injuries they wished the Celestines to heal. Among them were curse-hags and satyricorns, and Lilanthe was amazed that the gentle Celestines would extend their magic even to these malicious faeries.

All are welcome in the garden of the Celestines if they come with no thought of hatred in their hearts, Cloudshadow explained. *What they do once they leave our garden is a matter for their own character and conscience.*

When the Celestine laid her hands upon the little nisse's forehead, the tattered remnants of her wing wove back together until it was again whole, as brittle and diaphanous as a dragonfly's wing. Elala gave a piercing shriek and shot up into the air. High above their heads she soared and somersaulted, and all the other nisses darted up to join her, till the clearing resounded with their commotion.

It took some time to heal all the creatures of the forest, for squirrels, deer, woolly bears and wolves were among the many to crowd down into the clearing. Cloudshadow was not the only Celestine to heal by the laying on of hands, and she explained that all those that ate of the flowers were given restorative powers, as well as the gift of prophecy and clear-sight.

All Celestines carry the sap of the Summer Tree in their veins, for once swallowed it soaks deep into the very stuff of our bodies. Each generation that inherits the powers is less potent, however, and it is only those Celestines that have eaten of the flower itself who have the greatest powers, Cloudshadow said.

Lilanthe wondered at her ability to read her thoughts and the Celestine smiled wearily at her across the crowd. *I have only this hour eaten of the Summer Tree and its juice runs riot in my veins. I can hear the thoughts of all that are here and the thoughts of those that are far away. My ears are clamoring with the noise, and my heart thunders in my body.*

By the time all were healed, Cloudshadow was looking dangerously pale, dark marks like bruises under her eyes. She came to Lilanthe and held out one of the huge white flowers of the Summer Tree. A rich, spicy perfume rose from its golden heart and its silken petals were still stained with smears of blood. *This is a charge for you to carry and guard. You must protect and preserve it as you would your own life. When it is time, you will know what to do with the Summer Tree flower.*

Lilanthe shook her head involuntarily, thinking at once of Isabeau's braid of hair. The Celestine pressed it into her hands. *You will guard it well, I have no doubts or dread. You must trust yourself. Can you trust others if you do not have trust in your heart for yourself?*

The tree-shifter brought the flower to her nose and breathed deeply of its gorgeous perfume. The tears which had sprung to her eyes dried and the thickness in her throat dissolved. *Thank you, I will guard it well.*

The child, which had been laid in its bed of bloodied silk for all to greet and examine, was now wailing with hunger and tiredness. Cloudshadow lay on the flowering bank and let the child feed, saying wearily to Lilanthe, *Now is the time for you to speak, if you wish to win the faeries to peace. The Summer Tree makes all at harmony,*

*and we have exerted much effort and energy to bring so
many to be here for you. Alone among the people of the
forest do we the Stargazers trust you of the Coven, and
we have made many sacrifices, in lifeblood and love, to
help you today. Speak well, child of the sap and the blood,
and the world will make a turn to the sun.*

Panic washed over Lilanthe. She found the great mass
of creatures, both animal and faery, had turned to her
and were waiting, and she wondered what the Celestines
had said to them. Somehow she found the courage to
rise and face them. Niall rose too and stood at her shoulder, smiling warmly at her and nodding at the crowd.
Many growled or hissed at the sight of him, and that
gave Lilanthe the impetus to begin.

She did not know where the words came from but they
flowed as freely as water. All that she had seen and
learnt since her meeting with Isabeau the previous year
was woven through her own sense of alienation and her
intense desire to belong. Often she was mocked or
shouted down, but always she found the words to woo
them.

"No' all humans are evil," she insisted, "just as no'
all faeries are. Evil grows within the individual heart,
regardless o' kin or kind. They say all curschags are evil,
yet there are many here today and we all ken the evil-
hearted are no' welcome in the garden o' the Celestines.
Would the Stargazers have welcomed Niall the Bear if
they did no' ken he was a good man, with a kindly heart
and gentle spirit? Indeed there are many bad men, as
there are bad bears and bad tree-changers. Indeed humans have done much harm and have hurt many. Should
evil beget evil, though? If we should let blind hatred
flower in our hearts, then indeed Maya the Ensorcellor
will have done her work, and the whole land will be
steeped in blood and bad-wishing."

She reminded them of the golden days when Aedan
Whitelock had ruled, and men and faeries had abided by
the Pact of Peace, letting each live freely and without
interference. "Lachlan the Winged is the direct descendant o' Aedan Whitelock and he has pledged to draw

up another Pact o' Peace and return Eileanan to the days when faeries were welcomed in the courts o' the land, and their wisdom listened to and respected."

She told them how the dragons had pledged their support to Meghan of the Beasts, and how the armies of Lachlan the Winged were hunting down the evil Seekers of the Awl and making them pay for their evil deeds. Many in the audience had heard tales of the winged boy and how he had sung the summerbourne with the Celestines so that it ran stronger and more purely than it had in years. The forest rustled at her words, and faeries of all types turned to each other and whispered.

"Will ye no' give your support to the young rìgh?" she asked. "Like ye and me, he has been hunted and reviled, called *uile-bheist* and monster. He has wed one o' the Khan'cohbans and given birth to a wee laddie wi' wings like a bird. He received a tree-shifter and a cluricaun into his court, and paid us his respects, and bade us teach his people what we could about the faeries o' the forest. He has promised that those o' faery blood can again live without fear and sworn that any who lift their hand against us will be punished severely. But he needs our help if he is to enforce his rule—Eileanan is torn by civil war, and if Lachlan the Winged fails, so do all chances o' ever again living in peace."

After she had finished speaking, there was much argument and Lilanthe was disappointed to see there were many who thought she must have been misled or cozened by the human witches. But both Corissa and Carrick stood up and confirmed what she had said, describing their rescue from the Tower of the Mists. They too were only half-faeries, though, and many would not heed what they said. Another corrigan called Sann then described how she had met Meghan of the Beasts and the new rìgh in the Veiled Forest, and promised they were sincere in their intentions. Sann's words were listened to with respect, for she had been stoned and driven from her home by humans and had as much right to hate them as anyone there. Elala added her shrill cries to the chorus, and then the ancient Celestine they called the Stargazer came forward, so old and frail he seemed a mere bundle of bones and wrinkled skin.

He began to hum, deep in his throat, and the Celestines grouped behind him added their soft crooning. Where every other speaker had been interrupted and argued with, the Celestines were listened to with great respect. Tears gathered in Lilanthe's eyes and flowed down her cheeks as the Celestines spoke of their years of loss and exile, their struggle to keep their ancient culture alive, to tend the forest and its creatures as they had always done, and to stop their race from disappearing altogether. Many in the audience were as moved as she was. When the Celestines sang of forgiveness and friendship, Lilanthe saw many in the gathering were embracing or clasping hands, their cries and growls and murmurs almost drowning out the Celestines' thrumming melody.

When the Stargazer's song had murmured into silence, the Celestines withdrew into the secret heart of the garden, to grieve in privacy. The faeries and animals all gradually dispersed, many talking and arguing still. Lilanthe felt anxiety grip her, for she had hoped for a strong declaration of support from the crowd.

Niall laid his big, rough hand on her shoulder and said gently, "Ye must give them time to think, my lady. Ye spoke so wisely, I have no' a single doubt that they shall follow ye. Come and eat and rest, for it was a long night and an even longer day."

The next morning, however, when Lilanthe and Niall the Bear made ready to leave the serene beauty of the sun-gilded garden, they were bitterly disappointed to find the garden empty. They had hoped some at least would pledge their help and support. They walked down the avenue of moss-oaks with heavy hearts, unable to even smile at the antics of the cluricaun Brun, who danced and cartwheeled all around them, his tail waving joyously. Even Elala the nisse did not come to say farewell, and Lilanthe trudged along unhappily, miserable that she had failed again.

Then suddenly, beyond the borders of the garden, the bright-winged nisse came flashing through the trees, shrieking loudly, hundreds of her kin darting and soaring behind her. She seized Niall's hair and tugged it sharply, then hung off his nose, gibbering away in her shrill language. Lilanthe's face lit up. "She says the forest tread tramps!"

They could hear a rustling and soughing like a storm through pine-branches, then they saw a great army of faeries marching toward them. Through the forest of tree-changers prowled slinky shadow-hounds and sharp-horned satyricorns, while a screech of gravenings circled overhead, their harsh shrieks echoing. Leathery-skinned corrigans grasped clubs of stone, hobgoblins scampering behind, while the horse-eel pranced at their head, swollen to his largest size. It was an army the like of which had never been seen before in Eileanan.

A huge grin split Niall's bearded face and he bowed to Lilanthe and said, "Indeed ye have worked miracles, my lady! Will His Highness no' be pleased to see the magic ye have wrought?"

They seek revenge on those men who have hurt and hunted them, Cloudshadow explained, stepping out of the shadow of a moss-oak, her child in her arms. *They will march with you against the Seekers of the Awl who hide out near the fringe of the forest and seek to raise a false banrìgh. They will help you make the forest free again, hunting down all those soldiers who shelter in her shade and driving them far away. When it is time, they will come and make a pact of peace with your rìgh and will watch to make sure he is true to his promises.*

"I thank ye," Niall the Bear said, drawing his claymore and holding it high. "And I swear by the blood o' my own body that Lachlan the Winged shall be true!"

Lachlan and his retinue were at dinner when one of the soldiers who had traveled with Finlay Fear-Naught was admitted to the great hall of Dùn Eidean's castle. He was dusty and sweat-stained, his hair disheveled, his leather armor rent and torn. He strode up the side of the great hall and bowed before the thrones.

"Your Highness, sorry I am indeed to be disturbing ye at your meal, but I have news. The forest has marched!"

"Have a seat! Cameron, pour the man some whiskey. What do ye mean, the forest has marched? Have ye lost your wits?"

"No indeed, Your Highness. I saw it with my own eyes. The forest marched on Glenmorven, where we had laid siege to Renshaw the Ruthless and his Red Guards. I have never seen such a sight! They made a sound like the ocean, or like thunder. I have heard tales o' walking trees, Your Highness, but never did I think I would see it happen!"

"Lilanthe has roused the tree-changers," Meghan said softly. "What wonderful news indeed!"

"We would have tried to fight them if we had no' seen Niall the Bear riding at their head, carrying the Mac-Cuinn stag. Seeing him and the tree-faery, Laird Finlay ordered us to lay down our arms and so we did, though I am no' ashamed to admit my legs were trembling wi' fear. Then we were surrounded on all sides with the trees, as if in the midst o' a great forest. Running all through the trees were wolves and bears and strange creatures with horns and claws and gnashing teeth and hair like snakes and tiny winged creatures that stung like bees . . ."

"So what happened?" Lachlan cried, his dark face alight. "Meghan, do ye think it means the faeries have thrown their lot in with us?"

The old sorceress nodded and smiled, as the soldier went on to describe the battle. "The Red Guards had the gates shut tight against us, Your Highness, but the trees cracked them open as if they were made o' matchwood and no' the stoutest o' oaks. They all swarmed into the town—there were dogs wi' flaming green eyes, Your Highness, as did tear out the throats o' the guards, and faeries wi' horns that stabbed them and rent them. It was magnificent!"

"What o' Renshaw?" Lachlan demanded. "Was he taken?"

The soldier shook his head. "Nay, I be sorry, Your

Highness. Once it was clear Glenmorven would fall, he and a company o' his men hacked their way through with axes and flaming torches. The tree-faeries would no' face the flame, and so he won clear. Most o' his supporters were killed or taken prisoner, though. We have them under our charge, awaiting your instructions. Lilanthe o' the Forest said the army o' tree-faeries would now sweep through all o' Aslinn and make sure there were no camps o' Bright Soldiers hidden within."

"It would be a wonderful thing if we could plug that hole," Duncan Ironfist said with satisfaction. "All summer long they've been falling on our backs like ravening wolves, and we havena been able to throw them off. If they canna cross the Great Divide and come in through Aslinn, that means we have only to guard against Arran and the sea."

"Renshaw fled south, Your Highness, and we fear he has sought sanctuary in Arran."

They all exclaimed in surprise. Lachlan said, "Are ye sure?" and Meghan asked urgently, "What o' my apprentice Isabeau the Red, any news o' her or the babe?"

"Laird Finlay chased the ruthless one all the way to the borders o' Arran, but turned aside at the edge o' the marsh. Renshaw had the babe with him, there's no doubt o' that, for Laird Finlay saw her wi' his own eyes. He saw no sign o' the lady Isabeau though, but that does no' mean she was no' with them, for Laird Finlay said Renshaw had gathered together over two hundred supporters and Isabeau the Red could easily be among such a large party without being seen."

"I see," Lachlan said slowly. "Well, thank ye for the news. Ye must have ridden hard indeed to get here so quickly. Will ye have a wee dram with us to celebrate? In the morn ye can tell one o' the dispatch riders where Laird Finlay is and send to him to come home. It is dangerous indeed so close to the marshes and we need him here."

The man nodded and saluted. Lachlan gestured to Dillon to pour him some whiskey. They all drank a toast to the victory at Glenmorven and the rising of the forest faeries, then the tired, hungry, dusty dispatch rider went gratefully down to the kitchen to be fed. A buzz of conversation rose as soon as he had left the room.

"Renshaw gone to Arran?" Gwilym asked. "I do no' believe it! It must be a trick."

"Is it so impossible that he c-c-could have sought sanctuary in the m-m-marshes, taking the babe with him? We know M-M Maya and my m-m-m-mother were allies o' a s-s-sort," Iain replied.

"This is laughable!" Meghan cried. "The Grand-Seeker o' the Awl, in cahoots with one o' the most powerful sorceresses in the land! Surely he would no' seek sanctuary in Arran?"

"Why would he no'?" Elfrida asked. "Is she no' your bitter enemy?"

"Well, yes, there has always been bad bluid between the MacFóghnan and MacCuinn clans, ever since the days o' the First Crossing. But Renshaw is leader o' the Awl and so sworn to stamp out witchcraft. He hates and fears sorcery; it does no' make sense that he would go to Arran."

"But if they both see ye as their enemy, will that no' make them allies?" Elfrida said.

Iseult flashed her a look. "Likely enough," she agreed, unable to suppress the note of surprise in her voice. "There is a Khan'cohban proverb," and she spoke a few harsh syllables in the guttural language of her homeland. "Your friend, my enemy; your enemy, my friend," she translated.

"Still, they are strange bedfellows," Meghan said. "Though I thought Maya and Margrit bizarre allies as well. I wonder what game it is the Thistle plays."

"Whatever game it is, I wish those blaygird marsh-faeries o' hers would leave us alone," Lachlan said wearily. They had been attacked again only a few weeks earlier, right in the great hall of Dùn Eidean's castle. This time there had been more than twenty Mesmerdean and they had lost almost thirty soldiers and servants in fighting them off. All of them had had trouble sleeping since, starting at shadows and waking from uneasy dreams with a feeling of suffocation. "Will we never be free o' them and their thirst for revenge?"

"Or free o' the Thistle and her machinations?" Meghan too looked and sounded weary, her old face haggard.

"I am sure she would be glad to have Bronwen in her hands," Iseult said. "What a weapon she would be!"

"Och, I hope the poor wee babe is safe," Latifa said piteously, clasping her fat hands together.

"Margrit would no' harm the babe," Meghan reassured her. "She is too valuable alive. It is Isabeau I fear for."

"But surely Margrit would have no use for Isabeau?" Matthew the Lean asked.

"Isabeau has great Talent," Meghan replied somberly. "Margrit has already shown she wants bairns with Talent—why else did she steal away all those children and keep them imprisoned in the Tower o' Mists? I just pray to Eà that Isabeau is no' in her hands, for she is a cruel and ruthless woman indeed!"

THE CUTTING OF THREADS

THE CURSEHAG

Maya hurried through the busy streets of Dùn Eidean. It was dusk, and the rattle-watch was making his rounds, chanting: "The sun has set, and all is still; time to go home to eat your fill."

The stonemasons rebuilding the houses were packing up their tools, the merchants were closing the doors to their shops, and already the Inn of the Green Man was doing good business, the crowd spilling out onto the pavement to enjoy the balmy evening air. Maya smiled and nodded to a few of the soldiers she knew. One seized her arm with a ribald remark, but she merely shrugged herself free, smiling and saying lightly, "Och, give it a rest, my laddie, even fancy ladies need an evening free sometimes."

"Let me buy ye an ale, Morag," the soldier pleaded, "and happen that'll put ye in the mood for some fun."

"Thanks for the offer, laddie, but I have my plans for tonight."

He slapped her bottom and let her go, and she hastened her pace, afraid he and his friends may decide to pursue her. She rounded the corner and saw ahead of her the great wall of the castle, built in the very center of the town on the crown of the hill. Her heartbeat quickened, even though the glamourie spell she wore had grown so comfortable she needed very little effort to maintain it. There was always a chance she may run into one of the witches stationed at the castle, who would be able to see through the disguise with ease, and so she always felt a small quickening of fear when she kept a rendezvous with her spy.

The girl was pacing the courtyard impatiently, wringing her hands together. "Ye're late, I was feared harm had come to ye, Your Highness," she gasped.

"Do no' call me that, ye fool," Maya snapped. "I was held up coming through the town. Quickly, tell me your news before someone sees us together. It be dangerous indeed to be meeting here in the castle."

"It is so hard for me to get away," the girl explained. "There is always someone wanting me to do something, and the Keybearer seems to have eyes in the back o' her head. I thought ye would want to know that they think the Grand-Seeker has fled to Arran, taking the wee ban-prionnsa wi' him."

"To Arran?" Maya exclaimed. "Are ye sure?"

"That is what they said. I do no' ken if it is true."

"Renshaw did ken I had had dealings with Margrit o' Arran," Maya mused. "He acted as my go-between for some years, before I promoted him to Grand-Seeker. I suppose it could be possible." She gave a small, triumphant smile. The waiting for news had been hard, and sometimes she had grown so impatient it was all she could do not to scream or cry or hit out at someone. Her disappointment at Lachlan's string of victories had been acute. As the Graycloaks' fortunes had eddied like the tide, so had her spirits. News of defeat had her gloating, news of victory plunged her back into depression, and all the time she did not know where Renshaw had taken her daughter. So she had stayed at the tail end of the army, despite her frustration, knowing that any news of the Grand-Seeker would immediately be reported to Meghan and Iseult, and so would eventually find its way to her. At last her patience had paid off.

She thanked her spy warmly, taking care to bind the girl even closer to her, then waited in the dark courtyard till all was quiet, making plans. She would set out for Arran the very next day, spending some of her hard-won money on a horse and carriage and some fine clothes. She must not turn up on Margrit of Arran's doorstep looking like a beggar. It was imperative that the Nic-Fóghnan did not realize just how desperate Maya's straits

really were. They had been allies before, but Maya had
never deluded herself that Margrit assisted her out of
friendship or a kind heart. The Banprionnsa of Arran
had some plan of her own. Maya would have to be very
careful indeed, for if her daughter was in Margrit's hands,
the Thistle would be in the position of power and Maya
her supplicant. Maya's nostrils flared in annoyance at the
thought, and she began to think what she could offer
Margrit in return for her aid.

Deep in thought, she left the courtyard, hurrying down
the narrow passage to the lancet gate through which she
had come. Unexpectedly she collided with a large, soft
form. She staggered back and flinched as a lantern was
raised, spilling light full into her face. For a moment she
could not see, then terror flashed through her as a well-
known voice cried, "Maya! It canna be!"

It was Latifa the Cook. Her round, brown face was
horrified, her small mouth opened in a perfect O of surprise. Maya had not seen Latifa since Samhain Eve, when
she had left her in the garden surrounding the Pool of
Two Moons. If she had thought about Latifa at all, Maya
would have supposed her to have been executed for
treachery. That was what Maya would have done in
Lachlan's place. She certainly did not expect to find Latifa here, in Dùn Eidean.

Before Latifa had time to do more than exclaim, Maya
reached into her sleeve and withdrew her sharp dagger.
Gritting her teeth, she plunged it into the old cook's
breast. Latifa grasped the knife in both her hands, her
eyes round in shock, then she staggered and fell.

Maya ran down the corridor and out into the town,
her heart pounding with excitement and dismay. She had
always quite liked the fat old cook. She wished it had
been someone else who pierced her glamourie. Meghan
of the Beasts, for example. It would not worry Maya to
sink a knife into that old witch's heart. Latifa, though,
had been kind to Maya and had cooked her little delica-
cies of seaweed, rys seeds and raw fish, knowing how she
hated the fat-dripping roasts usually served up at the
royal table.

As Maya ran past a street lamp, she saw her hand was red with blood and for a moment she was giddy with horror. She clenched her fingers together, and ran on. Nothing could be allowed to stand in her way, not even a fat, kind-hearted old cook.

The spinning wheel whirled steadily, Isabeau's foot pushing rhythmically on the pedal, her hands guiding the thread through the spindle automatically. Propped up before her was a book which she was reading intently, each leaf turning itself over as she reached the end of the page.

Isabeau was studying a very ancient book called *De Occulta Philosophia Libri Tres,* one of the many books in the library which the Coven of Witches had brought over from the Other World. Sometimes she frowned as she read, other times she smiled in disbelief, but every now and again she stopped reading to say a line over again and commit it to her memory.

Bronwen was sitting on the floor behind her, singing to the ragdoll Isabeau had made for her. Scattered around her were some of the beautiful and amazing toys that Isabeau had discovered in one of the rooms in the south tower. On the same floor as the main bedroom, it had been furnished beautifully with two little cradles and a rocking seat carved in the shape of a flying dragon. The satin canopy and quilts had been used as nests by mice and were tattered and filthy. The flying dragon rocker was as perfectly balanced as ever, however, rocking back and forth with the slightest motion and painted with amazing realism. It stood behind Bronwen now, its wings stretched wide, its eyes gleaming with gilt paint.

Lying on the floor behind the little girl were a rainbow-painted spinning top, two rattles carved in the shape of bluebirds, a wheeled horse that could be pulled along by a string, a beribboned hoop, a collection of painted building blocks, and a miniature drum and flute.

Despite the beauty of these toys, Bronwen preferred the ragdoll Isabeau had made and took it everywhere with her, crooning to it and pretending to feed it bits of bread and cheese. The flute was her next favorite and the little girl showed an amazing aptitude for the instrument, especially surprising considering neither Feld nor Isabeau had any musical ability with which to guide her.

Suddenly the spinning wheel faltered and the thread snapped and unraveled. Isabeau looked up, her eyes vacant. "Latifa?" she whispered. "Oh no, Latifa!"

Meghan had slipped into a doze by the fire, Gitâ curled on her lap, when she suddenly woke, her black eyes snapping open. "Latifa?" she murmured, trying to shake off her stupor. She got to her feet rather stiffly and went to the door. She could hear nothing, but still a sense of unease persisted. She called to one of the guards standing at the end of the corridor. "Is all well?"

"Aye, my lady," he answered. "All is quiet."

She hesitated, then leaning heavily on her flower-carved staff, made her way past the guards and down the stairs. She passed through the great hall and into the maze of narrow corridors that led toward the kitchens. A scullery maid was hurrying up the hall, a bucket of steaming water in one red-chapped hand, a scrubbing brush in the other. Meghan stopped her with one gnarled hand. "Elsie?" The maid nodded, her fair skin reddening. "Have ye seen Latifa?"

"She was just going to get something from the storerooms," the little maid answered rather breathlessly.

Meghan thanked her and hurried on, unable to shake her deepening sense that something was wrong. Her breath was sharp in her side, but she ignored the pain. The cavernous kitchen was crowded with servants and she asked for Latifa again. Another of the young scullery maids was directing her out to the storerooms when suddenly there was a hubbub from outside. Meghan put her hand on the table to steady herself. She showed no surprise when a young pot-boy came running inside, his cheeks drained of all color.

"Murder!" he cried. "Latifa the Cook, she's been murdered."

Snapping out orders, Meghan followed him out into

the inner bailey and down a dark side-alley toward the
privy yard. Even her old eyes could see the great bulk
of the cook lying on the stones. With difficulty the sorceress knelt beside her, feeling for a pulse. Under her fingers
was a faint, erratic flutter. "Latifa!" she called. "Can ye
hear me, auld friend?"

Weakly Latifa's eyes opened, and she stared up at
Meghan's face without recognition. Very low she said,
"Maya . . . the Banrìgh . . . what does she do here?"
Then her eyes closed, and the pulse died. Tears running
down the seams of her face, Meghan tried to pump her
heart into life, but there was no response. Latifa was
dead.

The murder of the old cook threw the keep into chaos.
The chambermaids huddled in corners, weeping; the apprentice cooks spoiled the dinner; the steward sat with
his hands hanging, muttering, "But who could want to
kill Latifa? But why?"

Meghan was shocked to her core. Latifa was one of
the few of her friends from the old days to have survived
the Burning. She had known her as a plump baby with
dark curls and fat hands, and a cheeky young student
who refused to concentrate on her lessons at the Tower
of Two Moons, wanting to lie around on the grass and
eat gingerbread instead.

Meghan had wanted the young Latifa to take her Tests
and be admitted to the Coven as an apprentice witch,
but she had gone to work as an apprentice cook in the
kitchens instead, following in the footsteps of her mother
and grandmother. As a result, she had survived Maya's
Day of Reckoning when so many of her former class
mates had not. Maya had never suspected the palace
cook was a gifted skeelie, with a Talent for fire magic
and close ties with the Coven of Witches. For sixteen
years Latifa had spied for the rebels, risking her own life
daily to keep Meghan informed of the Banrìgh's movements and intentions.

Although Latifa had betrayed them at the final moment, Meghan knew it was because Maya's charm had
slowly and insidiously worked upon Latifa's own fears

and uncertainties until she had not known what to think or what to do. The old sorceress knew just how powerful Maya's compulsion could be. After all, the Fairge had ensorcelled Jaspar into massacring the witches, and Jaspar had been far more powerful than Latifa. So Meghan had pleaded with Lachlan and saved the bewildered old cook from a traitor's death.

Latifa had spent the two years since working to overcome Lachlan's suspicions and regain her trusted position in the Coven. To her great pride, she had sat her Tests and been admitted into the Coven as a fully accredited witch, wearing on her plump fingers moonstone and garnet rings to show she had passed her Test of Fire as well as her apprenticeship test. She had worked tirelessly to stretch their scanty supplies far enough to feed thousands, and had begun teaching her kitchen magic to some of the eager acolytes in the Theurgia. Meghan did not know how she was to manage without her.

The town guards searched every inn and house in Dùn Eidean but there was no sign of Maya the Ensorcellor. And even though Dùn Eidean's gates were closed and only those on the Rìgh's business allowed inside or out for close on a week, still Latifa's murderer was not found.

The sun beat down on blackened fields, the sky overhead a hard, bright blue. A few trees still raised black, angular branches in stark silhouette. Most had fallen and lay charred in the ashes. A small boy searched through the ruins of a cottage, his sooty face streaked with tears. As the carriage swayed along the road, he raised his face in hope, only to wail thinly in disappointment as the vehicle kept on its way.

Maya sat back on the cushioned seat, biting her lip. She remembered these fields as lush and green with clover and barley, with thick copses of trees on the hills and pretty cottages surrounded by flowers in the valleys. She and Jaspar had often driven through these gentle hills to stay with the MacThanach at his country estate. She was shocked by the devastation. On an impulse she put her head out the window and gruffly commanded one of her outriders to turn back and give the little boy one of her gold coins. He took the coin, saluted her and spurred his horse around, and she sat back against her cushions again, wondering at her moment of weakness.

A squad of soldiers, demanding to know her name and destination, stopped them some miles down the road. Their gray cloaks and leather breastplates were torn and stained, their shields badly battered. Maya recognized the uniform with a sinking heart. She had not expected to see any of the Rìgh's army this far east.

Maya leant from the gilded carriage, smiling at the sergeant and answering his questions in her low, melodious voice. She was dressed in crimson velvet, with a long, narrow skirt edged in gold, and a high collar that was cut away from the base of her throat to the cleft of her breasts.

"I travel to my country home in eastern Blèssem," she said. "My husband went there some weeks ago following reports the wicked Tìrsoilleirean had marched through that part o' the land. We were worried about our servants and crofters, and about the house. I have had no word from him and I was so overcome with anxiety that I decided I must come down and see for myself what is happening."

"Ye would be best staying and waiting for word, madam," the sergeant said gruffly. "All the land beyond that hill is held by the Bright Soldiers, and by all accounts they have little respect for person or property."

"I thank ye for the warning," Maya replied, "and I am glad I hired so many guards. My house is no' so very far from here. I am sure I will have no trouble and if I do, I shall send one o' my men to find ye, such a strong, sturdy man that ye are." She smiled at him winningly and he blushed.

"I think ye had best have a word to my captain, madam," he said.

She gritted her teeth. Her voice huskier than ever, laying the gentlest stress of compulsion on her words, she said, "My house is no' so far. I am sure I shall be safe. I shall drive on."

His fair skin reddening, he said stubbornly, "I think ye had best have a word to my captain."

Again she repeated her words, the stress stronger this time, but although he felt uncomfortable, he did not waver, opening the carriage door for her and holding up his hand to assist her out. She knew a stubborn, inflexible nature when she saw one and gave in gracefully.

The captain of the company was in his tent. The sergeant lifted the flap for her respectfully but inexorably, and she ducked her head and went in. At once her heart lifted. She recognized the captain, a young, handsome man with a discontented expression. He had been one of her customers at the House of Wanton Delights, a young laird who had given her every coin he had to spend a whole night with her. He had grown obsessed with her, visiting her many times before riding out with the Young Pretender's army. Much of Maya's hoard of gold had been seduced from his pocket.

The captain looked up as she entered and was immediately transfixed. She smiled at him and gave him her hand.

"Well met," she said huskily. He said nothing, just brought her hand to his mouth and kissed it passionately.

Maya fanned herself and rested her head on her hand. It was hot and stuffy within the confines of the carriage and the road here was rough, so that she had been badly jarred as the carriage rattled and shook its way forward.

It had been a long and wearying journey through the soldier-occupied fields of southern Blèssem. Once she had traveled beyond the battlefront she had at least seen green fields and blossoming orchards again, for the Bright Soldiers only burnt the land when it was lost. She was grateful for that, for the sight of the charred and ruined meadows had made her sick at heart.

Maya had been stopped several times by squads of Bright Soldiers but had simply told them she was the Dowager Banrìgh on her way to see her ally, Margrit of Arran, and they had waved her on her way. Their instant deference had pleased her. She knew it was Margrit's reputation that caused them to bow and speak humbly, but it had been so long since she had commanded such respect that she had almost forgotten how it felt.

Maya leant forward and looked out the window, hoping to feel some breath of air on her face. Beyond the road stretched rough, uncultivated land, with only occasional clumps of low, thorny shrubs relieving the gray-brown monotony. Here and there stretched shallow lochs, glimmering a brilliant blue under the burning sky. Overhead the sun beat down, hot and unrelenting, as if it were still summer and not the last month of autumn. Then she saw a glimpse of the sea, half hidden behind the sand dunes. She felt a rush of longing so intense she had to grip the carriage windowsill to stop herself from calling out to the driver. She sprayed her face and wrists with salted water instead, and urged him to hurry.

At last they came over a low hill and saw, far down the road, a wavering wall of mist, drifting like thick streamers over the swamp. Maya smiled, though her neck was stiff with tension. She felt the carriage falter as the driver unconsciously tightened his grip on the reins. She leant out of the window and urged him on again.

The road disappeared into the mist as if into a tunnel of white. The horses hesitated, and the driver had to crack the whip over them before they went on, shaking their heads nervously. The postilions all drew close about the carriage and Maya herself was unable to help a shiver of apprehension.

Suddenly the horses neighed and reared in terror. The driver shouted and cracked his whip, and the postilions wrenched at their horses' reins. Maya tried to see out the window but she could see nothing but writhing tendrils of mist. Then tall, gray shapes loomed up out of the gloom, their huge eyes glittering oddly, their multijointed, clawed arms reaching out as if to grasp. The horses plunged and screamed and Maya was flung to the floor as the carriage pitched. She heard a high-pitched humming then a sharp rap on her carriage door.

She cried out, biting her lip immediately afterwards in chagrin. The door was opened and a man with a long

gray beard and a crooked nose looked in. "If it is no'
the Dowager Banrìgh herself," he said. "Welcome to
Arran, my lady. May I assist ye off the floor?"

After swinging himself uninvited into Maya's carriage,
he introduced himself as Campbell the Ironic, a warlock
in the service of Margrit of Arran. He was a tall, lean
man with a sarcastic twist to his mouth. His stringy gray
hair hung halfway down his back, tied back with a leather
thong, and he wore a long, rather grubby purple robe
inscribed with mystical symbols around the hem and
sleeves. Leaning out the window, he tersely ordered the
Mesmerdean to retreat back into the mist, for the horses
were shying nervously at their dank, swampy smell. Maya
reseated herself, smoothing her crimson velvet and staring down her nose at the warlock, who had rather a
swampy smell himself. He was not at all discomposed by
her haughty look, rapping on the wall to order the coach-
man to drive on, then turning to rake her with black
eyes almost hidden under shaggy gray eyebrows.

"This is unprecedented, indeed," he said. "So many
visitors to Arran at once. And witch-haters and witch-
hunters at that. What do ye do here, Maya?"

"That is a matter for me to discuss with your mistress,"
Maya replied icily. "And who gave ye leave to call me
by my name, sirrah? Ye shall address me as 'my lady,'
if ye address me at all."

"Obh, obh!" Campbell replied. "Anyone would think
ye were still the Banrìgh, with your haughty looks and
manner. No' that that means anything here in Arran. We
never recognized the MacCuinn as Rìgh and I canna say
we ever will."

"Is that so?" Maya looked out the window, though all she
could see were dripping tree branches. "Is that why Iain
o' Arran fights at Lachlan the Pretender's command and
does his bidding like any o' his other squires?"

Campbell scowled and folded his arms. Maya smiled
thinly and continued to stare outside. The road wound
through the swamp, the mist occasionally clearing enough
for her to see banks of flowering sedge and the straight
arrows of bulrushes. Once she saw several pairs of pale,

bulbous eyes floating just above the surface of the mud and she recoiled involuntarily.

"Mudsprites," the warlock said with morbid satisfaction. "They'll pull ye under if ye set foot in the marsh."

"As I have no intention o' walking through the marsh, they are unlikely to concern me," Maya replied coldly, pulling her furred cape around her shoulders. She was beginning to think she had made a major mistake in coming to Arran.

At last they came to a great stretch of water, glimmering gray beneath the drifting mist. The horses came to a jittery halt, sweating under their harness despite the coolness of the air. Maya could see her driver and outriders were looking decidedly edgy, and she frowned at them even though she could understand their unease. Gliding smoothly across the loch was a long pinnace, its prow curved high into the shape of a swan. The boat was empty, and the sail was furled tightly, yet it moved as swiftly as if its oars were manned.

Maya allowed Campbell the Ironic to assist her out of the carriage and looked about her calmly. Built on the shore of the loch were several low buildings, their roofs thatched with flowering sedge. From the doorways peered several bogfaeries, their black, wrinkled faces expressing an anxious curiosity, their huge lustrous eyes as bright as jewels. Several other small boats were moored to the jetty, most of them rough dinghies without the grace of the swan-carved pinnace. There was one large, flat-bottomed barge, piled high with sacks of rys seeds and jars of honey. As Maya watched, a crew of bogfaeries slowly and laboriously poled the barge away from the jetty, heading north up the river.

"My lady," Campbell said, indicating Maya should climb into the pinnace.

She regarded him haughtily, and said, "Ye will have a care for my men and my horses?"

"Indeed, they shall be cared for," he replied, with a sneer that did not make her feel comfortable. She thanked him calmly, however, and watched the little, black-skinned faeries as they apprehensively helped unhitch the carriage, being too small to reach the harnesses of the horses. Her driver, a large, placid man, nodded at her reassuringly and said, "Never ye mind us, my lady, we'll wait here for your orders."

Maya smiled and thanked him, passing him a small bag of coins, then climbed into the pinnace, allowing none of her perturbation to show on her face. Campbell climbed in after her, and she faced away from him, staring across the loch. The swan-boat glided away from the jetty, its wake stretching behind as straight as a plough furrow.

The mist above the loch was thin and drifted away from the boat, revealing huge water-oaks crowding down the shore, their leaves beginning to color at the edges. Ahead of her was an island crowned with tall, sharp-pointed towers, each carved into spiraling forms and painted in pale, opalescent colors so they shimmered like hazy rainbows. Despite herself, Maya was overawed by her first sight of the Tower of Mists. She had thought Rhyssmadill beautiful, but this was like a palace out of a faery story: graceful, extravagant, magical.

"Tùr de Ceò," Campbell said reverently, and she frowned to hear the old language, the tongue of witches, outlawed seventeen years ago. He glanced at her sardonically and said a long phrase lilting and beautiful, which she did not understand. "Oh, the Tower o' Mists, mysterious beauty, beauteous mystery," he translated for her. "How does it feel to see it, my lady? The one Tower ye could no' topple?"

Maya gritted her teeth. Indeed it was ironic to be coming to the Lady of Arran for help when for many long years she had sent her Red Guards into the marshes in a vain attempt to destroy the NicFóghnan's magical power. Many a company of Maya's soldiers had been lost in the marshes, and the Tower of Mists was the only witches' Tower not to have been burnt to ruins. It made her feel very odd and off-balance to be approaching one of the most powerful sorceresses in the land with her hand extended in friendship.

Smoothly the swan-boat came to a halt at a wide marble platform. Maya gathered her crimson skirts together and climbed out as gracefully as she could. Standing to one side of the broad steps was a tall, strong-looking man dressed somberly in gray. His mane of coarse white hair was bound back from his brow with leather, so that the two heavy horns curling down on either side of his forehead were emphasized. Across each angular cheekbone were three thin white scars.

Maya stared at him in some surprise. She recognized him at once as a Khan'cohban, having met one of the mountain faeries at the Tower of Two Moons many years before. She knew they were a fierce warlike race, much like her own people, though they lived in the inhospitable snowy wastes at the top of the world. She wondered what he was doing here, in the soft airs of the coast, and knew him to be dangerous. The six scars on his face proclaimed him as a skilled warrior, and she remembered the one she had known. He had tried to kill her and had almost succeeded. Only her transformative magic had saved her, for she had turned him into a horse and broken him to her whip and spur. She knew how much it would have galled him to be a beast of burden, for the Khan'cohbans were fiercely independent. Breaking him to her will had given her intense satisfaction, for she had seen it as a symbol of her supremacy over all the peoples of Eileanan and the Far Islands. Idly she wondered what had happened to the ensorcelled horse, and thought he must have died years ago.

The Khan'cohban bowed and greeted her courteously. He escorted her up the stairs, passing two more Mesmerdean nymphs standing guard outside the great arched door. Maya stared at them in fascination and they stared back with greenish, multifaceted eyes, their beautiful inhuman faces showing no expression. Engraved on either side of the double door was the badge of the MacFóghnan clan—a flowering thistle with the clan motto curling above it. *Touch not the thistle*, Maya read, flaring her nostrils in disdain.

She was led through a grand hall hung with bright tapestries and decorated with marble statues, ancient shields and weapons, and silver bowls and pitchers. On the floor were rugs of exquisite workmanship, crimson and blue and gray, and a magnificent staircase swept down from the upper gallery, a streak of red carpet falling down the center like a river of blood. Servants hurried to take her cape and feathered hat, and to offer her mulled wine to warm her after the chilly journey. Maya sipped at it and was astonished at its honeyed tang. Its warmth raced through her, flushing her skin and bringing with it a slight giddiness. She drank no more, remembering that Arran was famous for wine sweetened with the honey of the golden goddess flower, a most intoxicating and heady brew.

The Khan'cohban flung open the massive doors into the throne-room and announced Maya in ringing tones; Campbell the Ironic bowed so deeply his beard brushed the floor. Maya held her head high, refusing to be daunted by all this servitude.

At the far end of the room was a daïs with an ornately carved throne piled with purple velvet cushions. Reclining upon it was a dark-haired woman dressed in black velvet, a silver brooch in the shape of a thistle upon her breast. Her skin was very fine and pale, her mouth colored a dark purple. As Maya slowly approached down the length of the room, she noticed the woman's long, curving fingernails were colored the same damson purple. Slowly and rhythmically they tapped against the dark wood of the throne, as long and sharp as scimitars.

Maya reached the area below the dais and inclined her head. "It is a pleasure indeed to meet ye again," she said. "I trust ye have kept well?"

"Indeed I have," Margrit replied. "Both well and amused. It has been an interesting few years since we last met."

"Interesting is no' quite the word I would have chosen," Maya replied, only the flaring of her nostrils betraying her anger. "It is true a great deal has happened."

"Aye, who would have thought the rebels would have triumphed and the Coven o' Witches be restored?" the banprionnsa said suavely. "Your husband dead, your daughter dispossessed and ye an outlaw and fugitive."

"Hardly," Maya replied. "There are many who resent the heel o' the Pretender and wish to restore my rule. It is only a matter o' time."

"The young MacCuinn has shown himself more able than one would have suspected," Margrit said. "The victories o' Blairgowrie and Dùn Eidean were cleverly done and my reconnaissance staff tell me supporters have flocked to his flag ever since."

"Fair-weather friends," Maya said lightly. "They will go wherever they think their best interests lie. Once my daughter wins back her throne, they will pledge their support to us once again."

Margrit regarded her rings. "Happen that is true," she replied. "But are they the sort o' friends one would wish to have?"

"Och, there are many whose support o' me and my daughter has no' wavered." Maya grew tired of standing before Margrit's throne and sat gracefully on one of the chairs set against the wall. "But I am sure your spies have told ye that as well."

"Spies is a harsh word," Margrit replied, smiling.

Maya felt herself tensing, and smiled sweetly in response. "My pardon. Your reconnaissance staff."

For a moment their gazes locked, then Margrit glanced away, saying affably, "But I forget my manners. Ye must be weary indeed after your journey. Let me offer ye some refreshment and a room in which ye may rest, and then perhaps ye shall tell me why ye have done me the honor o' this unexpected—but most delightful—visit."

"Why, I have come to be with my daughter, o' course," Maya replied urbanely. "I knew she would no' be o' much use to ye without my endorsement and support, and so once *my* reconnaissance staff informed me she had come under your protection, I naturally came to join her. I have no need to enquire after her health, I am sure, knowing what a caring and nurturing mother ye are yourself."

Margrit's smile deepened, dimples flashing in her

cheeks. "Your reconnaissance staff are efficient indeed, my dear. Ye must tell me how ye found such capable servants. Foolishly I had thought what went on within the mists o' Arran was impenetrable to those o' the outside world. I see I am no' so well protected as I thought."

Maya found fear was creeping down her spine like a trickle of icy water. Margrit's smile was as frightening as her Fairgean father's angriest bellow. She drew herself up, staring at the banprionnsa haughtily. "I am sorry if ye think my interest invasive," she said coolly. "The safety and wellbeing o' my daughter, the Banrìgh o' all o' Eileanan and the Far Islands, is naturally my greatest concern."

"Naturally," Margrit replied silkily, once again tapping her long fingernails slowly against the gilded wood of her throne. "And naturally ye will wish to see her." She rose and descended from the throne, her black velvet skirts trailing behind her. "Come, my dear. I ken ye must be longing to be reunited with the wee lassie, so many months it has been since ye last embraced her."

There was such subtle mockery in her tone that Maya flushed and clenched her fingers together. She followed the banprionnsa out of the throne room and up the stairs, Margrit suavely describing the history of many of the treasures displayed on the walls.

Maya murmured politely in response and then nodded at the chamberlain preceding them up the stairs. "Tell me, my lady, how is it that ye have one o' the horned mountains faeries as your servant? Are they no' a wild, independent people? What is one doing here in the depths o' the marshes?"

Margrit frowned in pleasurable remembrance. "I saved his life and under the Khan'cohbans' strict code o' honor that means he is in debt to me and must serve me as I demand, for as long as I demand. It was quite a few years ago, but I refuse to release him from his *geas* for indeed he is one o' the best servants I have ever had, fearless, intelligent and utterly faithful."

"But how did ye come to save his life?"

"I was traveling to Tìrsoilleir in my swan-carriage

when we were caught in a freakish hurricane. The swans
could not fly against such a strong wind and so I managed
to surround us with the calm eye o' the storm. Storm-
magic is no' my strength though, so we had to travel
with the wind. We were carried high into the mountains
and thrown at last onto a high field o' snow. My swans
were exhausted and some were injured and I myself was
worn out with controlling such a tremendous, elemental
force.

"We rested there until our strength returned, and I
became aware of birds o' prey circling a high plateau o'
rock. With nothing better to do while I waited for my
swans to recover, I climbed the ridge and found Khan'tirell there, naked and staked out to die. He had killed
someone in a fit o' jealousy over some lover and they
had condemned him to death. That is how they execute
their criminals on the Spine o' the World. Barbaric, is it
no'? Somehow he had survived the bitter cold, though I
think the wildness o' the storm must have kept the
wolves and snow lions away long enough for me to find
him. I knew o' the fighting skills o' the mountain faeries
because o' that savage young warrior that was at the Tower
o' Two Moons for a while, do ye remember?"

Maya nodded and the banprionnsa continued, "So I
freed him and bound him to me with his ridiculous code
o' honor and he has served me ever since. He has been
useful indeed and has told me much about the lost land
o' Tìrlethan that had been forgotten."

At last they reached the nursery wing of the palace,
and Maya could hear a child's soft babbling. She tensed
in anticipation, wondering how her daughter had changed
since she had last seen her. She knew there was no chance
Bronwen would recognize her, for the little girl had been
only a month old when Maya had fled the Pool of Two
Moons, and she was now almost two years old.

Margrit opened the door and ushered Maya through.
Within was a long room furnished with a cot all hung
with cream and gold satin, delicate gilded cupboards and
chests, and a tall rocking horse with wild eyes and a
luxurious mane and tail. Sitting on the floor playing with

a china doll was a little girl with dark ringlets hanging to her neck. A white curl at the front was tied back with a pink bow that matched her flounced dress.

She looked up as the door opened, and her chubby face puckered up at the sight of Margrit's black dress. She began to wail and Margrit smiled. The little bogfaery sitting nearby leapt up and hurried to soothe the little girl, her wrinkled face anxious. The child was inconsolable, however, and Margrit's dimples deepened. "If ye canna control the lassie, I may have to find another nursemaid," she said gently, and the bogfaery whimpered a little, rocking the little girl in her furry arms.

Maya came forward and bent to take the little girl from the bogfaery's arms. The nursemaid clutched the baby closer, and Maya smiled and said reassuringly, "Come, I mean the lassie no harm. She is my daughter and cruel circumstances have kept us apart for many long months."

Reluctantly the bogfaery allowed her to lift the little girl up. Maya cuddled the child close, crooning a lullaby so she quietened. Maya sat down in one of the dainty gilded chairs and held the little girl on her lap so she could examine her. The full bottom lip still trembled but the blue eyes stared back at her with interest. Maya frowned and lifted the curls from the baby's neck. Her frown deepened, her nostrils flaring in barely controlled rage. "What trickery is this!" she cried. "This is no' my daughter!"

Margrit's whole body stiffened. "What did ye say?"

"This is no' my daughter!" Maya cried in bitter disappointment. "Ye think to deceive me? What have ye done with Bronwen?"

Margrit came swiftly across the room. "Ye think to cheat me?" she hissed. "Do no' forget ye are in the heart o' the Murkmyre. Many enter the marshes o' Arran and never leave again. Who will ken if ye are one o' them?"

"Ye threaten me?" Maya cried imperiously, rising to her feet and holding the child out at arm's length. "Do ye forget who I am! The winged *uile-bheist* may have seized

the throne for now, but I am still Regent and ruler o'
this land till my daughter comes o' age."

"No' in Arran," Margrit smiled. "We have never recognized the right o' the MacCuinn to rule, and certainly
do no' recognize ye or your daughter. We gave sanctuary
to your Grand-Seeker only because it served our pur-
poses to have the so-called NicCuinn under our hand.
Ye are all here at my forbearance and I shall no' suffer
any double-dealing."

"If there is any double-dealing here, it is no' me that
is doing it!" Maya cried. "What have ye done with my
daughter?"

Margrit stared at her consideringly. "Are ye telling the
truth when ye say this is no' your daughter? I hope so,
for your sake, for I will no' forgive such a falsehood
easily."

"Do ye think I do no' ken my own daughter?"

"Well, ye have no' seen her for nigh on two years and
children change a great deal in that time. How can ye
be sure she is no' yours? She has the white lock, as she
should if she were a true NicCuinn."

Maya laughed. "Bring me a tub o' salt water and I
shall prove it to ye."

Margrit stared at her, speculation in her eyes, then
nodded brusquely. She snapped her fingers and the bogfaery went scurrying from the room. "Also, tell our other
guest to attend us here," she called after the little faery.
"If there is deceit and double-dealing here, I think it
must be Renshaw who has dealt it."

In the long minutes it took for the bogfaeries to return
with a hipbath, a bag of sea salt and jugs of water, neither
woman spoke. Maya had dropped the little girl back on
to the floor, and she sat clutching her doll and sucking
her thumb, the long white curl dangling down the left
side of her face. Margrit sat and regarded her rings, smiling equably, and Maya endeavored to match her poise,
even though her pulse was racing.

Once the bath was set up and filled with warm, salty
water, Maya nodded to the bogfaery. Hurriedly the
nursemaid undressed the little girl and lowered her into

the bath. She laughed and kicked her chubby legs, splashing water across the floor.

"Well?" Margrit said. "What does this prove?"

"I have heard ye called the mistress o' illusions," Maya replied. "Surely your eyes have pierced my glamourie and seen me for what I am?"

Margrit frowned in pleasure. "Truc," she admitted. "Ye never deceived me, though your first spell o' illusion was powerful indeed. This glamourie ye wear now is naught but a frail disguise, so much so that I wondered why ye bothered to wear it."

Trying not to show her chagrin, Maya let the illusion drop away from her. "Force o' habit," she replied, shrugging her shoulders. "It does no' suit my purpose to let all ken I am descended from the Fairgean king."

Margrit tapped her teeth with one long, purple nail. "So the rumors are true," she said. "Ye are a Fairge. I wondered when I saw the webs between your fingers, which ye so feebly tried to hide from my eyes. I could no' be sure though. They say many o' those born in Carraig have webbed fingers and toes like a frog, and ye seemed human otherwise."

Maya undid the high collar of her dress so that Margrit could see her gills.

The banprionnsa's eyes widened slightly, and a small frown flitted across her face. "So all your witch-hunts and faery persecutions were on behalf o' the Fairgean. I often wondered what was behind them, though I assumed ye and I shared a lust for power." Her frown of enjoyment deepened. "A most subtle and devious plan, though surprised I am indeed to find ye a mere pawn in your father's schemes."

"I act on my own behalf," Maya said coldly.

"O' course," Margrit replied urbanely. "Do we no' all? But tell me, how is it ye managed to disguise your true self for so long? I never heard that casting an illusion was one o' the Fairgean's Talents? And even with clearseeing I could no' be sure. Ye still look very human to me."

"My mother was human, and I inherited much from

her," she explained. "I look more human than Fairgean, as does my daughter. She is still one quarter Fairgean, though. She was born with fins and gills like any Fairgean babe, and should have transformed into her seashape as soon as she was lowered into the water. I have seen my daughter do it and know she has the gift. This human babe is no daughter o' mine."

Margrit smiled unpleasantly. "So I have been tricked and lied to," she murmured. "No doubt your former Grand-Seeker hoped to win the throne with his fake Nic-Cuinn and rule the land through her. He should no' have lied to me, though, or hidden his purpose. I dislike cheats."

She gestured to the bogfaery, who hastily dried and dressed the little girl and took her away. Maya wondered briefly what would happen to the child. From the deep curve of Margrit's mouth, she did not think it would be a kind fate.

The door opened and Renshaw swept in, his face gaunt and pale above the crimson gown. His step faltered when he saw Maya, and his skin turned the unwholesome color of a dead fish. He had never seen her without the mask of illusion and it was clear her appearance was a shock to him.

"Your Highness! What an unexpected pleasure," he said and bowed deeply. When he stood upright again, his eyes were hooded so it was hard to know what he felt, but Maya could see his fingers were rigid.

"The Dowager Banrìgh has come to visit me and has brought some very interesting news," Margrit said affably. "Very interesting indeed."

Renshaw assumed an expression of interest.

"She tells me the young bairn ye brought me is no' her daughter, as ye claim, but an imposter. Both she and I would be very curious to know who the lassie is and where the real Bronwen NicCuinn is. We both have some interest in the matter, as I am sure you can imagine."

Renshaw was silent for a moment. Although his face and hands were still, Maya had the impression he was thinking fast. "Ye shock me, Your Highness," he said at last. "Surely ye can see the young lassie is your daughter. Why, she has the white lock and your blue eyes."

"Any fool can bleach in a white lock." Margrit's dimples flashed across her cheek.

"True, Your Grace, if they had the knowledge. Dressing hair is hardly my area o' expertise, though. How can Her Highness be certain? She has no' seen her daughter for nigh on two years, surely?"

"Do ye think I do no' ken my own daughter?" Maya replied silkily, lifting one webbed hand to play with the wedge of hair that fell onto her neck. Renshaw stared at her, a faint sheen of sweat springing up on his high brow as he saw the gills that fluttered gently just below her ear.

"But, my lady . . ." Renshaw stammered, his fingers working nervously at the buttons of his crimson gown. "How can this be? I had no idea . . ."

"Ye lie," Margrit said sweetly. "Do ye think ye can deceive the Thistle?" Her smile was like the grin of a snake, full of malice. The Grand-Seeker fell silent, licking his dry lips, eyes darting from face to face.

"Ye have been false with me, Renshaw, and that is something I do no' forgive lightly," Margrit said affectionately. "Ye came to me, seeking sanctuary and offering me a chance to strike a blow at the MacCuinn clan that they would no' recover from easily. I took ye, fed ye and sheltered ye, and gave ye servants to wait on your every whim. I made plans that gave me much pleasure in the contemplation, and find now all my schemes are hollow. What would ye have done if we did overthrow the young Pretender and your impostor had been given the Lodestar to hold? It would have killed her, and ye would have been exposed as the charlatan ye are."

"I never expected ye to let the child live that long," Renshaw admitted. "The enmity ye hold toward the MacCuinns is legendary."

She laughed. "True," she admitted. "True on all counts."

"Ye have brought me here on a wild sardine chase," Maya hissed. "I have been searching for Bronwen for

months, and ye laid a false trail that led me here! Where
is my daughter?"

"I have no idea, Your Highness," Renshaw replied.
"This was a mere crofter's daughter who had a close
resemblance to your daughter. I kent the country folk
would flock to my standard if I said I had the true
banrìgh under my hand. With her disappearance, many
would have supported the winged monster simply because he was all they had to look to. They might have
suspected him o' murder and regicide, but who was to
prove it? With the country plunged into war, they had
to look to someone to save them, and the tales they were
telling o' ye, Your Highness, were far worse than what
they may have suspected o' him." His pronunciation of
her former title was made with such a sarcastic intonation
that Maya drew herself upright, her mobile nostrils flaring in anger. Margrit was also angry but for a far different reason.

"Ye brought a peasant's daughter to my palace and
told me she was the NicCuinn?" she said sweetly. "That
was a very bad mistake, Renshaw, a very bad mistake
indeed." Her smile deepened, and she held out her ringladen hand, pointing two fingers at him.

The Grand-Seeker's hands flew to his throat. Gasping
for air, he fell to his knees, his distorted face turning
a strange purplish color. Maya looked on, repelled and
fascinated, as he fell forward onto the floor, writhing and
choking as his own hands throttled the breath from his
body. His heels drummed against the floor, and spittle
flew from his purple lips. He turned desperate, bulging
eyes her way, then fell back limply. Renshaw lay where
he had fallen, his engorged tongue protruding from his
mouth, his hands still locked around his throat.

Margrit called to the terrified bogfaery. "Call the
guards to remove the garbage and throw it to the golden
goddess," she instructed. Then she turned and smiled at
Maya, who found herself quite unable to move or speak.
"One does not touch the Thistle without pain," the Banprionnsa of Arran said sweetly. "Ye would be advised
to remember it."

*   *   *

The cursehag stank so foully that Maya almost gagged. Margrit gave her an apple studded with cloves to hold to her nose, and Maya took it gratefully, drawing herself away. The cursehag chuckled evilly, staring at her through the matted rat's nest of gray hair that fell over her wrinkled, grimy face. She was a thin, bent creature, dressed in a strange collection of rags so filthy it was impossible to tell their original color or texture. Her hands, tipped with black, broken nails, scrabbled in the sack she carried over her hunched shoulder as she muttered nonsense to herself.

Maya glanced at Margrit doubtfully, and the banprionnsa frowned reassuringly. "Do no' worry, my lady, Shannagh o' the Swamp can cast the most potent o' curses. She has lived in Arran since I was but a bairn, and did much work on behalf o' my mother."

The cursehag giggled and gave Maya a look of surprising intelligence as she laid various twisted roots and branches on the table. "Indeed, the NicFóghnans have always found auld Shannagh o' use, no' wanting to dirty their own fine hands with curses and calamities. Shannagh knows what plants to gather to make the vilest poisons and what time o' the moon it is best to pick them. It was Shannagh that made the dragonbane for ye when ye were Banrìgh. It was Shannagh that concocted that bold brew, and I ken ye found it o' use."

"Enough, auld woman!" Margrit cried.

Maya could tell she was angry that the cursehag had revealed where the banprionnsa had got the dragonbane Maya had used in her attack on the dragons in the spring of the red comet. Maya had paid dearly for that poison and was interested indeed to know who had had the courage to distill it.

The three women were locked in a room at the height of Margrit's own tower. It was Samhain, night of the dead, and outside an eerie wind moaned. On Samhain the veils between the world of the quick and the dead were at their thinnest, and Margrit had chosen this night as the most auspicious for casting a potent curse against

Lachlan MacCuinn. The room was all hung with black curtains painted with strange symbols in silver and crimson paint. Tables were crowded with peculiar instruments and there was a strange odor to the room, like old blood. Maya resisted the temptation to huddle her cloak about her, standing tall and proud in one corner of the room.

Maya had been loath to reveal the feather and lock of hair to the Thistle and had kept them hidden for some weeks while she tried to decide on her best course of action. The discovery that the little girl was not her daughter had left the Fairge in Margrit of Arran's hands without a card to play. She had desperately needed the sorceress's help in locating Bronwen but was aware that Margrit wished her daughter only ill.

For three weeks the women had been charmingly polite to each other, all the while an undercurrent of menace and threat keeping Maya tense and wary. She had told Margrit about her spies in the very heart of Lachlan's camp and that had intrigued the sorceress sufficiently to prevent her from ordering Maya thrown to the golden goddess. Margrit had quickly seen how such spies could be of use to her and they had hastened to set up lines of communication so that Maya could easily contact her spies.

Next Maya had brought out the thick braid of red hair, using all her wit and wiles to convince Margrit to help her track down Isabeau the Red and the lost banprionnsa. Margrit had clearly seen how much better it was to have Maya's daughter under her own hand rather than out in the countryside, a wild card that could be used against her at any time. So she had used her own powerful magic to locate Isabeau through her scrying pool. She had seen the young woman in a shining world of snow that could only be found on the Spine of the World. There was no sign of Bronwen but Margrit's Khan'cohban chamberlain had been able to recognize the shape of the peaks towering behind the red-haired apprentice witch. "They are the Cursed Peaks," he had said in his harshly accented voice. "She is in the Cursed Valley."

Margrit's interest had quickened visibly. "Indeed?"

she had purred. She turned to Maya with a sweet, dangerous smile, saying, "But o' course I shall help ye find this lass! Why, as soon as the winter storms have subsided I shall give ye my swan-carriage and ye can fly up the mountains as swiftly as the snow geese. And I shall send Khan'tirell to guide ye! He knows those mountains like his own scarred face. Ye would never find the way through without him. He and all my servants shall be at your disposal."

Wondering what double game Margrit was playing, Maya had thanked her effusively and promised to return to Margrit's protection with the little banprionnsa, a lie she had no compunction in uttering. Only then, when her path had become clearer, had she brought out the feather and lock of hair. Margrit had been pleased indeed. Her whole body had quivered with eagerness, her face set in a scowl of joy.

"At last!" she had cried, reaching out for them. "With these we'll be able to cast a curse o' such power! The MacCuinns shall truly rue the day they scorned the Thistle."

Maya had held on tight to them, saying warily, "I give these to ye only on the condition that ye do as ye promised and help me find Bronwen. If ye betray me, it is ye who shall rue the day!"

"O' course, o' course," Margrit had smiled. "It shall be your blood that seals the curse. I shall be merely your humble instrument."

The cursehag grinned, singing to herself as she sewed a little doll out of cloth. With a stick of charcoal she drew features uncannily like Lachlan's upon its face, then stuffed it with wilted rue leaves, deadly nightshade berries and water-hemlock. As her gnarled fingers worked quickly and expertly, she explained to Maya what she was doing and the Fairge watched in fascination.

Shannagh sewed the doll closed with black thread, then wrapped it in a scrap of green plaid torn from the kilt of the young rìgh. She sewed to its head the tangle of dark hair Maya's spy had stolen from his comb.

"What sort o' curse do ye wish me to cast?" she asked.

"Do ye want him to be hurt or maimed, or merely ruined? Do ye wish him to lose his wits or his strength, or do ye wish to bind his mouth and silence him forever? Do ye want him to die, and if so, straightaway or a slow, lingering death? Do ye wish me to curse his blood, and all that are born o' it? What is your desire?"

"I want him to be ruined, as he ruined me," Maya replied slowly. "I want him to lose all he has gained, and know defeat and weakness and cold, as I have. I want him to be cruelly hurt, to suffer and slowly die in pain and misery, his power returned to me."

Shannagh nodded her matted gray head. "Ye had best pay me well for such a curse, or I shall make sure it is the Clan o' the Thistle that suffers so," she warned. Margrit smiled contemptuously and tossed the old faery a large bag of coins. She counted it obsessively, at last revealing her broken stumps of teeth in a smile and stowing the money away in her sack.

The cursehag then pulled out thick black candles that smelt strongly of belladonna and rue and set them into a squat iron holder. A snap of her fingers and flame burst into life at the ends of the wicks. The smoke smelt strange, and shadows danced over the room with their own fey life.

In her stained cauldron the cursehag mixed together urine from a black cat, a few pinches of dried dragon's blood, a handful of grave dirt, yew leaves and berries, and a few globùles of sap from the elder tree. With her pestle and mortar she ground a mandrake root to dust and added that, then she took Maya's finger and pierced it with a slender dagger, squeezing until three drops of her blood dropped into the cauldron. The cursehag then stirred the foul concoction with the dagger, muttering under her breath,

> "By the power o' the dark moons
> I make potent this brew,
> Fill it wi' coldness
> Fill it wi' darkness
> Fill it wi' hurt and sharpness.

By the power o' the dark moons
I make potent this brew,
Fill it wi' nastiness
Fill it wi' ugliness
Fill it wi' shame and sadness.
By the power o' the dark moons,
I make potent this brew."

Maya watched, both repelled and fascinated, as Shannagh drew the long, sable feather plucked from Lachlan's wing through the dark, sticky fluid until it was wet and bedraggled. Then the cursehag passed it to her, telling her to snap it in two and repeat after her:

"I curse thee, Lachlan MacCuinn,
By the power o' the dark moons,
And wish ye the harm ye have done me;
I curse thee, Lachlan MacCuinn,
By the power o' the dark moons,
And wish ye the harm ye have done me;
I curse thee, Lachlan MacCuinn,
By the power o' the dark moons,
And wish ye the harm ye have done me;
By the power o' the dark moons,
I curse thee, I curse thee, I curse thee."

Maya did as the cursehag said, bringing all her anger and hatred to the fore as she did so. The feather snapped with a sound like cracking bone, and she passed it back to the old hag with a peculiar sensation in her stomach. Shannagh had been soaking a length of black ribbon in the cauldron. She bound the broken feather to the poppet's body with it, winding the ribbon round nine times as she repeated the final line of the rhyme. Obediently Maya chanted it with her. "I curse thee, I curse thee, I curse thee."

Shannagh then wrapped the poppet in black cloth, tying it securely into a knot. From Maya's finger she squeezed another three drops of blood onto the knot, and the Fairge said, her voice quavering despite herself,

"Bound to me are ye by blood, none may free ye from this spell but me." Then she snuffed out the candles so the room sank into darkness.

"That will make sure none but ye can break the curse, no matter how powerful they be," the cursehag whispered. "Ye must keep the poppet wi' ye, for ye are bound tightly to the MacCuinn now, your fates entwined. Be careful though. Curses are like chickens—they come home to roost. Ye must guard yourself carefully against negative forces. Ken also that the MacCuinn may be able to resist the curse if he is strong enough, and if he keeps his spirits positive. Though by all accounts he is a man o' dark moods and quick temper—that will make it easier."

Maya nodded, stowing away the poppet in its black bag. She was conscious of a shadow on her spirits, and a strange smell to the air. The cursehag removed the black candles, lighting an incense brazier and waving it in all four corners of the room, and kindling fresh white candles that smelt sweetly of angelica. She washed out her cauldron and dagger and carefully packed away the jars of dragon's blood, mandrake root, cat's urine and grave-dirt. Once the room was purified, Maya was able to breathe more easily, though she still felt oddly afraid. The poppet seemed like a tangible presence, hot and breathing in her pocket as if it were alive.

"Well, 'tis done," Margrit said with satisfaction. "I look forward to the day when I see the MacCuinn clan broken forever. A thousand years they have sought to rule over Arran and make us subject to their will. It was Fóghnan who was the daughter o' kings in the Other World, no' Cuinn. He was naught but an enterprising alchemist who taught Fóghnan and her sisters in the palace and was paid a tutor's pittance by her father. Yet it was Cuinn that called himself the master o' the First Coven, and Owein MacCuinn that sought to lead once his father lay dead, broken by the magic they had wrought to cross the universe. A mere lad, and no more royally born than any o' the Thistle's servants, yet he tried to subject her to his will. Well, many a MacCuinn has rued the day they sought to order the Thistle, and now they shall truly suffer."

THE TOMB OF RAVENS

Clouds hung heavy over the valley, shrouding the hills and the sky and casting a gray gloom over the river. Muddy snow lay under the trees and thin rushes grew from beds of ice. Through this bleak landscape moved a company of cavalry in tight formation. Behind them trudged the infantry, their gray cloaks wrapped tightly about them against the cold, while the baggage carts and supply herds were kept under close guard at the rear. Last of all came the great destriers, for each of the cavaliers needed at least three horses, all specially trained to fight at their master's command. Far overhead a great falcon soared, its white wings almost invisible against the snow-laden clouds.

Lachlan reined in his horse. "Stormwing says the Bright Soldiers are camped just over the hill, near the banks o' the river. Are we to feint with them again, or shall we slip past?"

Iseult smiled coldly. "Is the plan no' to keep them guessing? Let us send the horses in to cause chaos and confusion while our men cross the river again. Then the cavalry can retreat back into the countryside and rejoin us further down the river."

Lachlan grinned. "Why do we no' call the birds to our aid once more, *leannan*? They sent the Bright Soldiers scurrying in terror last night, and soon we shall have them ducking whenever a bird flies overhead, ally or no'."

Iseult nodded, then wheeled her horse around to trot back to the head of the infantry. As she issued crisp orders, Lachlan lifted his wrist for the gyrfalcon. Stormwing dropped from the leaden sky like a bolt of white light-ning and perched on the young rìgh's wrist, turning its fierce eyes to meet Lachlan's gaze.

The Rìgh had spent all his few moments of leisure over the autumn taming and training the young gyrfalcon and had found the bird's keen eyesight and swift wings invaluable.

The long-winged bird had been a gift from Anghus MacRuraich, sent in his stead to the last Lammas Confer-ence. It was a kingly gift indeed and had to some extent alleviated Lachlan's disappointment that the Prionnsa of Rurach was still unable to join the army.

While Lachlan had tamed his gyrfalcon, the Greycloaks had spent the autumn months consolidating their position in Blèssem, rebuilding Dùn Eidean and planting the fields about with wheat, oats, barley and rye so that they would have crops to harvest in the spring. With the Fair-gean swimming down the coast with the autumn tides, both the Greycloaks and the Bright Soldiers had been careful to stay away from the firths and rivers. Lachlan and Iseult had been free to concentrate their forces on keeping the Tìrsoilleirean back and rebuilding their strength after the hard fighting of the summer.

Traditionally winter was a time for rest, and the Bright Soldiers had certainly not expected Lachlan to launch another initiative against them. It was now more than two years since the Lammas invasion, however, and Lachlan knew that Rhyssmadill had only been provis-ioned for two years. The besieged palace garrison would be close to starvation, and Lachlan was eager to have the wealth of its treasury in his hands. He knew the palace would fall if it was not assisted soon, for the garri-son had no loyalty to his rule, having been appointed by his brother Jaspar. If it was a choice between starvation and being prisoners-of-war, he had no doubt what choice the defendants would make.

So the Greycloaks had only waited for the Fairgean to swim north again before striking west. They had con-tinued their highly mobile tactics, riding circles around the enemy, engaging in feigned retreats and luring the

Bright Soldiers into traps and ambushes. As the Tìrsoil-leirean were driven back toward the Rhyllster, the fighting grew fiercer for the river was still the lifeblood of the land. Barges loaded with produce were poled down from the highlands to feed Lachlan's army, and fresh troops trained in the safety of Lucescere crossed the river to march down into Blèssem. The Bright Soldiers had been smarting over the loss of Dunwallen for almost two years. They were determined not to lose their grip on the river south of Lochbane, the eighth loch in the chain of lochan called the Jewels of Rionnagan.

Lachlan's army had confounded the Bright Soldiers only that week by crossing the river just south of Dunwallen and striking at their troops on the western bank of the river. Since the Rhyllster flowed swiftly even in the dead of winter and there were no bridges until well past Lochbane, the Tìrsoilleirean army had certainly not been prepared for an attack from that direction. By the time they had gathered their wits and their weapons, the Greycloaks had disappeared again, retreating back across the river.

The berhtilde in charge of the beleaguered battalion had pursued them to the very banks of the river, but had had to rein her horse in sharply to avoid being pitched into the icy waters. Clearly she could see the hoofprints of a large company of riders disappearing into the river then emerging again on the far side, yet she knew that to enter the roiling water was to risk death. Nonetheless she ordered some of her men to spur their horses on, and watched them being dragged under and drowned.

Iseult smiled thinly as she remembered, dismounting so she could stand on the bank of the river. Closing her eyes and holding out her hands, she concentrated on the void, as Meghan had taught her. This was the second half of the challenge of the flame and the void, the skill of lighting a flame and winking it out with merely the power of the mind. When Iseult had first been asked to try it, she had not known how to snuff out the flame, for on the Spine of the World the fire was never allowed to go out. At last she had brought a cold so intense the

sacred fire had turned to ashes and the water in the
scrying bowl had frozen over. It had occurred to Iseult
that the ability to conjure ice would be useful in this
winter campaign, so she had practiced the skill until she
had perfect control over the element.

Slowly the ice at the edge of the river thickened and
spread. She clenched her fists and brought all the
strength of her will to bear on the rapidly moving river.
The ice spread further, rose in delicate arches, spun itself
into a fragile and gleaming bridge. Iseult slumped back,
exhausted, managing to lift one hand to wave the soldiers
on. The infantrymen, who had been watching with awe,
marched quickly across, all holding their breath in case
the ice should crack and throw them into the treacherous
water. The baggage carts trundled after, the drivers whipping the carthorses on in fear, and then the herds of
goats and sheep were urged across, the herdsmen salut-
ing Iseult as they passed.

The Banrìgh struggled to her feet, clinging to her
horse's bridle, her legs shaking. She wondered briefly
how Meghan managed to work such acts of magic every
day without killing herself from exhaustion, then she
mounted again with the help of one of the Blue Guards.

The cavaliers came over the hill in a galloping charge,
whooping and shouting, clanging their lances against
their shields. Activity broke out in the Bright Soldiers'
camp as they scrambled to defend themselves. The
horsemen rode through, knocking down tents, scattering
campfires, striking left and right. As they wheeled to
charge once more, a flock of birds suddenly descended
from the sky, screeching and tearing with their claws and
beaks. There were birds of all shapes, sizes and colors,
from sharp-beaked hawks and ravens to curlews and
swallows. There was even a great golden eagle who had
heard Lachlan's call and flown down from his lonely
eyrie in the Whitelock Mountains.

The Bright Soldiers cursed and ducked, dropping their
swords to lift their cross-emblazoned shields above their
heads. Again the Blue Guards charged through, one of
the enemy toppling at every stroke. The berhtilde screamed

orders, and Lachlan raised his bow and shot an arrow straight through where her left breast had once been. She fell, and the Bright Soldiers cried aloud in consternation. They fought back desperately, and Finlay Fear-Naught's horse was dragged down. Duncan Ironfist wheeled around his great destrier and pulled the young laird to safety. Lachlan called the retreat and they galloped away, catching up burning brands from the fires and throwing them into the tangle of canvas and ropes that had been the Bright Soldiers' pavilions. Iseult summoned the last of her strength and sent fireballs shooting into those tents missed by the cavaliers, so that flame blossomed all around them.

The majority of the horsemen retreated back into the countryside, while Lachlan, Iseult and the Yeomen of the Guard galloped back to the river. Despite the chaos of the camp, thirty or more of the Bright Soldiers pursued the Blue Guards and tried to follow them across the bridge of ice. Iseult, safe on the other side, raised her hand and thought of the warmth of summer, the warmth of a roaring fire. Water began to drip from the arches. Before the Bright Soldiers were more than half-way over, the bridge of ice sagged and collapsed into the raging torrent beneath. Iseult saw only a few despairing faces swirling past, the weight of their armor sucking them down, their horses struggling to keep their heads above the choppy surface. A few horses made it to shore and were lashed in with the other mounts at the end of the train. Most drowned with their riders.

They rode on down the river, elated at the success of their stratagem, but encountered another battalion of Bright Soldiers where the river curved out into the wide waters of Lochbane. Again there was fierce fighting, Lachlan's forces aided once more by the flock of sharp-beaked birds. By sunset they had slashed their way through the ranks of the Tìrsoilleirean and were sheltering in the small town of Balbane. The settlement had been built on a high hill behind stout walls, but over the last few hundred years of peace it had spread out along the shores of the loch. Most of Balbane was now a smok-

ing ruin, invaded and occupied by the Bright Soldiers
and the Fairgean turn and turn about over the past two
years. There was little left but ruined houses and a few
bedraggled hens, which the soldiers ate for their supper,
with thanks to Eà for her providence.

Before dawn, Iseult again conjured a bridge of ice at
the far end of Lochbane, where it narrowed into the
river. They crossed in haste and in silence, leaving behind
a ghost town to puzzle the Tìrsoilleirean troops who arrived with the sun. Three more times they crossed that
day, though Iseult was white and shaking with the effort
of creating bridges of ice sturdy enough to bear so much
weight. So at last they came to Dùn Gorm, the city which
had once been the most magnificent in all of Eileanan
and the Far Islands. Most of it was drowned now, or
filled with sea wrack from the floods, or demolished by
the Bright Soldiers' cannons, or burnt. The broken ruins
that remained bore little resemblance to the great city of
blue marble which had once stood there. Many in the
troops had tears in their eyes as they made their silent
way through the twilight streets.

They were once again on the western bank of the river,
where the barons and rich merchants had built their man-
sions on the high land, giving them a view across the
harbor and firth. The soaring towers of Rhyssmadill
could be seen above the burnt rafters and collapsed
walls, the soft blue of its stone blurring into the sullen
evening sky. The Graycloaks took shelter in the ruins,
Stormwing flying over the park to scout out the position
of the Bright Soldiers. It was cold rations that evening,
despite the chill, for no one was willing to risk lighting
campfires. All were conscious that they were hidden in
the very heart of the territory occupied by the Tìrsoilleirean army. They had won their way through by trickery and guile, but the enemy was all around them and
retreat would be near impossible.

The gyrfalcon reported an army of more than twelve
thousand Bright Soldiers was camped in the palace park,
opposite the great finger of stone on which the palace
was built. The Tìrsoilleirean had their trebuchets, can-

nons and mangonels lined up along the ridge, their tents and pavilions crowded behind. It had been too dark to see how much damage the outer walls of the palace had sustained but the morale of the Bright Soldiers was low.

With a mocking laugh, Stormwing said the ravens had caused much unease among the troops by hovering over the camp, their melancholy cries causing many a superstitious soldier to shudder and make the sign of the Cross above their breasts. Ten of the night-winged birds had been chosen for this task, for the old Tìrsoilleirean superstition that began "one for sorrow, two for mirth" ended with the line "and ten for the devil's own self." It was Lachlan's intention to use every means possible to unnerve the Tìrsoilleirean army.

The size of the army drawn up outside Rhyssmadill alarmed Lachlan a little, for he had only five hundred men-at-arms, five hundred archers and the fifty mounted cavaliers of the Yeomen of the Guard. The other two thousand soldiers of Lachlan's division had been left to guard Dùn Eidean and to engage with those remnants of the Tìrsoilleirean army still occupying Blèssem. The eight hundred cavaliers who had accompanied Lachlan had been left on the eastern shore of the Rhyllster to badger the Bright Soldiers camped along its length. Their aim was to drive the Tìrsoilleirean soldiers back toward Rhyssmadill, straight into the arms of the MacThanach, who was marching toward the Berhtfane with the majority of the Rìgh's army. Even so, the Rìgh's forces would be outnumbered, for the MacThanach had only seven thousand men under his command, their numbers swelled by those who had deserted the Tìrsoilleirean army.

"Let us hope the horsemen o' Tìreich are even now riding through Ravenshaw," Lachlan said grimly, huddling his wings about him. "We will need every man we can muster to break the siege o' the palace."

"Happen I should scry to Meghan and tell her to send the MacSeinn's division to our aid," Iseult said, cuddling close to his side so his wings could warm her as well.

"It would be a month or more before they could get

here, and ye ken they are keeping the Bright Soldiers at bay to the east," Lachlan replied. "We canna risk another few thousand pouring in through the marshes and attacking us from the rear. Nay, we had best hope the MacAhern remembers his duty to the Crown and is riding to our aid. We will ken soon enough! We meet Dughall at dawn—that is, if he can sneak past the Bright Soldiers' sentries into the Tomb o' Ravens."

The ten ravens perched on the broken wall above them gave a bone-chilling cry, and the squires huddled against the wall shivered and hunched their shoulders.

"Happen we should be worrying whether *we* can make the meeting place," Duncan Ironfist said somberly. "We shall have to make our way through the park to reach the tomb ourselves, do no' forget!"

In the gray chill before dawn, mist began to rise from the river, winding through the charred skeletons of the merchants' houses and floating across the park. The tents and pavilions of the Bright Soldiers, the trees lining the long avenue, the muddy, churned-up meadows, all were shrouded in ghostly white. The Tìrsoilleirean sentries huddled into their long white cloaks, stamping their feet on the frozen ground and blowing into their steel-gauntleted hands. Through the mist came the melancholy *tok* of a raven and they shuddered and crossed themselves, shrinking back into the shelter of the tents.

On the far side of the palace park, a long line of men crept through the broken wall and into the gardens, darting from tree to bush to shrubbery, their gray cloaks almost invisible in the gloom. Barnard the Eagle led the way, his sharp-sighted eyes scouting the best route. He saw a Tìrsoilleirean sentry standing against a tree, and quietly and efficiently killed him, the sentry dying without even seeing the hand that killed him. They slipped past a small encampment of guards and made their noiseless way down a long avenue of yews to a great hulk of a building surrounded by the tall evergreen trees. It lay in the very heart of the park, the long, oblong pool that

stretched before it reflecting the dark shapes of the trees
and the white shapes of statues.

Silent as shadows they crossed the paved forecourt and
eased open a great arched doorway surmounted by the
brooding shapes of two stone ravens. Barnard the Eagle
stood guard as the Blue Guards filed past him into the
dank gloom within. He bowed as Lachlan and Iseult went
through, and nodded as Duncan Ironfist whispered a
terse command in his ear. Once all of the soldiers had
gone through the door, he closed it and stood guard with
Finlay Fear-Naught, their claymores drawn.

Lachlan had cupped the Lodestar in his hands and
brought to life the soft light in its heart. Now he raised
it high so they could look about them. A few of the men
muttered in fear as the darkness retreated and revealed
a long hall lined with iron gates leading into smaller
vaults. The ceiling above was arched and domed, with
stone ravens perched above each thick pillar. On either
side were lines of high, stone tombs, each topped with a
figure lying as if asleep, arms crossed over their breasts.
In the uncertain light it was hard to tell whether they
were stone or dead flesh, and the men unconsciously
moved closer together, their murmurs growing louder.
Lachlan shushed them and looked about him curiously,
unable to help his wings lifting and rustling in apprehension. Iseult had her dagger drawn, though her pale face
was expressionless.

They lit torches and began to explore, thrusting the
flame into the smaller vaults to make sure no one hid
within. Dillon, Anntoin, Parlan and Artair stayed close
to Duncan Ironfist's side, clutching the hilts of the small
swords they wore at their sides. Jed whined, slinking
close behind his master, his tail between his legs. They
all rather wished they had stayed behind with the men-
at-arms rather than accompanying Lachlan and the Yeomen on this dawn venture. This dark, echoing hall with
its silent stone figures and watching ravens made their
flesh creep.

Hamish the Hot, at the head of the party, suddenly
gave a cry and stepped back involuntarily. The flickering

light of his torch had found a set of broad steps leading
up to a dais on which stood an ornate sarcophagus. The
stone was all carved with ravens, some in flight, some
sleeping with their heads under their wings, others peck-
ing at the ground. On the lid reposed the figure of a tall
man in archaic dress, a sorcerer's staff in the hands
crossed on his breast, a stone ring on every one of the
stone fingers.

Standing silently on the steps was a tall, cloaked figure.
Lachlan's bodyguard brought their swords up, gathering
closer about their young rìgh. He disregarded them, striding forward with his hands held out. "Dughall!" he cried.
"Thank Eà! It's worried indeed I have been about ye. Is
all well?"

The cloaked figure threw back his hood, revealing
smooth, olive skin, an aquiline nose and a black beard.
Usually exquisitely curled and pointed, Dughall Mac-
Brann's beard was now tangled and dirty, while the
rough clothes under the enveloping cloak were those of
a hunter and trapper. He smiled and moved forward to
embrace Lachlan.

"All is well, as ye can see, my sweet," he said. "I have
been here for some days and am hungry indeed, so hope
ye have brought me some food. Have ye seen the park?
Seething with soldiers, and all bent on breaking
Rhyssmadill."

Lachlan nodded. Dughall smiled sardonically. "It
seems they have bruised their heads, ramming them
against Rhyssmadill's walls these past few years. Indeed
they would have done better to sit on their heels and
starve the garrison out, for all their pretty cannons have
had no effect that I can see."

"Ye must have had trouble coming here from Ravenshaw. Ye would have had to cross the very encampment, surely?" Lachlan said, spreading his cloak to sit
on the steps as Dillon and Anntoin hurried to bring them
food and wine.

His cousin nodded and said, "Aye, we came out o' the
forest with a clutch o' coneys and birds and sold them
to the soldiers. They are as hungry as the palace garrison

must be, having eaten every goat and hen for miles about, and finding the hunting in the forest scarce this winter. Indeed, so they should, for we've had a few lean winters."

His squire had come out of the shadows to stand behind him and serve him. Dughall thanked him, saying, "Lachlan, ye remember Owen, do ye no'? He was one o' the lads Iain MacFóghnan brought out o' Arran with him. He's a cousin o' sorts, and ye may remember I took him with me to Ravenshaw."

Lachlan glanced at the boy, a tall lad with dark hair and solemn gray eyes, and nodded, while Iain smiled and said, "Owen, good it is to see ye. How are ye yourself?"

As the boy replied shyly, the Rìgh settled himself more comfortably on the cold stone steps. "Speaking o' Ravenshaw, I am anxious indeed to hear all the news," he said. "How is your father? What o' the MacAhern? Tell me how your mission went."

While they all broke their fast, the squires only sitting down to eat once their masters had finished, Dughall brought Lachlan and Iseult up to date with his adventures.

"We had a fierce time throwing off the Bright Soldiers from Ravenscraig," he finished, "but with my father peppering them with boulders from the castle walls and the thigearns attacking from the rear, we were at last able to drive them off. I am sure that many o' them fled here to swell the forces camped outside Rhyssmadill. The Bright Soldiers have had a taste o' the MacAhern's fury—I think they will no' be best pleased to see the horsemen on their tail once more."

Lachlan smiled rather grimly, then asked for many logistical details, which Dughall supplied as best he could.

"My father has also been gathering together his forces to bring to your aid," he continued once the Rìgh was satisfied. "Ye ken Ravenshaw is no' heavily populated, and most of the lowland villages and towns were hit hard by the Tìrsoilleirean. He should be able to gather together a thousand men or more, though, most of them archers. Ye ken the longbowmen o' Ravenshaw are fa-

mous for their skill. There is no' much else to do in
Ravenshaw save hunting."

"Let us hope they can make it in time," Lachlan said
grimly. "Still, ye have done well, Dughall, and I am
grateful indeed."

His cousin made a mocking bow. "Shall we go on?"
he said. "It is past dawn and the tide is full. I am anxious
that we make it through the sea caves before the tide
turns again and fills the caves. We have only a short time
if we do no' wish to be drowned."

Lachlan stood and stretched, his wings extended to
their full height, then held out his hand to help Iseult to
her feet. "Come, *leannan*," he said. "I am curious indeed
to see these mysterious sea caves o' the MacBranns. I
remember my brothers and I spent a whole summer exploring Rhyssmadill trying to find the entrance. That was
before the new palace was built, o' course. In those days
it was just an auld, gray castle, half in ruins. The Mac-
Branns had no' lived there for a long time syne. I am
most intrigued to be here in the Tomb o' the Ravens.
We never thought o' looking here for the entrance."

"Tell the truth," Dughall said sardonically, "ye would have
been afraid to explore the tomb in those days."

"No' just in those days," Lachlan said, looking about
him with a shudder of his wings. "Indeed, it is an eerie
place, with all these stone coffins. Those figures look
as if they might just decide to get up and walk around.
That one up there has a most unpleasant expression on
his face. I certainly would no' like to meet him on a
dark, stormy night."

"That, my sweet, is Brann the Raven himself," Dughall replied with a spurious note of reproof in his voice.
"A most powerful sorcerer, by all accounts, and no' one
known for his benevolence. It was said he spent most o'
his life exploring the darker mysteries o' the One Power.
Come, ye shall have to get a lot closer to auld Brann if
ye wish to explore the sea caves."

He led the way up the stairs to the dais and, keeping
his body between the sarcophagus and the soldiers,
twisted the sphere at the head of the stone staff. There

was a grinding noise and the sarcophagus swung sideways, revealing a set of very steep steps leading in a tight spiral downward.

Dughall cast them a mischievous look. "Come on down into Brann's grave," he invited. "I canna promise ye the auld laddie does no' walk—it was said he was a master o' the forbidden arts and spent most o' his last years trying to outwit Gearradh. I do no' know if he succeeded, but in his last days he swore he would reach out from the very grave itself and pull her warty nose."

Even Iseult looked grave at this light-hearted reference, in this place of death, to she who cuts the thread. Casting apprehensive looks about them, the first of the Blue Guards clambered down into the tomb. Duncan Ironfist insisted that the Rìgh and Banrìgh wait until Hamish the Hot and Hamish the Cool had assured the way was safe. At last the word came up that all was clear, and Lachlan and Iseult began the descent, closely followed by their four rather white-faced squires and the miserable dog. Duncan Ironfist came last, finding it difficult to squeeze his shoulders through the narrow aperture.

The spiral staircase descended deep into the earth below the mausoleum, emerging at last in a small room with three crude doorways. Built into the walls of the room were deep shelves piled high with yellowing bones and skulls. Parlan gave a cry and pressed close to Duncan, who gave him a little pat on the shoulder. "Och, my laddie, no need to fear," the big captain whispered. "They've been dead a very long time and it'd take more magic than we have to string those auld bones together and make them walk. Do no' listen to Dughall MacBrann, he just likes to scare ye and the other lads."

Dughall turned and smiled enigmatically. "What do ye think o' your ancestral tombs?" he asked of Owen, who was trying hard not to show his own superstitious fear.

The boy shrugged. "Rather cold and smelly," he answered, and Dughall laughed.

He led the way through one of the doors into a passageway, the fifty Blue Guards following with their smoky torches; Iseult, Lachlan and the boys in the center of the procession. They found themselves in a labyrinth of passages and antechambers, some with faces and magical symbols inscribed on the doors, others with gravestones carved with epitaphs in the floors or walls. Occasionally they reached a long corridor lined with open shelves like those of the first room, heaped with crumbling skeletons, some still clad in shredded rags of clothes or tarnished armor.

"I wonder that the MacBranns allowed their bones to just lie like that," Dide said with a shudder. "Ye would have thought they would have demanded a wee bit more respect."

"Och, those bones are no' those o' the MacBranns," Dughall replied with a grin, enjoying the expressions of fear and horror on the faces of those around him. "They are servants and bodyguards and even pets. The Mac-Branns are properly interred, never ye fear."

Parlan caught hold of the end of Duncan Ironfist's plaid, his face rather green. The big man smiled at him, and said briskly, "Let us go on, all these auld bones are giving me indigestion."

They walked for close on an hour, the passageway often sloping downward or leading to several rough-cut steps, slick and dangerous with water. A dank smell like that of a freshly dug grave flowed over them. The stench was so like that of the Mesmerdean that Iseult felt sick and giddy.

At last they came out onto a wide platform with steps that led down into a reservoir. As far as the eye could see the water stretched, lapping against thick pillars which rose into a vaulted and domed ceiling. The stone of the pillars was stained almost to the roof, though the water level was now slowly dropping. Moored at the edge of the platform were six long rowboats.

"The tide is going out now," Dughall whispered, "and we have almost twelve hours before it reaches its height again. We want to use the flow o' the ebb to carry us— once it turns, it's a hard fight to carry on. Luckily it is winter and the tides are no' at their height. In spring, it is dangerous indeed to attempt to go through the caves."

The light of the torches reflected off the surface of the water, making it look inky black and sending ripples of light dancing over the pillars and vaulted ceiling. Quickly they climbed into the punts, ten or so to a boat. They set the oars to the rowlocks but Iain smiled and called, "No need to row, I can propel the boats without any need for your sweat and strain."

Smoothly the boats glided away from the platform. Iseult put out her hand and touched the stone of a pillar as they slid past. It was cold and slimy, and she wiped her fingers on her breeches in distaste.

Dughall held an old, stained parchment on his lap and consulted it with a frown. He counted the pillars as they passed them and once called over to Iain in the leading boat. Iain nodded and the boats silently changed course, as instantly and instinctively as a school of fish flashing away from the shore.

Soon the platform was lost behind them and Iseult could sense everyone's tightening nerves as they sailed on into the silent forest of overarching stone. Each pillar and curved vault of the ceiling came toward them from darkness and then sank back into darkness, all of them exactly the same. Without the stars or sun to guide them, there was no way to tell direction so deep underground. They began to feel they were drifting in one big circle, destined never to see daylight again.

Dide began to sing a bawdy tavern song but the words echoed so alarmingly that his voice soon faltered. Dughall leaned over the side of the boat, whispering across the expanse of water that separated the boats. "I would no' sing down here, my lad. We are right underneath the Bright Soldiers' camp, and who can be sure the sound would no' be magnified and somehow carried to land above? We do no' wish them to know we sail right beneath their feet."

Dide cast an amazed look up at the vaulted ceiling and sang no more. Dillon kept his hand on Jed's rough

head to keep him quiet, though the dog gave the occasional soft whine.

Just when Iseult thought she could stand the dark and
the silence and the dank smell of enclosed water no
longer, she heard a strange roaring, rushing noise over
her head. The carved pillars gave way to rough-hewn
stone, bulging close on either side and above them. The
boats slipped on through the tunnel, the taller of the
men having to duck their heads to avoid knocking them
on the uneven roof.

"We are under the firth now," Dughall whispered,
more out of awe than any fear of being overheard. "Hear
that noise? That is where the sea rushes through the
ravine which separates Rhyssmadill from the mainland."

They all stared upward, and many of the Blue Guards
gripped their sword hilts a little tighter, thinking of the
great power and volume of water thundering overhead. On
and on through the low, dark, dank-smelling tunnel they
slipped, then suddenly they emerged into a broad cave,
and the boats came to rest below a narrow rock shelf.
Hamish the Cool saw a row of iron rings screwed into
the shelf and swiftly clambered up the rusty, barnacle-
encrusted ladder to tie his boat to one, the soldiers in
the other boats following suit.

By the time the two Hamishes had ensured the way
was safe, the water was beginning to rise. They all hurried up a narrow passageway, the smoke from the torches
stinging their eyes. The stone underfoot and on either
side was slimy and wet. By now all were anxious to see
daylight again, and they trod on each other's heels in
their haste.

Suddenly there was a startled cry, and the procession
came to a halt. "What is it?" Lachlan called.

"The passageway just comes to a complete end, Your
Highness," Cathmor the Nimble replied. "There's some
kind o' pit at the end. I canna see any bottom to it
at all."

Iseult came up behind them and peered over Cathmor's shoulder. He was lying on his stomach, his torch
thrust down as far as he could reach into a deep, round

hole. It dwindled away into darkness, the walls smooth
and mossy.

"Drop a pebble down," Lachlan ordered.

Finlay Fear-Naught scrabbled beneath his feet but there
were no loose rocks to be found. He passed Cathmor a
coin, and Cathmor dropped it into the pit. After a long
wait they heard, very faintly, a small splash.

"Raise your torch, Cathmor, let us see what lies
above," Iseult said. The soldier obeyed. Just above their
heads was a rusty ladder, climbing up into the darkness.

"That's our way free," Lachlan said with satisfaction.
"Cathmor, my nimble one, that looks like a task for ye."

Cathmor grinned and swung himself up, climbing
swiftly up the wall. Soon his boots had disappeared into
the gloom, and Lachlan again brought the light to life in
the heart of the Lodestar, holding it high so they could
see Cathmor's agile progress. Even its silvery radiance
was not strong enough to illuminate the end of the ladder, and they watched their companion climb out of sight
with misgiving in their hearts.

After a long wait they heard a faint scuffle and a heartfelt curse, the sound magnified greatly by the enclosing walls.
Then there was a grating noise and suddenly a small circle of
light appeared far above them. They saw the dark shape
of Cathmor's body blot out the light as he swung himself
out, and then he was gone.

Finlay Fear-Naught, beside himself with impatience, was
begging Lachlan to allow him to go and see what had happened when the circle of light was again blotted out. They
heard Cathmor whistle the all-clear, and Finlay swung himself up and began to climb. The hot-tempered Hamish followed swiftly, then Hamish the Cool and Barnard the Eagle,
then Duncan Ironfist. Only when the big captain was himself satisfied that it was safe were Lachlan and Iseult permitted to follow, though the Banrìgh was as always
impatient with his excessive caution.

Iseult swung herself out of the hole, ignoring Duncan's
proffered hand, and looked about her with interest.
Above her was a peaked, shingled roof held up by four

wooden posts. A large wooden bucket had been tossed aside, its handle secured by rope to an iron rod above her head.

Lachlan was standing beside the structure, laughing. "Who would have guessed it!" he cried. "How many times did we beg one o' the servants to draw up some water for us, never realizing the well hid the entrance to the secret caves! Dughall, did ye know?"

His cousin was just clambering out of the hole. Unlike Iseult, he did not scorn Duncan Ironfist's help, allowing the captain to pull him free. "Nay, my sweet, I only found out the secret to the sea caves this past month. My *dai-dein* was never one for giving away secrets to a snotty-nosed lad, ye ken that. Besides, do ye no' remember that time Donncan and Feargus tried to beat the secret out o' me? Ye think I would have held out if I had known?"

Lachlan smiled, though his expression was tinged with melancholy. The young Rìgh still grieved deeply for his brothers, and any mention of them brought a dark mood that often lasted for days. Seeing his face, Iseult laid her hand on his arm and sought to distract him.

"What do we do now, *leannan*?" she asked.

Her husband was scanning the overcast sky. He uttered the harsh shriek of a falcon, and waited until Stormwing had flown down to his gauntlet before turning to answer her.

"We find the captain o' the garrison and send out some carrier pigeons to Meghan and the MacThanach, just to let them know the plan is progressing as it should," he said. "Come, I'll wager they'll be happy indeed to see us here."

Lachlan would have lost his bet if Iseult had taken him up on it. The captain of the palace garrison was a tall, lean man with a hard, suspicious face and hard, suspicious eyes. Two years of short rations and constant vigilance had honed him to a fine point and, unlike the besieged of Dùn Eidean, he was not at all overwhelmed with joy at the sight of his rìgh.

"What foul sorcery is this?" he cried, drawing his

sword and striding forward to meet Duncan Ironfist. His red cloak swung as he moved, causing the Blue Guards to draw together in scowling formation. Behind the captain stood his officers, also clad in the blood-colored cloaks of the Red Guards, their swords singing as they drew them. "How do ye come here?"

For a moment it seemed as if Red Guards and Blue Guards would come together with a clash. Then Lachlan strode forward. "How dare ye draw swords against your rìgh! We come to relieve ye and this is how ye greet us!"

For a moment the captain's sword remained thrust forward, then he lowered it, saying rather defensively, "Forgive me, Your Highness, but we were no' looking for ye to materialize out o' nowhere. We've been watching for ye for days, ever since we received your carrier pigeon, but could no' see how ye could come to us through such an army that is camped on our doorstep."

Lachlan stepped forward and dropped his hand on the man's shoulder. "This auld place has many secrets ye canna know o'," he said. "It is no reflection on your sentries that ye did no' see us coming. Indeed, we passed right through the blaygird Bright Soldiers and they did no' see us either. Ye have done well, holding Rhyssmadill for so long, with no surety o' help. I ken few soldiers who could have done so. Indeed, ye have proved yourself loyal and true to the MacCuinn clan and so I thank ye in my dead brother's name and in mine."

The captain's stern face relaxed a little, though he could not help eyeing Lachlan's wings with distaste. The Rìgh's mouth thinned a little but he motioned to his squires to bring forward the supplies he had brought with him. "I wager it has been some time since ye've enjoyed a wee dram," he said. "Ye and your men are relieved o' duty from this moment. Ye may eat and drink your fill, and sleep peacefully, knowing that Rhyssmadill is safe and that your rìgh is pleased with ye."

The weary-faced officers broke into relieved talk and laughter, accepting the silver flask that Dillon gave them and passing it between them. The captain remained stern-faced, however, his hand still firm on his sword hilt.

"Will ye no' tell me how ye and your men could just appear out o' thin air?" he said. "What vile act o' magic was this, and if it was so easy for ye, why have ye waited so long to come?"

Lachlan clenched his fists but managed to control his temper. "It was no act o' magic," he answered. "Have ye never heard o' the sea caves beneath Rhyssmadill? We have only just learned the secret o' the caves' entrance. Indeed, my cousin traveled to Ravenshaw at considerable risk to himself to find out the secret from his father, the only living man to ken it. We have had hard fighting indeed these last two years. We have won back all o' Rionnagan, Aslinn and Blèssem from those damned bloodthirsty invaders and have driven them from Ravenshaw and Tìreich, at a great cost to us all and with many lives lost. I know ye have been trapped here for many months, without news or succor, but I assure ye we have no' been just sitting around twiddling our thumbs!"

Despite himself, the Rìgh's voice had risen in anger and the captain flushed, dropping his eyes and muttering a sullen apology. Lachlan took a deep breath then said, more gently, "But ye must ken ye are likely to see sorcery performed in the defense o' this palace, for our reign is loyal to Eà and the Coven o' Witches. I know ye were a captain o' the Red Guards but the cruel reign o' the Awl is broken. Ye have shown yourself loyal to the MacCuinns, rightful rulers o' Eileanan and the Far Islands. I ask ye now if ye wish to remain loyal to me and serve me. If your conscience dictates otherwise, there will be no castigation, for it is the belief o' the Coven that all men are free to think and worship as they please, as long as they do no harm to others. Once we have won the day ye will be free to go where ye please and ye will receive your pension in thanks for the many years o' service to my brother Jaspar. Until then ye must remain under guard for we canna risk betrayal, as I am sure ye must understand. I hope that ye will stay and serve me and swear to me, though, for indeed dark days are upon us and I need all the good men I can find."

As he spoke Lachlan fixed all of the men in the room

with his unwavering yellow gaze and though some looked away and fidgeted nervously, many responded with ardor. The whiskey had warmed their thin, tired, over-strained bodies; but more intoxicating than the liquor was the hope and relief the Blue Guards had brought them. Most of them had expected to die slowly and painfully from starvation and disease or, if their will had finally been ground down or their walls broached, in agony as the besiegers took their inevitable revenge.

Like most soldiers they cared little for religion or politics, content to swear fealty to their overlaird and obey the orders of their superiors. The fact that Lachlan and his Blue Guards had managed to creep through the ranks of the Tirsoilleirean army impressed and heartened them and, to a man, they knelt and swore to serve the Mac-Cuinn and be faithful to him.

The captain of the garrison was last to swear and his thin, stern face was grimmer than ever. "I canna like your witch tricks, Your Highness, and am afraid yon Coven has cozened ye, but ye are the MacCuinn and my rìgh and so I will swear fealty to ye and promise to serve ye faithfully."

"That is all I can ask o' any man," Lachlan said, his voice rather thick for the man's words had moved him. "Come, strip off those red cloaks and kilts for indeed they make me sick to my stomach, and let my squires serve ye some food. Ye look like ye've eaten nothing but air for days."

A glint of humor appeared in the captain's hard eyes. "Indeed, there's no rat left living in the cellars and the sea birds have learnt no' to rest on our roofs," he answered. "We even thought about throwing a line and hook over the walls to see if we could catch a fish, but could find no line long enough."

Lachlan smiled and led him to the table. "Well, eat your fill now and then go and catch some rest, man. Indeed, ye deserve it! Duncan, we are going to have to start ferrying the rest o' our troops in through the sea caves, along with fresh supplies and weapons. We will need Meghan and Jorge too, and they must be guarded carefully. How long do ye think it will take till we have everything ready?"

Duncan frowned and counted slowly on his thick, brown fingers. "At least two weeks, Your Highness," he replied after a while. "Let us say three weeks to be sure. There are only two low tides a day, and only those six small boats. It will be difficult to manage it without attracting attention. We had to kill one Bright Soldier today to make it ourselves—they will be extra wary now and will have set extra patrols."

"We have to make sure they stay well away from the Tomb o' the Ravens," Iseult frowned. "I know Elfrida said the Bright Soldiers are superstitious indeed about graves and cemeteries, but if they suspect anything, they will be bound to investigate the mausoleum. I ken I would."

"Call Gwilym the Ugly in," Lachlan said, grinning. "I think it is time we made auld MacBrann walk again."

Mist hung heavily over the dark trees, and the sentry crossed his arms over his breast and rubbed vigorously. His armor was ice cold to the touch and his white cloak did very little to warm him. He peered out into the thick, wooly whiteness and wished he were back at home. He heard a twig crack and shrank back into the shelter of the hemlock tree.

Unlike the berhtildes and the priests, he had no desire to convert these witch-loving heretics to the One God. He himself was no great lover of the Kirk, but all Tìrsoilleirean had to do their military duty, and he had been unlucky enough to be conscripted into the invading army. Here he was, enduring a bitter winter camped outside the tallest, stoutest walls he had ever seen in his life, when he could have been toasting his toes in front of his own fire. For two years they had been besieging this fortress and none of their attacks had made the slightest impression on Rhyssmadill's walls. Most of their cannonballs fell harmlessly into the ravine or knocked a few boulders flying from the rocky walls of the crag on which the palace was built. Their catapults and mangonels were just as useless. The only fighting they had seen in two years was against the ferocious sea-faeries who twice a year rode into the firth on their sea serpents and forced them to scramble to safety in the hills or countryside.

He and his fellow soldiers were cold, hungry and more than a little apprehensive. Rumors of ghosts and curses and spells were being whispered around the campfires, making them all edgy and unhappy. Only a few days ago he had himself seen the walleyed prophet who had been plaguing their troops. He had appeared out of the mist, pointing his frail, shaking hand directly at the soldiers and intoning, "Doom to those who disturb the peace o' the dead. Doom to those who dare defy she who cuts the thread. Doom!"

By the time they had gathered their wits together and gone after him, the strange old man had gone. Although they searched the parklands with drawn swords and flaming torches, he had simply disappeared. Their berhtilde ordered a party of twelve soldiers to once again search the tomb that lay in the heart of the park. They did so reluctantly, their swords trembling in their gauntleted fists. The Bright Soldiers had a profound respect for prophets. All there remembered Killian the Listener and knew he had foretold the downfall of the elders of the Kirk. Everyone knew about the riot at Dùn Eidean, and the appearance of the angel of death. They knew many of their comrades-in-arms had thrown down their weapons and defected to the army of the winged warrior, and only the threat of the berhtildes prevented them from defying their officers and doing the same.

The tomb was cold and silent, though all felt as if the stone ravens perched on the rim of the scrolled pillars were watching them. Thrusting their torches into every antechamber, the soldiers suddenly heard a weird swishing sound and spun around, swords raised. Floating down the steps was the figure that had been lying on the dais. His eyes glowed with unearthly green light, and he moaned eerily. His mouth was stretched into a travesty of a grin, and his hands groped for them. As one the twelve soldiers turned and fled.

The sentry shuddered at the memory. That ghostly figure still haunted his dreams. He just hoped it was not an omen of coming death, for he greatly wished to see his home again and drink apple cider on his porch on a long summer evening. He shifted his shoulders, still raw from the whipping he had endured. Half their number had been executed for their cowardice. He was just grateful that he was one of the six who had survived, even though they had been severely beaten and given night duty around the tomb, much to their horror.

Again he peered out into the mist. For several hours he had heard soft sounds—hurried footsteps, leaves rustling, a horrible dragging sound. He shivered and huddled back against the hard bole of the tree. Although he hated and feared the berhtildes, he feared ghosts even more. He would stay quiet and still and hope the phantom sounds disappeared with the night.

Trumpets sounded with a flourish. A white-clad herald strode to the edge of the ravine, carrying a pennant marked with a scarlet fitché cross. He unrolled a scroll and began to read out the Tìrsoilleirean army's demands. He had done this many times over the past two years and his voice was flat and rather hurried. Once he reached the end of the scroll, he turned to go back to the meager shelter of his tent without waiting for any reply. The faint sound of a shout from the palace on the opposite side of the ravine stopped him in his tracks.

The captain of the garrison was leaning over the battlements of the gatehouse, his hands cupped over his mouth to try and make his words carry further. Even so, the dawn wind caught the sound and carried it away. The herald cupped his hand to his ear and the captain made a sweeping motion with his hands, as if inviting them in. Then his head disappeared from view. To the herald's complete astonishment, he soon heard a loud grating as the drawbridge began to lower. He turned and ran ponderously back toward the pavilions, his heavy armor and the rough ground making his progress difficult.

By the time the drawbridge had crashed down, a company of cavaliers and infantry had hurriedly been ordered into place. Caught between suspicion and elation, the Tìrsoilleirean seanalair ordered them to cross the drawbridge and investigate.

"We know there can only be a handful o' defendants left and they must be weak indeed from hunger, but we had best make sure they have no tricks up their sleeve," he said to the captain of the berhtildes, a massive woman with one pendulous breast.

She nodded, saying, "Aye, they must be desperate by now, so many dead they've thrown over the cliffs this past winter. They have sent no emissary out, though, which makes me doubt they mean to surrender."

"Then why open the drawbridge?" the seanalair answered, waving the soldiers forward. "They must have seen the size o' our encampment. They canna hope to withstand us."

The foot soldiers marched across the slender stone bridge and then onto the wooden drawbridge, their boots sounding like the rattle of hailstones. As they passed under the sharp points of the portcullis they glanced up apprehensively as if expecting it to come crashing down upon their heads. It did not move, however, and they disappeared into the barbican.

On their signal the cavalry trotted forward, their horses as heavily armored as the riders, who had their helmets lowered over their faces.

Beyond the portcullis was a long tunnel running through the thick enclosure wall and under the barbican. It led out into a courtyard surrounded by the solid, fortified walls of the gatehouse. The only windows were long, narrow slits and the ironbound oak doors leading into the watchtowers were all locked. All was quiet.

The horses shifted uneasily and the captain of the cavaliers dismounted, issuing terse orders to ram the doors open. Then one of the foot soldiers tried the inner gate and found it unlatched. With shouts of excitement, they flung it open and ran through to the outer bailey. Beyond was the palace, enclosed within the inner wall. Its tall

spires and towers soared above the walls, which were of
much older and cruder workmanship.

Confident now, the soldiers spread out, searching
through the maze of stone walkways beyond. The original keep had been designed to withstand just such an
attack as this, however, and a complicated arrangement
of towers, protected gates and ramps forced the attackers
to follow a route devised by the defenders. Before they
knew what was happening, the soldiers were picked off
by archers hidden behind the watchtowers' battlements
or by guards concealed within the walls.

Meanwhile, the soldiers milling around in the courtyard were suddenly deluged with boiling oil. There were
screams of agony as they fell writhing to the ground.
Flaming brands were tossed out the slit windows and
those soldiers to the rear leapt back in alarm as the oil
exploded into flame. The fallen soldiers were engulfed in
fire, rolling in agony on the cobblestones in a vain attempt to extinguish the conflagration.

Holding their shields above their heads to protect them
from the boulders now falling from the battlements, the
soldiers again tried to batter down the doors. Again boiling oil poured down from the windows, but the soldiers
below were protected by their shields and most of it
splattered on the ground without causing harm. The
Bright Soldiers ran back as flaming torches were again
tossed down and waited until the flame had spluttered
out before once more trying to batter down the thick
oak doors. At last they were smashed in, but the first
soldiers to venture through were speedily killed by the
defenders hiding within.

Within the confines of the gatehouse, the Bright Soldiers' advantage of numbers was lost. They had to fight
their way in over the bodies of their fallen comrades,
only to be met by soldiers far better nourished and rested
than they. The Bright Soldiers had been camped outside
Rhyssmadill for so long, hunger, disease and a depression
of spirits had weakened them, and the unexpected feroc-
ity of the defense took them by surprise.

More Bright Soldiers were pounding down the drawbridge, making the inner courtyard so crowded it was hard to move. The cavalry captain tried to wave the rein-forcements back but they misunderstood his gesture and surged inside, almost knocking him off his feet. A few of the great destriers reared, excited by the smell of blood and the sound of swords clashing, and there were screams as foot soldiers were knocked down and tram-pled underfoot.

At last the sheer mass of soldiers forced the defenders inside the gatehouse back, and they ran out onto the battlements, locking the doors behind them. The Bright Soldiers down in the outer bailey saw them and ran with yells of rage and excitement to engage them. The doors into each watchtower were tightly locked, however, and as the soldiers tried to break them down, they too were deluged with boiling oil and ignited with flaming brands.

Lachlan and Iseult were watching from the battlements of the inner wall. Every now and again one would issue a crisp command, and soldiers would run to obey. A squad of Tìrsoilleirean soldiers fought their way through the chaos of the gatehouse, carrying the sharpened trunk of a felled tree with which to pound the gate into the inner bailey. With a ferocious snarl, Lachlan snapped at the archers hiding behind the merlons. They leapt to their feet and fired through the embrasures. The soldiers below fell beneath the rain of arrows, the heavy ram crushing many as it crashed to the ground.

More Bright Soldiers came running to pick up the ram again, but again and again the arrows rained down. Soon the ground beneath the inner wall was piled high with the bodies of the Tìrsoilleirean, but still they kept com-ing, climbing over the corpses of the slain to try and ram the gate down.

Great cauldrons of boiling oil were tipped over the battlements, drenching the thick tree trunk and splat-tering those who struggled to carry it while still holding their shields over their heads. Then the longbowmen dipped their arrows in barrels of burning pitch and shot them into the ram. The oil ignited and the ram began to

smolder. Soon the flame had crept up its length and it
was burning merrily.

Meanwhile, the doors from the watchtowers onto the
rampart had been broken down and fighting now surged
all along the top of the outer wall. Although the
Graycloaks were well rested and well prepared, they
were vastly outnumbered and were slowly being forced
back, overwhelmed by the number of white-clad soldiers
still pouring in over the drawbridge.

The Bright Soldiers carried tall ladders with them,
which they tried to raise against the inner wall. At first
the defenders were easily able to throw them down, but
soon there were so many men climbing the rungs that
those above had trouble pushing them off. The defenders
poured burning oil down the rungs and many of the soldiers jumped off, willing to risk broken bones rather than
being burnt to death.

Then sharp-eyed Iseult saw a wagon piled high with a
hastily dismantled siege tower being whipped across the
stone bridge. Behind it trundled another wagon armed
with a massive trebuchet, capable of catapulting huge
iron balls and boulders nearly three hundred yards. It
would certainly do a great deal of damage to Rhyssmadill's defenses if the Bright Soldiers were able to get it
through to the outer bailey.

Iseult gripped Lachlan's arm and pointed. "Time, do
ye think?" she said. They looked about them and saw
that the sheer force of numbers was slowly overwhelming
their own defense. Grimly Lachlan nodded. "Aye, I think
so," he answered. Lachlan beckoned to Parlan, who ran
to his side, his face white with fear. "Call the Keybearer," Lachlan snapped. "It is time for her and the
witches to do their work."

Meghan, Jorge and Gwilym hobbled out of the corner
turret where they had been sheltering and Dughall came
striding along the battlement, Iain on his heels. They had
already prepared a circle of power and each of the five
witches hastily took up positions at the points of the
pentagram drawn within the circle.

They held hands and, as the wheels of the first wagon

clattered onto the wooden drawbridge, shut their eyes and
concentrated. Suddenly the drawbridge disintegrated beneath the weight. With screams of terror, the carthorses
were flung down into the chasm, the wagon plunging
after. The horses pulling the second wagon had already
set foot on the drawbridge and they too fell, the weight
of the great catapult propelling the wagon over the edge.
Down, down, into the raging torrent the wagons fell, to
be smashed to pieces on the rocks below.

"Shame about the horses," Lachlan said tightly.

Iseult nodded, her face grim. She could see the rage
and consternation of the troops left on the far shore, and
the sudden panic of the soldiers trapped within the palace. Without hope of reinforcements or retreat, they
could be slowly and comfortably slaughtered at the defendants' leisure.

For the next hour there was close hand-to-hand fighting all through the outer bailey and along the rampart,
but gradually the Bright Soldiers were overcome and
those who were not killed were taken prisoner and
herded down to the palace cellars where they were left
under lock and guard.

Meanwhile, the Bright Soldiers on the far shore had
not been idle. With renewed fury they had rearmed their
cannons and trebuchets and begun firing at the palace
perched on its finger of stone. Most of the boulders and
cannonballs fell harmlessly into the ravine, but a few
pounded into the outer walls; then the witches brought
rain sweeping in from the sea to dampen their fuses and
gunpowder and render the cannons useless once again.

The Bright Soldiers tried to make a ramp to cross the
open space between the edge of the bridge and the yawning gateway, once closed off by the drawbridge. Once
or twice they almost succeeded but the witches simply
disintegrated the ramps with a thought and those soldiers
manning them fell screaming into the ravine.

Iseult and Barnard the Eagle had climbed to the top
of the highest tower and were watching anxiously for any
sign of their own reinforcements. At last Iseult saw a
great, dark mass sweeping in from the east. Inexorable

as a flood, the Rìgh's army marched through the rolling
meadows until it finally reached the Rhyllster. She saw
the columns and squares break up as the Bright Soldiers
defending the bridges moved to engage. She sent Dillon
running to Lachlan with the news, excitement thrilling
through her. The MacThanach had seven thousand men
under his command, three thousand of them Tìrsoilleirean prisoners-of-war or deserters who had sworn allegiance to the MacCuinn. It was their hope that many
among the Bright Soldiers camped in the park would
join their comrades, the ground well prepared by Jorge's
prophecies and the tales of miracles and marvels.

Iseult watched until it was clear the Graycloaks had
seized the bridges over the Rhyllster and were advancing
through the ruined city, then she turned her attention to
the north and west, where Barnard was leaning out over
the battlements, his hand shading his eyes. They were
expecting fresh troops from Lucescere to attack the
Bright Soldiers from the rear, having marched through
the Ban-Bharrach hills and along the foot of the
Whitelock Mountains. Murdoch of the Axe had been
sent to guide them and had promised to bring Lachlan
and Iseult nearly a thousand men and women, though
most were untried and only half trained. The element of
surprise would be their greatest weapon, and Iseult
hoped that all the activity at the palace would distract
attention from the back gate.

Lachlan had sent Stormwing to fly over the palace park
and the gyrfalcon soon circled down to report Murdoch's
company had crept in through the back gate and were
advancing stealthily through the woods.

With a brief but heartfelt prayer of thanks, Iseult and
Barnard then hurried to the west wall and gazed out
anxiously.

The great forests of Ravenshaw stretched away to the
west and it was impossible to see anything through the
tangled branches, but Iseult watched until her eyes ached,
nonetheless. Dughall had promised them the MacAhern
would come but they had had no word, and since they
did not know him, they could not scry to him for news

of his approach, nor could the falcon's keen eyes pierce the forest's thick canopy. Dughall was down with the other witches, bombarding the white tents on the far shore with fireballs and making sure all attempts to cross the chasm failed. Iseult had just decided that she would ask him to try and reach the MacAhern that evening at sunset when Barnard touched her arm respectfully.

"Look, Your Highness," he said. "There is some disturbance at the forest's edge."

She glanced where he pointed and saw a small white figure running toward the western boundary of the Bright Soldiers' camp. Then white-clad soldiers were frantically gathering together their weapons and scrambling into defensive formation, their faces turned to the forest. Her heart lifted, and then she saw a wide column of cavalry trot out from under the shelter of the trees, pennants flying.

For a moment they paused at the edge of the open parkland, surveying the vast tangle of tents and pavilions that stretched before them, large as a town. Then the horses broke into a gallop, streaming down the slope toward the Bright Soldiers' camp.

"Quick!" Iseult called to Anntoin. "Run and tell Lachlan the MacAhern is here as promised! We shall surely win the day now!"

By sunset it was all over. Seven thousand Bright Soldiers lay dead on the field, their white surcoats torn and reddened. The churned-up soil was wet with blood, and smoke from the burning siege machines hung heavy as fog, half obscuring the trampled tents and tattered flags. The moans of the injured rent the dusk, and as Meghan and her healers moved through the tangle of overturned wagons and broken picket lines, hands reached out to them, pleading for succor.

All were tended, whether dressed in white surcoats, gray cloaks or the black cassocks of the Tìrsoilleirean clergymen. By the light of flickering torches, the healers washed and bound, stitched and splinted, administered healing potions and pain-numbing drugs. Soldiers, many of them bandaged themselves, helped carry the worst injured into the shelter of the palace.

Tòmas walked among them, laying his hands on all he passed, even though his fingers trembled and great, purple bruises hung beneath his eyes. He wept as he worked, the tear tracks running white down his grimy, blood-smeared face.

After a while Johanna came and led him away. "Ye will kill yourself if ye lay hands on them all," she scolded. "Come and eat and rest a while, and ye can touch them again when your strength has returned." He dragged against her hand, protesting, but her grip was firm and he was too worn out to fight her.

The little boy was too late to save the MacThanach, who had died at the crossing of the Rhyllster. The death of the bluff, hearty man weighed on them all, for the MacThanach had proved most staunch and loyal over the past two years. Also among the dead were Hamish the Hot and Hamish the Cool, who had died in the defense of Rhyssmadill's gatehouse, and Cathmor the Nimble, who had been shot through the throat in the last furious minutes of fighting. Lachlan was distraught at the loss of three of his most faithful officers, and he wept with the other Blue Guards as they laid them out in state in the great hall, wrapped in their plaids with their claymores on their breasts.

"More dead for the Tomb o' Ravens," he said somberly. "Indeed, Gearradh has eaten well this day."

Although the army celebrated that night with what scanty supplies they had, the Rìgh sat sunk in a black melancholy, his face haggard with weariness and grief. Iseult sat with him silently, her blue eyes somber. Every now and again she poured him some more whiskey, and once she said with unusual gentleness, "The purpose o' battle is slaughter and the price o' victory is blood. That is the nature o' war."

He cast his glass away from him, saying, "Ye think to comfort me thus? Eà damn ye and your Scarred Warrior proverbs!"

She shrugged. "Who said I tried to offer comfort?

What comfort is there in lost friends and comrades? I do but tell ye what war is. Ye did always think it was like the songs o' the jongleurs—a game o' chivalry and tactics like that game o' chess ye play with Finlay. Well, it is no'. The purpose o' battle is slaughter and the price o' victory is blood."

When he said nothing, she rose and went to leave, but he caught her arm as she went by and pulled her to him, burying his face in her lap. He took a sobbing breath, like a child, and she smoothed his unruly black hair. "Come to bed, *leannan*," she said. "We have waded in death today; let us drown ourselves in love and forget. We at least are alive and there is something in that."

THE SOUL-SAGE

As swiftly and effortlessly as a bird, Isabeau glided down the snowy hillside. With a slight sway of her body she changed direction, curving round to leap off a mound, spinning in the air and landing gracefully with an arcing spray of snow.

As the slope steepened, her descent accelerated until the cold wind was rushing past her face like the brush of fire. Tears streamed down her face and she rubbed her eyes with her white gloved hand to clear her vision. Her skimmer hit a slick of ice and she skidded at a breakneck speed, spun and almost fell, before flying on at an even greater pace. Isabeau whooped in excitement, and swerved again to leap off another round hump of snow. The blue sky spun beneath her feet, the snowy mountains blurring as the blood rushed to her head, then she was upright again, her skimmer landing on the slope with a loud thwack. Her feet shot out from under her, for a moment her arms windmilled wildly, her body bending backward, then she regained her balance and the snow again hissed under the wood of her skimmer.

"Woah!" Isabeau cried. "That was close!"

She came to a curving halt under a copse of trees, wiping her streaming nose with her gloved hand and trying to catch her breath. Her cheeks stung and she felt extravagantly, thrillingly alive.

Above her, needle-sharp mountains stabbed their icy points into a clear, bright sky, while the smooth, white slopes fell down as far as the eye could see, broken only by the occasional copse of dark trees. The snowy hillside was marred with the swooping, erratic line of her descent, and Isabeau frowned a little, knowing her Scarred Warrior teacher would have a few scathing words to say about her style. She looked rather longingly at the steep white slope plunging ahead of her, then up at the sun which was slowly curving down toward the mountains. It was a long walk back up to the Haven, and if she wished to be back before nightfall she should turn back now.

Reluctantly Isabeau bent to unstrap the skimmer from her feet. Her eye was caught by a flash of gold, and she looked up, excitement and pleasure quickening her pulse.

A dragon was soaring above the mountains, the sun shining on her gleaming scales. Her clawed wings were spread wide, thin as parchment, and her long tail writhed behind her. Isabeau raised her hand and called: *Asrohc!*

Greetings, little human! The dragon responded mockingly, her mind-voice as always echoing through the chambers of Isabeau's body so that she felt rather nauseous.

Do ye fly for pleasure or are ye on a journey? Isabeau asked.

Flying is always a pleasure, the dragon replied, folding her wings and doing a graceful, plunging somersault.

If I skim to the bottom o' the mountain, will ye meet me there and fly me back to the top? Please?

Perhaps.

Please?

I will see how I feel when thou reachest the depths of the chasm. Perhaps I shall have a whim to be amused by thine odd human eccentricities, perhaps I shall prefer to gnaw on a wurm, bloody carcass. I have seen no deer or geal'teas running so it is probable I shall be in the mood for some diversion.

The dragon had flown down out of the peaks and was now gliding across the meadows, her huge shadow passing over the humps and dips like the shadow of a thundercloud. As the shadow passed over her, Isabeau felt her knees tremble and her stomach clench in fear, even though she had often flown on the dragon-princess's back in the past eighteen months.

The young dragon soared away over the valley and Isabeau watched her, indecisive. She glanced back down

the steep, pristine slope then gave in to temptation, following the dragon's shadow in long, swooping curves.

As her blood quickened, the snow flying away beneath
her skimmer, Isabeau forgot her guilty apprehension,
shouting in delight as she leapt and spun over the humps.
The slope steepened and fell away beneath her so that
she really was flying, rushed up to meet her so she fell
in a tangle of limbs, hissed away again under her skimmer, rolling and dipping faster than a horse could gallop.
She reached the bottom of the hill in a slither of snow,
having to turn so sharply to avoid crashing into the trees
that her velocity carried her curving back up the hill
again. Isabeau bent over, legs trembling with exhaustion,
breath sharp in her side, and rested her fists on her knees
until she had caught her breath. Then she looked up and
scanned the sky. There was no sign of the dragon.
Asrohc?

There was no answer. Anxiety leapt in her. *Asrohc!*

The sun was sliding down into the sharp-pointed peaks
and shadows were falling across the valley. The only
sound was the quiet stammer of water tumbling along
under ice. Isabeau felt panic squeeze her throat muscles
shut until she could hardly breathe. She had no chance
of reaching the Haven before night came. If the dragon
did not respond to her call, she would have to spend the
night out in the snow and she knew her chances of sur-
vival were low indeed. Many who lay down to sleep in
the snow never woke again.

Isabeau looked about her, trying to calm the panic
threatening to overwhelm her. She should have known
better than to have relied on the dragon's good nature.
Dragons were not known for their benevolence. Just because Asrohc sometimes let Isabeau fly on her back did
not mean the dragon-princess felt any more warmly to
her than a dog did to the fleas that rode on its back. No
doubt the dragon had seen a herd of *geal'teas* that she
could run to their death or simply grew bored with the
view and returned to Dragonclaw. Isabeau had to think
what best to do.

She unstrapped the skimmer and tied it to her back

then looked about her. The slope was steep, snow
mounding against the boles of the conifer trees. Round
humps concealed rocks and fallen logs along the narrow
base of the valley, where black ice showed where a
stream would run in summer. She looked back the way
she had come and her spirit quailed at the height of the
mountain. It would take many exhausting hours to clamber back through the deep snow to the heights and she
had to suppress a bitter thought against the dragon,
knowing Asrohc would probably hear it.

With a sigh she began to slog along the base of the
valley, looking for somewhere to set up camp. Although
her teacher had often warned her about the dangers of
the valleys, she thought she was more likely to find a
cave or hollow tree down here than up on the bare,
windswept slopes. Far better that she find some shelter,
build a fire and wait out the long, freezing night than
exhaust herself trying to climb the mountain. She could
begin the long climb home in the morning, when she was
rested and could see the many pitfalls of the mountain
clearly.

Isabeau found a fallen tree that had created a small cave
between the rock face and its snow-laden trunk. She
crept inside, swearing and shivering as her movement
sent snow slithering down onto her back. She huddled
her furs around her and scraped around for twigs and
branches with which to build a fire. Normally Isabeau
was not permitted to use her witch powers while on the
Spine of the World, the Firemaker and her kin being
constrained by strict laws and customs. The pride were
safe in the Haven, however, so Isabeau had no hesitation
in summoning a spark of fire and feeding it with her own
powers until the wood was dry and a cheerful fire
crackling.

As night fell and a bitter wind rose, Isabeau turned
her hands upward on her thighs and began to meditate
in order to distract her thoughts from her cold and hunger and apprehension. She had spent many hours meditating with the Soul-Sage during her first winter on the
Spine of the World, and her lessons had continued in

greater depth since she had returned to the pride a few weeks earlier. Isabeau slipped easily now into a light trance, the distractions of the outside world drowned beneath the billowing beat of her own heart and breath.

It seemed as if she slipped out of her body and hung in the night, as pale and insubstantial as her own frosty breath. Faintly she heard a voice, as if in a dream. *Child*, it whispered. *Child . . .*

She twisted, as if listening, and heard the voice more clearly. Instinctively she wavered toward the voice. She felt fear, for the soft vapor of her being was dispersing in the wind, but then she saw, dim and far away, the angular face of the Soul-Sage. She was haloed in silvery light, her thin body floating behind like candle-smoke, and a long, throbbing cord trailing behind her, twisting back through the starry sky. *We are coming. Beware . . .*

Isabeau came back to consciousness with a jolt, her head and heart pounding, a strong feeling of nausea almost overcoming her. Her fire had sunk down to embers and it took a great effort of will to bring it back to leaping life. She huddled her furred hood close about her face and tried not to think about food.

After a long period of silence when Isabeau nearly nodded off to sleep, she heard the sound of crashing branches and the pounding of heavy feet in the valley outside. Her fear returned in greater force. There were demons in the valleys, her teacher had said. She thought they must be the same creatures that she had heard described in *The Book of Shadows* as ogres, truly monstrous-sounding creatures. She seized a burning branch from her fire and gripped it tightly as the crashing came closer.

The wind shifted, bringing with it a foul stench. Suddenly a massive hand swept in under the tree trunk. Dark and scaly, it was tipped with curved black claws that caught Isabeau's leg. She scrambled back, thrusting the fiery branch against it. The ogre howled and the huge, scaly hand was snatched back. The reverberating howls died down into whimpers, then suddenly the ogre's thick fingers again swept in under the fallen tree trunk and

Isabeau was knocked flying. She scrambled back against the rock, panting with fear, and then the groping hand found her fire. The ogre screeched with pain again, and Isabeau brought the fire blazing to life so flames ran up the rough, scaled fingers. He snatched back his hand, dragging the tree trunk away at the same time.

Isabeau, crouched in terror against the rock, watched as the monster hopped around the clearing, nursing his burnt fingers. Over ten feet tall, he was a hunched, broad figure, his limbs covered with scales, his body bristling with hair. His huge, misshapen head was a grotesque shadow against the stars, tusked and knobbly, with huge eyes that burnt with a reddish flame. He whimpered and sucked his fingers, then turned again to search for her, but Isabeau had slipped away under the cover of the trees, her white furs blending in with the snow. He raised his hideous snout and sniffed the air, then gave a screech of excitement and bounded after her.

She could not run very easily, hampered by the deep snow and the darkness, and in a few seconds he was upon her. Luckily his hands were so large and clumsy she was easily able to evade his sweeping grasp, grateful for her Scarred Warrior lessons that had taught her to sway away from a blow as effortlessly as a willow in a breeze. She foundered in the snow, though, and fell and his hand came down upon her, trapping her within the cage of his claws.

Suddenly Isabeau heard wild yells. Flat on her face, almost paralyzed with terror, she was able to look up and saw through the bars of her prison a long chain of flaming torches swooping down through the darkness. Relief flooded through her. She scrabbled at her belt and unsheathed her dagger which she thrust up into the hard, scaly palm above her. Although it must have pained him no more than the sting of a midge, he yelped and lifted his hand long enough for her to wriggle out and slide into the shadow of a snow-heaped bush. He snuffled about looking for her, then smelt the torches and looked up. He gave a loud yell of challenge and reared up, shaking his fists. Catcalls and cries replied him, and then tall,

dark shapes came whizzing out of the darkness, snow
flying up from their skimmers. There was the zing of *reils*
being flung, and the ogre yelped and swiped out with his
fists. For a moment he stood his ground, but the Scarred
Warriors were too many and too fierce, and so he gave
one last cry of defiance and blundered off into the
darkness.

"Khan?"

"Yes, I am here," Isabeau replied, crawling out from
under her bush and shaking off the snow. "I am so glad
to see you all!"

The Scarred Warriors did not reply, just unstrapped
their skimmers and began to climb back into the snowy
darkness. Only one waited for her to retrieve her own
skimmer and she could feel his cold disapproval even
though he said not a word. "I am sorry, teacher," she
said tentatively.

"Fool!" he snapped, and gestured to her to follow him.

Tired and chastened, Isabeau followed, her heart failing within her as she thought of the long, hard climb
back up the mountain heights.

They came out of the copse of trees and Isabeau saw
a cluster of flaming torches thrust into the snow at the
bottom of the high, steep slope. There were several long
sleighs there, a team of shaggy, white *ulez* harnessed to
each one. Sitting bolt upright in one was the Firemaker,
wrapped up well against the cold, her snow-lion cloak
raised to cover her head so her pale, autocratic face was
framed by its snarling muzzle.

Isabeau fell to her knees, her head bowed, her hands
crossed over her breast. Amidst her chagrin and apprehension was a sudden spurt of happiness. The Firemaker
had left the safety and warmth of the Haven to come in
search of her. Isabeau's great-grandmother was so cold
and remote that the apprentice witch had come to believe she meant nothing to the old woman. The Firemaker must have some feelings for her, though, to ride
out into the bitter night.

"Fool!" the old woman said, in the same curt tone
that the Scarred Warrior had used, then she lifted her

hand, indicating her great-granddaughter should rise. When Isabeau had obeyed, she said abruptly, "Come here, stupid child."

Isabeau stepped up into the sleigh and the Firemaker embraced her fiercely, then drew her down and tucked the furs around her. "Have you no more thoughts in that fiery head of yours than one of these wooly-brained *ulez*?" she asked angrily, and gestured to the Scarred Warriors to proceed. The sleighs wheeled round and then the *ulez* began the long, slow climb back up the steep slope. Their hooves were flat and spreading, and the *ulez* were strong so the sleighs slipped along quite swiftly. Isabeau snuggled down into the furs, her cheek against the Firemaker's thin hand, and was content.

She was shaken awake much later, as the sleighs reached the heights. The Scarred Warriors gestured to her to climb out and sleepily she saw they had reached the valley of the Haven. Still half asleep she stumbled round the path and into the cave, and saw the Soul-Sage sitting by her fire at the back of the cavern, eyes closed. The Firemaker made a curt gesture of dismissal and Isabeau crept back to her own furs, careful not to disturb the Soul-Sage. As she closed her eyes and began to slip back into sleep, she heard the Soul-Sage whisper, "Have I not told you to never trust the dragon?"

Isabeau was punished for her folly, of course, and her Scarred Warrior teacher was very terse and curt with her when next she went to him for her lessons in *ahdayeh*. She was told later that he too had been punished for her stupidity, for as her teacher he should have impressed upon her the importance of never skimming so far that she could not return to the Haven. Her teacher had told her so many times, and warned her of the dangers of the valleys, so Isabeau was even sorrier that she had ignored his warnings. She worked harder than ever at practicing the thirty-three stances of *ahdayeh*, and at learning his snow-lore, and was glad when his sternness eventually began to soften. She had discovered that although the Khan'cohbans were habitually grave-faced and humorless, they were nonetheless capable of deep friendship and love and it had hurt her to lose some of her teacher's regard.

It was a cold, bitter winter that year and Isabeau wondered often how her family was faring back at the Towers of Roses and Thorns. Feld was so vague he often forgot to feed himself, and she had left the two-year-old Bronwen in his care, as well as Ishbel and the stallion. If her mother had been a different type of woman, Isabeau would not have needed to worry, but Ishbel often exasperated her with her helplessness. Luckily Bronwen was quite capable of demanding her dinner in such a loud and imperious voice that even Feld and Ishbel could not ignore it, and Isabeau knew her mother would have a care for the stallion if not for herself.

The long hours confined to the Haven were enlivened by the tales of the storytellers, some of the most respected members of the pride. The First Storyteller was an old man with a deep voice that could reach every corner of the massive cavern and wonderfully expressive hands. He told only the most important tales, the stories of gods and heroes. The everyday fables of animals and weather and naming quests were told by the younger storytellers, who strove hard to match the power and resonance of the First.

One night, when the wind outside howled like a banshee and the snow had sealed shut the mouth of the cave, the Second Storyteller rose and bowed to the Firemaker, touching his heart, his brow and then sweeping his hand out to the night. She bowed her head and he assumed the storyteller's position, legs crossed, back straight, hands resting on his lap. Most of the pride brought their furs to the central fire, children curling by their parents' side, heads in their laps.

"Tonight I shall tell the tale of the name quest of he who tamed the dragon and so became First among warriors in the Fire Dragon Pride. This is the tale of he who was the youngest to receive the seventh scar, he who crossed his leg across the dragon's back and flew away, to be lost in the land of the sorcerers."

Isabeau had already been sitting up eagerly, for she

loved the tales of the storytellers. Grand and tragic, the stories often made her weep or left her with a sense of awe and humility. At the Second's words, though, she leaned forward, her lips parting, eyes shining. This was the tale of her father and she had longed to hear it.

Her father had been born of tragedy, it was told. The daughter and heir of the Firemaker had died while giving birth to twins, and to the great sorrow and consternation of the pride, her baby daughter had died with her. Her son had lived but none knew what should be done with him, for in the custom of the pride, the male of the Firemaker's twins was given to the Gods of White as sacrifice and restitution. If he was left out in the snow as usual, however, the Firemaker's line would die out and there would only be the false Firemaker left, the descendant of the child rescued by the Old Mother of the Pride of the Fighting Cats so many years before. The hatred between the Prides of the Fire-Dragon and the Fighting Cats was cold and hard like glacial ice. The council decided to let the baby boy live.

The storyteller's intonation changed, his hand gestures quickened. The child had grown up quick and fiery and proud, and was beaten often for his impetuosity and de fiance. Though he was not as tall or as strong as others his age, he grew adept at the art of the Scarred Warrior. Only his proud temper held him back from true skill, for anger is often the flaw of the warrior that is beaten. His thirteenth long darkness came and it was debated whether he was ready to face his naming quest. The child leapt to his feet and swore angrily that he was ready, more than ready. He would come back with a strong name and a powerful totem, the strongest and most powerful of them all. He was mocked and the Firemaker frowned and said he was too young and undisciplined. Defying her, the child caught up his skimmer and weapons and went out into the night.

It was a bitter winter that year, the storyteller said, a winter of ice storms and the white wind, cruelest of them all. Hungry, the frost giants had raged across the meadows, every step precipitating avalanches. Hungry, the timber wolves had hunted in howling packs, and the saber leopards had snarled and savaged their mates over the corpses of birds that had fallen, frozen, out of the sky. It was a bitter winter that year, the Second said, his long fingers bent like claws.

The long darkness passed and some of the other children returned, wearing the furs of bear or wolf or boar to show their totem and their name. Proudly they told the tale of their name quest and with pride their parents scarred them. The kin of the Firemaker did not return, and her grief was deep and bitter.

The white wind had died away and the snow was softening when the people of the pride one day heard the bugling of a dragon. In terror and anger they seized their weapons and rushed out to protect their herds from the dreaded dragon, who could devastate the pride with one blast of his fiery breath. They saw a great golden queen-dragon circle down out of the sky. On her back rode the Firemaker's kin, his face alight with triumph. He sprang down from the dragon's back and she bowed to him and spoke to him in her own, terrible language. On the child's back was no animal skin to show his totem but in his hand he carried a handful of golden jewels, the rarest and most precious of jewels, the dragoneye stone. Turning to the pride he told them the tale of how he had found the queen-dragon's young daughter injured and helpless on the rocks, having been caught in the white whirlwind and flung to the ground. He could have killed her then, for she was young and sorely hurt, but instead he tended her wounds and shielded her from the ravening beasts that would have devoured her living flesh. There, on the Skull of the World, the Gods of White had spoken to the child and for once their words were not of slaughter and conquest, but of mercy. Child no longer, the Gods of White had named him Khan'gharad, Dragon-Rider.

A long sigh issued from the crowd and some turned and glanced at Isabeau, who they knew was the dragon-rider's daughter. Isabeau herself was entranced. She wondered what they would say if they knew this great hero had been ensorcelled, transformed into a beast of burden

and ridden cruelly with whip and spur. She was glad she
had never told them and wished desperately that she
could find some way to bring back her father, warrior of
legends, the dragon-rider.

So wild were the storms that the Scarred Warriors
were also confined to the cavern and, restless and dis-
satisfied, many fights broke out. Although the First Warrior organized daily fighting matches to relieve their
energy and keep their skills well honed, it was difficult
with so many people crowded into the Haven to keep
tempers under control. When blood was drawn one day
after a tall, beautiful weaver moved her furs from the
fire of one warrior to another, the First came to the fire
of the Soul-Sage, asking her to cast the bones and tell
them when the storm would end and his Scarred Warriors could go out and hunt again.

The Soul-Sage nodded and indicated that the First
could sit with her by her fire. Wrapped up well in his
spotted furs, he sat, giving no acknowledgment of Isabeau who was crouched on the other side of the flames.
Isabeau was careful to show no interest in him or the
Soul-Sage, though she was curious indeed.

The Soul-Sage brought the bulging bag out from her
clothing and spread the precious hoard out on the
ground. Isabeau covertly studied them, for she had been
longing to watch the Soul-Sage cast the bones and learn
the art herself.

There were thirteen of them, a rough lump of amethyst, gleaming black obsidian, pure white quartz crystal,
a fiery garnet, a dark blue stone with gold flecks, a finger
bone, a lump of petrified wood, moss agate with a fossilized leaf sketched on its smooth surface, another fossil
of some ancient fishlike creature with sharp teeth, the
huge yellow knuckle of some long-dead monster, a saber-
leopard's fang, a stone glittering with fool's gold, and a
bird's withered claw.

The Soul-Sage took a stick from the fire and drew a
large circle in the earth, quartering it with two swift
strokes. Isabeau's eyes widened, for the quartered circle
was a sacred symbol of the Coven and she found it inter-

esting that two such alien cultures used similar shapes
and concepts.

The Khan'cohban woman cradled the stones and bones
in her hands, her eyes closed, rocking back and forth and
murmuring, then she flung them into the circle without
opening her eyes. For a moment she sat still, while the
First Warrior scanned the circle anxiously, then she
opened her eyes and looked.

Most of the stones and bones had fallen in the upper
half of the circle, the amethyst the highest, almost on the
charred line. The fool's gold was in the bottom left hand
corner close to the curved fang of the saber-leopard and
the finger bone. The quartz crystal and the gold-flecked
blue stone were also high, lying side by side and touching.

The Soul-Sage turned to the First Warrior and smiled.
"The storm shall pass soon. Still weather shall come and
the hunting shall be good. Be careful, though, for other
hunters seek your prey and they are hungry and clever.
Be quiet in your hunting, for the peaks are laden with
snow ready to fall. Too loud and hasty and your warriors
shall be swallowed in avalanche. Be quiet and wary."

The First Warrior made the gesture of heartfelt gratitude, his grim face almost smiling. He rose and bowed
and went back to the central fire.

The Soul-Sage swept the stones together in her hand
and carefully, one by one, passed them through the
smoke of her fire before tucking them back in her bag
of animal skin. She looked up at Isabeau and said sternly,
"No, you may not touch them. No hand but mine can
touch them else they lose their power. If the Gods of
White decide to honor you with the talent of future-
seeing, you will in time find your own bones."

"Will you not explain to me what they all mean,
though?" Isabeau pleaded.

The Soul-Sage indicated the circle. "The universe, the
soul, the life." She pointed to the left half of the circle,
tracing its shape with her multijointed finger. "The night,
darkness, the unconscious, the unknown, the life of
dreams and desires, birth and death." She indicated the

right side. "Daylight, brightness, the known, the real, the achieved, everyday life, the family."

Then she drew the shape of the upper half of the circle with her finger. "Spirit, wisdom, the stars. The future." She traced the lower semicircle. "The flesh, the earth. The past." With a sweep of her palm she wiped the circle away.

"What about the stones? What do they mean?" Isabeau asked eagerly.

The Soul-Sage's eyes flashed beneath their heavy hoods. "Stones mean many things. It is where they lie in the circle, where they lie in relation to each other, what the question is—these decide what they mean."

Isabeau nodded, a little disappointed. The Soul-Sage clicked her tongue, then slowly put her hand into the pouch and withdrew the lump of amethyst. "Healing. Spiritual growth, wisdom. Creativity. A good stone, peaceful, strong." Again without looking she put her hand into the pouch, this time withdrawing the gold-flecked blue stone. Again she flashed Isabeau a glance, this time of surprise and interest. "Skystone. Very powerful indeed. Healing, clear-sight, future-sight. Very sensitive, changes the meaning of everything it touches."

Next she pulled out the lump of white quartz crystal. "Vitality, luck, magic, power. Strong healing stone, clear-seeing, future-seeing. Another powerful stone. After the skystone, this means great spiritual growth and wisdom." She pondered for a long moment, then thrust her hand into the pouch again.

The fourth stone she withdrew was the bird's withered claw. "Flying. Wind and change. Can mean death, can mean wisdom. Interesting." She looked Isabeau over with an intense, raking gaze. "Maybe the scar speaks truly and you indeed have been marked by the Gods of White as a soul-sage. Maybe."

The next stone was the red garnet and she said quickly, "Passion, love, power, jealousy, deep emotion. Good news, happiness. Or bad news, grief. A strong stone but changeable."

One more time she put her hand in the pouch and this

time she withdrew the fossilized leaf. She turned down the corners of her mouth, swayed her head from side to side. "Peace, growth, opportunity. Healing again. Compassion and mercy. Not a strong stone, not a bold stone. Can mean change, not always for the better. Can mean lying, to yourself or to others. Interesting with skystone and bird's claw, interesting indeed."

Isabeau was fascinated and waited eagerly for her to go on but the Soul-Sage gathered the stones together and let them trickle through her hand back into the pouch.

"What about the others? What do they mean?"

"Stones mean many different things. I just read for you. They mean different things for somebody else. One day you will find your own bones and then you will understand."

Isabeau nodded and bowed her head in understanding. The Soul-Sage reached out her long, four-jointed finger and placed it on the scar at Isabeau's brow. "You have traveled a long, dark road and it stretches still before you. There is light at the end, though, and healing, for you and for others. You have been given powerful gifts, the bones have said so. Indeed I think you may be a great soul-sage if you listen in silence and learn."

Tears sprang up in Isabeau's eyes and she made the gesture of heartfelt gratitude. The Soul-Sage accepted it and then settled into her familiar cross-legged position.

Two days later the wind dropped and the sky cleared, and the Scarred Warriors were able to dig their way out of the cave and take to the slopes again. They returned triumphantly a week later with several deer, and the bloody carcass of a timber wolf which one of the young warriors had killed, saving his comrades. He was able to throw off his furs of arctic fox and wear the shaggy gray pelt with pride, and with great ceremony his cheek was slashed with a knife, to show he had won another scar. There was feasting and the storytellers told tales of heroes and great hunts, some of the only stories with happy endings that they had.

Only Isabeau's teacher was grim and silent, regretting

yet another winter away from the joy of skimming and hunting. He continued to teach her the art of the Scarred Warrior with great patience, nonetheless. Isabeau found her mind and body were being trained into a precise coordination. As she thought so she moved, no pause or hesitation between one or the other. She had gone beyond mere exercises now to being taught how the thirty-three basic stances and movements could be combined into defensive and offensive maneuvers. She had watched the First and Second display their skills with thrilling pyrotechnics of leaps, kicks, somersaults and throws, and knew she would never be able to attain such heights of skill. She had grown to enjoy her lessons, though, and loved the morning ritual of *ahdayeh* which allowed her to face her busy day with a tranquil mind and a loose, limber body.

One dawn, the Soul-Sage wrapped herself up in her furs and gestured to her to follow. Isabeau caught up her thick hood and cloak with some wonderment, for she had never before seen the Soul-Sage leave her fire. They walked out into the snowy silence and climbed up to the crown of the hill above the Haven.

It was still dark in the valleys but the sky was a clear blue and the sun was shining in glorious colors of rose and golden on the snowy peaks that stretched as far as the eye could see in every direction. They faced the west and far, far away, Isabeau saw the great pointed peak of the Fang, the mountain the Khan'cohbans called the Skull of the World. Up there, the sun rising on their backs, Isabeau and the Soul-Sage performed their *ahdayeh* together.

The wind swept over Isabeau's face and body, blowing back her hood so her hair billowed behind her. Tears sprang to her eyes, brought by the chill of the wind and the beauty and grandeur of the panorama before her. She became aware of some force of power surging and heaving around her, a great tide of power that poured over her, through her, past her. It was like the beat of a great heart, pounding in rhythm with her own heart and breath, or the beat of a god's hand upon a giant drum.

Sometimes, while meditating in stillness with the Soul-Sage or meditating in movement with the Scarred Warrior, Isabeau had felt as if she was floating in some great, still darkness. Now she had the sensation again, but it was a sea of light, a sea of joy, its deep song resounding in the inner chambers of her heart.

The movements of the *ahdayeh* became a dance, and she was dancing for the sheer, inexpressible joy of being alive. When at last they had finished their last run and somersault, the Dragon Dives for the Kill, Isabeau landed lightly and easily on her feet then flung wide her arms, embracing the wind, the billowing current of energy, the whole world. She turned and laughed at the Soul-Sage, who smiled back at her and bowed. Isabeau bowed back and they sat, facing each other, while the sun flooded the mountains with light.

It was the winter solstice, Isabeau realized. This was the turn of the tides that she felt. She looked up at the sky and let herself be filled with the thrumming of power.

"Shut your eyes," the Soul-Sage said. Isabeau obeyed and she heard the Khan'cohban woman begin to, very lightly, tap on her drum with her fingers. Slowly the drumming increased in intensity until it seemed the beating of her heart, the thrumming of her soul, the beating of the drum, the thunder of the wind, the inhalation and exhalation of her breath were all one, were all the same.

Isabeau had a sensation of rising, floating. She could not feel the rock below her, or any part of her body at all. It was as if she had flown free of the prison of her bones and was drifting as she pleased. She felt a tremendous lightness and freedom of being. Although her eyes were shut she could see, as if through a silvery veil. Glancing down she saw herself cross-legged, eyes shut. A thin silver cord wound between her physical and spiritual bodies, and it throbbed and shimmered with power.

Gradually the drumbeat quickened and she felt her heart begin to pound again and her breath inflate her lungs. She slipped back down into her body and had a moment of giddiness, as if the rock spun and tilted.

"Open your eyes," the Soul-Sage said gently and Isabeau obeyed. The sky was very bright and she felt very disorientated, with a sick feeling of vertigo. "The first step," the Soul-Sage said. "Come, eat and rest and you will feel better soon." She had to help Isabeau down the rocks and into the cave, and Isabeau sank down, still feeling very sick and giddy. When she woke many hours later she was still dazed, and failed to hear when she was spoken to.

As the winter passed, Isabeau was taught to leave her body at will. At first she could not travel far, and found herself very distracted by the whistle of her own breathing and the thunder of her own heart, which kept drawing her back. Then, as she was able to drag her consciousness away from herself, she was fascinated by the sight of other people's spiritual being hovering just above their sleeping bodies or quivering, imprisoned, inside their bag of bones and skin.

On more than one occasion Isabeau followed the Soul-Sage as, insubstantial as a nisse's wing, she flew effortlessly out into the snowy darkness. Above the heavy clouds they soared, up into the celestial sphere where stars and planets wheeled, and curtains of fire crackled. This was called skimming the stars, and was as addictive as moonbane. Once Isabeau grew too confident and flew so far she was unable to find her way back, the silver cord so stretched and tangled she could not find where it led. That time the Soul-Sage had to come and find her, and Isabeau was not allowed to skim the stars until she had learned to keep her cord properly smooth and straight.

Isabeau would have spent all her days and nights skimming the stars if the Soul-Sage had let her, and for the first time she understood why it was the Khan'cohban woman spent so much time in a trance. The wise woman would not let her, though, saying, "Patience, Khan. One step only at a time. Better to learn too slowly than too fast. Listen in silence and learn."

LIGHTNING AT LOCHSITHE

The little prionnsa shrieked with excitement.

"Donncan, come down here *now*!" Sukey cried. He grinned at her and did a swift somersault, his golden wings fluttering madly. Then he patted the faces of the dancing nisses painted on the ornate ceiling. "Please, Donncan, come down," his nursemaid begged. "Your mam will be here soon and ye ken ye should be in bed."

Swift as a swallow, the little boy swooped down and caught at Sukey's cap. Trying to hold the linen cap on with one hand, she caught at his arm with the other, but he evaded her nimbly and soared to the mantelpiece where he perched, babbling excitedly. "Where mam? When she come? One minute? Six minute? Where *daidein*? I dinna want to go to bed. Canna I go 'n listen?"

A small figure dressed all in white with a nightcap on his head appeared in the doorway, rubbing his eyes. "What be going on?" Neil asked sleepily. Two years old, he looked more like his mother Elfrida than his father, Iain, with fair hair, gray eyes and a rather frail little body.

"Neil, get ye back to bed!" Sukey cried. "Look, Donncan, ye've gone and woken Neil. Ye're a wicked, wicked bairn!"

She climbed onto a stool and pulled Donncan down from the high mantelpiece. Although he tried to grab her cap again, he did not fly away and she clambered down again, scolding him all the while. With the heir to the throne tucked under one arm, she turned Neil around with the other and directed him back to his own room.

Just then the door opened and Iseult walked in, her pale face strained.

"Och, I be so sorry, Your Highness, indeed I've been trying to get them into bed for the last ten minutes but I couldna catch Donncan and then he woke wee Neil and I—"

"Never mind, Sukey, I know what Donncan can be like. Just put Neil back to bed and I'll look after my son."

The nursemaid nodded and shepherded Neil back to his own room. Iseult sat down with Donncan on her lap. He wound his chubby arms around her neck and pressed his cheek into her shoulder. "Ye're a naughty lad," Iseult said. "Ye ken it is no' fair to fly around the room when Sukey canna catch ye. Ye ken what time bedtime is."

"I was afraid I'd fall asleep afore ye came," he said with a yawn. "Ye promised ye'd come 'n tuck me up and tell me a story."

"I'm sorry, sweetling, but indeed the meeting dragged on and on, and I had to be there to make sure all those foolish lairds did no' decide to do something silly."

"Did they?"

"No' yet, sweetling, but give them time and I'm sure they will."

"Do ye and *dai-dein* have to ride to war?"

Iseult nodded. "Aye, I'm afraid so, darling."

He struggled to be put down and she let him slip to the floor, her face graver than ever. He marched across to his toy chest against the wall and got out the little wooden sword Duncan Ironfist had given him for his second birthday. "I come wi' ye."

"I wish ye could," Iseult replied, pulling him to lean against her knee. "Indeed I'd like to have ye at my back, sweetling, such a swordsman that ye are. But ye canna."

He pulled away, indignant. "Why no'?"

"Someone must stay behind and look after Neil and Sukey and help guard Dùn Eidean. Ye ken we canna leave the city unprotected, else the wicked Bright Soldiers may sneak up and try and take it back from us."

Donncan nodded and rubbed his eyes, colored the

same unusual topaz-yellow as his father's. Iseult picked him up and cuddled him closely. "I will miss ye though, my sweetling. Ye must promise me to be good and no' tease Sukey too much nor fly away from her."

He nodded his curly golden head drowsily and she tucked him up in bed, his sword still clutched in his hand. With a thought she extinguished the many-branched candelabra on the table so the room sank into darkness, only the glowing coals in the fireplace casting any light. "What story would ye like?"

He snuggled down into the blankets. "Tell me the story o' the daughter o' Frost 'n the North Wind again," he begged.

Iseult sat cross-legged in the wide-seated chair by his bed, her hands turned upward in her lap. With a long sweeping gesture she began in a sing-song voice, "The daughter o' Frost and the North Wind was born in the shadow o' the Skull o' the World, far, far away from the valleys where the people lived and hunted . . ."

The little boy was asleep before Iseult had finished but she did not stop her tale-telling, knowing the end of a story was as important as the beginning. She came back to the real world with a little start, becoming aware of Sukey leaning against the doorframe, listening raptly.

"That was bonny, Your Highness," the nursemaid whispered, her voice a little husky. " 'Twas so sad!"

"Most o' the stories o' the People o' the Spine o' the World are sad," Iseult answered softly, rising carefully to her feet so as not to disturb the sleeping child. "They do no' have much o' a sense o' humor, I'm afraid." She brushed a lock of hair away from her son's face and kissed him very gently between the eyes.

"Have a care for him, Sukey," she said somberly. "It hurts me to have to leave him again."

"I will, Your Highness," Sukey promised. "So ye ride out again?"

"Aye, I'm afraid so. Fresh troops have marched through Arran and into Blèssem again, to join those that escaped Rhyssmadill. Indeed, they are stubborn, these Tìrsoilleirean! We have had near four months to rest and rebuild, so that is something, I suppose. Still it is time we cauterized Arran and Tìrsoilleir once and for all. We shall be riding for Ardencaple in the morning."

She went to leave the nursery and Sukey said impulsively, "Ye look tired, my lady. Must ye go back to the war conference? Should ye no' rest?"

Iseult looked at her swiftly and one hand dropped to her abdomen. "I wish I could, but we are planning tactics and ye ken those woolly-headed lairds know naught about such things."

"But . . ."

Iseult looked at her sternly and Sukey's words faltered in her mouth.

"His Highness does no' ken," Iseult said, "and he must no' ken! Do ye understand me?"

"Aye, Your Highness," Sukey said meekly. Iseult's gaze did not relent and the nursemaid's color rose and she gave a little curtsey, dropping her eyes. Iseult walked to the door and said, "I must get back. I've been gone too long as it is."

"I'll bring ye a hot posset o' herbs that the lady Isabeau used to make for ye," Sukey said.

Iseult gave a shrug of exasperation and said, "As ye will then, but be discreet, I beg ye."

"Aye, my lady," Sukey answered as Iseult walked out the door.

The army marched down the highway, their gray cloaks rolled up on top of their heavy packs, enjoying the mild spring sunshine on their bare arms and heads. To the north thickly forested hills rose, while to the south a patchwork of fields, hedges and small copses of trees sloped down to a little river.

The fields were freshly tilled and planted, and already a fine green mist was covering the soil. A shepherd was grazing his sheep among the grass at the verge of the road. He fell to his knees as Lachlan and Iseult rode past and called Eà's blessing upon them, much to Meghan's satisfaction. The old witch was well pleased with how easily many of the common folk had shrugged off the teachings of the Awl and returned to the old ways of the Coven. Although she knew much of their compliance was due to gratitude at the Rìgh's success in driving the Bright Soldiers from the land, it was her hope that a more genuine reverence for Eà would soon be animated in their hearts.

The spring equinox had been celebrated all over the countryside with the burning of sweet-scented candles, the making of evergreen wreaths and the ringing of the bells in every village meeting-house. Meghan, Matthew the Lean and the other witches had spent the winter and early spring overseeing the planting of the fields and the procreation of new lambs and kids. It had been too late to plant wheat and rye, but they sowed mixed fields of barley and oats, with beans to grow up the oat stalks, and vegetable plots with peas, leeks, potatoes and cabbage. All over lower Rionnagan and Blèssem new cottages and barns were built, broken walls and hedgerows were mended, orchards replanted and drainage ditches dug.

Many skeelies and cunning men had flocked to join the Coven as the Rìgh's army had triumphed over the few remaining Seekers of the Awl. Among them were many of the witches who had been rescued during the Awl's reign of terror, and hidden away about the countryside. Although most stayed behind in the safety of Lucescere, learning new Skills at the Tower of the Two Moons, some had the courage and Talent to join Meghan and the other witches and lend them their strength.

Lachlan had spent the winter overseeing the repair of the gates that guarded the mouth of the Berhtfane, so that the Rhyllster was safe once more. Their reconstruction at first confounded them all. The river gates and locks had been designed and built by Malcolm MacBrann in the time of Aedan Whitelock, at the end of the Second Fairgean Wars. The lock system had maintained the water level in the Berhtfane, controlling the flow of the tide up the river, and allowing ships to be raised and lowered at will, while keeping the hostile sea-faeries out. The Bright Soldiers had stupidly blown them up during their attack on Dùn Gorm, destroying many of their own ships in the ensuing flood and making themselves vulnerable to attack from the Fairgean. Although there were signs the Bright Soldiers had tried to fix the gates, they had obviously been unsuccessful, the sea serpents having broken down their crude barriers with contemptuous ease.

Lachlan and his engineers puzzled over the remains of the gates for some time without being able to work out how to fix the great wheel that had opened and closed the gates. Then Dide the Juggler brought an old man with a crippled foot to see the Rìgh. Named Donovan Slewfoot, he had been the harbor master at the Berhtfane for thirty years and had worked on the canals since he was a mere lad. After the Lammas invasion, he had joined the rebels in Dùn Gorm, fighting the Bright Soldiers from the shadows. He had escaped the first Fairgean onslaught with Dide and Cathmor and had served in the Rìgh's army ever since as an engineer's assistant and jack-of-all-trades.

Donovan Slewfoot grinned when Lachlan explained their problem. "Och, that one is easy enough to fix," he said cryptically and lay down on his back to slide under the wheel, coiled with thick chains. When he struggled out again, he held a spanner in his huge, rough hand. "I jammed the gates wi' this when those blaygird Bright Soldiers first attacked the harbor master's tower. I never thought it would hold the gates open for more than two years!"

With Donovan Slewfoot's advice, it was not long before the harbor and the river were once again safe from invasion by the sea-faeries. Sadly it would take a lot longer to rebuild Dùn Gorm and none of them had had the heart to try. Instead Lachlan's men had spent the early spring months consolidating their hold on the land they had won and recovering their own strength.

Almost four thousand Bright Soldiers had surrendered to Lachlan's troops after the battle at Rhyssmadill, but close on a thousand had escaped the carnage and fled through Clachan, retreating back toward Arran. There they

had been met by fresh troops who had marched through
the fenlands at the first thaw, determined to continue the
war against the heretical witch-lovers.

With all of southern Eileanan again under their control,
Lachlan and Iseult were determined to drive the Tìrsoilleirean back to their own country and to unite both
Tìrsoilleir and Arran under the MacCuinn banner. Their
confidence was running high after the victories of the past
two years, and the comrades they had lost had only honed
their resolve. They had called the lairds and prionnsachan to Dùn Eidean to plan their summer campaign.

The Bright Soldiers had set up their headquarters at
Ardencaple, the closest major town to the border with
Arran, which was well able to supply provisions for the
Tìrsoilleirean battalions. Built on the Arden River,
Ardencaple was a well-fortified town surrounded by rich
fields and orchards. Since that part of the countryside
was quite flat, Lachlan and Iseult had puzzled for some
time about how best to approach their enemy.

"The trick will be to take the Bright Soldiers by surprise," Iseult said. "They must know our intention is to
strike against them before they march too far into Blèssem or Clachan. It is so hard to tell what the area is like
from these maps. Where is the NicThanach? She must
know this countryside better than anyone. Happen she
will know the best way for us to advance on Ardencaple."

Melisse NicThanach, the eldest daughter of Alasdair
MacThanach, was called to the war conference. A slim
woman in her mid-twenties, she had golden curls tied
back in a snood sewn with pearls, a wide satin skirt all
covered over with lilies and roses, and long trailing
sleeves of green velvet and gold net. Next to Iseult's
battle-scarred leather, she looked very feminine and
rather helpless. A soft murmur of appreciation rose from
the soldiers and Iseult had to work hard to prevent her
exasperation from showing on her face. She drew Melisse
to one side and explained to her in a low voice what she
needed to know.

Melisse had inherited the crown from her father upon

his death and, rather to her dismay, had been ordered from the safety of Lucescere so she could command her men. Half of the Rìgh's troops were from Blèssem and their allegiance was sworn to Lachlan through the chief of the MacThanach clan. Unfortunately Melisse had been petted and protected all her life and she had very little idea of what fighting a war entailed. The journey through the war-scarred countryside had shocked her deeply and she found both Lachlan and Iseult very intimidating indeed. Luckily her seanalair, the Duke of Killiegarrie, had fought at her father's side all through the war and he knew the Rìgh well. He had assured the NicThanach that she could trust the stern-faced Rìgh and Banrìgh and that she should do as her father would have wished.

So Melisse furrowed her brow and thought about the problem seriously. After a while she said hesitantly, "Ardencaple lies in a valley edged to the north by the forests o' Aslinn. We often used to stay there when we were traveling to my cousins Gilliane and Ghislaine in Aslinn. Their mother had a wee castle in the woods and we used to stay there when we went hunting. There is a little used road that runs through the forest. It comes out no' far from Ardencaple and few know o' it at all. If ye circled round and went through the wood, ye could approach from the northeast and happen they'd no' be expecting that."

"Well, it's something at least," Lachlan said. "We know Aslinn is free o' Bright Soldiers for the faeries have scoured the forests thoroughly and killed or driven out all who were sheltering there. Happen we can meet up with Niall and Lilanthe and they can bring the faeries to our aid as well. We'll be able to use the NicAislin castle as a base. If we send a strong force in from the west, they may no' expect us to strike from the east as well. We shall take just a small force but o' the very best men, and we shall keep all our plans secret indeed. Too often this past year it has seemed as if the Tìrsoilleirean have kent what it is we've been planning."

So they had split their forces, the Duke of Killiegarrie taking eight thousand men along the main highway

toward Arran, and Lachlan and his troops taking the
high road to Aslinn. The MacSeinn and his two thousand
men had been patrolling eastern Blèssem for the past
two years and had seen hard fighting trying to keep the
Bright Soldiers from heading back up into Rionnagan.
They had been ordered to head to Ardencaple as well,
striking at the town from the north.

Iseult and Lachlan had only two thousand men with
them, the others having been left behind in Dùn Eidean
or sent with the main body of the army. Still, the double
column of men stretched back along the highway as far
as the eye could see. When they made camp that night,
the campfires along the road looked like a chain of rubies, glimmering red in the cool spring darkness.

They reached Aslinn the next day and marched on
into the woods, much to the surprise of the soldiers who
had not been informed of their destination. The road
was badly overgrown and they had to clear the way with
axes. The NicAislin, Gilliane and Ghislaine's mother Madelon, had sent some of her men to guide them and they
scouted ahead, tall, taciturn fellows dressed in rough furs
and leather.

They reached the little castle of Lochsithe within a
week. It was built on a small stretch of water and had
four round turrets with mossy pointed roofs. Three of its
sides rose straight out of the water, the other being protected by a stout outer wall. The trees grew thickly down
to the very shore of the loch, their branches hanging in
the water. It was a quaint little building, nowhere near
large enough to house all of the troops, who made camp
in the forest. Only Iseult, Lachlan, the witches and the
Yeomen of the Guard were able to rest within the castle's walls and even they were rather crowded.

An old couple who had lived there all their lives maintained the castle. Meghan noticed the piercing brightness
of the old woman's slanted green eyes and said know-
ingly to Jorge, "It would no' surprise me if she proved
akin to Lilanthe o' the Forest. They used to say there
were many born in Aslinn who had tree-changer blood."

They stayed there a week, for it had been arranged to

attack Ardencaple a month after Beltane, when both the moons were dark. They had reached Castle Lochsithe more quickly than expected, thanks to the fair weather, and so had time to scry to Lilanthe, hunt for fresh provisions and enjoy the tranquility of the forest.

Their last evening at Castle Lochsithe, Iseult and Meghan sat out on the balcony that ran the length of the central building, enjoying the dusk falling over the loch and watching the tiny sliver of the blue moon rise. "Tomorrow Gladrielle will be dark," Meghan said, "and it will be time to attack Ardencaple. Let us hope we find them unprepared, though I ken it is a vain hope."

Iseult said nothing, resting her head on her hand.

The old sorceress leaned forward and touched her shoulder. "Why have ye no' told Lachlan?"

Iseult did not pretend to misunderstand her. "He would have tried to make me stay behind in Dùn Eidean if he knew."

"Would that have been such a bad thing?" Meghan said. "Ye must have a care for the babes ye carry within."

"Babes?"

"Aye, twins again," Meghan replied.

Iseult's face was shadowed. "I have a misgiving in my heart about this campaign," she said. "I have to stay near Lachlan and protect him as best I may. I have had strange dreams . . ."

"Jorge too has had uneasy dreams," Meghan said. "Tell me what ye've seen."

Iseult shrugged. "When first I wake I can remember clearly but always the dreams slip away from me in the light o' day. Last night I dreamt I saw Lachlan walking away from me down a strange, flat, shadowy road and though I called to him he did not turn or look around."

"That is no' such a bad dream surely?" Meghan said. "Happen it means ye must just be separate for a while— which indeed I think would be a good idea, Iseult. Ye must have a care for the babes ye carry."

"It was no' so much what happened in the dream as the way I felt," Iseult said in a low voice. "Such despair . . ."

Suddenly the warm blue of the twilight was split apart

by a great crack of lightning which irradiated the sky from horizon to horizon. The pattern of twigs and branches sprang out black against its white shock. When the lightning was gone they could see the black fretwork imprinted against the fizzle of their vision. So unexpected was the flash of light that they heard involuntary cries from the camp out in the woods and from inside the castle hall. Again the lightning came and they heard the distant rumble of thunder.

"Lightning from a clear sky," Meghan murmured. "Indeed, no good omen the night before a battle."

"But for us or for them?" Iseult asked, getting wearily to her feet.

"Who kens?" Meghan replied. She let Iseult help her to her feet and went back inside the keep. The Blue Guards had been sitting drinking at the long table, Dide entertaining them with his songs and juggling, Finlay and Lachlan playing a game of chess. With a sinking of her heart Meghan saw the old servant woman was mopping up wine which had been spilled across the table like a stain of blood. "Who spilled the wine?" she whispered.

"I did," Lachlan replied with a grin. "That crack o' lightning had me and the lads just about jumping out o' our skins. Let us hope the men had the forethought to camp under a thorn tree and no' under an oak."

"Why?" Iseult said.

"Do ye no' ken that auld rhyme?" Lachlan said. "No, happen ye wouldna. It says:

" 'Beware o' the oak, it draws the stroke,
 Avoid the ash, it courts the flash,
 Creep under a thorn, it'll save ye from storm.' "

He saw Meghan still looking at the stain of wine and said, "Whatever is the matter, Meghan?"

"Ye who remember auld rhymes should know," she said harshly. " 'Tis a bad omen indeed to spill your wine thus."

"Drink up your cup but do no' spill wine, for if ye do, 'tis an ill sign," Duncan quoted.

"Och, ye and your omens!" Lachlan said. "Everything is an omen to ye! What about the bee sting in Lucescere? Nothing bad has happened to me yet, ye ken."

"No' yet," Meghan said but Lachlan only laughed at her and ordered the old servant woman to pour him a fresh cup.

The next morning the Blue Guards rose early and prepared themselves for battle, checking their weapons and armor, and washing themselves carefully. Meghan spoke Eà's blessing over the soldiers' heads and watched them mount up with a frown etched on her brow.

"I canna help being afraid," she said to Jorge, "even though I ken they must go. Ever since I saw that flash o' lightning yesterday, my heart has been uneasy. I shall no' stay here with ye and Tòmas and the healers as planned. I shall ride out with Lachlan and Iseult and keep them under my eye."

"Is that wise, my dear?" Jorge said wearily. In the bright morning light he looked frailer than ever, his face heavily lined, his hand clutching his staff like a bird's claw. He had not slept well, his dreams troubled with strange visions he could not or would not decipher. "Ye are no warrior, and ye ken ye could be a distraction to the bairns—they will be worried for ye and trying to protect ye. Will ye no' stay here in the peace o' this wee castle and wait for news with the rest o' us?"

"Happen they will need my magic," Meghan replied. "I am too far away here. How can I call the beasts o' the field and forest to their aid if I'm stuck away here in the forest? Nay, I shall ride out with them."

Despite Iseult and Lachlan's protests, she would not be swayed from her decision and at last one of the spare horses was led out for her. She clambered up quite nimbly for someone of her immense age, the little donbeag clinging to her long gray plait as usual.

The cavaliers trotted down the road, talking lightheartedly. The sun fell dappled through the canopy of leaves and birds sang all around them. It was hard to remember they were riding to battle and not on a hunt for sport,

particularly with Stormwing the gyrfalcon perched on
Lachlan's wrist, a leather hood tied over his head.

By mid-afternoon the forest was thinning and there
were signs of human society—a few felled trees, a great
patch of blackened ground where charcoal burners had
been flaming, a hunters' hut. The road ran through an
avenue of tall trees, with a rocky cliff to one side.

Suddenly Iseult reined in her horse, sensing the brush of
hostile minds. "Lachlan, *leannan*!" she cried. "I fear—"
Behind her she heard Meghan calling a warning.

Lachlan wheeled his horse around, scowling, and called
to his men. "Back, back! An ambush, by the Centaur!"
With a quick tug he released the ties of the falcon's head
and flung the bird into the air.

Startled, his men pulled in their horses, a few drawing
their swords from their scabbards. Duncan Ironfist cried,
"Call the retreat!" and the startled herald raised his
trumpet to his mouth and blew.

On the narrow road all was confusion. Lachlan spurred
his horse back, shouting to the men to retreat. Then the
quiet forest sounds were torn apart by the zing of long-
bows being let loose. A blizzard of arrows fell upon the
cavaliers, piercing leather armor, bone and flesh. Men
screamed and fell from their horses. The birdsong was
drowned by a cacophony of shrieks, shouts and terrified
whinnies. Everywhere Iseult looked she could see
wounded men and horses floundering. She drew her dagger and looked for the enemy but there were only the
deadly rain of arrows, the dying men and horses, the
great trees towering overhead. The falcon shrieked and
she looked up, seeing archers hidden in the branches and
along the top of the rocky crag. She yelled orders but
no one listened. All were too busy dying.

She pulled her *reil* from her belt and sent it whizzing
into the trees. Screams and a falling body showed she had
hit her target. It came back to her hand and she flung it
again. An arrow caught her in the arm and she dragged it
from her flesh with a curse. Ignoring the throbbing pain,
she wheeled her horse around, looking for Lachlan. Her
heart thudded painfully as she saw his black stallion lying

on its side, legs thrashing, a dozen or more arrows studding its breast and side. "Lachlan!" she screamed.

She saw Duncan Ironfist swinging up into the trees and threw her dagger straight through the heart of a Bright Soldier about to plunge a sword into his back. The Tìrsoilleirean fell with a scream. Without taking the time to acknowledge her, Duncan clung to the tree trunk with one hand and laid about him with his sword. Three more Tìrsoilleirean fell and he swung from the trees onto the rocks and began to fight a duel with three archers hidden there, his great claymore whistling with deadly grace.

Iseult called back her dagger and used it to kill a Bright Soldier trying to drag her down from her horse. As she stabbed him, another of the enemy used his mace to smash her horse's skull. The mare dropped like a stone. Only quick reflexes saved Iseult from being trapped beneath her horse's weight. She somersaulted high over the head of her attacker, landed lightly on her feet and killed one soldier with the *reil* in her left hand and another with the dagger held in her right hand. She gave a small smile of satisfaction, lashed out with her foot and knocked down another Bright Soldier. Then, as three tried to rush her from the bushes, Iseult somersaulted high over their heads and into the trees.

Looking everywhere for her husband, she unhitched her little crossbow from her back and wound it on with the hook on her belt. Though small, the crossbow was powerful and Iseult deadly accurate. She was able to kill or wound about fifteen Bright Soldiers in the branches about her before she ran out of arrows. She then flung down her bow and unsheathed her dagger again, somersaulting down to fight her way through the mayhem on the ground. Dead or dying Graycloaks were everywhere. Taken completely by surprise, many had not even had time to draw their swords or remove their shields.

Crouching behind a dead horse, Iseult tried to locate her husband with her mind. To her relief, she felt him nearby and she ran in that direction, killing six or seven Bright Soldiers on the way.

Lachlan was backed against the rocks, his bow discarded at his feet, his great claymore whistling all around him as he fought like a demon.

Stormwing fought with him, plummeting from the sky to strike with his clenched talons, then using his powerful hooked beak to tear at any unprotected flesh. As the Bright Soldiers were heavily armored, it was the force of his blow which was most effective and he soared away and plunged down again so swiftly that none of the archers were able to shoot him out of the sky.

Meghan was crouched beside him, her hair falling from its plait, the donbeag shrieking in rage from her shoulder. Piles of dead Tìrsoilleirean lay on either side, but ten more were fighting to reach them and Lachlan was only just managing to keep them off. Intent on their prey, they did not notice Iseult running up behind them. She killed two before they heard her, and the distraction of her arrival was enough to allow Lachlan to slice through two more. For a few seconds there was hard fighting, then all were dead.

Lachlan leaned on his sword, panting harshly, blood pouring from a cut to his brow and shoulder. "Where is Duncan?" he cried. "And Iain? Are they well?"

Iseult shrugged, trying to catch her breath.

"We've been betrayed," Lachlan raged. "Somehow they knew we were planning to ride down this road. We have a spy in our camp!"

Iseult nodded. "Without a doubt," she replied, then ducked so that an arrow which would have caught her in the throat flew overhead and embedded itself in the rock.

Another group of Bright Soldiers had swung down out of the trees and was advancing on them. Lachlan fought them off with a snarl. When all had fallen, he flew effortlessly and unexpectedly into the branches, the gyrfalcon leading the way. There were screams and then the thud of falling bodies. One almost fell on Iseult and Meghan, and the Banrìgh helped the old sorceress to her feet.

"Meghan, are ye all right? Ye're no' hurt?"

The old sorceress nodded, her face grim. "We are hard pressed," she said.

"Can ye help us in any way? They are slaughtering us! We are so confined among all these trees, we canna see where they are or how many o' them there are."

"I have already called for help, but we are so close to the fields here, there will be no woolly bears or timber wolves nearby, only squirrels and donbeags. Calling fire would only hurt our men as much as theirs." The old sorceress suddenly turned and flung up her hand, catching an arrow in mid-air.

"Come, auld mother, ye are no' safe here!" Iseult said. "Let me take ye to safety!"

They ducked down among the bracken as a mob of Bright Soldiers ran past, shouting triumphantly. "Who could have betrayed us?" Iseult cried. "Only a few kent our plans and I canna believe any o' our men would have led us into such a trap. The Bright Soldiers no' only kent where we would ride but when."

Meghan's eyes glittered with anger. "Once I find out, I swear on Eà's green blood that they will be sorry!"

Dillon sat on the stone wall and kicked his legs angrily, his dog Jed lying curled by his side. Below him the loch gleamed in the bright spring sunlight but Dillon was in no mood for enjoying its beauty. He was angry that Lachlan had, at the very last minute, decided to leave his squires behind with the healers and the servants. Dillon had been looking forward to the battle at Ardencaple, which many said would be the final confrontation before the Bright Soldiers were sent back to Tìrsoilleir with their tails between their legs. He had dreams of so dazzling Lachlan with his fighting prowess that the Rìgh knighted him there and then on the battlefield. Although he knew fourteen was rather young to win one's spurs, such speedy advancement did sometimes happen in times of war and Dillon saw no reason why it could not happen to him. He had practiced his fighting skills every day and listened fervently to all that was said by the soldiers, filing it away for future reference.

Dillon scowled at the dazzle of light. He knew his fellow squires were relieved at the Rìgh's decision, and were down in the castle kitchen at that very moment, begging the caretaker's wife for bits of candied peel. He scorned them for their childishness. He bet Duncan Iron-fist had not been so silly when he was fourteen.

His fingers found a loose piece of paving, and he prised it loose, tossing it in his hand. Then he scrambled to his feet and tossed it out into the loch, counting the number of skips it made across the water's surface. Five, he counted, pleased with himself, and looked about for another bit of rock. Out of the corner of his eyes he saw a flash of white and he stared in that direction, wondering if it was the tail of a deer. City born, Dillon was not too old to get excited at the idea of seeing a wild stag.

Then his eyes widened. Running low along the edge of the loch was a man in a long white surcoat. The next instant he had ducked out of sight but Dillon had seen all he needed to. He dashed back into the keep, calling, "Master! Master!" Jed bounded along, barking in excitement.

Jorge was dozing by the fire, his beard flowing over his lap and down to the floor. He woke with a start and said irritably, "I do wish ye would stop calling me that, lad. I was born the son o' a thief in Lucescere, same as ye, and I am no man's master but myself."

"Master, soldiers come!" Dillon cried, almost beside himself. "I saw them creeping along the shore."

"So this *is* the place," Jorge murmured. "I wondered when I felt that shiver o' lightning last night . . ."

He got slowly to his feet, fumbling for his staff. The lump of crystal at its apex caught the light of the fire and flashed suddenly red. Dillon helped him up impatiently, saying: "We should make sure the gates are shut and see what weapons they have here, should we no', master? Though it is naught but a wee castle, it is stout. We should be able to hold them off for a while, though there are only a few o' us and most naught but silly lasses."

"Aye, do what ye can to hold them off," Jorge said. "I shall try and reach Meghan and let her ken we are under attack. Though if we are being attacked, I think she must be also. Indeed I have been feeling uneasy all morning but thought I must be growing auld and foolish to feel so ill at ease in this peaceful place."

Dillon went running to alert the handful of soldiers that had been left to guard them, first making sure the gate in the outer wall was securely fastened. The soldiers were down in the kitchen, talking and laughing with the squires. At Dillon's hurried explanations, they were on their feet in an instant, alarm and stupefaction on their faces.

"How could they ken to attack us here?" one exclaimed, drawing his sword. "We did no' ken we were coming here ourselves!"

"Someone must have betrayed the Rìgh!" another cried, buckling up his breastplate.

They ran out of the kitchen, the healers crying aloud in fear and dismay. Dillon ran after them, then suddenly veered and bounded up the stairs to the south turret in search of his own sword. After only a moment's hesitation, he opened the door to the chamber where Meghan had slept and rummaged through a chest against the wall. If he was to fight, he wanted the sword he had chosen in the relics room, not the little flimsy play-sword he and the other squires had been given.

The sword was wrapped in a black bag and hidden at the bottom of the chest, along with Antoinn's sword, Artair's dagger and Parlan's goblet. Dillon had seen Meghan hide the gifts in the chest back in Lucescere when she had decided the boys were far too young and irresponsible to use them. The old witch had given the young Rìgh a severe tongue-lashing for giving them to the boys in the first place and Lachlan had been rather sulky as a result and would not listen to their pleas or arguments.

When he and the other boys had been appointed as the Rìgh's squires, they had been given small swords to wear at their belt so had been so pleased they had not minded the loss of their gifts so much. Those swords were only flimsy though, and rather ineffectual. Now that

Dillon was fourteen and almost a man, he thought it was time to wear his real sword.

He had no time to withdraw it from its scabbard, much as he would have liked to, but instead hastily buckled it to his belt and ran from the room again, the other boys' gifts still bundled up in the bag and slung over his shoulder. He flung the bag at his fellow squires as he ran through the great hall, calling to them to follow.

The view from the guards' tower gave them all a shock. A sizable force had converged on the little castle, with siege machines and cannons carried on wagons. Already ladders were being dragged to the walls and the cannons were lined up, ready to fire. This attack had been carefully planned and timed.

"I am no' sure how long we can hold against those cannons," one soldier muttered to another, his face pale. "This castle is no' built to withstand a major offensive. I wonder why in Eà's name they have brought such firepower against us? There is naught here but a few healers and the Rìgh's squires."

"Jorge," Dillon said, understanding dawning. "They want Jorge."

"And the lad wi' the healing hands too, I'll be bound," another soldier said.

Dillon nodded, alarm on his face. "We must keep Tòmas and Jorge safe," he cried. "Wha' would the Bright Soldiers do to them if they fell into their hands?"

No one replied but by the looks on the soldiers' faces, Dillon knew they too feared the consequences.

"Ye must try and get them away from here," the lieutenant ordered one of his men, a burly sergeant called Ryley o' the Apples. "We shall hold them off as long as we can, but I fear it canna be long. There must be some way ye can escape. Ask the caretakers!"

As he and Ryley ran back down the stairs to the tiny inner bailey, Dillon heard a large bang, followed soon after by the smash of a cannonball into the outer wall, which shook under the impact. Foul-smelling smoke drifted over the wall, making him feel rather sick.

They found Tòmas in the main hall, gripping the edge

of Jorge's robe with both hands. His thin, white face was frightened. "I can feel such hatred!" he whimpered. "They hate and fear us, Jorge, I can feel it. Why? Why do they hate us so much?"

Jorge smoothed back the little boy's blond hair with a trembling hand. "They do no' understand our powers," he answered gently. "What they do no' understand, they fear, and they hate what makes them afraid, for they think it is a sign o' weakness."

"They want to do us harm," Tòmas cried, tears brimming in his cerulean blue eyes, far too large for his wizened little face. "We have to flee, Jorge. They mean to break in and hurt us, I can feel it."

Jorge nodded. "Indeed, ye are right, laddie. I too can feel they mean us no kindness. They are witch-haters, thinking our powers are born o' evil. They are angry because o' their defeats, and long for a chance to have their revenge. I would rather it was no' ye that they wreaked their revenge on, my lad."

There was another resounding bang, and the whole building seemed to shake. They heard a malevolent shout of glee and excitement, then there was the sound of metal clashing.

"Have they breached the wall?" Dillon cried.

Ryley nodded. "I fear so, laddie. We must seek some way out. We canna sit here waiting for them to come and find us. There is a dinghy moored down by the kitchen. We shall have to try and escape in that."

"Where is Johanna?" Tòmas wailed. "We canna leave her!"

"She was with the other healers in the kitchen," Dillon answered, hurrying down the stairs, Jed at his heels as always. They heard shouting and the clash of arms grew louder. "Quick, master, they come!"

Jorge's face was drawn and gray. As they hurried down the passage toward the kitchen he whispered, "Let us hope it was no true sighting."

"What, master?" Dillon cried, urging the old sorcerer along.

"But my heart misgives me," Jorge continued, not

heeding him. "Indeed, my heart grows cold within me."
He gave a shudder and faltered, and Dillon had to push
him to make him continue.

They reached the kitchen, a long room that ran the
length of the building, almost level with the water. The
caretakers were hovering by the door, their old faces
anxious, while Johanna and her team of healers had gathered together their belongings and were waiting calmly.
Occasionally one whimpered in fear but Johanna repri-
manded them with a glance.

"Thank Eà ye have come!" she snapped at Dillon.
"Ye have been such an age. Come, they search the main
building. We must get Tòmas and the master away. I
have readied the dinghy."

Dillon looked at her in some amazement. He had always known her as an anxious-faced girl with long,
skinny plaits who had been scared of everything. Now a
tall girl of sixteen, her plaits were wound round her head
and her face was set in an expression of determination.
Preoccupied with his own dreams and duties, he had not
noticed how much she had changed in these past few
years.

At one end of the kitchen was a great iron-bound door
that led out onto a stone platform. Tied at one end was
a shallow dinghy, used for sculling about the loch. Piled
next to it were some sacks with supplies and cooking
utensils spilling out of them.

Dillon gazed at the little boat in consternation. "There
is no way we can all fit in that!"

"I ken," Johanna said calmly. "Ye must take Tòmas
and the master, and Kevan and his wife, and the youngest o' the lassies. And Parlan, o' course, he is still only
a laddiekin and shouldna be here at all. Then ye will
need Anntoin and Artair to help ye and Ryley row, they
are the strongest. The rest of us shall swim alongside
the boat."

Dillon cast her a quick glance of admiration. "But ye
canna swim," he answered.

She nodded and met his eyes fiercely. "I ken that!"
she snapped. "But if we hang on tight and kick our legs

as hard as we can, we should be just grand. Stop with
your blither-blather and help me!"

The smell of smoke was thick now in the air and they
could hear the cries of dying men. Dillon cast one look
back up the hall, saw soldiers running toward him with
their swords drawn, and slammed shut the kitchen door.
Hastily he bolted it then pushed the kitchen table across
it with the help of Anntoin and Artair. He ordered
everyone to climb into the boat, and they obeyed with
alacrity, some of the younger healers sobbing with fear.
Johanna stripped off her dress and petticoats and unlaced
her boots, and three of the older healers copied her,
leaving their clothes on the platform.

Kevan and his wife hung back. "We canna leave," the
old caretaker said. "Her ladyship the NicAislin entrusted
us to have a care for this castle. We have lived here all
our lives." To all their rapid entreaties, he simply replied,
"We do no' wish to go. We shall stay and hide in the
cellar. Happen they shall no' find us."

They did not have time to argue. Jorge said simply,
"Eà be wi' ye then."

"And also wi' ye," the caretaker answered with a lifted
hand, before hurrying to hide.

They could hear heavy boots trying to kick in the door,
and then there was a small explosion, so that foul-smelling
black smoke poured out of the kitchen. They pushed the
dinghy off from the platform, Johanna and the three eldest healers slipping into the water and clinging rather
desperately to its side. Jed rushed back and forth, barking madly, then jumped into the water at Dillon's imperious whistle. He swam right behind the boat, his head
held high.

Dillon heard shouting and saw soldiers standing on the
platform pointing after them. Then more soldiers came,
propping strange long weapons on shoulder-high prongs
and squinting down their length. Then there was a loud
bang and puffs of white smoke issued from the mouth
of the weapons.

"Get down!" Ryley cried. "All o' ye! Lie flat if ye
can."

He tried to push them down into the dinghy but one of
the healers suddenly cried aloud and toppled backward, a
crimson star opening in his forehead. Everyone screamed.

"Those long things be harquebuses," Ryley said, trying
to row while keeping his head and shoulders down. "We
fought against them at Rhyssmadill. They are like arrows
o' lead and smoke. Keep down, all o' ye."

The dinghy was shallow, though, and overcrowded. It
was difficult to row while trying to hunch below the sides
of the boat's hull, particularly since the healers were
crouching as low as they could get. Again the harquebusiers fired their weapons. Artair gave a high-pitched scream
and fell forward, blood streaming from a wound in his
throat. Almost simultaneously Ryley cried out and clutched
his shoulder. For a moment the boat veered wildly, then
Dillon lifted his oar clear of the water, calling to Anntoin
to do the same. Keeping his body low, he leaned over
Artair, his pulses thumping. The boy was dead, his eyes
glassy. For a moment Dillon could not move or think.
His heart beat so loud he could hear it in his ears. He
had grown up with Artair on the streets of Lucescere
and he counted him as a brother.

The sharp bang as the harquebusiers fired again roused
him, although he felt cold and shaky. Without a word he
tipped Artair over the side of the dinghy, first removing
the little sword and the jeweled dagger at his belt. Anntoin cried out and Dillon turned a fierce gaze on him.
"He's dead. We need to lighten the load," he said
harshly. Parlan crouched down, sobbing, and Dillon
turned to him. "Do no' start greeting now," he said in
the same angry voice. "Get ye to that oar, Parlan, and
row as hard as ye can."

Sniffling, Parlan obeyed as Ryley bound up his shoulder with his shirt and seized his oar again. The boat shot
forward over the sun-dazzled water, Johanna and the
other healers still swimming valiantly along behind.

Again and again the harquebusiers fired, but the dinghy was out of range. When Ryley was sure they were
clear, they pulled the swimmers and the wet, frightened
dog aboard and rowed on, aiming for the far shore. Dil-

lon could see soldiers racing out from the little castle and he yelled at them all to row faster. At last they came in under the shelter of the trees and scrambled out of the boat in some confusion, Jed showering them all with water as he shook himself dry.

"We must head through the forest toward Ardencaple," Dillon said. "We must see what has happened to the Rìgh! He may be hurt, wounded! He may need us. Johanna, can ye walk?"

The girl was exhausted, her bodice and long bloomers dripping wet, her face white, but she nodded, snapping, "Aye, I be fine! Let us get moving!"

They pushed the dinghy back into the loch, then, carrying the sacks of supplies and medicines, hurried on into the forest. Ryley was losing blood fast, but he said nothing, pressing the swab deeper into the wound.

It was not long before they heard the sound of pursuit as the Bright Soldiers came crashing along the side of the loch. Frantic with worry, Dillon kept trying to urge them to walk faster, but Jorge was old and very frail and could barely totter.

"Ye must leave me," the old seer said, but Johanna cried, "Dinna talk that way, master, we shall no' leave ye!"

"Ye do no' understand," Jorge said, stopping to lean on his staff and catch his breath. "I have seen the time and manner o' my death and this, I fear, is the time."

"But the Bright Soldiers will hurt ye horribly," Tòmas cried. "I can hear their thoughts, I ken what it is they plan!"

"As do I, my bairn," Jorge replied. "Do ye think I do no' wish to avert my fate? I feel it rushing hard upon my heels, though. I feel Gearradh's cold breath on my neck. If ye leave me, ye shall all be able to escape. If you wait for me, we shall all die. This I can see clearly."

Tòmas seized the old man's sleeve. "Come on, master, they come, they come!"

"We shall no' leave ye, sir," Ryley said respectfully, although he could not help glancing back at the ever louder pursuit. "Come, let us try and find a place to hide."

Jorge shook his head. "Dillon, have a care for Tòmas. He must be your charge. I would gladly give myself up to save his precious life. Go, my bairns."

"No, no!" Johanna wept, pressing close to the old man, taking his delicate, clawlike hand and pulling on it urgently. "Please, master!"

The children of the League of the Healing Hand all clustered close around him, begging him to come, all sobbing. Even Anntoin and Dillon wept in grief and terror. The shouts and crashing of the Bright Soldiers was so close now, they knew they would be within sight in just a few minutes. The old seer would not move, though, gripping tightly to his staff with both hands.

"I have just one wish," he said gently. "Tòmas, will ye touch me before ye leave me? Now that my time has come, I find I long to see the world all clad in brightness again. It has been many years since I last saw the sky."

"No, no," the little boy sobbed and buried his face against the seer's blue robe.

Jorge patted his head with one thin, trembling hand and said, "Grant me this, my laddiekin. It would give me great pleasure to see all your faces, when your voices and hearts are so dear and familiar to me. Please."

Choking with tears, Tòmas slowly raised his wet face, peeled back the black gloves he wore and raised his two small hands. Jorge bent his head and the little boy laid both hands on the old man's forehead, one on either side. A rush of color flowed over the old man's ashen skin and the cloudy eyes cleared and brightened. He straightened, a peaceful smile on his old mouth, and looked about him.

He gazed at the overarching trees, all clad in green, with catkins hanging or nuts swelling along the branch. He looked up at the sky, a brilliant blue between the shifting canopy of leaves, then raised his blue-veined, liver-spotted hands and gazed at them wonderingly. A bright-winged bird flashed past and his smile widened in response.

Then he looked round at them all, smiling gently. They stared back, smiling through their tears and clustering close about him. His gaze lingered on their faces and he put out a shaky hand to pat their cheeks or shoulders.

"Eà bless ye all," he said, his eyes shining with tears. "Go now, my bairns, and keep yourselves safe, I beg ye."

Tòmas buried his head again, refusing to let go, but Johanna pried his fingers free. "Come, laddie, we mun do as the master wishes. Come along, dearling."

They had to drag him for the first few steps, the little boy sobbing despairingly. Jorge stood calmly in the middle of the clearing, no longer having to lean so heavily on his tall staff, looking around with simple wonder at the butterflies dancing in the shadows, the birds flying sapphire-winged through the air. As they plunged again into the undergrowth they all looked back at him with tear-stained cheeks and he gazed after them and raised his hand, smiling.

Iseult lifted her head above the rocky outcrop and threw her *reil* with a flick of her wrist. It sailed in a wide circle, cutting one soldier's throat as it passed, before embedding itself in the breast of another. He fell with a clatter and the *reil* extricated itself and flew back to Iseult's hand. The soldier left standing turned with an oath and started for them and Iseult threw her *reil* again.

Meghan glared angrily at an archer in the rocks above them and he suddenly cried aloud, his hands clutching his breast, as he fell backward. Another aimed directly for the old witch but she caught his arrow with ease, just inches from her face, the archer tumbling head over heels as if thrown by an invisible hand.

Suddenly the sorceress's eyes lost focus and she stared off into the forest, a horrified expression on her face. "Och, no!" she cried. "Jorge!"

From the corner of her eye, Iseult saw another archer leap to his feet above them and take aim. His arrow sped straight toward Meghan's heart. Lost in her thoughts, the sorceress did not notice. With a cry Iseult dived forward, pushing Meghan out of the way. The arrow plunged

through her leather breastplate and into her shoulder.
She staggered and fell back. Meghan scrambled to her
feet, her black eyes snapping with rage, and clapped
her hands together. Suddenly the rocky crag collapsed
with a roar and a shower of small stones and boulders.
The bodies of many Bright Soldiers were flung down,
screaming.

"I hope none o' our own men were up there," Meghan
said as the whole cliff subsided into a pile of boulders
and broken slabs, only a few scraps of white cloth or
dented armor showing where the Tìrsoilleirean had
been buried.

"Duncan was up there last time I saw him," Iseult
panted, trying to pull the arrow out with both hands. "I
hope he got off . . ."

A wave of red-hot pain swept over her and she almost
fainted. Meghan stopped her, saying, "It'll be barbed,
dearling, let me . . ." She cauterized the point of Iseult's
dagger with her finger and cut the arrowhead out. Iseult
bit her lip till the blood flowed but did not scream.

"I thank ye for saving me," Meghan said gently. "I
did no' see that arrow coming." Her brows drew together
and she looked away again, searching the forest with
fearful eyes. "I am afraid . . . I think Jorge is in danger,
dreadful danger. I have felt . . ." Her voice faltered and
she shuddered, drawing her cloak around her. "Please,
Eà, let it no' be true," she whispered.

Lilanthe hurried through the thick undergrowth, heedless
of brambles or thorns. Brun bounded along at her heels,
his triangular face anxious.

"What is wrong, my lady?" Niall called, having to jog
to keep up with her, despite her lame leg.

She paused, waiting for him to catch up. "I do no'
ken, but I have a very bad feeling indeed." The tree-
shifter looked off into the forest. "There are soldiers,"
she murmured. "They are filled with hatred . . ."

Brun swiveled his furry ears. "Crash smash bang
clang," he said.

"Ye can hear fighting? Come, let's hurry!" Lilanthe

turned and looked behind her, raising her arm in a beck-
oning motion. Behind her the forest surged forward.
There were tall tree-changers with swaying manes of
leafy branches, crowned with golden berries. Corrigans
lurched forward, waving their clubs of stone, looking like
rolling boulders all covered with lichen. Hairy araks
swung through the undergrowth, shrieking hoarsely. A
stag trotted close behind Lilanthe, nisses clinging to his
proudly raised antlers. Galloping off to one side was a
herd of sharp-horned satyricorns, their necklaces of teeth
and bones bouncing on their naked breasts.

Lolloping toward the end was the horse-eel, his green-
black skin glistening, his webbed feet leaving slimy puddles behind him. Riding on the horse-eel's back was a
seelie, his beautiful face turned dreamily to watch the
sun strike through the leaves. They had come across the
seelie in the deepest heart of the forest and, overtaken
with wonder at the strangeness of their cavalcade, he had
joined them.

A woolly bear raised her snout and called mournfully,
and without realizing what he did, Niall called back in
reassurance. In the ten months that they had been patrolling the forests, the big man had grown close to all the
creatures of the forest but closest to the bear. He had
confessed to Lilanthe one night that his grandfather
had lived with a woolly bear he had saved from a trap
as a cub. Niall had often seen the huge creature lumbering around in the forest outside his grandfather's cottage
and had come to be called "the wee bear" after his
grandfather. The nickname had stuck, probably because
of his great size and thick, brown hair.

The past ten months had been the happiest of Lilanthe's life. She had been able to wander through the
forests at will, enjoying their peaceful beauty and sinking
her roots in rich, dark soil. She was never lonely for she
had Niall and Brun to talk to, the antics of the nisses to
laugh at, and the quiet, wise presence of the tree-changers
to teach and inspire her. At first there had been many
confrontations with encampments of Bright Soldiers scattered through the forests, but the satyricorns, gravenings

and shadow-hounds had done most of the fighting. As the months passed, the Bright Soldiers had all been driven out of Aslinn and their days had fallen into a more peaceful pattern. In the depths of the forest they encountered many other faeries and Lilanthe spoke to them all, convincing them of Lachlan the Winged's integrity and peaceful intentions.

Two weeks earlier she had been bathing as usual in one of the many calm, green pools strung through the forest when she had seen Dide's face slowly appear in the ripples of light dancing over the surface. The jongleur had been calling her name rather anxiously, and Lilanthe had responded automatically.

The tree-shifter had never scryed before but she had seen Dide talk to Lachlan through water and once she had spoken mind-to-mind with the young jongleur when he had been lost in the marshes of Arran. She stared at him in mingled pleasure, perplexity and embarrassment. The last time she had seen him was in Isabeau's bed two and a half years ago, the memory bringing color to her face in a hot rush. She could not help smiling at him, though.

The young jongleur showed no sign of embarrassment, though his gaze lingered on her slender form so intently that she had to quickly sink below the water so that all he could see of her was her face and the green floating tresses of her hair. He asked after her affectionately and she told him all the news. He asked a few questions about the movements of the Tìrsoilleirean army through Aslinn and she told him that they had seen no sign of any of the Bright Soldiers since the previous autumn.

"The Graycloaks ride on Ardencaple to drive the Bright Soldiers out o' Blèssem once and for all," he said. "Meghan asked me to try and reach ye to see if ye could bring the forest faeries and join us there. Indeed, we will need all the help we can get, for hordes more o' the blaygird witch-haters have been pouring through Arran, seeking revenge for all their losses. How far away are ye?"

"I do no' ken where Ardencaple is," Lilanthe an-

swered, "but we're a couple o' weeks' march away from
the edge o' the forest at least, I'd say."

Dide lowered his voice, saying, "We march on Ardencaple in the dark o' the moons after Beltane. Can ye try
and reach us by then? Indeed it would be good to see
ye, Lilanthe."

She blushed again and answered rather awkwardly,
"And ye, Dide. It has been a long time."

"Aye," he answered. "Hard to believe it's been two
and a half years! I've missed ye though."

Words tangled in her throat. Not knowing which ones
to choose, she said nothing. He waited a moment expec-
tantly then bid her farewell, his reflection slowly dissolving into the ripple of the water's surface.

After that the army of forest faeries had turned and
marched for Blèssem, pleased at the idea of seeing more
fighting after their quiet winter. Lilanthe had not been
so pleased, though she thought often of Dide in the ensuing two weeks, oscillating between pleasure and anxiety
at the idea of seeing him again.

The pack of wolves howled the scent of blood and
Lilanthe's pace unconsciously quickened. Soon afterward
they heard the clash of arms and all the forest faeries
raised their weapons and rushed forward. They came
across a thin road winding through the forest. Bodies of
horses and men lay all along its route, some still crying
out in pain. Small groups of men were fighting desperately through the trees, those in gray jerkins greatly outnumbered by their armor-clad attackers.

The stench of blood was thick in the air and the satyricorns screeched in excitement. Lilanthe called to them
to restrain their blood-lust. "Kill only those in white
cloaks," she cried, but the horned women were already
running, shrieking in frenzied anticipation.

Afraid of what they might do, Lilanthe called again in
distress and suddenly the seelie lifted his golden head and
called out a long ululation. The satyricorns turned their
heads and howled in protest, but they did not spear
the wounded men with their sharp horns or fight over
the bodies of the dead, as Lilanthe had feared. Instead

they ran on, surprising a group of Bright Soldiers who
were walking along the road, killing any that lay injured.
With cries of ecstasy, the satyricorns stabbed and thrust
with their horns and laid about them with their clubs
until all the Bright Soldiers were dead, then they ran on
into the thick undergrowth in search of more.

The faeries of the forest surged after them, surprising
the Tìrsoilleirean soldiers fighting all through the trees.
Some were pulled down by wolves or clubbed to death
by corrigans. A screech of gravenings swooped down,
their filthy hair trailing, disease-carrying claws raking at
their eyes. Slinky and silent as giant cats, the shadow-
hounds poured through the trees, tearing out the throats
of the enemy. Another band of Bright Soldiers were
seized in the great arms of tree-changers and their
backs broken.

Lilanthe and Niall hurried to offer what aid they could
to the injured men, many of whom had not even had a
chance to unsheathe their swords.

"Where is the Rìgh?" Niall asked anxiously.

One man pointed up the road, saying hoarsely, "His
Highness rode at the front o' the cavalcade. I canna think
he could still be alive. I canna see how any could be, so
sudden and fierce was the attack." His head fell back on
the cloak Niall had pillowed beneath him.

The big man rose, saying reassuringly, "Our attack is
fiercer yet, I promise ye. Rest awhile and we'll be back
to succor ye when we can."

Lilanthe bid the nisses to carry water to the wounded
soldiers and the little faeries went flying off down to the
stream, carrying tiny cups made of leaves back to the
road. All brimming over with water, each cup was only
a sip for the thirst-tortured wounded, but so swift were
the nisses and so many that soon their parched throats
were soothed.

Meanwhile Lilanthe and Niall ran on up the road,
leaping over the bodies of the fallen. Amongst the trees
they saw Dide and Gwilym fighting back to back, a wall
of dead Tìrsoilleirean building up around them.

The jongleur's knives were whirling through the air as

if they had minds of their own, darting and flashing like hummingbirds. Dide was badly hurt, one leg hanging uselessly, one eye obscured with blood flowing from a wound to his head. He was only able to keep upright with the help of the one-legged warlock, who had his club propped under his armpit. Blue light flashed out from Gwilym's fingers, disintegrating one soldier after another. Still the Bright Soldiers fought on, two replacing each one that fell. An archer fired arrow after arrow at them, but always Dide managed to deflect them, sending them spinning into the bodies of his attackers.

"Do no' kill the witches!" an armor-clad sergeant standing in the middle of the road cried. "We will want them for the fire in Ardencaple. Subdue them now, though, and quickly!"

Dide staggered as the onslaught intensified, and Lilanthe cried aloud in alarm. With a loud roar the bear launched into action, charging up the road and killing the sergeant with one swipe of her massive paw. Lilanthe called for help and a grove of tree-changers came striding through the forest, branches swinging, stormy voices singing. Their great, gnarled roots tore up the earth, tripping up the terrified soldiers who tried in vain to run. One by one they were caught up and crushed in the tree-changers' mighty embrace. Those who did escape were brought down by the shadow-hounds, their green eyes as bright as lanterns in the dim forest.

Dide wiped the blood from his brow with his hand. "It seems ye are to make a practice o' rescuing me," he said hoarsely and hugged Lilanthe fiercely. "Thank ye again!"

Lilanthe hugged him back, as Gwilym said, "I do no' think we could have held them off another minute. Thank Eà ye came when ye did!"

Lilanthe emerged from Dide's embrace to see Niall the Bear watching. Unaccountably she flushed and stepped away from the jongleur's arm. Dide sat down rather abruptly, his leg giving way beneath him. Ruefully he examined the gaping wound, then gazed up at the tree-changers swaying away through the woods.

"So ye found your own kin," he said softly.

Lilanthe flushed, feeling suddenly angry. *Why does he always think o' me as more faery than human,* she thought. *I am both!* She said nothing, nodding brusquely.

"I'm glad," he said, and her anger left her.

"So am I," she answered.

"Can ye walk?" Niall said to the jongleur rather abruptly. "The Bright Soldiers flee before us but I fear for His Highness. One o' the wounded said he was at the head o' the cavalcade. We must hurry and see if we can help him."

"He's alive," Lilanthe said, casting out her mind. "And so is Iseult. I can feel pain though . . ."

Dide tried to stand and fell again, too exhausted from the battle to bear weight on his uninjured leg. Niall gestured curtly to the bear and she swooped Dide up in her great paws and carried him as tenderly as a child. Gwilym swung along after them, using his crutch with great dexterity.

"Ye limp?" Dide said, seeing Lilanthe's halting step. "Ye've been injured?"

"Someone attacked me wi' an axe in Lucescere," she replied shortly and, at his expression of horror, felt a certain grim satisfaction.

"Who?" he demanded.

Lilanthe shrugged. "It all happened so fast and I was sleeping. I only saw a glimpse o' him . . ." She put two fingers in her mouth and whistled and the shadow-hounds swarmed to her heels, their jaws dripping with bloody froth.

The Bright Soldiers were gradually retreating before the advance of the forest faeries, fighting obstinately every step of the way. However, with the shadow-hounds writhing at their back and the great woolly bear at their side, Lilanthe and her companions were not challenged.

There were so many dead soldiers that it was difficult to make progress. They had to climb over the bodies as if they were logs swept downstream after a flood. There were many among them that Niall and Dide knew, and their faces were rigid with grief and horror. Lilanthe knew only a few, but she wept as she clambered and staggered through the corpses, seeing the contorted limbs and faces of violent death everywhere she looked.

Suddenly they heard the clatter of many horses traveling fast. Round the bend of the road came a company of Bright Soldiers, whipping their horses into a lather. They rode unheedingly over the bodies lying on the road, not caring if any they trampled were still alive. The satyricorns turned and charged them with shouts of glee. Without slackening pace, the soldiers laid all about them with their swords. Many of the horned women fell beneath their blades or were knocked down by the galloping horses. A few of the riders fell but none of their company even looked back, disappearing around the corner.

"Did ye see!" Lilanthe cried. "They carried someone wi' them. I think . . . I'm afraid . . ."

"Aye," Niall answered somberly. "It was the old seer. Even above all their bonds I could see him. This is bad news indeed."

Around the next bend, Niall and Lilanthe came upon great piles of dead and dying. Niall saw the mangled bodies of Bald Deaglan and Barnard the Eagle and could not help crying aloud in distress. "These are Blue Guards," he said. "His Highness must be near!"

Lilanthe said urgently, "I can sense Meghan. Quick! They are hard pressed, I can feel it."

Meghan threw up her hand and caught an arrow only inches from her breast. With a curse she flung it from her, catching another with her other hand. As she ducked her wild gray head, three more zinged through the air and stuck quivering into the rock behind her.

Then a Bright Soldier charging them suddenly and inexplicably tripped, his pike falling from his fingers. With a rustle the pike slithered across the ground and into Meghan's hand. The old sorceress used it to stab a soldier who had leapt over the pile of boulders. He fell back with a cry and Meghan threw the pike with unnatural strength, spitting the tripped Bright Soldier who had just managed to regain his feet.

They crouched down again, Iseult only just managing to ride out the waves of dizziness threatening to overcome her.

"Look, there is Iain!" Meghan cried. She sent a bolt of blue lightning from her hand, sizzling two soldiers about to split the prionnsa's skull with their swords. They fell in a scatter of ashes and Iain looked round, bemused.

"T-T-Thank Eà!" he cried. "Or rather, thank M-M-Meghan o' the Beasts."

He ran to their side, ducking and weaving through the scatter of arrows still falling from the trees. He was wounded in the leg and side, but his sword was clotted with blood and flesh.

"Where is Lachlan!" he cried. "Is His Highness s-s-safe!"

Iseult pointed dumbly upward. Iain gasped as he saw the Rìgh flying through the branches, his sword darting and flashing almost too fast to be followed. Behind him body after body fell.

"Look!" Iseult cried.

Meghan and Iain looked where she directed. Deep in the forest they saw a vine rear up out of the ground and throttle a Bright Soldier to death. Another vine whipped out of the trees like a giant snake and dragged a berhtilde down, strangling her in a few swift, agonizing seconds.

"Matthew!" Meghan cried. "Look, it is Matthew the Lean!"

They saw the lanky witch crouched in the shelter of a dead horse, his fingers working frantically as he commanded the very weeds of the forest.

"He always did have to use his hands," Meghan said censoriously. "A sorcerer should be able to command by thought alone, without all those finger-wavings and noisy grunts."

"We're in the middle o' a fight to the death and she still finds time to criticize," Iseult said, her face deathly pale, the plaid she clutched to her shoulder stained crimson.

"Ye're hurt, m-m-my lady!" Iain cried.

She said sternly, "Only a wee. Have ye seen Gwilym or Dide? And I'm worried indeed about Duncan, he was on the cliff last time I saw him." She waved behind her at the mass of broken slabs and boulders and Iain's face creased with concern. "Nay, my lady, it all happened so fast I do no' ken what has happened to anyone!"

Suddenly they heard the clatter of horses' hooves traveling fast. "M-M-More Bright Soldiers!" Iain cried, growing even paler. He lifted his sword but Iseult drew him down behind the pile of rocks.

"There are thirty or more there, Iain," she whispered. "Let them pass if we can."

Meghan stared down the road. "Jorge!" she cried. "No!"

The riders galloped around the curve of the road and straight for her. Although Iseult cried aloud in alarm, the old sorceress stepped right in their path, lifting her hand as if she thought to stop them by the gesture alone. The horses reared and plunged, trying to throw their riders, but cruelly the soldiers whipped them on. In horror Iseult realized one carried a tightly bound, unconscious form across his pommel. She saw briefly a flutter of a pale blue robe and the end of a long white beard, then the horses had galloped past, veering around Meghan like a stream of water around a rock.

One of the soldiers cracked his whip at her but she caught it in her thin old hand, pulling him from his saddle. He hit the ground with a thud and a crack and lay still. Iseult bent and caught up a bow, firing arrow after arrow. Although six of the riders fell with screams and one horse dropped in its tracks, the other riders raced on and disappeared from sight.

Tears were flowing down the old sorceress's face. She fell to her knees, rocking. "No, no," she cried. "We must save him! Iseult! We must save him!"

Iseult drew her dagger as seven Tìrsoilleirean foot soldiers charged them from the bushes. "Let us save ourselves first if we can," she cried.

Meghan did not rise. She raised her grief-contorted

face to the sky and cried, "Come to me, Caillec Aillen Airi Telloch Cas! It is time!"

Lachlan clung to the bole of a tree, trying to catch his breath. He swung behind the trunk as one of the archers hidden in the branches shot at him, and he had to use his wings to stop from falling. From this vantage point he had a clear view down the road and could see how many of his men lay dead or dying. A black misery and rage consumed him. With a shriek like a falcon, he spread his wings and soared above the canopy of leaves, dropping down behind the archer who had shot at him before and strangling him with his bare hands. The man's death brought Lachlan no relief.

The Rìgh heard the thunder of horses' hooves and looked down through the leaves to see the Bright Soldiers galloping over the bodies of his men. He saw Meghan try and stop them and recognized with a jolt of his heart the bound figure flung over one of the saddles. Lachlan had known and revered Jorge all his life. Horror pierced him like a knife. He gave an unearthly cry of despair and grief which rang through the forest like a clarion call. Without thinking, he spread his wings and swooped down through the trees in pursuit. An archer hidden in the branches took careful aim and fired. The arrow took the Rìgh full in the breast and, with a scream, he fell. Through twigs and branches he crashed, tumbling down and down until he slammed into the ground below, his wing snapped and bent beneath him, blood from a wound in his temple creeping out through the grass.

FIRE LEAPING,
SNOW WHIRLING

The shadows of the trees were growing long when Dillon led his little band out of the forest and onto the battlefield.

Ryley had died during the march, suddenly falling as he walked, his bandage bright with blood. The children were all shocked and distraught, for the soldier had made no complaint, no groan of pain. The Tìrsoilleirean had been so close on their heels they had had no chance to pause for Tòmas to lay his healing hands upon him. Numb with grief, the little boy had for once not noticed the pain emanating from the burly soldier and his sudden, unexpected collapse broke his tender heart. He sobbed uncontrollably and Anntoin had to lift him and carry him, as Johanna picked up Ryley's sword and buckled it around her waist, then hefted his heavy shield. In her grubby white bodice and pantaloons she could have looked a comic figure, but instead she looked stern and rather noble. "Let us go on," she had said simply, and they had left Ryley there in the shelter of a tree as if he was merely sleeping.

The healers were all drooping with exhaustion after their desperate flight, but as soon as Johanna saw the injured lying among the trees and bushes, she began to issue swift, clear orders and the healers obeyed her instantly, forgetting their own fear and weariness. Tòmas struggled to be put down, running from body to body, laying his hands on them all, not willing to wait for Johanna to see whether they were alive or not. So many of those he touched did not respond that the little boy grew even more distressed, and Johanna had to try and restrain him.

Then Parlan cried out in horror and they all came running. The boy had found Duncan Ironfist lying crushed beneath a great pile of broken boulders. Only his bruised and bloodied head and shoulders were free of the mass of stone. Miraculously the big captain was alive, although his every tortured breath bubbled with blood. All of the squires were distressed indeed, for they loved the huge, kindly man who had taken so much time to teach them their swordsmanship. Many small, willing hands cleared away the rocks and then at last they dragged him free, the unconscious man groaning in pain.

Every part of his body was crushed and broken and it seemed a miracle that he lived. Trembling and weeping still, Tòmas knelt and laid his thin little hands on the bloodied head, and slowly each cut and stab-wound healed over. The captain did not regain consciousness and Tòmas was visibly harrowed by the effort to heal him. The little boy shook and retched, trying to catch his breath. Johanna knelt behind him and supported his frail body, giving him some restorative potion to drink. At last some of his strength seemed to return to him.

"He be strong," the little boy said, slumped over, his shoulders still heaving. "He will recover, though I had to take much o' his vitality for the healing."

"And too much o' your own," Johanna scolded. "Ye will kill yourself in trying to save others. Ye must have a care for yourself."

Tòmas stared around at all the torn and bloodied bodies and said with a break in his voice, "I can feel their pain, I can feel it!"

Suddenly a flock of nisses swooped down, buzzing around the healers' heads like hornets, scolding them in their high-pitched voices. Most had never seen a nisse before and they stared at the rainbow-winged little faeries in wonder, half afraid. Then Lilanthe emerged from the trees, her green dress torn and blood-stained, her narrow face smeared with dirt. The healers stared at her, drawing back a little, but Johanna knew her and started forward with a cry.

"What has happened?" she begged. "Was the Rìgh ambushed? How did they ken where the Graycloaks rode?"

Lilanthe said somberly, "The Rìgh was betrayed. Come, Tòmas, the Keybearer will be glad indeed to see ye, I ken. The Rìgh is sorely hurt. He needs your powers desperately."

Johanna exclaimed in consternation and seized the little boy by the hand as he struggled to touch another of the thousands of bodies littered through the trees. "Come, laddiekin, ye canna touch them all. We shall do what we can for them and once we ken who are quick and who are dead, we shall bring ye back, I promise."

Tòmas was too weak to walk and so Dillon carried him on his back, leaving Parlan and Anntoin to watch over Duncan. They followed Lilanthe up the road, unable to control their cries of shock and dismay as they saw the extent of the carnage. They found Meghan stooping over the still form of Lachlan. Her face was ravaged, her eyes red-rimmed. The donbeag was huddled into her neck, crooning miserably, but for once the old witch paid him no heed. She was trying to staunch the wound in the Rìgh's breast, but there was little she could do. She saw Tòmas and her black eyes lit up with hope.

"Thank Eà!" she cried. "Oh, Tòmas, my lad, can ye save him? His back and wing is broken, and his head. He is close to death indeed."

Dillon set the little boy down. Tòmas could not stand unaided, his sticklike legs folding beneath him. He drew a trembling breath and looked up at Meghan. "I do no' ken," he said, "but I will try."

He leaned over and placed his hands on the Rìgh's forehead. For a long moment nothing happened and then the lips of the bloody wound at Lachlan's breast began to knit together. The little boy frowned and made a grunting noise, and his hands began to shake. The broken arc of the wing slowly wove back together; the bruising on Lachlan's temple sank and faded, the jagged cut in

its heart slowly congealing. Tòmas breathed harshly,
swaying. Suddenly he went limp and fell sideways.

"Is he dead?" Dillon cried as Johanna screamed and
scrambled to the little boy's side. Jed whined and nudged
him anxiously.

"Nay," she said, tears pouring down her cheeks. "No'
quite. He breathes—just."

Meghan dropped her face into her hands. "No, no,"
she whispered hoarsely. "It is too much! Both Iseult and
Lachlan—and now Tòmas."

Johanna cradled the little boy in her arms. "Is Iseult
hurt too?" she said in dismay.

Meghan raised her harrowed face. "She was with babe.
She was sorely wounded and when we found Lachlan
like this, it was all too much. She lost the babe."

Johanna laid Tòmas's head in Dillon's lap and rose to
her feet, her face grim. "Where is she? I will go to her."

Meghan pointed to one side. Through the uncertain
light of the dusk, they saw Iseult lying wrapped in cloaks
under the trees, Iain kneeling beside her. Johanna hurried to her, a ghostly white figure in the twilight.

Gwilym bent and seized a branch from the ground,
lighting it with a thought and setting it in the ground so
Johanna could see her patient. "Night comes," he said,
his voice hollow.

The Banrìgh lay still, her knees to her chest, dry-eyed
and grieving. Nothing Johanna said would make her look
up or respond, and so at last the healer made her drink
some poppy syrup and Iseult fell asleep, hunched over
still.

Lilanthe had gone beyond exhaustion to a strange,
floating state. She stood, hands hanging limply, tears hot
in her chest. Vainly she tried to rouse herself to go on
helping the injured, but it seemed she could bear no
more of the smell and sight of death.

The nisses flew all around her head, trilling loudly.
Elala caught hold of one of her flowering tresses and
swung, both diamond-bright wings fluttering madly. Lilanthe wiped her eyes and tried to swallow her grief. She

cupped the little faery in her hand and looked into her green-flame eyes. *What is it?* she asked.

Time for the eating devouring of the bloom blossom? Time for the healing unharming?

Lilanthe stared at the nisse in complete stupefaction, her tired mind refusing to work. Then suddenly her hand flew to the pouch at her belt where she had hidden the flower of the Summer Tree. In the confusion of the battle she had never given it a thought.

"Ye want me to eat the flower?" she whispered.

The nisse hissed and bared her sharp fangs. *Bloom blossom belongs to the Stargazers. It is their lifeblood bloodlife that is spilled to bless the tree, it is the child's loved beloved who dies.*

Lilanthe stared at the tiny faery. It took a while for her to understand, then her breath caught. *I see,* she said and went over to where Tòmas lay. She knelt by his side and withdrew the great flower from her pouch.

Although they were brown and crumpled, a fragrant odor still clung to the petals. Lilanthe held it under Tòmas's nose and the rich, spicy perfume roused him, faint color coming again to his cheeks. He opened his eyes and gazed blankly at Lilanthe.

"Ye must eat this," the tree-shifter said.

Tòmas looked at it, puzzled, then obediently he took it from her hand and began to eat the wilted petals. He asked no questions nor showed any revulsion. For a moment he lay still, then hectic color washed over him and he began to shudder, clasping his thin arms about his body. He cried out as if in pain and his pupils dilated until his eyes were black, not blue. He cast one wild glance at Lilanthe then he rolled over, kicking his legs, shaking his head uncontrollably, all his limbs twitching.

"Wha' is wrong? Wha' have ye done?" Johanna cried and sprang to hold him, her eyes accusing.

Lilanthe could not reply, watching Tòmas's convulsions with horrified eyes. She heard Meghan come hurrying, barking out orders and questions, then watched as they held Tòmas down, putting a stick between his teeth to prevent him biting off his tongue.

Meghan turned to Lilanthe and said harshly, "What did ye give him? I saw ye feed him something."

"It was a flower o' the Summer Tree. Cloudshadow gave it to me."

"Did she tell ye to feed it to Tòmas?" Meghan snapped.

"No, it was the nisses," Lilanthe replied, terrified.

They turned and stared at the little faeries, hovering nearby. In the flickering light of the newly lit torches, their triangular faces looked oddly malevolent. Johanna made the sign of Eà's blessing, beginning to weep.

"He is o' Stargazer blood," Lilanthe cried. "Can ye no' feel it?"

Meghan turned sharply and stared at Tòmas. He lay still, panting harshly. The old witch nodded. "Happen ye are right," she answered.

After a long time of stillness and silence, the little boy sat up, his cheeks still crimson, his eyes unnaturally bright. "Bring me the wounded," he said in a mere croak of a voice. No one moved and he cried, "Bring me the wounded!"

The first person he touched was Lachlan but although all the Rìgh's wounds healed over till there was not even a scar to mar his smooth, olive skin, he did not wake. "There is something more than mere physical hurt." Tòmas frowned, running his hands all over Lachlan's face and body. "He is bound down by black threads o' hatred that I canna cut through. He struggles to be free but he canna escape. He has been cursed, I think."

"Cursed?" Dide cried.

"Cursed and betrayed," Meghan whispered. "If I find out who has done such a thing, I shall cast a curse the like o' which has never been seen in this land!"

"How can we break the curse?" Lilanthe cried, and Meghan shook her straggly white head.

"We canna," she replied. "If it is a curse o' any potency, only they who cast the curse can break it."

"Then we must find out who it was that cast it," Dide cried, seizing Lachlan's hand in his and kissing it. "Och, master, who would do such a thing?"

"I wager if we ride on Arran we'll find our answer,"

Meghan replied, looking off into the darkness, her face set like stone.

They spent the night working to save the few who still lived and dragging the dead into grim piles between the trees. The tree-changers and other faeries helped, the horse-eel dragging litters through the undergrowth, the corrigans carrying the wounded on their broad backs. Tòmas walked among the injured, bringing miraculous strength and wellness back into their damaged bodies. Those he touched were able to stand and help carry others, and by the time dawn came, all who still lived were as if they had never been harmed.

In the morning light they made the terrible tally. Of the two thousand men who had followed Lachlan through the forest, only a scant few hundred still lived. Barnard the Eagle, Murdoch of the Axe and Bald Deaglan were among the dead, and Finlay Fear-Naught was missing, bringing Lachlan's staff of officers down to a mere four. They all feared Finlay had been taken prisoner, having been betrayed into some foolhardy action by his impetuosity.

Matthew the Lean too had disappeared, one of the wounded reporting he had seen the witch being dragged away after he had been struck down from behind.

"Please, Eà, let them no' be taken to the fire," Meghan prayed, rocking back and forth in despair. Some time during the night her hair had turned as white as snow and it hung down around her body in leaf-matted knots and straggles. "Please, let us reach them in time!"

Their only hope was that the other divisions of the Rìgh's army had won through to Ardencaple and had prevented the Bright Soldiers from taking their captives back into the shelter of the town's walls. Duncan Ironfist organized the remaining men into columns and made sure all were armed and provisioned. Then they lost no time in marching on through the woods, Lachlan and Iseult huddled together on a litter drawn by the horse-eel, swollen to his largest size. The great, white falcon perched near the Rìgh's head, occasionally nudging him with his curved beak.

It was a glorious day, all green and gold and fresh and singing. Lilanthe found herself so oppressed by the beauty of the forest that she could hardly see for her tears. Why should the sun shine or the birds carol when there was so much evil in the world?

They had reached the forest's outskirts when Meghan suddenly screamed. She flung up her hands and fell to her knees, the terrible, echoing cries going on and on. "Jorge!" she shouted. "Oh, no, Jorge! Matthew!"

Tòmas too was shrieking and writhing, beating at himself as if to stamp out invisible flames. For a moment all was confusion, Johanna flinging herself on Tòmas and trying to hold his hands still, Lilanthe trying desperately to comfort the old sorceress, although she herself was almost overwhelmed by the emotions that assaulted her.

Meghan would not be comforted. On and on she screamed, tears pouring down the furrows of her wrinkled face. Lilanthe dashed the tears from her own cheeks and went to the litter where Iseult still lay, her arm across her husband's back and under his wing. Her eyes were open but without any sign that she saw or heard a thing.

"Your Highness," Lilanthe called, shaking her arm a little. "Please, the Keybearer needs ye. Please." She shook her a little harder and Iseult turned and looked at her with a hard, flat, angry stare. "Meghan needs you," the tree-shifter said.

Only then did Iseult seem to hear Meghan's cries. "What?" she whispered, then an odd expression flashed briefly across her face. "I see. The auld blind man dies."

She rose a little gingerly, seemingly surprised to find that her body moved without pain, and crossed the clearing to where Meghan crouched, rocking and wailing. Iseult knelt by her side and, for the first time since meeting the old witch three years earlier, freely and willingly touched her in affection. She put her arms around Meghan's shaking form and pulled her wild, white head into her shoulder, crooning to her as if she were a child.

"There, there, Meghan, dearling, do no' greet, do no' greet."

Meghan rocked back and forth, keening. "Why, Eà, why?" she pleaded. "Why such a death? He was a good man, a dear, sweet, kind, loving man. Why should he die such a horrible death? And Matthew too, who never harmed a flea?"

She raised herself upon her staff and lifted her contorted face to the summer sky. "Ye who have betrayed us so, I lay this curse upon ye! Let the good earth refuse ye her fruits and the river his cool waters, let the winds deny ye their breath and flame deny ye warmth and comfort, let the moons turn their dark faces upon ye. May ye wander outcast and impoverished, and haunt the doors o' others, and beg for food with trembling mouth, and be turned away with kicks and curses. May neither your body nor your mind be free from querulous pain; may night be to ye more grievous than day, and day sore grievous indeed. May ye be forever piteous but have none pity ye; may ye long for death but have death elude ye! By the power o' the dark moons, I curse thee, I curse thee, I curse thee!"

All were greatly affected by the old sorceress's sorrow. Many found themselves so choked with sobs they could hardly breathe. Parlan, Anntoin, Johanna and Dillon were wracked with grief, tears flowing down their faces.

"He saw what was to come," Dillon choked, "yet still he smiled at us as we left him. How could we? How could we?"

At last Meghan composed herself, her hand creeping up to cup the little donbeag who cuddled under her chin. "What is done is done," she said harshly. "Let us ride on and teach those Bright Soldiers a lesson they shall never forget!"

So they marched on into the fields, not caring that their boots were trampling fresh, green crops into the ground. Behind them surged the faeries, so that it seemed as if the forest itself marched at their command.

Ahead, Ardencaple rose from the plain. Built on a small hill circled on three sides by the river Arden, it

was a pretty town with pointed roofs and round turrets
set at regular intervals about the outer wall. The white
pennants of the Tìrsoilleirean army fluttered from the
towers and the Graycloaks set their jaws and gripped
their hands into fists at the sight.

A column of dark smoke rose from the center of the
town straight into the still air, and as they marched, the
Rìgh's army fixed their eyes upon it in a sort of horrified
fascination. All were unable to think of anything but the
old man who had died in that fire, and all hoped that
the few people unaccounted for among the dead had not
been lashed in with him.

As they came nearer to Ardencaple they saw with dismay that the rest of their army had been lured into a
trap too and was slowly being obliterated. The Bright
Soldiers had lined up their cannons along the outer wall
and, with the day so still and warm, were having no
trouble in lighting their fuses. Again and again the attacking Graycloaks were bombarded with cannonballs,
men and horses falling screaming at every shot. It was
clear the Tìrsoilleirean had been fully prepared for their
attack and had lured the Duke of Killiegarrie within firing range by leaving their gates open and their men hidden. Although the Duke was trying to call the retreat,
the bridge behind them had been blown up and the
Graycloaks were trapped between the town and the
river.

Meghan and her party came to a halt at the crest of
a slight hill which gave a view across the battlefield. Beside them the Arden River flowed through willows and
alder trees, shading them from the hot sun.

Iseult bit her lip thoughtfully, examining the lie of the
land and the extent of the Tìrsoilleirean defenses. Although she felt as if her body was a cup overbrimming
with rage and pain, she had herself under tight control.
She fixed Iain and Gwilym with her grave stare and said
shortly, "Any chance o' calling up rain to dampen those
fuses? We canna hope to win the day if we do no' disable
those blaygird cannons o' theirs!"

They glanced at each other and then at Meghan. "If

we all work together, happen we could," Gwilym said hesitantly. "This still, warm air will work against us though."

"We are c-c-close to Arran," Iain said. "I f-f-feel my m-m-m-mother's hand behind this hot weather. We are n-n-near the coast and should be f-f-feeling a sea wind."

"Very well. Call the other witches. Do we have enough to make a circle o' power with Jorge and Matthew gone?"

Again Gwilym glanced at Meghan. The old sorceress was staring up at the sky, her face crumpled and worn with grief. With her white hair and haggard face, she looked every one of her four hundred and thirty years.

"I do no' ken if Meghan is up to much works o' power," Gwilym said in a low voice.

Even though she was some distance away, Meghan turned at that and limped toward them, saying harshly, "Worry about your own powers, Ugly! I have more power in my little finger than ye have in your whole body, never forget that!"

He gave a wry grin, saying, "How could I possibly?"

"I shall stay with ye and lend ye my powers, then ride to join the men when we are done," Iseult said. "Indeed, my will and my desire are strong today. I long to strike at those foul, loathsome, slimy maggots that call themselves men. Bright Soldiers! Better that they should be called filthy, black-hearted, mud-dwelling, blood-sucking scum!"

She paused, getting control of her temper again while the others stared at her in some amazement, never having heard Iseult raise her voice or utter anything but the most well-considered words. They saw the muscles in her jaw clench, then she said calmly, "Wait while I talk with Duncan and work out the best approach, then I shall be with ye."

Gwilym found a clear patch of earth near the water and carefully laid a fire, using a bough of each of the seven sacred woods, which the witches always made sure were included among the supplies. Then he drew a wide circle around the fire with his witch's dagger, leaving a

small gap to act as a doorway. Within he drew a hexa-
gram for, with Iseult joining them, they had six witches,
including Dide and Dughall. Neither Iseult nor Dide was
fully trained but both had power and would be able to
supplement the strength of the others. Working weather
was always difficult unless you had a Talent for it and
so Gwilym was doing everything he could to focus and
augment their strength.

The one-legged witch then sprinkled the circle with
water, earth, ashes and salt, chanting: "I consecrate and
conjure thee, O circle o' magic, ring o' power, symbol o'
perfection and constant renewal. Keep us safe from
harm, keep us safe from evil, guard us against treachery,
keep us safe in your eyes, Eà o' the moons."

He did the same along the crisscrossing lines of the
star. "I consecrate and conjure thee, O star o' spirit,
pentacle o' power, symbol o' fire and darkness, o' light
in the depths o' space. Fill us with your dark fire, your
fiery darkness, make o' us your vessels, fill us with light."

The army marching past watched solemnly as the
witches prepared themselves to work their magic. They
washed themselves in the river and performed calming
and centering exercises, breathing deeply and slowly, focusing their minds. Meghan would have liked them to
have undressed completely, but here on the edge of the
battlefield they were vulnerable enough already and so
they simply stripped off their plaids and jerkins and
rolled up their sleeves.

Iseult joined the little group by the river and washed
herself and unbound her red-gold curls. When she was
ready she stepped within the gap in the circle and sat at
one of the six points of the star.

Gwilym closed the circle behind her and they all held
hands and closed their eyes. The sun beat down on their
heads but they ignored it, chanting softly: "In the name
o' Eà, our mother and our father, thee who is Spinner
and Weaver and Cutter o' the Thread; thee who sows
the seed, nurtures the crop, and reaps the harvest; by the
virtue o' the four elements, wind, stone, flame and rain;
by virtue o' clear skies and storm, rainbows and hail-

stones, flowers and falling leaves, flames and ashes; in the name o' Eà, we call upon the winds o' the world, in the name o' Eà we call upon the waters . . ."

Then at a counterpoint to the other witches' voices, Gwilym began to chant:

"Come hither, spirits o' the west, bringing rain,
Come hither, spirits o' the east, bringing wind,
Come hither, spirits o' the west, bringing rain,
Come hither, spirits o' the east, bringing wind."

On and on they chanted and felt the first stirring of a breeze against the hairs on their arms. Their spirits lifted and the force of their chanting increased. Iseult gripped Meghan's and Gwilym's hands tightly, focusing every ounce of her strength of will and desire upon the words. A bitter wind lifted their unbound hair, blowing it about wildly. Icy wetness touched their cheeks. Their chanting slowed and then stopped. The witches opened their eyes to see snow whirling all about them.

Dillon hurried down the road, bent over from the waist so his body would be hidden behind the hedgerow. His freckled face was set in an expression of determination and his hand gripped the hilt of his sword tightly.

The squire had been ordered to stay behind with the healers and the unconscious body of Lachlan in the little grove by the river, but Dillon had waited only long enough for the Graycloaks to march out of sight down the road before following close on their heels. Behind him Anntoin and Parlan ran, doubled over as well with the big shaggy dog bounding close behind. No one had noticed them go, for the witches were busy casting their spells and Johanna and the healers were busy stripping bark from the willows. The battle in the forest had depleted their healing stores greatly and Johanna had been too well trained not to take advantage of such an abundant source of pain relief.

Soon Dillon could hear the sound of swords clashing and men shouting. The air stank of gunpowder smoke,

making his eyes sting. Behind the acrid smell of smoke
was the smell of blood, an odor he had grown too used
to.

The squire hesitated at the end of the hedge, watching
the battle with dismay. Several companies of Tìrsoilleirean knights had ridden out to engage with the broken
remnants of the Rìgh's army, wielding their swords and
lances with contemptuous skill. Most of the Graycloaks
were on foot, their horses either shot dead or too spooked
by the noise and smell of the cannons to be ridden. Row
upon row of harquebusiers were firing from the walls, aiming for the Eileanan leaders and flag-bearers so that the
foot soldiers were completely demoralized. The river was
choked with dead men and horses, overturned wagons
and broken barrels. A pall of smoke hung over everything and several trees were aflame, their blackened
twigs looking like pain-tortured fingers.

Despair and rage flooded through Dillon and he drew
his sword with a curse. It sprang free of the sheath with
a hissing noise. He waved it above his head and ran
yelling into the heart of the conflict.

Swords sprang at him and, yelling still, Dillon knocked
them away, a straight cut, a downward slash, a high
thrust, an extended lunge, a jab under his arm. A red
mist rose through his brain. The sword danced in his
hand. He parried and thrust, feinted and riposted. Men
screamed, falling before him. He heard their shrieks and
gurgles only dimly. The stench of burning was in his nostrils, the smell of blood. He was icy cold. He shook with
cold and fever. All he could see was Jorge's sad, sweet
smile, the bloody gash at Lachlan's temple, the sound of
Tòmas's screams, and his flailing, desperate hands. As
Dillon stabbed, slashed, hacked and dismembered, he
wept tears that turned to bloody icicles on his pale, freckled face.

Iseult stared at the thickly driving snow in stupefaction,
then turned and looked at the other witches. They were
all staring at her.

"We call rain and she brings snow—in the middle o' a heatwave!" Gwilym said with a twist to his mouth.

"Indeed, I wish ye'd worked with us last summer w-w-when we were trying to break my m-m-mother's hold on the w-w-weather," Iain said. "We could've done w-w-with a snowstorm or two then!"

Meghan smiled grimly. "Well, well, lassie, snow in the middle o' May!"

"Will it do the job?" Iseult said harshly.

They could not see through the whirling snowflakes but listened intently. Although the sound of arms clashing continued, there was no cannon fire.

"I think so," Gwilym said, hastily rolling down his sleeves. "Brrrrr, but it has turned cold!"

"Then open the circle and let me join my men," Iseult said.

Gwilym complied and they all gladly stood up, stamping their feet and huddling into their plaids. So swiftly did the snow fall that the ground was already covered and the river was icing over. The narrow green leaves and hanging catkins of the willows were tinkling with ice, and the sky to the north, so blue and sunny only a scant ten minutes earlier, was leaden with snow clouds.

Johanna and Lilanthe were trying to cover Lachlan's sleeping body with their cloaks but the bitter wind kept blowing them up into the air. Both girls had blue lips and nails, having been dressed for summer. The horse-eel was stamping and shivering miserably, shrunken down to the size of a goat. Even the seelie looked miserable, icicles forming at the end of his pointed ear lobes.

Gwilym snapped his fingers and the fire at the heart of the sacred circle sprung up into a roaring bonfire. Gladly the healers huddled close to its warmth, holding out their hands to its blaze. The seelie crept closer, his desire for warmth overcoming his instinctive fear of fire. For once even Lilanthe dared to come close to the flames, feeling her sap slowing and thickening in her veins in response to the cold.

Iseult ignored the bitter wind, strapping on her weapons' belt and cradling her crossbow in one arm. She bent and kissed her unconscious husband between the eyes, smoothing back his black curls, then set off down the road without a word. Iain and Dide caught up their weapons and hurried to join her.

Suddenly Meghan cried out and pointed up at the sky. "The dragons come!"

Iseult whipped around, her eyes flying up to the turbulent sky. Flying out of the maelstrom were seven great dragons, gleaming gold in the sun which shone on the clouds from the south. Their wings were spread wide as they battled against the storm and they bugled aloud in defiance and joy.

"Dragons!" Gwilym cried in alarm. "Eà forbid, the dragons fly!"

The healers screamed in terror and fell to the ground. Even Iseult, who had flown the dragon's back, felt dragon-fear quicken her pulses and loosen her bowels.

Meghan was exultant. "The queen-dragon has kept her promise!" she cried. "Come, Iseult! We must call for our men to retreat, lest they be flamed to death as well."

The old sorceress did not wait for a response but began to run down the road as nimbly as if she were nineteen like Iseult. The Banrìgh ran after her, Iain, Dughall and Dide on her heels. Gwilym stared after them longingly, leaning on his club, then looked up with fearful awe as the dragons wheeled around, bugling still.

Dide reached the edge of the battlefield first. He lifted his hands to his mouth and gave the call for the retreat as loudly and clearly as if he held a trumpet to his lips. Again and again he called, and all over the field gray-clad soldiers heeded the call, disengaging and retreating back toward the river. As they ran, the dragons wheeled one more time, then they folded their wings and plummeted toward Ardencaple, fire streaming from their mouths.

Flames billowed up the turrets and walls, casting lurid shadows over the battle scene below. The dragons dived and soared, shooting great screaming balls of flame into the center of the town. Barrels of gunpowder exploded and a terrible shrieking rose as the townsfolk and soldiers trapped within the walls began to panic. The Bright Soldiers out in the field were aghast, turning to watch, their swords dropping from their fingers. Some wept and shook their fists. Others were too shocked to move.

Only one small figure fought on. Covered in blood from his thatch of sandy hair down to his boots, Dillon battled on, disregarding the dreadful, magnificent sight of the flaming dragons. He was breathing in harsh, gasping pants, his chest heaving, his wrist wavering in exhaustion. Even though the soldiers he attacked had to wrench their attention away from the burning town to protect themselves, he did not falter. Jed was at his heels as always, his white fur stained and rusty, his jaws red.

Meghan saw the boy and the dog and her gaze sharpened. "Och, the foolish lad! He's taken Joyeuse."

The old witch strode through the dead and wounded, her plaid wrapped close about her against the cold. Behind her were the remnants of the Righ's army, standing on the frozen river, their faces upturned to the sky. All were watching in fascination the aerial maneuvers of the dragons as they rode the storm winds with spreading wings as thin as beaten gold.

"Dillon!" Meghan called. "Dillon, sheathe your sword. The battle is won. Sheathe your sword." Again and again she repeated the words but he ignored her, killing one then another then another. "Dillon, sheathe your sword. The battle is won. Sheathe your sword!"

He killed the last and looked about him blindly.

"The battle is won. Sheathe your sword."

Slowly the boy looked at her and raised the sword. His eyes were blank. Iseult wound on her little crossbow and raised it to her shoulder. "Ye have won," Meghan said kindly. "Ye need kill no more. Sheathe your sword."

Blindly Dillon looked around him. He was shaking with grief and exhaustion. Some sense returned to him. His dazed eyes took in the ruin of the meadow, the blazing town, the black smoke and whirling snow. Then he saw the fallen bodies of Anntoin and Parlan lying among the dead. He fell to his knees, looking at the bloodied sword and his arms, red to the elbows. He threw back his head and howled aloud in anguish. The shaggy dog howled with him.

"Sheathe the sword," Meghan said gently when his cry had shuddered away into silence. "The battle is won. Ye need kill no more."

Dillon looked at Meghan dumbly, his face contorted with grief and bewilderment. Slowly he obeyed, wiping his sword on his green livery and sliding it back into the sheath.

"Ye should no' have taken the sword," she said gruffly, bending to lay her hand on his shoulder. "Joyeuse is no ordinary sword. Once it is drawn it cannot be sheathed until it has drawn blood and it will continue fighting until the battle is won. Although it will never be defeated, like so many things o' magic it is as much a curse as it is a blessing. Those that carry Joyeuse come to dread it and rarely draw it. Most die early, even though the sword makes them invincible, for it will never yield and never retreat. I am sorry indeed that ye chose it, Dillon, for ye canna be rid o' it until ye are dead."

He looked at her without comprehension. "It's a magic sword?"

She nodded. "Some say it is cursed, though indeed it was forged with the best o' intentions. Normally those that bear it die o' exhaustion before its blood-lust is satisfied. When he dies, someone else will be compelled to pick it up and keep on fighting until the battle is won. It has been known to kill six owners in the one battle before it is satisfied. Joyeuse is a cruel sword indeed."

Dillon looked down at the sheathed weapon, so tired and numb with grief that Meghan's words made little sense. She beckoned to Dide. "Take the lad back to Johanna," she said in an undertone. "Tell her to give him some mulled wine with poppy syrup in it and make sure he is clean and warm. He will sleep. He is only a bairn still. Some o' the horror will fade in time."

Dide nodded. He bent, pulling Dillon to his feet, and put his arm around his shoulder to support him. Jed whined piteously and limped after.

Meghan looked back at Ardencaple. Despite the snow

swirling all around them, the town was aflame still. Above the conflagration, the seven sons of the queen-dragon soared and swooped, bugling in triumph.

"Let us hope they have no' enjoyed wreaking their revenge on humankind too much," Meghan said bitterly.

Iseult looked rather surprised. "Are ye no' glad?" she asked. "We have won the day now, and the war too, if I am no' mistaken. They will think twice about marching on us again."

Meghan nodded and drew her plaid up to cover her white hair. "Aye, happen you are right. Nonetheless, they are fellow human beings burning alive in there, innocents among them. I am sick to the very depths o' my soul with all this slaughter. Can ye no' feel their terror, their agony?"

Iseult looked back at the town. She nodded slowly. "But I'm glad. Glad! My *leannan* lies as if dead and many I knew and cared for are gone. I hope the one who betrayed us was sheltering within that town and I hope he does no' die too quickly!"

Meghan nodded her head brusquely and turned away from her into the snow.

Lilanthe stood within a grove of tree-changers, her roots deep in the delicious soil, her body swaying as she enjoyed the warmth of the breeze that blew down the valley. She could hear little rills of water trickling down into the river as the snow and ice melted, and the susurration of the tree-changers' leaves. They were talking among themselves in their deep, thunderous voices and she listened with pleasure. It was time for them to return to the forest, they were saying. *Green grow glad free flow ramble . . .*

Free grow ramble, she replied and they bent their leafy heads toward her, murmuring in welcome and appreciation. Then a few strode away toward the forest, none looking back or making any gesture of farewell. Tree-changers were solitary creatures. They wandered at will through the woods and rarely felt any need for social interaction. Those that stayed did so only because the soil was tasty and the sun warm.

Lilanthe remained with them until the sun was close to setting. Then quietly she pulled up her roots and walked away toward the fires glimmering beside the river. She did not look back or wave or say a word, though it wrenched her heart to be leaving the company of her kin. Lilanthe was half human though, and she longed for companionship.

Dide was sitting on a fallen log, playing his guitar and singing.

> "O Eà let me die,
> wi' a wee dram at my lip,
> an' a bonny lass on my lap,
> an' a merry song and a jest,
> biting my thumb at the sober an' just,
> as I live I wish to die!
> So drink up, laddies, drink,
> an' see ye do no' spill,
> for if ye do, we'll all drink two,
> for that be the drunkard's rule!"

The soldiers cheered and laughed, singing along with the chorus. Lilanthe sat with her chin on her knees, her bare feet tucked under the hem of her gown, watching him. All round her weary soldiers sat, singing and drinking their weak ale. Many were bandaged and bruised, for Tòmas's strength had been reserved for those hundreds of soldiers maimed by the cannon fire. Those men were now unmarked and strong, for Tòmas's healing powers were more potent than ever. The restored soldiers worked to bury the dead and sort through the ashes of the town, now a smoldering heap on its hill, while those with minor injuries sat and rested and recuperated their strength with ale and song.

Lilanthe sat in the midge-buzzing dusk and wondered what she was to do now the faeries of her army had returned to their forest home. Strangely she did not feel apprehensive of the future. *What Eà wills will be,* she thought. She accepted a mug of ale with a shy smile and watched as shadows flowed over the serene landscape.

She smelled the strong odor of bear and turned her head as Niall came up the curve of the river, his familiar lumbering along behind. The soldiers made room for him by the fire and he sat, his arm in a sling, his head bandaged. The bear lay down beside him, moaning to herself as she licked her wounded paw. Lilanthe smiled at them.

"Ursa has decided to stay?" she whispered.

Niall nodded, teeth flashing through the darkness of his beard as he reached out to pat the bear's massive, woolly shoulder. "Aye, though I told her she was free to go with the others. For some reason she wants to stay."

"I thought she would," Lilanthe answered.

Niall bent forward and looked at her intently. "Ye stay also?"

She nodded. "Though I hope to dance with the treechangers again," she replied softly.

"Happen we'll see the Summer Tree bloom once more," he said, rather sadly.

"Happen."

They sat in silence for a while. Dide got to his feet and began to walk around the fires, strumming his guitar and singing.

> "Och if my love was a bonny red rose,
> Growing upon some barren wall
> And I myself a drop o' dew,
> Down into that red rose I would fall."

Niall nodded in Dide's direction. "He be an auld friend o' yours?"

"Aye, an auld friend and a guid one," Lilanthe replied, turning to look in Niall's direction. "It was Dide who convinced me to join the rebels. He and his grandmother have been kind indeed to me. They risked their own lives for me and Brun."

The little cluricaun sitting on the opposite side of the fire swiveled his ears at the mention of his name but did not speak or join them, too busy emptying a flask of whiskey he had found somewhere.

"A good friend indeed," Niall answered and sighed.

Lilanthe said rather hesitantly, "What do ye do now, Niall? I mean, now we've won the war?"

"We may have won the battle but ye canna say we've won the war, while the Rìgh lies under the shadow o' a curse and our enemies still plot against us!" he answered rather sharply. "Her Highness has sworn to ride for Arran as soon as we can gather together our forces. She says the Thistle must be behind the curse and she shall no' rest until it is broken and Arran has signed the Pact o' Peace with the rest o' Eileanan." He paused for a moment then said more gently, "But once my Rìgh needs me no longer, well then, all I wish for is a wee cottage in the woods, with my own garden for herbs and vegetables, and happen some beehives for Ursa and . . ."

He stopped and Lilanthe said rather wistfully, "What?"

He said nothing for a long while, then said gruffly, "And someone dear to me to love me and live with me till I'm auld and gray."

"It sounds wonderful," she said softly. He turned to look at her, his eyes shining in the dancing firelight. He hesitated then leant forward as if to say something, but just then Dide came to stand beside them, smiling at Lilanthe and singing:

> "Och, my love's bonny, bonny, bonny,
> My love's bonny and fair to see."

The soldiers all cheered and laughed, some clapping, and Dide bowed to Lilanthe with a flourish and moved away, singing still. Her cheeks felt hot and she curled her toes, digging them into the earth. She could not help giving a little, embarrassed smile and risked a quick glance at Niall. He was watching her but immediately glanced away, calling for more ale and leaning back against Ursa's great bulk. The bear moaned and nudged him with her snout.

The singing went on until the camp cooks were ready

to serve up the hard bread and stew that was the usual soldiers' fare. Niall said no more to Lilanthe and she was conscious of a constraint in their usual ease. He sat and spoke instead to the other soldiers and after a while Lilanthe rose and walked away, her earlier contentment vanished. It was a balmy night, the sky dazzled with stars. She wandered along the river, wondering where Dide had gone and what he had meant, if he had meant anything at all.

She went away from the town, repelled by the smell of ashes and the aura of pain and terror that lingered there. Soon the campfires were left behind her and there was only the soft motion of the river, the green smell of willows and waterlilies. She came to a thick copse of trees and stood among them, letting little rootlets creep out from her feet and bury themselves in the soil. In this state of half tree, half woman, she stood and let the earth soothe her again.

Lilanthe's extrasensory perceptions were at their most sensitive in this state and so she became almost instantly aware of a clamor of emotion from further up the river. She knew at once who it was who felt such fear and confusion, such bitter shame. She wriggled her roots free of the earth and moved silently upstream.

He was crouched in the shelter of a bush of flowering may, rocking back and forth and keening silently. The tumult of his emotions beat at her and she knelt beside him and said hesitantly, "Laird Finlay?"

At once he sprang around like a cornered animal, crying aloud in surprise and fear. She saw his white face and startled eyes and then he scrambled backward and stumbled to his feet. For an instant she saw his tall figure silhouetted against the sky, then she heard his running footsteps as he fled through the trees. In that moment she recognized him.

"It was ye!" she cried. "Ye're the one who attacked me! Why? Why?"

There was only the rustle of the leaves and the sough of the river. She felt him running away over the fields, half mad with grief and shame, and knew at once what

Finlay Fear-Naught did there and why he ran. Tears choked her and she turned and hurried back to the campfires, knowing she must tell Meghan and Iseult.

The Keybearer was in the royal pavilion, for once sitting still, her hands idle in her lap, her face fallen into lines of bitter grief. Gitâ was snuggled up under her chin, his paw tucked under her collar, his plumy tail wrapped round her throat. Lachlan lay unconscious on his pallet, Iseult holding his hand and watching his face. He could have been dead, he was so white and still, his chest barely rising and falling at all. Duncan Ironfist and Iain sat at the table, drinking whiskey and looking over the maps, their faces set with grim determination.

They looked up as the tree-shifter came in and at once Meghan's gaze sharpened. "What is it, Lilanthe?"

She told them what she had seen and felt, and they all exclaimed in dismay.

"Nay, no' Finlay Fear-Naught!" Duncan Ironfist cried. "He canna have been the one to betray us! No' one o' Lachlan's own guard. He wouldna. He couldna!"

"Lilanthe, are ye sure?"

"W-W-Why? Why w-w-would he do such a th-th-thing?"

"But he was so eager, so loyal," Iseult said, remembering how the young laird had come to them after the Samhain rebellion, his eyes alight with ardor, pledging the new Rìgh his life and his sword. He had been the first of the highland lairds to throw in his lot with Lachlan and his support had encouraged many others to join also.

"He was thinking o' a woman," Lilanthe said softly. "His heart was twisted with longing and shame. He was sick to his very heart at the massacre in the woods and the burning o' Ardencaple, but still all he could think o' was this woman, her white skin, her voice, her silvery eyes."

"Maya!" Meghan got to her feet, black eyes flashing. "I should've kent!"

"When? How?" Iseult cried. "He was on the march with us for months! How could he have communicated with her?"

"Spies always have their ways," Meghan said harshly. "Carrier pigeons, or a note slipped to a dispatch rider. Who knows how deeply the rot o' betrayal has set in?" She paced the room, her brow deeply furrowed, her hands clenching and unclenching. "Finlay must have told her where Jorge and Tòmas would be too. The attacks came simultaneously. I should have guessed when we found him missing from the forest. To think I feared he had come to some harm at the hands o' the Bright Soldiers!"

Duncan buried his head in his hands. "So many good men dead," he said harshly. "How could he?"

"Eà d-d-damn him!" Iain said thickly.

The captain of the Blue Guards got to his feet abruptly. "I will send men out to hunt for him. We will question him and find out exactly how and why he broke faith with us, and then we shall put him on trial for treason. He shall suffer for this betrayal!"

Finlay James MacFinlay, the Marquess of Tullitay and Kirkcudbright, Viscount of Balmorran and Strathraer, and the only son and heir of the Duke of Falkglen, was found hiding under a bush at the edge of the forest, his blue jacket torn and muddied, his beard matted with thistles. He was dragged back to the army camp behind the horse of the soldier who found him. As he was hauled into the center of the camp, he was greeted with boos and catcalls and gobs of spit. He covered his face with his hand and sobbed.

Iseult stood pale and stern-faced outside the royal pavilion, dressed in her battered armor, her hair hidden beneath her long-tailed white cap. Duncan Ironfist and Iain of Arran stood to one side, Niall the Bear and Dide the Juggler to the other. They were all that were left of Lachlan's officers. They stared at Finlay with cold contempt in their eyes.

"I'm sorry, I'm sorry," he sobbed. "Please forgive me. I did no' ken what it was I did. She asked me to send her news o' our plans and movements . . . I thought it was so we could arrange to meet . . . I so longed to lie with her again . . . I did no' think. Och, please, in the name o' Eà's green blood, forgive me."

He raised piteous eyes but saw no pity in the eyes of those who condemned him. He cried for them to kill him but the mercy of death was denied him. He was branded with a T for traitor and condemned to wander as an outcast, begging for food and mercy, and having all know that he had betrayed his Rìgh and fellow soldiers. Even his own father would not offer him succor, driving him away with kicks and oaths. So Finlay Fear-Naught became Finlay the Cursed, a man without home or friends or honor, a man with the shrieks of the dying forever resounding in his ears.

THE FAIRGE

The dragon soared high over the snow-clad mountains, her scaled body shining a gilded green in the sunshine. Isabeau clung on tightly, tears streaming down her face from the sharp wind, her face alight with exultation. She gave a whoop of excitement as Asrohc plunged downward, her stomach lurching as the horizon blurred. Then the dragon twisted her body into a graceful roll, so that Isabeau was upside down, her hair hanging like a curtain. Despite herself Isabeau shrieked, clinging to the dragon's spines desperately, then the dragon was upright again, her wings spread.

I wish ye would give me some warning when ye do that! Isabeau said.

The young dragon-princess gave a mocking bugle which shook the snow from the crag of rock below them. Isabeau watched it fall hundreds of feet like handfuls of white feathers, gradually melting away in the wind. She could not help giving a shiver of fear at the vast distance beneath them. She gazed down at the green alpine meadows so far below and suddenly her eyes sharpened. Far below was a crumpled pile of red.

Asrohc, would ye fly lower for me? I think I see something . . .

Obligingly the dragon folded her wings and they dropped as fast as an eagle plunging for its prey. Isabeau gasped and clung on, grateful yet again for the complicated leather straps that kept her secure on the dragon's back. The heap of red she had seen rushed toward them. Isabeau had just realized that what she had seen was a

body, when the dragon suddenly changed direction and
was soaring again into the sky.

Nay, Asrohc, go back!

It is nothing I wish to touch ground for, the dragon
responded.

*Please, Asrohc! They may be hurt and in need o' my
help. Even if they're dead, I canna leave them for the
wolves. Will ye no' take me down?*

*The human lives, but not for much longer. Better that
ye let the breath fail in her body.*

She be alive? Asrohc, take me down!

*If thou so desirest, though why thou wouldst wish to
help one such as she, I understand not.*

Puzzling over the contempt in the dragon's mind-voice,
Isabeau leant forward, trying to see over the scaled
shoulder as the dragon slowly descended in ever decreas-
ing circles. Asrohc landed lightly in the meadow, coiling
her tail around her claws as Isabeau unbuckled the straps
and climbed down. It took her a moment to regain her
balance after the giddy descent, but once the world had
stopped whirling, Isabeau crossed the meadow and knelt
at the side of the woman lying facedown in the grass.

She was wearing a torn and muddied gown of red velvet, and her face was obscured by dark hair. Isabeau felt
for her pulse, which was very light and uneven, then
carefully rolled her over so that she could clear her
mouth and nose. The mud-matted hair fell back and Isabeau sat back on her heels in amazement. It was Maya.

The former banrìgh was breathing harshly, and the
gills at the side of her neck fluttered weakly. Her skin
was dry, its fine scaling rough to the touch, her narrow
lips blue. There was a bruised, inflamed wound at her
temple, thick with dried blood, and the soles of her slippers were in tatters. Isabeau felt her forehead and it was
burning hot. The apprentice witch chewed her fingernails
in anxiety. She knew she had to get Maya into salt water
as quickly as possible if the Fairge was to live. She glanced
back at the dragon. Asrohc was resting her great, angular
head on her claws, regarding Isabeau with enigmatic

golden eyes. Her long, spiked tail twitched from side
to side.

*Asrohc, she will die if I do no' get her to water quickly.
Will ye fly us back to the dragons' valley so I can immerse
her in the bubbling pools?*

The dragon yawned widely, curling her slender, sky-
blue tongue.

Please, Asrohc! I canna let her die!

Why not? The dragon responded. *It is she who sent the
red-robed soldiers to our valley and harmed my brother
with her poisoned spears; it is she who made the killing
of dragons a sport and rewarded those that murdered my
kith and kin. It will give me pleasure to watch her die.*

Isabeau did not know what to say. She knew she could
not allow Maya to die. She could not help thinking of
her as Morag, her friend of the seashore, who had taught
her about sand-scorpions and doom-eels and the flow of
the tides. Besides, Maya was Bronwen's mother and Isabeau could not be the one to deprive the little girl of
that, having been motherless herself. She looked about
her consideringly.

They were in the long, flower-strewn meadow that
stretched from the base of Dragonclaw down to the valley where the Rhyllster began to carve its way through
the hills. Isabeau's eyes brightened, for this was familiar
territory. She looked back at the dragon, and saw the
dangerous glint of an eye through the slitted eyelid.
Dragons were not noted for their mercy. Despite the
centuries of friendship between her family and the great
magical creatures, Isabeau dared not ask for assistance
again. She bowed and said, *It gives me no pleasure to
stand against your will, but I canna allow her to die. I
was taught always to heal and help, and swore I would
never use my powers to harm another. I beg your forbearance and hope that ye will forgive me.*

Asrohc's tail swayed back and forth. Gracefully she
rose and stretched, supple as a cat, and yawned again,
showing rows of very sharp, pointed teeth. *My mother
the queen says I must let thou do as thou wishest, even
though I abhor your weak human folly. She says the*

*Fairge queen has yet a role to play in this charade. So do
as thou wilt, Isabeau NicFaghan, and when thou wishest
to fly the heavens again, call my name. I may come, if I
am bored.*

Isabeau bowed her head in acquiescence, though her
spirits fell at Asrohc's cold tone. She watched as the
dragon launched off into the sky, the long sinuous body
rapidly dwindling as she soared toward the bent tip of
Dragonclaw. Then Asrohc was gone, and the sky was
empty again. Isabeau sighed and bent over Maya.

After a moment she straightened and looked about
her. From a copse of trees at the edge of the meadow
she called fallen boughs and green vines, and magically
wove them together into a stretcher. Lifting Maya carefully onto its length, she picked up a small wooden chest
that lay a few paces away and tucked it in beside her.
Isabeau then cast out her mind until she located a herd
of alpine goats clambering down from the mountain
heights to graze in the sweet meadows. She called them
to her and begged their help. Remembering her from the
old days, when she had run barefoot with them over the
rocks, they agreed to pull the stretcher for her. Using
vines as reins, she harnessed them up and they dragged
the injured woman through the fields.

The day was growing late when Isabeau at last reached
the rocky ridge that hid Meghan's secret valley from the
outside world. The cliff-face was dotted with caves. Most
were shallow apertures that led nowhere, but a few penetrated deep into the rock. The goats helped her maneuver the stretcher up the ridge, then bounded away in a
wave of mottled gray, tossing their horned heads.

Isabeau dragged the stretcher inside the narrow mouth
of the cave, then checked to make sure no one was
watching. Even though these mountains were wild and
remote, the occasional hunter penetrated its maze of ra-
vines and gorges in search of snow lion or woolly bear,
and she had been taught to take no chances. The
meadow below was quiet, though, and so she pushed on
into the darkness.

Although Isabeau could see as well as an elven cat,

the blackness within the mountain was so dense she had to conjure a witch's light to see. It hung before her, casting an eerie blue illumination over the fantastic stone formations that arched about her. There were thick, grooved pillars, taller than any tower. Clustered here and there on the ground were nests of gleaming pearls as big as hailstones, while rapier-thin hanging rods fell in tiers down the walls. Draping here and there were delicate lace shawls of stone, some rippled with pale color, most cloudy white. Here and there calcified tree roots hung down from the ceiling, weird and uncanny.

The stretcher was too unwieldy to drag through the caves, and so Isabeau untied the vines that bound Maya's unconscious body. With a great effort of will she raised Maya up until she floated before her, then pushed her along as if she was a boat upon water. The apprentice-witch had never used the One Power in this way before, and Isabeau found she was sweating, despite the chill within the caves.

Down into the heart of the mountain she climbed, pausing often to rest. Some of the tunnels were so narrow and low that she had to creep, others so lofty she could not see the walls. Occasionally she could hear the babbling of water and once had to splash through an icy stream, the stone beneath her feet so slippery she had trouble keeping her feet. Otherwise all was quiet, with an aura of deep peace and mystery.

Isabeau had never known the secret ways through the mountain as well as Meghan, and she frequently had to stop to get her bearings. Remembering what the old sorceress had taught her, she laid her hands upon the stone walls, listening, trying to feel through her palms what lay beyond. Whenever she sensed a great darkness and density in one direction, she would choose that way at the next branching of the path.

At last the steep descending gallery widened out and she sensed a vast space. Feeling rather giddy from her exertions, Isabeau raised the witch's light so cold radiance spread before her. She was standing at the edge of a huge cavern, its roof lost in shadows above her. An underground loch spread before her, its waters inky black. Every now and again a ripple spread, as if something stirred beneath its surface. All around her were tremendous columns and arches of limestone, intricate as any sculpture. At one end was a crystalline waterfall of stone, plunging hundreds of feet into the water. All round delicate white icicles hung like dragon's teeth, and the ground was frosted over with limestone flowers. The only sound was a slow dripping.

Maya floating beside her, Isabeau clambered over the slippery damp rocks. It was cold, and she huddled her plaid closer about her. Maya was ashen faced, her breathing rattling in her throat. Isabeau said a quick prayer to Eà and lowered the unconscious woman into the water. At the last moment, her control slipped and Maya fell with a splash. She sank out of sight and Isabeau's perturbation grew. She was just about to dive into the water in search of her when the water roiled, green bubbles bursting into life. She stared at them anxiously, suddenly afraid the underground loch contained some monster or serpent that would devour the unconscious woman. There was a flash of silver just under the surface, then a long tail with a great frilled fan broke through, splashing water into Isabeau's face. She stepped back with a cry of alarm.

From the depths a red velvet dress came floating.

Isabeau wrung her hands. "What have I done?" she cried. "Maya! Maya!"

Then the waters parted and Maya shot out into the air. Her face was serenely smiling, her dark hair plastered to her skull. She rolled, water streaming from her silver-scaled body, and plunged again, her tail smacking the loch so spray drenched Isabeau from head to foot.

For a moment Isabeau could not believe what she had seen. She watched, flabbergasted, as Maya sported in the inky black waters, her body gleaming like pewter. She had seen Maya change shape before, when the former banrìgh had dived into the heart of the Pool of Two Moons to escape Lachlan's vengeance. Then her wrists and ankles had been braceleted with flowing fins, like the frills the young lairds at court wore on the ends of their sleeves. She had seen the same fins on Bronwen when she gave the little banprionnsa her bath. She had never seen anyone with a tail like a fish before, however.

Maya swam to the shore and floated there, looking up at Isabeau, her scaled arms moving through the water slowly. "Thank ye," she whispered. "I would have died if ye had no' brought me here." She looked up wonderingly at the arches of stone icicles, which looked like the closing jaws of some great monster. "Where are we?" she said hoarsely. "How can this be, a sea beneath the ground?"

"It is an underground loch," Isabeau said. "It is bitter like the sea—I thought it would help."

Maya rolled, her tail twisting up through the water and away again. The silvery scales were spotted black along one side.

"Aye, it is like the sea, only dead," she said when her face emerged again from the water. "The sea zings with life while this is stagnant, without life. It is salty though, salty enough for me to transform to my seashape. It has been a very long time since I was last able to fully transform and so for that too I thank ye."

Isabeau nodded. "What do ye do here?" she asked brusquely. "How did ye come to be lying in the meadow and how did ye hurt yourself so?"

Maya lifted one webbed hand to her forehead. "My head aches terribly," she said huskily. "And I feel very faint. It is a long time since I last ate."

Isabeau saw with concern that blood was pulsing again from the wound at the Fairge's temple and that she was indeed very white. "Come," she said roughly. "I will take ye somewhere where ye can rest and eat, and then ye shall tell me how ye came here and why."

Maya looked at her steadily. "But I came for my daughter," she said softly. "How could ye think anything else? It has taken me all this time to track ye down. Where is she? Where is my Bronwen?"

Isabeau flushed and bit her lip. Determined not to feel ashamed, she shook back her red curls angrily and said,

"There is no one here but me. Come, can ye walk? We have quite a way to go." And although the Fairge asked her again and again where her daughter was as they made their slow, tortuous way out of the caves, Isabeau would not reply.

At last they stumbled out of the darkness into the cool dusk. Stars were beginning to prick the sky above them and the moons were rising, looking frail and insubstantial in the twilight sky.

Above them ancient trees towered. Their thick trunks looked like pillars of jet, their sun-touched leaves like the gilded ceiling of some grand hall. Through their outspreading branches Isabeau could see the dark, bent shape of Dragonclaw rearing against the sunset sky. Despite her misgivings she could not help giving a little sigh of contentment. She had lived in this little valley for sixteen years and she had missed it sorely. It was grand to be home.

Their progress through the woods was slow. Maya, still faint and rather dizzy, had to stop often to rest. Her filthy velvet skirts were sodden with water and she had lost the tattered remnants of her slippers, her bare feet bruised and scratched. Isabeau knew the Fairge would not be able to climb into the trees. When they reached the shore of the little loch that stretched toward thc eastern rim of the valley bowl, she bade her brusquely to stand still while she blindfolded her. Although the Fairge protested, Isabeau was adamant. It was betrayal enough taking Meghan's archenemy into her secret tree-house, without revealing the hidden entrances as well. Blindfolding Maya was the only way Isabeau could salve her troubled conscience, though still she hoped Meghan would never find out.

Isabeau led Maya to the base of the tallest tree in the forest, which grew on a rocky outcrop above the loch. Its roots were protected by thorns, and Isabeau scratched her hands badly holding back the branches for Maya to go through. The narrow passageway wound through the rock and the blindfolded woman had to grope her way through with hands outstretched, though Isabeau had lit a witch's light so she could see her way. They reached a little aperture and Isabeau felt for the concealed catch, lifted it and swung open the hidden door. They stepped out into the kitchen.

It was a small, dark room cut into the rock with the great tree growing up one side, its roots writhing out and providing many natural shelves and cupboards filled with bottles, jars and books. A fireplace was built into the rock, a crack, much stained with soot, providing a natural chimney. Before the fireplace were two high-backed chairs, with carved arms and headrests, and a rickety wooden table. The secret door was hidden behind a rack of shelves, which Isabeau swung shut behind her and secured close again. She led Maya to one of the chairs and then laid a fire and lit it with a snap of her fingers. Only then did she allow the Fairge to remove her blindfold and look about her, which she did with great curiosity.

"Och, what a funny wee place!" she cried. "It looks as if we're inside a hollow tree. Where are we?"

"This is where I live," Isabeau said, crossing her fingers behind her back even though it was only a partial lie.

"Then ye're a sloppy lass indeed," Maya said with amusement in her voice. Isabeau glared at her in indignation and the Fairge wiped the arm of the chair with one finger. It was thick with dust. Isabeau flushed and could think of nothing to say.

Maya grinned at her and kept on looking around. "So this is where the Arch-Sorceress hid for all those years. I must admit we would never have thought o' looking inside a tree."

Isabeau crimsoned even further. She had hoped Maya would not guess that this was Meghan's home and she could not think what had given it away so soon. Maya was looking up at a little crest above the fireplace, which sported a leaping white stag, a crown in its antlers. The motto above read: *Sapienter et Audacter*. Isabeau followed her gaze and consternation filled her. She had seen that crest and the motto, *Wisely and Boldly*, every day of her life and had never thought to wonder about its significance. Yet it was the proof that Meghan was no mere wood witch, but no less than a banprionnsa of the MacCuinn clan.

Isabeau said nothing, just busied herself around the kitchen. She shook out some quilts and sheets and hung them before the fire to dry, then searched through the jars and tins for food and medicines. She found enough herbs and grains to make a thin porridge and some tea, telling herself with a frown that she would have to go out foraging in the morning. It seemed she would never be free of this most mundane of tasks.

She washed and anointed the nasty gash on Maya's head and checked her pulse, which was erratic still, and her temperature, which was high. "I think ye will have to swim in the underground loch a few more times before ye are fully recovered," she said, ladling out the porridge and sinking down into her chair with a sigh. Indeed it had been a long day.

"That will be no hardship," Maya said. "I have had much trouble these last few years finding water salty enough to survive. Finding somewhere deep enough to immerse myself in and near as briny as the sea, that is a luxury indeed."

Isabeau nodded to show her understanding, though a strange sense of unreality was creeping over her. How could she be possibly sitting at ease in Meghan's treehouse with Maya the Ensorcellor, talking openly about how difficult it was for a Fairge to survive above water? She scrutinized Maya's face surreptitiously, noting the mother-of-pearl sheen of the skin, the narrow mouth and mobile nostrils, the flat ears and constantly fluttering gills. The firelight glowed on the left side of her face, revealing the spider web of fine, pale scars that marred the silken scales.

"How in Eà's name were ye ever able to conceal your real ancestry for so long?" she burst out.

"I had the Mirror o' Lela," Maya replied. "It was a very auld, very powerful artifact o' my father's family and I had been trained in its use since I was a mere bairn. I spun the illusion twice a day, at dawn and sunset, and never let it falter. Over the years it grew to be more than a mask, it was indeed like a second skin that had grown over my own face.

"I was careful to wear high collars and long sleeves that hid my gills and fins too. Ye never knew when someone would have the gift o' clear-seeing powerful enough to see through the glamourie, thick and strong as it was. It amused me that it became the fashion to wear collars closed up at the throat and sleeves that covered the hands."

She smiled a little in reminiscence, then said with a shrug, "Besides, people see what they expect to see, and once the witches were gone, I did not need to be so careful. That was one reason why I had to strike swiftly, do ye understand? I could not risk exposure. Anyone with witch senses was a danger to me."

She held out her hands, looking at the deep webs that ran from knuckle to knuckle, and gave a rueful smile. "I was startled indeed to see my face once the mirror was broken. I had near forgotten what I really looked like, or that I was no longer a young woman in the first flush o' my beauty."

She sighed. "Indeed, young Lachlan did no' ken what he did when he broke the mirror. Much o' my powers came from it and I was near helpless without it."

Isabeau could not help feeling sorry for her. The Fairge looked so thin and pale, and there was true sadness thrilling through her deep, expressive voice. Maya looked up at her pleadingly. "All I want is to find my daughter and somewhere we'll both be safe. Ye do no' understand what it is to be a hunted creature, hated and feared by all, with our lives forfeit if we are discovered."

Isabeau's heart hardened. "Yes, I do," she said harshly and spread out her own hands for Maya to see. "I lost these fingers in the torture chambers o' your Grand-Questioner and would've lost my life too, if your Grand-Seeker had had her blaygird way! I was hunted all through the highlands and nearly died several times from fever and exhaustion."

"Then ye do understand," Maya said unexpectedly, leaning forward and fixing her silvery-blue eyes on Isabeau's face. "Happen I deserve to be hated and hunted, though indeed I had no choice in what I did, but no' my wee Bronwen! She is naught but a babe and innocent. Ye ken they will kill her if they know she is born o' the sea people."

Isabeau looked away, troubled. Was that not why she had taken Bronwen in the first place, because she feared for her safety? She sidestepped the issue, saying rather harshly, "What do ye mean ye had no choice? There is always a choice."

"Aye, but can ye always see that? What if the only choice is to submit your will to others or die? What if ye had been trained since birth to obey without question and that the slightest hesitation resulted in the cruelest o' punishments? What choice do ye have then?"

Isabeau remembered the queen-dragon's words. *Fate is woven together of will and the force of circumstances. It is one thread spun of many strands.*

"Is that how it was for ye?" she asked hesitantly.

Maya nodded. "Aye. I was naught but a half-breed daughter, less important to my father than a good dinner o' fish. I had to struggle and fight to stay alive even as a babe, and once the Priestesses o' Jor knew I had Talent, they took me into the sisterhood. The priestesses are no' like your weak, soft witches, they are hard and cruel and relentless. I was a tool to be honed and sharpened and they made o' my life a grindstone. It never occurred to me that it could be any different. I did as I was told and thought I was happy to submit my will and my life to the god o' the seas."

There were tears in her eyes and in her husky voice. Isabeau was overwhelmed with pity, thinking of her own happy, carefree childhood.

"But why?" she asked. "Why did they make ye a tool? What for? All this death and persecution, all these years o' witch-burnings and *uile-bheistean* hunts. Why?"

"Ye took our lands and our seas," Maya replied simply. "Your people came from somewhere far away and

just took what was ours. When we protested we were
killed. Ye befouled the rivers and the sea with your
towns and cities and your filthy animals; ye hunted the
whales and sea stirks and left us hungry; ye took sport
in killing our people, ye even made a fashion o' wearing
our skins!" Her lip curled in distaste. "We were driven
from our winter homes on the coast o' Carraig and your
witches built their Tower above the king's own sea cavern, which was blasphemous! The sea caverns are royal,
and sacred, yet ye humans used it to moor your ships as
if it were some kind o' stable! My people were driven
away, only surviving by building rafts to cling to in the
icy, stormy seas. The only islands left to us were those
so bare and wild that even birds could not roost there.
'Why?' ye ask. Ye wonder why we hate ye and plot for
your downfall, aye, even for your annihilation. That is
why!"

Isabeau was silent. She knew what Maya said was true.
She was ashamed and embarrassed, not knowing what to
say. Words of both regret and indignant justification jostled in her mind. That was a long time ago, she wanted
to say, and it's no' our fault what our ancestors did. But
she knew even the smallest action could have a great
consequence, like the turning over of a pair of dice.

At last she said, "But did Aedan Whitelock no' try
and reach a settlement with the Fairgean king? At the
end o' the Second Fairgean Wars?"

"Pah!" Maya made a sound of disgust. "Humans steal
our lands and then think they are merciful and kind by
offering us the right to pay for the use o' our own
beaches and rivers! My grandfather swore he would
never bow his head before a human king and my father
was made to swear the same before he inherited the
black pearl scepter and crown."

She sat back and took a deep breath, then said in a
softer voice, "Ye see I was taught to think all humans
were evil and arrogant and that they deserved to suffer
for what they did to the Fairgean. I was glad that I had
been chosen to perform this great deed for my people
and that I, an unworthy half-breed daughter, had a

chance to justify their mercy in allowing me to live. It was only later, when I came to realize that no' all humans were evil, that I began to doubt what I had been taught and to wonder . . ."

Isabeau waited but Maya had fallen into a reverie, her face sad and weary. "Wonder what?" she prompted at last.

Maya sighed and turned back to her. "Wonder how different my life could have been if only I'd been allowed to love my Jaspar freely and live without the dread o' failing my father and the priestesses. I tried, ye ken. When Bronwen was born I left Sani in the shape o' a hawk and I did no' contact my father as I should have. I tried to pretend I was free, but it was too late. Far too late."

She leant forward, putting out one hand to touch Isabeau's knee. "Can ye no' see that all I want is to find my daughter and live in peace somewhere? Some place where my father canna reach me and where Bronwen will be safe?"

Isabeau was torn. She had to fight hard to resist the wistful pleading in the other woman's voice, reminding herself of the hundreds of witches and faeries that had died horribly because of Maya's machinations. The sight of her own maimed hand firmed her resolve and she said neutrally, "Ye can see your daughter is no' with me."

Maya sat back, exasperation flashing briefly across her face. "But I ken ye took my baby!" she cried. "Where is she? What have ye done with her?"

"How do ye ken?" Isabeau asked. "And how did ye ken to find me here?"

Maya was silent. When she did not answer, Isabeau busied herself clearing away their dirty bowls. The water barrel was empty so she wiped the dishes out with a cloth, adding filling the barrel to her list of things to do in the morning. She was very tired and her head was full of all that she had been told. She needed time to sort through her emotions and reactions. She turned back to the other woman and said, "We should rest. It is growing late. In the morning I'll take ye back to the loch and ye can swim again."

Maya nodded wearily and put her hand to her head. Isabeau unhitched the ladder from its hooks and put it up to the trapdoor in the roof. She climbed up and passed her hand over the lock, searching for wards. As she had expected, the trapdoor was guarded and it took her some time to work out the sequence of enchantments. She was familiar with Meghan's system of warding, however, and so eventually was able to make a series of complicated signs with her fingers. A symbol of green fire flared up for a moment and then disappeared. With her arms full of the fire-warmed quilts, Isabeau led the way to the room above, which was much smaller and quite round in shape.

A narrow bunk hung with green velvet curtains was set into one curved wall, and a carved wooden chest stood on the other side. There was barely room to stand between the two pieces of furniture, particularly since books were piled everywhere and the ladder came up through the middle of the floor. Maya had to press her back against the curve of the wall to make room while Isabeau set up the ladder to the next floor.

"Ye can sleep upstairs," Isabeau said brusquely, not wanting to put the Fairge in Meghan's own bed. She knew there was nothing in her old room that Maya should not see, but this room was filled with Meghan's books and artifacts and Isabeau did not want to risk the Fairge fingering through them. "Do no' try and reach the floor above for the trapdoor will be guarded and ye could lose a few fingers, if no' your life. I will wake ye in the morning. There are some clothes in the chest there that may fit ye. Throw down those wet rags when ye are ready."

Maya nodded and clambered up the ladder, her arms filled with quilts. Isabeau climbed into the little bunk, surprised at how hard and narrow it felt, and winked out her candle with a thought.

For the next few days she and Maya feinted and bluffed, each seeking to trap or beguile the other into revealing what they knew. Isabeau found it hard not to succumb to the Fairge's charm for Maya had a winning way about her and stirred the young witch's sympathies. She kept her maimed hand always before her, though, finding the sight of the ugly scars enough to keep her resolve strong.

She could not help feeling an increasing sense of uneasiness about Bronwen and she hoped the little girl was not teasing the old sorcerer too much. She knew Feld would not be overly concerned about her absence since Isabeau often went on foraging trips into the mountains, though usually she gave some notice. Bronwen always missed her badly, though, and tended to mope until Isabeau returned.

One afternoon, as they walked down through the towering trees, Maya again begged Isabeau to take her to her daughter. "Ye canna know how much I've missed her and longed to find her," she said pitifully.

Isabeau snapped, "I canna see why, when ye wouldna hold her or suckle her when she was naught but a wee babe. Ye havena seen her since she was six weeks auld and she's now almost three!"

At once she regretted her words but Maya turned to her imploringly. "I ken ye took her, Red, and I ken ye have no' been living here all this time. She must be nearby, though, for we saw yon mountain in the scrying pool, though with another just like it. Why will ye no' let me just see her?"

Isabeau said, "Ye saw Dragonclaw? Who did? In what scrying pool?"

The Fairge lifted her hands and let them fall. "I had some spies in the winged *uile-bheist's* retinue," she said. "They told me how ye had taken Bronwen and disappeared, and none kent where ye had gone. One stole a braid o' your hair and I took it with me to Arran. I went there to seek help for I knew the NicFóghnan was as much an enemy o' the winged *uile-bheist* as I."

"Someone stole my hair?" Isabeau whispered. "What about Lilanthe? Did they hurt her?"

Maya shrugged. "I do no' ken. He did no' tell me."

"Ye used my braid to track me down?" Angrily Isabeau wished she had burnt the plait when she had the chance.

Maya nodded. "Margrit o' Arran used it to spy ye out through her scrying pool. Her chamberlain, a Khan'cohban warrior, recognized the shape o' the mountains as the Cursed Peaks. I kent ye had taken my wee Bronwen and so the NicFóghnan promised to help me track ye down. She lent me her swan carriage and the Khan'cohban to guide me and we flew all the way. I should've kent she meant me only ill, though! I was wary and canny all the way, but without being able to bathe very often I was giddy and light-headed. The blaygird Khan'cohban waited until I had dozed off and so couldna transform him, then he threw me from the swan carriage as we came up the side o' the mountain. If ye had no' found me I would've died for sure."

"I thought ye said your powers were broken with the mirror!" Isabeau instantly picked up on the word "transform," her suspicions flaring into life once more. She had wondered over this question ever since she had found the Fairge unconscious on the mountainside, but had not dared ask her directly. She had seen no sign of any power and in reality it seemed impossible that this thin, pale, scarred-faced woman could be guilty of half the atrocities ascribed to her.

Maya lowered her eyes. "I did no' want Margrit to know I had lost my power for I would truly have been at her mercy then and she's a cruel, cunning woman who wishes me and my babe only ill. So I let her think I could turn her into a swamp rat or a frog as easy as clicking my fingers, and she was careful never to rouse my anger."

Isabeau was thinking carefully about what Maya had said when they reached the tree-house. She took the blindfold from her pocket and bound up the other woman's eyes, despite her exasperated protest, and led her down the passage to the kitchen. Once the secret door was safely hidden behind the shelving again, she untied the blindfold and let Maya sit.

"Meghan always said the craft is o' no use if ye do no' have the cunning," she said conversationally as she lit the fire and put the kettle on.

Maya stiffened. "I do no' understand."

"Witchcraft is the use o' the One Power through spells, incantations and magical objects like your mirror. Witch cunning is the use o' the One Power through will and desire. The spells and magical objects act as conduits for the witch's own power. The more ye use them, the more magical they become so that in time they can greatly enhance and focus the witch's inherent powers, and indeed they can become magical in themselves. But if ye have no powers o' your own, they canna work. O' course, all people have some Talent, most just never tap into it. This means anyone can get some use out o' objects that are deeply saturated with magic. If their Talent is only minor, however, their use will only be minor."

Isabeau made the tea and poured it out into the cups and sat down opposite the Fairge. "So ye see, no matter how potent the enchanted mirror was, ye could no' have used it if ye did no' have Talent o' your own, and for it to have worked so well, you must have a lot o' power. Transforming people into animals is no minor Talent, nor is maintaining for so long a glamourie which is so real that even powerful sorceresses like Meghan o' the Beasts canna see through it."

"I was always careful to stay away from Meghan and Tabithas," Maya admitted, "and to keep my hands and neck well covered."

Isabeau sipped her tea, refusing to be sidetracked. "Margrit would have known this even better than I. O' course, if ye are used to working magic through a particular object, ye may find it difficult to draw upon the One Power without that crutch and it may take ye time before ye are as strong in it again. Meghan always used to say ye should learn to work magic without any crutches at all, but most witches use something, from circles o' power to crystals to their witch rings." She looked down at her own rings, pale moonstone and bright dragoneye, then regarded Maya again with steady blue eyes. "So ye see, ye canna have lost all your powers when the mirror was broken and I think ye ken that."

Maya shook her head, her mouth trembling a little. "Nay, I told ye . . ."

Isabeau's gaze did not falter, though her mouth compressed a little. "It has been nigh on three years since the Samhain rebellion and ye have moved at will through the land in all that time without being discovered? I think no'. Nay, ye must have found some way to cast a glamourie without the mirror."

Maya suddenly smiled, a rather cruel smile, and passed her hand over her face, which changed to the pleasant, rather worn features of a middle-aged woman. Isabeau scrutinized her carefully. The glamourie was not perfect. There was a vague wrongness about it. As the light flickered over her face Maya's own features seemed to press out of the shadows and then sink back again. Then the Fairge swept her hand over her face again. This time the glamourie was much stronger.

Isabeau knew the face well. It was the face that had been celebrated as the greatest beauty in the land, the face of Isabeau's seashore friend Morag and of the Banrìgh Maya the Blessed. Although she did not know it, it was also the face of the whore Majasma the Mysterious. The opalescent shimmer of the scales was merely soft white skin, the lipless mouth merely thin, the flaring nostrils a mark of pride and temper. The scars were gone and the gray that had wrinkled through the glossy black hair. Because these features were much closer to Maya's own, and because she had worn the face for so long, it was almost impossible to tell that it was a mask and not the real thing.

Isabeau could not help being impressed. "A mistress o' illusions indeed," she said rather tartly.

"It took me some while to get used to doing it at will," Maya admitted. "I had to use a spell for quite a time and then I managed one day to cast the glamourie without chanting the words and after that it became easier and easier."

"And what about the spell o' transformation?" Isabeau asked, every nerve in her body coiling tight.

Maya hesitated. "If I could have, I would have used it," she admitted. "There have been a few people I would have loved to have turned into frogs or spiders, Margrit o' Arran among them, but I do no' know how. I have always used the mirror . . ."

Isabeau started to say something then changed her mind. Already there was a look of calculation on Maya's face and Isabeau was afraid that once she realized she still had the power locked away inside her, she would decide to practice on Isabeau herself. The young witch's thoughts had been on her father, still trapped within the shape of a horse, and her longing to release him. Having Maya in full control of her powers could well be dangerous, though, and so Isabeau bit her thumbnail and thought back over all that Maya had told her.

"Why did Margrit o' Arran help ye then, if there was so much ill feeling between ye?" she asked curiously. "By all accounts, she has no' got a sympathetic bone in her body."

Maya shrugged. "I went to Arran because I thought she had Bronwen there but it turned out to be a trick o' Renshaw's. He fled there seeking sanctuary and she took him in because she thought it would be useful to have Bronwen in her power. She was angry indeed when she found out Renshaw had deceived her." She described the Grand-Seeker's macabre death and Isabeau exclaimed in horror.

"And ye say she sent a Khan'cohban warrior with ye?" Isabeau was puzzled. She could not think what a Khan'cohban was doing in Arran or why he was in service to the NicFóghnan. Khan'cohban warriors would never serve another unless they were in *geas* to them or unless that person was higher in the social hierarchy. Only the First Warrior and the Firemaker were of higher status than a fully scarred warrior. "O' how many scars?"

"Six," Maya answered with curiosity in her voice. "Why?"

"And ye say he recognized the Cursed Peaks?" Alarm

suddenly ran through her. "So ye think the NicFóghnan wants Bronwen for her own ends? Did the Khan' cohban throw ye out o' the swan carriage so that ye could no' stop him from seizing her?"

Maya nodded. "Aye, I think so. But Bronwen is no' here with ye and I have the plait o' hair still, so I canna see how he could find ye, or her for that matter . . ."

"But did ye no' say he recognized the mountains in the scrying pool as the Cursed Peaks?" Maya nodded and Isabeau went on, her voice rising in alarm, "And if he comes from the Spine o' the World, he will know about the Cursed Towers." Unconsciously she used the Khan'cohban term for the Towers of Roses and Thorns. She got to her feet and began to pace in her agitation. "He threw ye out because he did no' need ye or the plait o' bluidy hair to locate her. He knew where he was going!"

Maya stiffened in response. "Ye mean he knows where Bronwen is?"

Isabeau nodded and wrung her hands. "It's been almost a week since I found ye—could he fly the swan carriage over the peaks? Do swans fly so high?"

Maya shook her head. "The plan was to alight some way up the mountain and send the carriage back to Margrit. Apparently they canna fly over the highest peaks." She looked at Isabeau with speculation in her eyes. "So ye have got Bronwen hidden away somewhere nearby?"

Isabeau said, "He must ken some other way to cross the mountains for he would no' dare go through the dragons' valley, that I am sure o'. The dragons would know that he is in Margrit's employ and that she was the one who provided the Red Guards with dragonbane and commanded the Mesmerd that was here in the spring o' the red comet."

She paused in her ruminations then said, "Meghan always thought that was odd. Why did Margrit help ye then and why did she send the Mesmerd here?"

"I do no' know," Maya replied. "She sent me an emissary saying that if I wanted to strike at the dragons and get rid o' them forever, then she had the means to do so. She's always full o' smooth plausibility, that witch. The Mesmerd was to help and guide the Red Guards to the dragons' peak—"

"But the Mesmerdean are creatures o' the marshes, they would no' ken the way through the mountains any better than anyone else," Isabeau replied. "She must have had some other reason . . ."

She paced back and forth, chewing her thumbnail. "The Cursed Towers . . . I wonder . . . She would've known they still stand, for the Khan'cohban would've told her . . . and Iain said she asked for the books from the Tower o' Warriors as part o' Elfrida's dowry . . . She must have wondered if any o' the auld books and artifacts from Tìrlethan still existed, for the Towers o' Roses and Thorns were famed for their library . . ."

Maya grew impatient with Isabeau's musings. "Are ye trying to tell me Bronwen may be in danger?" she snapped. "I do no' want that wicked witch getting her hands on my daughter, do ye hear?"

"No' just Bronwen," Isabeau replied. "I very much fear they're all in danger! Oh, Eà! If only ye had told me all this at first! We've been wasting our days here while all the time that blaygird Khan'cohban has been getting closer and closer to the Cursed Valley."

"What are all these cursed places?" Maya cried. "Ye have taken my daughter somewhere cursed?"

Isabeau did not bother answering her. She caught up her plaid and tam-o'-shanter and said sharply, "Stay here! Do no' try to follow me." Then she hurried down the secret passage, for the first time not bothering to conceal the entrance. It was growing dark outside and cold, and the red moon hung huge and swollen above the far horizon. She went swiftly through the trees to the shelf of rock on the far side of the loch, where the water poured away over the lip of the bluff. She stood and faced Dragonclaw, dark and sharp against the red-streaked sky.

"Caillec Asrohc Airi Telloch Cas," she called. "Come to me, I beg! Caillec Asrohc Airi Telloch Cas."

The words rolled out into the evening with all the

force and solemnity of the roar of the ocean. She waited anxiously and then whispered, *Please, Asrohc, I need ye truly . . .*

Over the past three summers she had called the dragon-princess whenever she felt the urge to escape her usual round of duties at the Cursed Towers and fly the dragon's back. At first she had done so hesitantly and with a sick flutter in her stomach. By her third year she had called confidently, and together she and Asrohc had flown over much of Tîrlethan and even up to the Spine of the World where the glacier stayed white even in the middle of summer.

Isabeau had known when Meghan had called the dragons to aid her at the Battle of Ardencaple. She had heard the queen-dragon's name in every hollow of her body, booming until she was near to fainting with the resonance. She had seen the seven sons of the queen-dragon fly gladly and triumphantly out of the heart of the Cursed Peaks, at last set loose to wreak their revenge for the death of their kin. Asrohc had been consumed with jealousy, longing to soar and flame and slay too, but constrained because she was the last young female in the land and the responsibility of breeding up many new dragons was hers. Isabeau had heard all about the victory at Ardencaple and the many who had died in the flames, until finally she was sick of it.

That week had been one of great pain and sorrow for her. She had felt her twin's injury as keenly as if an arrowhead had plunged into her own breast and then felt the terrible pain and grief of her miscarriage. If Asrohc had come to her call then, she would have left the Cursed Towers and flown to her twin's aid, but the dragon-princess was too excited by Meghan's summons and would not come. By the time the dragon-princess could be bothered to answer Isabeau's call, the young witch had felt the faint agonized echo of Jorge's death, and then the reverberations of the battle at Ardencaple.

Isabeau had felt the whole gamut of Iseult's anger, grief and fear and she had been nearly frantic with her need to know what was happening. So she and Feld had hurried down to the Scrying Pool, which Isabeau had only discovered under the brambles and weeds a few months earlier. She had cleared it out and unblocked the pipes so that water could again fill the round, shallow pond. Isabeau and the old sorcerer had watched the final stages of the battle through the far-seeing lens of the scrying pool, and Isabeau had thrown all her will and desire behind her twin to help with the conjuring of the snow storm.

So Isabeau knew about the strange fit which kept Lachlan in a state closer to death than life and she knew that Iseult had shouldered the command of the army and was planning a winter invasion of Arran. Several times in the past few months she had slipped down to the scrying pool to watch Iseult and make sure she was well, for Isabeau missed both her twin and Meghan sorely. She was distressed to see how old and drawn the Keybearer was now, and how sad her face. If Isabeau had not made a commitment both to Bronwen and the Firemaker, she would have risked the long and arduous journey back down into the lowlands or tried to persuade Lasair to travel the Old Way again.

Once more Isabeau called the dragon's name, despair filling her. If Asrohc did not come, the only way Isabeau could get back to the Cursed Towers was to climb the stairway up Dragonclaw and beg permission to cross the dragons' valley. That was a journey of at least a week, if not more. She wondered again how the Khan'cohban planned to cross the mountain, thinking with a sinking of her heart that he probably had a skimmer. With the little sleigh the Khan'cohban would be able to travel extremely swiftly once he was on a downward slope.

Suddenly she heard a great whoosh and a hooked, clawed wing crossed the round orange of the moon. Her heart leapt and she gazed up joyously as Asrohc swooped down out of the green-lavender sky, the wind as she passed almost knocking Isabeau over. "Ye've come, thank ye, thank ye!"

The dragon snorted bad-temperedly and landed lightly on the rock, her tail splashing into the water. *Thou hadst best be properly grateful, human, for I was just enjoying a nice haunch of venison when thou called and my brother will have eaten it all by the time I return.* The dragon's mind-voice was cold.

Isabeau knelt and made the Khan'cohban gesture of deep, humble gratitude. *I beg your forbearance and hope that ye will forgive me my temerity in asking, but I need ye badly! Please, Asrohc, ye must fly Maya and me to the Cursed Towers.*

The dragon lashed her tail, so that the surface of the loch was whipped into waves. *Thy red-robed witch shall never cross her leg over my back!*

Then could ye no' carry her in your claws as ye would a goat or a deer? Isabeau asked desperately. *Ye see, they are all in danger at the tower. An enemy stalks them. I must get there quickly and warn them. He is a Khan'cohban warrior o' six scars, a formidable enemy indeed. Maya must come so she can transform my father back into a man. He is the only one that can fight such a warrior. I have no' been found worthy o' even one scar and Feld is auld. Please, Asrohc! Do ye no' wish to help the man who saved your life when ye were a babe? The Khan'cohban will kill him if he stands in his way and ye ken Lasair, I mean Khan'gharad, shall if Ishbel or Feld is threatened.*

The dragon's tail swayed back and forth but it was a thoughtful movement, not one of rage. *Very well,* she said at last, *but only because I grow bored with all thy words and know I shall hear many more unless I take thee.*

Thank ye! Isabeau cried, and bade the dragon wait until she went to get Maya and a few things she would need. The dragon yawned and twitched her tail, examining her claws with slitted eyes.

Isabeau ran back to the tree-house and curtly told Maya that she had decided to take her to see her daughter on the condition she transform her father back from a horse to a man. "Ye must submit to being carried in the dragon's claws though," she warned. "It is the only way so do no' argue with me. Hurry now, for I have such a feeling o' foreboding."

She ignored Maya's questions and protestations, gathering together the books she had been studying, some of Meghan's potions and medicines, and some pots and pans and a griddle—the Cursed Towers were not well equipped with cooking utensils and Isabeau had no other way of getting any. With the bulging sack over her shoulder, Isabeau urged Maya down the secret passageway, unable to help feeling an odd frisson as she remembered the last time she had left the tree-house in a mad scramble.

"What do ye mean I must change your father back into a man?" Maya cried, as Isabeau hurried her through the forest. "Ye canna mean that the Khan'cohban I changed into a horse still lives—and that he is your father!"

"Indeed that is what I mean!" Isabeau snapped. "Ishbel the Winged is my mother, and Iseult's too, and Khan'gharad the Scarred Warrior is our father. He is the only one who will be able to fight off a warrior o' six scars for he has seven scars and is famous among the prides for his fighting skills. Ye must gather your will and transform him back, for he is our only hope o' defeating Magrit's Khan'cohban."

"But I canna!"

"Ye must!" Isabeau cried as they reached the edge of the loch where Asrohc sprawled, gleaming like polished jade in the light of the setting sun. The dragon whipped round and fixed the Fairge with her dangerous, cold gaze and the Fairge stared back, hypnotized with terror. Isabeau clambered onto the dragon's back, and with a mocking cry, Asrohc rose into the air, catching up Maya in her claws as she swept by.

As they flew through the sky, the mountains below them spread out in an amazing panorama of sunset-colored peaks and shadowy valleys, with the occasional glint of ice turned to fire dazzling Isabeau's eyes. The wind was bitterly cold and she huddled her mittened hands under her plaid and wondered how Maya felt with that great, terrible distance below her and only the untrustworthy cradle of the dragon's claws preventing her from falling. There was no sound from her and Isabeau could only hope Asrohc had not misjudged the tightness of her hold.

Then they were over the ridge of sharply pointed mountains and soaring over the Cursed Valley. Isabeau could see the tall spires of the Towers rising from the forest, the loch lying dark and mysterious before them.

Asrohc landed lightly at the edge of the trees, dropping Maya roughly on the ground. Isabeau leapt off her back and made a hasty but heartfelt genuflection. Reluctantly the dragon lifted her claws from the Fairge, who lay still though her eyes were wide open. Her dress was torn and bloodstained from deep scratches where the dragon's claws had scored her flesh.

Asrohc turned her angular head toward the Towers and gave a dragonish grin. *Lifeblood spills,* she said.

Isabeau dropped her sack and ran down the avenue she had cut through the brambles. Her heart felt like it was being squeezed between giant hands. *No' Bronwen,* she thought desperately, then, *no' my mam, please.*

The avenue led her straight up to the great stone door of the Tower, which stood ajar. It was dark under the arching branches but light spilled out from the doorway, illuminating the steps. Isabeau could hear the shrill screams of the stallion and the pound of his hooves, and she leapt up the stairs two at a time.

Within was a long hall with tall pillars holding up a vaulted ceiling. The walls were exquisitely painted with trees and flowers and faeries, while the ceiling above was painted with gilded suns and moons and comets, which glimmered in the light of the torches flaring the length of the hall. When Isabeau had first come to the Cursed Towers, this hall had been filthy with cobwebs and owl guano, but she had spent weeks scrubbing it out and now it was clean and empty.

At the far end of the hall was a broad spiral staircase, intricately carved with a fretwork of roses and thorns. Feld lay at the first curve of the stairs, blood spilling from a deep gash in his abdomen. He was feebly trying to keep off a tall, gray, winged creature with his staff while clutching the wound with his free hand. The stallion was rearing and plunging at the base of the stairs, his frantic whinnies echoing around the cavernous hall. Ducking his flailing hooves with contemptuous ease was a tall, horned man dressed all in gray, his brown cheeks clearly showing six thin scars. He held a long dagger in one hand and slashed at the stallion with it, while in the other he gripped a handful of long, fair hair which fell down the side of the stairs like a banner.

Isabeau's eyes flew upward. Ishbel was struggling desperately to fly up the stairs, screaming with pain as slowly but inexorably she was dragged back down by her hair. Bronwen was clutched under her arm, sobbing with terror.

The Khan'cohban lunged forward, his dagger flashing toward the stallion's breast. With a cry Isabeau threw up her hand and the dagger twisted in his hand and fell to the ground with a clatter. He ducked, the stallion's hooves missing his head by mere inches, and Ishbel screamed as the movement almost tore the hair from her head. She gripped onto the carved fretwork with one hand, but her fingers were pulled free and she fell back.

Without even thinking, Isabeau lifted both hands and clenched them before her breast. Her face contorting with the effort, she sent out a thin, hissing ray of blue fire which cut through Ishbel's hair like a knife. Released like an arrow from a bow, Ishbel shot up the stairs and out of sight as Isabeau's ray of light cut on through the stone of the stairwell, sending a large block of marble tumbling down to the hall below.

The Khan'cohban only just managed to fling himself out of the way, the block shattering into myriad pieces on the floor. In great dexterity he rolled one way then another, narrowly escaping Lasair's hooves, then bounded to his feet. In one swift motion he unhooked a bright star-shaped weapon from his belt and flung it at Isabeau. Instinctively she ducked, but without pausing it swung round and flew back to the Khan'cohban's hand. He threw the *reil* at her again, at the same time seizing a sharp skewer from his belt and hurling that at her as well. Isabeau jumped up in the air, bringing her knees to her chest. Both weapons sliced through the air just inches away from her body, the skewer clattering to the ground, the *reil* returning to the warrior's hand and then flying out again in a smooth arc so swift it could only be seen as a glittering blur. Only Isabeau's magic saved her. She deflected it with a scream, scrambling backward as the Khan'cohban leapt forward into a somersault that took him well clear of the stallion's savage attack.

Isabeau saw with dismay that the Mesmerd had darted easily past Feld's ineffectual staff and had flown swiftly up the stairs in pursuit of Ishbel and Bronwen. The Khan'cohban had seized his dagger again and was advancing on her, Isabeau backing away until she was stopped by a pillar. Her knees were shaking with terror and she gripped her sweaty palms together and tried to anticipate his attack.

Lasair dashed forward, teeth bared, but the Khan'cohban smashed his fist into the horse's cheek, causing him to scream and dance away. Isabeau took this momentary break in the warrior's concentration to run back, sheltering behind another thick pillar.

"Maya!" she called. "Can ye transform the stallion back? Ye must try!"

"I do no' ken if I can!"

"Ye must try! Maya, try, for Eà's sake!"

"Will ye give me back my baby?"

"If ye do no' do something, we shall all die!" Isabeau screamed back.

The Fairge clenched her hands into fists, her cheeks turning scarlet, her jaw clenched so tightly the muscles could be seen bunching up in her throat and cheeks. "I canna!" she grunted. "I canna!"

"Ye can!" Isabeau replied as another gray, winged creature darted at her out of the shadows. She only managed to evade it by falling flat on the floor, the Mesmerd's gray draperies brushing her as it flew over her. She was almost overcome with its swampy smell, covering her nose and mouth with her hands and scrambling to get out of the Khan'cohban's reach.

"Ye can!" she cried again, gathering fire into her hands and flinging a flaming ball at the Mesmerd. It darted away and the sphere of fire smashed into the wall and was extinguished. "Come on, Maya, ye ken ye can do it!"

Maya closed her eyes, pointed both hands at the rearing stallion, her fingers rigid, and said with a deep grunt of effort, "Change!"

The stallion did. His skin shivered and rippled, red hide, white flesh, red hide. His hooves stamped and spun, the sharp tattoo softening into the slap of bare feet. The great dark eyes glared blue, glazed over with shadows, glared blue through a tangle of red hair. The long, delicately boned nose flattened and shrunk into the face of a horned man, wild eyed and mad with confusion. Khan'gharad neighed and shook his wild red mane and stamped his bare feet and tried to rear, only to fall in a tangle of naked limbs, his body no longer that of the great, strong, four-legged horse but of a man who no longer knew how to walk.

The Khan'cohban warrior smiled and bent to pick up his dagger. As it turned in his hand it glittered in the light. Isabeau shrieked and tried to twist it out of his grasp but he had too firm a grip on the shaft. Casually he turned and sent the *reil* whizzing toward her, then bent to seize Khan'gharad by his hair, forcing his head back to expose his throat to the dagger.

Isabeau was barely able to avoid her own throat being cut by the eight-pointed star, so swiftly did it fly. She fell back on to the floor and then the Mesmerd was upon her, its great clusters of shiny eyes and out-thrusting proboscis filling her vision. The stench of the swamp was in her throat, a strange giddiness like that of love or lust or intoxication filling her veins. Pulses hammering, senses swooning, she clenched her hands together and blue fire leapt from her fists, drilling through one of the Mesmerd's compound eyes. Its head exploded into dust, and she was enveloped in its soft gray draperies. Choking and coughing she fought her way free, the Mesmerd's body dissolving into a fine gray dust that stank of mud. She tried hard not to breathe in the odor, reeling away across the room to stand against a pillar, coughing and trying to shake her hair and clothes free of the all-pervading dust. Her vision was obscured by dancing lights and her ears roared. She tried desperately to shake away the darkness overwhelming her, peering down the hall, expecting to see her father fallen in a pool of blood and the Khan'cohban warrior advancing on her with bloody knife.

Instead she saw her father scrabbling on all fours, his eyes staring blue and mad through the tangled red hair and beard, trying to rear and buck as strange neighing sounds issued from his contorted mouth. The dagger lay on the floor.

Coughing, her hands pressed against her painful chest, Isabeau stared uncomprehendingly. There was no sign of the Khan'cohban warrior. She heard a loud croak and looked down. A toad was crouched against the pillar, its lustrous black eyes staring unblinkingly. She looked involuntarily at Maya.

The Fairge smiled. She came down the hall, bent and picked up the toad. "He looks much nicer like this, does he no?" she remarked. She raised it to her face and looked in its bright, jewel-like eyes. "If only your blaygird mistress had been here too," she said, "ye could have both lived happily ever after together in the swamp. It would have given me as much satisfaction to turn her into a toad as it gave me to turn ye." She put it back down on the floor and it hopped a few steps away, hunching its square, ugly head down between its shoulders.

"Bronwen!" Isabeau cried and started for the stairs. Then she saw the old sorcerer lying on the steps, his hands clutched over the wound in his abdomen. "Feld!" she cried. "Oh, no, Feld!"

His eyes were shut but he opened them at the sound of her voice and smiled feebly. "Ishbel?" he asked in a reedy voice. "Is Ishbel safe?"

Isabeau sent a pleading look back at Maya but the Fairge was already hurrying up the stairs. Isabeau knelt beside Feld, feeling for his pulse. Tears choked her. She could hardly breathe with grief and guilt and the taste of the swamp still in her mouth. "Oh, dearling Feld, are ye all right?"

"Aye, lassie, no' so bad," he answered and lifted his bloodstained hands for her to see. She bit her lip at the sight of his bruise-colored entrails pressing up out of the wound, pulsating slightly with every hoarse breath he took. She tore a strip from her shirt and bundled it into the wound, feeling an unfamiliar helplessness. "Ishbel and the babe?" he asked and she said reassuringly, "Maya has gone after them."

His look of horror and the frantic scrabbling of his fingers suddenly made her realize that Feld still thought of Maya as the enemy, while she had, imperceptibly, come to think of the Fairge as something more like a friend and ally.

"Save them," Feld whispered, gripping Isabeau's arm with surprising strength. "Ye mun save them."

"But—"

"Nay, Isabeau, go! Do no' worry about me, I beg ye! Save Ishbel and the babe!"

Isabeau did not stop to argue, nodding her head and stumbling up the stairs, dizzy and confused. She could feel her mother and Bronwen were at the Tower's height and so she kept running up the stairs, not bothering to search each floor. She saw Maya searching desperately through the corridors of the third floor and called to her to follow.

Isabeau reached the chamber at the top of the Tower and staggered through the doorway, black dots obscuring her vision. She saw that Ishbel had flown up to the tall, stained-glass windows that lined the walls and was struggling to escape through one mullioned pane. Hampered by the wailing baby, she had not been fast enough to escape the Mesmerd, who hovered just behind her, its claws grasping her skirt. Ishbel was trying to kick the Mesmerd in the face but it evaded her easily, its translucent wings whirring. It sensed Isabeau's arrival and leant forward, bending its head over Ishbel and breathing directly onto her face. She faltered, and her hold on the struggling baby weakened. With a cry, Bronwen fell.

The Mesmerd swooped and caught her in its claws. Isabeau dared not try and shoot it down with her witch's fire, in fear of hurting the little girl. She could only watch helplessly as the Mesmerd darted away like a giant dragonfly, Bronwen kicking and struggling in its grasp. This image suddenly gave her an idea. She shut her eyes and concentrated on the heavy loops of filthy cobwebs strung across the high, domed ceiling. She felt a keen pleasure as the cobwebs dropped like a sticky, dirty net over the Mesmerd, entangling its wings so it could not fly.

With a strange hoarse sound it fell and Isabeau's fists flew to her mouth in dismay. Ishbel somersaulted down from the window ledge where she had been clinging and caught handfuls of the web, managing to slow its precipitous descent enough to stop the Mesmerd from slamming into the floor. It fell hard, nonetheless, and Isabeau dragged away the sticky mess from it with frantic hands.

Luckily the little girl had been cushioned by its hard, segmented body and although she clung to Isabeau with both hands, sobbing, she seemed unhurt. Isabeau soothed her, watching apprehensively as the Mesmerd struggled to rise. She knew she should blast it to powder while it lay helpless at her feet, but she could not bring herself to destroy it so heartlessly.

Then Maya came up beside her, looking at the creature curiously. She bent over it and said coolly, "Do ye understand me?"

It gazed back expressionlessly. She said, "If we release ye from your bonds, will ye promise no' to try to take my daughter again? We wish ye to take that loathsome toad back to your mistress and give her this message from me. Tell her that stepping on a thistle may sting your foot, but stepping on a sea urchin will cause ye to die in agony. Can ye tell her that?"

Slowly it bowed its head, just once. Maya nodded to Isabeau, but the young witch refused to relinquish her hold on Bronwen to do the Fairge's bidding. Maya was forced, very reluctantly, to strip the filthy cobwebs from the Mesmerd's body herself.

"Ye will find the toad downstairs," Maya said, fastidiously wiping her hands on her skirt. "Go now, else this witch will blast ye to dust as she blasted your kin. Understand?"

It stared back at her with glittering eyes and flew with some difficulty out the door and down the spiral staircase. Maya turned to Isabeau and held out her hands. "Give me my daughter."

Isabeau cuddled Bronwen closer. "Ye canna have her!" she cried.

At that moment Ishbel started forward, crying, "It is ye! Foul witch! Ye're the one that ensorcelled my beloved."

She flew at Maya, nails raking. The Fairge stepped back, raising her hands high as if to cast a spell of transformation. Isabeau thrust herself between them, keeping her mother back and shielding her from Maya with her own body.

"Stop it!" she cried. "Mam, it's all right. She's changed *dai-dein* back. He's a man again. He thinks he's still a horse but we can teach him again, I know we can."

"Khan'gharad? A man?" Ishbel faltered. Isabeau nodded and her mother turned and flew down the stairs without a word, swift as a snow goose.

Isabeau turned back to Maya, Bronwen still clinging to her, face buried in her neck. "Ye canna take your daughter," she said firmly. "Ye may stay here with me and learn to ken her again, but ye canna take her away. This is the only home she kens and I'm the closest thing to a mother she's ever had. Besides, ye will both die in the snows. Winter is coming and ye do no' ken the ways o' the mountains or where the hot mineral pools are. So do no' think ye can steal her and run away by transforming me into some horrible wee animal, for if ye do, both o' ye will die. Do ye understand?"

Maya smiled at her warmly. "O' course I understand and indeed I canna think o' anything I want more than to stay with ye and my daughter, and get to ken and love ye both again. For we are friends, are we no'?"

"Nay," Isabeau said steadily. "Ye are the enemy o' my people and ye have done more evil than anyone I know. We are no' friends at all."

Maya's smile faded and she looked away wistfully. "Still, I canna think o' anything that would make me happier," she said gently. "I thank ye. Now, please, may I hold my daughter? I have longed to have her in my arms again."

Reluctantly Isabeau unclasped Bronwen's chubby arms from around her neck and gently, with soft reassurances, passed her to Maya. The Fairge cuddled her close, crooning to her, and jealousy struck through Isabeau like a knife. She said abruptly, "I must see what I can do for Feld, who is sore hurt, and for my father. Ye may sleep in the room across from mine. Remember what I said. Ye do no' ken the way through the mountain and there are many dangers. Frost giants and woolly bears, avalanches and evil ogres. Ye would both die if ye tried to escape."

"But I do no' want to escape," Maya said with a smile in her husky voice. She rested her cheek on Bronwen's dark, silky head. "I have what I came for."

THE WEAVER'S
SHUTTLE FLIES

IN THE MIRROR

Khan'gharad tossed back his wild, red hair and scrambled across the room on all fours. Porridge was smeared all over his face and ran in clumps and dribbles down his tangled, red beard. He was barefoot, dressed only in an old robe of Feld's that had not been buttoned up properly so it gaped in odd places.

Isabeau stood by the table, holding a spoon dripping porridge all down her shirt. At her feet was a broken bowl. Bronwen was bouncing up and down in her chair, throwing her porridge around too, while Ishbel covered her face with her hands, sobbing.

"It's no use," she cried. "He will never learn to be like a man again! Look at him."

Isabeau ignored her. She said gently but firmly, "Come, *dai-dein,* I shall no' let ye eat on all fours like an animal. I know ye are hungry but ye must learn to act like a man again. Watch what I do."

She turned and sat down at the table, just as a globule of porridge from Bronwen's spoon hit her full in the face. "That's enough, Bronwen!" she snapped. "This is no' a game. Just because my father does no' remember his manners does no' mean that ye can forget yours!" She wiped her face clean and took a deep breath, trying to control her temper. "Now watch, *dai-dein.*" Slowly Isabeau ate from her bowl, exaggerating her movements. Her father neighed and tossed back his head and galloped across the room, thrusting his face into the oatmeal spilt on the floor.

"It's no use," Ishbel said again, her face wet with tears. "He has been a horse too long. He shall never—"

"Yes, he shall," Isabeau snapped. She got to her feet again and knelt by Khan'gharad's side, whickering in reassurance as he shied away from her hand. Gently she pulled him up to a standing position. "Try and remember, *dai-dein*."

He stood, swaying slightly, his blue eyes so dilated from fear and confusion that the blue was almost blacked out. She encouraged him to take a step and then another, but then his courage failed and he fell onto his knees. Ishbel covered her face again, weeping, and Isabeau turned on her in exasperation. "Mam, why will ye no' come and help me? Come and put your arm under his shoulder and show him how it is done."

"I just canna bear to see him like this," Ishbel wailed.

"Greeting will do none o' us any good!" Isabeau cried. "He has been a horse for so long he does no' remember how a man should walk. We must teach him again."

Ishbel dried her face with her napkin and came to Khan'gharad's side, helping him rise to his feet again. Together they helped him walk across the room, his lip gripped between his teeth, his shoulders hunched.

"Straight, *dai-dein*!" Isabeau seized his shoulders and pulled them back. "Remember ye are a Scarred Warrior and walk proud!"

For the first time it seemed her words penetrated the mists of his mind, for he stood tall, shaking back his hair and striding out like a man. Isabeau cried, "Good, good!" and Bronwen clapped her hands. Isabeau guided him to the table and helped him sit, giving him the spoon to hold. It fell from his fingers and she gave it to him again. This time he managed to grasp it, and she passed him her bowl of porridge, by now cold and congealed. Holding his fingers in hers, she tried to scoop up a spoonful but he could not manage it. At last he flung the spoon away from him in frustration and grabbed a handful of food and carried it to his mouth, cramming it in before Isabeau could stop him.

When she tried again to make him use the spoon, her father sprang up in a rage, knocking over his chair, stumbling and falling to his knees. There he crouched, grunting, his shoulders rigid with frustration.

Ishbel knelt by his side, stroking his hair and saying, "Never mind, my dearling, never mind."

Isabeau bent and pulled him up again. "Try again, *dai-dein*!"

"Canna ye see he canna do it? Leave him in peace."

"If I leave him in peace, he'll be like this forever." Isabeau turned on her mother, thoroughly exasperated. "Ye may be content to have a husband that thrusts his face into a bowl to eat and walks on all fours like a beast, but I am no'! I want my father the way he should be."

Khan'gharad tried to say something but his mouth only contorted in odd shapes, a strangled whinny coming out instead of words. One hand swept out and up, coming back to rest on his breast.

Isabeau stiffened for a moment in surprise, then slowly, with carefully defined gestures, said in the language of the Khan'cohbans, "Try, my father, try. I swear we can teach you to be a man again but you must try."

"I am!" he replied with an emphatic gesture.

Isabeau's eyes lit up, for it had not before occurred to her to try and talk to him in his native language. Castigating herself for a fool, she smiled and held out her hand and he struggled again to his feet.

The morning was well advanced by the time Isabeau had at last managed to coax her father into eating some of the porridge with a spoon clenched awkwardly in his large hand. It reminded her of Bronwen as a babe and she looked over at the little girl with a little smile of reminiscence. Bronwen immediately glanced up from her toys, smiling back. Isabeau bent and ruffled her hair, which hung as straight and glossy as a black silk curtain, with one silvery white stripe on the left side.

"Wanna swim," the little girl said. "When we go swim?"

Isabeau nodded wearily. "I know, sweetie. Soon, I promise. I must just tidy up a little, and get my father cleaned up, and make sure the goats have enough fodder.

Why do ye no' pack up what ye want to take to the valley while I finish what I need to do?"

She nodded eagerly and began to pack up her favorite toys while Isabeau did her best to clean up her father's face and rebutton his robe.

"Mam, will ye be able to manage? I need to take Bronwen across to the valley now. Bronwen needs to swim and so does Maya . . ."

"No, I canna manage!" Ishbel cried. She had been watching Isabeau and Bronwen jealously and now set her mouth stubbornly. "Look at him! He is more horse than man and I have never been one to mess around in the stables. That is what we had grooms for. Ye should stay here where we need ye, no' go running off to look after that wicked Fairge woman! What am I meant to do wi' him?"

"Feed him and wash him and have a care for him," Isabeau said gently, smoothing her hand over his great mane of vigorous red hair. "He is like a child now that has no' yet learnt to walk or talk or eat wi' a spoon. Ye must be like a mother to him."

"But I do no' know how," Ishbel cried, gripping Isabeau's sleeve.

Her daughter disengaged herself, trying hard not to lose her temper. "Well, ye should ken how," she answered sternly. "I ken ye were only just eighteen when ye gave birth to us and ye've been asleep ever since, but you're a woman grown now. I was younger still when I took on the care o' Bronwen and I had no one to guide me or help me but Feld, who kent less than I did." Her eyes filled with tears at the thought of the old sorcerer, who had been dead on the stairs by the time she had got back to him. Although seven months had passed since the battle with the Khan'cohban warrior and the marsh-faeries, Isabeau's grief and sense of guilt were still raw. She dashed her tears away with the back of one hand and went on gruffly, "He is your husband and ye say ye love him more than life itself. Well, care for him then and teach him, as ye should have cared for Iseult and me."

Ishbel's eyes dropped, color sweeping up her throat and over her pale cheeks. "I ken . . . I'm sorry . . ." she tried to say.

Isabeau said, "Ye ken I shall come back as soon as I can, but Maya and Bronwen need me too."

It was the wrong thing to say. Ishbel's mouth thinned and she said angrily, "To think my own daughter would shelter and help our greatest enemy, the sorceress who did this to your father and to me! Do ye no' understand that she and her evil Awl murdered hundreds o' innocent men and women?"

Now it was Isabeau's turn to blush and stammer. She could say nothing to explain her strange sense of connection and empathy with the Fairge, so she merely turned away, saying tiredly, "I must go, Mam. I said I would be back as soon as I can."

Maya had been living alone in the tree-house ever since the battle with the Mesmerdean the previous summer. Isabeau had moved her back to the secret valley only a few days after Feld's death, for neither Ishbel nor Khan'gharad could bear to have Maya anywhere near them. In their eyes the Fairge was their implacable enemy, the one who had taken their lives and smashed them into a thousand irreparable pieces.

Their condemnation hurt Isabeau and she wished she could see some way out of the tangle. She could not abandon the Fairge, much as she sometimes secretly longed to, for she knew Maya could not survive in the mountains. Even though Maya was her enemy, she could not help feeling a stir of sympathy for her. The fact that this empathy was spiced with a fierce jealousy only made it harder. Isabeau may have been able to condemn Maya to a cruel death to save everyone she loved further hardship and heartbreak. To do so because she wanted Bronwen all to herself was to truly become a murderess. Although Isabeau had killed before, she had never done so lightly. It had always been in extreme circumstances, when she had had to choose to kill or be killed. Abandoning Maya to die from the bitter cold or from the fierce mountain animals and faeries was to murder delib-

erately and Isabeau could not take that final, incontro-
vertible step.

So she compromised. She left Maya as a prisoner in
the hidden valley, opening the secret passage from the
kitchen so the Fairge could get in and out as she pleased.
Isabeau moved all of Meghan's books and potions into
one of the higher storeys and warded it off so the Fairge
could not learn any more of Meghan's secrets. Then she
divided her time between her parents at the Cursed
Towers and Maya in the hidden valley, taking Bronwen
with her wherever she went.

Isabeau foraged for all their food, cooked their meals,
taught Bronwen her letters and numbers, and Khan'gharad how to behave like a man. She took Maya and Bronwen through the caves to the underground loch to swim,
spun wool, knitted and wove all their clothes, dug and
weeded the vegetable gardens, milked the goats and
tended the beehives. She sometimes felt as if she was a
mother hen with four helpless chicks, rather than a young
woman just turning twenty and rather in need of some
mothering herself.

The winter had come and gone, the snow storms making Isabeau's self-imposed task even more difficult. She
had not gone to the Spine of the World as usual, worried
about how her charges would manage without her and
not trusting anyone else to look after Bronwen now Feld
was gone. Ishbel did not have a strong enough nature to
deal with the situation well. The daughter of a Blèssem
laird, she had been brought up with servants to wait on
her hand and foot and was not used to having to cook
or clean up after herself, let alone tend to Khan'gharad's
needs. She leant on Isabeau very heavily and resented
Maya for taking Isabeau away from the Cursed Valley
so much. Even Asrohc was bored with the situation and
often failed to come to Isabeau's call, leaving her
stranded and anxious about whomever was waiting for
her.

Isabeau left the warmth of the kitchen, huddling her
plaid close about her as she went out into the cold to
feed and milk the goats. It was a chill, gray day with an

ominous sky and a nasty, bitter wind that nipped at her
ankles and tugged at her plaid. She leant her head
against the nanny goat's warm flank and milked her
swiftly, her eyes hot and stinging. It was Candlemas, the
day of her twentieth birthday, and none had thought to
wish her happy birthday. She had had no time nor inclination for chanting the rites of spring and so for the first
time in her life, Candlemas had come without Isabeau
celebrating the end of winter and the beginning of the
season of flowers. She made a silent apology to Eà, did
her tasks with a weary step and heavy heart, then turned
back to the old Tower.

On a sudden impulse she turned aside and went instead to the scrying pool, which lay in the center of the
gardens. Completely covered over with rose briars and
brambles when Isabeau had first found it, the little round
gazebo that protected it from the elements was now clear
of all shrubbery. With a verdigris dome and arches all
carved with the pattern of roses and thorns, it was a
beautiful little pavilion with views across the garden to
the loch. Inside the pool glimmered blackly. A stone
bench at each of the points of the compass had legs
carved like dragons' claws, with a ferocious dragon's
head at one end, their wings folded back to form the
seat. Isabeau sat on one of the benches, staring into the
water which reflected her face back like a dark mirror.

She thought wistfully of her sister. It was Iseult's birthday too, and it had been some time since Isabeau had
last looked to see how her twin fared. It had been such
a busy winter, and the weather had been so cold, she
would have had to have dug a path through the snow to
even reach the scrying pool. Isabeau wondered whether
Iseult had managed to march on Arran as she had
planned and whether they had found the means to break
the curse that held the Rìgh in such an unnatural sleep.

The water's still surface seemed to darken, then Isabeau saw her sister's face as clearly as she had seen her
own reflection moments before. Only the difference in
their clothes and stance showed it was not her own face
she was staring at.

Iseult was crouched beside Lachlan, who lay still, barely breathing, on a low pallet, his wings folded beside him. He looked like a statue in a tomb, a white cloth draped over him, his aquiline profile looking as if it had been carved from marble. Iseult was holding his hand, chafing it between both of hers, talking to him in a low voice. Her face was harrowed with grief. Isabeau's heart was wrung with pity, for she had never seen her sister so distressed, not even when her baby daughter had died.

The Banrìgh was dressed in her leather breeches and breastplate, and her weapons belt was hanging over the chair behind her. As Isabeau watched, she stood up and buckled it round her waist, and came to stand before a mirror on a stand to check it was straight. She looked at herself in the mirror and the twins' eyes met.

"Isabeau," she whispered.

"Iseult, dearling."

"I was just thinking o' ye," Iseult said. "It has been so long and no word o' ye. Are ye well?"

Isabeau nodded and said, "And ye?"

Iseult's face was grim. "I have had happier days."

"It's our birthday."

Iseult nodded. "Yes, and today I march to war. Already the frost is melting and yet we still have no' set foot in Arran. May the White Gods blast those stupid lairds to dust!" Her voice and face were bitter.

"And Lachlan? The curse still holds?"

Iseult nodded, though surprise flashed briefly across her face. "Ye ken o' the curse?"

"I have watched ye through the scrying pool before. I saw what happened at Ardencaple."

"I thought I felt ye then, and other times as well. I tried to reach ye once through the scrying pool at the Tower o' Two Moons but ye were too far away or too preoccupied, or something. It was cold, snowing, and ye were crying. I thought, I had a feeling that ye were at the Haven but surely no' . . ."

Isabeau nodded. "I spent the previous two winters there. They shake their head over me and say I shall never be a Scarred Warrior like ye."

A smile flashed across Iseult's face. "I should think no'!" She paused and frowned and fingered her weapons' belt. "The Ensorcellor's babe?"

"Bronwen is safe wi' me at the Cursed Towers," Isabeau replied, rather defensively.

Iseult straightened her back and smiled with relief. "I knew ye had no' betrayed us! They were saying ye had given the Ensorcellor's babe to Maya and the Awl but I knew ye would no'."

Isabeau's smile faltered but Iseult did not notice, saying, "I canna stay. It is time for me to march out and we have already tarried too long. Glad I am indeed to see ye and speak wi' ye this way, peculiar as it seems. I was just thinking that all whom I love are far away or lost or cursed, and indeed they were unhappy thoughts."

"Meghan?" Isabeau cried in sudden alarm, and Iseult smiled in reassurance. "Auld mother is here and safe. I know no' what I should've done without her these dark months. Have a care for yourself, Isabeau . . ."

"And ye," Isabeau whispered. "I hope all goes well wi' ye and that ye win this war and break the curse."

Iseult's face darkened. "Auld mother says the curse can only be broken by the person who cast it. If it was Margrit o' Arran as we suspect, then I just hope we can win through and force her to our will. It seems so unlikely though. She is a powerful sorceress and rules the marshlands."

"Beware the Mesmerdean," Isabeau whispered, filled with dread. There was so much she wanted to say but could not find the words.

Iseult said with a little shudder, "I do, believe me, I do. I dread them more than anything, such a spell they can cast over me . . ." She squared her shoulders, blue eyes somber. "Let us no' think o' them. I must go."

"Happy birthday, twin," Isabeau said, her eyes stinging with tears. "Eà be wi' ye."

"And wi' ye."

Iseult's face blurred away as Isabeau's tears fell into the pool, breaking the image up into little, dark ripples. She sat back, wiping her face with her hands. "May Eà's

bright face be turned on ye this day," Isabeau whispered,
and rose to go back to the Tower.

Iseult stood at the doorway to the royal pavilion, looking
out across the army camp to the curtain of mist that
hung at the far edge of the paddock. She had to resist
the urge to turn back into the tent, lie down behind her
still, cold husband and pull the blankets over her head.
It was nine months since Lachlan had fallen and broken
his back and his wing, nine months since his restless vitality had been smothered beneath this unnatural sleep.

Nine months, spent arguing with the lairds, trying to
raise funds from the merchants, and gathering together
an army to march on Arran. They had suffered such
losses at Lochsithe and Ardencaple that it had taken this
long to recruit enough new soldiers and train them up.
Worst of all, many of the lairds were reluctant to invade
the fenlands, having heard so many stories about Margrit
of Arran's sorcerous powers and the dangers of the
marshes. With Lachlan still lying asleep, unresponsive to
all their pleading and shaking and pricking with pins, the
lairds were quick to find excuses to withdraw their men.

Although the three divisions of the army had been
under the command of the MacSeinn, the MacCuinn and
the MacThanach clans, the majority of the foot soldiers
owed fealty directly to their own lairds. This meant that
if the lairds withdrew their support and went home to
their own lands, the majority of the foot soldiers would
leave too. Although the lairds all admitted Iseult was a
skilled warrior and witch, it was quite a different thing
to put themselves and their men completely under her
command.

"A whistling maid and a crowing hen is fit for none,"
they said to each other with a grin and a shrug.

Lachlan had refused from the very beginning to use
any kind of forcible conscription, since that had been
one of the most hated tactics of Maya and her Red
Guards. So they had to rely on volunteers and the support of the lairds to swell their numbers, and after more

than three years of constant warfare, both wells were running dry.

Only the fear that more Tìrsoilleirean would come creeping through the marshes kept the lairds and prionnsachan faithful to Iseult and the Coven, and so the young Banrìgh was conscious that they needed a swift victory in Arran if they were to hold the army together. Luckily Anghus MacRuraich had marched to her assistance with close on three thousand men, and his loyal support had stiffened the resolve of the MacSeinn and the MacAhern.

Iain had advised them that the best time to attack Arran was in the winter. If it was cold enough, parts of the marsh would freeze over, making it easier to move large numbers of men through its twisting, tortuous paths. Most importantly, in the winter months the golden goddess lay dormant and the Mesmerdean were in hibernation, removing two of Arran's biggest dangers.

But the stags had begun to bellow in the woods and pigs to hunt for fallen nuts before new agreements between the Crown and the lairds were drawn up, and the snow was already beginning to melt by the time the Rìgh's army reached the borders of Arran.

They had made camp along the edge of the marsh, no one able to help feeling a shudder of apprehension at the wall of whiteness which hid the fenlands from their view. It was so uncanny the way the mist just hung there, never dispersing, never blowing over into Blèssem, marking the exact border of the two lands like a curtain between adjoining rooms. Those soldiers with imagination found it constantly preying on their minds, as if it were forming into spectral fingers reaching out toward them. Even those of a more pragmatic nature could not help wondering what it hid.

Iseult had tried to cast her witch senses into the fog but it baffled her extrasensory perceptions as completely as it did her eyesight and so she too felt her apprehension mounting as the time to venture within approached. The fact that none of the witches, not even Meghan, could sense what lay beyond, only increased her misgivings. She knew, having been told over and over again, that

not once in the history of Eileanan had an invasion of
Arran succeeded. The treacherous terrain, the dangerous
inhabitants of the marsh and the sorcerous powers of the
MacFóghnan clan caused every attempt to fail with many
casualties. In response to her troops' misgiving, Iseult
had only said, over and over again, "Where others failed,
we shall succeed. Do we no' have Iain o' Arran himself
to guide us? It is our only chance o' restoring Lachlan
and winning lasting peace. Do no' tell me why we shall
fail. Tell me instead how we can win."

Iseult sighed and slowly picked up her crossbow and
slung the quiver of arrows over her shoulder. Then she
walked out into the army camp, rehearsing in her mind
what she had to say to the soldiers. At the sight of her,
they raised a ragged cheer and beat their daggers against
their shields. She acknowledged their reception with a
raised hand, though her stern, cold face did not relent.

She faced them, saying calmly, "We go today to punish
Margrit o' Arran for her treachery. Too long the Nic-
Fóghnan has stood out against the other lands o' Eileanan, plotting to undermine the Crown and win power for
herself. It is time Eileanan was a united country, where
all are free to live in peace and amity. Margrit o' Arran
has helped our Tìrsoilleirean enemies invade our lands
and bring great suffering to our people. She has stolen
our children, encouraged insurrection and cast a curse
upon our rightful laird and Rìgh. We canna and willna
stand for such faithless and traitorous actions! So in Eà's
name we go forth with sword and spear, and in Eà's
name, I pray that ye fight with courage and strength so
we may all live with peace and mercy. May Eà be with
ye all."

"And wi' ye," the soldiers murmured in response.

Iseult nodded and gave the command to advance. Dillon brought Iseult her shield and she took it onto her
arm, saying sternly, "I wish ye to stay behind, Dillon,
do ye hear me? And keep that blaygird sword o' yours
sheathed. Too many o' the League o' the Healing Hand
have been lost already. It is your job to stay and guard
Tòmas and Johanna and the other healers. Understand?"

He nodded mutely, rubbing Jed's black-patched head. Although the past nine months had helped the horror and grief of that day at Ardencaple fade, Dillon had not fully recovered his usual cheeky energy. Despite all that Meghan and Johanna said, he blamed himself for the deaths of Parlan, Artair and Anntoin and missed their companionship keenly.

Iseult walked to join Duncan and Iain at the head of the double column. Meghan and Gwilym were waiting there for her too, both leaning on their staffs, both with very grim faces. They fell into place behind Iseult as she led the advance into the marshes, the young prionnsa of Arran pointing the way. Behind came Dide and Niall and the Yeomen of the Guard, most newly appointed and eager to prove their worth. Marching along behind them were the other lairds and prionnsachan, each leading his own company of men, their pennants drooping in the still air.

After long argument the lairds and prionnsachan had all agreed to leave their horses behind, for the paths were narrow and treacherous. This had been a sore point with the lairds, for only common soldiers walked into battle. It was a sign of wealth and position to ride to war. Purchasing and maintaining a cavalier's armor and horses cost as much as the plough teams for a dozen peasant families. There were many lairds who virtually bankrupted their families to pay for their horses and none of the cavaliers took kindly to the suggestion they leave such valuable commodities behind. Common sense had won out in the end, though, and so the lairds and prionnsachan walked with their men-at-arms, swords at the ready.

At first all was quiet, the drifting mist concealing nothing more than banks of sedge and bulrushes. Forced by the thick undergrowth and the patches of bog to keep to the path, the army advanced in long columns, four by four. All were grateful for their long, gray cloaks. Not only was the air damp and chilly, but the magically woven cloaks offered more concealment here than they had in the green, sunlit fields of Blèssem. With the fog

pressing close about them, each man was only able to see
the men a few paces ahead, the others simply merging in
with the winter-gray landscape.

They had walked for several hours when Gwilym suddenly paused, listening and smelling the air. Iain stopped
abruptly too, his knuckles on his sword-hilt clenching
white.

"Can ye smell them?" Gwilym asked rather hoarsely.

Iain nodded. "I hope my sense o' smell d-d-deceives
me, though," he whispered back. "It's m-m-much too
early for the nymphs to have shed their w-w-winter
husk. Unless . . ."

"Could your mother have somehow hastened the last
instar?"

Iain shrugged. "If she rigged up some kind o' incuba-
tor, I suppose it is possible. All they need is the coming
o' warmth."

Iseult stared around apprehensively. The mist smelt
dank and heavy, like a freshly dug grave. She said softly,
"Mesmerdean?"

"I'm afraid so," Iain replied grimly. "Let us do what
wc can to see." He closed his eyes and concentrated, his
hands gripped into fists. Slowly the mist swirled away.
The sky above emerged a pale blue, the bushes and trees
all about gray and colorless in its thin warmth. Before
them lay an open stretch of evil-smelling swamp. Floating
in the mud were hundreds of pale, bulbous eyes, staring
unblinkingly. Those nearest the edge of the swamp had
reached out long, skinny, mud-smeared hands. One was
only a few scant inches away from the toe of Iseult's
boot and she stepped back with an involuntary cry.

"Mudsprites," Gwilym said gloomily, then added even
more glumly, "and Mesmerdean, Eà curse them."

Floating above the swamp were hundreds of the tall
marsh-faeries, their veined, translucent wings whirring,
their great clusters of eyes fixed with implacable intent
on the little group of soldiers and witches that had just
emerged from the undergrowth. The only sound was the
slight humming their wings made, and their very silence

was far more intimidating than the usual loud bravado projected by an opposing army.

"Another few steps and we would've been in the swamp!" Dide exclaimed, his face white.

Iseult retreated a few more steps as the bony, muddy hand crept further out of the bog. "Look, there are men there too, and witches," she cried, her uncannily acute eyesight penetrating the gloom at the far side of the swamp. "They lie in wait for us. This is no' the place for us to fight a battle, Iain. We'll be all drowned by those blaygird sprites o' yours before we even reach your mother's army. Is there a better spot for us to retreat to? Firm ground, away from those creepy things?"

Iain opened his mouth to answer, but the tense silence was shattered by the blast of a war-horn. It seemed the creatures of the marsh had only been waiting for the signal. Immediately they surged forward and the battle was begun.

Iseult, the witches and the Yeomen of the Guard took the brunt of the attack, most of their soldiers still back on the path. With swamp before them and thick, boggy undergrowth behind them, the Yeomen had nowhere to go. So they stood their ground and fought like madmen, hacking off the hands and heads of the mudsprites that sought to drag them into the swamp, and seeking to impale the Mesmerdean that darted past like huge, evil-eyed dragonflies. As fast as the marsh-faeries fell, more rose to replace them and then the Thistle's army rushed from the sides to engage. Tall, surly-faced men armed with poles and scythes, they did not have the weaponry or skill of Iseult's troop but they knew the terrain far better. Where many of the Blue Guards slipped in the mud and fell, they stood firmly on their hobnailed boots or leapt easily from one hassock of grass to another. All around were the screams and gurgles and groans of dying men.

Anger and despair filled Iseult and she conjured a great, hissing ball of flame and flung it across the swamp. To her amazement, the very air took flame. Mesmerdean darting overhead were incinerated into ash in a moment and the mudsprites shrieked and dived beneath the mire. The sphere of fire exploded into the hordes of men concealed on the far side of the swamp and they heard agonized screaming and saw a few flaming forms leap and run.

"Marsh gas!" Gwilym cried. "O' course, it burns!" Lifting his staff, he conjured another ball of flame and flung it to where the Mesmerdean buzzed as thick as a swarm of midges. Meghan followed suit, and in seconds those Mesmerdean not incinerated had fled.

They could not flame the Thistle's men, though, for to do so would have been to incinerate their own soldiers. As Iseult and Duncan fought on, side by side, the big captain panted, "We need room . . . to move, Your Highness. Can . . . ye bring ice . . .again?"

Iseult swallowed. She was so tired that only her years of training kept her on her feet, ducking, leaping, thrusting, evading. She found the working of magic far more tiring than fighting hand-to-hand and the gigantic ball of fire had drained her completely. She said abruptly, "I will try. Guard me?"

Duncan nodded. "O' course, Your Highness," he replied with great respect and affection in his voice.

She smiled at him rather grimly, bent her head and concentrated all her will upon the mire. Slowly, slowly, the ooze of the swamp congealed and froze, hard as diamonds. The Blue Guards were able to leap backward to avoid a thrust without being afraid of stumbling into the mud and drowning. The fighting spread out and those soldiers still lined up back on the road ran out to engage.

"Fire and ice," Duncan said respectfully. "Indeed, ye have an unusual Talent, Your Highness."

The mist was swirling up again, and it had grown bitterly cold. With a shout Margrit's soldiers turned and ran back into the swamp, disappearing into the thick fog. Swiftly Duncan shouted orders and the Blue Guards plunged on in pursuit while the rearguard organized litters to take the injured back to camp. Within minutes the chaos of the battlefield had been restored to order, and the Banrìgh's army was again marching on into the swamp.

Suddenly there was a faint hissing sound and men began to fall with screams. They thrashed about on the ground in agony, their faces turning a mottled purple, a discolored foam covering their lips. Thin black thorns extruded from their necks.

The hissing sound came again and Iain cried, "Get down! Get down!" All along the path men dived for cover, some using the still thrashing forms of their comrades as protection. Then Iain called, "Aaiiieeeeeeeeee!"

Immediately there was silence, and then they heard a tentative, "Aaiieeee?"

"Aaaaiiieeee," Iain called back reassuringly.

"Ee-ann?"

"Aye, it's Iain. Who goes there?"

From all round them dark, round heads popped up out of the marsh, showing their fangs in broad grins. They clambered out onto the path and clustered round Iain, hugging their arms around his waist which was as high as they could reach. In their four-fingered hands they carried blowpipes made of reeds and over their shoulders were tiny quivers stuffed full of black thorns.

Dressed in an odd collection of cast-off clothes, their skin was the dark purple of sea grapes, rippled all over with short, plush fur. Their anxious faces were dominated by huge, black, gleaming eyes. They all chattered away in their high-pitched language and Iain patted and stroked them as he answered in the same wailing speech.

The soldiers waited warily, their weapons at the ready, while those who had been stung by the poisoned darts slowly twitched into silence.

"Relax, lads," Gwilym said, leaning on his staff. "They're bogfaeries and would never do anything Iain did no' want them to do. They'd never have attacked us if they had known Iain was with us."

Iain looked up, smiling. "They tell me my m-m-mother has set up an ambush n-n-no' far from here. They will show us another w-w-way through the m-m-marsh. Some m-m-more good news. My m-m-mother's blaygird chamberlain, the one I was so w-w-worried about, M-M-Maya turned him into a toad! A f-f-fitting end, do ye no' agree, Gwilym?"

The warlock smiled grimly. "One I would have devised myself. Who would've guessed the Ensorcellor was capable o' so much insight?"

By sunset they were deep in the marsh. Although there had been many minor clashes with both soldiers and marsh-faeries, the major confrontation was between the forces of weather. Margrit of Arran fought to keep the air currents warm, moist and still so fog would hang above the swamp. Iseult and the witches had bent all their skills to bring a cold wind to blow away the mist and harden the earth. For a while they succeeded, and the Mesmerdean flew no more, hating the cold and retreating to warmer waters. The deeper they penetrated into the marsh, however, the more difficult it was for the witches to hold back the mist. This was Margrit's terrain and her greatest skill, and she had a team of trained witches to help her.

As the sun went down the breeze died away and the stifling atmosphere of the swamp rose up all around them. The smell made Iseult feel sick and apprehensive and she could not rest, staring out into the gloom with a frown etched between her brows. She was so tired she had gone beyond sleep, feeling as finely drawn as a thread of silk. Meghan brought her a cup of valerian tea and ordered her to drink it.

"Do ye think we will be able to find the way to break the curse here in this blaygird bog?" Iseult said, sipping the fragrant tea obediently.

"I hope so," Meghan said. "I have tried to break it but it is tightly bound, and I canna trace its source. I feel Margrit o' Arran is behind it somehow, though it was no' her who cast it, that I'm sure o' it. Margrit has a subtle, devious mind, and though this curse has a cunning twist, it does no' have the stamp o' Tower training. It is more like a cursehag's work, or maybe a skeelie with strong powers. Whoever cast it had something o' Lachlan's, though, something heavily soaked with his life force."

"Finlay again?" Iseult asked heavily.

"He swore he knew nothing about the curse and that he never gave Maya anything o' Lachlan's that may have helped her cast it. Strange as it may seem, I think he is an honorable man and would no' lie . . ."

"Honorable as a swamp rat," Iseult said harshly. "He is so under Maya's spell, he would lie through his teeth, the green-bellied snake."

"Ye're mixing your metaphors," Meghan replied with a smile. "Come, try to sleep, Iseult. It'll be another hard day tomorrow. Ye'll need your strength."

Iseult leant her head on her hand. "Let me be, Meghan. I'm too tired to sleep."

Meghan leant over and touched her between the brows. Iseult's eyelids fluttered and closed, and her head fell onto her knees. Meghan very gently laid her down, then took the plaid from her own shoulders and tucked it around the Banrìgh. "Sleep, dearling," she said softly.

Sunrise the next morning brought with it a horde of freshly emerged Mesmerdean nymphs. Still damp and glistening, their wings curled at the end, they hung all round the clearing where the soldiers had made camp, humming softly. Mist hung low over the swamp but the sky was clear so their great clusters of eyes shimmered with iridescent green and their translucent wings shone. The soldiers simply stood and stared, overcome with fear and awe. Iseult and Meghan stood with them, unable to believe how many of them there were.

"M-m-my m-m-mother has s-s-somehow h-h-hastened the h-h-hatching," Iain said. As always, when talking about his mother, his stutter became much more pronounced. "This is n-n-no' n-n-natural, this early e-mer-mer-mergence."

"What can we do?" Iseult said bleakly. "We canna fight off so many, no' here. There is no marsh gas to ignite and no room to maneuver. We shall be slaughtered."

"Enough is e-n-n-ough!" Iain cried. "I think it is time. I shall go and t-t-talk with them."

"Nay, it is too dangerous!" Iseult cried.

He smiled at her. "I've been talking to M-M-Mesmerdean since I was n-n-naught but a laddiekin," he answered. "Do no' fear for me."

He gestured the soldiers back with his hands and walked over to the first phalanx of the winged creatures. He held out his hands, palm outward, and stood silently. The Mesmerdean stared back, and the humming of their wings died away into silence as they simply hung there, hovering, watching him with their great clusters of eyes.

"What is he doing?" Duncan whispered after a long period of silence. "I thought he said he was going to talk to them."

"He is," Gwilym said, watching closely, his hands clenched on his staff. "Mesmerdean have no spoken language. They have no ears and no tongue."

"But Iain said he would talk to them—and he's just standing there, staring at them."

"They read his thoughts, or perhaps it would be more exact to say they read his energy fluctuations. Iain knows that the Mesmerdean elders will be watching and listening too. It is they he wishes to communicate with. These newly emerged nymphs are still immature and canna make decisions about affiliations or actions. It is the elders that will decide whether to continue to uphold Margrit, to withdraw their support, or even to aid us."

"But are the Mesmerdean no' servants o' the Thistle?"

"The Mesmerdean are servants to no one," Gwilym said in exasperation. "They are free and powerful, and give their service to Margrit only because o' centuries-auld treaties between their people and the MacFóghnan clan. Many times they have withdrawn their support and Margrit works hard to keep them happy."

"If they canna talk, how can Iain ken what they intend?"

"They will tell him," Gwilym replied, clearly still exasperated. "Just because they do no' speak our language does no' mean they canna communicate. If they wish to woo a female or warn another male away from their territory, they rub their wings and claws together, and that is how they communicate with us too, though contemptuously. They think humans very crude and unsophisticated."

Suddenly the humming began to rise again, and the Mesmerdean moved, some rearing back with their claws extended, others lowering their heads and dropping their wings. Some of the buzzing was so shrill the Graycloaks had to cover their ears.

"No' good," Gwilym said. "Some refuse to give up their vendetta."

Iain continued to stand still, facing them, and the humming quavered, grew in intensity. Long minutes passed, and then the Mesmerdean melted back into the mist. The prionnsa came back to them slowly, his face thoughtful and rather grim. He sat down and called to one of the soldiers to bring him some food.

"So what happened?" Iseult demanded impatiently. "Why have they gone?"

"We have an amnesty o' sorts," Iain replied. "I simply sat and thought about my m-m-mother and how tricky and t-t-treacherous she can be. This impressed upon them forcibly. Then I thought about who was truly the p-p-power in the land, able to decide on b-b-borders and territory. Ye ken my m-m-mother has been promising them for ages that once she had the reins o' p-p-power in her hands she would make sure the m-m-marshlands spread out across the land again. I made it clear that only the M-M-MacCuinn had the power to do that. I said that we have already spoken with the NicThanach and that she agreed to give up the l-l-land the MacThanach clan reclaimed for farmlands and allow the s-s-swamps to spread once m-m-more."

"I hope ye made them realize how many concessions we had to make to the NicThanach before she would agree," Iseult said with an expressive snort. "Who would have guessed such a milksop could bargain so shrewdly?"

Meghan smiled. "The MacThanachs are always shrewd when it comes to protecting their own interests. They are a practical clan indeed."

"Still, we are p-p-paying highly for land that has never

been very fruitful," Iain said. "The s-s-soil was always sour and is even m-m-more so now that the bulwark has been b-b-broken down and the tide runs as it wills. The NicThanach w-w-would have had a hard time making it fertile enough for crops anyway. This way, she gets rich t-t-trade concessions with Arran as well as Rionnagan and Clachan."

"No' to mention rich dowries for her five sisters," Meghan said with a little laugh. "Indeed, she is a canny bargainer, that lassie. I have hopes she will make a fine NicThanach."

"So what did the Mesmerdean say? Did they agree to give us their assistance in return for no' rebuilding the bulwark and letting the water seep back? It is a significant concession."

Iain shook his head wearily. "They are interested but n-n-no' convinced. After all, my m-m-mother has promised them the s-s-same result and they at least k-k-ken and respect her. Ye are strangers in their l-l-land and they resent that. The only f-f-factor in our favor is that they are angry with my m-m-mother for waking them early. M-M-Mesmerdean dislike the cold and all this ice ye've been conjuring m-m-makes them very irritable."

"So what do we have to do to convince them? We have little hope o' victory without their help." Iseult tried hard to keep the despair out of her voice. She had hoped against all odds that they would be able to bargain for the Mesmerdeans' neutrality, at the very least. Iain had explained that the marsh faeries only supported his mother because she had promised to restore the lands the MacThanach clan had drained back to swampland. It seemed the Mesmerdeans' loyalties to the Thistle ran deeper, however.

"They will n-n-no' give up their q-q-quest for revenge so easily," Iain said grimly. "They have ye and L-L-Lachlan marked as kin-killers, no' to mention M-M-Meghan, Gwilym and Isabeau . . ."

"Isabeau?"

"Aye, I think that is who they meant. It is hard to understand every subtle nuance o' their humming, but they certainly indicated one who was kin unto ye, and Isabeau was all I could think o'.''

"But how could Isabeau have killed a Mesmerd up on the Spine o' the World?" Iseult said without thinking, immediately attracting Meghan's fierce gaze. The sorceress made no comment, however, twisting the rings on her gnarled fingers thoughtfully.

"If we w-w-want their help," Iain said, "they w-w-want the lives o' those who have killed M-M-Mesmerdean. I said that was n-n-no' possible. They l-l-leave us to think about it. If we do n-n-no' agree they shall return when the sun is high and t-t-take all o' our lives."

"But why?" Iseult cried. "They attacked us, we were all merely defending ourselves. Does that count for nothing?"

Iain was silent for a moment. "I'll try and explain," he said at last. "The Mesmerdean do no' have the same respect for life as we do. They live only a few years anyway and most o' their existence is ruled by the copulation wheel." He blushed, his prominent Adam's apple bobbing. Not looking at Iseult or Meghan he went on rather rapidly, "This no' only means the actual act o' copulation, called the wheel for the shape they make, but for the whole cycle o' birth, life, and death. Only the nymphs have the freedom to travel far from their territory. Once they are fully mature, the Mesmerdean elders live very close to the swamp and their own patch o' water, where they breed and lay the eggs and watch over the naiads. So the elders live through the nymphs. They see what they see and experience what they experience. Nymphs can travel quite widely and have many adventures."

Iain paused, trying to find words. "It is hard to explain but Mesmerdean are rather like . . . spiritual leeches. When they kiss someone to death they swallow their life essence, all their memories and knowledge. Mesmerdean do no' kill for food or even sport. It is a sort o' intellectual hunger. What they learn from those whose lives they take is transmitted to all Mesmerdean. What one Mesmerdean sees, all Mesmerdean see. When a Mesmerd dies, however, that transmission is lost and all that they have learnt is lost too, unless they have had a chance to procreate. A Mesmerd's memories are passed down to its children and so preserved generation after generation. If a Mesmerd dies before it procreates, however, all that they have learnt is lost to the entire race—which o' course is what happens if they die while still nymphs. Do ye understand?"

"The auld ones get bored, live through the young ones; if a young one dies, they lose the connection, get bored again and want revenge for the knowledge they've lost," Iseult said swiftly. "Is that right?"

Gwilym laughed harshly. "Bang on the nail, Your Highness."

Iain smiled reluctantly. "Ye see, the Mesmerdean elders are fascinated by what ye ken and have done. They want that . . . life knowledge. The Mesmerdean nymphs ye killed had traveled far and wide and learnt a great deal about life beyond the swamp. The elders were angry to lose that knowledge; having had it once, they want it back. Add this to the very strong kinship they feel for their own kind . . . Well, the fact is, they will only accept your lives in return for the lives o' their dead kin." He hesitated then turned to Meghan. "Ye in particular. They are greedy for your life. It has been very long and very interesting. They will no' give up the chance to taste it. Besides, ye have been responsible for the deaths o' many nymphs. They hate ye and are fascinated by ye, and that is a potent combination. I do no' think the offer o' swampland is enough."

"I see," the sorceress said, getting to her feet. "I suppose I should think o' it as a compliment. Are they merely trying to bargain for more concessions or are they adamant?"

Iain shrugged. "Who can tell? They are enigmatic creatures. And very dangerous. Mesmerdean never forgive and never forget. I have known o' vendettas that have been carried on for centuries."

"I see," Meghan said again. "Well, let me think on it. I think I have a solution but it is one that needs careful thought." She began to pace the clearing, her forehead furrowed, her mouth grim. The little donbeag nestled under her ear, chittering in agitation. Meghan stroked him in reassurance, though her expression only became bleaker.

The others watched her unhappily, Iseult frowning. "What does she mean to do?" she asked Gwilym uneasily.

He shrugged. "I can think o' no solution," he said harshly. "The Mesmerdean are vengeful creatures and care little for things that may sway men, like land or gold or beautiful women. I canna think what she means to offer them."

Meghan beckoned to Iain and he went over to her, his face troubled. Iseult watched him shake his head, watched Meghan speak low and compellingly, saw the prionnsa shake his head again. Meghan grasped his doublet in both her hands and spoke to him earnestly. Again Iain shook his head, his face miserable. At last he gave a gesture of resignation and nodded his head. She pointed her finger at him forcefully and he lowered his eyes and nodded again.

"What does she mean to do?" Iseult asked again, feeling her heart sink in her breast. Gwilym said nothing, though she saw by his face that he feared as she did. Iseult clenched her hands, feeling rather sick. She ran to Meghan's side, grasping her by the arm. Even through her agitation, Iseult was shocked by how thin the old sorceress's arm was.

"Auld mother!" she cried. "What is it that ye mean to do? Ye canna mean to . . ." Her voice faltered.

Meghan covered Iseult's hand with her own, gnarled, liver-spotted and knotted with veins. She nodded.

"Yes, o' course I do," she answered. "Can ye think o' any other way? We have no' fought so hard for so long to die here in this swamp. I am very auld and I am tired. Ye are young and your lives stretch before ye."

Iseult was astonished to find she was weeping. Scarred Warriors never wept. She said fiercely, "No!"

"I am four hundred and thirty years auld," the sorceress said gently. "I should have died long ago. If I had no' tasted o' the waters o' the Pool o' Two Moons when my father wrought the Lodestar, so many years ago, I would be dead. We all must die some time. I am luckier than most because I can choose the time and manner o' my dying. They say to die in the Mesmerd's arms is to die in bliss."

"No," Iseult wept. "Ye canna! We can fight them, we can kill them all. If there are no Mesmerdean left, there will be none to carry on this stupid vendetta. We will wipe them off the face o' the earth!"

"Annihilate a whole race to save one auld witch?" Meghan's voice was gently mocking. "A witch who should've died long ago? Nay, Iseult, this is the best solution. Besides, I do no' mean to let them have me now. There are still a few things I need to do. Iain says the Mesmerdean are patient. They can wait awhile."

Iseult shook her head, too choked with tears to speak. Meghan smiled and stroked her wet face with one finger. "Glad I am to see ye weeping, dearling. I thought ye must have been born without tear ducts. Come, ye o' all people must understand. Death is as much a part o' our existence as birth or life. There is nothing to fear in death."

Iseult could only stare at her. Meghan put her hand up and stroked Gitâ's soft, brown fur. The donbeag was almost strangling her, he had crept so close about her neck, quivering and keening in distress. "We all must die," Meghan repeated, a touch of impatience in her voice. She glanced at Gwilym and Duncan, who had come up behind Iseult, their faces full of distress.

"Did my beloved Jorge no' sacrifice his life to save his loved ones? Why should I do any less? If I can save ye, well then, I shall go gladly into the Mesmerd's embrace."

They protested, Duncan reaching out his huge hand to seize her arm. She wrenched her arm free, snapping, "There is no need to weep and wring your hands. Why should we all die if one o' us shall suffice? Iain admits that they have said they will willingly pledge us their support and release ye all from their vendetta if they

may have me. Well, let them have me! All I have asked
for is time. Time for Iseult and Isabeau to reach their
full potential, time for me to teach Lachlan to use the
Lodestar, time for me to make sure the Coven is restored
to all its strength and wisdom."

"How much time, auld mother?" Iseult cried.

"Till the red comet has risen and sunk again," Meghan
said, rather heavily. "Four years. Jorge said that was
when the Fairgean come, with the rising o' the red comet.
So I shall wait till then, to make sure ye are all safe."

Again Duncan protested, pleading with her not to sacrifice herself. The old sorceress sighed and rolled her
eyes. "There is no need for all these dramatics. We all
must die." She reached out and took Iseult's hand between her own, holding the Banrìgh's gaze with her own,
black and snapping with vitality between their wrinkled
lids. "Death comes to us all," she repeated gently. "It is
like birth, a door into another place, another life. It is
nothing to be afraid o'. Ye ken that, Iseult."

The Banrìgh nodded. "Yes, auld mother. I ken."

SWANS OVER THE SWAMP

Isabeau sat in her chair by the fire, her chin in her hand, her eyes on the flames dancing in the hearth. Bronwen played at her feet, while Maya rather sullenly chopped herbs and mushrooms at the table for their evening meal. It was her turn to cook dinner but the Fairge had never grown resigned to helping Isabeau with the daily chores. The apprentice witch was always having to remind Maya that she was no longer her servant and she had to be careful not to respond instinctively to the Fairge's haughty orders.

The firelight wavered over the tangle of tree roots, all crowded with jars and tins, and strung with herbs hung up to dry. Isabeau was very weary after her labors of the day and rather dispirited.

Staring into the flames, she remembered how she had sat here herself as a little girl, helping Meghan spin the winter away, being told stories about the Three Spinners. Meghan had said they gave three gifts at the birth of a child. The spinner Sniomhar, the goddess of birth, gave joy. The weaver Breabadair, goddess of life, gave toil and its contentment. And she who cuts the thread, Gearradh, the goddess of death, gave sorrow. Isabeau gave a slight, wistful smile and told herself she had to strive now for contentment. She had had joy in her brief, happy childhood, she had had sorrow. Now was the time for her to toil and be content.

Isabeau was roused from her abstraction by the lilting sound of music. She smiled and glanced lovingly down at Bronwen's dark head, constantly amazed at how beautifully the little girl played her flute. Her eyes widened

as she saw the child's ragdoll dancing about on the floor
as if it had come alive. It waltzed and curtsied in perfect
time to Bronwen's playing, spreading its little skirt and
bowing its raggedy head as the tune came to an end.

At the sound of her mother's in-drawn breath Bronwen glanced up, and the ragdoll collapsed into a heap
on the floor. Isabeau looked up too and was shocked at
the expression on the Fairge's face. It was not amazement or even pride at her daughter's cleverness but
rather calculation, almost greed. Isabeau frowned, troubled, as Maya became aware of Isabeau's scrutiny and
smoothed her expression.

"Who's a canny lass then," she said brightly, "making
your dolly dance to your tune."

Bronwen smiled and said, "I can make them all dance,
Mam, watch!"

She lifted her flute to her lips again and played another
infectious tune and all the toys scattered around the floor
began to waltz around. The spinning top whirled faster
and faster, the dragon rocked back and forth, the
wheeled horse ran round in circles and the two bluebird
rattles swooped about, touching wings and then beaks.
The ragdoll and little wooden puppets Isabeau had made
all pranced about, bobbing up and down and touching
hands in a perfect imitation of a waltz. Even the two
little drumsticks danced up and down upon the drum,
marking the tempo in perfect time.

Isabeau watched enthralled and clapped her hands as
the tune reached its end and all the toys bowed to each
other and then sat down with a plop. Even as they both
exclaimed over Bronwen's cleverness, Isabeau was wondering rather uneasily what she was to do with a child
who showed such early promise of an extraordinary Talent. She was conscious of a glint in Maya's eye and reminded herself yet again that the Fairge could not be
trusted. Despite all her warm endearments and caressing
ways, Isabeau was not convinced that Maya loved Bronwen as deeply and sincerely as she did herself.

Early the next morning the three of them went to the
underground loch so that Maya and Bronwen could swim

and transform. Although it was a beautiful spring day and Isabeau would much rather have been out in the sunshine, she refused Maya's offer to take Bronwen by herself, replying curtly that she did not want them getting lost underground.

"Och, I think I know the way by now," Maya replied silkily, which only made Isabeau more determined to stay close to her side.

The two Fairgean left their clothes on the rocks and dived into the water, changing almost immediately into their sea-shapes. As always Isabeau was fascinated by this process, so different to all the other magic she had ever studied. She watched closely and rather jealously as they sported together in the icy-cold loch, splashing each other with their tails. Then Maya dived beneath the surface and Bronwen immediately followed, her little tail flipping out cheekily before disappearing from sight.

Isabeau waited for them to emerge, feeling anxiety tightening her chest muscles as the loch stayed calm and empty. Water dripped, occasionally stirring the mirror image of the stone waterfall. She began to pace and then to call their names, not knowing whether to fear for their lives or be furious at Maya for attempting to escape. Anger won over anxiety, for she knew Fairgean rarely drowned. She began to search the shores of the loch, stumbling over the slippery rocks. To her consternation she found the little bundle of clothes had disappeared. She hesitated only a moment, then stripped off her own clothes and dived into the water.

It was bitterly cold but strangely buoyant so that Isabeau had to work hard to swim into its depths. Even with her uncanny eyesight she found it hard to see under the water, it was so dark. She cast out her witch senses, searching, but the water distorted everything so that she could not be sure which way they had gone. She felt the faint flow of a current against her skin, however, and followed it. Strange white shapes loomed up at her and every now and again she scraped her skin against rock. She found the current quickening and swam faster, her chest beginning to hurt with the strain of holding her breath. She sensed the rock overhead lifting and swam to the surface, finding just enough room to put her mouth above water and breathe. The air was dank and stale and cold but it tasted like wine to her air-starved lungs. She took another deep breath and dived again.

This time she emerged in another cavern, with the river running through its center. She conjured witch's light and looked about her. There was no sign of either Maya or Bronwen but she trusted her intuition and swam on.

The river ran on through low caverns and lofty halls, sometimes so shallow Isabeau scraped her elbows and knees. At last it emerged in a dimly lit cave and Isabeau was elated to see two pairs of webbed footprints in the mud, leading toward the light. She followed hastily, anxiety now completely swallowed by anger. Then she heard Bronwen's high voice saying, "But Mam, why? Where Is'beau? Why canna she come too?"

Isabeau came up behind them so silently that when she said, "But Bronny, o' course I came too! What an adventure, exploring down the river!" Maya started and screamed involuntarily.

Isabeau smiled at her and took Bronwen's hand, saying, "We canna go far though, else we may get lost and we willna be able to find our way back again. That would no' be such an adventure, would it?"

"But Mam said ye couldna come," Bronwen objected.

"Happen she thought I could no' swim so far, no' being a quarter Fairgean like ye," Isabeau replied, "but I was taught to swim by otters and they are wonderful swimmers indeed."

They were standing in the mouth of the cave, looking out across the valley below. The underground river poured down the steep slope of the cliff and joined what Isabeau recognized as the Rhyllster below. She looked back at Maya and saw the Fairge's nostrils flare and her mouth compress until it was a mere thin line. Her fingers twitched and Isabeau said conversationally, "Are ye planning on turning me into an otter? Or maybe a toad? Now would be a good time to do it, for I warn ye, I will no' let ye take Bronwen and use her against Lachlan and my sister. That is no' why I took her from Lucescere."

The Fairge's fingers gripped into fists, then she laughed, rather artificially. "Nay, ye ken I do no' want to ensorcel ye unless I have to. I meant it when I said I thought o' ye as a friend. Indeed, ye are the only one to ever offer me the hand o' friendship and I'd be loath to reply in such a way. Ye make me very angry though. Why did ye follow us? Ye must know I canna stand being shut up in that blaygird wee valley any more. I always feel like all those animals are staring at me and condemning me . . ."

"They probably are," Isabeau replied swiftly and then wished she had held her tongue, for the Fairge's mouth thinned again and her mobile nostrils flared out like little white wings. "Ye said all ye wanted was to stay somewhere where ye and Bronwen can be safe," she went on before Maya gave in to the temptation to turn her into something small and slimy, as she so clearly wished to do. "I gave ye that sanctuary. Why do ye wish to leave it? Ye ken ye and Bronwen will both be in grave danger if ye return to Rionnagan."

The Fairge said nothing, though the little girl said rather fretfully, "Wha' do ye mean? Why are ye fraitchin'?"

Isabeau smiled at her and stroked the wet hair away from her cheek without replying. Maya scowled and said, "Bronwen is the rightful banrìgh! Jaspar named her heir."

"Only because he did no' believe Lachlan was truly his brother," Isabeau replied swiftly. "And ye ken the Lodestar chose Lachlan. It knew Eileanan needed a strong Rìgh and warrior. The land is already in chaos, Maya. The people do no' need more doubt and confusion in their hearts and ye ken Bronwen is too young to rule."

"She is the rightful heir," Maya said obstinately.

"Admit that ye wish to be banrìgh again and have everyone adoring ye and obeying your every command," Isabeau said tartly. "If ye canna be banrìgh, regent is close enough, is that no' so? Well, I will no' let ye sacrifice my sister or the Coven or the people to your selfish ambitions. Ye canna take Bronwen away."

"I dinna want to go 'way," Bronwen said, suddenly beginning to cry. "Wanna stay wi' Is'beau. Wanna stay."

"It's all right, my lassie, ye do no' have to go anywhere ye do no' wish to go," Isabeau said, drawing her close and looking Maya defiantly in the eye. She could only hope that Maya would not want to upset her daughter and change Isabeau into a toad before her very eyes. Seeing the Fairge gather in her will, she tensed, ready to throw up her defenses or to try and dive behind the rocks, futile though both actions would probably be. Bronwen was clinging close, though, and Maya hesitated then relaxed, unable to risk losing her daughter's tenuous affection.

After a moment she said softly, "Will ye give me my daughter and let us leave if I remove the curse from Lachlan?"

Isabeau stiffened all over. "Ye cursed Lachlan? That is why he sleeps so? How?"

Maya said, "Will ye give me Bronwen and no' follow us or try to stop me? Will ye let us go and no' follow?"

Isabeau shook her head, resisting the urge to let her will be submerged beneath Maya's. "No! No, I canna! Meghan would never forgive me."

"Ye mean she'd rather have Lachlan lying more dead than alive?" Maya said silkily. "What about your sister? He's no' much good to her like that."

Isabeau's emotions were in a tumult. She clung to the little girl, saying, "Nay! Ye canna take Bronny away from me!"

"She's no' your daughter!" Maya snapped. "She's mine! Ye wonder why I do no' want to stay with ye when ye act like ye're her mother and I'm some kind o' interloper. How can she come to love me with ye always snatching her away from me?"

"Ye do no' want her because she's your daughter and ye love her, ye just want her so ye can get the Throne back!"

"She's my daughter! If ye do no' let her go, I shall
turn ye into a toad, I swear it!"

"I do no' believe ye really cursed Lachlan!" Isabeau
cried, adroitly distracting the Fairge's attention. "Ye are
just saying that to make me agree to let Bronny go."

Maya rummaged through the bundle of clothes she
had dropped on the ground and unwrapped the wooden
chest Isabeau had found beside her on the mountain.
Isabeau was filled with consternation. Although small
enough to carry, it was still heavy and unwieldy. She
wondered how Maya had managed to conceal it from
her as they had walked through the valley that morning,
and then she realized Maya must have hidden it near the
underground loch previously. This then was no impromptu decision—Maya had been planning this escape
for some time.

Maya unlocked the chest and drew out a little black
bag made from a square of cloth tied up with black cord.
Isabeau stared at it, conscious of its throbbing, malignant
power. Using only the tips of her fingers, an expression
of distaste on her face, Maya held it out for Isabeau to
see. "A cursehag cast the curse for me," she whispered.
"It is bound by my own blood. None can break the curse
but me."

Although there was nothing to see but a black bag,
Isabeau believed her. She said in a low voice, "But where
would ye go? How would ye survive?"

Maya said, "All rivers run to the sea. That is one thing
I was taught as a child. All rivers run to the sea, and so
shall we."

"But the Rhyllster is fresh water," Isabeau objected.
"Ye need salt."

Maya nodded. "I ken. We shall have to swim fast.
Besides, I brought some salt for emergencies." She lifted
a small sack out of the chest and Isabeau recognized it
with chagrin. She had carefully gathered that salt from
the hot mineral pools in the Cursed Valley and stored it
for Bronwen. It angered her to see it.

"What shall ye eat?" she said tightly. "Did ye steal
provisions too?"

Maya looked at her, oddly anxious, and nodded. "Aye. I hope ye do no' mind."

The incongruity of the statement jarred with Isabeau. She frowned, soothing the anxious, questioning child absent-mindedly and thinking over what Maya had said.

"But where will ye go?" she asked again. "Do ye return to the Fairgean?"

Maya shook her head emphatically. "How can I return there? They will feed me to the sea serpents. Nay, I will try and find somewhere safe at first. Maybe one o' the islands. I do no' ken what I will do then."

"But ye are safe here," Isabeau objected.

"Ye do no' understand," Maya said. "Swimming in that loch is like being buried underground with dead things. I want to swim in the open sea where everything is free and alive. I want Bronwen to ken what it is to swim in the sea. She is three years auld and has never seen the sea!" The tone of Maya's voice expressed clearly how strange and horrible that was to the Fairge.

"But it will be so dangerous—how can ye take Bronwen into such danger?" Isabeau drew the little girl closer, her hands shaking. For the last three years she had looked after the banprionnsa as if she were her own child, and the idea that she might be about to lose her opened up the future as a gaping emptiness. Isabeau searched desperately for ways to keep Bronwen with her but the black bag was a palpable presence between them, hot and sinister.

Isabeau had seen her sister's distress as the months passed by and Lachlan still did not recover, and she knew how difficult it was for Iseult to try and rule while her husband lay under such an odd affliction. Isabeau knew she had to give Bronwen up if that would lift the curse, but the decision had rushed too suddenly upon her, it was too great for her to make easily.

"I will have a care for her, I promise," Maya said gently.

"Only because ye want to regain power through her," Isabeau said bitterly, pressing her cheek against Bronwen's.

"No' only," Maya said rather haughtily. "She is my daughter."

Bronwen had been following the conversation intently and now she flung herself on Isabeau, sobbing, "No, no, stay wi' Is'beau, stay wi' Is'beau!"

Reluctantly, tears so thick in her throat she could hardly speak, Isabeau held Bronwen away from her. "Ye must go with your mam, dearling. I wish I could go with ye but I canna, I must stay here with my mam and my *dai-dein*. Ye must be good, and mind your mam and remember what I've taught ye, and hopefully the Spinners will bring our threads together again very soon."

"No!" the little girl wailed. "I dinna want to go! Stay wi' ye!"

Isabeau crouched down beside her and said, "Remember, my Bronny, that I love ye very, very much and that ye can always come back to me if ye need me. But now ye must go with your mam. She loves ye too and it is time for ye to be with her. Do ye understand? Remember what I have told ye—everything in its rightful time and place."

The little girl nodded tearfully, though her grip on Isabeau did not lessen. Through her tears Isabeau looked up at Maya, saying, "Ye must remove the curse now! And ye must burn it all so ye canna cast such a hex again. Do ye promise?"

Maya nodded. "I do no' ken how to do it, though," she said. "Shannagh o' the Swamp cast the actual curse, using my blood. I do no' know how to break it. I am no' a witch."

Although Isabeau bristled up at the Fairge's contemptuous tone she did not protest, toying with the wet straggles of Bronwen's hair and murmuring, "If we only had *The Book o' Shadows*! That would tell us how to break the curse." She looked back up at Maya and said, "Ye must return with me to the valley. I canna break the curse here. I need to read Meghan's books and find out the right time and method. I need to know the best phase o' the moon, and to make some candles scented with angelica and St. John's Wort, with clover perhaps, or rosemary. And Meghan has some dragon's blood, power-ful indeed for spell-making . . ."

"So do I," said Maya surprisingly. "And other things too, I'm no' sure what." She indicated the chest, saying with an odd fluctuation of color, "It belonged to a wizard I kent . . ."

"Please, will ye no' come home with me? I promise to let ye go again if only ye'll let me cast off this curse properly. I give ye my word."

Maya nodded. "Very well. But do no' try and trick me for I ken the way out o' the valley now and if I have to, I will transform ye, I warn ye."

Isabeau bit back bitter, angry words and said merely, "I ken."

Mist swirled all around the resting army, making the stark trees look as if they were swaying forward, reaching out with skeletal hands. When the marsh-faeries drifted out of the haze, the sentries all gave strangled shrieks before composing themselves enough to call the alarm. Most of the soldiers leapt to their feet, hands on their weapons, but a grim-faced Iain gestured them back and went forward to meet the Mesmerdean alone.

There were hundreds of them, their inhuman faces strangely beautiful. Their multitonal humming filled the air, thousands of many-veined wings whirring, thousands of claws rubbing against their hard abdomens. Iain looked very small and very alone, standing before them. There were long, long minutes of silence and then the humming changed. It deepened, softened, harmonized, sounding much like the satisfied purr of a cream-fed cat. The Mesmerdean's wings lowered and folded back, and they dropped their claws.

Gwilym's grim face lightened a little. "The Mesmerdean have accepted Meghan's offer and have pledged us their support! Who would have believed it was possible? They must want ye very much indeed, Keybearer."

Iseult's expression only became more somber, and she put her hand on Meghan's shoulder. The little donbeag Gitâ clung to the old witch's collar, his whole body quiv-

ering in distress. Meghan nodded her white head a few
times and twitched her grim old mouth, soothing Gitâ
with a hand that trembled.

Duncan gave swift orders to pack up the camp and
advance, and all round the clearing the rigid stance of
the soldiers relaxed. Swiftly they rolled up their blankets
and shouldered their packs, while the ranks of Mesmerdean slowly and deliberately stripped off their fluttering,
gray draperies and flung them into the bog. Without their
covering they looked more alien than ever, with a long,
hard, segmented body that curved forward, ending in a
sharp point. They had six legs, the highest also the lon-
gest and most maneuverable, the others curling back into
their body. Their stiff wings were in constant motion and
they darted about in unexpected directions, causing many
of the soldiers to jump, startled and alarmed.

With the bogfaeries scouting ahead and the Mesmerdean flying all about, they were able to press on into the
swamp at a much faster pace. Many times the Thistle's
men tried to ambush them but, despite the fog which
rose up thick and stifling all around them, the Graycloaks
were forewarned and able to beat them off. As the day
passed, most of the army's casualties were due to mudsprites, who reached their bony hands out of the bog and
dragged unwary soldiers in, drowning them before their
frantic comrades could rescue them. A few were bitten
by poisonous snakes, dying quickly but painfully, despite
the attempts of their companions to suck out the poison.

Most of the Graycloaks learnt to carry their ropes tied
at their belts, not coiled in their packs, for the ground
was treacherous and many of the soldiers slipped into
bogs or quicksand and had to be dragged free before
they were sucked under.

Now that they had the Mesmerdean as allies, Duncan
and Iseult had decided to abandon any attempts at
stealth and so were making their way toward one of the
few roads that wound through the marshes. The Thistle
needed a solid highway for the wagons that carried Arran's exports out to the world and brought in the many
luxuries the banprionnsa required. The Banrìgh had not

attempted to use the highway previously, knowing it was heavily guarded, choosing instead to trust to Iain and Gwilym's knowledge of the secret ways through the swamps.

They camped that night uncomfortably and uneasily but managed to survive with only a few casualties, thanks to the Mesmerdean who drifted along the chain of camp-fires like ghosts, thwarting any attack by the Arran soldiers. They went to sleep in dense fog and woke to the same close, impenetrable dampness, so thick that each man could barely see the soldier marching a scant few paces ahead.

As they neared the road, the fighting grew much fiercer and many Graycloaks were lost, despite the assistance of the marsh-faeries. Nebulous flickering lights led the soldiers astray so that they stepped into quicksand or were killed from behind by a quick dagger thrust. The men of the swamp knew the terrain and were easily able to conceal themselves in the clumps of rushes and sedge grasses, or in the huge water oaks that grew out of the many patches of still water. Suddenly a rain of arrows or poisoned darts would hit the marching columns of men, killing or injuring many before the soldiers could bring up their shields or take cover.

Although the witches could sense the minds of the hiding men, they were all marching at the head of the column and so the Thistle's men simply waited until they had passed, then poled silently through the watercourses in flat-bottomed boats or crept up through the hidden ways to attack the men marching behind. After several such silent attacks, Iseult sent Gwilym, Iain, Niall and Dide to walk with those of the prionnsachan who did not have any witch senses, and asked the Mesmerdean to fly out through the marshes and disable any of the Thistle's men hidden some distance away. After that they had no more major casualties, although the attacks continued in increasingly desperate forays.

They reached the highway just on dusk. It was a narrow, winding road, built on a firm base of stones and shale which was continually having to be shored up to stop the highway sinking back into the bog. The mist continued to shroud everything in a pale gloom and many of the Graycloaks were jumpy and anxious, so that Iseult ordered an extra ration of whiskey to be passed around, to warm their chill bodies and settle their nerves. They camped on the road itself. Although hard and stony, it was a far more comfortable camping spot than the treacherous bogs had been. They were able to camp close together and set up sentries to patrol the perimeters rather than being scattered through the marshes on whatever patch of firm ground they could find, with the constant fear of being dragged into the quicksand by a mudsprite.

The alarm was called just before dawn. Iseult woke from uneasy dreams with a start and leapt to her feet, staring out into the misty darkness. Duncan was by her side, his claymore drawn, and they listened in dismay to the sound of marching feet on the road. It sounded as if hundreds of legions were advancing toward them, their hobnailed boots ringing on the stone.

"Can we have light?" Iseult called.

Torches were lit from the embers of the fires, and Gwilym summoned witch light at the end of his staff and raised it high. Iain gathered together all his strength to blow away the fog which hung over them still, but to his surprise the mist parted easily. The red light of the torches and the blue blaze of Gwilym's light illuminated the road ahead of them, and sighs and groans of dismay were wrung from the Graycloaks.

An army of immense size was marching toward them down the road, weapons glittering in the torchlight, faces under steel helmets grim and determined. As far as the eye could see, the Thistle's army stretched in rows of a dozen men, all armed with long pikes and great, double-handed swords. Many more approached through the marshes on either side, making no attempt to conceal themselves.

Duncan began to shout out orders and hurriedly the Graycloaks jumped up from their blankets and gathered together their weapons. Iain frowned and rubbed his hands through his soft, brown hair. "Where could my m-m-mother have got so many m-m-men?" he wondered. "Arran has n-n-no standing army . . ."

Gwilym too was frowning. "Something does no' smell right to me," he muttered. He turned to Meghan, saying softly, "Keybearer?"

Meghan had been silent and distracted since the pact with the Mesmerdean had been made, but she roused herself now from her deep abstraction to gaze at the approaching army, almost close enough for the archers to begin firing. The mist drifted and wavered over the road, making it hard to see more than the dim shapes of the approaching men. As the archers ran forward to take up position in the first row, arrows set to their bows, she stroked Gità's soft fur thoughtfully then gave an odd little smile.

"The mistress o' illusions weaves her spells," she said softly.

Gwilym gave a harsh laugh. "O' course! So cannily she weaves I was no' sure." A master of illusions himself, he gave a negligent wave and suddenly the legions of men disappeared like smoke. The Graycloaks gave a triumphant yell and ran to engage, while Margrit's men—revealed now to be no more than a few hundred—groaned in dismay. They fought savagely, however, knowing it was far better to die here on the road than to run back to the Thistle with the Graycloaks at their heels.

League by slow league, the invading army pushed their way down the road, the Mesmerdean patroling the swamps on either side. The sun rose but the mist had descended again, so thick it was like trying to breathe through cotton wool. They heard groans and sighs all around and strange shapes drifted toward them out of the mist—ghosts of horribly maimed warriors, huge slimy monsters with gaping jaws and groping tentacles, wailing banshees, giants with flaming eyes. The soldiers faltered, some crying out in fear and horror, but Dide began to sing a rousing battle song.

> "Behold I am a soldier bold,
> And only twenty-four years auld,
> A braver warrior never was seen,
> From Loch Kilchurn to Dùn Eidean.
> The wind may blow, the cock may crow,
> The rain may rain and the snow may snow,
> But ye canna shock and ye canna scare me,
> For I'm the bravest lad in the whole damn army!"

The soldiers began to sing too, at first rather raggedly, then with great cheer and loudness, swinging their swords in time to the rhythm. With the song ringing in their ears and their eyes on their opponents, they did not see the strange monsters, and so after a while the wails and groans faded away and there was only the clash of arms and the sound of the soldiers' singing.

Then voices began to call out of the mist and many of the soldiers glanced up, glad recognition flaring in their eyes. They saw pretty young women with outstretched hands, old women with pleading faces, children begging to be picked up. Many of the Graycloaks would have stepped off the road and followed the illusions into the marshes if it had not been for the witches, who called out in warning voices or caused the glamourie to dissolve back into mist.

At last they saw a great stretch of water ahead of them, its far shore hidden by mist. The road widened out into a large square, surrounded on three sides by low warehouses, their roofs thatched with sedge. A long jetty thrust out into the loch, with barges and small boats moored alongside.

Here, on the shore of the Murkmyre, the tattered remnants of the Thistle's army made one last, desperate stand. There were witches among them, dressed in flowing purple robes, who fought with flame and wind and illusion, but Meghan, Dughall, Gwilym and Iain were easily able to combat their magical powers. One by one they fell, studded with arrows or slashed with gaping wounds, or were seized in the arms of the Mesmerdean and kissed to death.

With the Mesmerdean fighting at the Graycloaks' side, the men and witches of the marsh had little hope of winning, but they defended the last bastion of the fenlands with their lives. Despite all Iseult's offers of quarter, they fought to the very last man. Even the Banrìgh felt rather sick at heart when they had finally hacked down the last man and stood panting on the jetty, leaning on their swords.

Only then did the fog begin to drift away, and the Graycloaks saw the pearly spires of the Tower of Mists rising out of the serene water, built on an island in the center of the loch. So still was the water that the towers were reflected in perfect mirror image, stretching almost to their feet.

Iseult stood and stared, overawed. The palace was simply the most beautiful and fantastical building she had ever seen, its towers and minarets all painted in dawn pink and ice blue, violet and softest green, scrolled and pointed and domed. Rising as it did from the water, it shone like something spun from rainbows. She heard indrawn breaths all round her and saw Iain's hands clenched, his Adam's apple bobbing up and down.

"It's bonny," she whispered and he nodded, blinking away tears.

"I've been away far too long," he answered quietly. "The marshes get into your blood like a pox. I've missed them indeed."

"Well, let us take ye home then," she replied with a sigh of sympathy as she thought about her own snowbound home, long unseen. She nodded to Duncan, who gave the order to board the punts.

As the long, narrow boats were poled across the Murkmyre, Iseult heard a hoarse, drawn-out cry and glanced up. "Look!" she cried.

Flying up into the sky was a carved sleigh pulled along by twelve crimson-winged swans. Crouched in the sleigh, whipping them mercilessly on, was a tall woman dressed all in black. She turned and glared down at them and shook her fist, then the sleigh curved away, the swans' wings beating strongly.

"The NicFóghnan flees," Meghan said, her face losing its look of melancholy for a moment. Gwilym gave a swift order and a drove of Mesmerdean nymphs took flight in pursuit. They did not have the strength or speed of the swans, however, and were left far behind. The swan-carriage soared into the clouds and disappeared.

A ring of tall white candles encircled a fire built on the rock shelf near the curve of the waterfall, where the waters of the loch poured over the edge of a cliff. It was sunset, moonrise, on the night of the spring equinox. One of the key events in the witches' calendar, the vernal equinox marked the death of winter and the birth of summer, the first day of the year when the hours of sunlight lasted as long as the hours of night. An auspicious time for the breaking of a curse.

The smoke of the candles smelt sweet, rising into the dusk like blue, wavering ribbons. Maya sat at the point of the pentagram, naked. The firelight glittered on her scales and made strange shadows of her fins. On either side of her were Isabeau and Bronwen, also naked, while Ishbel and Khan'gharad sat at the opposite points of the star. They found it hard to look at Maya, bending their gaze instead to their clasped hands.

Isabeau said softly, "It is sunset. Time for the Ordeal to begin."

Obediently they all closed their eyes. Isabeau breathed deeply of the forest-scented air and tried to find peace. Despite the stillness, serenity eluded her and as the long hours trickled away, she found herself crying. Occasionally she heard a muffled gasp or sob from elsewhere in the sacred circle and knew she was not the only one to weep.

She felt the tide of the seasons turning within her, more clearly than she had ever felt them before. Isabeau opened her eyes and said, with a choke in her voice, "It is midnight and the tides turn. Let us chant the rites."

The husky voice of the Fairge, the sweet, weary stumble of the little girl, Ishbel's light voice and Khan'gharad's deep baritone all chanted with her:

> "Darksome night and shining light,
> open your secrets to our sight,
> find in us the depths and height,
> find in us surrender and fight,
> find in us jet-black, snow-white,
> darksome light and shining night."

The familiar chant soothed her as the long hours of meditation had not, and her voice grew stronger. She said in a low sing-song: "Ever-changing life and death, transform us in your sight, open your secrets, open the door. In ye we shall be free o' slavery. In ye we shall be free o' pain. In ye we shall be free o' darkness without light, and in ye we shall be free o' light without darkness. For both shadow and radiance are yours, as both life and death are yours. And as all seasons are yours, so shall we dance and feast and have joy, for the tides o' darkness have turned and the green times be upon us, the time for the making o' love and harvest, the time o' nature's transformations, the time to be man and woman, the time to be child and crone, the time o' grace and redemption, the time o' loss and sacrifice . . ."

Although tears came again, it was not the hot, stifled, painful weeping of earlier but a flood of cleansing tears which left her feeling pure and empty. Bronwen wept too, from sympathy and tiredness and fear at the coming separation. Isabeau had explained to her that she was to leave with her mother in the morning. At first the little girl had been distraught but all her tears and tantrums had not moved Isabeau to relent and say she did not need to go. So at last the banprionnsa had grown sulky, refusing to speak to Isabeau at all and clinging close to her mother. Her sullen anger had hurt Isabeau far more than her tears, and she had found the previous day one of constant heartache. It was some comfort to her to hear the child's weeping and to know that Bronwen would miss her as much as she would miss the little girl.

The chant came to an end and Isabeau let go of Maya and Ishbel's hands, wiping her face and pushing away the unruly curls from her face. "Maya, it is time to break the curse."

Slowly the Fairge lifted the black bundle from where it had lain by the fire. In the candlelight her eyes glittered oddly. She took her jeweled eating knife and slowly and deliberately cut the knot that bound the cloth together.

> "Darksome night and shining light,
> By the power o' the moons so bright,
> Words o' grace be spoken,
> Power o' the curse be broken," she chanted.

The cloth fell open, revealing the little poppet all bound up in its stained, crumpled ribbon, smelling of evil and poison. A wave of such malevolence passed over Isabeau that she almost gagged, and both Bronwen and Ishbel gave a little cry and shrank back. Khan'gharad's bearded face was stern and sad, and he looked at Maya with cold anger in his eyes.

The Fairge looked rather sick but she picked up the poppet in her fingertips and carefully cut away the ribbon so that the broken feather fell away.

> "Darksome night and shining light,
> By the power o' the moons so bright,
> Words o' grace be spoken
> Power o' the curse be broken," she repeated huskily.

Handling the poppet as gingerly as possible, she cut away the scrap of MacCuinn tartan and the lock of dark hair, repeating the chant with a trembling voice.

"In the name o' Eà, mother and father o' us all, shine your light o' white upon Lachlan MacCuinn and shield him from all forces evil, malevolent and baneful," Isabeau chanted, the others all joining in. "Oh divine power o' the moons and stars, the winds and breathing air, the sweet waters and fruitful earth, the life that is in all the universe, the life that is in all o' us, bless Lachlan MacCuinn, encircle his body and soul and bring him peace and protection from harm. Cast away the evil chains that bind him, cast away the darkness that presses upon him, unseal his eyes so he may see, unseal his voice that he may speak, let vigor and warmth flow through him, let life return to him in full. By the power o' the moons so bright, as we say, so let it be!"

Maya cast the poppet and all the scraps of ribbon and cloth and feather on to the fire, crying loudly:

> "Fire burn, ashes turn,
> Evil spirits disperse
> I now remove this curse
> By the power o' the moons so bright,
> I bless ye, I bless ye, I bless ye!"

The flames leapt up, green and foul smelling, and they watched as the poppet was burnt to cinders. Then Isabeau threw a handful of dried dragon's blood on the fire so the flames hissed violet and blue and green, then purified the circle again with salt and earth, water and ashes.

"So," she said softly. "It is done. In Eä's name let us hope it is enough!"

Iseult leant her head on her hand and watched as the early morning light fingered across the wall and through the bed curtains. Although she was tired, having endured the Ordeal with the other witches, she did not want to leave her husband's side and seek her own cold, lonely bed. In almost a year of sleeping alone, Iseult had not grown used to not having Lachlan beside her. Although she had slept alone the first sixteen years of her life and they had been married only two and a half years before he fell, still her body craved his beside hers, his wings curving over to cup her through her sleep. She lowered her head onto his slack hand and let unaccustomed tears seep through her lashes.

The sunshine crept down onto the pillow and then over the face of the sleeping man. His eyelashes fluttered and he turned his face away from the light. His eyes opened and he looked about him blankly. He was in a strange room, ornately furnished with tapestries and silken cushions. The double doors were carved with the shape of flowering thistles. He felt very light and weak. He looked down and saw Iseult's red-gold head pressed against the coverlet. Slowly, hesitantly, he turned his hand in hers and gripped her fingers. She looked up, startled, and he saw her eyes all wet and red-rimmed.

"Why, *leannan*," Lachlan said, surprised at the hoarse croak that issued from his lips, "why do ye weep?"

THE PACT OF PEACE

....

T he sun shone down warmly on the dancers, who
skipped and twirled their way through a long archway of upraised arms. Jongleurs played and sang
from the sidelines, and children ran screaming with
laughter through the crowd. It was Lammas Day and
everyone had come to watch the Rìgh being whipped
and the loaves blessed by the Coven.

Suddenly a small voice piped, "They come, they
come!" The music stopped abruptly and the dancers jostled to the side to make room for the merry procession
winding its way down the hill.

The Rìgh was there on his black stallion, his bonny
banrìgh riding by his side, the prionnsachan behind him.
All were dressed in their kilts with their badges pinning
up their plaids. The town's laird was there, rather flus-
tered to be in such grand company, while a young jongleur with a crimson cap regaled them all with song and
jests, his black eyes sparkling. The Rìgh's own bodyguard
rode with them, dressed in blue, and the children's eyes
opened wide to see a great bear lumbering along behind
one of the Yeomen and a lean black wolf loping at the
heels of one of the prionnsachan's horses.

Then a little flutter of excitement ran over the crowd,
for in a barouche pulled by two white horses were the
three elderly members of the council of sorcerers and
the little prionnsa, his wings fluttering as he sought to
soar out of the arms of his nursemaid. The crowd threw
flowers to him and he waved back, grinning happily.

Another barouche followed and the crowd muttered
in amazement, for it was filled with faeries. There was a

girl with long, leafy hair, a furry cluricaun all dressed up in velvet, a snow-haired Celestine with a little child perched on her lap, and a corrigan, looking rather like a mossy boulder with one curious eye. A bright-winged little nisse darted all about the open carriage, shrieking with laughter. First she pulled the tail of one of the horses, then she hung from the whip of the driver so she was flung around as he cracked it. The watching children squealed with delight and she darted over to tweak their noses and pull their hair, causing them to laugh even louder.

The procession reached the tall, white boundary stone and came to a halt. The Rìgh dismounted and called to the laird with a laugh. "Come, man, whip away! Never let it be said Lachlan MacCuinn was slow to be reminded o' his responsibilities!"

He was dressed only in a kilt and plaid, his chest bare. As he spoke, he drew the plaid down so it hung around his waist. His shoulders and arms were marked all over with red slashes.

The laird dismounted rather reluctantly. "Are ye sure, Your Highness?" he asked anxiously. "It has been many years since we had the Common Ridings. I do no' wish to offer any disrespect . . ."

"Whip away, my laird," Lachlan replied cheerfully. "Indeed, if I am to bring back all the auld rites and customs, I canna no' bring back the only one that hurts me and no' your pocket. My shoulders are broad; I can stand it, I swear."

The laird smiled ruefully. "As ye wish, Your Highness." He raised his riding crop and slashed the boundary stone three times, then brought the crop down hard on the Rìgh's bare shoulder.

"Cursed be any man who forgets the bounds o' the land, be he bondsman, laird or Rìgh," Lachlan cried. "By my blood, I swear always to respect the rights o' the people o' this county. With thanks I accept their Lammas tithe and promise to protect them as I would my own child. For as I am your Rìgh I am as your father, duty bound to honor and shield ye."

There was a roar of approval from the crowd as Lachlan stood back from the boundary stone. Three of the prettiest young lasses of the county then came shyly and proudly through the crowd, their hair all bound up with corn and flowers. One carried water and a cloth to tend his lacerated back, another a flask of whiskey for him to swallow, and the third a little doll made from corn sheaves and tied up with flowers. The Rìgh drank down the whiskey with a wink and a jest, then gravely accepted the Corn Bairn and anointed its forehead with a little circle drawn with his own blood. They washed his weals and he rather gingerly arranged his plaid over his shoulder again.

Then Meghan stepped down from her carriage and solemnly blessed the bread and apples and winter wheat brought to her by the children of the county, making Eà's sign over their heads with a sorrowful smile. Gitâ allowed them to pat his silky brown fur and then the old sorceress climbed stiffly back into the barouche, having to lean heavily on her staff.

"On to the next village!" Lachlan cried. "Indeed, I wish the MacCuinn's land-holdings were no' so wide. If I do no' fall off my horse from the whippings, I shall from all the wee drams they keep giving me!"

The prionnsachan laughed.

"Just as long as your hand is steady enough to sign the Pact o' Peace this evening, I'm sure we do no' care," Madelon NicAislin called.

"Ye may no' but I do," Iseult said with a smile. "Too much o' the water o' life and he'll no' be able to perform his duty to his wife."

They all laughed again and Anghus MacRuraich said, "By the looks o' ye, Your Highness, ye have no cause to complain!" The black wolf sitting by his horse showed her teeth in a wide grin as if she understood and enjoyed the joke too.

Iseult smoothed her hand over her swelling abdomen with a slight, dreamy smile. As they rode on their way, a wagon piled high with the Rìgh's tithes trundled along behind them, for not only was Lammas Day the celebration of the first harvest, but also the day when rents and taxes were paid. This was Lachlan's own land that they rode through, the hills and meadows all round Lucescere, and he had come to collect his dues.

Dide bowed to the crowd, cap in hand, and began to sing:

> "Harvest home! Harvest home!
> We've ploughed and sown,
> We've reaped and mowed,
> Eà's blessing on hearth an' home,
> Harvest home! Harvest home!"

The afternoon shadows were growing long when they at last rode home to Lucescere, all rather merry from the whiskey the crofters and landholders kept pressing upon them. The palace gardens were strung with lanterns and as the Rìgh's party rode up the long, tree-lined avenue, they sprang into life with a wave of Meghan's finger.

All round the great square striped stalls had been set up, giving out Lammas cakes and Lammas ale. There were bellfruit jellies and roasted apples for the children of the Theurgia, and wild pigs were roasting on spits for those that did not prescribe to the vegetarianism of the Coven. Lachlan smiled as the children ran alongside the horses, calling out to him and Iseult. He dug his hand into his sporran and threw a handful of gold coins to the children, and they ran squealing to catch them.

Tòmas was waiting for the Rìgh by the front steps, Johanna by his side, but Lachlan waved them away, saying, "What good is it letting them whip me if I come running to ye to heal me the moment I get home? Nay, they're honorable wounds. Let me suffer them in peace."

He dismounted with a wince and said to Iseult, "The only care I want is ye, *leannan*. Come and help me change for indeed these cuts sting!"

Iseult only waited for the witches' barouche to come trotting up behind them. "Donncan, dearling!" she called. "Come to mam. I'll feed ye and bathe ye this night. Let poor Sukey go and enjoy the fete."

"Och, thank ye, your Highness!" Sukey cried. "Are ye sure? I do no' mind tending Donncan first . . ."

"Nay, ye go," Iseult said. She caught up the little boy and ruffled his red-gold curls. "Come along, ye wee ruffian! Ye think I did no' see ye trying to fly away from Sukey again. Indeed, ye're a wicked lad!"

The Lammas Congress was to be held before the feast and so once they were bathed and changed, Iseult and Lachlan went along to the great hall where the prionnsachan were all gathered. There was a warm buzz of conversation that ceased as the Rìgh and Banrìgh came in, and then the silver and blue room echoed with the sound of cheering and clapping.

"Long live the Rìgh! Long live the Banrìgh!"

"Slàinte mhath!"

"To peace and happiness!"

The Lammas Congress that year was the most tranquil and harmonious in many years, and in many ways, the strangest. As well as the prionnsachan and greater lairds, there were representatives from all of the major faery folk except the Fairgean.

Cloudshadow was there and her grandfather, the Stargazer. Sann the corrigan was there to represent her people and a grove of tree-changers that had kept the servants busy sweeping up all the twigs and leaves they dropped through the corridors. A Mesmerdean nymph hovered in one corner, his multifaceted eyes transmitting all that happened to the elders back in the marshlands.

The seelie had ridden up to the palace gates on the horse-eel and had insisted on bringing the creature in, despite the slimy puddles it left behind it. Hobgoblins, bogfaeries and brownies played chase-and-hide among the furniture, and cluricauns entertained the crowd with an impromptu performance of music.

The nisses had all been banished outside after causing a rumpus with their tricks. They now caused havoc throughout the fair set up in the gardens, overturning pitchers of bellfruit juice, snatching Lammas cakes and stealing the flowers out of ladies' hair. Only Elala remained, swinging on Lilanthe's hair and making mocking comments about the smelliness, hairiness and ugliness of the men and women gathered within. Although none but Lilanthe and Niall could understand the little nisse, still the tree-shifter blushed crimson and tried to shush her.

There was even the leader of the satyricorns, a wild-haired woman with a single, rapier-sharp horn and a thick necklace of teeth and bones that hung between her three pairs of breasts. She had been kept well supplied with bloody meat and had confounded the soldiers earlier in the day by winning the annual wrestling match with ease.

Months had been spent negotiating the Pact of Peace and so the gathering tonight was really a formality. Nonetheless, the herald read out the long scroll of terms and conditions, with the crowd cheering some and calling out satirical comments on others. The borders between the lands had all been renegotiated and agreed upon, with Brangaine NicSian, Gwyneth's niece, declared the absolute ruler of Siantan. The Double Throne was dissolved with Anghus MacRuraich's blessing. Melisse NicThanach reluctantly allowed her aunt, Madelon NicAislin, to again assume responsibility for Aslinn, admitting her grandfather had not really had the right to rule the land of forests simply because he had wedded one NicAislin and married his son to another. Since this had long been a point of contention within the family, its resolution was greeted with much joy and relief.

Elfrida NicHilde was to sign on behalf of her people, even though she was a banprionnsa in exile and Tìrsoilleir was still ruled by the Fealde and the council of elders. Both she and Linley MacSeinn had been promised help in regaining their lands and their thrones as soon as order had been fully restored elsewhere in Eileanan, and so they were glad to be accorded as much courtesy and respect as those prionnsachan still sitting their thrones.

Iain MacFóghnan was ratified as the ruler of Arran, even though his mother still lived. After escaping the invasion of the fenlands she had reportedly fled to the Fair Isles where she was trying to raise support to wrest back her throne from her son.

Kenneth MacAhern was just signing his name to the

pact when they heard screaming from outside. Immediately the atmosphere in the room changed. Iscult's hands flew to her belt, only to realize with chagrin that she was not wearing her weapons, and the Blue Guards drew their claymores. Lilanthe was standing near the windows, half hidden by the brocade curtains.

"A dragon flies down!" she cried in amazement. There were exclamations of horror and astonishment. Too many remembered the burning of Ardencaple not to feel fear at the sight of a dragon. Then Lilanthe cried, "Isabeau! Isabeau rides the dragon! And others as well. Isabeau has come!"

Iseult was on her feet with a glad cry. She did not bother going out the door and down the stairs. She ran lightly down the hall and with a quick bound leapt out the window, dropping the five storeys to the ground as lightly as a feather falling.

Asrohc was coming down to land in the garden, her golden wings spread wide, careless of smashed stalls and screaming, running spectators. On her back were crouched Isabeau, Ishbel, Khan'gharad and the Firemaker, all wrapped up against the cold.

Iseult's steps faltered. She smiled through her tears and held out her hands as Isabeau jumped down from the dragon's back and ran to meet her. The twins embraced tightly, Isabeau babbling greetings and explanations, Iseult not saying a word but hugging her twin so tight Isabeau feared her ribs would crack.

"... so ye see, once we saw through the scrying pool what ye planned, we all thought we should come and be part o' it. Indeed, an historic moment, the signing o' a Pact o' Peace by every land and every faery race ..."

"All but the Fairgean," Iseult replied rather grimly.

Isabeau's smile died. "I need to explain about Bronwen and Maya," she said rapidly.

Iseult nodded. "Time enough for that. Let me greet the Firemaker first and our mam. What are they doing here? And who is the Khan'cohban o' seven scars? I do no' ken him and I should, for indeed a warrior o' seven scars is rare enough."

Isabeau smiled radiantly. "He is our *dai-dein*! Indeed, I had forgotten ye did no' ken. He was ensorcelled . . . Och, I have so much to tell ye!"

Iseult stared past her in astonishment. Striding toward them was a tall man with a strong, arrogant face scarred with three slashes on either cheek and another that ran down between his brows. His eyes were a brilliant blue beneath lowering brows, and his thick red hair was tied back with a leather thong. On either side of his brow were two curling horns.

He brought two fingers sweeping to his brow, then to his heart, then out to the garden. Iseult bent her head and lifted one hand to cover her eyes, the other hand bent outward in supplication. Such was the proper way to greet a Scarred Warrior. He grunted and she dropped her hands, though her eyes remained lowered. Then he reached out and caught her to him, hugging her fiercely. For a moment Iseult was frozen in surprise, for Khan'-cohbans did not embrace. Then her arms flew round him and she hugged her father back.

There was a joyful reunion with Ishbel and the Fire-maker, neither of whom Iseult had seen since her marriage four years earlier, then she went to bow before the dragon-princess and exchange greetings. Isabeau turned in search of Meghan and her smile faltered as she saw Lachlan standing before her, his wings erect, his face stern.

"So, the miscreant has returned," he said. Tart words rose to her tongue but she swallowed them, curtseying respectfully instead, eyes lowered.

"What have ye done with my niece?" he asked.

"I gave her to Maya so she would remove the curse from ye, Your Highness," Isabeau replied equably.

Surprise flitted across his face. Then he laughed. "O' all the things I was expecting ye to say, that was no' among them! Ye continually astonish me, Isabeau. Ye and your sister, both. Come, who is that man my wife was just embracing so affectionately?"

Isabeau bit back a grin. "That, Your Highness, is my stallion Lasair, who ye wanted to have shot. He was really my father Khan'gharad, whom Maya ensorcelled on the Day o' Betrayal. Nineteen years he was a horse, Your Highness, and indeed he has found life as a man again very difficult."

"I can imagine," Lachlan murmured sympathetically. "I was only a blackbird for close on five years and yet still I find it hard sometimes. Come, I can see it's quite a story ye have to tell us! Will ye no' all come up to the meeting hall? We were halfway through signing a most historic piece o' paper when ye so rudely interrupted us. Ye can tell us your tale and make your excuses later."

Isabeau was torn between a smile and an angry refutation, but she saw the rueful twinkle in Lachlan's eyes and grinned in response. "Aye, Your Highness. Ye ken your word is my command," she answered and he laughed.

With her arm linked through Iseult's, Isabeau followed the Rìgh through the palace and into the meeting hall. She was greeted so warmly by so many that her cheeks crimsoned. She had dreaded returning to Lucescere, sure that her welcome would not be warm. But it seemed that no one was willing to let the good cheer of the day be ruined by old tensions.

Meghan was waiting impatiently in the long conference hall and Isabeau was shocked at how old and haggard she looked, with her long plait all white and her small frame gaunter than ever. The black eyes still snapped with vitality, however, and she pulled Isabeau into a fierce embrace.

"What do ye mean by sneaking off into the night like that and no' sending word for three long years?" she cried. "It's worried to death I've been about ye."

"I'm sorry," Isabeau said contritely. "Indeed it seemed the best thing to do at the time, and where I've been I've had no way o' sending ye a message."

"Ye were always a foolish, impetuous lass, but I had thought ye had begun to gain some sense," Meghan snapped. "Why did ye no' trust me to have a care for the wee lassie?"

"It was no' just Bronwen, it was *dai-dein* as well,"

Isabeau said defensively. "And that at least worked out for the best."

"Whatever do ye mean?" Meghan asked, but just then Iseult came in the door, her arm linked with the Fire-maker's. Following them, arm in arm, were Ishbel and Khan'gharad.

Meghan's mouth dropped open in astonishment. "By Eà's green blood! It's Khan'gharad," she cried. "How . . . ? Where . . . ?"

Isabeau tensed. Despite all her attempts to explain and justify Meghan's actions on the Day of Betrayal, Khan'gharad persisted in thinking the worst of the old sorceress.

"She never approved of me and tried many times to separate Ishbel and me," he had said angrily. "She wanted Ishbel all to herself—she was a jealous, possessive auld woman who could no' bear that Ishbel loved me best. She tried to kill me on purpose that day so she could have Ishbel all to herself—she saw the opportunity and seized it."

"Meghan is no' like that, truly," Isabeau had protested.

Even Ishbel spoke up on Meghan's behalf, saying, "She was truly sorry, my love. It was that blaygird Ensorcellor she was trying to kill, no' ye."

Khan'gharad had remained unconvinced, and so Isabeau was dreading this meeting between her father and her beloved guardian.

Meghan's face lit up, however, and she limped hastily across the room, her hand held out. "The queen-dragon spoke truly. Ye were alive! Och, Khan'gharad, can ye ever forgive me? I did no' mean for ye to fall into the chasm too. I was angry and I opened the earth too wide. The edge just crumbled beneath your feet and pitched ye in. I swear, on Eà's blessed name, that I never meant to harm ye. Where have ye been all these long years? Come, I can see there are many tales to be told. Will ye no' sit with us and tell us?"

Khan'gharad was stiff and proud but he acknowledged her apology with a curt nod and allowed Dillon to pull up a chair for him, Ishbel and the Firemaker and to pour them some wine.

The interrupted formalities resumed then, the Mac-Brann signing after the MacAhern, followed by the Nic-Thanach and the newly restored NicAislin. Isabeau gave Meghan and the royal couple a very quick account of her years at the Cursed Towers and explained how Khan'-gharad had been ensorcelled by Maya.

Lachlan then pleased her greatly by leaping to his feet and saying, "We have a new addition to our signatures which I have only just learnt about. My wife Iseult Nic-Faghan was going to sign on behalf o' her clan, but we are glad indeed to be able to welcome her long-lost father, Khan'gharad MacFaghan, Prionnsa o' Tìrlethan, the direct descendant o' Faodhagan the Red!"

A murmur of surprise arose and Khan'gharad bowed, his face quirking into an unaccustomed smile. He was passed the quill and ink, and he signed with a clumsy hand, still unused to having fingers again.

Once all the prionnsachan had signed, the representatives of the various faery races came forward to make their mark. The Firemaker signed on behalf of the Khan'-cohbans, the Stargazer on behalf of the Celestines, and Brun on behalf of the cluricauns. Elala dipped her tiny hands in the ink and pressed them on the paper; the oldest of the tree-changers made a twiglike inscription, and the seelie drew his own simple rune. Asrohc was brought a barrel of ink in which to dip her claw, signing her name in a strange, ornate flourish that took up a great length of the scroll. Asrohc had been sent by her mother to renew the promises the queen of the dragons had made to Aedan MacCuinn at the signing of the First Pact of Peace, more than four hundred years earlier. Then Tòmas carried the huge roll of paper down into the sewers so that Ceit Anna, the last of the nyx, could make her mark without needing to brave the light.

The palace was once again filled with music and dancing, the jongleurs and troubadours competing to see who could draw the greatest crowd to listen to their songs and stories, watch their fire-eating, juggling, acrobatics

and stilt-walking, and dance to their reels and jigs. Dide
was in his element, playing his guitar as he walked among
the throng. His eyes lit up when he saw Isabeau and
Lilanthe sitting together under the trees, deep in conversation, and he veered that way.

"My lady Isabeau," he said with a deep bow. "I see
ye have returned from wherever it is that ye've been.
May I have this dance?"

Isabeau smiled up at him. "I do no' feel much like
dancing, I'm afraid. I'm sure that Lilanthe would like to
dance though. I saw her feet tapping."

The jongleur dropped down on the grass beside her.
"Now I come to think on it, I do no' feel much like
dancing either," he replied. "Will ye no' tell me where
ye have been and why ye left like that? Three and a half
years without a word!"

"I'll leave ye two to talk," Lilanthe said, getting to her
feet, color washing up over her cheeks. She had seen the
expression on Dide's face when Isabeau had walked into
the meeting hall and she realized now that he had eyes
for no other. He nodded and waved his hand as she
slipped off into the garden, the nisse hovering above her.

Isabeau frowned at him. "Poor Lilanthe! Why are ye
always so mean to her?"

"Mean? To Lilanthe? When am I ever mean to her?"
he cried. "We're guid friends, I had thought, though I
have no' seen so much o' her in recent times. She spends
most o' her time at the Tower o' Two Moons, lecturing
in the ways o' the forest faeries. Ye can guess how I feel
about Theurgias! I'd rather be in a snug tavern, singing
and playing my guitar. But enough about me. Where in
Eà's green bluid have ye been?"

She told him rather stiltedly some of what had happened during her years at the Cursed Towers. As she
neared the end of her narrative, there was a sudden
cheeping sound and a round, feathery head emerged
from Isabeau's sleeve, regarding Dide with huge, golden
eyes. He gave a startled exclamation.

"What in Eà's name is that?" he cried.

"This is Buba," Isabeau said, laughing. "I found her a

few months ago, soon after Maya and Bronwen left. She had fallen out o' her nest and was too young to fly. I splinted her broken wing and carried her round with me while it healed, but even though she can fly well now, she will no' leave me. I think she thinks I'm her mother."

"But what is it? It looks like an owl but it's no' much larger than a sparrow!"

"She's an elf owl. They are the smallest o' all the owls. There are quite a few o' them at the Cursed Towers. They eat spiders and crickets—I had a horrible time trying to find food for her until she was auld enough to hunt for herself!"

The little owl crept further out of Isabeau's sleeve. Only six inches long from her tufted head to her feathery talons, she was almost a pure white in color with a few gray speckles on her wings. Her enormous eyes were fixed unblinkingly on Dide's face.

He looked back rather uneasily, saying, "Och, it's an uncanny gaze your wee birdie is giving me. It's almost as though she is reading my thoughts."

"Well, your thoughts are no' that hard to read," Isabeau replied with a laugh. "It's a most expressive face ye've got, Dide."

He seized her hand, color rising in his lean, brown cheeks. "Then if ye ken what it is I'm thinking . . ."

Isabeau squeezed his fingers and then drew her hand back. "I want to be a sorceress," she said gently. "Witches do no' marry, ye ken that. Or at least, only rarely and usually to other witches. Ye ken ye do no' want to give up the jongleur's life for the Coven. Ye said yourself ye hate Theurgias! Well, I do no' much want to travel around in a caravan, juggling oranges for a living. Ye ken I canna sing or dance or swallow fire or do somersaults like ye and Nina. I'd be no use to ye at all."

Dide was silent for a moment, and then his irrepressible smile broke over his face again. He leant forward and nuzzled under her ear. "Who said anything about marriage?" he whispered. "Tomorrow is a long way away, but tonight is here and now."

Isabeau laughed and pushed him away. "Aye, but if I

want to be a sorceress I canna be distracting myself with the needs o' the body, at least no' yet. Maybe one day, when I've won my staff and sorceress rings . . ."

Dide kissed her ear and then her cheek. "So your body has needs, does it? I canna be allowing those needs to be unmet. Would I no' give a wee dram to a man dying o' thirst?" He kissed her cheek and then her mouth. Suddenly he leapt back with an exclamation of pain. "Your blaygird birdie just pecked me!" he cried.

Isabeau gave a peal of laughter. "Buba!" she cried. "Wicked bird!"

Dide glared at the little owl, nursing his hand. Gingerly he sat down again, saying, "Canna ye tell it to go hunt some spiders?"

Isabeau smiled at him affectionately. "Nay, I think I need Buba here to protect me," she replied. "My chastity, if no' my health. Nay, go on, Dide, I meant what I said. I'm only here for a short time anyway. I must return to the Cursed Towers with my mam and my *dai-dein*. They need me there, and I have more to learn from the Soul-Sage and the Firemaker yet. I want to undergo my initiation and win my name and my scars. The queen-dragon said to know my future I must know my past. I think too much o' ye to merely dally with ye in the gardens . . ."

He laughed, rather bitterly. "That's a soft brush-off, if ever I heard one," he said. "Ye sure I canna get ye some wine? If only it was Hogmanay, I could try with the Het Pint again."

Isabeau laughed ruefully and got to her feet, shaking leaves from her skirt. "Go and play for the party, Dide," she said. "I have only a few hours and I want to spend some time with Meghan. I have no' seen her for a long time syne, and indeed she is looking auld and drawn."

Dide jumped up and strummed his guitar. "Och my love's cruel and cold, cruel and cold she is to me," he sang, bowing to her with his black eyes sparkling with mockery. "Made o' ice and snow is she, cruel and cold she is to me."

He wandered off into the crowd, singing, and Isabeau

lifted the little owl so she could brush her chin against its velvety feathers. "Come, Buba," she said. "I want ye to meet Meghan, who was my foster-mother as I am unto ye."

The little owl hooted softly in response. *Wise auld mother waiting,* she said.

Lilanthe stood in the darkness under the trees and watched Dide kiss Isabeau with a queer, soft pain around her heart. Then she turned her back deliberately and walked away. On the lawn before the palace, dancers were skipping round in wide circles within circles, while long chains of men and women danced under the lantern-hung trees. Lilanthe got herself a cup of mulled wine and sipped it, watching enviously, her foot tapping.

"Ye do no' dance, Lilanthe?" Niall came up beside her, Ursa the bear lumbering along behind him.

"No one wants to dance with a tree-shifter, they're afraid they'll trip over my feet," she said with a self-mocking smile, lifting her skirt so he could see her broad, gnarled roots.

"But I've seen ye dance, ye're a dainty dancer indeed," he cried.

She smiled gratefully but said, "That was in comparison to the tree-changers. Anyone looks dainty in comparison to them."

"Or to me," he said ruefully. "No one wants to dance with me because they're afraid if I step on their foot I'll break it!"

Lilanthe laughed. "They're probably more afraid that Ursa will get jealous. I'll wager ye that if ye send her off to bed with some honey, ye'll have flocks o' girls gathering round to dance wi' ye, hero that ye are."

He blushed and said awkwardly, "I'd rather dance wi' ye again."

"Really?" Lilanthe cried. "I'd love to dance. Do ye mean it?"

He bowed. "Madam, will ye give me the pleasure o' this dance?"

"Why, thank ye, sir." Lilanthe laid her twig-thin fingers in his huge, hard hand. Then she gave a little gasp as he swung his arm around her waist, sweeping her off the ground and whirling her around. "See, your feet do no' even have to touch the ground," he said. "That way I can be sure no' to break them."

"My feet are no' easily broken," Lilanthe replied when she had caught her breath. "They're tough as wood, I'm afraid."

The trees closed over their heads as he swung her away from the crowd. "What about your heart?" he said, very gruffly.

"My heart?"

"Is it easily broken?"

She flushed and did not know how to answer. "I do no' ken," she said at last. "It's never been broken—but I do no' think that means it's hard."

He said, very low, "I saw ye watching your jongleur friend. He seemed very intent on the bonny lass wi' the red hair like the Banrìgh. Do . . . does that upset ye very much?"

They danced on in silence. Then she shook her leafy hair. "No. I always kent Dide was no' for me. We are very different. He loves crowds and parties and smoky inns. I am a creature o' the forest, I'm afraid."

"So am I," Niall said, very low. She looked up, trying to read his face, but it was too dark under the trees. Then he surprised her by kissing her, very hard.

When at last he released her mouth, Lilanthe stood very still, leaning against his shoulder. She felt very safe in the circle of his arms. She said nothing, dazed and tremulous.

"Ye remember once ye asked me what I would like to do once the war was over?" Niall said. She nodded. "Would ye like that too? A wee cottage somewhere in the woods, with a garden and some beehives, and a pool for ye to bathe in and sweet earth in which to dig your roots? For I want ye, Lilanthe. It is ye I dream o' beside me in that cottage. Do ye think ye would like that too?"

She nodded again and leant her head against his broad shoulder. "Aye, I would," she whispered. "I'd like that very much."

Isabeau found her guardian waiting by the Pool of Two Moons, in the center of the labyrinth. It was very quiet there, with the stars thick as daisies in the dark sky. She came and sat at Meghan's side, leaning her head against the sorceress's knee. Meghan smoothed the unruly curls away from her face.

"Ye have learnt a lot since ye've been gone."

"Aye."

"Ye've lost all the veils over your third eye. Ye see clearly now."

"Aye."

"It's been a stony road for ye, my lass."

Isabeau nodded. "Aye, that it has."

"Tell me?"

Cuddling the little owl in her hands, Isabeau told Meghan everything she had done and learnt. For Meghan, there was no judicious editing or softening of the truth. Occasionally the sorceress asked a question or made an exclamation, sometimes of horror, more often of exasperation. Once she said, "Och, ye were always an impulsive lass! Ye'd think ye would have learnt some wisdom by now!"

Isabeau finished with the lifting of the curse and Maya and Bronwen's departure from the secret valley. "I watched them through the scrying pool. They reached the sea safely. I saw them swim into the waves." Tears choked her, then she went on with a catch in her voice, "I couldna see them after that, though. I do no' ken where they went."

"The sea distorts the far-seeing," Meghan said. "Like the mountains. Ye did well to see so far, even with the scrying pool."

"I hope I did no' do wrongly," Isabeau said, her voice rather shaky. "She could've just turned me into a toad and taken Bronwen but she did no'. I do no' ken why."

Meghan shrugged. "Who understands the heart o' a fairge? No' I." She brooded in silence for a while, then said, "And who is this wee white owl?"

"This is Buba," Isabeau replied with a tender smile. "Is she no' bonny?"

Meghan hooted, soft and low, and the elf-owl hooted back.

"I do no' ken what I should do without her now," Isabeau said. "It has been lonely at the Cursed Towers. Even though I ken she should be living with the other owls, I rather hope she does no' fly away, at least for a while."

"She shall no' fly away," Meghan said.

Isabeau smiled and rubbed her chin against Buba's tufted head. "I was sorry indeed about Jorge," she burst out. "Och, it was an awful week! I saw through the scrying pool . . ."

Meghan was silent, though her hand shook. Isabeau glanced up and saw tears shining on her guardian's furrowed face. "I do no' think there is any greater grief," Meghan said curtly, "than to outlive all those that ye love most."

There was a long silence, then she went on, "That is why I left the Coven all those years ago, sick at heart to be still alive when I should have died a comfortable auld age like my father and my sister and all my friends and lovers. Then I saw the Weaver still had a place for me in the pattern. I found ye, the bonny, naughty lass that ye were, and I saved Lachlan as best I could. I saw I must go on living and so I forged on, doing what had to be done. For Jorge to die like that, though, to die in agony in the flames when he was the gentlest soul alive . . ." Her voice shook and her little donbeag whimpered and clung tighter around her neck. She put up a thin, trembling hand and soothed him.

Very low, she said, "It is odd that I should put my faith in Eà all my life and only now, when we have triumphed against our enemies and restored Eà's veneration, have my faith falter."

"No!" Isabeau cried. "Meghan!"

The old sorceress nodded. "I ken it is weak and foolish to blame the universe for the evil o' humans. I o' all people ken that Eà is as much darkness as light, as much death as life. Still, since Jorge died, it seems I can see only her dark face."

"May Eà shine her bright face upon ye." Isabeau whispered the ritual phrase.

Meghan stroked her hair. "Indeed, with your bright face near me again, I find myself much comforted," she said. "I am glad ye came for the signing o' the Pact o' Peace."

"It is a wonderful thing indeed," Isabeau said.

Meghan nodded. "I think my father would be pleased. Even he could no' manage to bring so many o' the faeries to sign, nor Arran or Tìrsoilleir for that matter. It is no small achievement."

"It is odd how things have turned out," Isabeau said dreamily. "To think I once longed for adventure and now all I want is to be quiet for a while and enjoy the peace we have won."

"A precarious peace at best," Meghan said dryly. "Do no' forget the Fairgean. Each year they grow stronger and bolder and soon none o' the rivers or lochan shall be safe. And they are a bloodthirsty race—they shall no' be content to rule the waves but shall rise forth to try and drive us from the land. Jorge had disturbing visions o' waves that rose as high as mountains and swept over the land, drowning villages and cities alike. Indeed he had the gift, for so much o' what he saw has come to pass."

Isabeau gave a little shiver. "The Fairgean hate us," she said in a low voice. "They seek revenge for all the harm our people have done theirs."

Meghan shot her a curious glance but just then Isabeau heard a faint rustle in the hedges and tensed, her head whipping round. As the breeze shifted she smelt a dank odor, like a stagnant pool or a freshly dug grave. She clenched her hands, her pulse quickening, and would have risen, but Meghan pulled her back. "No need to fear, dearling," she said.

"But it's a Mesmerd," Isabeau whispered. "I can smell it—and look! There in the hedge. I can see its eyes watching us."

"I ken," Meghan replied. "It follows me around. I came through the maze because I thought I might lose it for a while, but I should have kent better."

"I killed one, up at the Cursed Towers," Isabeau said, troubled. "Will its egg-brothers no' seek revenge for its death? And ye? Have they no' marked ye as kin-killer too? Mesmerdean have come hunting ye before."

Meghan smiled. "Many times now. Indeed they are an intractable, vengeful race."

"Then should we no' . . ." Isabeau made to rise again, and again Meghan soothed her.

"No need to fret, lassie. The Mesmerdean have signed the Pact o' Peace. All wars and vendettas have been laid to rest. They shall no' seek revenge on ye, nor on Iseult or Lachlan."

Isabeau relaxed. "Really? Thank Eà for that! I can stop starting at shadows."

Meghan made no response and the donbeag laid his paw on her ear.

Isabeau sat up a little. "What is it?" she asked, then cried swiftly, "Ye said Lachlan, Iseult and I were safe. What o' ye?" Before Meghan could answer, Isabeau cried, "Nay, Meghan! Ye havena?" Tears rushed to her eyes and spilt down her face, hot and bitter.

Buba the owl hooted mournfully and rubbed her tufted head against Isabeau's hand. For once Isabeau paid her no heed, reaching up to grasp Meghan's thin hand. "No, no, ye canna," she said pitifully.

Meghan stroked back her unruly curls. "I want to," she replied gently. "Death is nothing but a door into another place, another life. I am no' afraid o' stepping through the door."

" 'Eà, ever-changing life and death, transform us in your sight, open your secrets, open the door. In ye we shall be free o' darkness without light, and in ye we shall be free o' light without darkness. For both shadow and radiance are yours, as both life and death are yours. For ye are the rocks and trees and stars and the deep, deep swell of the sea, ye are the Spinner and the Weaver and the Cutter o' the Thread, ye are birth and life and death, ye are shadow and brightness, ye are night and day, dusk and dawn, ye are ever-changing life and death . . .'" Isabeau quoted, stumbling over the words as her breath caught in little sobs she could not control.

Meghan smiled. "I knew ye would understand." They sat in silence for a moment, watching the stars in the dark sky and breathing in the fresh, green darkness. Tears slid down Isabeau's face but she did not break the silence.

Then Meghan said, very low, "They have given me till the time o' the red comet, time enough to see ye come into your full powers. I would like to know your path lies straight before ye."

Isabeau said, rather shakily, "Four years, anything can happen in four years."

Meghan just stared into the shadow of the hedge, where the Mesmerd hovered, his huge, multifaceted eyes glittering in the moonlight.

Isabeau sighed and rested her wet cheek against Meghan's knee again. The little owl hooted and she hooted back, low and melancholy.

The Mesmerd hovered in the shadow of the hedge, watching and listening and smelling. There was no expression on his beautiful face, dominated by the great clusters of iridescent green eyes. Very lightly he rubbed his claws against his wings. Soon he would have to return to the marshes, to lie in the mud and slowly metamorphose within his hard shell. When spring came he would emerge from his winter husk as an elder. Then there would be no more flying, no more adventures. Then he would fight for his own territory and a mate, and the copulation wheel would begin again. His mate would lay their eggs in the water and he would watch over them and guard them. And every one of his spawn of little naiads would carry within them the face and shape and smell and emotional aura of the Keybearer Meghan. Mesmerdean never forget.

(0451)

THE BLACK JEWELS TRILOGY

by *Anne Bishop*

"Darkly mesmerizing . . . fascinatingly different . . . worth checking out."—*Locus*

This is the story of the heir to a dark throne, a magic more powerful than that of the High Lord of Hell, and an ancient prophecy. These three books tell of a ruthless game of politics and intrigue, magic and betrayal, love and sacrifice, destiny and fufillment, as the Princess Jaenelle struggles to become that which she was meant to be.

❑ **DAUGHTER OF THE BLOOD:**
BOOK ONE (456718 / $5.99)

❑ **HEIR TO THE SHADOWS:**
BOOK TWO (456726 / $5.99)

❑ **QUEEN OF THE DARKNESS:**
BOOK THREE (456734 / $5.99)

Prices slightly higher in Canada

Payable by Visa, MC or AMEX only ($10.00 min.), No cash, checks or COD. Shipping & handling: US/Can. $2.75 for one book, $1.00 for each add'l book; Int'l $5.00 for one book, $1.00 for each add'l. Call (800) 788-6262 or (201) 933-9292, fax (201) 896-8569 or mail your orders to:

Penguin Putnam Inc.
P.O. Box 12289, Dept. B
Newark, NJ 07101-5289
Please allow 4-6 weeks for delivery.
Foreign and Canadian delivery 6-8 weeks.

Bill my: ❑ Visa ❑ MasterCard ❑ Amex_____(expires)
Card# _____
Signature _____

Bill to:
Name _____
Address _____City _____
State/ZIP_____Daytime Phone # _____
Ship to:
Name _____Book Total $ _____
Address _____Applicable Sales Tax $ _____
City _____Postage & Handling $ _____
State/ZIP_____Total Amount Due $ _____

This offer subject to change without notice.   Ad # Bishp/BlkJelw (9/00)

More Great Fantasy from

PENGUIN PUTNAM INC.
Online

Your Internet gateway to a virtual environment with
hundreds of entertaining and enlightening books
from Penguin Putnam Inc.

*While you're there, get the latest buzz on
the best authors and books around—*

Tom Clancy, Patricia Cornwell, W.E.B. Griffin,
Nora Roberts, William Gibson, Robin Cook,
Brian Jacques, Catherine Coulter, Stephen King,
Jacquelyn Mitchard, and many more!

**Penguin Putnam Online is located at
http://www.penguinputnam.com**

PENGUIN PUTNAM NEWS

Every month you'll get an inside look at our upcom-
ing books and new features on our site. This is an
ongoing effort to provide you with the most
up-to-date information about
our books and authors.

**Subscribe to Penguin Putnam News at
http://www.penguinputnam.com/ClubPPI**